ALBERTA BRIDES

Hearts Seek a Secure Wilderness Home in Four Inspiring Romances

LINDA FORD

BARBOUR
PUBLISHING

Published by Barbour Publishing, Inc., P.O. Box 719, Uhrichsville, Ohio 44683, www.barbourbooks.com

Our mission is to publish and distribute inspirational products offering exceptional value and biblical encouragement to the masses.

 Member of the
Evangelical Christian
Publishers Association

Printed in the United States of America.
5 4 3 2

Dear Reader,

I grew up in a home rich with history. My dad always had a story about his growing up years and the struggles his parents faced as settlers on the prairie in Alberta, Canada. I loved the stories. They seemed full of romance and strength and perseverance.

My parents also introduced me to the rigors of pioneer life. My father gave up farming to move his family closer to schools and doctors and became a road maintenance man in a vast prairie setting. He spent the summers living in a bunkhouse in primitive conditions. My mother, brave woman, joined him with us children during the summer holidays. For me it was wonderful—wild open fields, discovering little secrets of nature, the bird nest huddled in the grass, the baby hawks learning to fly, the fragile flowers on a cactus.

These memories became the background for the stories I've written about pioneer women. I know it wasn't all glamour, but to me, that life held a charm of a different age when people faced overwhelming odds and discovered little pleasures; when they drew on their faith and found one of life's greatest treasures—love. I hope you enjoy these stories as much as I enjoyed writing them.

Linda Ford

Chastity's Angel

To my husband, Ivan:
Together we have journeyed many years,
faced many hardships, enjoyed many adventures,
and grown together in love.

Chapter 1

Everything seemed to happen at once that pleasant summer afternoon of 1909 at Brownlee's Boardinghouse in the thriving town of Willow Creek, Alberta, Canada.

Chastity stood in the kitchen, her nimble fingers rolling out dough, fitting it into the pie dishes, and laying aside perfect circles for the top crust. She breathed in the heady scent of the last lilacs of the season and listened to the cheery call of the robin in the backyard. Occasionally she glanced out the open window to drink in the brightness of the cornflower blue sky and the fullness of green in the row of poplar trees marching down the side of the yard.

As her hands worked, Chastity's thoughts flitted from one subject to another with no more concern than a butterfly tasting of the bounty of flowers in a summer meadow.

For a moment she thought of supper. The roast was in the oven; she had plenty of time to peel vegetables and finish the pies. A smile tugged at her lips as she anticipated the boarders' eager reaction to hot rhubarb pie. Then she remembered a conversation she'd had earlier with Emma, the hired girl, about mending the sheets from Mrs. Banner's room. From there her thoughts drifted to planning tea, then to Michael and how he—

Just then the back doorbell clanged. It would be her grocery order.

At the same time, she heard a crash from the dining room, where she had left her mother polishing the silver teapot.

"Come in!" she called to the back door and in the next breath to the dining room, "Mother?" And before she could gasp in more air, she cried out, "Emma!" She only hoped that Emma, out in the garden pulling rhubarb, would hear her.

The back door squeaked, but Chas didn't even glance at the delivery boy. Her throat constricting, she dashed for the dining room.

Her mother lay in a heap on top of the statue that ordinarily stood beside her chair. The teapot quivered against the table leg.

"Mother, what happened?"

Her mother groaned and tried to disentangle herself from the statue and chair legs.

"Wait, Mother—I'll help." She bent down to the stricken woman.

Footsteps thudded in the doorway, and without turning, the young woman called over her shoulder to the delivery boy, "Could you give me a hand, please?"

The boy stepped to her side. It flashed through her mind that the hands were awfully large for the boy Mr. Silverhorn usually sent, but glad for strong arms to lift her mother, she gave it no more thought.

Still on her knees, she ran her hands along her mother's legs.

"I'm all right, *cherie.*"

Chas looked into her mother's face and, seeing her pallor, found no reassurance in the words.

"What happened?" Chas narrowed her eyes. She'd left her mother strict instructions to call if she needed anything, but the polish and rag were on the table, too far to reach without leaving the chair. "What were you up to?"

Her mother sighed. "I only wanted to put the teapot on the sideboard." She leaned back. "My leg went out from under me."

Emma skidded through the doorway. "What on earth's going on? The door's wide open, and the groceries are spilled all over the table." She gulped. "Miz LaBlanc, what happened? You look as if you've seen a ghost." Before anyone could respond, Emma answered her own question. "Ah, I think you've been naughty again."

Chas stood to her feet. "Emma, run and get Doc Johnson, please."

Her mother waved her hand. "No, no, that isn't necessary." She moaned. "Chastity, please get one of those tablets he left."

Chas hesitated. As much as the sight of her mother in pain frightened her, a tremor of anger passed through her. *How can she so blithely ignore the doctor's warnings to let her hip heal before trying to use it?*

The woman shifted and flinched.

Chas turned and hurried down the hall toward their private suite. The pill bottle stood on her mother's bedside table. She shook a tablet into her palm and hurried back, pausing in the kitchen long enough to fill a glass with water. "Here, take this."

"Merci, my dear." The woman tipped her head back and swallowed, closing her eyes and resting her head on the back of the burgundy wing chair.

She slowly she opened her eyes, focusing them on something to the right of her daughter.

Chas turned to follow the direction of her mother's gaze and saw the delivery boy standing a few feet away. She swallowed a gasp. This was no boy. He had a thick mop of blond hair dipping over one eye. Dark blue eyes returned her stare. Chas's cheeks grew hot, but she couldn't stop staring.

"Why, it's Adam, isn't it?" Her mother's voice shattered her trance, and Chas pulled her gaze away. "Adam Silverhorn."

"Yes, ma'am."

"So you finally decided to return."

"Yes, ma'am." He grinned at her.

"About time, I'd say."

"Yes, ma'am." He chuckled. "I kind of thought so myself."

Chas studied him openly. The last time she'd seen him, he was a scrawny youth with a habit of plunging into trouble. Then he had up and disappeared, following the gold rush to the Klondike, or so the story went. She tried to think if she had heard where he'd been since then.

"So where have you been all this time?" her mother prodded.

Again Adam chuckled. "How long do you have?"

"Why don't you take tea with us and tell me?"

Chas jumped to attention. She had forgotten tea.

Behind her, Emma groaned. "The dearies will be here expecting everything to be ready." She hastened to the door. "I'll put the kettle on."

"I'd better hurry," Chas muttered and, turning to leave, stubbed her toe on the statue. She leaned over to set it upright.

"Let me." Adam bent over at the same time. Their faces were so close, she could see the glittering streaks in his irises.

She let him straighten the heavy statue. Suddenly she began to laugh. Adam regarded her with raised eyebrows. Out of the corner of her eye, she saw her mother's startled expression.

"Did I miss something?" Adam asked, looking at her.

Chas pointed at the statue. "It's Mother's protecting angel." Made of rough white pottery, the statue was an angel with wings folded at his back, a sword resting on the ground at his feet. She grinned. "Perhaps he was sleeping," she said to her mother.

"Away with you. You couldn't blame an angel for an old woman's foolishness."

Adam smiled at the woman. "Now, Miz LaBlanc, you don't look a day older than when I last saw you ten years ago."

Mother narrowed her eyes. "And I'm thinking you've developed a silver tongue to go with that last name of yours."

Chas headed toward the kitchen, scooping the teapot off the floor as she left.

Emma, busy placing china teacups on the big tray, turned as Chas hurried into the kitchen. "So that's Adam Silverhorn." She pressed her palm against her chest. "Be still, my racing heart." Fixing her eyes on Chas, she demanded, "Why didn't you tell me he was so dreamy looking?"

Instead of answering right away, Chas washed the teapot and warmed it with hot water. "Put some cookies on the flowered china serving plate." She scooped a handful of tea leaves into the warmed pot and filled it with boiling water. "I remember him with a nose that seemed too large for his face and arms too long for his sleeves." Her cheeks warmed again as she thought how she had stared unmercifully at the poor man. "He seems to have outgrown all that." She nodded. "I expect he'll set your poor young heart all aflutter."

Emma sniffed. "Oh, you old grandma. I declare. I don't know how you manage without your cane." Her voice wheezed and wobbled. Then she glared at Chas. "I am eighteen, you know. You make six years sound like a lifetime."

Chas sighed as she arranged the serving tray. "It feels like it sometimes."

Beyond the far door, hinges creaked, and a shuffling sound started down the hall.

"Hurry. Take in the serving tray." Chas grabbed the teapot and followed on Emma's heels to the sitting room. They set up tea on the small table reserved for this ritual. "You look after things while I get Mother." She hurried across the hall to the dining room, pausing in the doorway to take in the scene.

Adam had pulled a chair close to her mother's side and, leaning back, spoke to the older woman.

"It was like nothing you could imagine. In fact, if I didn't have the photos and drawings to prove it, many people would call me a liar."

His voice was low and lazy yet filled with a melody that told Chas whatever he was talking about gave him pleasure and excitement.

Mother turned and saw her daughter. "It's teatime, Adam. Do join us. You can tell me more." She nodded toward Chas. "Get my cane—will you, dear? I think I left it in the hall."

Chas retrieved it from outside the door. "I can't imagine what Doc Johnson is going to say when you have to explain you decided you could get along without this."

Her mother leaned forward, one hand on top of her cane. "Never you mind, young lady. I'm not going to cry over spilt milk. What's done is done. I'll just be more careful from now on." She reached a hand for Adam's arm. "If you'd be so good as to assist me to the other room—"

"My pleasure."

Chas grinned. Her mother had a way of bringing out the best and the kindest in people.

Following them to the sitting room, she glanced around. Mrs. Banner had eased into the armless padded chair where she always sat and peered over her glasses as the trio entered the room. Her head bobbed up and down as she watched the procession.

"Marie." She focused on Mother, then tilted her nose to study Adam. "Who is this young man?"

Mother lowered herself into the rocking chair across from Mrs. Banner, murmuring her thanks to Adam and waving him to the chair at her side.

"Ida," she leaned toward the older woman and raised her voice, "you remember Adam. Adam Silverhorn."

Mrs. Banner drew back in the chair. "Pshaw. Why would I want corn? This is teatime," she said with a huff.

"No, no." Mother's voice grew louder. "Not corn. Silverhorn."

Mrs. Banner pulled her handkerchief through her fingers. "I don't care if it is summer corn. All I want are tea and cookies." She looked down her nose at the other woman. "Now who is this young man?"

Chas turned away, hiding a smile. Sometimes there was simply no way of getting through to Mrs. B, but Mother never seemed ruffled from trying.

"Adam. Adam from the store."

Mrs. B bobbed her head, several gray hairs straying around her face. "Why didn't you say so? Now where's that girl with the tea?"

Emma set the cup at her elbow.

Even though Chas knew exactly what Mrs. B would want, she played out the ritual, carrying the creamer and sugar bowl to the regal lady. "Would you like milk or sugar?"

"I do believe I'll have a little of each. A rounded spoonful of sugar and a splash of milk, if you please."

Chas knew without looking that Emma would be silently mouthing the words, and she lowered her head to avoid the girl's knowing wink.

"Adam, would you like tea?"

His eyes flashed with bright spears of silver. For a moment his look seemed to isolate the two of them.

Emma shoved the plate of cookies under his elbow. "Cookies, Adam?"

Chas turned away, setting the creamer and sugar bowl on the tea table.

The clock on the mantel bonged three times. Chas straightened, listening, and met Emma's eyes. Upstairs a door closed with a muted thud, and footsteps could be heard crossing the length of the hall and descending the stairs.

Emma waggled her eyebrows. "You could set your clock by him."

A stiffly upright man stepped through the door, his gait measured and precise.

"Good afternoon, Mr. Elias," Mother murmured. "Tea is ready."

"Good afternoon."

His nod included them all. He took the cup Emma offered and sat ramrod straight on a hard wooden chair, the light from the window glistening on his head.

Chas sat on the overstuffed green sofa and glanced around. This was her home—the only home she had ever known and certainly a home like no other. But despite its unusual nature, she had been surrounded by love here. Every aspect of her life had been overshadowed by the knowledge of God's love. She turned and met her mother's gaze and smiled.

This ritual was almost as old as she was. Afternoon tea—punctually at two fifty-five. Over the years some of the regulars had gone, while others had come to take their places—some for a short time; others, like Mr. Elias, for longer periods. Mrs. B had been there longer than Chas or even her mother.

They each had their special chair—not by right of ownership but by silent consent. Teacups were arranged in their own fashion—her mother's on the stool at her knee; Mrs. B's at her elbow on the skirted round table; Mr. Elias's balanced in one hand.

The room itself was as unchangeable as the tea ritual. The same burgundy drapes were fastened back with the same faded wine-colored rope. Despite her subtle attempts, Chas had been unsuccessful in changing a single feature. Every knickknack was quickly returned to its original position as soon as she left the room, each chair shoved back to its precise placement. Even the angel picture hanging over the fireplace had remained unchanged since before her birth. She looked up at it. A kind-faced angel robed in a white gown caught the fingertips on the outflung hand of a child stepping on rocks as she made her way across a swiftly flowing river.

Indeed, the only thing different was Adam's presence, and every eye sought him.

"Mr. Elias," Mother said, her voice soft and gentle, "this is Adam, Ed Silverhorn's son."

Mr. Elias nodded his head in acknowledgment. "Pleased to meet you."

"He was telling me about his trip to the Klondike." She tilted her head to Adam. "And where else did you say?"

Adam stood and shook Mr. Elias's hand, returning to his seat before he answered. "I spent three years in the Klondike and two more in Alaska. From there I explored down the coastline and among the Gulf Islands. After that I spent some time in the interior of B.C." He shrugged. "Then I decided I was heading in the right direction and came home."

Chas let her breath out in a little whistle. "All that in ten years!" She shook her head. She had been no farther than the edge of town. "Did you find gold?"

He chuckled. "No. Found something better, though."

She squinted at him. "Better than gold?"

"Yes," he said, nodding. "I found life."

She studied him. Life was what you made of it. Life was here and now. It was found in making wise choices and adjusting. It was in being content where God put you. There was no need to chase off to the ends of the world to find life and live it, and his suggestion of it made her want to argue.

Adam spoke before she could do more than open her mouth. "I can see you're wondering what I mean." He leaned back and smiled up at the ceiling as if seeing something wonderful and elusive. "I got to see firsthand the events that are making history. I recorded them. And for the most part I lived them." He suddenly lowered his head and fixed her with a sharp look. "That's what I mean."

She pulled her gaze away, studying the brown liquid in her cup. "Some of us live life in the minuscule, seeing it and experiencing it and enjoying it through the tiny details of every day." She straightened, and her gaze locked with his. "The beauty of the sunset, the sweetness of the lilac blossoms, the sound of the birds singing. We learn to take what God has given us and appreciate it."

Emma sighed. "But how exciting to be able to see so many new and wonderful things. It thrills me. Tell me, Mr. Silverhorn—what was the most wonderful thing you saw?"

"Please call me Adam." His expression grew serious. "I guess I would have to agree with Chastity. It's the wonders of nature that are the most profound."

His blue eyes forbade Chas to turn away when she would have dismissed his pronouncement. "When I saw the sun glistening off the great glaciers of the Yukon and realized the challenge the snow-covered mountains would be to the puny men trying to scale them—" He half-laughed. "Well, I was so awestruck, I could barely breathe."

Chas tried to pull her gaze away. She tried to blink. But she was caught by his intensity.

Emma let out a whoosh of air. "It sounds wonderful."

"Adam," Mother said, "you mentioned photos and drawings."

He turned toward her, and Chas sank back against the cushions. "Yes, I have quite a collection. I tried to record everything I saw."

Mother nodded. "Perhaps we can see some of your recordings."

"Of course." He relaxed. "I plan to display some of them at my shop, but I have hundreds more than I can display. I'd be glad to bring some for you to see." His glance included Chas.

She pressed her finger to her lips. Adam Silverhorn might have grown from a gangly youth to a handsome well-built man; he might have seen life, as he put it. But she wasn't about to let him turn her life upside down with talk of faraway places and exciting events. She knew the boundaries of her life, and right now they were the four walls of Brownlee's Boardinghouse. And with that she was content. There was only one thing she wished she could change—

"A shop?" her mother asked.

"I'm planning to turn the side room Father uses for storage into a photography shop. That way I can help in the store and continue with my own business, as well."

Mr. Elias nodded. "It sounds to me as if you've had yourself a fine adventure, young fella." Without bending his back, he stood to his feet, setting his cup on the tea table. "Now if you will all excuse me, I must leave." And he marched from the room.

Chas did not have to listen to know his steps would lead up the stairs and into his room, where he would get his coat and then walk back down the stairs and out the front door. He would be gone exactly one hour and thirty minutes and return to his room until precisely fifteen minutes before the evening meal, when he would once again descend the stairs. The only variable was whether or not he would take a small parcel with him or return from his outing with one.

Emma's dark comments one time had sparked curiosity as to the contents of the parcels.

Mrs. B's fingers fussed at the variegated pink doily she had withdrawn from her cloth bag.

Chas caught the sorrow in her mother's look and swallowed back her own sadness. Mrs. B's joints were daily growing stiffer, and her eyes were no longer able to pick out the stitches as she crocheted. Chas was certain she worked as much by feel as by sight. The current project was knotted and curled.

Her mother reached out for the doily. "You've made good progress, Ida. This is lovely."

"I can't seem to get the pattern quite right," Mrs. B said, her voice thin. "Could you see what's the matter, Marie?"

Mother held the half-made doily in her lap and quickly pulled out several rows. "I think I can solve the problem." She took the hook from Mrs. B's lap, made a few stitches, and gave the handiwork back to the older lady. "It was only a knot."

Mrs. B bent close, examining it as much with her fingers as her eyes. She sighed and lifted her head. "Thank you, Marie. I'm sorry to be such a bother."

Mother patted her hand. "Ida, you are never a bother."

Emma stood up. "I guess I'd better get back to work." She paused in front of Adam. "I think your life sounds real exciting. I wish I could do something like that." Then she laughed. "But since it's doubtful I'll ever get the chance, I'd love to see your pictures."

Adam stood to his feet and smiled at her. "That's what they're for—to give people who can't be there the chance to see what it was like."

Chas followed Emma. As she started to pass Adam, he murmured, "It's good to see you again."

She stopped and turned to meet his gaze. Ten years ago she was barely more than a child. She narrowed her eyes. What did he remember of her back then?

"Thank you for tea," he said with a grin, as if guessing her thoughts.

"You're welcome," she said and fled to the kitchen.

But if she thought the kitchen would provide relief from thinking about Adam, she had forgotten to take Emma into account.

The girl grabbed her arm and whispered, "Isn't he something? Almost too good to be true."

"Emma! Just because he's been to the Klondike and back doesn't make him exceptional. Besides, what about his poor parents? I wonder how they felt about him disappearing into the wild blue yonder for so long?" She pursed her lips. "How old is Jack Silverhorn? Nine. Ten. Why, I'd venture a guess Jack was born after Adam left."

"And you'd be right." The deep voice behind her almost made her choke. "Furthermore, Ellen was only seven. That's part of the reason I've come back. I wanted to get to know my little brother and sister."

Chas swallowed hard and forced herself to turn toward him. "Forgive me," she murmured. "I have no right to concern myself with your affairs."

"It hasn't offended me," he said with a chuckle, his eyes shining.

"Matter of fact, I expect I'll be the center of a lot of speculation. And I expect I can handle it."

Emma stepped over to Adam, her face glowing. "I think it's wonderful you've come back. So will everyone else."

"More than likely most of them will think I'm crazy," he said, his gaze never leaving Chas's face. "Crazy for going, crazy for the work I do, and crazier still for coming home and bringing it with me. Isn't that right, Chas?"

At this Chas had to smile. She shook her head. "No, I don't think 'crazy' would be the word most people would use." She pressed her finger to her lips. "Let's see, maybe strange, unusual—" She blinked. Those were the same words she was sure people used to describe her life. "You're right. I think you'll be able to live with it."

He nodded and then turned toward the table. "I'm sorry I dumped your groceries like that." He picked up the sack of oatmeal. "Where do you want me to put this?"

Chas had been about to say he didn't need to bother, but Emma spoke up. "In the pantry—I'll show you."

Adam followed her. Chas turned to the pile of rhubarb Emma had flung on the table. It had to be washed, chopped, and hurried into the pies if they were to be baked in time.

After she and Adam returned, Emma picked up the basin of potatoes and grabbed a paring knife. Adam paused at the table, and Chas glanced up to see what he wanted.

"I'm sorry about your mother's accident. Will she be all right?"

Chas gulped. "I don't know if she'll ever be all right again."

"What do you mean?"

She looked down again, continuing her task as she talked. "She fell down the stairs almost two years ago. She was carrying an armload of washing and didn't realize how close she was to the first step." Chastity took a deep breath. "Doc Johnson said no bones were broken, but he thought she must have torn something inside. Her hip doesn't seem to want to get better."

She shrugged, her fingers trembling as she remembered the first days after the accident when her mother was black and blue and in so much pain.

"I'm sorry," Adam murmured. "I'm sure it's been difficult for you."

Chas stared at the pies for a moment, breathing slowly, letting peace fill her before she lifted her face and smiled at Adam. "The worst part has been seeing her pain. As for the rest of it—all my life I've been taught God is as close as a prayer and His angels ready to minister to us. It was a thought that carried me through my childhood."

At this Adam nodded.

"But this situation made it more than a teaching. I wouldn't have traded it for anything," she added.

Caught in his blue-eyed gaze, something inside her responded to his unblinking intensity. Not a word was spoken, yet she felt a volume had been said.

"It's as if living makes life real," he said, nodding slowly.

It was exactly how she felt. Life was not chasing adventure or seeing new and exciting things. It was experienced in the living of every day to the full. She tried to make it the motto of her life.

"But—"

He smiled. "I know. You thought I had to roam the edges of the world to find meaning for my life. But that's not how it is. Sure, I want to see and touch those far places. I want to witness the making of history." He shook his head. "But I know that is not where or how life gets meaning."

"So what have you discovered gives life meaning?" Chas realized she'd been holding her breath so that her words sounded airy.

Emma sat with knife poised motionless over the basin, her eyes wide and fixed on Adam's back. Her surprise was natural. Chas herself wondered how the conversation had taken such a serious turn.

"That's easy," Adam answered, his expression warming. "Meaning and satisfaction come from inside oneself." He tilted his head to one side. "It's in knowing that all is right with the world because God is in control, and all is right with me because I am one of His children."

Her jaw slackened. Chas couldn't tear her gaze from the look of peace and assurance in his face. Deep inside, something unfolded as she recognized a faith matching her own.

"That's it exactly," she murmured.

Emma's knife clanged against the basin. "My! To listen to you two, one would think life should be a safe, narrow existence." She grunted. "Adam, I thought you of all people would understand the need for something more."

His eyes lingered on Chas a moment longer before he turned toward the younger girl. "I guess there's no point in my saying there's no place in life for adventure." He grinned at her. "Life would certainly be dull without it. But that's not what I'm talking about." He faced Chas again. "With or without that sort of thing, peace is found inside."

"Hmph! Sometimes I think there's a tad too much peace around here," Emma retorted.

Chas had been working as they talked, and now she fluted the edges of the crusts and slashed the tops. She grabbed a pie in each hand and eased around Adam to slip them in the oven. Turning to get the other two pies, she almost collided with him where he stood at her elbow with a pie in each hand.

"Thank you," she half-whispered, glad of the excuse to lower her head and hide her confusion as she slid them into the oven. She closed the oven door, wiped her hands on her apron, and straightened a towel on the handle. She had no choice then but to face him.

His expression sober, he studied her face. "You've grown from a girl into a woman." His gaze lingered on her nose, then dropped to her chin before circling back to her eyes. "A fine woman. But in many ways I think you're still the same—serene and inscrutable."

His assessment both surprised and dismayed her. It made her sound like one of Mother's lifeless statues—like the one by the window of the dining room—smooth, cool porcelain.

Adam sighed. "I better get back to the store before Father thinks I've gotten lost." He dusted a speck of flour from his pants. "Thanks again. I'll be seeing you."

He turned and strode out the door before Chas could pull her thoughts together.

Emma watched her curiously. "Exactly how well did you know Adam?"

Chas shrugged, busying herself with cleaning up the table. "I barely remember him. He was"—she paused—"oh, probably three or four years older. Of course I knew who he was. After all, it's a small town."

Emma set the pot of potatoes aside ready to put on the stove when the time came. "He sure seemed to know a lot about you."

"I'm surprised he even remembers me."

"You must have done something for him to have such a definite opinion of what you were like."

Chas scowled as she tried to think of all she knew of Adam.

"He liked to draw," she mused out loud. "I remember him getting into trouble at school because he would waste his time drawing instead of listening." She chuckled. "I do recall he liked to see things real close so he could draw them better. One time he tried to see a beehive closer and got stung rather badly for his efforts."

Emma's eyes grew round. "Ouch."

"He swelled up all bumpy." She stared out the window at the memories from long ago. "Another time he climbed up a tree to look into a bird's nest." She gasped. "I remember now. He fell out of the tree and landed on top of Esther James and me." She giggled. "Esther was so mad, I thought she would hurt him. She might have if he hadn't hidden."

Chas remembered the rest of the incident to herself. Esther had thought Adam ran toward the store, but he had ducked behind the fence. Chas had seen, but she hadn't told. Later that day, or perhaps it was the next day, he had thanked her for letting him escape and handed her a sheet of paper. He was gone before she could look at it. It was a drawing of her—one that made her look grown up and beautiful with her fair hair circling her face and a bouquet of wild flowers lifted to her chin. She had treasured the drawing for years, hoping she would someday be as beautiful as he had made her look. She thought for a moment. The drawing was probably still tucked away among her school items.

Chas turned away from the window. "I'll clean up the tea things and check on Mother."

Emma nodded. "I'll get this mess tidied up." Already she was heading for the door to throw the vegetable peelings on the garden.

Mrs. B had returned to her room, no doubt eager to get back to her crocheting.

Mother sat in the chair, head tilted back, eyes closed. She heard her daughter approaching and opened her eyes.

Chas's heart tightened at the weary lines around her mother's eyes. "Come, Mama—I'll help you to your room. I think you should take a little rest before supper."

"*Merci*, my dear."

She let her daughter help her to her feet, and together they headed down the hall toward the bedroom. She stifled a groan as Chas helped her lie down.

"I don't know what I would do without you, Chastity," she murmured.

Chas pulled a quilt over her shoulders and brushed her hair back from her forehead. Here and there a few silver strands showed up in her mother's black hair, still thick and luxuriant. Again Chas wondered how her mother could be so dark-haired while she had hair as blond as bottled sunshine. The father she never knew must have been fair haired.

At one time she had resented her hair coloring. People would touch her head and make comments about it—"angel wings," "goose down." But as she had grown older, people had stopped touching, and her hair had become thick and heavy, no longer flying about her face like thistledown. Chas had learned to accept her fairness, tying her hair at the back of her neck and, for the most part, paying little attention to it.

She kissed her mother's brow, her hands lingering. Her insides tightened until she could barely breathe. Her mother had already suffered so much pain with her hip.

Please, God, don't let her suffer anymore.

Mother sighed and closed her eyes. Chas slipped away to the kitchen.

"I'm going to Doc Johnson's and ask him to drop by to see Mother this evening," she told Emma. "Keep an eye on the pies, will you?"

"Of course. Is she in a great deal of pain?"

"She's trying to hide it, but she can scarcely move." Chas took a trembling breath. "I'm guessing she's undone everything."

"Just when she was getting better." Emma shook her head. "It's too bad. But you run along. Take your time." She smiled. "Take the 'long' way home. I can manage here."

Chas laughed. "I know you can." Emma had proven herself capable since the day she walked into the kitchen shortly after her mother's accident.

Chas stepped into the sunshine, lifting her face to the warmth. She would never have managed running the boardinghouse without Emma's help—not after Stella, the woman who had worked for her mother for years, had walked out in a huff declaring she would not work for a young girl. Although dismayed by Stella's leaving, Chas had smiled at being described as a young girl, for she felt she was well on her way to being an old maid. She reached the sidewalk, squinting against the brightness of the sky. It was beginning to look as if she would spend her life running the boardinghouse for her mother—doomed to be a spinster for life.

For about the space of a heartbeat, disappointment swelled in her chest. Then she smiled, comforting herself with the assurance that God would work things out for her good.

In Your time, Lord—in Your time.

The streets of Willow Creek rang with summer. Chastity's steps held a little spring as she made her way to the doctor's office. A few minutes later, after leaving a message with Doc Johnson's nurse, she stood on the steps outside his office.

Across the street and up a few buildings was Silverhorn's Mercantile. At that moment Chas saw Adam walk out of the store with Jack following him. She couldn't make out what they were saying, but Jack was waving his arms and talking rapidly. Adam ruffled his younger brother's hair and nodded. Together they stepped into the shadowed doorway of the storeroom. Chas waited a moment longer, but they didn't reappear. Soon she could hear the sound of hammering. Adam must not be wasting any time getting to work on his shop.

Rather than turn her steps toward home, she decided to do as Emma had suggested and take the long way down the side streets past the elegant homes of Willow Creek's prosperous businessmen. She thought the three-story, turreted house and the two replicas farther down the street were beautiful. The yards were finely manicured. But in her mind, they were not places to spend time dreaming about, and she hummed under her breath as she strolled along the pleasant streets.

She glanced about her, noting how the flowers were thriving in one yard and admiring the new green trim on a house across the street. She breathed deeply of the familiar scents of lilacs, a freshly mowed lawn, and the distant underlying odor of a nearby farm. She had never been more than a few miles from this town in her whole life, and somehow she couldn't imagine why anyone would want to wander very far away.

She turned a corner. Her steps quickened until she neared the end of the block and slowed down. She took two more steps, then stopped, touching the white picket fence and staring at the low white house, surrounded by perennials and low bushes. Tall poplars lined one side of the yard, with a stately spruce forming the backdrop. A narrow veranda ran the length of the house.

After a moment, she made her way past the gate to the corner of the fence and turned down the sidewalk. She peered into the backyard, where a stone pathway led to a tiny lattice arbor under which stood a white wrought iron table and two matching chairs. A book lay turned over on the table, a cup beside it.

Her heart beat calmly when she finally turned away, a smile tugging at her lips as she made her way toward the boardinghouse.

Chapter 2

Emma carried in the gravy while Chas came behind with the potatoes. She checked to see if everything was in place then pulled out the chair at her mother's right.

As soon as she was seated, Mother took her hand. "Let's pray."

They all bowed their heads, and there was a moment of silence.

They had offered a blessing that way since Chas was nine years old—when Mr. Brownlee died and her mother inherited the boardinghouse.

At the time, curious about the change from her mother's asking the blessing, Chas had waited until they were in their own rooms, the rooms where Mr. and Mrs. Brownlee had previously slept, before she asked, "Mama, why did we have to pray like that?"

Her mother sat down beside her on the edge of the bed that had been moved from the upstairs bedroom. "Some of those men at our table would feel belittled to have a woman ask the blessing. This way nobody needs to be offended."

"Amen." Mother's word was the signal to begin, as hands reached for the dishes and spooned the food onto their plates.

Chas looked around the table.

Mrs. B sat across from her, where her mother could unobtrusively give whatever help she needed.

Next to Mrs. B was Beryl Hanes, her fan of dark curls emphasizing her plumpness. Beryl had been with them almost a year and worked at the bank. Catching Chas watching her, Beryl smiled.

Chas smiled back before continuing her quick assessment of the others at the table.

Carl and Orsby Knutsen were newcomers. They had come from the farm a month ago and managed to find jobs on the section crew of the Canadian Pacific Railway. Still too shy to say anything in front of the others, they kept their heads down, focusing on their food.

Louise, secretary to a lawyer, was the last one on that side. She had been at the boardinghouse a little longer than Beryl. Louise was tall, blond, and willowy. Chas admired her bearing. Even her name was elegant—Louise Leishman.

Mr. Elias maintained his post at the end of the table with quiet dignity.

Emma sat next to him so she could watch to see if anything was needed at that end of the table.

Between Chas and Emma were Roy Vandenberg, who worked in the drugstore, and John Nelson, who worked in the land titles office. They had been living in the boardinghouse since last fall.

Michael sat beside Chas. Besides Emma, who lived with her folks at the far edge of town, Michael, a teacher, was the only one who didn't live in the house. But he was regular enough not to be thought of as a guest.

"I stopped in at Silverhorn's on my way home from work," Louise said in her cool, controlled tones. "The place was in quite a state of confusion. I believe the older son, Adam, has returned. Seems he's going to set up a photography shop in conjunction with the store."

Beryl leaned forward. "I was there, too. And I saw the most amazing painting. You should have seen it." Her look included everyone. "It was huge. Even bigger than the one over the fireplace in the other room."

Chas knew she meant the guardian angel picture.

"What was it of?" Roy asked.

Roy had a need to know the particulars of everything. One time the discussion had been about a trip to Banff, and someone said it looked like Main Street sprung from the roots of Cascade Mountain. Roy kept asking how high the mountain was and how far it was from the administrative building to the Banff Springs Hotel until everyone became quite annoyed.

But this time Beryl showed no annoyance. "It was of a mountain but nothing like the mountains we have here. It was all ice with light glistening off it and the sun setting—or maybe it was rising, for all I know. Anyway, it tinted parts of the snow with pink." She waved a hand. "But pink isn't the right name for the way the color shone."

Louise broke in. "Goodness, Beryl. You make it sound mystical."

"It was. You'll have to see for yourself."

"Where was this mountain?" Roy demanded.

"I asked. Mr. Silverhorn said it was in the Yukon. Then his son—"

"Adam," Louise supplied.

"Yes, Adam. He came in and said it was Muir Glacier." She sighed. Her hands lay still, and she got a dreamy look on her face. "He said to think of Niagara Falls frozen stiff, add about thirty feet to its height, and you begin to imagine what it's really like." For a moment she stared across the table at nothing in particular then laughed a little. "It was very romantic."

Wondering if she meant the painting or Adam, Chas saw that everyone was caught up in Beryl's description. Even the Knutsen brothers lifted their heads and listened as if it were as important as food.

"Muir Glacier then. Not really a mountain—is that what you're saying?" Roy had to know.

Beryl shrugged. "Looked like a mountain to me. A mountain covered with ice."

"Remember she said the Yukon? Isn't it always frozen?" Even John, who usually avoided taking part in discussions unless they had to do with crops or farm prices, was drawn into the conversation.

Michael spoke up. "They have summer, too. The sun shines twenty-four hours a day."

"Adam was here today," Emma said. "He told us about his travels."

Emma made it sound as if they had been visited by royalty.

"Here?"

"Did he say where he'd been?"

"Who is this Adam?"

They were asking so many questions that Emma waved her hands in the air. "I wasn't the only one who saw him. Chas, Mr. Elias, Mrs. B, Miz LaBlanc—they all saw him. In fact, he picked Miz LaBlanc off the floor."

The young people turned to Chas's mother.

"Why were you on the floor?" Roy demanded.

"I fell."

Beryl reached for her hand. "Are you all right?"

Before her mother could answer, Chas said, "She's hurt her hip again."

Everyone but Mrs. B, muddling over her meat, looked at Mother.

"I'm so sorry," Louise said gently.

"I suppose this means you won't be wanting your job back anytime soon?" Michael murmured close to Chas's ear.

"Shh." She shook her head, not wanting her mother to hear.

He leaned closer and whispered, "We'll talk later."

She nodded and turned back to the conversation.

Emma told about Adam's visit. "He said he would give Miz LaBlanc a private showing of his pictures."

"I'm sure he didn't mean anything as formal as that," Mother said. "And he didn't mean only me."

Roy reached for the potatoes before he asked, "So he's planning to stay?"

Emma shrugged. "I guess. Sort of."

"Until something more exciting comes up." Chas smiled in an attempt to take any sting from her words.

Roy demanded to know how long Adam had been gone and where.

Emma did her best to supply the answers.

Beryl fairly bounced on her chair. "I heard him tell his father he was going to display some pictures from the Klondike. Doesn't it sound exciting?"

"I wonder if he would let the children see them." Michael strained forward. "Think of how educational it would be." He turned to Chas. "What do you think, Chas? Do you think he would give a talk at the school?"

"That's a good idea. Why not ask him?" She pushed back from the table. "I'll get the pie."

Emma gathered up the plates and serving dishes as Chas sliced pie and spooned on whipped cream.

When she returned, the conversation still centered on Adam Silverhorn and his adventures. Chas held her tongue as she passed the dessert. She longed to bring everyone back to reality, but everything she thought of sounded like the words of a bitter old maid. She certainly didn't want people to have that impression, but all this excitement about a man who had left his home and family without a backward look seemed uncomfortably out of proportion. It made normal life appear narrow and dull, which it wasn't. Life was full and satisfying.

Like now, for instance.

Chas slid Mrs. B's plate under her arm and set the fork where she would find it without searching. She felt pleasure in seeing Mrs. B happy; in the grateful comments of the boarders as they sampled the pie; in the closeness of her "family." She met Michael's dark brown gaze and smiled. No, she couldn't imagine why anyone would feel the need to seek adventure elsewhere.

Chas and Emma carried the dishes back to the kitchen and cleaned off the dining room table. Chas wanted to do the dishes right away, but Michael pulled out a handful of papers. "I thought you might like to read some of the essays the class wrote."

"Emma, I'll be a minute." She dried her hands and sat down again, taking the papers Michael offered. He often brought assignments and tests for her to help check, along with regular news of the class she had taught until two years ago—the class that was now his responsibility. "What was the topic?"

" 'The Importance of Being Trustworthy.' "

"Good topic." She read the first one. "Annie's developing her expression."

Michael leaned back. "She's improving, but I'm having a hard time deciding how to grade the essay."

Chas straightened. "But why?"

He pulled his tie to the center of his shirt and folded his long arms across his chest before he answered. "It's written well enough, but I don't think she's properly addressed the topic."

With a puzzled look, Chas read the essay through again. "She talks about truth a lot. Isn't that being trustworthy?"

"True. But she's missed the biggest part—doing what you say you will and what others are counting on from you. We talked about this a long time before I gave them this assignment."

Still feeling as if they were talking about different things, Chas asked, "So how did you explain trustworthiness to a group of ten- and eleven-year-olds?"

"I told them about my brother, Timothy, and me. When we were growing up, I tried to be honest about some of the things I felt, and it was perceived as a failure to do what I should. On the other hand, Timothy did what he was told while never agreeing with anything my parents believed. They felt they could count on him. And I learned my lesson: Sometimes it doesn't matter how we feel inside. We should simply do what's expected."

His reasoning troubled Chas. "You make it sound like believing and doing are different things. Isn't that hypocrisy of the worst sort?"

He shook his head. "Not exactly. Sometimes you have to do things even when you don't like or agree with them. Take yourself as an example."

She drew back. "Me?" When had she acted out of insincerity?

"Certainly. You were happy as a teacher. You had plans."

He read the denial in her expression and added, "You know you did. You told me how you hoped to get yourself a little house someday."

She wanted to explain, but he continued before she had a chance.

"Then you had to quit teaching to look after this place." His gaze swept the room, then touched on the ceiling including the rooms upstairs. "So what do you do? You smile and do your work as if it's all that matters."

"You make it sound as if inside I'm a quivering mass of resentment and unfulfilled dreams."

He didn't answer, only held her gaze.

"But I'm not. I was disappointed at first, but I wasn't unhappy about it. I'm not unhappy now."

"You certainly have maintained a good face, and that's truly admirable. Even today, after your mother fell again, you smiled and acted as if it didn't matter that you're stuck here even longer."

"Michael." She couldn't believe he had misjudged her so. Michael of all people. She began again on a quieter note. "I'm not pretending—putting on a good face, as you say. I'm content. And, yes, happy. Happy to be helping my mother and doing a good job running the house. But more than that, I'm convinced God is in control. He will work out what is best for me. He is totally trustworthy."

"You're right, of course. But I wanted the children to express something more than simply being honest. There's more to it."

She nodded. "I realize that. But shouldn't what we believe reveal itself in how we act?" Not waiting for him to answer, she bent her head and focused on the next essay.

It was true she had thought her life would be different. Before her mother's accident, Chas took it for granted the older woman would manage the boarding-house until she was too old to do so and then sell it. And Chas would teach until—she closed her eyes and breathed deeply. Her dreams had included love and marriage and a quiet little home that sheltered only her, her husband, and their children.

But she had fought her disappointment and won. She would leave her future in God's hands. And above all, she would not allow herself to become a bitter old maid with a razor-sharp tongue. She pictured Pastor Simpson's sister, Martha, with her puckered mouth and sour-apple comments, and shuddered. Even if she never married, she vowed she would not let bitterness turn her into another Martha Simpson.

Forcing her mind back to the papers in her hands, she read young Joel's comments about the dire results of being untrustworthy and chuckled.

The next piece belonged to Jack Silverhorn, and she read it with sharpened interest.

"Being trustworthy," she read, "means being honest all the time even when it's hard. It means being honest in what you say and do. It means doing what you said you will even when you change your mind and don't want to do it. It means always coming back. It's important to be trustworthy so people know what to expect from you."

She put her finger on her chin. *Always coming back.* Did Jack mean Adam, the brother he had met for the first time a few days ago? She hated to think of Jack's being hurt when Adam decided to leave again.

Michael pulled out another sheaf of papers, and Chas knew he was settling in for a night of correcting papers and working on lesson plans. But beyond the door, Emma rattled the dishes.

"Michael, I have to help Emma."

He barely glanced up. "Let her do it. It's her job."

"Not really," Chas said, sighing.

Emma had volunteered to extend her day until the supper dishes were done, but Chas knew Emma had a life apart from her job and would be eager to go home or out with friends.

"But I thought we would work on the lesson plan for next week."

He looked up with a pleading, wide-eyed look she found hard to resist, and she wondered, not for the first time, if he did it on purpose.

"If you want to wait until I'm finished—"

He grinned. "I have nothing else to do."

Chas hurried to the kitchen. "I'm sorry," she told Emma. "You go on home. I'll finish up."

Emma shook her head. "I'll stay, or you won't finish until time for bed." She plunged her hands into the hot dishwater. "Doesn't Michael realize you're busy?"

Chas shrugged. "I enjoy hearing about the children."

"I know you do, but he should have seen you had extra to do today."

Her mother had needed help back to her room. Mrs. B was fretful and wanting to talk. And there was still the dough to set to rise for tomorrow's bread. "It's just one of those days." She dried the dishes as fast as Emma washed them. "But then I guess every day has its share of good and bad."

"I guess overall it was a good day."

"I take it you mean Adam Silverhorn?" The younger girl was blinded by the man.

Emma sniffed. "You know I do. Stop pretending you weren't impressed."

"But I wasn't."

"You need your eyes checked."

Chas smiled. "Maybe I saw more than you think."

"So you're admitting he's handsome as a king?"

Chas's smile widened. "I didn't mean his looks."

Emma straightened to look at her. "What do you mean?"

"I saw a man who lives for adventure. How long do you think he'll be happy to hang around Willow Creek?"

Emma shrugged. "What difference does it make? I intend to enjoy his company as long as he's here—and see his pictures and ask him about his travels. If he goes again, at least I won't have wasted the opportunity. If he stays, so much the better."

Chas didn't answer. Emma's words held an element of truth, yet it wasn't enough for her.

Emma grabbed Chas by the shoulders, her wet hands making two damp spots, and pushed her toward the window. "What do you see out there?" she demanded.

Dusk had fallen, and the yard lay in gray shadows. "I can't see much. It's dark."

"You know what's out there. Tell me."

Chas shrugged. "Trees and grass and lilac bushes."

"Exactly. And how long do lilacs last?"

"Not nearly long enough."

"That's not the point. The point is, you enjoy them the little while they're in bloom." Emma returned to scrubbing the roaster.

"It's not the same."

Chas looked out for a minute longer. Trees and flowers were supposed to change with the seasons. She sighed and turned back to the chores. Michael was right. She longed for other things in life.

"Of course there's a very big difference between a bunch of lilacs and Adam." Emma sighed loudly to indicate her opinion in Adam's favor. "But you can enjoy it just the same and let it go when you have to." She paused. "As long as you don't fall in love."

Chas couldn't help the way she pulled back. "That would be begging for trouble."

Emma shrugged. "A person could always go with him on his adventures. Think of all the things you'd get to see."

It was so far removed from what she wanted that Chas's mouth went dry at the very thought. "I don't understand why anyone would want to go to those places."

Emma studied her. "Don't you find them interesting?"

"Oh, yes, I find them immensely interesting. They're like the different flowers of the seasons. Each season to be enjoyed and admired. It's just—" She didn't know how to explain that the mere thought of wandering from place to place, living from day to day, left her with an empty echo inside.

"Then I suggest you don't fall in love with Adam Silverhorn."

"You can count on that."

"Chas, are you finished yet?" Michael called from the other room.

"In a minute." She pushed back a strand of hair clinging to her cheek. She still had the dough to mix and a list of small things—like watering the African violets on the window ledge, putting away the clutter on the cupboard, wiping the table, checking to see if everything was handy for the morning. But those things could wait. It wasn't every night Michael called. Not quite.

She flipped off her apron. "You go on home now," she said to Emma. "I'll see you in the morning."

Emma shook her head. "Everything doesn't have to be done tonight."

"I know." Chas waited until Emma closed the door before she hurried to the dining room. "I'm sorry, Michael, but I'm finished now."

"Don't worry about it." He sat at the table, a fan of papers before him. "I understand." He grinned up at her. "It takes a lot of work to look after this place, and you do it very well. You should be proud of the job you do."

Tension slid from her shoulders. "Thank you. I like making sure things are well taken care of and doing little extras that make a difference."

"Just don't overdo it. You're only one person."

"I know."

He pulled out the chair next to him. They'd had this discussion before. She had explained how important it was to keep up the tradition her mother had started of running a boardinghouse that provided more than a room and meals. Her mother had drummed into her head from her earliest memories that they could never be certain of the identity of the people who lived in their rooms.

"Remember—some could even be angels we're entertaining unaware," she had said.

Chas lowered her head to hide a smile. She had to admit that to the best of her knowledge, she had never fed an angel, but the idea did make the work more satisfying.

As if reading her mind, Michael said, "Your mother places far too much emphasis on this angel business. A person can't turn around without running into a statue or a painting of one."

Chas laughed. "It's pretty hard to ignore, isn't it?"

"Downright impossible. It doesn't take all these paintings and things to be reminded of the angel's gift." He grabbed her hand, sending warm waves through her body. "One only has to look at you."

Chas knew her cheeks had blushed pink, and she shifted on her chair. With her free hand, she plucked at the papers on the table. "Michael, you're making me blush."

He squeezed her hand. "It's very becoming."

She returned his squeeze, relaxing under his gentle teasing. "You always make me feel better, you know."

He nodded. "Part of my job."

"I suppose the ad said, 'Besides taking over a classroom of nine- to twelve-year-olds, the applicant must be willing to keep former teacher informed of her students' progress and provide cheer and encouragement to said teacher.' "

He shrugged. "You have your standards for your job; I have mine."

She looked deep into his eyes, liking the steady warmth she saw, finding calmness settling into her bones. Michael was good for her. Steady as a rock. He would never pull up stakes and head for some far port in search of adventure. Not like Adam.

She blinked. *Where had that come from?*

"I thought of introducing some new arithmetic concepts next week. The grade-six class is ready to go on to. . ."

They spent a pleasant half hour discussing different exercises for the class before the bell sounded at the front door.

Chas hurried to answer it.

Doc Johnson, round as a toad, stood on the porch. He carried with him the slight odor of formaldehyde and disinfectant. "How's your mother? I understand she took another fall." His jowls shook as he talked. With a heavy tread, he stepped inside and hung his hat and jacket on a hook. "I warned her to take it easy."

"She isn't good at taking orders."

Doc chuckled, making his whole body jiggle. "She's always had a mind of her own." He rubbed his hands together a moment before picking up his worn black bag. "Though in all truth, it's what's made her such a strong woman. Now where is she?"

Chas waved down the hall. "In her room. I'll take you."

She led the way, pausing at the door. "Mother, Doc Johnson is here. I asked him to have a look at you."

Mother lay on her bed reading her Bible. She glanced over her glasses at the doctor. "Samuel, you needn't have bothered."

Doc stepped into the room. "Well, I'm already here, so let's have a look at what you've done to yourself."

"I'll be back in a few minutes." Chas pulled the door closed and hurried back to the dining room. "It's Doc. He's with Mother right now."

Michael shuffled the papers into a neat pile. "I'll be on my way."

She nodded. She really did need to look after things. She followed him to the door. "Thank you, Michael. It was nice to have your company."

"Saturday then?"

"Of course." It was a long-standing arrangement—every Wednesday and Saturday for supper and church on Sunday with dinner afterward.

"I hope it's nothing serious with your mother."

"Me, too."

They stood at the door, the silence between them as comfortable as a pair of worn slippers. He smiled at her, said, "See you then," and left.

"Bye." Chas pulled the door closed, her gaze resting on her hand curled around the knob, unable to identify the unsettled feeling in her stomach. She wished Michael had kissed her, but then he never had.

Pushing back her thoughts, she straightened her shoulders and hurried down the hall to knock on her mother's door.

"Come in," Mother called.

Doc sat on the edge of the bed, folding his stethoscope into his bag. He waited for Chas to close the door before he spoke. "Marie, I'd have to say you've probably undone all the good you accomplished over the last two years." He shook his head, his jowls swaying. "As I said before, you've torn a muscle or ligament or something. It's reluctant to get better."

Chas listened.

"I could suggest a trip to the city, where you could have surgery, but—"

Mother pushed herself up on her pillows. "It will get better, though, won't it, Samuel?"

Doc Johnson cleared his throat with the sound of a bullfrog in a muddy swamp. "Given time. Lots of time. I'm not one to say—sometimes things seem to improve when we least expect them to."

"How long?" Mother demanded. "How long will it take?"

The doctor shrugged. "There's always hope. You should never lose hope. I've seen my share of miracles."

"Samuel, you're waffling."

He heaved his bulk to his feet. "No doubt you'll have to put in another two years at the very least. Then there's your age."

She drew back. "What about my age?"

"All I'm saying is, you aren't as young as you used to be." He handed Chas a slip of paper. "Take this to the drugstore tomorrow and get some more tablets for the pain."

Chas walked him to the door. "Doc, how much chance do you give her of getting back on her feet?"

He shifted into his jacket and parked his hat on his round head. "My guess, and it's only a guess, is she'll gradually improve—if she takes it easy. But she'll never be strong again. As to running this house—" He shook his head. "I'll stop in again in a day or two. Call me if her pain gets severe."

After he left, Chas leaned on the door. Even though Doc Johnson had hedged his predictions, Chas understood what he refused to say: Mother would never be able to manage the boardinghouse again.

For two years she had willingly, happily done her job, always clinging to the knowledge, the hope, that at some point her mother would take over the task again.

Now she was faced with a harsher reality.

And she knew she must talk to her mother about it.

She silently prayed for wisdom as she returned to her mother's bedside.

"It doesn't sound too hopeful, does it, Mama?"

Her mother held a tiny angel carved from ivory. "I haven't given up yet."

"I would be disappointed if you did."

Squaring her shoulders, she faced the older woman. "Doc doesn't seem to think you'll ever be strong enough to run the boardinghouse again."

Mother's gaze veered to Chas's face. "Is that a fact?"

Chas refused to blink. "That's what he says."

"What if I prove him wrong?" Her voice was soft, but Chas recognized the stubborn lines on her face.

"I hope you do." She paused. "But it might take a very long time."

"Ah. But what seems long to you might seem but a passing thing to me." Her gaze had dropped back to the small ivory angel. "Who knows? Perhaps I'll get a miracle." Suddenly her dark eyes flashed at Chas. "I've had my share of them, you know."

"I know." Chas pulled a chair close and perched on the edge, leaning close to her mother. She waited for her hands to grow still, until she was sure she had her complete attention. "Mother, have you given any thought to selling the boardinghouse?"

The older woman pulled back and gave a little scream.

Chas half-rose, not knowing if it was the question that had given her mother pain or if the sudden movement had sent a spasm through her hip.

Mother shook her head, and Chas sank back.

"Chastity LaBlanc. How could you even ask such a thing?" Her mother clutched the angel. "This has been my home for twenty-five years. It's the only home you've ever known. Why, this is where a miracle led me." She tilted her chin. "No. I will not sell the boardinghouse. I'm not prepared to roll over and play dead. Not yet. Not by a long way."

"I don't mean for you to give up. I thought we could get a little house together, just the two of us. We'd have time to enjoy the things we've never had time for."

"And how would we live?" her mother asked abruptly. "Have you thought of that?"

Chas lifted her shoulders and let them drop again. "I could go back to teaching. And you'd have the money from the sale of this place. We would do all right."

Mother turned to her, studying her long and hard before speaking. "Have you been so unhappy here?" she whispered. "Have I done the wrong thing in raising you this way?"

"Oh, no, Mother." She grasped her mother's small, cool hand. "I've been happy. I still am. My life has been enriched by living here—seeing so many people and learning what pleases them. It's just—" She stood to her feet, paced to the end of the bed, then faced her mother. "I'm not unhappy. I'm not. I know God will take care of me and my future. But"—she sighed—"I don't want to live here the rest of my life. I don't want to run this house until the day I die."

"Now you're being melodramatic. No one expects you to stay here until you die. I just need you to keep things going until I'm back on my feet. Can you do that for me?"

Chas's shoulders sagged. "Of course I will. You know you can count on me."

"I know I can, *ma cherie.*" She held out a hand. "Come here."

Chas went to her side and allowed her mother to pull her down on the edge of the bed. "I know a couple of years seem a long time when you're young, but it isn't very long in view of a lifetime."

"I suppose not."

"I'll be better much faster than you think."

"I hope you are—for your sake, not mine."

Mother wrapped her arms around Chas. "I believe I'm doing the right thing. You know I wouldn't do anything I thought would hurt you."

"I know."

"You're the best thing that ever happened to me in my whole life, child. I love you."

Chas grinned. "Am I better than an angel?"

Mother chuckled. "Better by far. You're the gift of an angel." She paused. *"Ma cherie,* that is not quite correct. I know children are a gift of God, but in your case—"

Knowing how it upset her mother to talk about the past, Chas hugged her. "You're the best mother a girl could ever want. I love you lots."

Her mother gave her a little push. "Now away with you. Let your old mother rest."

Chas sighed. "I've still got bread dough to mix up. Then I'll be back, and we can read together." They always read the Bible together at bedtime.

Her mother smiled. "I'll be here."

Chas hurried from the room. She sang as she worked, but as she pounded and turned the dough, working it from a sticky mass to a smooth, elastic ball, a tear surprised her, trickling down her cheek and dripping off her chin. She dashed it away with the back of her wrist.

Chapter 3

Mr. Elias came through the door as Chas handed Mrs. B the cream and sugar. Mother was already sitting in her chair, sipping from her cup.

Chas had been up once in the night to give her mother a tablet for pain. She had managed to persuade her to take breakfast in bed, but she had refused to stay there for lunch. Seeing her face smooth, her eyes clear, the tightness across Chas's temples relaxed.

Her mother was strong and stubborn, traits that had stood her in good stead throughout her life. Perhaps she would, as she predicted, prove Doc Johnson wrong.

The bell at the back door clanged.

"I'll get it," Emma called from the kitchen, where she was getting scones.

Chas wasn't expecting any deliveries and wondered who could be calling. She didn't have to wonder long for Emma hurried into the room with the plate of scones in her hands and Adam at her heels.

"I've come for tea, if I may," he said.

"Why, how nice. Sit here beside me." Mother indicated the chair at her side. "Chastity, dear, get Adam some tea." She beamed as Adam pulled the chair closer.

"Of course," Chas murmured.

Mrs. B leaned forward for a better look.

Emma sprang to Adam's side, offering a scone.

Even Mr. Elias edged forward a couple of inches in his chair, his gaze lingering on the stack of papers in Adam's hand.

Chas grinned. Adam certainly had a way of making his presence felt.

He looked up as she handed him his tea and caught the amusement in her expression. For a moment they regarded each other openly. Then he shrugged and smiled.

"I thought they might enjoy seeing some pictures."

"Adam, how lovely of you to remember." Mother refused the scone Emma offered.

"We'll enjoy tea first," Adam said. "Then I'll show you what I've brought."

Mother made a wry face. "You're much too astute for a boy." She turned to Emma. "I've changed my mind. I'll have a scone after all."

Emma chuckled. "Miz LaBlanc, don't you go letting him turn your head."

Mother waved her away. "It's too late for me, but if I were your age"—she paused—"or Chastity's—"

"Mother!" Chas knew her cheeks were flaming pink. She turned a desperate look at Adam. "She thinks she's being funny."

Adam laughed—a low, pleasant sound—and met her gaze, his sparkling blue eyes never blinking. Then he turned away, allowing Chas to draw a deep breath.

"How are you today, Mrs. Banner?" he asked, raising his voice and leaning close.

"You're that nice young boy from the store, aren't you?" She squinted to get a better look. "You're very much like your mother, aren't you?"

"Yes, I am. Are you well today?"

"I remember when she first came here with her new husband and a little boy with a thatch of blond hair and eyes so blue—" She leaned closer, peering into Adam's right eye and then his left. "They're still as blue as God's great sky." She leaned back, satisfied.

Adam grinned. "Thank you, Mrs. B." He turned to Mr. Elias. "Good day, sir."

Mr. Elias nodded. "It's a fine day."

"You'll be going out later to enjoy the sun?"

"I take my daily constitutional every afternoon, rain or shine."

"Ah. But how much more pleasant on a day like today."

Mr. Elias tucked his chin in. "I've learned to forge ahead whatever the weather."

Adam studied him. "I'm guessing you were a soldier."

Mr. Elias pulled himself taller in his chair. "I was indeed in Her Royal Majesty's service for twenty years."

Chas gaped at the pair. Adam had discovered in five minutes something she hadn't known in the five years Mr. Elias had been there.

"Where did you serve?"

"Mostly in the East Indies."

Adam nodded, his expression thoughtful. "Someday I'd like to talk to you about your experiences, if I may?"

"That would be fine." Mr. Elias settled back, looking pleased.

"Are we finished with tea?" Mother asked, and everyone murmured agreement.

Chas quickly gathered up the cups as Adam untied the strings around his sheaf of papers.

"I thought I'd give you an overview of what it was like to go to the Klondike." He pulled out a photo. "You could take several routes, depending on where you disembarked, but all were treacherous beyond imagination. This series of photos depicts what is probably the most famous route—the passage to Dyea and then over the Chilkoot Trail."

Adam handed Mother a photo, which she studied before passing it to Emma. He then handed another to Mother.

"Men faced the most incredible odds. The strong overcame them. The weak turned back—or, worse, simply sat down and quit. Then there were the weak of a different sort who took advantage of other men's desperation and profited from it."

Chas found herself drawn to the tale of men against the elements—weather, terrain that would stop a mountain goat—things at once beautiful and terrifying.

"This picture shows the city of tents on the shores of Lynn Canal. Thousands of people arrived there." He passed around more pictures. "This is a group of men outfitted for the trail." He paused. "To reach the Klondike River, each man had to cross a formidable range of mountains."

Chas gasped as the enormity of the gold fever stared back at her in stark black and white. "It looks like half the population raced off in search of gold."

"The fervor these men displayed was incredible." Adam pointed to the picture in her hand. "These are the golden stairs."

She saw an unbroken line of men scaling a steep slope.

"The slope was thirty-five degrees, making it necessary for each man to walk so he bent over looking at his boots. It was a torturous climb."

Chas shook her head. "It's incredible."

Adam held up his hand. "That's only the beginning. At the top, the Mounties had a border check. In order to be allowed any farther, each man had to have two thousand pounds of supplies. You have to understand there were no supplies available until ships could navigate the frozen waterways. So each man had to carry in what he needed." He bent over the photo, his head close to Chas's. "A man could carry fifty pounds on his back. That meant he had to make the twenty-mile trip over this pass forty times."

"Forty times!" Chas stared into his blue eyes, dark and serious.

"Many men died trying to make it."

"But you made it." She couldn't take her eyes off him, thinking of the horrors he had faced as he forged his way to the Klondike. This was more than seeking adventure; it required the determination of a sort that awed her.

He shook his head. "I took the all-Canadian route. It had its own set of challenges." Finally he pulled his gaze away and straightened to address the whole room. "These photos I'm showing you now were not taken by me. They were taken by a man I met in the Klondike. I got them from him."

Curious about the tightness she heard in his voice, Chas asked, "Who was this man?"

"He was the man who taught me everything I know about photography. He was a very special person."

Suddenly Chas's desire to know more seemed insatiable. Who was this man? What had happened to him? What had he meant to Adam? And more. How had men survived such an ordeal? How many actually found gold? What about their families? But something in Adam's expression—a tightness around his eyes—made her wonder if he had painful memories he didn't wish to share, so she chose to keep her questions to herself.

The last of Adam's pictures had passed from hand to hand.

"Adam, those were truly wonderful," Mother said. "Thank you."

Emma sighed. "Now I'll know what people are talking about when they mention the Klondike gold rush and the Chilkoot Trail."

Mr. Elias nodded. "It's a wonderful documentary you have there, young fellow. I wish I had such a record of my own journeys."

"Yes, thank you, Adam," Chas said, her mind still transfixed by what she had seen and heard. It was a magical experience, like being transported to another time, another place.

"I can bring more pictures and maybe some sketches sometime, if you like. And maybe of other places." He gave a low chuckle. "I have ten years' worth of stories and pictures."

"We'd like that," Mother said for them all. "How wonderful to have such a collection."

Mr. Elias cleared his throat. "If you'll excuse me, I'll be on my way." He rose and marched to the door, his measured steps thudding up the stairs and then descending again as he headed outdoors.

Emma, clearing away the tea things, watched him through the window and then leaned over and spoke close to Chas's ear. "He's got a parcel with him again. What do you suppose he's up to?"

Chas frowned at Emma. If Mother overheard them discussing Mr. Elias's personal life, they would both be in for a scolding.

"Our boarders are entitled to their privacy," she had said over and over. "As long as they don't do anything illegal. We would then, of course, be obligated to report them to the authorities."

That was Emma's loophole. "How do we know what anybody's doing? For instance, maybe Mr. Elias is—I don't know—maybe he's making counterfeit bills."

Chas had laughed at her suggestion. "I suppose he sits up in his bedroom painstakingly drawing each bill."

"He could." Emma drew her brows together. "Or he could be making some other kind of forgery. He could be doing all sorts of things."

Chas had shaken her head. "Or he could be borrowing books from a friend."

At that Emma had pulled away. "That's real exciting."

Now Emma mumbled, "Makes you think, doesn't it?"

Ignoring her, Chas turned back to hear what her mother was saying to Adam. "You certainly have a fine collection of photos. I'm eager to see more of them. And the sketches you keep mentioning."

Adam's gaze circled the room. "You have a fine collection yourself."

Mother followed the direction of his look as did Chas, her heart dropping like a stone as he studied the angel figurine in the window, then the painting over the fireplace, then the framed drawing next to the hall of an angel looking as if he were listening for a call. Penned underneath were words Chas knew by heart: "But if these beings guard you, they do so because they have been summoned by your prayers."

Mother nodded with a bright smile. "I've collected angels since before Chastity was born. They serve as a constant reminder to me that 'the angel of the

Lord encampeth round about them that fear him, and delivereth them.' "

Adam looked at the older woman. "I sense a story."

"I'll say it again—you are much too discerning for a young man." She set-tled back.

Chas squeezed her hands together. She had heard the story many times throughout her life and was always uncomfortable when her mother told it. It made her feel like a spectacle. She edged forward in her chair, hoping she could slip out, but her mother lifted her hand.

"Stay, Chastity. You should hear this."

"I've heard it before, Mother," she said quietly.

"I know, but stay."

Her mother's gentle voice set Chas back in her chair more effectively than a brisk order. She clutched her hands together and refused to look up.

"I married young," Mother began, "and not wisely. I thought my husband was everything I'd dreamed of—a caring, principled man who would take gentle care of me." She took a deep breath. "Neither of us had much in the way of family, so it was easy for us to pull up stakes and move West."

Chas steeled herself for the next installment.

"I don't know if moving West changed him or if it revealed him for who he really was. He grew angry, demanding, and cruel. When I knew I was pregnant, I hid it, fearing what he would do." Her gaze rested on Chastity.

Her mother always found this part of her story painful, and Chas met her look, silently encouraging her and affirming her love.

"Your father's name was Simon LaBlanc."

Chas gripped her hands together so tightly her knuckles hurt. Never before had her mother given the name of her father or even said if LaBlanc was his name or her mother's maiden name.

"I promised to leave the past behind me when I came here," she had insisted when Chas questioned her.

"Simon LaBlanc," Chas repeated, her voice thin. "What was he like?"

"He was charming and handsome. His mother was Swedish, his father French. It's from his mother's side you get your coloring."

Her throat too tight to speak, Chas nodded.

"But he was a no-good scoundrel," her mother said with a sigh. "When he found out I was pregnant, he beat me." Her voice dropped to a whisper.

Adam cleared his throat. "You don't have to tell me. I didn't mean to pry into something personal."

Chas had forgotten he was there and blinked back the emotion rising in her eyes, striving to compose her face.

Mother waved aside his comment, addressing Chas directly. "I've wondered for a long time if I was right in keeping this from you. I decided a few days ago if someone were to ask me to tell them about the angels, I would take it as a sign to tell you." She turned to Adam. "It's a story most people around here have heard bits and pieces of. I'm not sure why, but having you here has given me the strength to tell Chastity about her father."

She continued. "He kicked me out and said he never wanted to see me again. He had hurt me so badly, I was afraid I would lose my baby, who was, of course, Chastity." Her voice quivered. "I knew no one. I had no place to go. I had no money. All I wanted was to get away. Far, far away. So I started down the road. A couple picked me up and took me several miles. That night I slept by the edge of the road with nothing but my shawl to keep me warm. I headed out again as soon as it was light. I don't even know what direction I was going. I walked all day. Toward dark, I was so weak, I kept falling down." Never once did her gaze flicker from Chas's face. "I hadn't eaten in two days, and I was bleeding."

She took a deep breath. "Finally I just couldn't get up. I thought I was going to die. I no longer thought I believed in God, but I remember thinking, 'God, if You don't help me, I'm finished.' " Her voice grew stronger. "That's when a buggy pulled up beside me. A young man came to me and lifted me into it. I seemed to float in his arms. He gave me some warm broth, washed my face and hands, and wrapped me in a warm quilt." She smiled. "I don't know if I slept or what, but we soon drove into town. The man stopped in front of a big house and took me to the door.

" 'You'll be safe here,' he said as he rang the bell. 'God wants you to know He sees your trouble and will surely rescue you. He wants you to understand how much He loves you.'

"And then the door opened. A sweet-faced older lady welcomed me as if she had sent me an invitation. When I turned around to thank the kind gentleman, he wasn't there, and there was no buggy in the street."

Mother smiled. "He had vanished into thin air.

"That's how I came to this house. Mr. and Mrs. Brownlee owned it. They took me in and cared for me until I regained my strength. I've lived here ever since."

The room was quiet.

"Mrs. Brownlee brought me my first angel," she added. "It's that little ivory one I keep by my bedside," she explained to Chas. "She said it was to remind me that when all hope is gone, we have endless hope in God's provision."

She sat back.

No one spoke.

Chas stole a look at Adam, wondering what he thought of the tale. Slowly he turned to face her, his eyes warm as a summer sky. "I always knew Chas had a special quality about her, and now I understand what it is: Her life has been touched in a special way."

"She's my gift."

Chas's cheeks grew warm, and she lowered her head to study her clenched hands. She knew the moment Adam shifted his gaze. She sucked in a deep breath to ease the tension crackling up her spine.

"That's a remarkable story, Miz LaBlanc. I don't know when I've heard a more powerful one." He tidied his bundle of photos and stood. "It's been a lovely afternoon, and I thank you for your hospitality."

"Anytime, Adam. Consider it a standing invitation."

Chas stood, as well. "Do you want help back to your bedroom?" she asked her mother.

"No, I'm quite comfortable here. If you'll bring me my Bible, I'll be fine."

"I'll do that. Then I think I'll go pick up some more of your pills." She turned to Adam. "Good-bye then. I enjoyed your stories of the Klondike."

"I'm glad."

Chas slipped from the room to get her mother's Bible. Adam was still there when she returned. Her eyebrows seemed to go up of their own accord.

He chuckled at her surprise. "Since we're headed in the same direction, I thought we might as well walk together."

She nodded, too confused to speak. Her emotions had been on a whirlwind ride from awe at the spectacular challenges the Klondikers faced, to reluctant admiration of Adam's experiences, to mouth-dropping surprise at her mother's revealing the name of Chas's father. She wasn't yet sure how she felt about it. She had never expected to be told and had long ago decided it didn't matter. Now that she had the information, she wasn't sure what she should do with it. She needed time to sort everything out.

Yet she wasn't reluctant for Adam's company. Something about him roused her curiosity. She had pegged him for an adventurer—bent on trying something new and exciting at every opportunity. But his stories of the Klondike had revealed something else—something she couldn't put her finger on.

"Are you ready?"

Chas smoothed a hand over her hair. She was acting as impressionable as Emma. "I'm ready."

They reached the drugstore first, and Adam accompanied her inside and waited while Roy dispensed the pills Doc Johnson had ordered.

"Why don't you come and see what I'm doing at my shop?" Adam asked as they stepped back into the sunshine.

Curious, Chas agreed.

Inside the room Adam had claimed for his shop, Chas saw at once he had been hard at work. The mahogany wainscoting glistened with polish. The odor of calcimine stung her nostrils from the upper half of the walls with their soft green paint.

She stood in the middle of the floor and turned full circle. "I see you've been busy."

"I haven't done it alone. The whole family helped."

"I suppose they're hoping they can convince you to stay." She crossed her arms in front of her and squeezed tight.

His hands shoved into his pockets, Adam leaned against the door frame and gave a slow smile. "Chas, you talk as if I've only paused here to catch my breath. Do you think I would go to all this work if I was only visiting?"

Chas let her eyes circle the room. Stacks of framed pictures leaned against the wall. Crates waited to be unpacked or stored. "No, I suppose not." She brought her gaze back to Adam. "Do you mean to tell me you're planning to stay and put down roots, as they say?"

He smiled wider, light filling his eyes. "I have no immediate plans to go anywhere."

Chas wondered about the quickening of the pulse in her neck. She could barely breathe and glanced around the room again, wondering if someone had lit a fire in the stove. But there was no stove. No fire. "Are you saying you plan to stay here?"

He nodded. "I need a home base for my business."

"So you might take off again someday?"

He didn't answer. He simply stared at her until she looked down, mumbling, "I'm sorry. It's none of my business."

He sighed. "You make it sound as if the only thing that matters to me is roaming new pastures."

She blinked. He had expressed her feelings very well. And yet it seemed the idea was contemptuous to him.

"That isn't it at all." He pushed away from the wall. "Let me show you some of my work." He knelt before a stack. "This is some of my early work." He handed her a drawing and waited.

It was a simple sketch of a man hunched on a pile of boards, looking as if he had lost all hope.

"This is very good. It reminds me of the sketches you made at school, but it's much more"—she searched for the right word—"it says something."

His eyes took on a light. He handed her more—portraits of vacant-eyed men, drawings of men bent over a sluice box, pictures of men leering at a palmful of gold.

She had thought the photos of the Klondike were moving, but these sketches caught the stark emotions of individuals. "They're very powerful."

He moved to another stack. "These are paintings I made down the coastline." He picked out one and handed it to her. It showed ribbons of fog and a shadowy shoreline.

She touched it, almost expecting to feel moisture, and laughed a little. "It's so real." She let the painting pull at her senses until she breathed the damp air and felt the calmness of the drifting fog. "I like this."

"I have hundreds more sketches and paintings." He rose to his feet. "But there's something I especially want to show you." He moved to the table at the back of the room and pulled a worn leather portfolio toward him, then he untied the strings that held it closed. Then he seemed to think better of it and walked toward her, pausing a few feet away.

She wondered why he had changed his mind and watched him, mystified at the serious expression on his face and the way his eyes probed hers, searching for what she did not know.

"I guess most people think it was like a hike in the mountains to go looking for gold." He paused, his eyes still looking deep into hers until she felt he was seeing right into her soul. "It wasn't. All those who went fought a tough trail and discovered truths about themselves." He turned to look out the window. "Some found ugly, weak things. Others developed a strength beyond their imagination." Again he faced her. Again his eyes blazed into hers. "Many finally reached Dawson more broken than whole—more worn out than alive."

He rubbed the back of his neck. "It was like nothing I could describe. Men lined the streets, vacant eyed, empty. Mere shells. They seemed to have survived the trip but forgotten what life was about."

Sensing he was talking about something that had a profound effect on his life, Chas waited for him to continue.

He shifted and looked past her. "I guess I was one of those who, having made the trip, couldn't figure out what was next. I wasn't interested in packing out to the gold camps. Gold wasn't the reason I had gone in the first place. Yet there seemed no place for me. I remember getting out my paper and pens and trying to draw, but I felt empty inside." He paced the room, as if he were experiencing again the emptiness he described.

"I remember walking along the river wanting to be by myself and figure out what I was going to do. I sat there for a long time, too weary and discouraged to move." He leaned against the wall, his look warm and knowing, as if he saw something in her she was unaware of. "I had taken my sketching materials with me."

Chas shifted her gaze away, but there was something compelling about his story—and the look in his eyes—that drew her despite her resolve.

He took a deep breath and continued. "I finally opened my materials and began leafing through them. I found a picture I had drawn long before I got there, while I was still in school. I looked at it for a long time while peace and purpose returned."

Chas felt caught like a moth before the lamplight, but after a second or two, she managed to ask, "What was the picture?"

He smiled then, a smile so warm it made her blink.

"That's what I want to show you." He returned to the table and, flipping open the portfolio, picked up a tattered piece of paper and held it toward her.

She stepped forward and took it, wondering what had so inspired him. She saw the picture and gasped. "It's me." It was identical to the drawing he had done for her all those years ago. "I don't understand."

"Look at it again. What do you see?"

She examined it. "It's the same drawing you did for me that time I let you escape from Esther James."

"I made one for myself at the same time."

"I don't understand," she repeated, bending over again to study the picture, wistful pleasure tugging at her thoughts. "You have no idea how many times I looked at that picture, wishing I could look like that."

It was his turn to look surprised. "That's how you do look."

She squinted at him. "Not now. Not ever. When you drew this, my hair was so flyaway it clung to my face and blew around my head like static. You've given me an expression that makes me look—"

"Serene, calm. And that's what you are and always were. I remember when the kids teased you about not having a father or living in a boardinghouse or even about your hair. You never let it upset you."

Chas laughed. "I told them I was special. My mother always told me I was and so surrounded me with love that I firmly believed it. When the kids teased me, I went inside myself to a place where I felt special and loved. Most days their teasing didn't bother me. I guess I was a solitary kid, but I was pretty happy most of the time."

For a heartbeat neither spoke. Chas tilted her head and studied Adam closely. "I still don't know why my picture would mean anything to you."

Shrugging, Adam looked past her. "I don't know if I can put it into words. Perhaps it was being reminded of your calmness." Embarrassed, he laughed a little. "All I can tell you is from that moment I knew I was going forward, and someday I'd come back home." He shoved his hand through his hair. "As you can see, I almost wore the picture out." He crossed to a stack of paintings. "I decided I better replace it before it was worn to shreds." He turned a painting around for her to see.

Chas gasped as she stared at another likeness of herself, her flyaway fair hair spraying out around her head like a halo against the sky blue background. Her eyes, which she considered ordinary hazel, blazed a warm dark green. He had given her a shy half smile instead of the sober look of the sketch. She touched the painting, uncertain what to say.

He paced back and forth. "I returned to the hustling, dirty, crowded city."

She pulled her thoughts back to his story.

"I walked up and down the streets looking for something. I didn't know what, but I was sure I'd find it." He stopped in front of her and smiled. "And I did. I saw a man with his camera set up. For a price, he was taking pictures of men to send back to their families or to keep for posterity. Even though most of them were broke and defeated, they wanted to prove they had made it.

"I watched for a while. The photographer noticed my interest and called me over to help." Adam shrugged. "He taught me the whole business." He looked out the window. "And when he died a few months later, he left me all his equipment."

Adam fell silent for a moment and then walked to the desk and picked up the tattered sketch of Chas. "I carried this picture of you in my heart all these years. I hoped you would still be here when I got back."

Chapter 4

Chas's world tilted. She caught flashes of Adam's blue eyes as her gaze darted around the room. Finally she forced her frozen voice to speak. "I don't know what to say."

"You don't have to say anything. I just wanted to tell you."

He was smiling and relaxed.

She couldn't look directly at him.

One blaring question resounded in her brain. What did his confession mean?

She hurried toward the door, mumbling something about how much she'd enjoyed seeing his work, and stumbled outside. Emma would be wondering what was taking her so long, but Chas needed time to think, to let her tumbled thoughts settle. Her steps took her down the residential street, past the big turreted houses, toward the white picket fence. As she passed, her eyes sought the arbor enclosing the table and chairs.

She choked back a sob. Her own father, Simon LaBlanc, had not cared enough to find out who she was. Yet a man she remembered only as a boy in school had carried her picture for ten years. *In his heart.*

She had told Adam she'd been raised to know she was special—a gift from God. But never had anything made her feel as special as this.

Later that evening, after her mother was settled and the house was quiet, Chas went to her little cubicle. It was barely big enough for her narrow bed, the tall wardrobe, and the tiny table she used for a desk; but it was her quiet haven. And how she needed to be alone and sort out her thoughts.

More than once after her return home, Emma had given her a strange look as she repeated a question Chas had missed.

"I get the feeling your mind is elsewhere." She had studied Chas carefully. "Perhaps on a handsome man who has visited recently."

Chas pulled up short. "Adam?"

"Who else? Even Mrs. B, half blind as she is, finds him attractive."

Chas laughed. "I'm not denying he's handsome."

"Nobody would believe you if you did." Emma bent over the pot of potatoes and leaned on the masher. "Don't forget he's also charming, considerate, and interesting."

Chas stirred the gravy. "And as likely to settle down in one place as I am to fly."

Emma straightened to look at her. "What's so wrong with a little adventure in your life?"

"I'm not opposed to adventure," Chas protested, trying to marshall her thoughts. "It makes life interesting and fun. But I think we need to be careful of the risks involved." She paused, wondering how to explain. "Take my mother, for instance. She thought she had found a handsome, charming man and decided it would be fun to join his adventure of moving West. Look where it got her."

Emma's eyes narrowed. "Seems to me she's happy enough with where it got her. She has this boardinghouse and you. I've never heard her complain. Not once."

"You're right, of course. God turned her mistakes into good. But that doesn't mean it's a good idea to rush headlong into things and hope God will send an angel to rescue you."

"You make it sound as if you expect Adam to rush off to the North Pole for a dozen years or more."

Chas shrugged. "Maybe. After all, he took ten years to go to the Yukon."

"Yes, but what better time to wander free than as a young man with no responsibilities?" Emma dished the potatoes into a large bowl. "I guess he's decided it's time to settle down."

"I doubt it, but it's neither here nor there to me."

Emma let out her breath. "You're already half in love with him. Not that I blame you."

Chas almost dropped the platter of meat. "Emma, I am not. When I fall in love and marry, it will be with someone I know will always be there."

Emma nodded. "Someone dull and steady and as predictable as the rising of the sun. Michael, I suppose."

"There's nothing wrong with Michael. He's not dull. He's comfortable and a good friend. Being content to stay in one place doesn't mean you have to be dull."

Emma had waited until she was halfway through the door to the dining room to mumble, "Maybe Michael's an exception then."

Now, in the sanctuary of her room, the troubling emotions of the day swept over Chas.

She hurried to the little table and sat down, pulling out a sheet of paper and dipping her pen in the ink. She wrote in neat letters across the top of the page: Simon LaBlanc. It was all she knew of her father. Her mother's parents had been dead many years before she married Simon LaBlanc, but Chas wondered if either of his parents was still alive. Could she have grandparents somewhere, perhaps the grandmother from whom she had inherited her fair coloring?

She sighed. They wouldn't even know she existed.

She ran her fingers back and forth across the letters of his name. He could be, and probably was, the worst sort of scoundrel; yet there was something comforting in knowing his name. Finally she folded the paper in half and slipped it between the pages of her Bible.

She dragged her chair to the wardrobe and reached to the far corner of the top shelf for a box. She carried it to the table and untied the strings. Inside was an assortment of essays and graded papers. About halfway down she found what she was looking for—a piece of heavier, grainier paper—and pulled it out. It was the drawing Adam had made of her. She stared at herself for several seconds and then carried it to the mirror on the door of the wardrobe and held it next to her face.

She looked from her own image to the reflection of the drawing, trying to see why Adam had found encouragement in remembering her. Had she even thought of Adam in the last ten years? Of course she had wondered at first, like everyone else, how he could leave like that and how long he would be gone. Then she'd forgotten him, except for the occasional reminder when Mrs. Silverhorn mentioned she had received a letter.

Yet he had thought of her all that time.

He had carried her in his heart.

The words fluttered through her along with Emma's announcement: "I think you're already half in love with him." Emma had also warned Chas that falling in love with Adam would mean excitement and adventure.

Chas shook her head. She wasn't opposed to a bit of excitement, but neither was she willing to risk losing the sort of life she had always dreamed of.

She pushed the drawing back in the box, retied the strings, and returned the box to the top shelf.

Falling in love with Adam was out of the question. It simply did not fit in with what she wanted for her life.

She opened her Bible and read a little then bowed to pray, promising God she would trust Him to guide her future and asking for strength to serve Him in her current situation.

And keep me from foolishness, she prayed, thinking how handsome Adam looked and how her heart had almost exploded when he said he'd carried her picture in his heart.

🖎

Tea was over. Mr. Elias had gone for his walk. Mother sat in the front room helping Mrs. B with her doily.

Emma pulled the roaster out of the oven. "I'll check the meat. Then I guess everything is ready. Looks as if we'll have a few minutes to spare today."

Chas poured a cup of tea. "I'm going to take this out to the veranda. Join me when you're finished."

Emma nodded in agreement as Chas stepped out the back door to one of her favorite spots, the bench at the end of the veranda. A latticed wall provided a feeling of privacy without shutting out the view.

She had taken a book with her and opened its pages. After a few minutes, she discovered she was restless and unable to concentrate and laid it aside.

"Hello, Miss LaBlanc."

She lifted her gaze to the sound, met three pairs of eyes over the gate at the bottom of the garden, and grinned at the wide-eyed look they each gave her.

Jack, Adam's younger brother, had greeted her. She addressed him first. "Hello, Jack." Then she turned to Adam and his sister. "Hello, Ellen and Adam. How are you?"

"We're fine," Jack answered for all three. "We're just out for a walk."

"Would you like to come in?"

Adam opened the gate before she finished asking, and the three trooped up the walk to the veranda. There weren't enough chairs, but Adam perched on the railing as Ellen sat in the wooden chair facing Chas.

Jack plopped down on the veranda floor. "Adam says we deserve a break because we've been working so hard. We got a lot done, didn't we, Adam?"

Adam ruffled the boy's hair and grinned at him. "We surely did." His gaze sought Chas's eyes. "We put up the backdrops for portraits, and then we set up the first display of pictures."

"First display?" Chas said.

"I have far too many photos and pictures to hang at once, so I plan to change them every month or two."

"We did the Klondike this time," Jack added. "But we only used the pictures that showed a broad view of the area."

Chas knew he was quoting Adam.

"I thought he should have shown all those gold rush pictures."

Adam chuckled. "Maybe another time, youngster."

Chas turned to include Ellen in the conversation and caught the adoring look she gave her older brother. "What did he have you doing, Ellen?"

The girl lowered her head, hiding her face, and mumbled, "I helped him pick out the pictures to hang."

Remembering the stacks of pictures, Chas shook her head. "It must have been difficult to choose."

Ellen looked up at Chas. "I wanted to show just paintings, but he said I had to choose photos and sketches, as well. His paintings are so wonderful." The girl's voice was filled with admiration.

"Ellen could be a bit prejudiced in her judgment," Adam said with a drawl.

Ellen spun on him. "Am not. Your paintings are good. You should be proud of yourself."

Chas drew in her breath, waiting for Adam's reply.

He leaned back, his legs crossed at the ankles, his hands resting on the ledge, smiling down at Ellen with an expression that caused Chas's throat to tighten. "I'm happy with my work. It gives me pleasure. But there's room for improvement."

"How can you say that?" Ellen demanded.

Adam shrugged. "There's always room for improvement. If I as an artist, or anyone else for that matter, sit back and accept things as being as good as they'll get, there would be little progress made in this world."

Ellen drew back. "Well, I think your paintings are perfect."

Adam gave a low chuckle. "Ellen, thank you for your loyalty."

Jack suddenly sat up and leaned toward Chas. "We came to invite you to see the display. It'll be ready Monday, won't it, Adam?"

Adam nodded.

Jack rushed on. "Tomorrow Adam is taking us to Sheep Falls. Have you ever been there, Miss LaBlanc?"

Chas shook her head. "I hear it's lovely."

"You should come with us."

Adam leaned forward. "Good idea, Jack."

"Yes, do," added Ellen.

Chas looked from Jack with his eager face, to Ellen smiling shyly, to Adam. At his dark searching look, her heart stalled.

"What about it, Chas?" he asked.

Her gaze darted away and then returned to Adam's eyes. Just as quickly, she pulled away again, unable to deal with what she saw there. "I couldn't," she murmured, choosing to study her fingers. "I have my work."

"Couldn't Emma manage for a day?" Adam asked, his low voice pleading gently.

"I couldn't ask her."

The back door squealed then slapped shut, and Emma joined them. "Why is everyone looking at me?" she demanded.

Jack scooted forward to face her. "We want Miss LaBlanc to go with us tomorrow."

"Adam's taking us to the falls," Ellen added.

"But she doesn't think she can leave for the day," said Adam.

Emma laughed. "And you want me to persuade her it's all right to go and let me run things for the day?"

Three heads bobbed up and down.

"It's fine with me." She turned to Chas. "I can manage. You run along and enjoy yourself."

Chas scowled at the knowing grin on Emma's face and the slight emphasis she put on the word *enjoy*.

"It's settled then," Adam said, leaning back.

"Yeah!" Jack yelled.

Ellen suddenly lost her restraint. "We'll have a lovely time."

It was late before Chas got to bed.

Sunday was traditionally a day of rest with cold meals, which meant preparing twice as much food on Saturday. Chas felt guilty leaving Emma with the extra work, so she had cooked potatoes and boiled eggs and diced them for potato salad. While the potatoes cooked, she had baked several cakes. Emma would cook the turkey and serve it hot Saturday, slicing the rest for Sunday's cold dinner.

Although pleasantly tired, Chas didn't go to sleep at once. Butterflies fluttered in her stomach.

She looked forward to seeing the falls—the local attraction. But forcing herself to be honest, she admitted she was also deeply curious about the man who said he had thought of her all those years.

The sky shone like a mirror as they made the two-hour journey to the falls.

"It's a perfect day," Ellen said from her seat behind Chas.

"Couldn't ask for better," agreed Adam, glancing at Chas.

She suddenly found the passing scenery required her full attention. During the night she had decided to forget he'd thought of her for the past ten years; it was simply some romantic notion born of loneliness and desperation. She would treat him as an old friend, nothing more. But the way his eyes continually sought her, at once compelling and proprietorial, made it difficult to remember her decision.

"Makes me feel like singing." And to prove her point, Ellen started: "Oh, my darling, oh, my darling, oh, my darling Clementine."

Glad of the diversion, Chas relaxed.

Ellen had a sweet, clear voice, and the others listened as she sang the first verse. As she started the chorus again, Jack's uncertain voice joined hers.

Adam smiled over his shoulder and then joined his siblings, his deeper voice rounding out the trio. They finished the song and laughed together.

Chas sat back, watching Adam with his younger brother and sister, enjoying the way he was at ease with them.

Ellen started another song.

"Come on, Chas." Adam smiled at her. "Sing with us."

She couldn't resist the twinkling challenge in his eyes, feeling all the while she was being sucked further and further from her decision.

They sang song after song.

Ellen and Jack taught them some new choruses they had learned at school.

"Remember this one?" Adam grinned at Chas and began a song they had learned in school.

"Where did you hear that?" Jack asked.

"At school." His warm eyes lingered on Chas's face.

"It must be really old."

Both Chas and Adam laughed. Then Adam reached back to squeeze Jack's knee.

"Are you calling me an old man?"

Jack grabbed Adam's arm and pretended to twist it up behind the seat. "You're pretty old all right."

Adam turned around and half-lifted Jack from his seat. "Not too old to handle you, sprout."

Jack clung to Adam's fist, giggling. "I'll grow up soon enough, and by then you'll be really old."

Chas watched the interplay, knowing Adam had already earned the innocent love of both his sister and brother, and she envied their mutual affection. Life as an only child had often left her wishing for a brother or sister, or both, to share secrets with or simply to enjoy the sort of play she saw here.

They edged down a narrow trail through the trees. Adam pulled the horses to a stop.

"Listen. Hear it?"

Chas tilted her head, catching the rumble of the falls. She leaned forward, straining for her first glimpse.

"Relax. It's still a distance before you can see it."

Jack bounced on the seat, rocking the buggy. "Hurry up, Adam."

Chuckling, Adam flicked the reins, and they rattled forward.

Suddenly sunlight flashed on the water, momentarily blinding Chas. Then she saw the falls, a mane of white water tumbling from the rocks above, crashing to the foaming cauldron before them. Chas tasted the cool mist on her lips. The roar drowned out all other sound.

Adam leaned close and yelled in her ear, "We're here!"

It was such an unnecessary bit of information that she shouted with soundless laughter.

"I noticed!" she exclaimed, grinning back.

He shook his head, indicating he couldn't hear, and leaned close. A whiff of spicy shaving soap drifted across her senses. She tasted the moisture on her lips again and tried to satisfy her lungs with the damp air.

"You'll have to yell in my ear," he roared, his breath teasing her hair, warming her cheek, making her acutely aware of his nearness.

Determined to remain unaffected, she nodded and turned to shout in his ear, instead staring into his eyes, the sunlight reflected in his irises. His eyes invited her—she swallowed hard—to what she couldn't say. But she knew the invitation carried with it risks she vowed she would not take.

She shook her head, indicating she didn't wish to repeat her statement, and sat back, her gaze on the falls.

The buggy bounced as Ellen and Jack jumped down.

Chas stared at them and then turned to Adam. "What—?"

Remembering he couldn't hear, she raised her eyebrows, silently asking what they were doing.

Adam draped the reins and jumped down, coming to her side to hold out a hand. Curiosity overcoming caution, Chas allowed him to help her down and lead her to the edge of the rocks, where the spray washed their skin.

Chas couldn't take her eyes off the boiling water. It was like standing in the pit of a storm.

She had almost forgotten the rest of them until Adam touched her shoulder. She started at his touch. He tilted his head toward the hill where Jack was scrambling up a narrow trail and Ellen was clutching at the bushes as she followed him.

Adam held out his hand. Surrounded by the deep-throated roar of the falls, she allowed him to take her hand and lead her up the path. Diamonds dripped from every leaf and clung to every blade of grass. A rainbow caught in the mist, and she pointed to it.

Adam nodded, then flashed a smile at her, mouthing words she couldn't hear. Shrugging, she took another step up the trail. Adam didn't move. On the narrow path, their shoulders touched; their still-clasped hands brushed her leg.

Moisture beaded on his lashes. One silvery drop splashed on his cheek. In the mist-shrouded scene, his blue eyes were warm and intense.

She welcomed the cool moisture and tore her gaze away, seeking the rising trail. He led the way, and she could finally fill her lungs with the heavy, moisture-laden air.

As they climbed, the noise of the water softened to a murmur. They struggled over a rocky bench and stepped into a wide, grassy meadow. The river here was wide and quiet.

Ellen sat close to the bank, tossing bits of grass into the water.

Jack explored the underbrush of the trees.

Chas dropped Adam's hand and stepped away. Welcoming the warmth after the dampness of the trail, she turned her face to the sun rather than meet Adam's eyes.

But she could not avoid him forever. Slowly she forced herself to turn. But he was gone. She turned full circle, wondering if he had joined Jack or Ellen, but he wasn't with them. She shrugged. But it was disappointment rather than relief she felt as she ambled to Ellen's side and dropped down on the grass beside her.

"It's so beautiful here," Ellen murmured. "I wish we could stay here forever, just Adam and us."

"You're really enjoying having him home, aren't you?"

Ellen beamed. "Oh, yes, it's wonderful."

The girl's words troubled Chas, but how could she warn Ellen her brother was only looking for a home base?

Ellen glanced over her shoulder. "Where's Adam?"

"I don't know."

"Here I am." Breathing hard, Adam stood at the top of the trail. "I went back to get my sketchbook." He held out a large black-covered book. "Too many good things to waste." He sat on a rock several feet away, his pencil already busy.

He occasionally glanced toward Chas and Ellen, but every time Chas looked, he had his attention on the page. She tried to forget he was there.

Jack bounded to Adam's side, peering over his shoulder. "Hey, that's pretty good."

"Thanks, sprout. What have you been up to?"

Jack shrugged. "Just looking around." He shoved his hands in his pockets and rocked back on his heels.

Recognizing his stance as an imitation of Adam, Chas lowered her head to hide a smile.

"I'm hungry," he announced.

Adam closed the sketchbook. "Me, too. Come on, girls. Let's go back."

Chas jumped to her feet, brushing her skirt with her hand. Jack was already leaping over the rocks.

"Jack, slow down," Adam cautioned. "I wouldn't want to have to fish you out of the water."

"Okay!" Jack called out, leaping over another rock.

Adam stood back, waiting for Ellen to follow her younger brother.

"Are you enjoying yourself?" he asked Chas, falling into step at her side.

"It's lovely," she murmured, keeping her attention on the path. The rocks proved difficult to traverse, and she admired Jack's nimbleness in jumping over them. Her foot slipped. She grabbed at a bush to steady herself and found instead a warm hand.

"Better let me help," he said. "Wouldn't want to fish you out of the water, either."

His touch did more to her than steady her steps—much more. Things she didn't want; things she had promised wouldn't happen. But the trail was steep and slippery, and she welcomed his help, while remaining vexed at the waywardness of her heart.

She blinked the mist from her eyes. He would be gone as suddenly as he had returned. A man with no roots. The roar of the water made conversation impossible, allowing her to concentrate on the trail as she scolded herself mentally. Her resolve returned, strong enough to enable her to cling to his hand without letting her emotions dissolve into a vapor.

The roar of the water made conversation impossible, allowing her to concentrate on the trail as she scolded herself mentally.

They stepped to level ground, and she pulled away from his grip, clutching her fingers together to prove her inner victory.

Ellen and Jack were already seated in the buggy.

Chas hurried over, but before she could step up on her own, Adam was at her side taking her hand. She nodded her thanks without meeting his eyes. She felt his surprise when she busied herself smoothing her skirt rather than looking at him.

Slowly he released her hand.

She drew a shaky breath. *Please, God, give me strength to be true to my convictions.*

They drove along the river's edge to a clearing, where they spread blankets. Ellen opened the large basket and began to set out the food.

As they ate, Chas turned to Jack. "How is school going?"

"Okay," he mumbled, his eyes downcast.

When he didn't say anything more, she prodded. "Jack, is there a problem?" She had always found him an eager student.

He shrugged. "It's just I don't like Mr. Martin as much as you."

"Why, thank you, Jack." She thought the children would have forgotten her.

"You said you'd come back."

She had explained to her class that she had to leave to take care of her mother, but she thought then it would be only a month or two. "I know I did—and I want to. But, you see, my mother still can't manage on her own. She needs me."

A thoughtful look crossed his face for a moment. "Yep," he finally said, "if someone you love needs you, you should look after them."

"I agree." She didn't dare look at Adam. She was afraid for all of them—Jack, Ellen, herself. What would happen to them when Adam left again?

Ellen asked, "You won't leave again, will you, Adam?"

Chas caught her breath, waiting for his reply.

"I can't promise I won't go see what's going on in another part of the country. But I can promise you I'll always come back."

Ellen lowered her head, but not before Chas glimpsed her look of disappointment. He didn't say when he'd come back. Ten years maybe? She twisted a blade of grass around her finger. A person would never be certain with Adam.

Jack sprang to his feet. "Can I go wading, Adam?"

"I don't see why not."

"Thanks." Jack sprinted to the river.

"Take off your shoes and socks and roll up your pants first."

Jack shot an adults-are-so-strange look over his shoulder. "As if I'd forget."

Adam laughed. "It's happened before."

Ellen tugged on Chas's hand. "Let's go."

She followed Ellen behind some bushes, where they took off their shoes and stockings.

She dipped a foot in the cold water and hesitated, but Ellen raced in, splashing and squealing.

She wondered if Adam would join them, but he sat on the bank, sketchbook on his knee. She felt awkward and not a little immature at his amused expression.

"Come on, Adam!" Jack called. "It's fun."

"I'll just watch."

"Aw, come on." Jack scooped up a handful of water and threw it at him.

Adam ducked and rolled away.

Laughing, Jack threw more water.

Adam tossed a handful of pebbles into the water in front of Jack, but the splash posed no threat to the boy.

Jack paddled his hands in the water, trying to soak Adam, and succeeded in drenching himself.

Adam retreated along the shore with Jack in pursuit.

"Enough," Adam ordered.

And Jack quit, more so, Chas was sure, because he was laughing too hard to continue than because he felt like obeying. He plowed through the water toward the girls, with Adam following more sedately at a safe distance.

Ellen trailed her fingers through the water, singing softly.

"Stop."

At Adam's sharp word, everyone froze.

"Don't move," Adam ordered.

"What's the matter?" Afraid to breathe lest she invite some lurking danger,

Chas kept her eyes on Adam's face.

A slow smile widened his mouth. "Stay right where you are."

She moved nothing but her eyes. "Jack?"

His eyes were saucers.

"Don't move," Adam said again, grabbing his sketchbook. "The sun has caught the moisture around your head. It looks as if you're wearing a rainbow halo."

Chas forced herself to stand still, though she inwardly squirmed at the way Adam stared, then looked down to draw a few lines.

After a moment he lowered the paper. "It's gone."

She longed to see what he had drawn, but his bright-eyed intensity made her keep quiet.

The cold seeped upward from her ankles, and, shivering, she hurried from the water.

"You were so pretty, Miss LaBlanc," Jack said, his voice squeaky.

Grateful for a reason to flee Adam's look, Chas ducked behind the bushes to pull on her stockings and shoes.

When she returned, Adam lounged against a tree, his sketch pad at his side. She chose a spot within easy talking distance but far enough away to give her some confidence.

Jack pulled himself from the water, soaked from head to toe. "Let's go exploring," he said to Adam.

Adam rested his head against the tree. "You go ahead, sprout. I think I'll stay right here."

Jack called over his shoulder, "Come on, Ellen. Let's go."

His sister hurried to put on her stockings and shoes, and the two set off. Chas wavered, not knowing if she should follow them or stay where she was.

"Chas and I will stay here," Adam told the others, settling the question.

Adam lay back, and Chas relaxed, enjoying the murmur of the water, the chatter of birds, the fresh pine scent. The sun was warm, and she let her tension seep away.

She had almost dozed off when Adam stirred, rustling the pine needles. She kept her eyes closed, not wanting to end the delicious sense of peace, but she could hear him turning the pages of his sketchbook.

He cleared his throat. "I thought you might like to see the sketch I did."

She sat up. "I would indeed."

He scooted over, laying the open book on her knees. She saw herself, face framed by spray, hair tossed up. She looked so ordinary.

"It's just a crude sketch," Adam murmured in her ear. "You can't see how the light broke into a full spectrum around your head. It was really quite unusual."

"I wish I could have seen it."

He chuckled. "Wait until I paint it—that is, if you'll give your permission?"

There seemed no reason to refuse. "What would you do with it?"

"Guess it depends on what you want. You could have it if you like, or I could add it to my collection." He hesitated. "I would love to do that."

Confused, she asked, "Do what? Paint the picture or add it to your collection?"

"Both."

He flipped a page. She and Ellen sat at the riverbank. He flipped another page, and she laughed at the drawing of Jack jumping in the water, his mischievousness captured perfectly.

Adam showed her several more sketches and then, leaning back on his elbows, looked at her.

She tried not to let her gaze jump about. Finally she demanded, "Why are you staring at me?"

He pulled his gaze away. "I'm sorry. I didn't realize I was."

She didn't speak.

"I had to come back," he offered.

She nodded. "I know a young boy and girl who are grateful you did."

"I suppose they're the only ones?"

Aware he was watching her closely, she made a great study of the pinecone she had plucked off the ground. "I'm sure a mother and father are equally grateful."

"Hmm. Anyone else?"

She looked down the trail. "You don't suppose they've encountered a problem, do you?"

"I'm sure they're fine."

She sighed, looking everywhere but at Adam. "This is a really lovely place. I'm glad Jack invited me along."

"I had to see if you were as I remembered."

It still amazed her he claimed to remember so much of her. She faced him, instantly regretting her action as his blue gaze caught and held her like a trap.

"I thought I might have actually created you in my imagination." The pulse in his throat beat with steady rhythm, echoing in her emotions. "I was in love with a memory and had to find out if it was real."

She jolted to her feet, half-running down the path in pursuit of Ellen and Jack. "I think we should check on them," she called, not caring if he thought she was acting strangely. She couldn't bear to hear any more.

Emma's words rang in her ears: "Don't go falling in love with him." She had promised she wouldn't, thinking it would be easy. He was just the opposite of what she wanted.

She tried to calm her pounding thoughts. She knew what she wanted. Someone steady, someone she could count on. Someone like Michael. Her insides settled.

Yes, Michael was exactly what she needed.

Chapter 5

She caught up to Jack and Ellen and called them to return.

On the way back, Jack poked into every tree stump while Ellen picked flowers. Chas followed slowly, welcoming the chance to settle her thoughts before she had to face Adam again.

When they marched into the clearing, Adam was intent on his sketchbook. He stood and stretched. "Good. You're back. It's time we headed home."

"Aww," Jack began, "already?"

Adam ruffled Jack's hair. "I promised Chas I'd have her back for supper." He scooped up his drawing materials and started toward the buggy.

Jack blocked Chas's path. "Couldn't we stay longer?" he begged.

Chas smiled down at the boy. "I'm sorry, Jack, but I promised Emma I'd be back."

"Couldn't you break your promise?"

"No, Jack, I wouldn't do that."

The boy studied her for another moment. "It wouldn't be honest, would it?"

"No, it wouldn't be. People should be able to trust what we say."

"Come on, sprout." Adam stood beside the buggy.

Jack nodded thoughtfully before he sprinted toward Adam.

Chas would have preferred to climb up on her own, but Adam waited, hands planted on his hips, leaving her no choice but to go to his side. Grabbing a deep breath, she reached for the hand he extended, keeping her eyes on the step. He released her hand quickly, turning to help Ellen.

Chas clutched her hands together in her lap, staring ahead as Adam took his seat and flicked the reins.

He didn't speak until they were away from the noise of the falls. "Did everyone have a good time?"

Two voices from the backseat chorused, "Yes."

"Thank you, Adam." Chas angled a glance at him.

He smiled. "My pleasure." His silver-threaded gaze returned to the trail.

At his impersonal response, Chas wondered if she had imagined the passion of his earlier confession. But the way he had looked at her—seeking—insisting—on a response she didn't feel able to give, had not been a fancy of her wayward thoughts. It had been there. It had been real.

The homeward journey was quiet. The two in the backseat, Chas suspected, were tired. She was content in her own thoughts, as long as she avoided remembering Adam's behavior at the river.

In front of the boardinghouse, Adam reached behind the seat to grab his drawing pad and pulled out two pages. "I want you to have these. To remember your first trip to the falls."

One sketch was of the falls. Even on paper, the water appeared to roll and churn. The other was of Chas and Ellen splashing in the river, their skirts tucked up to their knees. Ellen was attempting to catch a drop of water; Chas appeared fascinated with the splash her feet made.

A lump swelled in her throat at Adam's kindness, and she allowed herself to look at him. "It was a wonderful day, Adam. I'll cherish it always."

The taut lines around his mouth disappeared as he smiled. "Me, too."

She turned to bid good-bye to the others.

"Don't forget to come to Adam's shop on Monday," Jack reminded her.

"I won't," she said.

She stepped away from the buggy, waving good-bye to them, and barely had time to turn toward the house before Emma yanked open the door. "So? How was your date?"

Chas rolled her eyes. "It was an outing, not a date."

Emma tossed her head. "And I'm a chef, not a cook."

"Have you been to the falls?"

"A teacher took us once several years ago." She planted herself in front of Chas. "I don't want to know about the falls. I want to know about Adam."

Chas wrinkled her nose. "Then maybe you should have gone with him."

Emma waved her hand in dismissal. "I don't mean for me, silly. How did Adam treat you?"

"Like a gentleman, of course."

Emma stalked to the stove, checking to see if the kettle had boiled. "You are so dense sometimes."

Chas looked down. She knew what Emma was getting at, but she didn't want to think about it. His devotion to her memory made her uncomfortable. The sketches in her hand provided the perfect escape. "Here—look at these."

Emma snatched them from her hand, looking at one and then the other, then tossing them on the table. "So you played in the water with Ellen."

Chas chuckled. "What did you expect?" Before Emma could answer, she hurried on. "How was Mother?"

Emma lifted her shoulders in a deep sigh. "She's fine. Helped me ice the cakes and mix the potato salad."

Chas opened her mouth to protest, but Emma lifted a hand to stop her. "I put everything on the table within reach. Chas, she needs to know she's needed and that we appreciate her help."

Chas nodded. "But every time I allow her to do something, she overdoes it."

"I know. But she's learned her lesson. All she wants to do now is get better. I'm sure she'll do whatever she must."

"She said all that?"

Emma shrugged. "Sort of."

"Where is she now?"

Emma pressed her hand to her mouth. "Whoops. I forgot to tell you Michael is here already. She's visiting with him in the sitting room."

Chas groaned. She wanted to change her clothes and wash off the sand and dust. Then the meal needed to be prepared. "What still needs to be done?"

"Everything's ready and keeping warm in the oven. I just have to make the tea and put out the food."

"Give me a minute to change. I'll let Mother and Michael know I'm home. Then I'll give you a hand." She paused at the door. "Didn't you have plans for tonight?"

Emma nodded. "Pastor Simpson and Miss Martha have invited half a dozen of us over to meet a cousin of theirs or something." She wrinkled her nose. "Probably some old codger, but I promised Dorothy I'd go with her."

Chas nodded. "There's no need for you to stay. Run along and enjoy your evening."

Emma shook her head. "I have lots of time. I'll help clean up the meal before I leave."

"Emma, you're a gem. I don't know what I'd do without you."

Emma gave her a mischievous look. "You could ask Stella back."

Remembering those first days of Stella's criticism and refusal to accept Chas's authority, Chas shuddered. "I'm grateful to say she would never consider it." She hurried down the hall. "I'll be right back."

A few minutes later, everything was served. Beryl and Louise were out, having gone with their beaus; the Knutsen boys had left after work for a visit to the farm; and John was absent. But the rest settled around the table.

Mrs. B leaned over to Mother. "Your girl is back. Where did you say she was?"

"She went to Sheep Falls!" the younger woman yelled close to Mrs. B's ear.

Mrs. B looked annoyed. "What does she want with balls?"

"Not balls, Sheep Falls."

"What difference does it make if they are cheap?" She shook her head. "You better keep an eye on her, Marie." She unfolded her napkin on her lap and sat up straight, waiting for a signal to begin eating.

Mother laughed, winking at Chas. "I do my best, Ida." But everyone knew the comment was not for Mrs. B's ears. "Now let's pray." She took Chas's hand, giving it a little squeeze, taking away any sting Mrs. B's words might have carried.

Chas bowed her head, silently thanking God for His bountiful provision, adding a special thanks for her dear mother who made life special.

Mother murmured, "Amen."

For several minutes conversation was confined to getting the food passed around the table. When the bowls and platters had circled the table, Roy leaned around Michael.

"Were you able to estimate the height of the falls?"

Chas shook her head. "No, Roy, but we did climb to the top of them."

"Did it take long?"

"It didn't seem long. I guess I never paid it much mind."

Emma grinned. "She had other things on her mind."

Michael stiffened, and Chas glowered at Emma.

Mr. Elias leaned forward. "I expect Adam could answer your questions, Roy. He's a knowledgeable young man with a head for learning."

Satisfied, Roy leaned back. "Yes, I'll ask him." He glanced at Chas. "Though I can't understand how someone could go there and not notice anything about it."

Chas laughed out loud. "I noticed lots of things, Roy. I just didn't measure anything."

"It's all the same," Roy said, frowning. "Isn't it?"

Still smiling, Chas shook her head. "Not necessarily. For instance, I noticed how the mist from the falls made rainbows over the water. I noticed the way the flowers and vines clung to the wet rocks. I saw how the tumbling water churned around the rocks in a magical dance."

"How much water do you think flows over every minute?"

Chuckling, Chas shook her head. "I have no idea. How would one even measure it?"

Roy grew thoughtful. "You could set up—"

Emma put her fork down and wrinkled her nose at Roy. "How would you expect her to care about scientific nonsense when she was with Adam? I tell you, I would have had my eyes on nothing else. Not even trees and flowers."

Chas glared at Emma, silently warning her to stop.

"Now there's a young man with a bright future," Mr. Elias announced. "I assure you he will go a long way."

Michael held his fork halfway to his mouth and said, "Seems he's gone a long way already. The Yukon, Alaska—where else did he say he went?"

Roy supplied the answer. "He made the thousand-mile trip down the inside passage and then explored the islands of the passage."

"Thank you, Roy," Emma said. "I'm guessing he was more interested in the people and scenery than in how far it was from point A to point B."

Roy drew back. "He's the one who told me this."

Chas jumped up. "He did a couple of sketches at the falls. I'll get them." She hurried to the kitchen to retrieve them, handing them to her mother to pass around.

Mrs. B bent close to the one with Chas in it. "Isn't this Chastity?" She looked across at Chas as if she expected her to have sprouted a second head.

"She went there this morning!" Mother shouted.

"I know she wasn't here this morning. She was out playing ball." Mrs. B looked at the picture again. "Who are these girls playing in the water?"

Rather than try to make her understand, Mother handed her the other sketch. "Sheep Falls," she yelled, pointing to the words Adam had penciled at the bottom of the page.

Mrs. B studied the picture without comment before she handed it on.

"He's a good artist," Emma said, handing the pages on to Mr. Elias.

The pictures went around the table with no one arguing the point. Shortly afterward, the residents began to push away from the table. It didn't take long to clean up, and Emma was soon on her way.

Chas returned to the living room, where Michael sat visiting with Roy.

"Let's go out on the veranda," she suggested.

"Good idea." Michael sprang to his feet.

The cool night air held a hint of moisture, taking her, despite herself, to thoughts of the afternoon spent at the falls. Deftly she pulled her thoughts away, resting them instead on the man beside her on the bench. "It's a lovely evening."

"I guess sitting out here is rather dull after your outing this afternoon." His voice was mournful.

"Oh, no. It's peaceful and calm, and I like that. Besides, it's far from dull. Look at the way the moon glistens off the leaves. What more could I ask for than to sit on my own back step and enjoy the evening?"

He shifted about. "I've never taken you anywhere special." He cleared his throat. "I always thought you were content right here."

She grabbed at his arm, anxious to clear up this misunderstanding. "I always have been. I still am. I've never hankered after excitement." She wanted to tell him not to worry. The one thing she always enjoyed about her friendship with Michael was how comfortable they were together. *Not like Adam.* She jerked her thoughts back. He shouldn't have bothered to come back. All he'd done was disrupt her life. She wouldn't think of him anymore. Not with Michael beside her wondering if he had failed.

"He's full of adventure," Michael said, "and tales of faraway places."

"Yes, he is. He has wonderful stories."

"And he's very artistic."

"Yes, he's that, too." It felt like an argument with herself. He was all of these things, but— "I'm not looking for instability."

"I suppose he'll be around just long enough to turn everything upside down, and then he'll leave."

It was an echo of her own sentiments. "Some people prefer the predictable, the conventional."

"Put that way, it sounds deadly dull."

She squeezed his arm. "I don't mean dull. I mean stable and secure—knowing the one you love will walk through the door every day and sit across the table from you each meal. And be there every morning, every night. Go to church with you every Sunday."

At first, Michael didn't answer. Then he covered her hand with his own. "Have you fallen in love with Adam?"

She jumped to her feet, facing him in the cold moonlight. "Didn't you hear a word I said? He's not my sort. I don't want the kind of life he'd want. I want a home and stability. I want—" Breathless, she broke off and dropped down beside him again, her voice falling to a whisper. "I want a real home, a real family. I don't want to end up like Mother, alone in a big house that isn't even a home."

He took her hand and tucked it around his arm, holding her close to his side, and she relaxed, content to enjoy the comfort of his presence.

After some moments he broke the peaceful silence between them. "I'm not arguing with you, but I don't think you need to feel sorry about how your mother's lived her life. She seems very happy with her lot."

"I know. But I've always dreamed of more." In her mind she stood at the white picket fence looking at the little house and its pleasant yard. She laughed a little at the comparison. "Maybe I should say I've dreamed of something less—a little house of my own rather than the boardinghouse."

She could feel Michael nod. "Maybe it's time to think about fulfilling some of those dreams." His hand tightened around hers.

She held her breath.

"I always hoped we'd become more than friends." His warm breath flitted across her cheek, sending little thrills up and down her spine.

She pulled in air, forcing it down into her lungs, telling herself to be calm. "You never said anything." She didn't succeed in keeping the quiver from her voice.

He lifted their clasped hands a few inches. "I figured we'd grow close at our own rate."

She wondered how long it would have taken for him to announce all this without Adam's arrival to speed him up. Another two years? Then, shamed at her unkindness, she squeezed his hand. "That's so thoughtful."

"I believe in caution when it comes to relationships. They so often turn out to be something other than what we first thought."

She sat back a little. His words sounded like a warning. Or perhaps bitter experience. Suddenly she realized how little she knew of him, considering the length of time they had known one another.

"Did you have a relationship that went bad?" The words stuck in her throat, but she needed to understand him better.

He stiffened, almost pulling his hand away, and then, changing his mind, squeezed her fingers. "I was speaking generally. When we're young we approach all relationships with a wide-eyed trust. Time teaches us to be more selective."

He had avoided her question. The fact that he chose not to answer directly bothered her. She wanted him to trust her enough to be open and honest.

"I think there's more to it than you're admitting." Her voice was low, her words gentle. Despite her desire for honesty between them, she didn't want to force him into a discussion he wished to avoid. "But I know you'll discuss it when you feel the time is right."

Minutes passed. The pale moonlight cast gray shadows across the yard, ghostly suggestions of trees and objects. A cat howled. Somewhere a dog barked, the mournful sound echoing in her soul.

"I did have a bad experience," Michael offered, his voice slow and silvery in the quiet. "I thought we had an understanding, but Miriam thought differently. She walked away without so much as a good-bye."

She squeezed his hand. "Michael, I'm so sorry."

"I got over it. I guess in a way I wasn't all that surprised."

"Why didn't it surprise you?"

He drew in a breath. "My parents never cared for me as much as my brother. I guess I didn't expect she would be any different."

She gasped. "Miriam ran off with Timothy?"

"That would have been poetic justice, don't you think?" His laugh was short and bitter. "No, it was someone else. But I guess it proved to me no one would ever care for me enough to love me unconditionally." His fingers tightened around her hand. "But in all the time I've known you, you have always been honest and true."

"Thank you, Michael." A sliver of steel raced down her spine. She hoped she could live up to his expectations and never hurt his sensitive soul.

Muffled sounds came from inside the house. The light in her mother's room came on.

"I should go see if she needs any help." But she made no effort to remove her hand from where it rested on his arm, covered by his warm, possessive fingers. This new level of intimacy with Michael felt good and right.

"Yes, I suppose I should be leaving." He slowly released her hand. "Would you like me to come by and walk you to church?"

She restrained the desire to hug his arm. "That would be nice." They had sat together for months but always met at the church before the service. "Thank you." Her heart swelled.

They looked into the moon-draped yard, but Chas's thoughts were not on the scene; they were on the man at her side. She wondered if he was thinking about kissing her.

"I'll see you tomorrow." He was gone, like a man fleeing from a ghost.

Chas smiled, understanding how difficult he found it to trust any sort of intimacy, knowing the progress made in their relationship tonight constituted a giant leap for him. It was enough for now. A beginning.

She hurried indoors and down the hall.

Mother was ensconced upon her pillows, the quilt folded neatly across her chest. "Hello, *ma cherie*. Michael has gone home?"

Chas nodded. "He's just left."

Her mother patted a spot beside her on the bed. "Come here."

It was a ritual as old as her life, and Chas sat beside her on the covers. "How are you feeling?"

"I'm fine. I have to learn to be careful, that's all. Forget my old aches and pains. Tell me about your day."

Chas sighed. *Where to begin?*

"How was your outing with Adam?"

"The falls were lovely. Spectacular. Adam couldn't keep his pencil still."

"He's always so full of the joy of life. It's as if he lives life with a wing and a song."

"Mother," Chas said, chuckling, "you've turned poetic."

"Away with you now. I'm just making an observation." She rubbed her little ivory angel with one fingertip.

"Adam seems—he's such a gentleman. Always so kind to everyone from Mrs. Banner to Emma. Yet—" Again she paused.

"Yet what?"

"Maybe I see it only because I'm your mother." She let the ivory angel lie in her lap, holding it with fingers grown still.

A heartbeat strumming behind her eyes, Chas watched the still fingers, knowing it meant the problem had been sorted. Knowing, too, that her mother was pulling her thoughts into order, praying for wisdom before she spoke.

"Adam appears to have a special regard for you."

Chas said nothing.

"I realize it's none of my business, but has Adam spoken to you of his feelings? Has he expressed more than casual interest?" She rushed on, not giving Chas a chance to answer. "I mention this only because I wonder if I've prepared you adequately for such an event."

Chas laughed. "Are you talking of a man expressing interest? Because if you are, I learned to deal with that by the time I was fourteen years old."

"Chastity!"

"This place is hardly a convent."

"I realize that, but you never told me anyone had ever been—" She stopped, searching for the word.

"Inappropriate?" Chas supplied.

"Were they?"

"Nothing that wasn't handled by a word or two. About all I had to say was, 'Shall I call my mother?' and the miscreant would turn tail and run." No need to mention some of the bigger boys at school who had proved slightly more difficult to dissuade. She was thankful God had always protected her.

"There—you succeeded in making me forget what I was talking about. I suppose that was your intention."

"Not at all. Should I be wanting to?"

"Of course not. I was only wondering about Adam." Again she paused and then rushed on. "But don't feel you have to tell me if you don't wish to."

But Chas wanted very much to tell her mother. "He showed me a sketch of myself. You remember that one he did when I was twelve or thirteen?"

"Vaguely."

"He carried one like it with him all these years." Chas repeated Adam's story, leaving out only the part where Adam said he'd carried her in his heart. Just thinking those words turned her head into a whirlwind of confusion. She knew she would choke if she tried to say them aloud.

"Do you think he's interested in a special way?"

Chas pressed her finger to her chin. "He has no reason to think we're more than acquaintances."

"I wonder if that makes a difference to a man who has thought of you with such high regard for so many years."

Chas let out her breath sharply. "I should think if he truly had feelings toward me, it wouldn't have taken ten years to return and speak of them."

"I expect he thought of you as still being fourteen."

Chas refrained from mentioning one didn't have to be too bright to do the arithmetic. Instead she addressed the thing that mattered most. "It really doesn't matter because I have no desire to be a widow to a man's wanderlust. It isn't at all what I want."

The words fell into silence. Her mother plucked up the tiny angel and again rubbed her finger back and forth over it. After a moment she asked, "What do you want?"

Chas searched for the right words—a way of expressing her desires without making her mother think she was unhappy with the current situation. "I think, most of all, I want to be sure I don't make a decision that would leave me having to make the best of things. I want the very best God has available. And I'm content to leave things in God's hands for His will and His timing."

Her mother clasped Chas's hand. "Chastity, I expect you're talking about my life when you talk of making the best of things. I admit I made a rather big mistake in my youth, and to some it looks as if my life has been relegated to making do, but I don't see it that way. I never have. I feel privileged. After all, I had a firsthand experience with an angel. It turned my life around full circle and gave it meaning above and beyond the ordinary."

Chas was silent. She'd heard it before. She knew her mother believed life had given her a special bequest. But it wasn't enough for Chas. She wanted more. Or, as she had said to Michael, less.

"I never meant to raise you to be afraid of risks."

Chas stared at her mother. "What do you mean?"

"I suppose I'm thinking of Adam. I wouldn't want you to turn him aside simply because of the risks such a relationship carries."

Chas tried to assess her mother's words in light of her feelings about Adam—and Michael. Taking risks was one thing, but throwing everything away recklessly was something else. Besides, it was all a pointless discussion. It was Michael she was fond of—surely love would grow with time. It was Michael who shared a desire for the same sort of life she wanted.

"Are you suggesting Adam might be in love with me? Because if you are, you can put your mind at ease. We are worlds apart. Besides, there's Michael."

"Yes, of course, Michael. Has he given you cause for hope?"

Chas chuckled at her mother's phrasing. Although he hadn't said he loved her or asked her to marry him, he had given her cause for hope. "Yes, Mother, he has."

"Well, he's certainly a solid, steady man. And if that's what you're looking for. . ." Her voice trailed off on a thread of doubt.

"It's what I want—a life that is steady and predictable."

Mother smiled. "Then I can only wish you happiness—whatever you decide." She reached for the Bible. "I rest assured God will direct your steps in the way that is best."

Chas whispered, "That is my prayer, too."

Mother read several verses before turning to Chas. "Let's pray together about your future."

Chas let her mother's soft prayer brush clean the hidden corners of her soul like a warm Chinook wind blowing away the accumulated dirt and dust of winter.

Taking with her a fresh settledness, she kissed her mother and hurried to her own room to open her Bible and study the name written on the piece of paper, Simon LaBlanc. What would it have been like to have a father?

On Sunday morning Chas set a tray with coffee and toast on the bed beside her mother. "I wish you could come to church."

"I do, too, *ma cherie,* but I couldn't possibly walk that far." She smiled her reassurance. "Now don't you fret about it. Maybe you could mention to Pastor Simpson I'd like to see him when it's convenient." She waved a hand. "Don't look like that. I only want some spiritual refreshment."

"I'll ask him to call."

A few minutes later, she and Michael strolled down the sun-dappled street toward the church. Nothing special happened. Nothing of significance was said. Yet when they stepped through the double doors into the sanctuary, Chas felt as though a sweet bond had been forged. She let Michael lead her to a pew. He sat close enough that their elbows touched. Warmth centered in a place behind Chas's heart.

Emma caught her attention across the room and lifted her hand in greeting. Beside her sat a red-haired, pink-faced youth Chas had never seen before. Then her attention was diverted to the pew in front of them.

"Good morning, Chas." At Adam's warm greeting, she looked up to see the Silverhorn family filing into the pew. Adam was directly in front of her. It was impossible not to notice how his hair—sun-bleached on the ends—curled along his neck. Jack sat at his side, and Adam leaned over to mouth something in his ear, every movement so quick and graceful that, despite herself, Chas found pleasure in watching him.

He turned to face her, and she clenched her hands in a vain attempt to stop the guilty heat from rushing up her cheeks.

"I thought your mother would be here."

She shook her head. "It's too far to walk, and we don't own a buggy or any means of transportation."

"I see." His brow furrowed. "I expect she misses going to church."

"Yes, I'm afraid she does."

Michael said nothing, but the pressure increased along her arm where they were touching.

Pastor Simpson took his place behind the pulpit and called for the first hymn. Chas couldn't help thinking how symbolic it was that she and Michael were joined together by the hymnbook they both clasped. It spoke of so many things they had in common: their faith, their contentment in a quiet life, even their love of teaching children.

Then Pastor Simpson announced the title of his sermon, "The Steps of a Good Man Are Ordered by the Lord," and Chas's attention was riveted on the message.

A short while later, she left the service with her heart lighter, her convictions strengthened. *Thus far the Lord has led me,* she reminded herself. He would surely keep her on the right path.

Emma stopped Chas at the doorway, pulling her aside. "Did you see him?"

"I assume," Chas said, chuckling, "you mean the young man beside you."

Emma grinned. "Remember the old codger cousin of the Simpsons' we were going to meet?"

Chas smiled. "I'm guessing he wasn't so old after all."

"Not a bit old. His name is Gordon Simpson. He's from down east but wants to move west." She grabbed Chas's hand. "Come and meet him."

Chas allowed herself to be dragged to the blushing young man. As she turned to rejoin Michael, she came face to face with Adam.

"Don't forget my opening show tomorrow."

"I'm looking forward to it."

And surprisingly she was. His work, whether photos, paintings, or sketches, had the power to flood her senses with color and emotion. Which did not explain the alarm ringing up and down her spine at Adam's nearness.

"I promised your mother I would bring her more photos to look at. Tell her I haven't forgotten."

Chas nodded. "I will." And she hurried to Michael's side.

Outside in the warm sunshine, Michael asked, "What did Adam have to say?"

Surprised at his sharp tone, Chas said in her calmest voice, "He reminded me he's having his first display tomorrow, and he wanted me to tell Mother he hadn't forgotten his promise to visit her again."

"I suppose that's decent of him."

It was said so grudgingly that Chas giggled. "I suppose it is, though I don't think Mother would want to hear it put quite that way."

Michael had the grace to laugh at himself. "I was rather condescending, wasn't I? I'm sorry. I didn't mean to be."

She tucked his apology and the tiny bit of jealousy he'd shown into her thoughts. Michael was so right for her.

Chapter 6

Emma spent the morning extolling the virtues of Gordon Simpson, and, according to Emma, he abounded with them.

"He wants to start a new business," she said. "He says he'll spend some time deciding what the town needs." She barely paused as she stepped outside the door to hang the laundry to dry. "He thinks Willow Creek has a tremendous future since it's on the rail line between Calgary and Edmonton." She stepped back inside, the wicker laundry basket under her arm. "Of course the town council has been telling us that for years, and the paper has duly reported it. I just didn't pay them much mind."

Chas hid a smile. As far as she could remember, Emma had only looked at the gossip pages and household hints of the weekly paper. "I'm wondering if you've found Mr. Simpson has a bit more to offer than the local boys?"

It was a longstanding argument of Emma's that there could be no romance with a local boy. "How could I fall in love with someone I've known all my life," she would ask, "and seen with a runny nose or crying for his mama?"

Emma let out a sharp breath. "Do you see any of the local boys setting out to establish a new business? They'll do what their fathers have done and never see what's right in front of their noses."

"So Mr. Simpson is the answer to your prayers?"

Emma blushed. "It's rather soon to tell." She rushed on. "He's not at all like his cousins. He's so—so full of enthusiasm."

Remembering how the pink-faced Gordon could barely say hello, Chas wondered if Emma was the only one who brought forth life in the man.

Emma stopped to study Chas. "Of course I know he doesn't hold a candle to Adam as far as adventure goes, but Adam doesn't even see me. He has eyes only for you."

"Emma! How can you say that?" The room was steaming from the tubs of hot water, and the exertion of running the heavy sheets and towels through the wringer had caused the sweat to bead on Chas's forehead. She paused to wipe her face on a rag.

"I have eyes. And I'm not stupid."

"No, you're not, which is why I'm so surprised you should think such a thing. I could never be interested in a man with wandering feet. Besides, you yourself warned against falling in love with him."

Emma tightened her mouth. "The heart does not always go where the mind goes."

Chas giggled at Emma's stern expression. "True enough, but neither do we

65

have to follow the fickle desires of our heart. I believe in mind over matter—and emotions."

She dumped the rinsed sheets into the basket, and Emma hoisted it to her hip, heading outside to hang them.

"I only hope you don't 'mind' yourself right out of something special."

Chas glanced up. "Special?"

Emma nodded. "I might be young and inexperienced when it comes to love, but I have eyes, and it seems to me one would have to have a weak mind to pass up love—real love—for something 'reasonable.' " She practically spat out the final word and slipped outside.

Chas's startled gaze followed her, and she pressed her lips tight. Why was everyone determined that she and Adam should be romantically interested in each other? She ran a finger under the neckline of her dress to cool herself. Sure, he'd carried a memory of her, but it had nothing to do with reality. She wasn't the person he had carried in his heart all those years. Her dreams and wishes had grown in a different direction from his.

"So what are you going to do about Adam?"

Busy loading the washing machine, Chas spared Emma the barest of glances. "There is nothing to do about Adam. We're old schoolmates, I enjoy his work, and he's been kind to Mother, for which I am grateful. We're friends and neighbors. That's all."

Emma sighed, but Chas said no more. Let Emma think what she wanted. Chas knew her heart—and her mind.

But Emma continued. "I suppose you'll end up marrying Michael." She rolled her eyes. "I can see the two of you planning a school program and telling yourself what an exciting day you'd had."

Chas laughed so hard, she had to grasp the side of the rinse tub.

Emma glowered at her. "What's so funny? Sounds deadly dull to me."

Chas wiped her eyes on the edge of her apron. "Put that way—it certainly does."

"Believe me, it would be." Emma's forehead wrinkled as she stared into Chas's face. "I sometimes think you're so set on getting a little house of your own that you'd settle on Pastor Simpson himself if he offered it."

Chas giggled at the prospect. "I guess it would work if you marry Gordon and let Martha move in with you."

Emma shook her head. "Not me. Martha goes with her brother."

"I guess that's out then."

"I should hope so." Emma took the last load of laundry and headed to the door. "But I'm not fooling about what I said."

"You really think I should consider Pastor Simpson? He's old enough to be my father."

"No, silly. I mean about having your gaze so firmly fixed on the one thing you think you want that you're blind to everything else." The door slammed shut between them.

Chas shook her head. Young, impressionable Emma would settle for nothing but stars and roses. And gladly live with the consequences. But Chas wanted so much more. It was something Emma, having grown up as she did, would never understand.

⁂

The tea had been served and the laundry collected off the line before Chas said to Emma, "I promised Jack I'd go to Adam's opening display today."

"You go ahead," Emma said, glancing up from ironing a sheet. "And while you're looking at the display, have a good look at Adam."

Laughing at her friend's determination, she headed downtown to the shop. Inside she stared around the room. The once-bare walls were now colorful with paintings, drawings, and photos. Adam stood speaking to one of the older citizens of Willow Creek. When he saw her, his blue eyes darkened. Then a slow smile drove flashes of silver through his irises.

A sensation stirred in the pit of her stomach not unlike the feeling she had when staring at the whirling waters of Sheep Falls. She blinked to steady herself, blaming Emma for her reaction. She squared her shoulder and took a step forward. Her mind would rule her heart.

"I thought maybe you'd forgotten to come." Adam reached for her hand. "I'm glad you didn't."

An older couple called out, "Adam, where did you paint this picture? It's lovely."

He looked at Chas with regret then sighed. "Duty calls. Feel free to browse."

She studied the display, entranced by the beauty. Scenery of the Yukon. Weathered faces of its inhabitants. Fleeting glimpses of the wildlife. She circled the room twice and would have gone around again, but Adam was at her side.

"Ellen's going to watch the store for a while so I can get some air. I thought we might take a walk."

Caught in a web of color and sight and sensation, Chas nodded. If he had asked her at that moment to follow him to the Antarctic, she would have agreed. *So much for mind over matter,* she scolded herself inwardly.

She let him lead her outside into sunshine that was suddenly flat and streets that were colorless and ordinary. A wagon lumbered past, and a child ran across the street squealing in excitement. The spell broken, she planted her feet firmly on the wooden sidewalk. This was Willow Creek, where she belonged, where she longed to make a permanent home.

"Were you pleased with the turnout?" she asked, her feet leading her on a familiar route.

"Yes, very much."

"How did the people respond to your work?" She wondered if others had been as moved by his paintings as she had been.

"Mostly they oohed and aahed. A few asked if they could purchase a piece."

Somehow she couldn't imagine him parting with anything. "Are you selling them?"

"Not from this collection. In a week or two, I'll set up a display of work for sale."

They walked past the turreted houses and turned the corner into a narrower street.

"How about you?" he asked. "What did you think of the display?"

She oohed once and then aahed and smiled.

He chuckled. "That good?"

"Yes." She nodded briskly. "I'm not sure I can put it into words, but it was tremendous. I felt as if I were right there. As if I could feel the water's spray, touch the tiny flowers, even smell the sweat on that wizened old man."

"You're doing a good job of putting it into words."

She grinned. "The scenery is beautiful. Somehow I expected barrenness."

Her steps slowed of their own accord as they neared the picket fence. He halted and faced her squarely, blocking her pathway and her view of the little house. "It is beautiful, but in all my travels, I found nothing to compare to your beauty."

She raised her startled gaze to his and, at the sight of the glittering warmth in his blue eyes, immediately lowered her head, squeezing her hands into a tight knot.

"I wish I could hang the picture I did of you. Yet I really wouldn't want anyone else to see it. It's the most personal painting I've ever done."

She tried to move around him, but he touched her shoulder and stopped her. "Don't run away."

She nodded. Perhaps it was best to clear the air.

"I can't imagine life without you." His voice was low and strained.

She took a deep breath. "And I can't imagine living the sort of life you do."

"What do you mean? What do you know about the sort of life I want to live?" His hand was insistent on her shoulder.

She summoned the courage to look him in the eye without blinking. "No doubt, you'll be gone as suddenly as you've come. For how long? Perhaps another ten years?"

He stared at her, his eyes hard and unfathomable. "You're determined to believe that, aren't you?"

"I'm determined not to make a colossal mistake that would ruin my life and rob me of what I want—what I've wanted for a long time."

"I'm guessing you mean me when you use the word 'mistake.'" His words were dangerously low, but she forced herself to maintain eye contact. "And I suppose if I tell you I love you, you'll say I'm incapable of knowing what love is."

"Not at all." She forced the words out of a parched throat. "But it isn't me you're in love with—it's a memory. You don't know who I am or what I want."

His look was cold. "Perhaps you're right. The Chas I remember was never afraid."

She pulled back. "I'm not afraid."

He continued as if he hadn't heard her. "Remember the time you stood up to

Carl when he was tormenting little Sally? I can still see you planting your toes squarely in front of him, with your nose practically touching his. I'll never forget how you glared at him and said, 'I don't care if you are bigger than me. I won't let you hurt Sally anymore.'" Adam grinned. "You looked fierce enough to eat him. Poor Carl didn't know what to do. He sort of melted away."

Adam's smile faded, and he grew serious. "Now it seems you wear a pair of blinders so you can't see what's outside your safe little world. When did you become so scared of life?"

Chas had forgotten the incident with Carl, but now the feeling of angry defiance returned. She glared at Adam. "If you'd grown up without a father, always wondering if it was your fault he'd left; if you'd grown up in a houseful of strangers coming and going, asking questions, feeling free to touch your hair and make comments; if you could never have your mother to yourself because of the guests, then maybe you'd understand." She sucked in heated air.

"I am not afraid." She ground the words out. "I only want what I've never had." She stepped around him and pointed at the house. "I want a little home with a white picket fence. A house just for me and my family." With her hands on her hips, she looked at him. "I want a husband who is there for me and our children. I don't want to end up alone—for any reason." She gulped in some air. "I couldn't stand wondering if you would take off again."

Adam touched his finger to her cheek. She hadn't realized she was crying until he wiped a tear from her face.

"Oh, Chas. I can't promise I would never go away, but I would always come back. I love you, and I don't mean that tattered sketch I carried for years. I mean you, all grown up and fierce and gentle and sweet."

She shook away his hand. "You didn't hear a word I said. What we want in life is different." Her voice fell to a whisper. "I can't love you." And ignoring the protest from deep inside her heart, she mentally slammed a door in her mind.

"Can't or won't?"

His words were so low that she wondered if she had imagined them.

"I must go. I have work to do."

She spun around, not caring if he followed or stayed, every pounding footstep she made driving her determination deeper.

At the corner where she would turn one direction and Adam another, she paused.

"Adam, I don't mean to be rude or unkind, but I think it's best this way. I am not the person you think I am. We would never be happy together." She spoke as if he had asked her to marry him, but she had to make him understand. "You're a special person. You deserve someone who shares your dreams and goals, not someone who would always be fighting with them—and you—because of basic differences."

His eyes told her he didn't accept her words, but she still rushed on.

"I hope we can continue to be friends. And I wish you happiness." She held out her hand.

He stared at it as if she had offered a snake and then stuffed his hands in his pockets. "And I hope you come to your senses."

She wiped her palm on her thigh and swallowed hard. "I am being sensible."

He shook his head, a frown carved deeply into his cheek. "By burying your head in the sand? You could end up in a confining, dull existence if you do."

"I don't think that's going to happen."

She rushed toward home until she reached the final corner. She paused to let her racing heart slow down. She knew what she wanted. She would accept nothing else. She marched up the steps and into the boardinghouse.

"How was it?" Emma asked before Chas could close the door behind her.

Feeling as if she'd been caught with her hand in someone's change purse, Chas stared at Emma. "I suppose you could say we sorted things out satisfactorily."

Emma's eyebrows went up. "I meant Adam's show."

Chas adjusted a curtain. "The show was wonderful. He has a lovely collection of pictures of the Klondike. He says he'll leave it up awhile and then put up pictures on gold mining. He says he could pick a different topic every week of the year and change his display to suit the topic."

Emma watched with a wide-eyed expression. When Chas paused to catch her breath, Emma asked, "What was it you sorted out satisfactorily?"

"Things. Nothing. I'm going to check on Mother." She rushed from the room.

"Chicken!" Emma called after her.

The next day Adam appeared in time for tea, carrying a bundle of photos.

"What do you have for us?" Mother leaned forward eagerly.

"Pictures of the Queen Charlotte Islands and the Gulf Islands. I think you'll enjoy the mystic beauty of them."

Chas hung back, not wanting Adam to think she had changed her mind about what she'd said the day before, yet longing to get more than a glimpse of the pictures as they were passed from hand to hand.

"Look, Chastity." Her mother indicated Chas should come to her side. "Isn't this wonderful?"

Chas slid to the chair, hoping Adam would ignore her. The photo was a scene of spectacular mountain beauty and tall trees reflected in glass-calm water.

"I painted the same scene."

Adam handed Chas a small oil painting, and she gasped.

"Adam," Mother said, "I've never had a desire to travel, but these pictures make me want to go sit on this beach."

The beauty was so powerful that Chas felt her heart would explode from her chest. She stood to her feet.

"I have to make a pudding for dessert," she mumbled, fleeing to the kitchen, where she yanked the pot from the cupboard and measured in milk. It was wonderful to see the beauties of the world. She could understand why Adam wanted to travel and see more of them. But she didn't want to think about him leaving again. She was thankful Michael did not feel the same need. He was content to enjoy the pleasures secondhand.

Reason and purpose returned.

Emma joined her a few minutes later. "Why are you in such an all-fired hurry all of a sudden? Did something bite you?"

Chas answered calmly, "Just the need to get supper ready."

"Wouldn't be you're suddenly anxious to avoid Adam?"

Chas shook her head. "I told you there's nothing between us except friendship."

The girl began filling the basin from the bin of potatoes. "By the way, Adam is still in there with your mother."

She shrugged. "It's good of him to spend time with Mother. I know she appreciates it."

Emma sat on a stool and began peeling vegetables. "Why don't you get the rest of the tea things while I do this?"

Chas narrowed her eyes, studying Emma. But the girl was busy with her job, and Chas had no choice but to mumble, "Sure."

Adam and her mother sat with their heads close together, the pictures piled neatly on Adam's knee. As soon she entered the room, they stopped speaking and looked up, their expressions startled.

Chas looked from one to the other. "What are you two up to?"

"I'm going to help Emma," Mother said, struggling to her feet.

Adam jumped up. "I need to get back to the shop."

Chas stared at them.

That was the last she saw of Adam for some time, and life settled back into routine.

Michael joined them for supper on Wednesday. They had barely seated themselves around the table when he announced, "Adam has agreed to talk to the students, but he wants to know what subject I'd like him to talk about. What would you suggest?" He addressed the assembled group.

Beryl became dreamy eyed. "The glacier picture, for sure. The mountains and glaciers and rivers of the Yukon."

"That's too vague," Roy insisted. "I'd want to know more about his travels—how long it took him to reach the Klondike and how he did it. A bit about his travels down the coast."

Mother laid her fork down. "Michael, the Klondike gold rush will go down as a significant part of our history. I'm sure Adam could make it a real learning experience for the children."

The conversation went back and forth.

Chas, for her part, silently wished everyone would forget Adam.

Days passed, and Adam did not visit the boardinghouse. Days turned into weeks, and apart from the glimpses Chas had of him seated with his family at church on Sunday, he might as well have disappeared into the wild yonder.

Then one day Emma looked up from washing the dishes. "Adam has a new display at the shop. He calls it 'Faces of the North.' It's very interesting."

Chas nodded. Adam had obviously decided it was best for them to go their separate ways. She agreed. But why was she missing his visits?

"I hear his sales have gone well, too. Several parties have come from Calgary and Edmonton for the sole purpose of seeing his display and buying one of his paintings."

"I don't blame them. He's a very good artist."

Emma spun around to face her. "I don't understand you."

"What's to understand?"

"How can you be so dense?" Emma slapped the wet rag over the table. "I had you and him figured out for a sure thing, and now you avoid each other as if you both have something catching."

Chas kept her attention on the platter she was drying. "I tried to tell you we had nothing in common."

Emma exhaled loudly. "He adored you with his eyes. I can't believe you would let that sort of thing go to waste. I know I wouldn't. When Gordon looks at me like that, I'm ready to fall at his feet."

Chas laughed. "Somehow I don't see you turning into a docile slave for anyone."

Emma looked thoughtful. "Knowing someone thinks you're as special as the sun rising makes any task seem like a privilege."

It was Chas's turn to stare. "Why, I do believe you've fallen in love."

Emma's cheeks darkened. She angled her shoulders in an attempt to block Chas's view.

Chas laughed. "I hope he deserves you."

Emma nodded. "I hope I deserve him." Then she straightened. "But you're not making me forget what we were talking about. You must have said something to discourage Adam, for I know he saw nothing and nobody but you."

"You're always such a dreamer, Emma. You see romance in every look and conversation. Adam and I are friends, but we are worlds apart when it comes to what we want in life."

"Well," Emma sniffed, "it wouldn't do you any harm to expand your world a little."

"You're impossible. Number one, I have had a very broad experience in life from living in this house. I've met people from all walks of life and from all over the world. Why, right now we have under our roof a man who spent years in the East Indies."

"Oh, I'd forgotten." Emma rolled her eyes. "I suppose you're going to tell me it's been a real learning experience? None of us even knew about our Mr. Elias until Adam showed up." She shook her head, mumbling, "Wonderful things we've heard about the East, I'd say."

"That may be so, but there's something else."

"Yeah, what?"

"As far as expanding my horizons, I wonder how I could do that and still manage this house? You ever think about that?"

Emma was instantly contrite. "I'm sorry, Chas. Sometimes I forget you're stuck here."

"I'm not stuck. This is where I belong."

Emma nodded, her expression thoughtful. "I suppose that leaves Michael."

Emma made it sound like leftover breakfast.

"You are truly impossible." Chas turned away, not wanting her to see how her remark had stung.

Michael had visited regularly as before, but if Chas had expected their relationship to change, she was disappointed. He brought papers for her to help with and news of the children. He reported that Adam had given a talk of the Klondike, and it had been very good. But he had said nothing more about what he had called "being more than friends."

Chas took her restless feelings to bed with her and sat at her little table, pulling her Bible toward her. The page fell open to the piece of paper on which she had penned her father's name. Her heart twisted into a knot, and she rested her fingertip on her mouth. *Simon LaBlanc, who are you? Why did you never care enough to find me?*

Michael came as usual on Wednesday. It took Chas a few minutes to realize he had come without his usual armful of papers.

"Did you forget something?" She glanced down the hall, wondering if he had set them on the table in the entryway.

He shook his head and followed the direction of her look. "I don't think so. What have I forgotten?"

"Where is the children's schoolwork?"

His grin slightly lopsided, he held out empty hands. "No papers tonight." His expression sobered. "I thought we'd just enjoy the evening."

Her heart gave a sudden jolt, and hope swelled in a wave. Then her mother's voice called Chas back to her senses.

"Have a seat, Michael. Supper is served."

Chas barely heard the discussion around the table as they ate.

"Chastity." Her mother's voice was amused. "Have you forgotten dessert?"

Chas leapt to her feet, ignoring the curious stares of those across the table, and hurried to the kitchen. As she dished out rhubarb crisp, she hummed.

After the meal, Michael leaned back in his chair. "I know you like to get the meal things cleaned up right away, so go ahead. I'll have another cup of tea."

Emma followed on Chas's heels. "Don't suppose it occurred to him to help. I'll bet he doesn't even know what dishwater is for."

Chas chuckled. "He must do dishes at home. After all, he lives alone."

"You mean he hasn't invited you to visit him so you can do them?"

"Emma, shame on you. Besides, you know I'd never go to his house."

Emma shrugged. "I guess if you're happy with him waiting for you in the dining room, I shouldn't be concerned. If it was me, I'd want him at least to sit in the same room." She got a faraway look in her eyes, and Chas knew she was thinking of young Gordon, who came frequently to the back door to walk her home.

"I'm happy." It was enough to know Michael was content to wait for her, content to visit at the boardinghouse and not expect her to be free to take time for a bunch of social activities. It was enough he didn't resent her work.

Emma studied Chas's face. "I sincerely hope you are. You deserve every bit of happiness there is."

"Emma, that is so kind." Chas hugged the younger girl.

Emma nodded. "Let's get this finished so you can visit with your Michael." She glanced toward the back door.

"And so you can go out walking with Gordon."

Chas and Michael sat together in the corner of the veranda. The sun dipped toward the horizon, casting ribbons of red, orange, pink, and purple across the sky.

Chas sighed. "There's nothing much better than watching the sun go down on a summer evening." She brushed a strand of hair from her face. Sharing the sunset with someone special made it even more enjoyable.

"You are happy, aren't you?" It was half question, half affirmation.

"Yes, I am. What reason would I have not to be?"

He was silent a moment. "I wondered for a while if you were greatly disappointed because you couldn't return to teaching."

She continued to watch the sky, the colors dancing into different formations. "I love teaching and would gladly go back, but I'm content to leave things in God's hands and trust His timing. He knows what is best."

"Sometimes He sends unexpected events into our lives."

She nodded, her attention drawn to a sudden flare of orange over the roof of the house across the alley. "Mother always says the unexpected carries a special gift."

Michael laughed a little. "And she's usually referring to you."

Chas turned then to smile at Michael. "She does rather belabor the point."

His brown eyes darkened to the color of rich chocolate. "I don't think that's possible."

Her tongue suddenly uncooperative, Chas let herself float in the depths of his look.

He studied her, his gaze lingering on her hair, her chin, and her lips before returning to her eyes. Somewhat distractedly he said, "I wondered for a while if you were interested in Adam."

"He's just a friend." Her voice sounded strange in her ears.

"Does that mean I have the right to think you might be interested in me as more than a friend?"

"Didn't we have this discussion not long ago?" It was impossible to concentrate. His look did funny things to her mind.

"Might it be possible for you to consider marrying me?"

The moment froze. She was aware of color dancing across the sky, bathing Michael's features in a warm, golden glow. Her heart throbbed inside her chest. Her emotions curled for a moment and then erupted in a glorious burst of color and joy. She gave one low-throated laugh.

"Michael, if this is a proposal, I want it done right."

His features softened into a knowing smile. "You shall certainly have your wish." He fell to his knees at her feet and took her hands between his. "Chastity LaBlanc, may I have the honor of requesting your hand in marriage?"

She giggled. "Yes. Oh, yes, I'll marry you, Michael Martin." *I'll share your life. I'll enjoy your love. I'll be beside you always and you beside me.*

He stood to his feet and drew her to her feet, their clasped hands against his chest.

She tilted her head back so she could see his dear familiar features. *Michael of my heart.* The words filled her being.

He smiled gently and then lowered his head to touch his lips to hers. It was a kiss as soft and gentle as dew upon the cheek, as pure and undemanding as the summer sun.

And as Chas rested her head against his shoulder, her heart sang with joy.

Chapter 7

Chas bounced down on the bed beside her mother.

Mother lowered her Bible and smiled at Chas. "You're looking pleased with yourself, *ma cherie.*"

"That's because I'm so happy."

"Something special?"

Chas turned to her side. "Something very special indeed. Tonight Michael asked me to marry him."

Her mother nodded. "And I take it that you've accepted."

"Of course."

"Then I'm very happy for you. Michael is a nice young man, steady and dependable." She leaned over and kissed Chas's cheek.

The familiar scent of her mother's dusting powder filled Chas's nostrils. "I'm very lucky."

Her mother lay back against her pillows and sighed. "I guess we'll have to begin making plans. Have you picked a date?"

Chas laughed. "I never even thought of it."

"Yes, I suppose you had other things on your mind."

She gave her mother a startled look, but the older woman's face was innocently expressionless. "It was so unexpected." Chas stared up at the ceiling. "He was so sweet."

Her mother chuckled low in her throat. "One would rather expect him to be at this point."

Chas giggled. "One would, I suppose."

Mother grew thoughtful. "I hope you can put off your marriage until I'm well enough to take over the boardinghouse again."

Reality slammed into Chas's chest, driving her breath from her. For a moment she had flown away on her dreams—marriage, a little house of her own, raising a family with Michael. But now the cold, hard facts had to be faced. Her mother wasn't able to run the house on her own and may never be. If only she would sell the place—perhaps now she would consider it.

"I know what you're going to say. You want me to sell." Her mother picked up her little ivory angel from the bedside table. "To you it makes sense, but I can't. Not yet. It's too final a choice. I can't even contemplate it."

"I know how much it means to you," Chas said. "And to be perfectly honest, Michael and I never even discussed a wedding date. But I promise I will not leave you to manage on your own. Somehow things will work out. God will provide a way. Isn't that what you've taught me all my life?"

Mother grasped Chas's hand. "I have indeed, *ma cherie*. And I know He will. Let's turn it over to Him."

Chas closed her eyes and bowed her heart before God as her mother prayed aloud, first thanking God for sending Michael into Chas's life and then laying out the problem before Him. "God, from the moment You sent an angel to rescue me, You have never failed to provide my every need, and I know You won't fail me now. I'm asking You to meet our need, and I'm suggesting the best way would be for my leg to get better. Thank You. Amen."

Chas giggled.

Her mother raised an eyebrow.

Grinning, Chas explained. "I was thinking how funny it is for you to tell God how He should answer your prayer. Maybe He has a different plan in mind."

"If He does, I'm sure it's better than mine, so I won't have any trouble accepting it."

Chas laughed at her mother's pleased-as-a-cat expression.

They remained there quietly. Chas let contentment slide through her. The future was as bright as the stars in the sky. Suddenly she jumped to her feet, pausing to kiss her mother's cheek before she went to her own room, where she did a little dance across the narrow space, hugging herself as she drew to a halt in front of the table.

"Thank You, God," she murmured, picking up her Bible. Dropping to the chair, she read a few verses and let the pages fall open to the piece of paper bearing her father's name. She stared at it for a second and then picked up the bit of paper and pressed it to her chest.

The next morning Chas greeted Emma before the girl got through the door. "Guess what?"

Emma closed the door behind her and faced Chas, looking her up and down slowly. "Someone left you a fortune?"

Chas pulled herself taller. "Nope. Something better."

"Your mother sold the boardinghouse?"

"Not a chance." Chas stepped aside to allow Emma to unhook an apron from behind the door and tie it around her waist.

"Then Adam must have come calling."

Chas jabbed her fists to her hips. "You couldn't be further from the truth. Michael asked me to marry him."

Emma dropped to a chair and stared at her. "So he finally got around to it?"

"You make it sound as if I've been waiting for ages." She thought Emma would have been a little more enthusiastic.

But then Emma sprang to her feet and threw her arms around Chas. "I'm very glad for you. When's the big day? Where are you going to live? What's to happen to the boardinghouse? And your mother?" She pushed away and studied Chas with wide eyes. "Wow! I can't believe it."

Chas laughed. "He only asked last night. We haven't had a chance to discuss any of the details." She sobered. "I guess the most important thing is Mother's needs." She took a pot holder and removed six golden loaves from the oven. "Somehow things will work out."

"I'm sure they will." Emma picked up a pot and filled it with water. "I guess this means Adam is out of the question?"

"Oh, you." She flicked a towel at Emma. "He's a free man as far as I can tell. If you're so interested—"

Emma gave her head a toss. "I've already found what I want."

The girls grinned at each other.

"Life is good, isn't it?" Chas said, as she tipped the loaves onto a clean towel.

Around the table that evening, Emma, having asked Chas if she meant to keep her engagement a secret and being told no, said to the assembled group, "Chas has some very special news."

Every eye turned toward her. Chas wished Michael were there to share the moment, but he wasn't, and she had no choice but to answer the babble of questions.

"Michael and I are going to be married."

Beryl bounced forward. "Congratulations, Chas. I'm sure you'll be very happy."

"Yes, congratulations," Louise said.

John added more slowly, "He'll be staying on as teacher then?"

"Thank you." Chas smiled at the two girls then turned to John. "I would assume so."

Mr. Elias sat up straighter. "May I add my congratulations? Young Michael is a good man. I'm sure you'll be very happy."

Mrs. B tugged at Mother's arm. "What's all the fuss?"

Mother leaned close. "Chastity announced her engagement to Michael Martin, the young teacher who visits here."

"Michael Martin, you say? Isn't he that quiet young fellow who comes and goes all the time?"

"The teacher, yes."

Mrs. B sat back and squinted at Chas. "Well, I declare."

Chas smiled at the old lady, having no idea what her comment meant.

Roy cautiously leaned forward and asked, "What about the boardinghouse?"

The quietness following his question told Chas the answer was important to everyone at the table. "We have made no plans as yet, but selling the house is not something we're considering."

She felt the room swell with a collective sigh of relief.

"I'm planning to continue running this place even after Chastity marries." Her mother's look told them she would contemplate no other option.

"But, Miz LaBlanc, what about your leg?" Beryl asked, her voice filled with concern.

"We would make other arrangements if it came to that," Louise added, her voice soft.

Mother waved away their concern. "I'm expecting to get better faster than any of you think."

Even the Knutsen boys looked up with sudden interest.

"We all hope you do," Beryl said and asked for the bread to be passed.

As if by some signal, the conversation turned to other matters, and Chas knew no one wanted to argue with her mother about her chances of getting better.

Chas knelt in the warm dirt of the garden, plucking weeds from around the pea plants. The sun was warm on her back. The birds sang from the tree branches, their songs ringing through her heart.

After a while, Chas sat back on her heels, turning her head about to ease her muscles. The beautiful Saturday afternoon would soon be more glorious when Michael arrived. She hadn't seen him since he'd proposed. Each evening she had hoped he would come, and when he failed to appear, she had consoled herself with the knowledge he was busy with year-end tests and preparations. Suddenly she chuckled. It had been all of two nights since she'd seen him, and here she was acting as if it had been weeks.

She bent back to her task, a smile on her lips.

"Chas?" A familiar voice called her name.

Her heart leapt to her throat, and she turned around. Adam stood at the gate, his arms resting on the top bar, his hands hanging over into the yard. She stared at his hands—long fingers, flecks of red and blue paint under his nails.

She stood to her feet, dusting her skirt.

They were several feet apart, but not so far that Chas failed to see how dark his eyes were.

"Hello, Adam." She brushed her hair out of her face. Why was he here?

He watched her without speaking.

She took a step and another, bringing her within reach of the gate. She halted, twisting her hands together. Now she could see smudges of green on his thumb and a black mark on his index finger.

His hands pulled away, and she looked up. His eyes glittered with silver. "I had to come and hear for myself."

"Hear what?"

"That you and Michael are getting married."

The tension drained from her, and the sun was again warm. She smiled. "Yes, we are."

He nodded. "Then I wish you every happiness. I hope he loves you very much."

"Thank you." She paused. "How are things at your shop?"

He rubbed the top of the gate post. "Good. Very good."

She couldn't think of anything more to say.

He cleared his throat. "I've come to tell you I'm going away for a while. I'm taking my display on tour across Canada."

"I'm not surprised. I always knew you'd be leaving sooner or later." The news didn't upset her. She had Michael's love to protect her.

"I hadn't planned on leaving so soon, but suddenly it seems like a good time."

She knew he meant because she had agreed to marry Michael.

"I'll only be gone a few weeks. I have shows lined up down east, Winnipeg, Toronto, and a few other places." His eyes found hers.

She knew he still hoped she'd give him a reason to stay. But she couldn't. "I hope you have a good trip."

"Maybe you'll be married by the time I get back."

"Maybe. We haven't discussed a date yet." She shrugged. "There are a lot of things to consider."

"Of course." He glanced past her to the house. "Say good-bye to your mother for me, will you?"

"You're welcome to tell her yourself."

For a moment he looked at the house and then shook his head. "No, you tell her."

"I will."

His gaze found hers again, and she gasped at the stark emotion in them. Then he blinked, and his expression deadened. "I'll miss you."

She nodded. He meant more than the impending trip, more than her engagement to Michael. He was saying good-bye to a dream he had carried for the better part of ten years. She saw the pain in his eyes and wished she could do something. But there was nothing left except to say good-bye.

"Have a safe trip," she murmured.

He gave a tight smile. "And you have a good life."

He looked at her a moment longer, as if memorizing every feature, and then turned and walked away.

She stared after him a long time. Finally she muttered, "There was never anything to miss," and returned to weeding the garden.

Later, as she prepared for supper, she made frequent trips to the dining room window to check for Michael's arrival.

"Why don't you set the table while I mash the potatoes?" Emma finally said. "That way you won't have to make so many trips into the dining room." She shook her head. "I've never seen you so anxious for visitors."

Chas wrinkled her nose. "It isn't just any visitor. It's Michael." At Emma's raised eyebrows, she added, "I know he's been coming every Saturday for months, but now it's different. Now I can't wait to see him and see if he's still the same or"—her voice was muffled as she pulled aside the curtain—"if he's changed." Her voice dropped so low, she knew Emma couldn't hear. "As I've changed." Suddenly Michael was so dear, so important, she half-expected him to have grown several inches.

Finally she saw him coming. If he glanced at the house, he would see her waiting, but he turned in at the front gate and headed for the door without looking in her direction.

Chas raced for the door, throwing it open before he could give the bell a twist. "Michael. I thought you'd never get here." She leaned forward, lifting her face for a kiss.

"Am I late?"

"No, I was only eager to see you." She waited, her face upturned.

"Well, I'm awfully glad to see you, too." He dropped a kiss to her lips, warm but so short, she swallowed her disappointment.

"Come on in. Supper's ready." She pulled her hand through the crook of his arm as they walked to the table.

Besides her mother, only Mr. Elias, Mrs. B, and the Knutsen boys were there.

Mr. Elias stood and offered Michael his hand. "Congratulations on your engagement, my boy. You'll make a fine couple."

Carl and Orsby each mumbled their congratulations without lifting their heads for more than a moment.

Chas drew Michael to her mother's side. Mother took one of Michael's hands, looking at him with a keenness that made him stiffen.

"You're a fine young man," she said. "I'll expect you to take good care of my daughter. Always."

Michael held her gaze a moment. "Yes, ma'am. I aim to."

He smiled at Chas, and she knew she had never seen anything as wonderful as the way his expression softened as he looked at her.

"Good. Now everyone sit, and we'll have our supper."

Chas was grateful the others weren't with them. It allowed her and Michael to eat in peace without the questions she knew they would direct at him—questions she and Michael hadn't yet had a chance to discuss.

As soon as the dishes were put away and Emma had departed with a waiting Gordon, Chas drew Michael out to the veranda. They sat elbow to elbow on the bench, Chas letting the peace of the evening envelop her, hoarding to herself the joy of Michael at her side.

It was Michael who broke the silence. "Your mother sounded as if she doesn't like me much."

At the injured tone of his voice, Chas placed her hand on his forearm. "Oh, no, Michael. She likes you fine. She's just protective of me." Chas sighed. "I guess it comes from her being my only parent. She feels she has to do everything twice as well. But don't take it personally."

He nodded. "It's not as if I don't intend to take care of you."

"I know that. So does she. I told her about us last night, and she was pleased about it, so stop worrying."

He took her hand, sliding his fingers between hers. "I will then. After all, I don't want to ruin such a nice evening and the company of such a beautiful girl." He beamed at her.

His eyes were as warm and gentle as liquid chocolate, and she let herself float on her dreams. "Don't be looking at me like that, Chas."

He tweaked her on the nose, and she giggled, shifting on the bench to look out on the yard.

"Now that you've had time to think about getting married, are you having any second thoughts?" he asked.

"Of course not, silly. You and I will make a fine match." Only one thing would make her happier than she was this moment—for him to say how much he loved her.

"We will, won't we?"

She rested her head on his shoulder, sighing. "We have so many things to discuss."

He pulled back. "We do? Like what?"

"Now it's you who's being silly. We have to decide when we're to be married, where we'll live, what to do with the boardinghouse. All that sort of thing."

He remained quiet so long that Chas shook his arm and asked, "Have I over-whelmed you?"

"No. It's just—" He cleared his throat. "I sort of thought it was pretty obvious."

Her mind went round and round seeking answers. How could he have found them so quickly and simply? She shook her head. "It's certainly not obvious to me."

Smiling, he continued, "Probably because you're too close to see what's right in front of you."

"So explain to me what I'm not seeing."

"Let's take things in order. First, when should we marry? I propose we marry as soon as I've finished teaching for the summer.

"As to where we'll live—why, this house is ideal." He pressed her hand to stop her from arguing. "You and I can move into the private quarters. Your mother could move into the room she insists on keeping empty. It's time it was put to good use."

"It's for emergencies."

Her mother insisted the small room next to Mrs. B's be kept unrented so they could offer it to people in distress.

"We must be prepared to take in strangers," she insisted every time the sub-ject came up. "We never know when we might be entertaining angels. Or simply helping travellers in distress—'as ye have done it unto one of the least of these.'"

The room had been used numerous times over the years.

Once a young woman went into labor on the train, and Chas's mother had taken her in and cared for her and the new infant until the frantic husband could be contacted to come and get his wife and new son.

Another time, an elderly man rode into town, hungry and befuddled, and her mother had nursed him until he was strong again and could remember who he was. They never knew for sure what happened. Her mother said he must have banged his head somehow.

Then there was the young couple, their wagon on its last legs, their money gone. Her mother had allowed them to stay until he earned enough money for repairs so they could continue their journey.

Others had stayed there, as well.

Michael waited for her response.

"I don't know what Mother would say."

"I'm sure she'll see the reasonableness of it."

"You think we should continue to operate the boardinghouse then?"

"Of course. It makes good money, and it isn't too much work." He turned toward her. "You don't mind the work, do you?"

She shook her head slowly. It wasn't the work she minded. With Emma's help, she managed very well. No, it wasn't the work at all.

"Good. Then it's all settled. I told you it was simple."

He made it sound so reasonable—all the problems taken care of. Except one. "But, Michael, I thought we'd get a place of our own."

He turned and stared at her. "How would you manage the boardinghouse?"

She plucked at her skirt. "I hoped Mother could be persuaded to sell it," she mumbled.

He sat back. "I never even considered that. You've discussed this with your mother, and she agrees?"

Chas's heart sank through the seat of the bench. "She flatly refuses to sell."

"I'm confused. I don't understand why you think your mother should sell this place. It's a prospering business. Besides, how often have I heard you say you're perfectly happy here? Why would you want to change that, especially when it's plain that your mother has no intention of selling?"

She shrugged, at a loss for words. As plainly as Michael had just expressed them, her wishes appeared silly and juvenile. She swallowed hard.

"I guess it's only a childhood dream."

Ignoring his puzzled look, wanting nothing more than for him to understand her desire, she forged ahead. Even if they were left with no choice but to live here, she ached for him to acknowledge the yearning of her heart.

"All my life I've dreamed of living in a little house all my own, sharing it with no one but my husband and children." Her voice fell to a whisper. "All I want is a place of my own."

His brown eyes were puzzled. "I guess we wouldn't have to run the boardinghouse all our lives." He smiled gently. "Someday you'll get your little house."

She nodded, knowing she would have to be content with his promise of "someday."

"Don't look so disappointed." He pulled her close, tucking her head under his chin. "Things will work out. You'll see."

With a contented sigh, she relaxed against his chest. After a moment, she pushed away and lifted her face. "Michael, you have a way of putting things in perspective. You're so good for me."

He lowered his head and gave her a warm, gentle kiss that settled through her.

A few minutes later, he said good-bye, and Chas crossed the kitchen toward the rooms she shared with her mother and would in a few weeks share with Michael. Her steps faltered. What would Mother say about his proposed arrangement?

She paused in the doorway, half-hoping her mother had fallen asleep already, but she glanced up. "You have something you want to discuss, *ma cherie*?"

Chas lifted her hands in a gesture of resignation. "It's impossible to hide anything from you."

Her mother smiled. "Of course, I'm your mother." She patted the bed at her side, and Chas hurried over, sitting down so she could see her mother's face.

"Michael and I were talking."

"You've made some decisions?"

Mother's face was smooth, giving away nothing. Chas took a deep breath and began.

"Michael wants us to get married as soon as he has finished teaching for the summer."

Her mother nodded. "I see."

"He wants to move in here. He means for us to live here." Chas's throat tightened as she said the words.

Her mother looked at her, waiting for the rest.

Chas dreaded saying it. "He thinks we should make this our room. He says it makes sense for you to move to the guest room beside Mrs. B." Her words came out in a rush, and then she sat there, breathless, watching her mother's reaction.

Mother looked around the room. Her eyes widened. Then she sighed. "It will take some getting used to." Then she turned back to Chas. "How about you?"

Chas lifted her eyebrows.

"It's been all 'Michael says this' and 'Michael wants that.' Are you happy with the plans?" She patted Chas's arms. "Before you answer, remember I'm your mother and I see things others don't."

Chas swallowed hard, determined she would not make this any harder for her mother than it already was. "I don't suppose it will come as any surprise to you that I someday hope to have a little house of my own."

"I know, *ma cherie*. I've always known."

Chas waited for her emotions to calm before she continued. "I don't know why it seems so important."

Her mother stroked her hair. "Perhaps it's because so many things have been missing in your life."

Chas drew back. "I certainly don't think that. You've always been here for me."

Mother nodded. "Thank you. But you've missed a family. A father." She sighed. "And you've had to share everything with the boarders. Even your mother. And though you've always been sweet and nice about it, I can't help thinking it's created an emptiness inside you that may never be filled."

Chas lay back. Could it be true that this longing, this emptiness, would never be satisfied? "It doesn't make sense. I'm not unhappy. I feel as if I'm trusting God. I try to. Why should I long for things that will never be mine?"

Her mother tucked Chas's hair behind her ear. "Perhaps you are reaping the result of my bad choices."

Chas looked at her. "What do you mean?"

Mother shrugged. "I was so desperate for someone to love me and take care of me that I married Simon without knowing who he really was. If I'd taken more time to figure out what it was I wanted and to get to know him, things might have turned out differently. And you're the one who has had to pay for my mistake."

"Mother!" She grabbed her mother's hand and squeezed it. "I've never suffered. In fact I always thought I was luckier than most people to have a mother who cared so much and who taught me to trust God wholeheartedly. Things will work out somehow. I know they will."

Her mother gave a low laugh. "Now it's you who's reminding me to trust God." She picked up her Bible. "He will never fail us."

Mother read a few verses and then they prayed together.

Chas silently mouthed the words, *God, help me be content in the place You have put me.*

The days fled past. Michael kept busy in the classroom and Chas in the garden.

One morning, well into June, Chas returned to the house from weeding and pulled off her gloves when the front doorbell rang.

"I'll get it," she called to Emma, who was ironing sheets.

"Yes?" she asked, as she opened the door to a tall, thin man, neither old nor young. "May I help you?"

"Miss LaBlanc?"

"Yes." It wasn't unusual for people to have been given the name of the owners of the boardinghouse.

"I need to speak to your mother." He coughed—a cough that shook his frame and made him grasp the doorpost. He sucked in a rattling breath. "I have something for her—for you both."

Chas noted bright red spots in each sunken cheek.

The man swayed. Chas grabbed him, clutching at his sleeves.

"You're sick!"

She turned and called over her shoulder to Emma, hoping the girl would hear the urgency in her voice. Something clattered in the kitchen, and Emma was at Chas's side.

"Help me get him into the spare room."

Emma grabbed one elbow. Together they steered the tottering man down the hall and shuffled him through the door to the edge of the bed, where he collapsed on the covers.

"What is it?" Mother called from the kitchen.

"Just a minute, Mother," Chas said, then to Emma, "I don't want her coming in here until we know if this man has something contagious." She lifted the man's legs to the bed and pulled off his scuffed boots.

"Right."

They stood at the bedside looking down on the man.

He regarded them from fever-glazed eyes. "I don't want to put you to any trouble."

Chas smiled. "It would appear you're the one with the trouble."

He nodded, tried to say something, and had a coughing spell. Finally he gasped, "Thank you for your kindness."

Emma turned to Chas. "Do you want me to get Doc Johnson?"

"Yes, please. And if he isn't in, leave a message."

Emma hurried from the room.

Chas studied the gaunt man. Without his hat, she could see he had thinning blond hair. From the way his clothes hung, she guessed he had been sick a long time.

"What's your name?"

He tried to smile. "Colin Courtney. Please call me Colin."

"Do you have any family I should contact?"

He shook his head, too weak to speak.

Chas patted his shoulder. "You rest. I'll go tell Mother what's going on and then bring you some water. And not to worry. You can rest here until you're better."

"You're very kind," he whispered as she slipped away.

Mother was standing up from her chair when Chas hurried into the kitchen. "Mother, what are you doing?"

"I was going to see what all the commotion is about."

Chas explained about the visitor and that he was now resting in the spare room. "I want you to stay away until we know what's the matter. There's no point in everyone's coming in contact with him if it's something contagious."

Her mother gave her a hard look and pursed her mouth, preparing to argue, then relented. "I suppose you're right. Have you sent for Doc?"

"Emma's on her way."

"Good." Mother sat back. "No matter what is wrong with the poor man, he's going to need lots of fluids. And some broth. Do you still have the chicken bones from Saturday?"

Chas smiled to herself. She might succeed in keeping her mother from the sickroom, but she couldn't keep her from playing nurse from a distance.

"I'll take him water right now. By the way, his name is Colin Courtney." Chas paused, remembering. "He said he had something for us. I wonder what it could be?"

Mother looked up, interested. "I don't know the name." She turned away. "I can't imagine what it is."

As Chas supported Colin's shoulder so he could gulp the cold water, Doc Johnson trundled into the room. "You run along for a few minutes, Chastity, while I have a look at our patient." He dropped a dusty satchel on the floor and lay an equally dusty coat on top. "I found these on the step. I presume they belong to your guest."

"Thank you," the man muttered. "I guess I dropped them."

"Now you lay back and behave yourself while I check you over." Doc waved Chas aside and sat on the edge of the bed, his bulk making the springs protest shrilly.

Chas hurried back to the kitchen. Emma already had the chicken simmering on the stove. She glanced up at Chas's entrance. "Doc was full of questions, but I said I didn't even know the man's name."

"Colin Courtney."

Chas put the kettle on for tea and took out a tray, her hands busy even though her thoughts were centered elsewhere. When Doc called her name from the bedroom, she set the creamer down and hurried to the bedside.

"Besides being too thin, the man has pneumonia. He'll need some good nursing to pull through." Doc shook his numerous chins. "That's where you've found your bit of good luck, my man. You couldn't find a better place to get good nursing. Chastity and her mother have provided care to strangers many times over the years."

The weakened man nodded.

Doc turned to Chas. "I took it for granted you'd be taking care of him here."

"Of course. Where else would the poor man go?"

Doc rolled his lips like a bullfrog. "I've taken the liberty of removing his shirt and pants."

The man lay under a thin blanket.

Doc Johnson picked up his black bag. "I'll leave this syrup to calm his cough. Give him lots of fluids. Sponge him to bring the fever down. Call me if he worsens. Otherwise I'll drop by tomorrow. Good luck, my man."

When Chas started to follow him to the door, Doc said, "No need to show me out. You've got your hands full here."

Emma could manage tea and the rest of supper preparations, leaving Chas free to care for the sick man. As Doc had said, Colin would need good nursing to fight his illness.

She hurried to the kitchen for a basin of water and cloths to sponge him down.

Chapter 8

Colin coughed until it seemed his thin frame would break. Finally the cough syrup took effect, and he fell back on the pillows, the perspiration pouring from him.

Chas sponged his forehead, his neck, and his shoulders. "Your sheets are soaked again. I'll have to change them before you can rest." She hated to make him move for fear it would start another bout of coughing.

"I can't thank you enough." His voice was tight, and she knew it took an effort to say even those few words.

He rolled toward the wall, and Chas pulled out the sweat-soaked sheet, tossing it toward the door. Then she pulled the clean one tight and tucked it in place. He lay back, and she spread a light blanket over him and smoothed it across his shoulders.

She arched her back to ease her sore muscles and noticed the sky had turned slate gray.

Colin followed the direction of her gaze. "Almost morning," he whispered. "I've kept you up all night."

At the regret in his voice, Chas shook her head to clear away the fog of sleepiness. "It wasn't your fault." He had alternately shivered, sweated, and coughed. "Besides, I managed to get a little sleep." She nodded toward the armchair.

His smile was weak. "Not very much, I'm afraid." He took a heaving breath. "I think I'll be able to rest now, so you go and get some sleep."

Chas assessed his color. Despite the bright spots in his cheeks, his skin had a gray cast to it. He clutched the covers to his chin, and she knew it was the beginning of a chill that would lead to a rise in his fever. "I'll rest in the chair for a bit."

His eyes thanked her.

"Don't worry." She squeezed his hand. "I'll see you through this. You won't be alone. I promise you."

His eyelids closed, and he took a deep breath.

She tiptoed to the chair and stretched out, pausing only to ask God to heal Colin's frail body before she let sleep claim her.

She woke to the sun shining through the window and pulled herself up in the chair. Colin's covers were tossed aside. His skin glistened with sweat. He tried to stifle a cough, but when she stood, he let the cough rack through him.

His sheets were soaked again. As soon as he stopped coughing, she changed his bed and added the wet sheets to the growing mound outside the door.

A few minutes later, Emma came with hot tea. "How's the patient?" she whispered.

"About the same." Chas nodded toward the pile of sheets. "I'm afraid you'll have to do laundry today. I expect he will need nursing most of the day. Do you suppose you could get someone to help you?"

After a moment of consideration, Emma nodded. "I'll see if Dorothy can come. What about you? Did you get any sleep?"

"A bit." She pushed her hair off her face, realizing how rumpled she must look. "I'll relieve you after I get things organized."

Chas nodded, shutting the door behind Emma. Colin seemed quiet for the moment, and she again settled into the chair.

The day passed with Colin alternately shivering and sweating and always racked with coughing. Chas changed his sheets and continually offered fluids.

Early in the afternoon, Emma came to the room.

"Dorothy and I have everything under control. Run along and get some sleep."

Chas headed to her room, pausing only long enough to tell her mother about Colin's condition.

The second night was a repetition of the first.

The next day saw no change in Colin.

Doc Johnson came by to check on him. "You're doing all you can," he told Chas, shaking his head in a less than assuring way.

Chas prayed even harder for Colin.

His gaze followed her every time she stepped away from his bedside. Sensing he did not want to be left alone, she pulled her chair close and asked, "Would you like me to read to you, or would you prefer I sit quietly?"

"Talk to me." The few words triggered a coughing spell.

As soon as he quieted, Chas told him about the meal Emma was preparing, about Dorothy helping. She described the yard and the weather. He clung to every word. When his eyelids drooped, she thought he had fallen asleep; but when she stopped talking, he opened his eyes, silently begging for more.

So she told him about the boarders and her mother.

Again Emma came to the door in early afternoon to allow Chas a few hours of sleep.

She returned to the sickroom refreshed, and Emma hurried out to complete supper preparations.

"Talk to me some more," Colin begged.

So Chas told him about growing up in Willow Creek, about life in a small town, about going to school. Somehow she ended up telling him about Adam and his drawing.

A short time later, Emma returned to the door. "Michael's here asking for you."

Chas blinked. "Is it Wednesday already?"

Emma nodded.

"Where is he?"

"Cooling his heels in the sitting room." Emma paused. "I better warn you—

he wasn't pleased to hear you'd been nursing a stranger night and day."

"Really?"

Emma gave her a thoughtful look before she ducked into the kitchen.

"I'll be back in a few minutes," she told Colin, closing the door softly.

In the sitting room, Michael stood with his back to her, his arms crossed as he looked out the window. She watched him for a moment, seeing nothing in his stance to indicate displeasure.

"Hello, Michael. I'm sorry I was busy."

Michael spun around, his face wreathed in a wide smile. "You're here now. That's all that matters." He strode to her side, taking both her arms and pulling her close. His expression darkened as he looked down at her. "So what Emma says is right. You've been nursing that man night and day. I can see it in the dark shadows under your eyes."

She shrugged. "He's very ill."

"How did he end up here?"

"I have no idea." She recalled how he'd said he had something for them and wondered what it was. "Maybe someone sent him."

"I suppose they knew he'd be welcomed here even if he was sick with who-knows-what."

His tone made it clear he thought it was an imposition. He held up his hand. "Don't deny it. Everyone knows your mother has a reputation for taking in strays."

She faced him squarely. "It's a noble reputation."

"I suppose it is." He sighed. "Though not one I should think we need to continue."

She stared at him. Where did he get the "we"? Last time she checked, this was still her mother's house. Did he think he would become owner and operator when they married? She closed her eyes and took a deep breath. It was fatigue, she reasoned, making her overreact to his innocent statements.

"Never mind now." Michael led her to the couch and pulled her down beside him. "I've missed you."

Her annoyance fled. "And I've missed you." She settled back against the cushions and sighed.

"I don't like this." He frowned. "You're all tired out."

"I'm fine."

But at that point Colin coughed. Chas leapt to her feet. "I better get back to the sickroom."

Michael grabbed her hand. "Let Emma do it."

Chas shook her head. "She's got her hands full. Besides, it's not her responsibility."

Michael was insistent. "Nor is it yours."

"Mother has taught me well." Chas faced him. "I could not turn my back on a stranger in distress."

He stood to his feet. "Chas, enough of this foolishness!"

She stared at him, stunned by his reaction, longing for him to understand and support her. But all she saw was the tightness of his mouth.

"I'm sorry," she mumbled. "But it's something I have to do."

She tore from his grasp, racing down the hall. Michael would have to accept her decision. She pushed her disappointment to a dark shelf of her mind.

For three more days, Chas nursed Colin through raging fever, shuddering chills, horrific sweats, and hacking coughs, each day wondering how much longer his body could endure.

Her presence seemed to calm him, and he asked her over and over to talk to him. "I like the sound of your voice," he choked out between coughs, "and hearing about you as a little girl."

So she dredged her memory for stories of her childhood—the time she locked herself in Mrs. Allan's henhouse and had to wait, sneezing and scratching until Mrs. Allan came to free her. She laughed, remembering the louse bites she suffered.

She told of the time she had stood up for little Sally, the time Adam drew her picture, and so many things she hadn't thought of for years.

Michael came again Saturday, waiting in the sitting room for her to slip out.

"Michael," she began, "I'm sorry, but I can't leave Emma there for long. She has supper to serve."

He gave her his stern teacher look. "This has gone on long enough."

"I agree," she said, purposely misinterpreting his comment. "The poor man has endured enough."

"You can't wear yourself out taking care of him. It sounds to me as if he may not even make it."

"He's not going to die," she vowed, pulling in a deep breath. "And if he does, he'll not do it alone and uncared for."

Michael threw up his hands. "He's only a stranger."

" 'I was a stranger, and ye took Me in,' " she quoted, not willing to admit that Colin was more than a stranger. Over the past few days, a bond had grown between them. In many ways he was the father figure she had never known. She would not abandon him to the ravages of his illness. Not even for Michael.

"I'm sorry. But try to understand—this is something I must do." She paused. "You're more than welcome to stay for supper, but I won't be available."

She waited, hoping he would relent, but his face remained stern as he silently challenged her. She turned and left the room.

That night Colin worsened. Chas did her best to fight the fever, but it continued to rise alarmingly.

Having exhausted her resources, she could do nothing but fall at his bedside and pray. *God, You are the great healer. Please touch Colin's body and heal his illness.* She prayed for a long time until she rose and resumed her nursing, believing God would answer.

Toward morning the fever began to fall. Just as dawn threw pink banners across the sky, he took a deep, shuddering breath. She pressed her palm to his chest, relieved to feel it rise.

The worst was over.

Thank You, God, she breathed.

She sank into the chair and slipped into an exhausted sleep, not waking until Emma came in dressed in her Sunday best. Chas scrambled to her feet.

"I forgot about church."

Emma laughed and pushed her back down. "Too late now. It's all over."

Chas leaned her head against the back of the chair. "I can't believe I slept right through."

"You needed it. How's our Colin?"

Chas's smile felt as wide as the open sky as she studied him still sleeping peacefully. "His fever broke early this morning."

"Praise the Lord," Emma said. "I expect it will take awhile to get his strength back."

Chas didn't answer. It was enough for now that Colin was on the mend. She followed Emma from the room, joining her mother and the others for lunch. She was surprised to find Michael wasn't there.

"Where's Michael?" she asked Emma. "Wasn't he at church?"

Emma gave her an odd look. "He was, but he said there was no point in coming over when you were otherwise occupied."

"Oh." She couldn't help being disappointed. "Perhaps he'll come this afternoon."

"Could be." Emma opened her mouth as if to say more but stopped herself and set out the cold chicken.

Chas helped carry out platters of food. "By the way, what are you doing here today?"

Emma lifted one shoulder. "I figured you needed the help."

"Emma, you are such a dear."

The younger girl chuckled. "I know."

Michael called that afternoon, coming when Chas was in the sickroom spooning chicken broth into Colin.

She slipped away to speak to him, aching to smooth over their misunderstanding. "Thank you for being patient," she began as soon as she stepped into the room. "Colin is over the worst now."

"Does that mean you're finished looking after him?"

"Not exactly." She smiled gently. "He's very weak."

Michael turned away.

"Michael." Chas reached for his arm. "Please try to understand."

"That's just it. I don't understand. I'm sure Doc could find someone else to look after him."

"Michael, it's part of who I am. It's a culmination of my history and how I was raised."

He looked down at her a long time, his brown eyes dark and troubled. Finally he smiled. "I guess if that's who you are, then that's how it must be."

She longed for him to heal her trembling emotions with a hug and a kiss, but when he made no move to do so, she lowered her eyes, forcing herself to be content with the victory she had won.

Except to drink sweet tea and swallow a bit of chicken soup, Colin slept for two days. He woke the third morning to give Chas a slow smile. "So my nurse is still here."

"As long as you need me." She studied the steadiness of his pale blue eyes, the slight pink in his cheeks. Now that the fever had left, she could see that he was probably in his forties, a serious-looking man with a kind face.

"You've been a faithful nurse. I think I might owe you my life." His smile deepened. "Thank you."

"You're most welcome. Now how about some nourishment? What would you like?"

"Now that you mention it, I am hungry. Breakfast would be good."

"I think you'll have to start easy," she said a few minutes later as she returned with thin oatmeal and toast.

"This looks fine." He looked up from the tray. "Won't you sit down and visit while I eat?"

She welcomed his invitation. Over the passing days, she had found satisfaction in sharing the story of her life with him.

He waited until she sat down before he bowed his head and prayed out loud, thanking God for his healing, for Chas's faithful nursing, and for the blessing of food to replenish his strength. He took several mouthfuls of the oatmeal before he turned to her. "You've told me so much about yourself that I feel as if I know you. So forgive me if I seem presumptuous in the way I talk."

She smiled. "I feel the same—though I know very little about you."

"There's not much to know about me." He tilted his head. "I'm just a wandering old man."

"I expect there's more to it than that. How did you end up here?"

A strange light filled his eyes. "Divine intervention, I expect." He studied her seriously. "I notice Doc calls you Chastity though everyone else calls you Chas."

"Mother never calls me anything but Chastity."

"It's an unusual name."

"Very." She laughed. "You see, when my mother was expecting me, she ran away from a bad situation. Lost and alone, she was rescued by a man she declares was an angel. She vowed to live a life devoted to serving God and anyone He sent across her path. She named me Chastity to remind her of her vow."

"And your father?"

"I never knew my father. I didn't even know his name until a short time ago. Simon LaBlanc."

"What happened to him?"

"My parents married down east and then moved west." She twisted her hands together. "After they moved, Mother said my father changed. He started drinking and grew violent. She ran away from him and never heard from him again."

Chas had learned to live with it and accept it, but at the compassion in Colin's kind, steady gaze, she clenched her fingers.

"So you grew up wondering if your father was alive and if he knew about you. Wondering, too, I'd guess, why he didn't care enough to find you?"

Emotions she had hidden from all her life sprang loose, choking her, sucking at the depths of her soul. Hot tears poured down her cheeks. She dashed them away.

"Didn't I matter?" she gasped, unashamed for Colin to see her this way.

"Of course you mattered. You always did and always will. You are a special young woman. Kind and gentle, sweet yet strong. Not to mention beautiful. Everything a young woman should be."

She clung to his words, letting them ease through her pain like a healing balm. "I've never allowed myself to admit how much it hurt that my father didn't care about me."

"Perhaps it has affected you more than you think."

She blinked. "Why do you say that?"

"You grew up strong. Yet I think a tiny bit of you is locked away, afraid of the future."

She thought how similar his words were to what Adam had said. "I don't see how wanting security indicates fear."

"It doesn't, as long as wanting security doesn't disable us from embracing the future."

Again she shook her head. "Why would I want to choose anything but security?"

"You wouldn't want to necessarily, but remember—security means being free to take a risk."

Although uncertain what he meant, Chas nodded.

"Now I seem to recall a young man wanting to see you several times. Tell me about him."

"Yes, Michael. He's the teacher." She told him everything she could think of about Michael. "We're going to be married soon."

"Then he must be a very special young man. I hope he loves you very much."

"He is."

She faltered. Michael had never said the words, "I love you."

"I'm sure he loves me."

"Love is patient and kind. It always protects, always trusts, always hopes, always perseveres."

He spoke the words like a benediction, and Chas nodded, certain Michael loved her that way. Even as she loved him.

Colin pushed aside the breakfast tray. "I had a bag when I came. Do you know where it is?"

"In the closet. Would you like it?"

"Yes, please."

She set the tray on the floor outside the door and retrieved the bag.

"Would you get your mother, please? I have something for her."

Chas tilted her head. "Of course."

"Colin wants to see you, Mother," she said as she set the tray on the table.

Mother pushed herself to her feet and, using two canes, headed toward the bedroom. "Probably wants to discuss rent. As if I'd charge someone for being sick."

Her mother was gone a long time, and when she came out, she did not return to the kitchen, heading instead for her bedroom. She only paused to say, "Chastity, Colin would like to see you."

A sheen of tears coated her mother's cheeks, and her voice trembled.

"Are you all right, Mother?"

The older woman nodded. "Go see him, Chastity."

She hesitated. Then curiosity drove her toward Colin's room. She pushed open the door. The skin on his face was taut, as if the meeting with her mother had sucked out all his energy. He lifted a shaking hand.

"Come in, child." He waited until she perched on the edge of the chair. "I have looked for you a long time to bring you a message from your father."

A jolt raced through her veins. Could her father be asking for her after all these years?

"First, let me tell you what I know of him.

"When I met Simon LaBlanc," Colin began, his voice soft and low as if he meant to tell her a long story, "he was a broken man, sick and injured. But most of all his mind was not at ease. During the weeks I tended him, he told me his story.

"I will tell you it as I remember it."

Colin paused. "I ran into him way up north. He'd taken to trapping. Lived alone in a little cabin up along the Mackenzie basin. This particular time he had headed to the Hudson Bay post to trade his furs and get a few supplies for the winter. On the way he ran into some varmints of the two-legged variety who had tried to take his furs off his hands without offering to pay for them. He managed to dissuade them but was shot up. By the time he reached the post, he was more dead than alive with a bullet lodged inside his chest and one leg already gangrenous."

Chas stared as Colin told a tale of fighting and injury such as she had only heard of in tales of the Wild West. To think her own father had been involved in such was beyond her imagination.

"It took several of us to persuade him to let us take care of his furs and quite a few attempts before he would let them out of his sight so we could carry him to my cabin. I did the best I could for his injuries, but we couldn't do much for his leg or the internal wounds. I think he knew. That's why he insisted I hear his story. This is how I remember it.

" 'I've lived a life of regrets,' he told me. He was a big man, with a wild black mane of hair, who had fought every kind of danger known to man, but his eyes filled with tears as he spoke. 'I married a fine young woman, and I done her wrong. When she left me, I didn't even try to find her. I got me a child somewhere, and I don't know if it be a boy or a girl. Don't know if it's got black hair like me. Or maybe white blond like my own mother, God rest her soul.' "

Colin grew quiet a moment. "Before Simon died, he wrote a letter to his wife and child and made me promise to do my best to deliver them. For a while I wondered if I'd be able to keep my promise, but here I am." He reached into his bag and pulled out a worn and soiled envelope. "This is his letter to you."

Hands trembling, Chas took the letter. A tightness around her lungs made each breath difficult. One fingertip caressed the envelope. She closed her eyes as if doing so could contain the whirl of emotions racing back and forth through her like a washing tide. Having suddenly and unexpectedly found her father through Colin's story, she just as suddenly had lost him again. This small bit of paper was all she had left. She sought Colin's gaze, clinging to the steadiness of his light blue eyes.

He smiled and nodded. "Your father lived all those years wishing he had done things differently, wishing he could go back and undo his mistakes. In the end"— Colin's low voice deepened—"in the end he found his peace the way we all have to—he turned to God and sought forgiveness there."

The stillness around them was alive with images of Simon LaBlanc.

"I don't know what he said in his letter to you, but I do know he would have asked for your forgiveness."

Chas's vision blurred. Choking back a sob, she hurried from the room, seeking the shelter of her own narrow quarters. She flung herself across her bed and sobbed, but she couldn't tell if she cried over the pain of her father's death or the gladness that she had this bit of him to touch and hold.

She wiped away her tears and turned the envelope over. She ran a fingernail under the flap. The paper crackled as she drew forth the pages and unfolded them. Strong black letters marched across the yellowed paper. Chas drew in a shaky breath and began reading.

To my child,

I don't even know if you're male or female. All I know is I've thought of you so often over the years. You may wonder how I can say that when I never went lookin' for you or your mother. But it's true.

You might ask where I was and what I was doin' all this time. It's not a pretty story, but mostly I was drinkin' and soberin' up. When I got tired of that, I headed north. I found a little peace in the aloneness up here—a peace that was haunted by rememberin' a woman and child I had let go.

If you get this, you'll have met Colin. He told me I could make peace with God. I have, but my mind won't rest until I tell you I'm sorry. If I could go back, I'd do things a lot different.

I'm not thinkin' you can forgive me. Maybe it wouldn't even be right, and I don't deserve it.

I do wish for you to be happy. Maybe you never think about me, but if you do, don't have any regrets. And don't ever live your life lookin' back, wishin' things might have been different. Don't make the mistakes I made. I thought I could live without love. I was wrong. If you find someone to love, that is the most important thing you can find. Never let it get away from you.

God bless you.
From your father,
Simon LaBlanc

Chas pressed the page to her lips. "Simon LaBlanc," she whispered. "My father." A shuddering breath escaped. "I forgive you. I guess I always have." And someplace deep inside her, an empty and hollow place filled with warmth.

Someone knocked on her door. "May I come in?" her mother asked.

"Yes," Chas answered, suddenly anxious to know how her mother had received this news.

Mother shuffled in, leaning on her canes. "You have read your letter?"

Chas sniffled as she nodded. "How are you, Mother?"

"I'm fine," she said, smiling. "I'm so glad Simon found God in the end. He says he never quit loving me, and that makes me feel good. It's you I'm concerned about, *cherie*. To hear from your father so suddenly after all these years—it must be a shock."

Chas gave a tremulous smile. "It's a nice surprise. I'm so glad he wrote me a letter." She hugged the pages to her.

"Does it answer a need inside you?"

Chas, laughing low in her throat, hurried over and gave her mother a hug. "I suppose it does. But don't go thinking that means I've been unhappy, because you know I haven't."

"You have always been a happy, contented person." Her mother pressed a kiss to her cheek. "Always so sweet. I couldn't ask for more."

"I love you, Mama."

"And I love you, Chastity, *ma cherie.*"

Chas smiled at her. "Now do you suppose I should go see about supper?"

"I think Emma has it under control, but perhaps you should see if Colin can be persuaded to eat a bit."

Colin was watching the door as she entered. "I've been waiting for you."

She smiled. "I'm fine if that's what you're worried about."

"You've been crying."

She nodded. "But it was a good sort of crying."

"I never could understand that sort of thing." He chuckled, his pale eyes warm as the bright summer sun.

"Thank you for going to all the work of finding us and bringing us news of my father."

"It was not as difficult as you might imagine."

They heard a knock on the door, and Emma stuck her head in. "Michael's here asking for you."

"Ah. The young man. He's been patient long enough. You run along and visit him." Colin settled back and closed his eyes. "I believe I'll rest."

"Thank you, Colin," she whispered.

Michael sat in a hard chair, his feet planted on the floor. He smoothed his tie and straightened his lapels as she entered. "I take it the patient is on the mend?"

"Yes, he's much better. Thank God." She burst to share the news Colin had brought, yet the new feelings were too fresh. They needed a chance to mature and stabilize. And so she hesitated.

"Good. I didn't like having to share you with him." Michael crossed to her side and pulled her into his arms, his words muffled against her hair. "I want you all to myself."

His words trickled down her spine, vaguely troubling. How could he expect to have her all to himself if she were to run the boardinghouse? She smiled against his shoulder.

"I'd like that, too."

She hoped he would realize how impossible it was under the present circumstances and suggest they consider alternatives, but he only hugged her.

"So Colin will be leaving?"

"He's too weak to get out of bed."

"Are you telling me your nursing duties aren't over?" he asked, pushing her away so he could look into her face.

She stiffened. "They aren't as demanding as they were."

He dropped his hold on her and stepped away. "I hoped I wouldn't have to say this, but it seems I have no choice." His blunt fingers rubbed across his hair. "I cannot accept the way you devote yourself to him." Eyes cold, he faced her. "I will not play second fiddle to a stranger. I insist you find someone else to care for him."

She shrank back as if he'd threatened her. "That's ridiculous."

How could he be so high-handed? Caring for others was part of running a boardinghouse. Certainly, the time she had given to Colin's care was above the norm, but in some circumstances, more time than usual was demanded.

"What if it were Mrs. B who was sick?" Suspicion flared. "What if it were Mother?"

He refused to answer.

She refused to look away. "Is it Colin you object to or having to put yourself aside for an evening or two?"

"He's been here ten days."

Chas blinked. Since when did Michael keep track of her daily activities?

"Because if it's just Colin, you're being ridiculous. He's brought Mother and me a message."

Michael's contemptuous snort made her glad she hadn't told him anything more.

"How very convenient." He glowered at her and then took a deep breath and started to plead. "Chas, try to understand. I've hardly seen you in over a week."

She breathed hard. She should be flattered by his words, but suddenly they sounded petty, possessive. "If you'd needed me for anything, I would have done things differently, but—" She threw up her hands. "Colin, on the other hand, was very ill. I could hardly let Mother take over his care."

"He's better now. You said so yourself. So are you going to do as I ask and find someone else to give him the extra care you insist he needs?"

"It sounds very much like an ultimatum." She spoke quietly.

He half-shrugged. "I suppose you could look at it that way."

She took a step toward him. "Michael," she pleaded, "it doesn't have to be this way."

He drew back. "Are you refusing to do as I ask?"

She stood helpless and confused. Perhaps she could find someone to care for Colin, but she didn't want to; she wanted to spend as much time with him as possible, asking about her father. Besides, she'd grown close to Colin during his illness. She didn't want to turn his care over to someone else. For some unfathomable reason, she needed to do it herself.

Michael waited, stern and unrelenting. Michael, her dearest friend. How could he demand this of her?

She shook her head. "Michael, please understand. I must do it."

He stepped away. "Then you leave me no choice but to withdraw my offer of marriage."

Her knees gave way under her. She reached out to the tea table for support. "Michael, no."

"I fear you are not the person I thought you to be. When I marry, I will not share my wife with another man. Not for any reason." He walked out of the room without a backward glance.

Chas sank into the nearest chair, moaning.

Chapter 9

Fearing someone would come into the room and wonder why she was huddling in the chair, Chas squared her shoulders and headed for the kitchen to prepare a tray of chicken noodle soup and custard for Colin.

He gave her a surprised look when she entered his room. "The young man has left already?"

To her chagrin, she burst into tears.

Colin said nothing as he waited for her to stop crying.

"He said—it was—over," she managed to say between sobs. "He—doesn't understand."

"I see." Colin pulled himself up on his pillows. "What is it he doesn't understand?"

"Me," she said, fresh tears welling up in her eyes.

"Well, that is rather important in a relationship such as yours."

Chas, hearing the smile in his voice, took a deep breath. "I'm sorry," she muttered. "I didn't mean to do that."

Colin's smile was gentle, his voice soft. "I don't imagine it's the sort of thing one plans to do. Now tell me what happened."

She shrugged, suddenly discovering she had no idea how to answer him. "He withdrew his offer of marriage."

"Sounds like a lovers' quarrel. If he really loves you, he'll be back soon, apologizing for being so silly." He gave her a hard look. "One would assume he does love you?"

She couldn't meet his gaze. "I'm sure he does. He just never thought to tell me."

"What!" Colin exclaimed. "I should think it would be uppermost in his mind. I would expect him to be so overwhelmed by love, he couldn't stop talking of it."

Chas could feel his gaze upon her like hot flames, but she refused to meet his eyes, afraid he would see more than she intended.

"What about you?"

His soft tone did not deceive her. She knew he was probing her depths. She squirmed.

"What do you mean?" She made her eyes tell nothing as she faced him.

"Do you love him?" Before she could answer, he added, "Or does he feel safe to you?"

A wave of confusion swept through her.

"Ahh." Colin nodded. "So that's it."

"No. I don't know. Maybe. We are good friends. Michael and I have a lot in common. We think the same. Or at least I thought we did."

"Were you perhaps seeking the security you never knew from your father?" He didn't wait for an answer. He didn't seem to want one. "Don't be misled. Security is not necessarily found in taking the safe, comfortable path. God has created you with a heart full of dreams. Follow your heart. Don't quench your emotions."

Her thoughts swirled. Questions she had never dared to ask raced through her mind. Had she accepted Michael's proposal simply because it felt safe? Because Adam's confessed love frightened her with its inherent risks—and its intensity.

"I'm so confused."

Colin squeezed her hand. "Change is often frightening."

She clung to his hand. Life had turned on its side.

"Chastity, God will guide you, but you must be willing to step out in faith. Now you run along and let me rest."

She sprang to her feet. "I've taken too much of your time."

He laughed, a soft, pleasing sound. "I seem to have a great deal of time right now. I'll pray for you to be able to sort out what it is you want."

She murmured her thanks and hurried from the room.

❧

Chas sat on her mother's bed.

"Something's troubling you, *ma cherie*. Is it hearing from your father?"

Chas swallowed back a sob. "Michael says he's changed his mind about marrying me."

"But why?"

Michael's resentment and his ultimatum poured forth.

"Did you explain that it's always been our policy to care for strangers in distress?"

"I tried. He knows the angel story. He should understand. The really unfair thing is he insisted it was wisest for me to keep running the boardinghouse after we married. He wouldn't even discuss other options."

Tears pooled in her eyes, but she was too drained to cry.

Her mother pulled her into her arms, and Chas cradled her face against her neck, breathing in the scent of rosewater and powder.

"Chastity, I'm so sorry." She waited a moment. "But I have been praying you would make the right decision. I wouldn't want you to make the kind of mistake I made. Far better you sort these things out ahead of time. If he loves you, he'll be back."

"That's what Colin said, too."

In her own room, she sat at the little table, opening her Bible to the page where the name, Simon LaBlanc, stared up at her. She unfolded his letter and lay it beside the Bible. And over it all, she mentally placed the name Michael Martin.

How did it all fit together?

If you find someone to love, that is the most important thing you can find.

The sentence from her father's letter jumped out at her.

Love. Love protects, perseveres, trusts, hopes. Was it love she felt for Michael? Or safety?

Was she looking for something she had missed as a child? Was she afraid to take risks because of that lack?

Why did Adam keep popping up in her mind?

Because you refused his love out of fear.

The words blared through her thoughts.

She stared into her heart.

Adam had confessed a deep, passionate love for her, and she had run away because it frightened her. She didn't want to live with his need to visit strange new places.

He had never promised he wouldn't go away. He had only said he would come back.

And that had scared her.

But would Adam be Adam if he didn't have a hunger to see and know and record everything he saw? Could she ask him to be anything less?

Love trusts. Love perseveres.

She ran her fingers along the page of her father's letter, letting his words of counsel sift through her consciousness.

It was too late to think about how things might have been with Adam. But it was not too late to be honest about who she truly was and what she wanted.

She was her father's daughter as much as her mother's. She wanted love. She wanted trust. And while she was being truthful, she could not deny she wanted a little home of her own with a husband and children. Michael was comfortable, but it seemed he was not able to give her the things she wanted any more than was Adam.

Father God, You know my desires. You know me better than I know myself. Guide me in the right direction.

The days passed. Colin slowly gained strength and began getting up.

Michael did not return.

Chas admitted what she felt for him had not been love, yet she missed his visits terribly. She missed hearing about the children and discussing lesson plans. After several Sundays of seeing him at church and aching at the way his glance slid away from her, she sought him out after the service, catching up to him as he headed home.

"Michael, can we talk?"

He paused, his back to her. She thought he was going to walk away without answering. Then he turned around slowly. "Certainly."

She fell in step beside him, suddenly not knowing what to say to him. "How have you been?"

"Fine."

"I suppose you're preparing the final report cards for the class?"

"Yes."

She sighed. "This isn't going the way I'd hoped."

He stopped and faced her. "What had you hoped?"

She searched his face for some sign of what he was thinking, but his eyes were guarded, his expression controlled. "I was hoping you'd agree to be friends."

He stared at her.

"I've missed our visits." She rushed on. "I think we were both mistaken in thinking we could be anything more than friends. We want different things, but still we share a lot of common interests." She faltered. "I guess I hoped we could go back to before."

He laughed. "Before our ghastly mistake, you mean?"

She nodded uncertainly.

His eyes darkened. "You aren't mad at me for being so pigheaded?"

It was her turn to laugh. "Of course not. You only made clear what was happening. We're good at being friends but not much good at planning marriage." She waited as he relaxed.

"Friends?" She held out her hand.

"Yes, friends." He clasped her hand for a moment. "Now tell me how you are and how things are at the boardinghouse."

As they meandered home, they filled each other in on the events of the past few weeks. At the last corner, Chas drew to a halt. "Michael, be honest with me."

He nodded. "I'll try."

"You never really loved me, did you?"

He looked sheepish. "I was hoping to find someone who loved me more than anything else in the world—in a way I've never known." His voice grew husky.

"Michael." She hugged his arm. "I'm sorry I couldn't be that person, but someday she'll come along. And you'd better be waiting for her."

"I hope you're right."

"I'm sure I am."

She stared down the street. What Michael wanted was what she wanted. Probably what everyone wanted. Would she ever know that sort of love? A pair of glittering blue eyes sprang to her mind. Adam said he loved her. But was it only part of some fanciful dream he had carried for years? She closed her eyes and took a deep breath. What did it matter? She had turned him away, and he had left, perhaps for another ten years.

"Come for dinner," she said to Michael. It would help keep her mind occupied.

A few days later, Colin announced, "Thanks to the good care and excellent food I've enjoyed, I am fully recovered. It's time I was on my way. I'll be leaving on Friday."

His words echoed around the table. All eyes turned toward him.

Beryl bobbed forward. "Mr. Courtney, why must you leave? I'm sure there's something here you could find to do."

"I have things I must attend to."

The Knutsen boys dipped their heads in unison and resumed eating.

"Are you sure you're quite well?" Louise asked.

"I'm fit as a fiddle."

"A man must do what he has to do," Mr. Elias said. "We will certainly miss you."

"Where are you planning to go?" Roy asked.

Chas could see Roy's mind busy with how far, how many days, how long.

"I'm heading west." Colin's smile was gentle. "There's someone I must find." He looked into Chas's eyes. "I will certainly miss this place."

She lowered her head, afraid she would cry in front of everyone. It was impossible to imagine life without Colin; he had come to mean so much to her.

"Don't feel you have to rush away," Mother said.

Chas waited until supper was cleaned up and Emma headed home before she sought out Colin. He was sitting on the veranda steps, his back against the post, gazing into the sky.

She pulled her skirt around her legs and sat beside him. She didn't speak. There was no need. All she wanted was to be with him and cherish his presence.

After a few moments, she murmured, "I wish you didn't have to go."

"I do, too."

"Then why go?"

He touched her shoulder. "Because I must."

She drew in a breath.

"Chas, I will never forget you. I will pray for you every day. I wish you all God's best and every happiness."

"Thank you," she said faintly.

He squeezed her shoulder. "If I had a daughter, I would want her to be exactly like you."

A sob caught in her throat.

He smiled. "My dear, remember—follow your heart. It will guide you to love and happiness."

She nodded.

They sat under the stars for a long time. Then Colin rose.

"I think it's time to get some sleep." He helped Chas to her feet. "Don't be afraid of the future, my child. God will guide you."

"Good night, Colin." The door closed softly behind him before she whispered, "Good-bye."

On Thursday Chas and Emma prepared a special meal for Colin's farewell dinner. Michael and young Gordon Simpson had been invited.

"Isn't this exciting?" Emma put the finishing touches on the trifle she'd prepared.

Chas tried to smile. "You mean Gordon coming?"

Emma held her hands over the whipped cream a moment before she turned to face Chas. "I was forgetting about how you're feeling. You'll miss him, won't you?"

"It won't be the same with him gone." Chas lifted her shoulders. "It's like losing one of the family."

Emma's eyes softened. "I'm sorry."

"It looks as if everything is ready." Chas stirred the gravy. "Have our guests arrived?"

At that moment the back doorbell sounded, and Emma stepped over to admit Gordon. Then the front doorbell rang, and Chas hurried to open the door for Michael. Everyone was there. There was no delaying the inevitable, and she announced supper.

Somehow she got through the evening, and the next morning she managed to wave good-bye to Colin without breaking into tears. She watched him ride out of sight and for a long time stared down the road after him. Then she returned indoors, thankful she had a meal to prepare, the garden to take care of, and shopping to do.

Two weeks later, Louise announced, "I saw Adam at the shop today."

She gave Chas a long look, but Chas only nodded and smiled as her heart did a funny flip-flop. She hadn't expected Adam to return so soon.

Beryl edged forward. "I expect he's got lots of interesting tales to tell. I wonder if he'll come visit." She slid a look at Chas.

"I do hope so," Mother said. "He's such an interesting young man."

Mrs. B looked up. "Why do you want a fan? It's not hot."

Mother smiled as she leaned close and yelled in Mrs. B's ear. "We were talking about Adam."

Mrs. B's eyes widened. "I remember him. His folks run the store. Such a nice young man." Smiling, she picked up her fork and turned back to her food.

Mr. Elias perked up in his chair as if he'd been waiting for Adam's return. "I have some things I would like to discuss with him."

"How long was he gone?" Roy squinted his eyes, mentally figuring it out. "Six weeks. Say, he could have gone"—more mental measurements—"why, he could have gone to the East Coast and back in that time."

The Knutsen boys turned in unison from one speaker to the next as if they were of one mind.

John added, "I heard he's planning a big show here. Seems some VIPs are coming to town to see him."

Roy almost jumped from his chair. "How many are coming? When?"

"Who cares?" Beryl interrupted. "Goodness. One would think numbers are everything."

Roy frowned, shifting back. "I was only wondering."

"Perhaps Adam will come for tea, and we can all have our questions answered." Mother turned to Chas. "In fact, why don't you slip down to the shop and invite him? Tell him how much we'd like to see him."

At her suggestion, Mr. Elias beamed, but the young people looked disappointed because they wouldn't be present at that time of day. Seeing their reaction,

Mother chuckled. "I'll be sure and invite him for dinner the first evening he has available."

The Knutsen boys bowed their heads over their plates. Chas did the same, not wishing to face any questioning glances, not wanting to face her own swirling emotions.

She would have ignored her mother's directive to issue an invitation to Adam, but shortly after lunch the next day, Mother reminded her, "Be sure to drop by Adam's shop while you're getting the mail and ask him to come for tea."

She met her mother's look squarely, wondering if she were more eager to visit with Adam or to play the matchmaker?

Mother smiled, her eyes guileless. "I'm sure he's full of interesting stories of his travels."

"No doubt."

Chas shook her head. Her mother didn't fool her. But Adam was not the man for her; he was a wanderer at heart. Nor was Michael, who sought someone he wouldn't have to share. Was she doomed to live forever in a boardinghouse, caring for and serving strangers rather than having a family of her own?

Stepping into the sunshine lifted her spirits at once. God would guide her steps as surely as He had put the sun in the sky. It was hard to be patient, but she knew God's timing was best.

The door of Adam's shop was propped open to let in the summer breeze. Chas stepped soundlessly over the threshold and stopped.

His back to her, Adam was leaning over his worktable absorbed in some papers. He hadn't heard her enter, allowing her a chance to study him unobserved. His hair had lightened in the summer sun. A recent trim left a narrow white edge around his hairline. The way he leaned on the table made his shoulders seem broad while revealing his leanness.

Chas swallowed back an aching emptiness. He was good and kind. In many ways he was all her heart desired. Except for one fundamental thing. He had not nor, she suspected, ever would promise he wouldn't do any more traveling. And she could not give her heart to a man only to wonder every day when he was leaving. She couldn't love him. She wouldn't.

Follow your heart.

She had promised Colin she would, but it was a promise she couldn't keep. Squaring her shoulders, she vowed she would protect her heart. As she stepped forward, she spoke.

"Hello, Adam."

He lifted his head, staring at the wall in front of him a moment, and then turned slowly. "Hello, Chas."

His smile didn't quite reach his eyes. His eyes darkened as his gaze swept over her, taking in a wayward strand of hair, resting for a moment on her chin, then descending to her dusty shoes.

Her tongue stiffened, and no words came.

His gaze returned to her face, his eyes slightly narrowed. "What can I do for you today?"

She lowered her gaze to her twisting fingers. She noticed that her fingertips had turned white, so she relaxed her hold. Taking a deep breath, she forced her thoughts to the invitation she had come to deliver.

"My mother asks you to come to tea at your convenience."

He nodded his head in acknowledgment. "How is your mother?"

The tension seemed to leave her, and a slight smile formed on her lips. "Mother's fine. She's getting around with both canes and, as often as she can elude my supervision, using only one." Taking another breath, she smiled more warmly and went on. "I sometimes wonder if I were noncompliant when I was a child and now I'm reaping what I sowed."

Adam's smile brightened, and his eyes warmed. "Were you?"

"Not that I recall. I think I was more likely to retreat to my room than defy my mother."

"Not very confrontational, are you?" He leaned one hand on the table.

"Only when I feel it's worthwhile."

"Like defending someone else, I suppose?"

Not knowing how to answer, she chose to ignore his remark. "I didn't expect you back so soon."

He crossed his arms over his chest. "It was six weeks."

Her glance slid over the pictures on the wall behind him.

"Did you expect me to disappear into the beyond and never return?"

She shrugged. "I guess I didn't know."

"I told you I was going on tour. I didn't plan to be gone long."

Chas could think of nothing to say in response.

"How are your wedding plans coming? The big day must be close now."

She looked sharply at him. "I thought you would have heard." Everyone in town knew.

His face gave away nothing. "Heard what?"

"Michael and I have decided we're more suited to being friends than husband and wife."

His expression never changed.

"It was quite amicable," she murmured.

"Friends?"

She nodded.

"You don't love him?" He was so impassive that she wondered if he even breathed.

"Only as a friend."

"I see."

What did he see? she wondered, feeling compelled to explain. "We discovered we really had different goals and expectations."

"Are you saying you didn't love each other enough to reconcile those differences?"

Her eyelids twitched. He made it sound mean-spirited and selfish whereas it had been, as she said, amicable. "I guess you could put it that way if you want to." Her terse tone indicated he would be wrong to do so.

"It's none of my business, I know, but I'm curious to know exactly what you found to be such a big difference you couldn't work out."

For a moment she was tempted to tell him it was indeed none of his business, but something in his eyes made her answer. "I think Michael discovered I was not the malleable person he hoped to have for a mate." She shrugged. "And I did not wish to be confined to his set of parameters."

"It sounds to me as if you're saying neither of you was willing to accept the other as you are."

She nodded. "I suppose that sums it up."

He strode to the window. "Then I guess it was never true love." The light sharpened his features and painted streaks through his hair. "It seems to me that true love accepts the other person just as that one is and wraps love softly around the beloved without binding or constricting."

Chas couldn't breathe. A tiny pulse hammered against her left temple. Soft love. It sounded like a dream too good to be true. *Love trusts.*

At that moment Jack bounded into the shop. "I've done my chores, Adam. Dad says I can help you." He skidded to a halt. "Hi, Miss LaBlanc. How are you? What do you want me to do, Adam?"

"Hi, sprout. Give me a minute, will you?" Adam shoved his hand through his hair, looking as if he wanted to say more to Chas.

But she turned and dashed out the door.

Chas set out the tea things, wishing she could somehow avoid meeting Adam. His words haunted her; they condemned her. She understood that as Michael had wanted to confine her to his own expectations, she had done the same to Adam. Her fear wanted to bind him to certain rules. Yet she didn't know how she could do otherwise; her heart dreaded making a mistake she would regret the rest of her life.

She knew she must sort out the problem in order to love the way she wanted to love and be loved. If not with Adam, then with the man she would trust God to provide.

When the bell at the back door rang, she grabbed the teapot and hurried to the dining room, calling to Emma to let in their guest.

Emma mumbled something about running away and then called for Adam to enter.

Chas kept busy handing out tea, making sure Mrs. B's was quite correct and her mother had the little table close to her knee. She hoped if she took long enough, Emma would wait on Adam. But today Emma seemed inclined to passing out the cookies slowly, forcing Chas to hand Adam his cup.

"Thank you," he said quietly.

Unable to stop herself, she glanced up. His blue eyes glittered knowingly. She dropped her head, ignoring his low chuckle.

"I won't bite," he murmured for her ears alone.

His comment was so unexpected that she pulled back and laughed. "Then I promise I won't, either."

It was that easy to make a truce, and Chas relaxed and settled back to listen to his tales.

"I feel it was a very successful tour," he concluded. "Mr. Edwards of Calgary, a prominent businessman, has organized a group of other businessmen and notables to come here to Willow Creek and see more of my work." He managed to look uncomfortable and pleased at the same time.

"That's wonderful, Adam," Mother said. "I expect they'll want to buy as many pictures as you care to part with."

Adam laughed. "Thank you, Miz LaBlanc."

Mr. Elias excused himself, heading for the stairs. He surprised them all a few minutes later when he reentered the sitting room and marched to Adam's side. "I have something I want to show you." He unwrapped a parcel and pulled out a book, handing it to Adam.

Adam read the title out loud: *Memoirs of a Soldier*, by T. L. Elias. Why, Mr. Elias, you've had your life story published."

Mother sat forward. "How thrilling! You wrote it yourself, Mr. Elias?"

He nodded.

"So that's what you've been working at?" Chas asked, giving an I-told-you-so glance to Emma.

"It's taken me a long time," Mr. Elias said.

Adam was still examining the book, reading excerpts aloud, when Chas followed Emma to the kitchen.

"A book. Can you imagine?" Emma was obviously vexed no mystery was involved.

"It sounds as if he had a very interesting life."

Emma sighed. "I had so hoped it was something a little more dramatic."

Chas laughed. "Seems to me life is complex enough without looking for something to complicate it."

Emma considered Chas. "Are you referring to anything in particular?"

"No, just things in general."

What had once seemed so clear was now muddied. Somehow she had to sort out exactly what she wanted in life—and how much she was willing to risk.

But the days passed, and she found herself no closer to discovering the answers. And if life wasn't complicated enough, her mother seemed determined to make it even more so.

❧

"There is no reason to celebrate my being an old maid," Chas insisted.

Mother waved away her arguments. "My only daughter, my only child, is about to have a birthday, and I plan to celebrate."

"But, Mother," Chas complained, "I'll be twenty-five. Too old to have a birthday party."

"Fine. Then we'll call it something else. How about a celebration of joy?"

Chas shook her head. "I'd just as soon forget the whole business."

"It's important to me," her mother insisted.

Chas studied her mother's face, set in quiet, resolute lines. How could she deny her? Besides, what would be the point? She would find some way of doing what she wanted. "Promise me you won't invite anyone extra, and we'll have just a little celebration with the residents."

Her mother smiled and said, "We'll have a grand time."

Chas turned back to kneading the bread dough, troubled that she had not given her promise.

Chas was almost grateful when the birthday arrived, hoping it would put an end to her mother's furtive whispers behind Chas's back and her hiding things quickly when Chas would enter a room.

Emma baked a big cake and decorated it with icing roses.

"I feel like such a fraud," Chas complained. "All this fuss for nothing."

Emma finished the last rose before she straightened and answered. "It's fun to do something special." She washed the icing from her fingers. "I hope you don't mind, but I invited Gordon."

Chas shrugged. "I don't mind. He'll be the only guest."

Emma gave her a quick look then busied herself wiping the table. "Your mother is excited about the party."

"All I agreed to was a birthday supper." She studied Emma's bent head. "She didn't do anything I should know about, did she?"

Emma shrugged. "Not that I know of."

Chas waited, suspicion growing in her mind. "I said nothing special."

Emma looked at her, her eyes wide. "I'm sure your mother wouldn't do anything you wouldn't approve of."

"How I wish."

After a quick teatime, Emma ordered Chas out of the house. "You're the birthday girl. I don't want you doing the work, so go away while I finish up meal preparations."

Chas hesitated, but the turkey was cooking in the oven, and the potatoes were peeled. She had gathered lettuce and radishes from the garden earlier. There wasn't a great deal left to do.

"Thank you, Emma. A little time off is the best gift you could give me."

Emma shooed her away.

Chas wandered the streets of the town, enjoying the late summer display of flowers. Already some of the trees looked worn out. The evenings were growing short, the nights cold.

And I'm stuck in a rut.

For weeks she had battled a restlessness she couldn't identify. She had tried to ignore it, explaining it away as missing Colin. Even praying didn't ease it completely. As she walked around town, she determined to use the time alone to sort out her thoughts.

But an hour later, she stood in front of the little white house with the picket fence and now-dusty arbor, still searching for answers.

She stared at the house and yard. For so long this little house had symbolized everything she longed for. But now she derived no pleasure from her dreams. *What good are empty dreams?* she wondered. A little white house with a picket fence meant nothing if she was alone.

Neither the house nor the place provided the security she wanted.

Colin's words rang through her brain.

Love always protects, always perseveres, always trusts, always hopes.

She wanted love.

But she wanted so much more.

She wanted a little house filled with love and she wanted her mother to be happy, which meant keeping the boardinghouse.

The things she wanted seemed to oppose one another. It was impossible to sort out.

God, please show me what I need to know. Grant me wisdom and patience.

She breathed deeply, letting God's peace fill her, knowing He would lead her to what was best for everyone. After a moment, she turned her steps homeward.

The back door opened, and Emma called, "Supper is ready."

"I hope I haven't kept you waiting." Chas couldn't help feeling a little guilty at the amount of time she had spent daydreaming.

"No, silly. Perfect timing. Come on."

Emma pulled Chas toward the dining room. The first thing Chas noticed was that the connecting door was closed, an unusual occurrence. Then Emma threw open the door and pushed Chas inside.

She gasped. Red, white, and blue streamers hung across the ceiling to the corners of the room, and bouquets of bright flowers flooded the table.

"Oh, my!" she murmured, blinking.

No extra company, she had insisted. Nothing special. Gordon Simpson she had expected, but not Doc Johnson, Pastor Simpson, and Miss Martha, Michael—and Adam, grinning enough to split his face in two.

Chapter 10

H appy birthday!" everyone shouted.

Chas shot a scolding look at her mother, who only smiled and said, "You're to sit in my place tonight."

Emma pushed her toward the head of the table.

Chas spent several seconds adjusting herself before she looked at the group seated around the extended table.

Mr. Elias beamed at her from the far end.

To her left sat her mother, with Mrs. B at her side.

On Chas's other side, Adam was so close, she could say with certainty that he had very recently shaved with a soap reminding her of pine trees after a rain. Michael sat next to him with the others filling in the places on either side.

Michael grinned. "I think we succeeded in surprising you."

"I wasn't expecting this. Mother promised me she wouldn't do anything special."

Mother sighed. "What would be the fun in that? Besides, I never promised."

Adam chuckled. "Your mother has been planning this for weeks."

Chas had promised herself not to look at him until her surprise and confusion had settled. She feared her heart would be in her face, that he would see things she didn't want him to see. But her eyes seemed to have a will of their own and sought him. His blue eyes flashed with laughter, unblinking as they met her gaze.

Her pulse beat wildly behind her temples. She was trapped by his look, floating to the sky.

"It's such fun to surprise you."

Beryl's voice provided escape. Chas tore herself away from the sparkling fire. "It's so kind of everyone," she murmured.

Emma laughed. "I thought you would come home early and discover us."

Chas grinned. "And here I was feeling guilty about wasting the afternoon."

Mrs. B turned to Mother. "I thought it was mealtime."

Everyone laughed, and Emma sprang to her feet. "I'll serve things."

When Chas pushed back to help her, Emma frowned. "You sit. Gordon will help me."

The young man jumped to his feet with an eagerness that made everyone laugh.

After they had filled their plates, Mr. Elias asked Adam, "The delegation from the city has come and gone. Was it a successful visit?"

"Very. Besides making several purchases, they've asked me to set up a display in Calgary. They talked about renting a shop and having a more or less permanent place for my work."

Every word he spoke zinged along Chas's spine. If only she dared love him. If only she could accept the love he had offered her.

Had offered. Past tense. How perverse her nature was that, since he seemed to view her now as nothing more than an acquaintance, she was almost willing to admit she cared about him as more.

"You might be interested in the man who came to the shop today," Adam said.

Grateful to have something to divert her confusing thoughts, Chas forced her attention to his news, reminding herself her feelings could not be allowed to rule her heart.

"He put up a poster advertising hot-air balloon rides."

Everyone talked at once. One by one, Adam sorted out their questions, answering as best he could.

"He'll be in town next week. He's arranged for my father to collect the fee and set up a schedule."

"Time for the cake." Emma and Gordon hurried to the kitchen, where muffled giggling could be heard.

Emma came back bearing the cake. Gordon's arms were filled with gifts. Everyone sang "Happy Birthday!"

Chas groaned. "I'm too old for a birthday party."

Mother patted her hand. "It's not a birthday party—it's a celebration."

Chas laughed so hard, she had to wipe her eyes. "Mother, you are priceless. If this isn't a birthday party, I don't know what is."

Mother had the good grace to look sheepish. "You said no birthday party, so it's not a birthday party."

Everyone laughed. After that it seemed the room rang with laughter.

"Cake or gifts first?" Emma asked.

The guests called out, "Gifts!"

Chas nodded, allowing Gordon to pile them in front of her.

The first was from Mr. Elias, a monogrammed silk handkerchief. "Thank you. It's lovely."

There was a book of poems from Michael, a blouse from Emma, a crocheted doily from Mrs. B, who beamed when Chas thanked her. Knowing the pleasure and pain Mrs. B got from her handwork made the item more precious than she could have imagined.

Beryl and Louise had gone together to buy a lovely box of body powder. Pastor Simpson and Miss Martha gave her a tiny black devotional book.

"Sweets for the sweet," Doc said as Chas unwrapped his gift—a bag of toffees.

Chas giggled. As far back as she could remember, Doc had come on her birthday with the same gift and the same teasing words.

Two gifts remained. She opened the flat one from Adam first. Inside was a miniature painting of Ellen and her the day they had gone to the falls. Tears blurred her vision.

"Thank you," she said softly. She wished she could bring back the day with all its pleasure. It seemed so long ago.

Quieting the trembling of her fingers, she reached for the last package. It was a black lacquered box from John and Roy and the Knutsen boys. When she flipped it open, she gasped. It was filled with money.

It was all she could do not to cry.

"Now my gift," her mother said.

But before she could stand to her feet, Adam jumped up. "I'll get it."

He disappeared into the hall, returning with a large flat package covered in brown paper.

Chas looked from Adam to her mother. "What have you two been up to?"

As he pulled out his chair and propped the present on it, Adam grinned.

Mother fairly bounced in her chair. "Open it. I can't wait to see it."

Everyone laughed.

"I guess this explains all the whispering between the two of you." Chas ripped the protective paper away and gasped.

"It's beautiful!"

An angel, hidden in clouds so that he seemed a part of them, reached down, almost touching a young woman making her way along a winding country road. The young woman was Chas. A brass plaque at the bottom bore the title "Chastity's Angel."

She bent closer. The angel looked exactly like Colin. She glanced up at Adam.

"But you never saw Colin."

"Your guest, Colin?" At her nod he shook his head. "No, he left before I returned from my trip. Why do you ask?"

"Because this angel has his face."

Everyone leaned close to the painting.

"It *is* Colin," Emma murmured, her voice filled with awe. "How did you know how he looked?"

Adam seemed confused. "I never saw him."

"Maybe he was truly an angel," Mother said quietly.

Chas sat back in her chair. Was it possible? Had Colin been an angel? She cherished the thought—her own angel coming with news of a father she had secretly longed for her entire life.

After cake and tea, Michael left. When Chas rose to help with the dishes, Emma chased her from the room.

"You'll not be doing any work this evening."

Emma grinned at Gordon, who rose to his feet and said sheepishly, "I'll give Emma a hand with the dishes."

Beryl and Louise offered, as well, but Emma shooed them away. "You let us do them."

"Would you care to sit out on the veranda with me?"

Adam's voice was so close that she felt his breath. She turned to face him, instantly wishing she hadn't. His eyes, the color of rushing water, blazed through her reason. Swallowing hard, she blinked and forced herself to look across the room. She wouldn't let herself be foolish just because the evening had left her unsettled. But she let him lead the way out the back door to the narrow bench, where he sat down beside her. Neither of them spoke. Chas listened to the evening sounds—a child calling to another, a dog barking, a bird whistling in a nearby tree. Dusk draped them, soft and gentle.

Finally Chas broke the stillness. "You're sure you've never seen Colin?"

"I suppose I must have seen his face somewhere."

"Do you think it's possible he's an angel?"

Adam shrugged. "Do angels get sick? And why did he come here?"

"I don't know if angels get sick, but can you think of a better way of getting invited into this house?" She rushed on. "He came for a specific reason. You see, he brought Mother and me each a letter from my father."

Adam sat forward, turning to look at her. The light from the window behind them cast golden shadows over his features, drawing them sharply. "Simon LaBlanc? You heard from him after all these years? Where is he?"

She gulped back a sudden rush of tears. "He's dead now," she whispered, pausing. "Colin cared for him at the end. Father wrote the letters before he died."

Adam drew in a sharp breath and sat back.

"Colin says he repented and turned to God before he died." She blinked back tears as she met Adam's eyes. His gaze searched her face and studied her eyes.

"How do you feel about all this?"

She gave a tremulous smile. "Good."

Suddenly she was aware of how good it felt to hear from her father, to know who he was and that he had wished for healing between them. She searched for words to explain it.

"Hearing from him, even though he was already gone, has satisfied something inside me. Like suddenly something that's hurt all my life is healed."

He nodded. "I'm glad."

"Colin told me something else, too. He said I should follow my heart."

Adam's look never faltered. "What did he mean?"

She lowered her eyes, needing time to sort out all the things racing through her mind. "I think he saw how I feared so many things. I was afraid I would make a mistake and end up alone. I think not having a father has somehow made me feel I had to build a safe, predictable future for myself."

"And now?" His words were low, insistent.

Chas laughed, tossing her hands in a helpless gesture. "I don't know if I can put it into words, but I feel as if my heart is growing." She shrugged. "I know it doesn't make sense, but that's how I feel."

Adam continued to study her. "Was Michael part of trying to create a safe future?"

She looked at him and nodded, unable to tear her gaze away from his. "I think he was. Poor Michael."

Adam let out his breath sharply. Then his eyes seemed to darken. Or perhaps, Chas reasoned, it was only that the last of the light had faded from the sky.

"And now," he asked, "are you ready to step out of your safe place?"

Chas knew what he meant. His look was intense and probing, his eyes steady and unblinking.

"I'm not sure," she whispered. "Perhaps. I think I'm getting close."

A quick reaction flickered across his face—too fast for Chas to be able to tell what he thought. He stood to his feet and stretched.

"I should be getting home."

He faced her again, his gaze darting to her lips then resting on her eyes.

"Great birthday party," he murmured. "Happy birthday."

He stepped off the veranda and then turned back to her. "Chas, my feelings haven't changed. I still love you. You will be forever in my heart, but only you will know when you're ready to accept my love."

She nodded, her throat too full for her to speak.

He hesitated and then walked down the path and out of sight.

She waited until her pounding heart had calmed before she hurried to her room.

Her birthday painting stood on the chair. She sat on her bed and studied it. Adam was a wonderful artist. This painting was not only beautiful, it almost breathed peace and safety.

And he said he still loves me.

She hugged herself even as her mind struggled with the implications. Loving Adam carried with it risks. She had to be very sure she was willing to accept those risks before she allowed herself to love him in return.

Colin seemed to speak to her from the picture. "Follow your heart. Love protects, trusts, perseveres, hopes."

Was she capable of that sort of love? Was her heart strong enough to trust Adam's love even when he felt the need to wander? Was it strong enough to persevere when he took to the roads, to remain behind waiting and patient? Or to leave the security of her home and accompany him? These were questions she must answer. And until she could, reason must prevail.

The next night, sitting on her mother's bed, she asked, "How do I know the right thing to do?"

All day she had thought about the choices she faced and was no closer to knowing what she should do than she had been twenty-four hours earlier.

"What do you desire in your heart of hearts, *ma cherie?*"

Chas picked at a thread on the bedcover. "I love Adam, but I'm afraid of loving unwisely."

Her mother's hands grew still, and for a moment she didn't speak. Chas waited, knowing she was praying and thinking.

"Chastity, never fear love. The love of a good man is a precious gift from God."

"But what if—?" She couldn't bring herself to point out how it hadn't been such a good gift for her mother.

Lifting her hand to still Chas's words, her mother continued slowly. "Adam is a good man. He is nothing like your father was. Nor are you as senseless and headstrong as I was at your age. No, *ma cherie*, you have shown yourself time and again to be wise, steadfast, and strong."

Chas lay back and studied the ceiling. Was she wise, steadfast, and strong? Strong enough to face the challenges a life with Adam would bring?

Later, alone in her room, she paged through her Bible, praying for assurance about her future. She sighed. Life was so uncertain. She couldn't begin to guess what lay ahead. Of course, that was true no matter what choices she made. Or even if she let things continue as they were and refused Adam's love.

An ache grew inside her until the tears sprang to her eyes. Life without Adam was a bleak prospect.

But how could she prove to him—and to herself—that she was willing and capable of stepping outside her safe little world?

And prove it she must. For her own satisfaction. She had to know she could deal with the challenges Adam's way of life would surely bring.

❧

The poster hanging in the window of Silverhorn's Mercantile was large and colorful. Chas stared at it a long time, studying every detail.

The canopy of the balloon hovered over the basket in which two people laughed and waved.

It was so unlike her to want to do such a thing.

Always she had done the sensible thing. Suddenly it wasn't enough. She wanted to fly. Her fingers curled around the wad of money in her pocket. It was extravagant, but she was sure the boys would approve; and not stopping to analyze her motives, she marched to the counter and plunked the money down in front of Mr. Silverhorn.

❧

The balloon was bigger than she had thought it would be—and noisier. She listened to the instructions closely, excitement and fear combining to make her mouth dry.

She crawled into the basket. The burners hissed. And then they slowly lifted from the ground, rising gracefully. Chas looked down at the tops of trees and houses and the startled, upturned faces. Not a breath of wind stirred.

The burner puffed out hot air, the sound making her jump. A bubble of joy filled her heart, bursting forth in a shout of laughter. She could never have imagined flying was so freeing. It was like floating in God's hand.

"In God have I put my trust. I will not be afraid what man can do unto me."

The words swelled within her.

I will not be afraid of risk or change. I will not fear Adam's way of life.

Her heart felt ready to explode into a shower of light over the side of the basket.

They drifted across the treetops, leaves flashing like golden coins, over meadows dotted with cows and horses, over gardens with mounds of potatoes and carrots dug up ready to be put in root cellars, over yellowed stubble and pale stacks of straw that seemed as insignificant as a bubble in the surface of the earth.

The hour was up much too soon. The pilot masterfully brought them safely back to the ground.

Laughing, she let the pilot help her step from the basket. Preparing to take pictures of the balloon ride, Adam stood beside his camera, his jaw slack. He hurried toward her.

"You went up in the balloon?"

She laughed at his expression. "You make it sound as if I walked on water. All I did was go on a little balloon ride."

"Did you think about the risks?"

"It seemed perfectly safe to me." Her smile faltered at the stern look on his face.

"Well, it isn't. How could you do such a silly thing?"

She tried to keep back her laughter and failed. It ended up half guffaw, half giggle. "It was wonderful! I wouldn't have missed it for the world."

He glared at her.

"Now I can understand why you need to experience some things for yourself." She grew thoughtful. "No one could have described this for me."

He adjusted a knob on his camera and fiddled with the black cloth. "Sometimes there's no need for firsthand experience." He shuffled his feet. "We need to talk."

"All right."

"Let me finish here, and then we'll go someplace."

"Sounds good."

He nodded toward a buggy. "Do you mind waiting?"

"Not at all." Welcoming the chance to watch Adam work, she settled on the ground beside the buggy as a couple prepared to enter the basket.

Adam slid in a plate and ducked under the cloth. He took several photos as the balloon filled and rose gracefully.

While he was working, he glanced toward Chas several times, his expression puzzled.

She hugged her secret to herself.

Finally he folded the tripod and tucked it under his arm.

She jumped to her feet as he headed toward her, an unsteady pulse throbbing along her veins.

"Are you finished?" she asked, although the answer was self-evident.

He shook his head as if to clear it. "For now."

He packed his equipment in the back and helped her to the seat, the buggy dipping as he climbed up beside her.

Without saying anything more, he flicked the reins and headed down the road. Before they reached town, he turned into a side road.

Chas's heart began to dance.

He reined in near a thick stand of trees.

"Shall we walk?"

"I'd like that." He reached up for her, his warm hands lighting fires that sped along her spine to her heart, where they crescendoed into a mighty roar. Although grateful for his hands steadying her, she knew she wouldn't be able to stop quivering until his touch ended.

They fell into step. Chas clenched her hands together. This walk was as daunting as the balloon ride had been, full of promise, yet at the same time fraught with a sense of having lost her moorings. She fortified herself with the reminder of how exhilarating the balloon ride had been.

Adam stopped, turning to look at her.

She lifted her face, letting his gaze search hers until he found what he sought. She knew the moment he did, for his blue eyes glittered with triumph. Her heart swelled against her ribs.

"I can't believe you went on that ride," he murmured.

"I saw the poster and thought, 'I have to fly.' It was as simple as that." His look lifted her heart toward the heavens.

He trailed a finger down her cheek. "Are you really ready to fly?"

She knew he wasn't referring to another balloon ride. "I believe I am," she murmured, her thoughts scattering as she took in the rugged line of his jaw and his golden lashes. The musky scent of his nearness filled her senses until she could think of nothing else.

Slowly he lowered his head, his lips touching hers in the barest hint of a kiss. As he drew back, she strained forward, longing for more.

He gave a low-throated chuckle and pulled her into his arms, taking her lips in a breath-stopping, satisfying kiss that seemed to last forever yet ended far too soon.

She nuzzled her face into his shoulder. She could feel his breath sifting through her hair. She didn't want the embrace to end, but he sighed and lifted her face.

"We need to discuss some things."

She smiled into his eyes.

He lifted her chin. "Are you really ready for this?"

She knew what he meant: Was she ready for the sort of life he offered? But she pretended to misunderstand him and, closing her eyes, tilted her face, offering her lips.

He drew her to him and kissed her again.

Finally he pulled away. "Let's try again," he muttered and, guessing she would again misinterpret his meaning, drew back another inch. "And I don't mean that."

His eyes darkened. "We'll save that for later."

She smiled again, relishing the promise. "What did you mean?" she inquired, her voice full of pretended innocence.

He looked beyond her. "I won't make any promises I don't intend to keep. There will be times I go on trips either to show my work or to see something." He looked deep into her eyes. "Though I can't imagine ever wanting to leave you, even for a minute. You'll simply have to come with me."

His confession went straight to the depths of her heart, and she cradled it there, knowing she would forever remember the way he looked at her.

"I promise you this, Chastity LaBlanc—I will love you forever with all my heart. And if I have to travel for some reason and you can't accompany me, you have my assurance I will hurry home to you as fast as I can."

"Adam Silverhorn, I love you."

Light flooded her gaze until the rest of the world vanished, and she saw nothing else but Adam.

He cupped her face in his hands and kissed her gently and reverently.

"I have dreamed of this for so long," he murmured between kisses. "What made you change your mind?"

"I suppose you could say I grew up." She smiled, thinking of the path her maturing had followed, the role Colin had played. "I've learned security isn't found in a place or a position or even promises. It's found in God and the love He provides. Love protects, perseveres, trusts, hopes."

His expression was hungry, asking for more.

"I understand about your having to travel. I can live with it, knowing you will hurry back. I believe my love is strong enough to accept that. Just as your love was strong enough to wait for me."

Her heart was so full. She had so much she longed to say to him, but she could not find the words. Then his lips found hers again, and she knew sometimes words were unnecessary.

Chas lay on the bed beside her mother, only half-listening. Her thoughts lingered on Adam's good-night kiss. They had agreed they would delay their marriage until after Christmas to give them time to sort out the details of their lives. But sometimes it seemed impossible to wait.

"We need to discuss the boardinghouse," Mother said.

Chas gathered up her thoughts. From the day she had told her she and Adam were to marry, her mother had wanted to know their plans regarding the boardinghouse. Chas had been honest. "We haven't planned that far ahead." Now she rolled to her side so she could look into her mother's face.

"I don't want you worrying about it, Mama. Adam and I are both content to leave things in God's hands."

Mother nodded. "I've come to a decision. I'm going to sell the house."

Chas sat up straight. "Sell?" She gulped. "You always said you wouldn't."

"Doc and I have been talking. He says I might as well accept the facts. Chances are I'll never get well enough to run this place on my own again." She held up a hand. "And I saw when you were thinking of marrying Michael that making the house your responsibility would never allow you to have a normal married life."

"But, Mother, Adam is not Michael. We've discussed it and feel sure things will work out."

Mother smiled serenely. "And they have. Gordon has made me a very pleasant offer." She nodded. "I've accepted it."

Chas fell back on the bed. "Gordon Simpson?"

"He's an astute young man. He'll run the house efficiently, and I've no doubt he'll make a tidy profit."

"Emma?" Was there another wedding in the future? A tiny thought troubled Chas. Would Emma end up being worked to death?

"No one has said anything, but I've got eyes. Emma is very capable, and Gordon has already shown himself to be useful."

Chas relaxed. "You're right. He doesn't seem to mind helping."

He had peeled vegetables, washed lettuce, iced cakes. Until now Chas thought it had been simply a way of spending time with Emma, but now she could see he truly liked the work.

"He's good at fixing things, too." He had saved Chas a call to the handyman by repairing the washing machine and fixing the front step. "He's perfect for the job, Mama."

"I thought so myself."

They laughed together, but one thing still troubled Chas.

"What about Mrs. B?"

"Why, that's the best of it. Gordon has made inquiries about a little house for me. He says the Mellon house on the corner is for sale. He's going to make an offer for me. Mrs. B will live with me."

Chas thought of the cozy house, tucked away behind some trees with a front veranda close enough to the street to visit from the front gate. "It's lovely." She sighed. So many changes. All good, but so much to deal with.

"I think it will be good for Mrs. B. I'll have more time to spend with her. Perhaps I can get her to sit outside on the veranda on nice days. She'd enjoy that."

"And it will also make it easier for you to leave the boardinghouse."

Mother took her hand and squeezed it. "I'm looking forward to the move."

Two weeks after she had told Adam her mother's decision, he came to the house to ask Chas if she had time for a walk.

"Go ahead," Emma said. "Gordon and I can manage."

"Thanks." Chas smiled, but Emma had already turned back to Gordon.

The days had been filled with making arrangements for the sale, deciding what to take, what to leave, painting and preparing her mother's house. Through it all, Emma and Gordon had shown themselves more than adequate to run the boardinghouse.

She and Adam sauntered along the streets. Autumn had made her flashiest show and now seemed spent. When Chas would have followed her regular pattern and headed past the big houses to the white picketed yard, Adam turned toward the street paralleling Main Street. Chas was too busy telling of the packing and arranging to give it more than a passing thought.

"I want to show you something." He pulled her to a stop.

"What?" She searched his face for a clue.

"This," he said, pointing. "This house," he added when her expression remained puzzled.

"What about it?"

"I want to buy it, but I want your opinion first."

She lifted her gaze to the house. It was large, two full stories. Her first thought was that it was large enough for boarders. Her spirits dropped.

"I know it's not the little white house with the picket fence, but come inside and let me tell you what I have in mind."

She followed, waiting as he unlocked the door. He closed the door behind her and pulled her into his arms. "I've discovered how much I want to be close to you all the time, so I thought of moving my shop to the front of the house." He trailed kisses along her cheek, sending waves of delight through her. "That way I can slip out and kiss my sweet wife whenever the shop is quiet."

She nestled closer.

"The rest of the house will be ours and ours alone. Except"—he paused to shower more kisses upon her face—"except for the little ones who will fill the rooms."

Tears welled up in the back of her eyes at the thought of little Silverhorns.

"Do I get to see the rest of the house?" she asked him, smiling.

"In a minute." He kissed her soundly.

It took much longer than a minute to see the house with their having to pause for a kiss in each room and to congratulate themselves on how happy they were.

Then he led her to the backyard. She gasped. The yard was so sheltered by trees that it was entirely private. Tucked away in the far corner, surrounded by almost bare bushes, stood a tiny gazebo, still shining with newness.

"It's perfect," she murmured.

He pulled her back into his arms. "My sweet Chas, I will love you forever and do everything in my power to make you happy."

She cradled his face in her hands. "Adam, all I need to make me happy is you."

She kissed him gently and then took his hand and led him to the gazebo. Under the latticed shadows, the now leafless vines crackling merrily around them, she faced Adam, their intertwined hands pressed to his chest.

"There's something I want to do," she whispered. "Something I promised myself I would do if I ever had a place like this."

He smiled down at her, waiting.

"I want to dedicate this place and our marriage to God. I truly believe He sent Colin to guide me, to show me how to go ahead in my life."

" 'Chastity's Angel.' "

"That painting will always have a prominent place in our home."

"Let's dedicate ourselves and this place to God. I owe Him my deepest thanks for your love." He took her hands, adoring her with his eyes, and then they knelt side by side in the damp leaves.

She closed her eyes as Adam prayed aloud. A whisper of warm breeze swirled around them. She knew it was only the wind, but for a moment, she felt as if Colin stood beside them, smiling his approval.

"Thank You, God," she said softly.

Crane's Bride

Chapter 1

Crane had figured out everything else before he headed west. The farther west he went, the more the neglected detail bothered him.

He leaned forward in his saddle and stared at the town ahead, a fair-to-middling-sized place, looking as if it had sprung helter-skelter from the land with half-finished buildings and a wide dirt street.

"Ain't much," he muttered to the ever-patient Rebel.

The horse tossed his head. Town meant a warm stall and a good grooming, and he sidestepped in an effort to get his rider moving.

"Ain't much," Crane repeated. "But it ain't going to get any better." Towns were meaner and farther apart with every passing day.

He pushed his dusty cowboy hat back from his forehead and scratched his head. "About time for a bath." And to take care of this other business plaguing his thoughts ever since he'd made up his mind what he was going to do.

"Let's go." He flicked the reins and tugged the lead rope of the packhorse. He pulled in under the sign COLHOME GENERAL STORE, turning his back on the curious stares of the two old codgers who lounged on the wooden chairs. They were watching him as he secured both horses to the rail.

Crane wiped his palms along his thighs and stepped to the lean-to veranda. One old coot spat on the boards close to Crane's boots. Crane drew to a halt, glaring at the old man until he wiped his grizzled mouth and turned away.

Inside, Crane paused for his eyes to adjust to the dim light then ran his gaze over the store interior. Nothing but the usual dusty shelves and two old women fingering some yard goods. The rail-thin storekeeper studied Crane over the top of his wire glasses, as if examining some rare and unwelcome bug. Crane fixed him with a steady, narrow-eyed look, forcing the man to lower his gaze.

His boots thudded on the oiled boards as he crossed to the counter. "I want to put up a notice." His lazy drawl gave no hint of the way his insides were knotted up, as if he were scared.

Only he wasn't scared. He'd thought on this and knew exactly what he was doing. Besides, near as he could figure, there was no other way.

"Go ahead." The storekeeper jerked a thumb toward the pocked board and busied himself with a handful of bills.

"Got a piece of paper?"

"Sure. Cost you a penny."

Crane dug a coin from his pocket and flicked it to the counter. The man swept it into his palm and drew a square of paper from under the stained boards then turned back to his bills. Crane waited, scowling at the top of the man's head. "Can I borrow a pencil?"

"Sure thing." He offered a pencil stub on the tip of stained fingers. "No charge."

Crane licked the lead and carefully wrote the message he'd composed. Finished, he pulled a jackknife from his pocket, dug out a tack, and put up his notice.

The storekeeper stretched his neck like a chicken so he could see Crane's note. He mouthed the words then glared at Crane.

Crane cared little what the man thought. He retreated to the nails and saws, pretending to examine the merchandise.

"Can I help you?" The bespectacled man watched his every move.

"I'll let you know." He edged around so he could see the door.

A gray-haired matron bustled in, conducted her business, and left. One of the old codgers from the veranda shuffled to the door, peered in, then returned to his post. Two schoolgirls came in, whispering and giggling, selected two cents' worth of candy, and giggled their way out.

Crane waited, ignoring the looks he got. His stomach rumbled.

He'd about decided to come back later when the door opened and another lady hustled in. Crane squinted, but against the bright window, he couldn't determine whether she was young or old, ugly or otherwise. All he could say for certain was that she was reed thin, wore a dark dress, and moved as if she were in a hurry. He tensed and drew in his breath.

The girl, or woman if she was that, rushed to the counter, bent over it to make a low-spoken request, then turned as the storekeeper chose an item from behind the counter. The girl checked the room in a sweeping glance and, with nothing to detain her interest, studied the notice board, bending forward as she saw Crane's notice.

Crane began to sweat. His stomach had been kissing his backbone for a spell and now groaned so loud he was sure it could be heard across the room.

She tore the notice from the board and shoved it toward the storekeep. "You know who put this up?"

The man behind the counter jerked his head toward Crane. She whirled to face him. He wished he could see her better, but before he could figure a way, she marched across the floor, her steps crisp and quick.

"You the man who wrote this?" She shook the note in his face.

She's not very big. In fact, she looks as if a stiff wind will blow her away. His mind whirled without lighting on another thought. Again his stomach growled. "Yup," he managed through the confusion of his thoughts.

She studied him from head to toe, taking her time about it.

He wondered what she saw. A dusty cowboy, lean and tough as shoe leather? Another saddle bum with too-long blond hair darkened by days in the saddle?

Suddenly his arms felt too long, and he crossed them over his chest. Her gaze lingered on his boots. He followed her stare, wishing he'd taken time to remove the evidence of the last trail ride.

She jerked her head up and boldly met his eyes.

He braced himself.

"I'm a God-fearing woman. I'll be your wife." Never once did she blink.

His thoughts exploded. He didn't know what he'd expected. Nor could he explain why he'd worded the notice the way he did, but something inside insisted she must be God-fearing. Her gaze bore into his until he clenched his jaw. Her look demanded an answer, and he croaked, "Yup."

Her brow puckered, and she glanced at the note in her hand. "You write this yourself?"

"Yup." His mind spun like the wheel on a runaway buggy. Now would be a good time to find the back door and use it, but her eyes riveted him to the spot. The light caught in her hair. *Black,* he thought. *Black and shiny.*

"Then I guess you can read and write. But can you talk?"

Beads of sweat collected on Crane's forehead. He managed another "Yup." At the sound of his own voice, thick and slow, his brain slammed its fist. He grabbed her elbow. "Let's get out of here."

There was no resistance in her arm as they hustled from the store. Outside, desperate for a retreat from the prying eyes following his every move, he turned in the direction of the river. Despite her shortness, the girl had no trouble keeping up with his hurried strides. He liked that, he decided.

Neither of them slowed until they ducked through the sprawling willows and faced the tumbling river. He dropped his hold on her arm and stared at the sparkling water.

"I'm headed west. Going to start a new life. I need a woman—a wife." He'd said it badly, but the fine words he'd practiced for three days had fled.

"Fine. I'm willing."

He looked at this woman who had agreed to marry him. He could see over her head without a hair in his view. *Small,* he thought again. *And thin.* He narrowed his eyes. She looked downright starved. But he liked the way the light caught in her hair, trapped in the black strands.

He met her eyes then. Blue as ink and unblinking. Full of defiant challenge. Even the way she stood, hands clenched at her side, feet gripping the ground, spoke a warning. He couldn't help but admire her spunk.

As he studied her more closely, he wondered if he'd made a dumb move. He had no desire to get hitched to a dirty woman, and this was one of the dirtiest he'd seen. Although her hair had been brushed smooth and tied at her neck, her dress was ragged and soiled, and—he wrinkled his nose—she desperately needed a bath. Her eyes narrowed as if reading his mind, and again her gaze traveled his length as if to remind him of his own condition.

"I meant to have a bath as soon as I hit town," he said.

She nodded. "I'm dirty, and I know it. Don't need no reminding. The dirt will come off with a dip in the river, but I won't pretend I'm something I'm not. This dress is all I got." Her eyes amazed him. Never once shifting away from his, they darkened, and he saw—no, he felt—her pride like a fist driven into his chest.

Pushing his hat back, he rubbed his forehead. Clothes and bathing were easy to solve, but other things needed to be sorted out. "First things first," he murmured.

She nodded.

"Are you running away?" All he needed was an angry father or husband barking at his heels.

Her jaw tightened. "Not running away—running to."

"And what would you be meaning by that?"

"Same as you. I'm looking for a new life."

"I'm not promising you anything but a home, a fair share of whatever I have, and probably lots of hard work." He'd struggled for three days for a way to say this, to make plain what he wanted and at the same time let her know what he did not expect. He did not expect love or passion, only a wife and a home to complete his new life.

"You trying to say this is to be a businesslike arrangement?" Her clear voice was brittle.

He nodded.

"You're wanting to make sure I'm not expecting romance?"

He grimaced at the way she spat it out but silently thanked her for putting words to his thoughts. "I'm looking for a partner for my new life, nothing more."

Her blue eyes flashing, she drew herself straighter and fixed him with a hard look. "Fine. I'm willing to work, and I don't need much. There's only one thing."

He raised his eyebrows and waited.

Her scowl was dark. "You ever hit me and I'm gone."

Crane jerked back at the thought. He wasn't a fool. He knew some men figured women were no better than a cow or a dog, but he had been raised differently. His frail mother would have dissolved at his feet if he'd even raised his voice in anger.

He studied the creature glowering at him and decided she could hardly be considered frail despite her small size. She had the bearing and boldness of a born fighter, and he wanted to know more about her.

"I will never hit you," he promised, but her shoulders remained hunched. "And if I ever do, you can leave without any questions asked."

Slowly she relaxed, and Crane let out his breath. Again they studied each other.

"My name's Crane." He held out his hand.

She hesitated then grasped it and gave a quick shake. "I'm Maggie."

Her hand was very small, yet her grip firm.

"We'll go back to the store and get enough for the coming months." He felt her shift in emotions even before he saw her eyes darken with what he figured must be acceptance, even anticipation. "We're both needing a bath. We'll go to the hotel and shed ourselves of this dirt."

"I'd as soon bathe in the river," she announced.

He searched her eyes for a clue to her meaning, but she continued to stare at him fiercely.

Finally he shrugged. "Suit yourself. Now let's get fixed up." He strode in the direction of town, leaving Maggie to follow at his heels.

They proceeded directly to the store. The uncooperative storekeeper's attitude changed quick as a wink when he saw the coins Crane clinked to the counter. "We'll be needing a few things," Crane muttered, his gaze following Maggie as she plucked two dresses from the ready-made rack. He'd instructed her to buy all she would need without regard for cost. "No telling what we'll find ahead of us." Within minutes she had gathered a number of items, hesitating before she added a cake of soap and a length of toweling.

He would have preferred to lie back in a tub of hot water, but he followed her back to the river, leading the horses and carrying the bundle from the store. With a murmured explanation, she pointed toward a canopy of overhanging willows. Crane nodded and followed the river in the opposite direction until he found another secluded spot.

The water was still icy from the spring thaw. Crane lathered up quickly, then held his breath as he plunged under the surface, shaking his head and shuddering as he emerged. The brisk rubdown restored but a fraction of the heat he'd lost in his dip. Running a comb through his hair, he wondered if he had time for a barbershop cut and as quickly dismissed the idea. He wanted only one thing, and that was to get this done with and get back on the trail.

He waited for Maggie to reappear. When she pushed aside the willows, his mouth fell open, and he stared. *She cleans up real nice.* Her scrubbed skin held the pink glow of a sunset.

"You look good," he murmured, amazed when the pink in her cheeks deepened, and he understood it was because of what he said.

"You, too," she said.

He shuffled as warmth crept up his neck and hoped his cheeks didn't darken in the same telltale way.

They retraced their steps to the heart of town and a low building offering food.

"I bringee man big breakfast?" offered the waiter of uncertain origins.

"What would you be wanting, Maggie?"

Maggie perched on the edge of the chair, her glance darting about the room. Crane knew the moment she'd checked every person and knew, too, she had been looking for something or someone. Finding them absent, she filled her lungs and relaxed. "The same."

After days of campfire cooking and gulping from a tin cup, Crane savored the hot coffee served in heavy white china. His concentration eliminated the need for conversation yet gave him a chance to study his soon-to-be bride, suddenly struck by how young she looked.

"How old are you?" He had no intention of playing her nursemaid.

"Eighteen." Again that blue-eyed directness. "But I know how to work and take care of myself if that's what's bothering you. How old are you?" She drummed her fingers on the table.

He had to think. "Twenty-seven, near as I can recall." He chuckled. "And I know how to work and take care of myself."

She blinked then laughed, low and musical. Her blue eyes sparkled with splinters of light. Crane stared like an idiot.

Heaping plates of steak, eggs, fried potatoes, and flapjacks were set before them. Crane dug into the food without a second look. By the time he cleaned his plate, he knew he'd enjoyed a hearty breakfast and figured Maggie would surely be stalled by now, but she steadily plowed through the mound, finishing up shortly after he did.

"You ate the whole thing."

Her cheeks bloomed pink. "I was hungry."

"I guess so." If she ate like that every day, he would spend all his time foraging food.

"I haven't eaten in three days," she whispered. "Since I walked away from—" She didn't finish.

He rubbed his forehead. "You better explain yourself."

"It's not what you think." She took a deep breath. "I was working at the hotel in exchange for a place to sleep and some food." Her fingers twisted around each other. "My job was to clean up rooms after the guests." She shuddered, and Crane could only guess at the things she'd done.

"When the hotel owner wanted me to do other things"—her eyes grew stormy—"I left." She squirmed forward until she balanced on the edge of the chair.

Finally he nodded. "And you left everything you own."

She shrugged. "It weren't much."

Seems like what he had to offer, no matter how slim, was an improvement. He felt rather pleased with himself. He pushed his chair back, and she sprang up, bouncing on the balls of her feet. He clamped his hat on, and they ambled toward the livery barn, where Crane ran his practiced gaze over the available mounts, choosing a well-built mare for Maggie.

She slid her hands along the mare's neck and whispered to the animal in a way that assured Crane she was at ease with the horse. "I shall call her Liberty."

The significance of her choice was not lost on Crane, and he smiled, hoping they would both find what they wanted in their new life—sweet liberty for her and, for him, help in building a home. A vague yearning tugged at his thoughts, but it disappeared as swiftly as it came, and he had not the time or patience to search after it.

They repacked the animals, Maggie working alongside Crane with a quiet quickness he found comforting. Then they headed toward the little church where the man who sold them the horse said they would find a preacher.

With every step, Crane's resolve strengthened. It was what he had decided to do; Maggie seemed pleasant enough and, now that she was cleaned up, not hard on the eyes. Whatever there was to discover about each other, they would have plenty of time to find it out on the trail.

And so he stood before the preacher with Maggie at his side.

"Do you Byler Thomas Crane take Margaret Malone to be your lawful wedded wife?"

He answered, "I do."

The short ceremony ended, and they stepped outside into the bright afternoon sun. "Well, Mrs. Crane, are you ready to set out?" He grinned down at her.

She nodded, keeping her head bent. "The sooner the better."

In order to pick up the trail to the west, they traversed several streets, dirtier with each step, the buildings increasingly ugly. The whole place smelled of trouble, and Crane kept sharp attention.

As they drew abreast of a narrow alleyway, he heard a high-pitched scream followed by gasping fear-laced wails, then a sudden flash of pink and white to his right.

A child. The small body rocketed across his path, with thundering steps in pursuit. Crane had his hands full, holding Rebel, who snorted and reared.

Out of the corner of his eye, he saw Maggie drop to the ground and wondered if she had been thrown, but he was too busy with Rebel to offer help. As soon as he'd calmed his horse, he dismounted, searching for the figure he was sure had been battered by Rebel's hooves, but a man scooped up the small child.

"Let me go!" the child shrieked. "I won't go back!"

Crane saw it all in a heartbeat. The swelling arms of a blacksmith tightening around the tiny body clad only in skimpy white undergarments. The anger darkening his face. Crane clenched his fists at his side. He was no match for this bulk of a man, and it was none of his business, but his gut wrenched.

A figure in a blue-flowered dress he recognized as being one he'd purchased just a few hours earlier skidded to a halt in front of the struggling pair. Maggie planted herself in the man's path, her hands on her hips. "This your child?"

"He ain't my father. He ain't nothing." The child's sobs tore at Crane's mind like a cold winter gale.

"Get out of my way." The burly man pushed Maggie aside with a thick arm. She swayed but held her ground.

Cold steel filled Crane, and he stepped toward them with casual deliberateness.

"Put her down," Maggie growled, her fists clenching and unclenching at her side.

"Lady, you best mind yer own bizness." He lifted his hand.

Crane pushed the hand away, at the same time shoving Maggie behind him.

"What seems to be the problem?" He balanced on the balls of his feet, his words low and lazy.

"No problem." The burly man dropped his arm. "Just claiming what's rightfully mine."

"Put her down." Maggie again faced the man.

A gleam jerked at Crane's nerves, and he stared at his Colt .45 gripped in her hands.

"Where'd you get that?" Something akin to knifepoints scraped along his nerves.

She didn't answer, but there was no need. He'd hung the revolver on the pack animal. He was not a fighting man, but neither was he naive as to the need for a gun.

"Maggie, what do you think you're up to?"

"I'm doing what any decent person would do," she answered without shifting her gaze. Again she ordered the man, "Let that child go."

With a volley of curses, the man lunged at Maggie. She neatly sidestepped and fired.

Dust at the man's feet kicked up, and Crane saw a hole in the toe of his boot. His muscles coiled to spring. "Why you—"

"Let her go, or I'll shoot you." She jerked away as he swung a fist at her.

She fired another shot, removing his hat. He gingerly rubbed his head.

The child squirmed from his grasp, skidding out of reach of the three adults, her glance darting from one to the other. Crane had seen that hunted look in wild animals. The child seemed not far removed from a wild animal with her matted hair and scruffy appearance.

"Honey, who is this man, and what does he want with you?" Maggie kept the gun trained on the man as she addressed the child.

The child shook like leaves before a wind. "He thinks he owns me 'cause I don't have no folks."

"That so, mister?" The voice, so sweet and gentle when speaking to the child, carried a hard, warning note.

Crane smiled at the contrast.

"She's mine. I owned her mother, and I own her." He jerked his head down the alley. At the end of the lane, Crane saw a mean building and knew it for what it was—a place of disrepute. He shuddered to think of anyone, least of all a child, having to live there. *You don't own people. Nobody can own another.*

"You got any papers to prove that?" Maggie pressed the man.

He spat. "Don't need any. Nobody gonna argue about it." He spat again, his spittle landing at Maggie's feet.

A small crowd had assembled, and their mute silence proved his words.

"Nobody but me," Maggie snarled, turning to the child. "You want to come with us?"

Her eyes bright, the child nodded.

Unmindful of Maggie's gun, the man roared and reached for the quaking child.

Quicksilver-like, Maggie grabbed her and, in a swift movement, sprang for her horse, lifting the child behind the saddle and jumping up in front of her.

"Let's go!" Maggie called.

Crane didn't have time to think about who was right. "Ride!" he called, but he could have saved his breath. She was already leaning over the neck of her horse, urging it forward. They raced toward the open trail. Shots rang out behind them, and Crane ducked lower.

Chapter 2

Crane narrowed his eyes, forcing them to focus on bits of the racing landscape to examine them for danger. He saw speeding trees and one lone shack—the only visible occupant a brown-speckled hen, flapping and squawking a protest at the clattering trio.

The only other sounds were pounding hooves and the heaving breath of his horse. The flying mane stung Crane's cheeks as he kept his head low to avoid any bullets aimed at them, but he heard no more. His thoughts galloped at a pace every bit as swift as their flight. *All I wanted was someone to help set up a home in the new West.*

The last few minutes were giving him pause for thought. Not in his wildest dreams had he considered he might be biting off more than he could chew.

He kept at a gallop until they crested a hill some miles from town, where he slowed Rebel, turning him to face the back trail. For several minutes he squinted toward town, now a low cluster in the distance. Maggie pulled up beside him.

"I don't see nobody after us."

Crane held his peace, willing their dust to settle so he could be certain.

Maggie stood in her stirrups and shaded her eyes. "You see something?"

Finally he eased back and lifted his hat to let the breeze through his hair. "Don't see nothing. Don't necessarily mean there ain't nothing." But they'd had plenty of time to mount a party to ride after them. Perhaps the townspeople had refused to help the burly man. Maybe they'd decided one little child wasn't worth the effort.

Maggie murmured to the mare as it pranced nervously and settled again, half a head in front of Rebel, allowing Crane to study Maggie without turning his head. She clutched the child's arm around her waist. Her skirt flowed around her legs. She strained forward, still watching for pursuers. Every muscle seemed taut, every nerve alert, yet he sensed no fear.

A suspicion grew. He could have sworn she was enjoying this inordinately much, and again he wondered what he had gotten himself into. He slapped his hat to his head, pulling it low. "Let's go." He paused, his gaze fixed to the front. "We'll put some space between us and them. Then we'll talk." He looked squarely at Maggie and the child. These were not saddle-hardened men at his side. "You both up to this?"

Maggie's eyes snapped. "We certainly are." She dipped her head to the child. "Aren't we?"

Eyes wide, the child glanced at Crane, turning away quickly, her whispered yes barely audible.

They kept a steady pace for another hour or more, riding in silence. Crane wondered if Maggie's thoughts were as confused as his; as for the child, he had no notion what such a little thing would be thinking.

The sun had passed its hiatus when Crane reined in. "There's a good spot over there. We'll give the horses a break." He wasn't going to invite any more surprises, and he led the way to a thick grove of trees close to the river. They could water the horses and still be able to see the trail.

Maggie swung down, pulling the child after her, then stiffly turned her horse to water. Crane did the same, taking his time. It wasn't until the horses had been led to a grassy spot and left to graze that he faced Maggie.

"Do you mind telling me what you think we're going to do now?" His voice was low.

She shuffled her feet in the sand.

Crane waited, his gaze lazily resting on the top of her head. Could be she was regretting her haste.

She snapped her head up so suddenly, he jerked back. "What else could I do?" Her eyes flashed.

"Besides shoot the man dead, you mean?" Perhaps he should count himself lucky she hadn't. "Where did you learn to shoot like that?"

She grinned. "A boy taught me."

He held up his hand. "I don't want to know. Next thing you'll be telling me you're part of a gang of bank robbers."

She laughed, a sound echoing the bubbling water behind him. "It wasn't near that exciting. I was about twelve or thirteen, and a neighbor boy begged his dad to teach him to shoot. His dad gave him an old pistol and told him to go practice." She shrugged. "I tagged along."

"I can't say whether or not it was good you did. Seems like it's given you call to get yourself into a heap of trouble."

She looked past him, a distant longing in her expression. Finally she turned her blue eyes toward him, direct and challenging. "What would you have me do?" She shivered. "It don't take any imagination to guess what kind of life she's had." Her eyes darkened. "And what's in store for her. Somebody needed to help her."

He couldn't argue that. "Why'd it have to be you?"

"You see anyone else rushing in?"

"No." He wanted to tell her the code of the West: Keep your nose out of other people's business. But her chin jutted out, and he was pretty sure she would have told him that was all well and good in most situations, but this wasn't one of them.

The child sat with her toes in the water, peeping out from under a curtain of tangled hair. Seeing him look at her, she ducked her head.

"What do you expect to do with her?"

"Why, I figured she would go west with us."

"How do you figure? You don't just ride into town, snatch a child, and ride away without so much as a 'do you mind' or 'if you please.'" Crane kept his voice low, disguising the tension stiffening his spine.

"A body shouldn't ignore a child in need, even if it means stepping on toes." Her taut voice made Crane wonder why she cared so much. How little he knew about this woman who was now his wife. He had a wife! In all the excitement, he'd almost forgotten. Not only a wife, but now a child, as well.

He looked more closely at the child. "She ain't very big."

"Size means nothing." She spat the words out.

He guessed she meant something by that, but he wasn't about to go nosing down an unfamiliar trail.

She answered him even though he hadn't asked. "It's your heart that counts. How you look at things."

They stood side by side watching the child. He pushed his hat back. "She got a name?"

"I 'spect so. Everybody's got a name." She paused. "Sweetheart, come here."

The child slowly turned toward them, looking at the ground, her toes clenching in the sand. She studiously avoided eye contact with Crane.

He looked at her—really looked at her—for the first time. Big brown eyes, a mat of blond hair, a hunted look. "I don't know much about little ones."

Maggie motioned the child closer but directed her words at Crane. "You got no brothers and sisters?"

The little one inched toward them, her tiny limbs stiff. He could smell her fear. It made the skin on the back of his neck tingle. "No, I was the onliest one."

Maggie looked at him for a moment. "Huh," was all she said before turning back to the child, rocking back and forth just out of reach. "You got a name, child?"

Big brown eyes stared unblinkingly at Maggie. "My mamma"—she swallowed hard—"my mamma done call me Betsy." Her words carried on the breeze.

Maggie nodded. "That sounds like a right nice name to me."

A trace of a smile transformed the child's face for a heartbeat.

"You got another name, a last name?" Maggie prodded.

The child shook her head. "I don't know. My mamma not tell me."

"That's fine," Maggie said as the child's fingers plucked at the material around her waist. "Betsy, do you know how old you are?"

"Maybe five. Maybe six." She twisted the material into a knot.

Maggie turned to Crane. "What's today's date?"

"I believe the preacher wrote May tenth, eighteen ninety."

"Look at that, Betsy. Your birthday and our wedding are on the same day."

Crane stared at the child's tiny fingers and pint-sized feet.

"Well, what you going to do with her?" Maggie's question jerked at his senses.

"Me? Seems this is your doing." His slow words hid his turmoil.

She flung her hands out. "You played a part, too."

He watched the river gurgle by; he saw the trees whispering in the breeze. He could not think.

"You got to choose—either we take her with us, or you have to ride back to town and give her back to that horrible man." She spat out the last few words.

He blinked and turned on her. "Ride back there? Why me?" She sure had a funny notion of what was right for him.

"I'd go with you if you want."

He didn't want, and he had no intention of taking the child back, which left him few choices.

"Wash her up," he told Maggie. "I'll get a shirt for her. She can't ride around the country half-naked."

Maggie looked at him openmouthed. Then a slow grin spread across her face, and her eyes flashed bright blue before she led Betsy to the water's edge.

Crane stared after them. How had he managed to end up this far from where he was only this morning? With a shake of his head, he trudged toward the horses, rifling through his pack to pull out a faded denim shirt. He shook it, trying to imagine the child wearing it. His mental powers failed to produce any sort of image. He'd have to buy her some proper clothes at the next town. And shoes. You needed shoes to head west.

He grabbed the bar of soap and towel and returned to the river. Maggie stood beside Betsy in water to their ankles. Betsy. He turned the name over in his mind, trying to get used to the feel of it. The child shook enough to rattle her bones.

Maggie spoke to her, but Crane did not catch what she said. The child nodded, clutching her hands in the hem of her undershirt.

Maggie acknowledged Crane. "Good. You've brought the soap." She took bar and shirt. "We're going to stand right here to wash. Betsy says she'll take her clothes off, if you don't look."

Warmth rushed up his ears. "I'll wait over there." He jerked his thumb toward a wide, sandy spot. "Thought I'd build a fire and make some coffee." The idea hadn't entered his mind until this very moment, but now it seemed good. He saw no sign of pursuit, and the child would want to get warm after her wash.

Crane lit the fire. He filled the coffeepot, opened a can of baked beans, and hunkered down on his heels.

Maggie carried the towel-wrapped child close to the fire and set her down on a grassy spot before she hung the wet underthings to dry and fetched a comb from her saddlebag. She perched behind the child on a fallen tree and combed the tangles from Betsy's wet hair.

Big brown eyes watched Crane as he stirred the beans, but as soon as he turned toward the child, she dipped her head and pulled the towel closer.

Maggie rested her hands on her thighs and looked across the fire to Crane. "She's nervous of you."

Crane thought on the notion, but before he could draw a conclusion, Maggie added, "She don't trust men." Her voice hardened. "She ain't got much reason to." She picked up the comb and ran her fingernail along the teeth, making an annoying insect sound.

Crane watched a play of emotions across her face. A look of determination settled. "Don't worry, child. This man won't hurt you. I promise." And the look she gave Crane was direct. He understood her meaning. *I'm making it my business to see you don't.*

He wanted to say not all men are the same, not all men want to treat her like that, but the child's frightened gaze stopped him. Instead he seated himself on a tree stump across the fire from Maggie and Betsy.

"Betsy," he began, the name awkward on his lips. "My name is Crane." She looked at a spot in the middle of his chest. "Maggie and I got married this morning." Now was not the time to wonder if he'd done the right thing. "We're headed west to the Territories, where we can get free land. We're going to build us a home and a new life. There'll be lots of work and not a lot of people. You're welcome to come with us if you want."

Maggie had finished combing Betsy's hair, and the girl turned to look into her face. "It's all right," Maggie said, rubbing her hands along the small arms. "We'll take good care of you."

Crane nodded.

"Now turn around, and I'll braid your hair." The child obeyed instantly, plucking at the edge of the towel as Maggie worked on her hair and talked in a soothing tone. "I hear tell the grass is up to a horse's belly, and the mountains are giants topped with snow. They say the winters are cold, but the summers are so nice, it's worth the winter just to get the summer."

Wondering where she'd picked up her information, Crane added, "There are ranches with thousands of cows. And deer and antelope." He'd seen many deer but was itching to see his first antelope.

"And flowers?" The child's eager question was so low, Crane wondered if she'd really spoken. For a heartbeat he caught a glimpse of her big eyes before she ducked her head.

"Yup. Flowers, for sure." Though he'd never heard tell of them. But a country as pretty as the West was sure to have its share of flowers.

"And birds." He heard her sigh and met Maggie's solemn glance over her head.

Finished with Betsy's hair, Maggie stood and checked the garments. "Not dry yet," she announced. "That coffee ready?"

He filled two tin mugs with steaming coffee, then hesitated. "What about—?" He glanced toward Betsy. Maggie took her cup. "She can have water. Is there another cup?"

He shook his head. He never thought he'd have call for more than two.

"Doesn't matter."

He gulped some of the hot brew then spooned beans onto the two plates, leaving his share in the can. He handed Maggie and Betsy each a plate and a biscuit. Maggie caught the child's fingers before they dug into the beans and wrapped them around the handle of a spoon.

As he ate, Crane kept a guarded eye on the pair across from him. Betsy licked up every crumb on her plate before turning to watch each mouthful he took. He swallowed hard. Betsy licked her fingertips. He tossed the almost-empty can at her.

"Here—wash this, and it can be your cup."

She dove after the can and cleaned it thoroughly with her fingers before she ran to the river and washed it.

"She's hungry," Maggie observed. "Wonder when she ate last."

"I'll open a can of peaches." He ambled to the packhorse and found what he wanted. When he returned, Betsy's eyes widened at what he held. He opened the can with his knife and poured almost half in her now-clean tin can and divided the rest between Maggie and him, keeping barely a taste for himself.

While he relaxed with his coffee, Maggie plucked the wisps of clothing from the nearby branches and took the child behind a curtain of trees to help her dress. When they emerged, Crane smiled. Betsy had all but disappeared in his shirt. The sleeves, rolled into a lump, hid her hands. Her bare toes flashed from under the garment. The neck hung over one shoulder. He glanced at Maggie, and seeing the amusement in her eyes, his smile widened.

Maggie washed the dishes and packed them away as Crane doused the fire. A few minutes later, they were back on the trail.

"I guess no one's after us," Maggie said, studying the back trail.

" 'Pears that way." But he knew he wouldn't relax for several days.

They headed west, Crane slouched in his saddle in the loose way that made the miles easy on the body. Used to long days in the saddle, he prepared to settle down into his own thoughts.

They had gone a mile or so when Betsy asked Maggie, "You got a mamma and papa?"

Crane strained to hear the conversation without indicating he listened, sensing neither Maggie nor Betsy would converse freely if they thought he could hear them.

Maggie didn't answer for a few minutes. "I had a mamma and papa."

"They was nice?" Her little voice quavered.

Crane eased back on the reins, dropping back half a gait.

Maggie lifted a hand and tugged at a strand of hair at her neck. "My mamma was real nice."

"What happened to her?"

Maggie shivered like a cold wind had torn across her neck and whispered, "She died two years ago."

"My mamma died, too." Betsy twisted round and round the cuff of Crane's shirt she wore.

They rode on, the silence broken only by the thudding hooves of three horses and the cawing of a pair of crows disturbed by their presence.

"What happened to your papa?" Betsy asked.

Maggie's shoulders lifted and fell as she sighed. "He weren't the same after Mamma died."

"He beat you?" As much statement as question, the words made Crane clench his teeth.

"Sometimes." Maggie hesitated. "But I didn't mind that so much."

Betsy leaned around so she could look into Maggie's face. "What else he do?"

Maggie shook her head and refused to answer.

Crane's jaw started to ache.

"Guess he just didn't want us anymore," Maggie said after they had ridden several minutes.

"He was a bad man," Betsy said. "Like Bull."

"Bull?"

Betsy nodded.

"That man who—?" Maggie began.

Betsy nodded, and again they rode in silence.

Finally Maggie spoke. "Well, Bull ain't never going to hurt you again. Ain't that right, Crane?"

Crane jerked to attention, meeting Maggie's challenging look. Betsy's glance slid away as soon as she saw him looking at her. "Yup. That's right."

Maggie stared at him a second longer then nodded.

Satisfied he had given them the assurance they sought, Crane settled back. But something rattled at the back of his mind, something he'd missed, but he couldn't find it.

Betsy's thin voice broke the silence. "I never had a papa." She pulled Maggie's face close to whisper, barely loud enough for Crane to hear. "He have a mamma and papa?"

Maggie cast him a quick glance. "I don't know. You'll have to ask him yourself."

But the child hunched down. The horses walked on. When Crane determined neither female was going to ask the question of him, he gave his answer. "My parents are gone."

"Dead?" the child whispered.

He kept his eyes on the trail. "My mother died this winter past." He couldn't remember when she'd quit living.

"Your papa, too?"

It seemed the child had a hankering to know about parents. He supposed he couldn't blame her, but it was something he no longer thought about. Finally he answered, "I don't know."

She nodded. "We's all orphans."

No one said anything different, and they rode on into the afternoon, passing scattered farmyards, houses, and barns set back from the road. Used to the quiet of the trail, Crane thought nothing of the silence until, turning to look toward one of the farms, he saw the child drooped over, her head wagging against Maggie.

She's sleeping. She's hardly bigger than a minute.

Maggie's head lulled from side to side. They were both asleep.

His first instinct was to rein in right now. But it wasn't a place to make camp.

Ahead he saw a farmhouse close to the trail and, hoping to get some supplies, turned toward the house.

When Maggie would have kept going straight ahead, he called her. She jerked up, saw his intent, and reined in to follow. Betsy lifted her head. Her face wrinkled as if she were going to cry, then she took a deep breath and pressed her quivering lips tight.

The woman of the house came to greet them, and a few minutes later, they purchased eggs, potatoes, fresh bread, and a pie. As Crane secured the items in the packs, Betsy's round eyes followed him. Finally she could contain herself no longer.

"That all for us?"

He grinned. "You think we can handle it?"

Her stare greedily consumed the pie. "I only ever had pie once before."

"Didn't like it, huh?"

"Oh, yes. I did. It was so good." Her look said volumes more than her words did.

Until now Maggie had been silent. Now she grinned at Crane as she said to Betsy, "Don't suppose bread interests you?"

Betsy sighed in ecstasy. "I love bread."

"And eggs and potatoes?" Maggie prodded.

"And eggs and potatoes." The child swallowed hungrily.

"And just about anything you can put in your mouth," Maggie added, shaking her head.

Betsy gave Crane a desperate look. "I'm awful hungry."

Maggie's bubbling laughter caught Crane by surprise, sending tickling fingers up and down his spine. He ducked his head, mumbling, "We'll stop as soon as we find the right spot." He flicked the reins.

Behind him he heard Betsy. "We'll eat then, right?"

Crane grunted. It didn't take long before he saw what he wanted. "Over here." He pointed toward a bunch of trees.

He found a grassy spot close to the river and dropped from his horse. It was easy to see Maggie was about all done in, and he reached up to take Betsy, his hands completely encircling her tiny waist. As he lifted her, he made the alarming discovery she weighed even less than he'd estimated and swung her in a high, wide arc. His heart did a quick dogtrot. He felt her sharply indrawn breath.

I've scared the wee mite half to death! And just when we was starting to be friendly.

Her ribs quivered beneath his fingertips, and her voice quaked in a soft sound.

Now you done it. You made her cry.

He set her down, holding her until she gained her feet, but she hung limp in his arms, the same sound and the same quivering under his fingertips. He didn't know what to do and shot Maggie a look.

She stared at the child.

"I didn't think she'd be so light." He hoped Maggie would understand and forgive his stupidity.

She dragged her gaze to his.

But Betsy straightened, commanding his attention. She twisted in his grasp to look up at him, her tiny fingers clutching at his hands. "That was fun. Do it more." Her eyes shone, and she beamed up at him.

The thin sound and the shaking had been laughter. She wasn't scared; she had enjoyed it and begged for more.

"Again. Again." She bounced in his hands.

He didn't know what else to do, so he swung her up again, feeling the thistledown weight of her and hearing her thin laughter. When he finally released her, she spun around to face him. "I like that."

Crane rubbed his hands on the sides of his pants. He wondered if he should say something, but nothing came to mind. "Huh," he grunted finally, reaching up to help Maggie as she eased herself from the saddle. She didn't weigh a whole lot more than the child, but he felt something reassuring about her hands on his arms as she let him lower her to the ground. She tightened her grasp and bit her lip as she straightened.

"Didn't realize how hard I pushed us today," he murmured, knowing her discomfort was his fault.

"I'll be fine." And to prove her point, she dropped her hold on him.

They faced each other, a hum of thoughts knotting in the back of Crane's mind. "Guess I don't know nothing about traveling with a woman and child."

"You ever done it before?"

He pushed his hat back, trying to remember. "Can't say I recollect another time."

"Then don't guess you'd know."

He nodded. It was all new to him. And not at all what he'd had in mind.

"Mind you," she continued, "I've never ridden west before." She paused. "And I've never had a husband before. So I guess we'll all have to learn as we go along."

"Right." He liked the sound of it. Kind of like easing into the whole thing.

Chapter 3

He left them building a fire while he went to find meat, relishing the quiet of the open country. It gave him time to think. He was treading unfamiliar water. There was no guessing where the current would carry him next.

A brace of partridges shattered the air. He managed to bag two of them and carried them back to camp to prepare them.

Betsy ran to the water's edge to watch. "That for supper?"

"Yup."

"How long it gonna take to cook it?"

He glanced up and saw the pinched look around her mouth. "You hungry?"

She nodded, her eyes big.

"Think you can wait 'til it's cooked?"

"Maybe." She paused. "If it ain't too long."

He finished washing the carcasses, carried the birds to the fire, fixed them on a spit, and crouched down to tend them. Maggie dug a hole near the fire and put in three good-sized spuds, covering them with sand, then a layer of hot coals.

Betsy watched their every move, her hand twisting the bunched-up material at her wrists. "We have to wait now?"

Maggie answered. "It won't be long, sweetie."

Still the child jittered inside Crane's too-large shirt. "We wouldn't have to wait for the pie to cook."

Crane stared at her then looked at Maggie for direction, but Maggie only shrugged as if to say it was up to Crane.

"Why not?" he said.

The child's hands relaxed. Her smile was blinding.

Poor thing, he thought. *She must be starving.*

In an instant, he was a child again, older than she by a few years but still looking to his parents to provide food when necessary. He had climbed down the rough ladder to the basement and searched the bins for any overlooked vegetables, but he found nothing except a rotted carrot. The cupboards upstairs were as bare. His stomach hurt, though he couldn't be certain if it was from fear or hunger, and he huddled at the bottom of the ladder, hating to climb up and tell his mother nothing was left. No food and no money to buy it with.

He shook his thoughts aside. That was too long ago to think about. With the child's eager brown gaze on him, he retrieved the pie and cut it into six pieces. Betsy hung close, watching his every move.

"It's red," she said, leaning over as juice oozed out of the cut lines.

"Pieplant," he explained. "First fruit of the spring." His own taste buds were springing to life at the tangy smell of the pie.

"I like pieplant."

"You ever tasted it before?" he asked, lifting a piece to a tin plate.

"No, but I like it." Her eyes never left the wedge of pie.

Crane waited as she bit into it. At first taste, her mouth puckered, and her eyes grew round. Then the sweetness came, and she chewed greedily. He smiled. "You still like it?"

She raised her brown eyes to him and nodded, her mouth too full to speak.

Grinning, he served a wedge for Maggie and another for himself. "And a piece each for later," he said, setting aside the rest of the pie.

Crane thought Betsy would devour the delicacy in a gulp. Instead she lingered over every bite. He could almost feel her delight in the flavor and texture. When done, she licked her lips and handed the tin plate to Maggie. "That was good," she announced then scampered to the river to cast stones in the water.

Maggie's clear laugh rang out. "My mother used to say, 'A child with a full tummy is a happy child.'"

Crane nodded. Hunger had a way of making everything else unimportant.

Maggie's smile faded. "I'm sure she meant children in a normal, happy family."

Again Crane nodded.

"Doesn't matter how full you are if you're scared to death." Her blue gaze drilled into him. "She'll never be afraid again," Maggie vowed.

"Not as far as it depends on us," Crane likewise vowed, meeting her piercing look with matching firmness.

Betsy played as Maggie and Crane turned their attention back to supper preparations. The partridges were soon spitting on the fire, the aroma bringing a flood of saliva to Crane's mouth and Betsy back to the fire.

"They almost ready?" she asked.

He looked up from turning the spit and, seeing the longing look on her face, laughed. "I thought you had enough pie in you to last awhile."

"It was good." She squirmed inside the too-big shirt. "But it's gone."

He knew she meant the feel of it in her stomach and nodded. "Guess you don't like nothing better than eating."

Her gaze lingering on the golden carcasses, she absently replied, "That's 'cause I'm hungry."

Struck by the simple wisdom of her words, he smiled. "You ever not hungry?"

With a look of fear making her brown eyes even browner, she faced him and solemnly shook her head.

He wanted to assure her everything would be all right now; yet sensing her fear of him, he settled for asking, "You ever had spit-roasted meat?"

She shook her head.

"Or roasted potatoes?"

Her eyes grew rounder, and she shook her head again.

He figured he could list a hundred things, and she'd continue to shake her head. "Well, get your plate. It's ready."

She dove for the plate.

"Slow down, honey," Maggie crooned. "It's not going to disappear."

Crane cut a hunk of meat for Betsy. Maggie dropped a hot potato beside it. They ate in silence, both Maggie and Betsy eating as if there were no tomorrow. They finished and waited expectantly for him to pass the rest of the pie. Food took on an importance that hadn't existed for him since he got his first job. He wasn't paid much for sweeping the floor, carrying in wood and coal, and taking out ashes at the general store back home, but Mr. Brown had been only too happy to give him part of his wages in groceries. And after he moved on to bigger things, he always made certain his mother had a full pantry. Now all of a sudden, he was faced with a child who was constantly hungry and a woman who ate like a workingman.

He ate his pie and straightened. Thank goodness they were passing through a country with plenty of game. He promised himself he would never let them go hungry.

Maggie and Betsy took the dishes to the river to wash, and Crane piled more wood close to the fire.

Dusk tiptoed in. It was time to get ready for the night. He untied the bedrolls from the pack, looking uncertainly at the bundles. He'd brought enough for two—man and wife—but what about the child? He could feel Betsy's stare boring into his back. The tension-filled air crackled.

"Betsy and I will sleep together, right, Betsy?" Maggie murmured. He could sense the child's relief as he handed Maggie a roll of blankets.

"Here you go, honey." And giving her the bedroll, Maggie said, "You decide where we'll sleep." Crane chose a place close enough to the fire so he could throw on more wood if he got cold and against a fallen tree so he wasn't completely exposed. With a flick of his wrists, he spread the roll on the ground.

When he returned from checking the horses, Betsy still stood clutching the blankets. Her glance darted away when he looked at her. He poured himself another cup of coffee and took it to his pallet. He removed his boots, setting them carefully against the tree trunk, put his hat on top, and stood the rifle close before he settled down on the pad to enjoy the coffee.

"You pick a spot?" Maggie urged the child.

She nodded.

"Well, then?"

Still Betsy stood rooted there, her big eyes watching Crane. He made a point of ignoring her, letting her feel her space and decide what she wanted. He heard a little sigh before she silently eased in his direction. She halted so close, he could tell she was breathing through her mouth. Then she knelt down and set the blankets next to his, struggling to unroll them.

Maggie knelt beside her to help. "You sure this is where you want to sleep?"

It was the same question Crane wanted to ask.

Betsy nodded without looking up.

"There's lots of other places," Maggie insisted.

"I know," the child whispered. "This is the best."

Maggie stared at her.

Crane watched them both from beneath his eyelashes.

"This is a fine spot all right," Maggie agreed, "but can you tell me why you picked it?"

Betsy glanced sideways at Maggie and whispered, "So we can be close to him." She flung a quick glance at Crane. "He takes care of us."

The child's words slammed into him. He steadied his cup, keeping his eyes lowered.

Maggie jerked to her feet. "You need anything before you go to bed?" she asked the child.

"Can I have a drink?"

Maggie handed her a cup. "Run and get some water from the river. Mind you, don't get your clothes wet."

The child scampered away.

Crane lifted his head to face Maggie. Her fists thudded against her hips, and she glowered at him.

"What?" he asked, having no notion what had made her angry.

"It seems you've earned the trust of the child."

She made it sound as if he'd done something wrong. "So?"

"So?" she repeated. "The trust of a child is a precious thing."

He nodded.

"Some people act like it's nothing. They don't take it into consideration." She was breathing hard.

Again he nodded, having no idea what she was trying to say but figuring it wasn't a good time to point it out.

"You have a child. You got to always be there."

It was a sucker punch, but he knew what she meant. "I ain't going no place."

Betsy sang as she returned.

Maggie's eyes narrowed as she drove her words home. "You earned the trust of that child. See you live up to it." And as Betsy stepped into the light, she turned to her. "You ready for bed now?"

He crawled under the covers, turning his back to give the other two privacy, aware when Betsy crawled in next to him, the cold from her bare feet reaching out to the small of his back. Maggie settled in next to the child.

"Go to sleep," she murmured, hands brushing along Crane's spine as she pulled the covers around the child.

Crane let his body settle into the shape of the ground and waited for sleep to envelop him, but tonight sleep did not come instantly. Instead his thoughts hovered on the day. He'd been so confident of what he was doing when he rode into town. Now he couldn't say exactly what he'd expected; only it wasn't anything like this.

He guessed he thought he would marry, and somehow, come nighttime, they would crawl under the covers together, and the rest would come natural. But instead they lay under separate covers, a child between them. Perhaps it was as it should be. After all, what did he know about being married? He couldn't even look at his parents for an example. His father had left when he was eleven. He could only remember what it was like afterward. And his adult life had taken him on the trail with other drifters and cows. He hadn't had a lot of women in his life.

The feeling he had was not unlike grabbing on to the tail of a stampede.

He was awakened by an unfamiliar sound and something touching him. He jerked up, reaching for his rifle before he realized it was a pair of bare feet kicking at him. And the sound was the child sobbing. He waited for Maggie to do something, but by the gentle snores from her direction, he knew she hadn't been disturbed by the noise.

How much did it take to wake her? he wondered.

The sobs bordered on hysteria. Betsy must be having a nightmare.

"Betsy." He touched her shoulder. She jerked away, choking on a scream.

"Betsy." He shook her. "Wake up."

Still sobbing, she reached for him, pulling herself to his lap, huddling against his chest.

He stiffened, afraid to touch her. She was so small. But her sobs shuddered through him, and not knowing what else to do, he wrapped his arms around her, cradling her. "Shh. You're safe now. Stop crying. Stop crying."

Maggie grunted and sat up, rubbing her eyes. "What's going on?"

"The child was having a bad dream."

Maggie reached out to rub Betsy's back. "It's only a dream, honey."

Together they comforted the child, and her sobs quieted. Crane held her as her breathing deepened.

"She's asleep again," he whispered.

Maggie pulled the covers back so he could lower Betsy to her bed. Their hands brushed as they smoothed the blanket over the sleeping girl.

"She'll be fine now," Maggie whispered.

Crane went to the fire and shoved wood into the embers. Sparks flared, and he saw Maggie standing close, her arms wrapped around her middle, her eyes watchful. He shook the coffeepot. It rattled with dry grounds.

"I'll make more," Maggie offered.

"No need." He settled on a stump, staring at the flames.

Maggie pulled a piece of log close and sat beside him. "Are you having regrets?" she asked, her voice low.

"About what?"

"About everything. Getting married." She hesitated. "To me." Another pause. "About the child."

He laughed. "More like confused. Not in my wildest dreams was this what I expected. I'm wondering what's going to happen next."

"Bet you thought your first night as a married man would be a little different, huh?"

He could feel warmth creep up his neck and thanked the darkness she couldn't see it. "I really hadn't given it a lot of thought."

The soft night noises settled around them.

Finally Maggie said, "I guess it's my fault."

He shrugged. "You didn't force me to do anything." Then he added, "Tonight is only the first night of the rest of our lives. We got lots of time."

He felt her sigh and looked across the fire to the sleeping child, barely a ripple under the blankets. "You think she'll be all right?" he asked.

"I don't know. What do you think?"

"I know nothing about little ones, but she seems eager to find good things and enjoy them. I think she'll do fine."

"I think you're right. Besides, she's young. The younger you are, the easier it is to forget."

He thought about that. For certain he didn't remember much about his younger years. In fact, he'd thought about his youth more today than he had in a long time. Maybe, he admitted, he'd done his best to forget those early years. Meeting this child had driven his thoughts to those forgotten places.

"We best get some sleep." He waited for her to cross to the child's side then followed.

Throughout the night he was aware of the child beside him, her little snufflings and sighings and her feet pressing into his side. He couldn't decide whether or not he liked it, but he was certain it kept him half-awake all night.

&

He tensed at the humming sound close to his ear and dragged his eyes open. Betsy sat cross-legged almost at his head.

"I'm hungry," she announced when she saw his eyes open.

He groaned. "You're always hungry."

She waited and, when he made no move, asked, "Aren't you hungry?"

"Where's Maggie?"

"She's sleeping. I tried to make her wake up."

He grunted. That left him to deal with this persistent scrap of humanity. "You got coffee ready?"

She giggled. "I can't make coffee."

"Time you learned." He rolled to his feet and stretched. "First thing you do every morning is make coffee."

She nodded and scampered to the ashes of last night's fire. Grabbing the coffeepot, she turned with a questioning look.

"Take it to the river and wash it out and fill it with fresh water."

She was gone in a flash, and he set about getting the fire going. The wood was dry and caught instantly.

As he waited for the child to return, he looked at Maggie's sleeping form, again wondering what it took to waken her. She lay on her side, her hands curled together under her chin, her black hair fanned out around her face. In repose she looked even younger. He felt a swell of doubt; then he reminded himself she'd proven to be more than resourceful and strong. The way she had gone after that man back at Colhome—he grinned. She was like a bantam rooster.

Betsy nudged his leg. "I got your water."

"Thanks." He took the pot and dumped in a handful of grounds and set it over the fire. "Now we wait."

He hunkered down. Betsy did the same.

For a moment she was content to watch. Then she looked at him. "Isn't it time to start some food?"

He chuckled. "What would you like? Eggs or"—he paused, smiling at the eager look on her face—"or eggs?"

"I like eggs."

"I bet you do." He'd gamble she'd never met a food she didn't like. He glanced at Maggie, still breathing deeply. "Looks like you're my number one helper."

Betsy quivered with anticipation. "I can help."

"Right." He went to the packs and pulled out a spider. "You take this to the fire."

"It looks funny. What is it?" she asked, holding up the cast-iron skillet.

"Spider. See the legs on the bottom. Works real well over a fire." He grabbed the rest of the biscuits and carried the eggs himself. With Betsy sticking close as an August fly, he set the spider over the fire and checked on the coffee.

"You better get Maggie awake before I start the eggs."

Her response was instantaneous. "Maggie, Maggie!" she yelled, racing over to pummel Maggie's arm. "Get up so we can have breakfast."

Maggie moaned. "I'm awake, Betsy. You can stop pounding me."

"Your eyes aren't open." Betsy shook her.

One eye squinted open. "There. That suit you?"

"You got to get up. Crane says we can't eat 'til you do."

"He does, does he?" She squinted at him. "You sure it's morning already?"

"Yes, it is. See—the sun is coming up." Betsy pointed to the east.

Maggie closed her eyes and pulled the covers to her chin. "That settles it. It isn't morning 'til the sun is up all the way."

"Maggie, please." Betsy pulled at the covers. "I'm hungry."

"And I'm so tired." Her voice was muffled.

Betsy gave Crane a look of desperation, and he said, "Maybe I should get a bucket of water from the river and dump it on her."

Betsy sprang to her feet, silently urging him to do it, and Maggie jerked upright.

"You wouldn't." She glowered at him.

He chuckled. "Looks like I don't need to."

With a scowl darkening her features, she sat in the midst of her rumpled blankets.

"Guess I can start the eggs now," he said to Betsy, who hurried to his side, watching his every move as he cracked shells and dropped eggs into the sizzling pan.

Behind them Maggie groaned and stood to her feet, shuffling to the river to splash cold water on her face.

When she returned, Crane offered her a cup. "Coffee's hot and strong."

For several minutes she nursed it without speaking. He observed her out of the corner of his eye, amazed as she slowly came to life. Like a flower opening to the sun!

"Get the dishes," he told Betsy, and she ran to obey.

"She sleep the rest of the night?" Maggie spoke low.

"Yup. And woke up before the birds, complaining she was hungry."

Maggie chuckled. "Did you see how she ate last night?"

Crane raised his eyebrows.

She nodded. "I know. I ate a lot, too." She ducked her head. "I was hungry."

He grinned. "You hungry now?" Taking the plates Betsy had fetched, he dished up their breakfast.

She grimaced. "It's too early to eat."

Betsy cleaned her plate, ate three biscuits, and, when she saw Maggie hadn't eaten all her eggs, asked, "You finished, Maggie?"

Maggie handed her plate to Betsy.

The sun was completely over the horizon, and already Crane could feel its heat. "Let's get moving."

Betsy and Maggie cleaned the dishes, rolled up the bedrolls, and filled the canteens while Crane caught and saddled the horses and fixed the packs. Then they were ready. But when Maggie reached for Betsy, the child ducked away to stand at Crane's side.

"I want to ride with you."

With studied calmness, Crane continued checking the cinches and determined no one would see how her request had surprised him. How could she have changed so suddenly from the child who wouldn't even look at him yesterday? He didn't understand it, but it made him feel warm inside. He kind of liked the feeling. But he didn't know if he could trust it.

"Come on then." He scooped her up, bringing a squeal as he tossed her to Rebel's back before climbing up behind her. He flashed Maggie a look, watching to see if she'd been hurt by Betsy's choice.

Maggie smiled. "It's fine by me."

"Let's make tracks," he called, heading down the trail with the sun warming their backs.

Betsy squirmed from side to side, trying to take in everything around her. "Crane, Crane, look—a rabbit!" she called as a brown jackrabbit sprang from the grass. And a few minutes later, "Crane, Crane, look. A whole bunch of yellow flowers."

"Yup," Crane answered. "You better sit still before you fall."

"You'd catch me, wouldn't you, Crane?"

"*Depends.*" *How do you catch thistledown?*

For a few minutes, she sat still then looked at him over her shoulder. "Crane, does everybody have a papa?"

"Yup. Everybody's got to."

"Why do papas go?"

The question flashed down the pathway of his mind to a bewildered boy who asked himself a similar question. *Why did my papa leave?* There had never been an answer, and he had soon found life went on, leaving no time to dwell on it.

"Not all papas leave."

She shook her head. "Mammas die. Papas leave."

How could he convince her otherwise? He flung a desperate look at Maggie.

"She's only going by what she knows. We've all lost our mothers." She paused. "I told her my pa didn't want me around."

Crane watched her through narrowed eyes. Did he see a flash of pain just then? Or had she, like he, learned to accept the reality of a father who didn't care? Was two years long enough to grapple with the problem and learn to leave it be? Maggie looked directly at him. "I don't recall for sure what you said about your father."

He stared into her blue eyes, again struck by how little they knew of each other. "He left when I was eleven. It was a long time ago." The future beckoned. Let the past be past.

Maggie nodded, her eyes intent for another heartbeat. Then she said, "Guess you can hardly blame her for how she thinks." She dropped her gaze to Betsy, who strained to catch their every word. "Honey, Crane's right. Not all papas leave."

"They stay forever?" Her whispered awe tugged at an unfamiliar emotion in Crane.

"That's right," he agreed.

"Forever," she whispered. "That sounds nice."

They rode for several minutes before she asked, "There a house where we're going?"

"Not yet. We'll build one when we get there."

"A real house with rooms?"

"Yup."

"A kitchen?" she persisted.

"Yup."

"A parlor?" She rolled the word around in her mouth. "And a room for me?"

"A house just right for us."

"Us." Her chest heaved, and she settled again.

They continued in comfortable silence until Betsy asked, "How long to get there?"

Up until now, Crane hadn't given it a great deal of thought. He'd estimated it to be about eight hundred miles from Manitoba to the plains facing the mountains in the Territories. But now, as he explained the distance to Betsy and saw her look of disbelief, he realized how far it sounded to a child. "I hope we'll find a place by the end of June."

"Not tomorrow?"

"No."

"Not the day after?" Her shoulders slumped.

Maggie came to his rescue. "We'll see lots and lots of things. It's like a picnic every day."

Betsy nodded. Crane sensed her disappointment and longed to say something to dispel it, but he could think of nothing to make the trip seem shorter. Her head nodded. At first he thought she was still quietly thinking about the trip. Then, as she slumped to one side, he realized she had fallen asleep and, pulling her toward him, let her rest on his chest. Maggie smiled at the sleeping child then at him, and Crane felt something unfamiliar, yet not altogether unwelcome, burgeon in a spot slightly below his throat.

He let Betsy sleep until it was time to stop. They had cold leftover partridge and the last of the bread. Not wanting to take time to build a fire, they settled for a drink of cool water.

As soon as she had eaten, Betsy ran along the riverbank, yelling tunelessly with her arms outflung. She ran until a pile of rocks stopped her progress. Then she turned and ran back, still yelling and waving her arms.

Maggie watched, grinning. "She's glad to be feeling her legs under her."

Crane turned from checking the cinches and stared after the child. He hadn't given the long hours in the saddle a thought, finding riding more comfortable than walking. Again he realized how little he knew about traveling with a child and a woman. He turned to Maggie. "You getting pretty sore of riding, too?" He'd noticed her awkward way of walking.

It was a moment before she faced him. "I'm not used to it." Her blue gaze held steady, making it clear she wasn't complaining.

He ducked behind Rebel. "I 'spect we could walk some."

Crane led the way. With a narrow path along the river, they had no need to return to the trail.

Betsy ran ahead then stopped suddenly, turning toward him, her face bright. "Listen to the birds," she whispered. "They sound so happy."

Crane halted. He'd never bothered to listen much unless the birds raised a fuss; then he would check to see why. But now he really listened.

The child stood with her face lifted, her eyes closed. It made his chest tighten just to watch her.

"It must be great to be so young and be able to forget your past as easily as she does." Maggie tugged Liberty's reins. "Let's get moving."

"Yup," he drawled. "I'm looking forward to crossing into the Territories." But it was nice walking, he decided. Betsy ran and skipped like a heifer released from the barn. Even the silence between him and Maggie was pleasant. And it was cooler next to the river. They walked until Betsy's steps began to slow. Then they returned to the trail. Crane knew enough now to begin planning the evening camp early in the afternoon. So when he saw a farm close to the road, he turned in.

A thin, worried-looking woman came from the house.

"I'm looking to buy some food," Crane called. "You got anything to spare?"

Before she could answer, an overalled man came from around a low building. "We got some pork and eggs." He named a price that made Crane raise his eyebrows.

"You be fixing to skin us?" Crane asked.

"I've no mind to leave my own family short," the man growled. "But you're mor'n welcome if you've a mind to pay."

Crane stared hard at the man. If he'd been alone, he would have turned his back and ridden away, but with two hungry females to feed and them already wilting, he jerked his head in agreement.

"Run and get it, missus," the farmer ordered his wife, and she scurried inside, returning with a hunk of meat and a sack of eggs. Crane unwrapped the paper from the meat and sniffed. Satisfied it was unspoiled, he handed a fistful of change to the man and turned to leave, passing between several low outbuildings.

"Phew. It stinks." Betsy wrinkled her nose as they neared a pigpen, knee-deep in muck.

"Hush," he ordered, determined not to offend the man he sensed thrived on trouble.

"Look at that boy," Betsy said. "He's stuck in it."

"No, he's not," he said, though it took a great deal of effort for the lad to carry two heavy buckets of feed through the slop without upsetting them.

With a muffled gasp, Maggie slid from her horse and rushed to the fence. "Ted!" she called as she struggled to unlatch the gate.

The boy looked at her with blank eyes.

"Ted, Ted." She pulled on the heavy gate. "It's me. Maggie."

Chapter 4

The boy changed his grip on the handle of the bucket and continued toward the trough, pigs squealing at his heels.

"Ted, wait!" Maggie called, jerking at the gate and squeezing through the wedge opening.

"Maggie." Even as he uttered the low warning, Crane figured she'd ignore it. "Here we go again," he muttered, pushing his hat back.

"What's she doing?" Betsy asked, her voice thin and shrill as Maggie lifted her skirts and plunged into the muck. "Oh, yuck, yuck!" Betsy pulled her face down into the neckline of the shirt she wore.

The smell stinging his eyes, Crane shifted so he could see Maggie and watch for the farmer.

Maggie reached the boy. "Ted, listen." Her voice was taut. "It's me, Maggie. I thought I'd never find you."

When the boy acted as if she hadn't spoken, she wrenched the bucket from his hands and flung it away. The pigs oinked after it, their noise drowning out her words as she grasped his shoulder.

The boy raised his head, but his eyes stared away as if sightless.

Crane, wondering if the boy was deaf, watched the farmer approach, a shotgun tucked under his arm. Crane eased his hand toward his rifle.

The man stood before the twisted gate. "Leave the boy be," he growled. "He's got work."

"He's my brother." She grabbed the boy's hand and tugged at him to follow. "I've looked for him for so long."

"Your father sold him to me fair and square. Said he was mine to do with as I wanted."

Crane's jaw tightened. From the boy's bony thinness, he guessed feeding him wasn't one of the things the man did. In fact, he'd guess the boy was treated worse than the animals. "How much?" Crane growled.

The man jerked toward him. "How much what?"

"For the boy." It stuck in his throat to say it.

A gleam brightened the other man's eyes. "I paid twenty dollars for him." He scratched his nose. "Figuring all I put into him, he should be worth twice that."

"He's my brother," Maggie cried, approaching the gate. "He belongs with me."

The farmer lifted his shotgun and pointed it at her. "Don't see him agreeing."

"Ted, tell them. Tell them you're Edward Malone, my brother."

The pigs squealed, the man snorted, but the boy made not a sound. Crane pulled out a twenty-dollar bill. "This should do it."

The man lowered the gun, snatched the money, and put it in his overalls. "He ain't much use anyway," he snarled. "The boy's addled."

"He ain't!" Maggie cried. "He's fine."

"He can ride with you." Crane led the mare to Maggie's side, holding the reins as she pulled herself into the saddle. She reached down for the boy, but he neither looked at her nor lifted his hand.

Crane reined closer and lifted the boy up behind Maggie. "Ride downwind," he ordered as they rode from the farmyard.

But even with two lengths between them, the smell was almost unbearable. Betsy clung to him, her nose buried in the neckline of her shirt. The distance between him and Maggie made conversation impossible. Crane was more than willing to wait.

He led them into the river, not turning until Liberty stood knee-deep in it. Then he reined back to shore. "Get rid of that smell." He set Betsy down and dropped to the ground beside her.

"What they going to do?" Her voice was thin.

"Wash, I hope." He removed the saddle, took the packs from the other horse, and led both animals to water. When they'd had their fill, he tethered them to graze.

Betsy's wide eyes followed his every move.

"You gather up some branches for the fire. Mind you, don't go too far." He dug a curry brush from the pack.

"Then we'll have supper?"

"Soon." He trod back to the river to catch Liberty and set to scrubbing the manure from the stirrups. "No need to carry this smell west with us," he muttered.

Satisfied the saddle was clean, he carried it to shore and hung it over a stump. Then he returned and scrubbed Liberty, sparing a glance at Maggie and her brother.

She faced him, hands on hips. "Ted, you got to take off those clothes. Let me help you." She reached out. His arms tightened at his sides. "I'll wash them, and you can have them back," she pleaded. He remained stiff. "Maybe Crane can give you something to wear while they dry." She shot a glance toward him.

He nodded and retraced his steps to the saddles, digging out a faded blue shirt and tossing it beside the towel on the bank. "It's my last one," he mumbled, turning his back, running his hands over the horse, watching without appearing to. "Your sister only wants to help, young man." He bent and rinsed the brush. "And a bath wouldn't do you no harm."

He put his attention on washing Liberty's flank but could see out of the side of his vision as Maggie grasped the boy's shirt and pulled it over his head. The boy did not resist; neither did he help.

"Ted, you imagine how scared I was when I came home and found you was gone." She urged him out of his trousers. "Pa was gone, too. No one seemed to know where you was." She turned him around and gasped, flicking a glance at Crane.

Crane saw what she had, the angry red welts across the boy's back. As his pants lowered, he took in the gaunt ribs, the bruises across the buttocks. Crane's insides twisted into a knot.

Maggie shuddered then gently lathered soap over the thin body. She talked as she worked. "It took me three days to find Pa in a back alley. He didn't much like it when I tried to make him tell me where you were." She paused to splash clean water over the boy. "Well, you know what he was like after Ma died, and he took to the bottle." She led him to the sandy bank. "He said he sold you, but he couldn't remember the man's name or where he lived."

She picked up the towel, draping it over his shoulders. But when she would have hugged him, he shrugged away and stared past Maggie without so much as a blink. Maggie drew in a sharp breath.

Crane led Liberty to the other horses. The river murmured past. Betsy added more branches and twigs to the pile she'd made. Her voice carried on the gentle breeze, and Crane paused to listen. She was singing a song she had made up.

"Pie, pie, I like pie. I like flowers and the birds that fly. I like everything. But I like pie the best of all." Her voice was clear and sweet.

Crane smiled as he tethered the horse. He cut off thick slabs of the hunk of pork and fried it in the hot spider. The rest he put into a large pot, covered it with water, and threw in a handful of salt and one bay leaf.

"Why'd you put in a leaf?" Betsy demanded.

He settled back on his heels, and Betsy squatted beside him. Across the fire Maggie nursed a cup of coffee, her expression troubled. The boy huddled on the ground in Crane's shirt, his body turned away from the rest of them as if to shut them out. "It's a trick Biscuit taught me." He stirred the pot and put on a lid.

"Biscuit?"

"Yup. The best camp cook I ever knew." He glanced around the circle again. No one seemed to have anything to offer, so he continued. "He was as mangy looking as an old dog. Not one you'd pick to cook your meals. But he made the best biscuits I ever had." He bent his glance to Betsy's. "That's how he come to be called Biscuit."

He paused to scratch his chin. "Never did know what his rightful name was."

Betsy bounced on her heels. "He the one who told you to put a leaf in?"

"Yup. It's a bay leaf. Adds a little flavor." He lifted the lid to see if the water had boiled yet.

"For sure?"

"Yup."

"Then I like leaves." She skipped around the fire to Maggie. "You, too, Maggie?" She leaned close, touching Maggie's face.

Maggie smiled at her and nodded.

"You sad?" the child asked. "About him?" She nodded toward Ted, who gave no indication of hearing.

Again Maggie nodded.

Betsy straightened and walked to Ted's side. She put her face close to him. "You don't need to be afraid anymore. Maggie and Crane will take care of you."

The boy jerked away, turning his back to her. His foot thrashed out, catching Betsy in the ankle and knocking her to the ground.

Whimpering, Betsy jumped up and backed away.

Maggie stood to her feet. "Ted. What are you doing? You mustn't hurt Betsy." But when she lifted a hand to touch him, he shrank back. Seeing his fear, Maggie turned to let her hand fall on Betsy instead. "Are you okay, honey?"

Betsy nodded. Crane reached out and turned the frying meat before he walked around the fire to face Ted. "I think it's time we introduced ourselves. I'm Byler Crane, but everyone calls me Crane. You can, too." He paused, waiting. "Me and your sister are married."

The boy gave no sign he heard.

"We's headed west to start a new life."

Still nothing.

"We found Betsy in a town back there. She needed someone. She's coming with us." He was beginning to wonder what he would have to do to get the boy's attention. "You're more than welcome to throw in with us." He waited. "Unless you've a mind to go back to that pig farmer."

The narrow shoulders hunched forward just enough for Crane to nod. At least he could be certain the boy understood what was said.

"I thought not. Then I guess you're stuck with us."

He turned back to the fire, pouring himself a cup of coffee. "On a long trail, every hand has to do his share." He downed the scalding cup of coffee, poured his cup full again, and shook the pot. "Almost empty," he announced. "Guess we need some more water."

Betsy sprang to her feet, but Crane said, "Ted, how 'bout you fill it at the river? Mind you, go upstream from where the horses are." He held out the pot.

The boy stiffened.

Maggie half-stood, but Crane shook his head, hoping she'd understand this was something he had to settle with Ted.

The boy jumped to his feet so quickly, Crane blinked. He snatched the pot and raced toward the river.

Crane could almost hear the boy's thoughts. *You can make me do it, but you can't make me like it.* He smiled. If beneath those glassy eyes was a fighter, so much the better.

He opened two cans of beans and set them to heat.

"Is it almost ready?" Betsy hovered at his side.

He studied her. She seemed none the worse for having been knocked down by Ted. "As soon as Ted's back."

She squatted beside him. "Ted's mad?"

He met Maggie's eyes. "I'm not sure," he answered. Maggie stared after her brother.

Betsy spoke again. "I think that man hurt him."

Crane stiffened, wondering if she had seen the marks on Ted's back.

The child continued, "He's a bad man. Like Bull."

"He'll never hurt him again," Maggie muttered.

Ted returned, holding the coffeepot toward Crane without looking at him.

"Thanks, boy." Crane poured in the coffee then dished up the food. He'd eat his own out of the spider.

He handed the plates around. Betsy dug into her food without hesitation, but Maggie waited, watching as he handed a plate to Ted. The boy jerked back as if expecting to be hit.

"Food," Crane said. "Enjoy."

Ted grabbed the plate, turning away his shoulders as if to shut them out again.

Maggie sat close to him. "You're safe now, Ted," she murmured. "We'll take good care of you, Crane and I."

Ted gobbled up his food without any indication he'd heard.

Betsy scampered down to the water to play, her laughter and singing whispering through the dusk. Ted disappeared into the trees, gathering more firewood. Crane filled Maggie's cup then hunched down to enjoy his own coffee. She edged closer.

"I couldn't leave him."

He watched her in the dancing light. A shower of sparks hissed, their light flashing through her hair. "Any more surprises?"

Her eyes grew round; her cheeks darkened. Then she smiled. "Don't think so."

He'd noticed before how a smile made her look so good he could hardly breathe.

"Ted used to be—" Her voice was tight. "He used to be—"

He nodded. "How old is he? How long since you saw him?"

Maggie sniffed. "He's ten now. It's been eight, no ten months, since I've seen him." She shuddered. "Did you see his back?"

He nodded. "Met a few men who liked to hurt others. Just a few, but that was a few too many."

"He was eight when Ma died, and Pa—well, Pa changed. We never saw much of him, and when we did, he was mean. I was glad when he left us alone."

Maggie threw the rest of her coffee in the fire. Over the hissing protest, she growled, "I don't care if I never see our pa again."

Crane drained his cup. There wasn't much he could say to that. Best to get on with life, he always figured. He was about to remind her about the new life in the West, freedom and all that, when she asked, "Why didn't anyone help him?"

"Most people don't want to start trouble."

"Seems to me it was already started."

He kept his gaze on the fire, but he could feel her stare knifing into him. He gnawed on his bottom lip, wondering how her mouth would feel to kiss. Here he was a married man for two days now, and he hadn't even kissed his bride. Come to think of it, this was the first time they'd been alone since the wedding. And about high time he had his first kiss. He set his cup down at his feet and twisted toward her.

Her blue eyes caught the flare of light from a leaping flame and shot silver spears. Her lips were parted, but as he turned, she spoke. "Would you ignore a child in trouble? Would you have ridden past Ted?"

He pulled in a cooling breath and swallowed hard, dismissing the idea of a kiss. Later, he promised himself. "I don't know." *Of course I would and never give him a backward look.*

"What if it was you?"

"Me?"

"Yes, what if you needed someone to help? What if you were that child?"

He twitched, feeling like a knife had been plunged into his solar plexus. The occasional word of Betsy's song reached him. Behind him in the brush, he could hear the crack of branches as Ted stepped on them. Flames licked the air. Sparks exploded, sizzling through the night.

"I was that child." He hadn't meant to say it out loud, but it couldn't be lassoed back.

"What?"

"Things got tough after my pa left. Some days we didn't have enough to eat." *Never enough and lots of times nothing at all.*

"And no one helped you?"

"I don't remember thinking they should." And once he started to work, they always had food. He never looked back.

"I will never walk by a child in trouble and not stop to ask if I can do anything." Crossing her arms, she glared at him.

"It's a mighty good thing you told me this." He narrowed his eyes. *Wonder what other little philosophies she has hidden up her sleeve.*

For a moment more, she glared at him. Then she giggled. "Guess you already figured it out." She sobered. "I didn't mean to cause you so much trouble."

He shrugged then refilled their cups. She moved over on the log, making room for him. They sat side by side, staring into the flames. Her shoulder whispered against his arm. She seemed so small beside him. He was certain he could wrap his arms around her with plenty of room to spare.

Her hair had a fresh summer-day scent, and he breathed deeply. He wanted to draw her close. But he sat as still as the log on which they perched, uncertain how she would react. A nerve twitched in his arm. Maybe she was wanting this as much as he.

"Do you believe in God?"

"What?" If she wasn't the blamedest one for talking all the time.

"I said, do you believe in God? I guess you must, seeing as you wanted a God-fearing woman for a wife."

He sighed. " 'Course I do. My mother taught me it was so."

Maggie nodded. "Mine, too. What all did she tell you about Him?"

Crane tried to remember. "She said things like God made everything. She said He would take care of us. Other things." It was so long ago.

Maggie grabbed his arm, sending warm waves along its length. "What did she say about Him taking care of us?"

Pa had been gone a few days, maybe a week—he couldn't remember for sure—but long enough that Crane had grown suspicious.

"Where's Pa?" he'd demanded yet again.

His mother turned away but not before Crane caught the flash of pain in her face. "He's away."

"Is he coming back?" Crane insisted. He had to get rid of the awful feeling in the pit of his stomach.

But she had turned slowly. "Come sit by me, Byler. I've something to tell you."

Inside he had screamed, "No! I don't want to hear it!" But he let his mother draw him to the big old armchair and pull him to her lap.

"I don't know when your pa is coming back."

The pain in his stomach erupted.

"But I know he will come back." She smiled as she brushed his hair from his forehead. "Because I prayed about it. And God has said He'd take care of us, so I know He'll send Tom back. I promise you." She stroked his forehead, her words driving back the pain.

But Pa had not come back.

That was the last time his mother had held him. It was the last time he believed a promise.

Maggie tugged at his arm. "Tell me what she said, what she meant."

Ignoring the stabbing in his belly, Crane said, "After Pa left, she prayed. She said she knew God would bring him back. She hoped and hoped, but when he didn't come back, she began to die inside."

At first, he had thought she was angry with him, that somehow it was his fault Pa had left. That was why she no longer laughed with him, or tickled him, or told him jokes. It was years before he figured out it was because of her own heartbreak. Not until now did he realize she simply couldn't survive without hope.

In happier times, she had read the Bible and talked about God. In his mind, he was certain the two were connected.

"I got something you might like to see." He pushed to his feet. Digging in the saddlebags, he found a paper-wrapped parcel and took it to her.

She turned it over in her hands. "What is it?"

"Open it and see."

Maggie's fingers danced at the knots; then she unfolded the crackling paper. "It's a Bible," she whispered, trailing her fingertips over the black leather.

"It was my mother's." A smile tugged at the corners of his mouth. "She wanted me to take it." He'd been home on one of his visits. In the months since he'd last seen her, she had failed noticeably.

"One of these days, you won't be needing to come back here. You can follow those cows and that trail as far as you like," she'd said. "Son, I wish you all the best. I wish life could have been better for you, but"—she sighed—"keep my Bible with you always. Read it. Maybe you'll do better than me in learning God's ways."

After her death, he had disposed of her meager belongings but, remembering his promise, had packed the Bible for the trip west.

Eyes wide and bright, Maggie stared at him a moment then turned back to the Bible. "My ma always wanted a Bible. She said her folks back in the old country had one." Slowly she opened the pages. "I can't believe I'm actually holding one." She turned page after page, letting her hand slide over each. "It's so beautiful."

The pages fell open at the center, and she tipped the book toward the flames so she could see better. Crane watched as she read the black spidery names in the family tree. "Thomas Crane was your father."

"Yup."

"Powell Crane?" She looked at him again.

"My brother. He was born four years before me. He only lived six months."

She looked away. "How awful." A shudder shook her. Then her finger trailed up the page. "Imagine being able to see all your family like this for all these years gone by." She fixed a searching look on him. "It must make you feel good."

Crane rocked back on his heels as he considered it. All his life he'd been a loner. He hadn't given family a lot of thought, except occasionally to acknowledge to himself that his mother's dependency tethered him to his home. But Maggie's words hit a mark. "I guess it's kind of nice."

Satisfied, she nodded. The sound of crashing wood echoed across the clearing, and Crane turned to see Ted wipe bark and leaves from his arms, a pile of branches at his feet. In the dimming light, the boy looked even bonier, his face all sharp angles. Crane glanced toward the trees. Darkness had fallen as they talked.

"Time to call the children in," he murmured even as Maggie called, "Ted, stay here now. That's enough wood, thanks."

On the heels of her voice, Crane called out, "Betsy, come in now."

"Coming." The light voice carried through the dusk; then she could be heard singing, the words and voice growing more distinct as she skipped toward them.

"Look what I found." She knelt at Maggie's side and unwound her objects from the rolled-up shirttail. "A shiny rock and this one all full of holes." She set them at her knees. "And look." She held up a twisted piece of driftwood rubbed soft by the water. "It's so pretty." She lifted it toward Crane. "Isn't it, Crane?"

He smiled. "It sure is." Even so young, she was quick to let go of the past and rush wholeheartedly into the future.

Scooping up her treasures, Betsy sprang to her feet and scampered to the far side of the fire, where Ted sat as still as a stone. "Look, Ted. See all the nice things I found." She held them out for him to examine. "There's lots of good things down there. You should come with me next time."

Ted lifted his face and scowled at her. "It's dumb junk," he muttered.

Crane pulled himself taller. Those were the first words he'd heard the boy speak. *I guess it's a good sign.* Though he didn't like the way the boy spoke to Betsy.

Betsy seemed unaffected as she skipped back to Maggie's side and arranged her things in a neat row, humming as she played.

"It's time to get ready for bed," Maggie announced, springing to her feet.

Crane handed Betsy a bedroll. She waited as he flicked his into place then spread hers beside him. He smiled as he ducked to put more wood on the fire. He carried his coffee to the bedding, where he stretched out, his back to a tree.

Betsy watched him, waiting until he was settled before she crawled under the covers at his side.

"Ted," Maggie called. "Come over here."

Ted's shoulders tightened, and he shifted toward the darkness.

"It's all the bedding we got," she called again. "You'll have to share with us."

His shoulder drew closer to his ear.

Maggie turned toward Crane, her look begging him to do something. He shrugged.

"He'll get cold," Betsy whispered.

Crane nodded. "He's got to make up his own mind."

A heavy, waiting silence settled uneasily around them. Finally, with a sigh from as low as her shoes, Maggie shifted her attention back to the Bible, still lying on her knees. "Do you suppose I could read some?"

Crane nodded. "Go ahead. Read it out loud."

She bent her head and carefully opened the pages to the front and began, " 'In the beginning God created the heaven and the earth.' " Her voice was low and musical.

Crane eased back into a more comfortable position and, beneath his eyelashes, let his gaze skim over the others.

Betsy, her eyes wide and glimmering, a finger wrapped in a corner of the blanket, squirmed around so she could see Maggie.

Maggie's hair fell around her face like a curtain, moving just enough for the golden light to catch in its strands.

As she read, Ted's shoulders relaxed, and he stared at his toes, the light from the fire making sharp angles across his features.

Crane let his gaze return to Maggie. He got the same feeling in his chest he got when Rebel nuzzled his nose against his neck. He let the words take him back to the distant rooms of his memory to a time when they had been a happy family—before Pa left and Ma lost hope. Evenings had a special ritual of their own. Pa settled down before the fire with pipe and coffee. Crane sat on a stool, close enough to lean against Ma's knees. And Ma read aloud from this same Bible.

He drank his cooling coffee. Strange how he had forgotten. Maybe it was why he had kept the Bible; the reason he had put God-fearing as a requirement for his future wife.

Maggie closed the book. "I reckon I better stop for tonight." She sighed deeply. "It's so beautiful. I wish I could read it all right away."

"Me, too." Betsy flipped over on her back. "God made everything. Crane," she said, fixing him with a demanding gaze, "did He make me?"

Crane struggled to find the words to explain how a baby was made. "It took a mamma and papa to make you, child."

"Of course He did," Maggie interrupted. "My ma always said God made every sparrow and every flower in the grass. He made every one of us. She said little children are the most special, so He made an angel for each one to watch over them." She turned to Ted. "You remember that, Ted? You remember our mamma saying that?"

Ted shrugged his back toward them, his narrow shoulders creeping toward his ears.

Maggie ducked her head. Carefully she rewrapped the Bible and returned it to the pack before she crawled in beside Betsy. "Ted, it's getting colder by the minute. Come and lay beside me like we used to do." But Ted didn't respond.

Crane tossed out the last drop of coffee and pushed to his feet. He set the empty cup on a rock, then caught up his heavy gray blanket and wrapped it around Ted's shoulders, ignoring the way the boy stiffened and leaned away. From his saddlebag he pulled out his long black slicker and lay down, huddling under the coat.

"Thank you," Maggie whispered. "I hope you'll be warm enough."

"I'll manage." He'd survived worse.

"You're a nice man," she whispered.

Crane wasn't sure he'd heard her correctly. He grunted and waited until Betsy dug her feet into his ribs before he squirmed into a more comfortable position and waited for his thoughts to quiet.

Out of the darkness, a little voice spoke. "I guess his died."

Chapter 5

He heard Maggie's sharp intake of breath even as his thoughts flared like a hot burst of flame.

"Who died?" Maggie asked, the tension behind her low, calm words ringing in his head.

"Ted's angel," Betsy answered calmly.

"What makes you say that?"

"Well, he was dead or sleeping when your pa sold Ted to that pig man. Otherwise he would have helped Ted."

Smiling, Crane digested the idea, but it wasn't her statement that made him smile; it was the quick way her mind worked, assessing information, evaluating it against her experience, trying to fit it into her world. And he couldn't wait to hear what Maggie would say.

"Far as I know, angels don't die," she muttered. "I don't know about sleeping. Doesn't seem they should need to."

"Then what was he doing?" Betsy demanded. "Maybe playing with someone?"

Crane chuckled deep in his chest. The little minx wasn't going to let it go easily.

Out of the darkness, Maggie's voice challenged him. "You like to answer her?"

"No. You're doing fine."

"Thanks." Maggie grunted. "Maybe angels play. Guess I really don't know. But I don't blame the angels or God for what happened to Ted." She paused and drew a trembling breath. "Or me." Another pause. "My ma told me God loved me no matter what. She said He loved me so much, He sent His Son, Jesus, to die so we could have our sins forgiven and be part of God's family. And she said He would never leave me alone. All I had to do was decide whether I wanted it or not."

Silence descended for a moment.

"If I blame anyone, I blame my pa. Him and his bottle."

Crane stared into the darkness. People did what they did probably not even thinking how it might hurt another. It was useless to blame. It tied you to the past, controlled the present, and pinched the future.

"Best to forget it," he murmured. "What's done is done. We have the rest of our lives ahead of us."

"I suppose you're right. Not much any of us can do about what's already happened. Except learn from it." Her voice hardened. "I know I've learned a few things."

Crane wondered what lessons Maggie had learned, but Betsy snuggled close to his side, her breathing slow and even, and he didn't ask for fear of waking her.

Then out of the darkness, Betsy's soft voice asked, "You'll never leave us, will you, Crane?"

It was as much statement as question and drove Crane's breath from him in a gust. "Don't see no reason to." Awkwardly he shifted to one hip so he could drape his arm over Betsy's wee body, letting her know she was safe. He stiffened as his hand touched Maggie's warm fingers. She tensed momentarily, but her hand remained beneath his. Inch by inch he relaxed, letting his hand rest on hers. He liked the warm rush of blood through his veins and wondered what Maggie's reaction would be if he pulled her close. How could he with the child curled between them?

"You never answered her question," Maggie whispered.

"What question?"

"About leaving. Will you ever leave us, Byler Crane?" Her words whispered through the darkness.

"Like I said, I don't see no reason to leave."

"What would constitute a reason?"

He withdrew his hand and threw himself on his back. They were married. Wasn't that promise enough? He said as much.

"Your pa was married, and he left."

He didn't need her pointing it out. His jaw tightened. "I can't answer for my pa, but I recall back in Colhome I promised ' 'til death do us part.' I ain't changed my mind and don't plan to."

She sighed. "That's something, I guess."

"Yup." What more did she want? Theirs wasn't a romantic liaison; it was a business arrangement—one they both stood to benefit from. His parents had married out of love and passion, and look how that turned out. He decided he was more'n happy to do it his way.

"And we'll take care of Ted and Betsy?"

"I ain't about to leave them to fend for themselves." He'd learned to take what life handed him without asking too many questions, but it seemed Maggie wasn't so inclined. "No point in trying to figure out everything. It only boggles you down with worry."

"I'm not trying to figure out everything." She sounded annoyed. "Only where I stand and what I should expect." A minute later she added, "I feel like I've been swept into a whirlwind."

He chuckled. "Mostly of your own making."

"I can't seem to help it."

"I suppose not." Not if she meant to rescue everyone she thought was in trouble.

"I guess I act before I think."

"Umm."

He heard a tiny sigh. "But even if I sat and thought about it a week, I wouldn't put either Betsy or Ted back where they was." Her voice hardened. "It wouldn't be right."

"Nope."

"It's just—" She sounded uncertain. "I only—"

He waited, letting her sort her thoughts.

"You said you needed a God-fearing wife to begin a new life in the West. And now here you are with me and two young 'uns. It's not what you bargained for." She took a gusty breath. "I guess what I'm trying to say is, I'd understand if you said you wanted out."

He thought he'd made it clear he was going ahead as planned. What more did she want? He wriggled away from a lump under his back. He could not promise the future; he could only say, as he already had, he was prepared to continue their journey.

Again he shifted so he could drape his arm over Betsy's sleeping form. Maggie's arm was still there. He found her hand and rested his own on top of it. She curled her fingers away but made no attempt to pull her hand out.

"The past is best left behind, and there's no point in trying to guess what the future might hold. So we make plans as best we can and take each day as it comes."

Her fingers tightened into a ball. "Together?"

He squeezed her hand. "I meant what I said."

The tension in her arm eased. Slowly her fingers uncurled to lay warm and relaxed in his grasp. The child between them snored softly. Maggie's breathing deepened, but he couldn't be certain she slept. Across the fire Ted shifted in his sleep and moaned, the sound choking off as if he'd tied a rope around it.

Crane lay with the child under his arm and Maggie's hand in his. *No promises other than the one I made in front of the preacher. And no assurances.* It was enough to be like this—husband and wife united to face the future. As to the rest of it— His chest tightened so it hurt to breathe. The rest would come later.

The next morning, anxious to be on the trail, Crane silently urged everyone to hurry. Breakfast complete, he left Maggie to clean up as he went to get the horses ready. He was tightening the pack in place when a sound stopped him. He paused to listen. It was a high-pitched keening sound.

Silent as a shadow, he slid between the trees toward the sound. Through the leaves he glimpsed the gurgling water of the river, and as he lifted his gaze to the shoreline, the skin on the back of his neck crawled.

Betsy stood waist deep in the slow, persistent current, her arms flung out as she struggled to keep her balance. The water caught the too-big shirt she wore, tugging her downstream. Her face was contorted with fear. The keening sound rose from her lips.

Ted stood on the shore facing Betsy, the expression on his face sending shudders across Crane's shoulders. As Crane watched, Ted pitched a rock into the river, splashing water in Betsy's face, forcing her to draw back.

Crane held his breath as she stumbled and righted herself. She took a step toward the shore. Ted threw another rock and forced her back again. The keening sound raced through Crane's veins. Crane's jaw ached from clenching his teeth together. He eased toward the pair then pulled back as Maggie broke through the trees. She skidded to a stop behind Ted, her hands clenched, her mouth widening. Her gaze flicked from Ted to Betsy, and she took a deep breath.

"Ted, Betsy," she called, as if trying to locate the children. "Where are you? It's about time to leave."

The handful of rocks slipped from Ted's fists, and he plopped down on a boulder, looking detached and disinterested.

Betsy struggled toward shore.

"There you are," Maggie crooned, stepping into the river to help Betsy. "You best be careful around the river. It can be dangerous." She held the child's hand.

Ted studiously avoided looking in their direction.

"We wouldn't want anything to happen." Her voice carried a hard, warning note. "Would we, Ted?"

Slowly he turned toward her. Brother and sister stared at each other. Crane couldn't see Ted's expression, but he could see the set of Maggie's shoulders and the challenge in her face.

Just when he thought Maggie would have to relent, Ted moved his head. It was barely a nod, but Crane sighed.

She smiled grimly. "Then let's get ready to go."

Betsy clung to her hand as they hurried back to the campsite. Ted waited a moment then jerked to his feet and followed.

His fists clenched at his side, Crane watched until they were out of sight. It was several minutes before he led the horses to the campsite, where Maggie had built up the fire to dry Betsy's clothes. Crane moved slowly and deliberately, his calm exterior giving no indication of his troubled thoughts. Out of the corner of his eye, he studied Ted, but the boy sat on his former perch, peeling a branch and looking as ordinary as an April shower.

As they rode west, Crane's thoughts knotted, again and again replaying the scene at the river. He barely heard Betsy's chatter or Maggie's replies. He'd have to keep a more careful eye on Ted and wait to see what the boy was made of.

"I recollect the day you was born," Maggie said to Ted. "After you was washed, the midwife wrapped you up and put you in my arms while Ma rested. I remember Pa said, 'I reckon he's going to be as much your baby as anybody's.'" She paused, a faraway look in her eyes. "You were so sweet. You was smiling before you were more'n a few days old. Ma said it was just gas, but Pa watched you and said, 'I declare. He does seem to know when it's Maggie talking to him. There's something special between the two of them.'"

Crane knew what Maggie was doing, trying to bring the boy out of himself and back to the child she remembered. But thinking of the way Ted had treated Betsy, Crane wanted to warn Maggie the brother she once knew might be forever gone.

"Ted," she continued, "do you remember the time Ma and Pa decided to take us on a picnic down to the river, and Pa made sure you could swim good—then he hung a rope from that big tree and taught us how to swing over the river and jump in?"

Crane turned to look at Ted where he rode behind his sister. Expecting to see him with head ducked as usual, Crane was startled to see Ted's face lifted to watch Maggie. Crane stared. Perhaps something was redeemable in this child after all.

"Your pa sounds like a right nice man," Betsy said, her voice full of awe.

Maggie nodded. "He was until Ma died, and he took to the bottle. After that he changed." Her voice hardened. "I guess you can never be certain someone won't change from one day to another as they ride down the trail."

Crane sat up straight. He didn't have to look at Maggie to be certain she meant him. But how could he promise her tomorrow and tomorrow? Today was all they could be certain of. Today was all he could promise.

By midafternoon they rode into a town. "We'll get more supplies here," Crane announced, turning in at the general store. Maggie followed. "You all better come in and help get what we need."

The four of them marched up the steps toward the door.

"We need clothes for Betsy. Maggie, you look after that," he said. "I'll see to Ted's needs." He pulled open the door and stepped in.

He selected several blankets and asked for a bag of flour and another of cornmeal before he led Ted to the men's section. He chose three shirts and some overalls then had Ted sit while they tried on boots. Ted did as he was told without any interest in the proceedings until Crane looked over the pile and said, "I suppose a young fella your age will be needing a pocketknife."

Ted glanced up, giving Crane a chance to see his wide eyes before he ducked his head again. It was long enough for Crane to see a gleam of interest, and he smiled.

"Let's see what they got."

They returned to the counter and asked to see the knives. The storekeeper pulled out a tray with eight knives on it and set it before them.

Crane lifted each knife, feeling the weight of it in his palm then flicking open the blades before he handed it to Ted, who did the same. One by one, they examined each knife then stared at them lined up on the counter.

"It's your knife—you'll have to decide which is best," Crane said. He felt Ted's sharp intake of breath, then the boy reached out and picked up a plain black knife with two solid blades.

"Good choice," Crane said, pleased the boy had chosen the sturdiest one rather than going for the flashy red one with all the doodads. "Add this to the tally," he told the storekeeper. Ted held it uncertainly in his palm. "It's yours," Crane said. "Carry it in your pocket, and use it wisely."

Ted pushed the knife into the pocket of the new overalls he wore. "Thank you," he murmured, flashing Crane a quick look.

"You're welcome, boy."

Maggie and Betsy joined them, adding more articles to the pile.

"Look at my new shoes." Betsy pranced before Crane.

"Nice," he said, pleased at how much better she looked in a dress her size. "Looks like we're all set then." He paid the bill. "Now let's go see what we can find for a horse for Ted."

Again the boy flashed him a wide-eyed look. Crane felt compelled to explain himself. "We don't want to overload our mounts and have them wear out before we get where we're going."

Under the watchful but guarded eye of Ted, he purchased a small Morgan gelding and a saddle. Crane was certain Ted sat taller in the saddle as they left town. His glance met Maggie's, and she smiled and mouthed, "Thank you."

He felt heat rush to the tips of his ears. "Let's make tracks." He turned his attention to the trail, his thoughts scattering like the dust at Rebel's hooves. The wind had picked up while made their purchases, tearing out of the northwest with a hunger that made Crane grab for his coat. Maggie did the same, while he handed the children each a new coat. He'd wanted to ride for three or four hours yet, but after an hour, he couldn't abide the misery on the faces of those under his care and pulled in at the first sheltered spot.

"We could be in for a storm." He led them into a stand of trees that cut the wind. "Let's set up camp." Betsy huddled close to a bush while Maggie hunched against the wind. Crane dropped his gaze to Ted, pleased that the boy didn't look away.

"Ted, we'll build a shelter. Maggie and Betsy, you gather up as much wood as you can." He stared at the cloud-darkened sky. "Looks like we might need a good fire tonight."

"Come on, Betsy." The child sniffled as Maggie took her hand.

Crane got his axe and bent thin poplar saplings, cutting them close to the ground, then showed Ted how to weave them into a lean-to. The boy proved a good help despite his shivering.

Crane brushed his hands off. "Think that will do?" he asked Ted.

"Guess so," the boy murmured.

Crane smiled. "Let's get the saddles and bedrolls."

Ted jumped to obey, helping pile the saddles and packs at the edge of the lean-to and shoving the bedrolls into the shelter.

"Come here and get warm," Crane called to Maggie and Betsy, and they hurried inside the shelter.

Ted helped Crane build a fire and stacked wood close by.

"Good boy," Crane murmured. "Now get in out of the cold."

Ted hesitated, looking at the tight quarters, but a cold gust of wind tore through the clearing. The boy crawled in close to the saddles, keeping a space between himself and the others.

Crane had built tree shelters before but always for himself, and although he'd tried to build a larger one this time, only a narrow space was left for him to squirm into. Betsy edged forward to make room for him, resting her elbow against his knee. His left shoulder rubbed against Ted's slight body. Maggie's warmth raced along his other side, and as he shifted, his arm brushed her.

He could hardly breathe. Was she likewise feeling a response to their closeness? Was that why her breathing was so shallow? He wanted to say something, let her know he wanted more from marriage than a physical presence. But he sensed she was as frightened as Ted, and he didn't know how to tell her she didn't need to be afraid of him. Although he wanted a proper marriage, he was willing to bide his time until she was ready.

He hunched over. Betsy's hair tickled his lips as he pulled items from the saddlebags for supper.

After the meal was cleaned up, Maggie asked, "Would it be hard to get the Bible?"

"No problem at all." He leaned across Ted and lifted it from the pack.

"Would it be all right if I read it again?"

"Yeah, yeah!" Betsy cheered.

"That would be nice," Crane agreed. He shoved more wood into the flames and settled back.

Maggie read story after story. Occasionally, Crane leaned forward to throw on another chunk of wood, and the flames flared, bathing them all in a warm glow.

She read until her voice cracked.

"Guess we should go to sleep," Crane murmured.

She carefully rewrapped the Bible and handed it to him. He tucked it back in the pack.

The children had snuggled down behind them. He was certain Betsy was already sleeping. Maggie tugged her bedroll around between Crane and the children and crawled in. He waited until she was settled then spread his blankets so he slept across the opening. He lay stiff, afraid his movements would disturb the others.

Betsy kicked a little.

The leaves rustled as Ted shuffled as far away as possible.

Beside him, separated only by the blankets, Maggie lay quiet and still.

Crane filled his lungs slowly and held the air in his chest for a moment then eased it out through his teeth and forced himself to relax. The night noises settled around him, comforting in their familiarity.

Out of the darkness, Maggie said, "I didn't know I'd forgotten so much."

Crane waited for her to explain.

"All the things my ma told me, the stories she read from the Bible and how she explained about God." She took a deep breath, making her body touch Crane's in several places.

His breathing jerked to a halt.

"I forgot so much. It's like I shoved it all from my mind."

He grunted.

"Guess I let my anger get in the road." She stiffened. "I was so angry when Ted disappeared. And when Pa left me in town, not caring what happened to me. I guess it all made me forget."

He couldn't say much to that and lay still as a deep sigh eased through her. A muffled sound came from Ted's corner then a barely audible whisper. "Me, too."

Maggie wrapped her arms around the boy. "Oh, Ted, I love you so much."

Relief washed through Crane. It was a time of healing for brother and sister. Maggie's words were a faint echo of the things his mother had said to him.

"I let other things get in the road. I don't want you to forget like I did," Maggie said. "I feel like I can hear Ma's voice again."

They hadn't been on the road long the next morning when they saw a tilted wagon. A woman sat on the ground, rocking back and forth. A man stood over her, waving his arms. As they drew closer, Crane heard soft cries from the woman and the deeper tones of the man.

"Now, Marta. It be okay. Somet'ing come off, but we be okay. Now you not cry."

Crane pulled to a stop beside the pair. "Looks like you got problems, mister."

"Ya, t'at we got. For sure. Dis here wheel come wrong."

Crane dismounted. "Bet you could use a hand fixing it."

"Ya. Dat we can. Dat we can."

The woman on the ground groaned. Her husband turned to watch her. "My missus. . .I t'ink the baby come soon." The man turned imploringly to Crane. "Your missus, she help my missus?"

Crane looked at Maggie. She was so young. And not very big. But she had proven to be spunky. "Can you help?" he murmured.

She grabbed his arm and leaned close. "I ain't never done this before." Her hand slipped down and buried itself in his grasp.

"You never seen a baby born?"

"I seen Ted born."

He squeezed her hand. His heart quickened as she clung to him. "Do what you can."

She looked around. "She needs someplace quiet and clean. A place to lay down."

"Ya. I get 'ta bed off the wagon." And the man jumped into the wagon box, handing Crane a roll of blankets.

Maggie called, "Over here." He took the bedding to her and saw she had found a grassy spot behind some bushes.

"My missus, she have this ready, too." The worried man held a satchel toward Maggie. "It have 'ta clean cloths, scissors, and a blanket for the baby."

Maggie returned to the laboring woman. "Can you walk that far?"

"Ya." Marta grunted to her feet and waddled to the spot. Maggie disappeared with her.

Eyes big, Betsy and Ted stared after them, Betsy plucking at the hem of her dress. Ted's arms hung stiff and straight at his side.

"Come on, you two," Crane called. "I need some help." He handed the reins to Ted. "Hold the horses while I have a look." He crawled under the wagon. The axle was cracked. He eased out and spoke to the man. "You got a spare axle, Mr.—? Sorry, I don't know your name."

"I ban Mr. Swedburg." He held out his hand. Crane introduced his group.

"I not got spare axle."

"Then we'll have to patch the old one. You'll have to go back to town and get it done proper."

"Ya."

"Now let's see if we can get the wheel back on."

But when Crane put his back to the wagon, it would not budge. He checked inside and saw a stove, a trunk, and several boxes piled in the corner. "We'll need to move some of this stuff."

Swedburg disappeared in the back of the wagon and returned with a basket. "We better move Mamma and her babies first. Maybe the little girl like to play with dem."

The basket held a purring cat with four half-grown nursing kittens. "Betsy, you want to look after this bunch while we fix the wagon?" Crane placed the basket on the grass out of harm's way, grinning as Betsy bent over to pet the kittens.

He and Ted helped the man rearrange the contents of the wagon, distributing the heavy objects away from the broken wheel. "Be careful not to put all your big things over one wheel," Crane told Swedburg.

"I not t'ink very good. I just t'ink about getting free land. I want to get dere before baby born." He paused and listened to his wife's moans. "I t'ink it be too late now."

"Now there'll be another reason to get there."

Crane showed him how to grease the wheel and reinforce the axle. "Now there are three of you. You're a family." Even as he had gone from being alone to a family of four. The thought made him feel warm inside. And at the same time, a little apprehensive. It was an awesome responsibility for one who had spent his life alone.

"Ya. We start new life." The man smiled at Crane. "You, too, ya?"

Stepping back from the repair job, Crane nodded and wiped his hands on a rag. "It should get you back to town."

"I t'ank you."

Whatever reply Crane had thought to make was drowned by a scream that ripped through his brain. Swedburg's face blanched. For a moment Crane thought the man would faint; then the color seeped back into his face.

"Da little one not want to come, maybe."

Crane pushed his hat back. "I'm sure everything's all right."

Chapter 6

The children each held a kitten, but Crane could sense their fear as they turned to him.

"I'm sure everything is fine," he said again, ignoring the shiver racing up his spine. He turned to Swedburg. "Let's get the wagon repacked."

But the man let Crane do most of the work of putting crates along the wall.

"Mr. Swedburg," Maggie called, and the man rubbed his hands on his pants and looked toward the bushes then back at Crane. "You have a son!" Maggie's voice sang out as she stepped into sight, a small, blanketed bundle in her arms.

The baby wailed as Maggie placed him in his father's arms. "Congratulations."

"Marta?"

"She's fine. Resting for a few minutes."

Crane dropped his hand to her shoulder and squeezed. "Good job," he murmured. Feeling her trembling, he pulled her close. She almost collapsed against him.

After a moment, she straightened. "I'd best go take care of Marta." And she slipped away, leaving an empty coldness at Crane's side.

They stayed long enough to get Marta settled in the wagon with the infant at her side.

"Now we must put the cat back."

But Swedburg looked from the basket to the two children. "Ve have too many cats. You take one, ya? Let the children choose."

Two pairs of begging eyes turned to Crane.

"A cat is good when you build new house. Keep the mices out. Ya?"

"Please, Crane. Please," Betsy begged. "We'll take good care of it, won't we, Ted?" She looked to Ted for confirmation.

Ted nodded.

But it was not Betsy's eager pleading that convinced Crane; it was the resigned look in the boy's eyes that said he expected to be denied.

"You two will have to agree which one you want."

Betsy whooped her delight, but Crane's reward was Ted's wide grin before he turned back to the cats.

Betsy lined them up, petting each. "I like them all."

"We can only take one," Crane warned.

"I know," she whispered.

Maggie joined the children. "They're adorable. How will you decide which one to take?"

"I can't," Betsy wailed, turning to Ted. "You choose."

Ted had been sitting back, watching, and now he nodded and began to draw little circles on the knee of his pants.

The others watched quietly.

"What we want is a kitty that is alert. One that's smart enough to know what's going on," Ted said.

Crane narrowed his eyes and studied the boy. It was difficult to see this lad as the same one who had tormented Betsy not much more than a day ago. But he'd sensed a difference in the boy all morning. The stiffness was gone. And the guarded fear. Crane chewed his bottom lip. Seems a door had been broken down last night. Whether it was the memories sparked by Maggie reading the Bible or her talk about their ma, he didn't know, and it didn't matter. He only hoped the boy could leave the past behind and get on with the future.

A gray-striped kitten detached itself from the others, tail lifted like a flag, and stalked toward the circling finger. It sprang to Ted's knee, grasping the finger in its paws. Ted laughed, tickling the kitten's tummy. He played with the animal a minute then cradled him to his face. The kitten licked Ted's cheek. Crane could hear the cat purring even where he stood.

"That the one, Ted?" Maggie asked.

The boy nodded.

"Here's a blanket for him." Swedburg handed a scrap of gray material to Ted. "You wrap him up, and he travel good."

Ted bundled the kitten up and rose to his feet. He held the bundle out to Betsy. "We'll take turns carrying him. You go first."

Amid a flurry of thank-yous and good-byes, Crane, Maggie, and the children again headed west.

❧

It was two afternoons later as Crane returned from hunting that he heard high-pitched squealing and the sound of splashing water. He angled toward the river and saw Maggie and the children playing in the water. Ted was several feet from Maggie, and he sang a little tune, "Baggy Maggie, you're so shaggy. Raggy, raggy, raggy." He laughed.

Maggie swept her cupped hand through the water, spraying an arc of water in Ted's face.

Crane's gaze lingered on Maggie as she laughed. She had stripped down to some sort of lace-trimmed undergarment rounded at the neck. Her arms were bare. Gems of water glistened on her skin.

Ted continued his teasing. "Raggy, baggy, shaggy Maggie."

Betsy joined the chorus, jumping up and down in the water. "Baggy Maggie, baggy Maggie."

She sprayed them both with water, calling, "Ted, Ted, your head is red. Ted, Ted, go to bed." She turned to Betsy. "Miss Betsy, you're so pesky."

Then she saw Crane watching them, and her words sputtered to a halt. She sank into the water. "We were just playing," she muttered, her gaze never leaving his face.

He took a step closer, drawn by an indescribable force.

"Come in the water," Betsy called. "It's lots of fun."

Crane shook his head and stepped back. Maggie's gaze dropped but not before Crane caught a flash in her blue eyes. Was it a wish for their relationship to progress to the next step, or was it simply the reflection of the sunlight off the water?

The children flung water at him, and he ducked away, catching his hat on a branch, tipping it over his forehead. As he pushed it back, his gaze returned to Maggie. He knew what he wanted. He wanted to be man and wife in more than name. He ached to hold her to his chest and kiss her lips, red and moist from playing in the river.

"Come on," Betsy called again.

Crane considered the idea, half-deciding to join them, then thought better of it. He might know what he wanted, but he had no notion what Maggie was feeling. He could afford to be patient. He'd let Maggie find her own way in her own time. They had the rest of their lives.

"I got us a rabbit. Best get it roasting." And he walked away, feeling strangely hollow inside. And it wasn't from hunger.

By the time the others joined him, he sat on the ground tending the rabbit on a spit over the fire and, looking up, caught Maggie watching him, her eyes wide and steady. She held his gaze for a moment before turning her attention to the cup of coffee in her hand.

He reached around Betsy to turn the meat. His own words condemned him. *No love or passion,* he'd told himself. But now he wanted both. He longed for physical closeness, but even more, a place deep inside him ached for her love.

He set Betsy aside and pushed to his feet. "I'm going to see what Ted's up to." He stalked into the dusk.

Ted wasn't difficult to locate. He sat near the river's edge, holding the kitten, which the children had named Cat, and staring into the distance. Although Ted had changed dramatically in the passing days, Crane noticed he often sought solitude. He crossed to Ted's side and sat beside him.

The silence settled around them, broken only by Cat's purring and the murmur of the river. They had no need for words. Sometimes a man had to work things out inside himself. He was sure it was as true for Ted as for him.

"Crane, Ted." Betsy raced toward them. "Maggie says it's ready to eat."

"Better not keep Betsy waiting," Crane murmured out of the side of his mouth. "She'll think she'll starve if we do."

Ted rewarded him with a flash of a smile. "Bet she's been pestering Maggie steady, wanting to know if it was ready."

Crane chuckled as he scrambled to his feet. "Nothing quite so important as food, is there?"

Seemed Ted liked his food almost as well as Betsy, but Crane wasn't about to point it out.

"Not so far as Betsy knows." Ted followed Crane toward the fire. "It's hard being hungry." His voice was thoughtful. "But there are harder things."

Crane wanted to ask what the other things were, but Betsy tugged on his hand, chattering like a magpie as she hurried him along.

Later, having eaten their fill, the children played with Cat, tossing a knob of wood back and forth between them, getting her to chase it.

Maggie brought the coffeepot and refilled his cup. She set the pot back and sank to the ground, her face upturned to him. "I've been thinking."

He had been about to take a swallow, but at her words, his throat tightened and he lowered his cup.

"I think I should write Pa and tell him I got Ted. And when we get settled, I'll let him know where we are."

The coffee sloshed in Crane's cup. "You think he might want Ted?" He watched the boy playing with Betsy. He was quiet compared to the girl, but underneath the scars left by the hands of the pig farmer, Ted seemed to be a nice boy. Crane's fist tightened around his cup, and he admitted he had grown fond of him.

"I wouldn't think so. He knows I'll take good care of him. But maybe someday he'll put his bottle down and remember how much he cared about us. Maybe he'll wonder how we're doing."

Crane's gaze shifted to Betsy. "Will someone claim Betsy one day?"

"I thought about it some." Maggie's face caught the flare of the fire, making her eyes bright. Her moods flashed across her face as quick as the light from the fire. She was open and direct. If she wanted a change in their relationship, she would come right out and say so. But she hadn't.

She looked at him steadily, and he forced his thoughts back to the conversation. "Ma knew someone who had a foundling child. She said the lady got a lawyer to make some inquiries, and when no one turned up, she adopted the child, legal-like. Maybe we should do that, too."

He nodded. "Soon as we find a place to settle, we'll contact a lawyer."

She smiled. "It's funny, don't you think? All of us have lost our families, and now here we are together. A new family." Her expression flattened; her voice grew harsh. "A forever family."

Crane stared into the fire. Was there such a thing as forever?

Taking his silence for disagreement, she shifted her back to him. "I know we can't see what the future holds." Her voice was low. "But we can promise ourselves and each other that as far as possible, as much as lies within our power, we won't change our minds."

Until death do us part. He'd promised it when they wed; he'd reiterated it since, but she wanted more. Trouble was, he didn't know what it was or if he could give it. "What is it you want me to say?"

For a moment, she didn't reply. Then she shrugged. "I don't know. It's just—" She hesitated. "I no longer believe in happy ever after." Her voice dropped to a whisper. "But I want to." She lifted her head again. "I want to believe we will ride west and find a place we like and build a new home where we will be a true family." She rubbed her clenched hand against her knee. "But I'm afraid when we get to the end of the trail, it will all fall apart."

Crane reached out and squeezed her shoulder. For a spell he was silent; then he said, "A man is only as good as his word." Beneath his hand her shoulder slumped. His answer had disappointed her, but he didn't know what else to say. Seemed some people could make promises easily. And forget them as easily. He had no wish to be one of those men.

He rose and called the children, handing them each a bedroll. "Time to settle in."

Betsy spread her blankets next to his as always. Maggie unrolled her blankets on the other side of the child. Ted waited until the others were finished then flipped his bedroll next to Maggie's.

Crane poured himself and Maggie another cup of coffee and handed her the Bible. He lounged on his bed, sipping his coffee, but she hadn't read long when her voice thickened, and she choked. Tears washed her face, and she dashed them away.

"My ma told me I could be a child of God. He loved me enough to send His Son, Jesus, so I could be forgiven. All I had to do was ask. And I did." She sniffed. "She said He would always be my Father, no matter what happened to me." Again she sniffed and took a long, shuddering breath. "How could I forget so much?"

The children watched her—Ted's face pinched, Betsy's eyes big and her mouth round.

Maggie jerked around to face them all. "Ted, Betsy, Crane, listen to me. We can each be a child of God. He will always take care of us. It doesn't matter where we go or who tries to hurt us—God will love us forever."

Although her fervor made him squirm, Crane couldn't turn away from the dark gleam in her eyes.

"Ma said we could never for sure count on men, but we can always count on God."

Crane clenched his mug, certain her comment held a note of censure. But then he could hardly fault her if she held no confidence in men. Her experiences had not given her cause. It would take time for him to prove himself.

She leaned toward the children. "I know bad things happened to you. They happened to us all, but God will help us. From now on I'm going to trust God to take care of me. He promised He would. Forever."

Crane leaned back, staring at the stars. His own mother had said much the same thing the last visit he'd had.

"I've failed to prepare you for the future the way I should," she'd said. He could still feel her frail hand clasping at his arm. "Remember—no matter how your pa and I have failed, God never changes. He is the same forever."

He scrubbed a hand over his face. He simply couldn't believe in forever. Seemed like a man was better off doing his best and letting the future take care of itself.

The next morning, Maggie sang loudly as she worked. Betsy laughed, and soon they both sang.

Ted wore a longing expression. He turned toward Crane, and the moment their eyes met, Crane knew Ted wasn't ready to trust anyone. Or anything.

"Come on, Ted," he murmured. "Let's get the horses ready."

Ted leapt to do his bidding. He had proven to be a quick learner and worked efficiently at Crane's side. Neither of them spoke until they were cinching the saddles.

"What'd you think about that stuff?" Ted asked, his words muffled as he reached under his gelding.

"What stuff?" Crane stalled.

"The stuff Maggie says about God." Ted straightened to look directly at Crane. "About being able to go to heaven and all that."

Crane secured the pack on the spare horse before he answered. "Well, I reckon it must all be true. It's in the Bible, isn't it?"

"But what do you think about it?" He pinned Crane with his question. The boy deserved honesty.

"I guess it's hard to separate out things. Things people do get mixed up with what God says. Seems like they should be closer together."

"Yeah, I know what you mean."

"Don't mean it's not true. Don't mean I don't believe it. It's just real hard to sort it out. I need to do some heavy thinking on it."

But it seemed thinking wasn't something Maggie was prepared to let him do. As soon as they hit the trail, she started talking. "It's your mother's Bible. She'd underlined lots of verses. She must have known this."

"I reckon she did."

"She tell you about it?"

"Yup. I reckon."

"Well, my ma said it was a gift, but a gift don't do you no good if you don't take it."

"I reckon that's so." He was beginning to wish they'd run into the Swedburgs again, if only because it would give them something else to talk about.

The cat lay curled in Ted's lap. Cat had turned out to be a good traveler, content to spend hours on the saddle. And now, when Crane longed for a diversion, she slept as if life held nothing else.

"I know," Maggie continued. "You're afraid."

Crane interrupted before she could finish. "Men have been shot for saying that," he growled.

"Crane ain't afraid," Ted yelled. "He needs time to think."

She waved little circles with her hands. "I don't mean afraid of somebody or something. I mean afraid to let go and trust."

"Maggie's right," Betsy insisted. "I did what she said. I prayed like she said. She's right."

Ted looked at Crane and said, "We need time to think about it. Don't we, Crane?"

Crane shifted in his saddle and stared dead ahead. It was two against two, a divided camp—a situation that made his nerves crackle. He turned to Maggie. "You was the one who didn't want nothing to change."

Her smile faded, and her face tightened. "Nothing's changed. We're still headed west, ain't we?"

Their gazes locked. Neither of them shifted away. Finally he grunted and kicked his horse into a trot.

After a few minutes, he allowed them to settle into a steady walk.

"Crane?" Betsy's voice was thin.

"Yup."

"You mad at Maggie?"

"Mad?" Had she taken his silence for anger? "No, I was just thinking." Though for the life of him, he couldn't recall one thought.

"Good." Her voice rose, and she began to chatter to Maggie about Cat and birds and asked what they would have for lunch.

Crane grinned at Maggie.

"I 'spect we'll find something," she muttered with an exasperated glance heavenward.

They made good progress that day. As they pulled up to make camp, Crane said, "We're in the Territories now. Tomorrow we'll leave off following the river and drop down to the new rail line." He'd heard the travel was easy with settlements along the new tracks. And although he had no interest in the towns, he understood it was the fastest route to the new West.

With camp set up, Ted wandered down to the river. Crane watched him. All day he'd felt the boy's withdrawal and knew he needed to be alone to sort things out. But the meal was ready, and Ted had not returned.

Maggie called him again then hurried down to the water's edge. "Ted," she called and waited. But Ted did not answer. She hurried back to the fire, twisting her hands together. "He should have been back."

Crane nodded. "Yup. I was thinking the same." He pushed to his feet. "I'll go get him."

He followed the river, occasionally seeing Ted's track in the soft ground. He walked for the better part of a half hour with no sign of the boy. The muscles in the back of his neck tensed. The boy couldn't have disappeared into thin air. He searched the now rocky ground and found no tracks, but as he edged his way around some willow branches, he sucked in his breath. Ted floated in the river, bobbing with the current.

Crane's thoughts crashed like a wave. A groan rose from deep inside him. Then Ted turned toward him, and Crane saw the muddied streaks down his cheeks and his quivering lips, and he leapt forward.

Ted saw him. "Crane, help." His words rattled over his teeth. "I'm stuck."

"I'm coming. Hang on!" He ran into the water, grabbing the boy under his arms. But he couldn't lift him.

"It's my foot." Ted choked back a sob.

"It'll be all right." Crane swooped his hand down the boy's leg and found it wedged between two boulders. A trickle of pink fled downstream from his foot.

Crane wrapped his arms around one rock and heaved. But it refused to budge. "I'll get something to pry with."

He plowed his way through the water and ran to the trees. The closer trees were willows with only thin wisps for branches. He had to find a sturdy branch.

He pushed through to the heavier growth and grabbed the first sizable branch he saw then raced back to the river. Grunting, he pried the end under the boulder and heaved, bending the branch with his weight. He grunted and pushed again. The branch snapped, but the rock did not move.

"I'm gonna have to force your foot out."

The boy nodded, gritting his teeth. "I can take it."

Crane bent over, feeling underwater, locating the best angle to free the foot. If he twisted and pulled at the same time—it would hurt like fury, but he had run out of ideas.

"Hold on now." He shut his mind to the pain he was about to inflict. "Take a deep breath and hold it." He grasped the foot with both hands and pulled. It stuck. He continued to pull, and it came free with a sickening jerk. Ted's scream tore through his brain.

He grabbed the boy, crushing him to his chest, and plunged out of the cold water. "Are you all right?" He held the boy a moment then set him down and looked deep into his eyes.

Ted nodded, then Crane bent to check the foot. A nasty gash bled profusely, but the foot and ankle seemed otherwise sound.

Ted's teeth chattered. "I was so scared," he whispered.

At the look of misery on his face, Crane pulled the boy back into his arms and held him tight. He wanted to say something to comfort and soothe the boy, but no words came. He pressed the small head against his chest and held him, letting his own fears slip away.

"You're freezing. Slip out of those wet things."

But Ted's fingers were clumsy from the cold, and it was Crane who undid the buttons and pulled the clothes off. With nothing dry to wrap him in, Crane stripped off his water-blotched shirt and wrapped it around Ted. He wrung as much water as he could from Ted's wet clothes then tied them in a bundle and hooked it to the back loop of his pants.

"Let's get you back to camp." He swept the boy into his arms. Ted allowed himself to be carried, clinging to Crane as if he feared he was still drowning. They could see the fire ahead and Maggie peering into the darkness.

"I found him!" Crane called.

Maggie raced toward Ted. "He's hurt!" she cried as she saw Ted in Crane's arms. "Oh, baby, say something."

"It's just my foot." Ted's voice quavered. "I slipped and caught it between two rocks."

Maggie reached for Ted, but Crane shook his head. "Get some blankets ready. He's cold."

She sped to the bedrolls, yanked up the blankets, and raced back.

At the fire Crane lowered Ted to the ground. Maggie had the blankets around him before Crane finished pulling away the damp shirt. She grabbed the shirt and saw the blood on it. "He's hurt." Her gaze settled on his foot, and she bent to examine it.

"It's a nasty cut."

"It's clean." Crane put on a fresh shirt. "Right now we need to get him warmed up."

"I made some tea." She hurried to get a cupful, ladling in several spoonfuls of sugar. "Here, sip this." She held it to the boy's mouth.

"Is he all right?" Betsy whispered.

Crane turned to the child. She stood apart from them, pinching the seams of her dress.

"He'll be just fine. He's cold now, and he has a cut on his foot." He reached for her, and she sprang into his arms, burrowing against his chest.

"I didn't want anything to happen to him."

"I know," he said softly. "None of us did."

"I asked God to help you find him." She snuggled closer, relaxing in his arms. "I guess He did."

"Maybe He did at that." Crane was grateful for whatever help God had offered.

Maggie brought some material from her pack and tore it into strips, bandaging Ted's foot.

"Here, Cat," Betsy called the animal to her. "You come keep Ted warm." She parked Cat in Ted's lap.

"Thanks," he whispered.

Crane and Maggie smiled at each other. Crane wondered if she was thinking the same as he: *These two have come a long way.*

184

Betsy climbed back into Crane's lap. Suddenly she cried out.

"What's the matter?" Crane asked.

"Your hands." She pointed, tears welling up in her eyes. "They're hurt."

Crane looked at his hands. Blood dripped from the backs of both of them. "I must have cut them pulling Ted's foot out." Strange, he never felt a thing. He was about to wipe his hands on his shirt when Maggie grabbed them.

"Here—let me clean them."

His hand rested in her palm as she wiped the back with a damp cloth then wrapped his hand in clean rags. Her touch was gentle as the warm summer rain, warming him all over. He shivered, not from cold but from some unfamiliar longing flooding through him.

She looked up from her task. "You're cold," she muttered. "You should take better care of yourself." She turned to the child. "Betsy, get Crane a blanket."

The girl ran to do as she was told, tenderly wrapping the blanket around Crane, patting his shoulders. He wasn't cold; yet their touches calmed his insides better than a hot drink.

They finally got around to having their supper.

Crane kept a close eye on Ted, but he seemed none the worse for his accident. He sat close to the fire, laughing at Cat's antics. In fact, Crane decided, Betsy seemed more affected by the incident than Ted. She hovered at his side, trying to anticipate his needs and satisfy them.

Maggie, having finished her chores, wandered down to the river. Crane watched her from his spot near the fire and, seeing the children were playing happily, sauntered down to join her. He knew she was aware of his presence, but she stared out across the water without speaking.

After a while, she let out a shuddering breath. "Thank you. You saved his life. I can never thank you enough."

"It was nothing," he murmured.

"I don't know what I would do if anything happened to Ted."

He kept his gaze on the trees across the stream. There she was wanting assurances about the future again. He couldn't promise her nothing would ever happen to Ted. He couldn't promise that for himself. Not for anybody.

"Ted kept his head."

"Poor boy." She swallowed a little cry. "Oh, Crane. He must have been so scared. I was so scared." And she flung herself against his chest, almost toppling him over.

Chapter 7

Crane wrapped his arms around her, promising himself he would do his best to see nothing ever hurt her. He rubbed her back, feeling her leanness, her toughness, and her softness.

"Everything will be fine," he murmured.

No sooner had he spoken the words than he wished for them back. He couldn't be making promises he didn't know if he could keep. The feel of her in his arms had turned his mind to mush.

He cupped a hand over her hair. It was so silky. Like nothing he could remember feeling before. He lowered his head, letting his lips caress her hair. He was drowning in the scent of her, the feel of her, the pound of his heart against her slight form.

"God took care of us today," she murmured, her voice muffled against his chest.

Her breath was sweet and tempting, and he lowered his head a fraction more, willing her to lift her face and offer her lips.

Instead she pushed away.

Crane's hands lingered on her waist until she dropped to her knees. He crossed his arms, striving to still the wild emotions raging inside him. She knelt beside him, her hands clasped before her. "Thank You, God, for taking care of Ted today. Thank You for sending Crane to help him." She paused. "Thank You for sending Crane to help us all."

He squirmed. *She must think I'm something I'm not.* Yet it made him think of something his mother used to say when he did something she appreciated.

"Why, bless you, Byler," she'd say. That was the feeling he got listening to Maggie thank God for him. A sense of being blessed.

Maggie got to her feet and stood close to him. A flash from the fire threw sharp angles across her face, then her features disappeared in the darkness.

He could feel her breath against his chin. She was watching him. But he didn't know what she wanted. Then she grabbed his hand, sending a wave of warmth up his arm.

"Let's go have coffee." He could hear the smile in her voice.

Her hand felt small and soft, and he let her pull him toward the fire, a smug smile widening his mouth.

They stepped into the circle of light, and she dropped hold of his hand, rushing toward the coffeepot. His arms hung at his sides, and his stare followed her movements. Had their touching affected her the same way it did him?

After they'd settled the children in bed, Crane handed Maggie the Bible. Betsy leaned across his legs, her focus on Maggie, while Ted sat cross-legged at his other side.

Maggie began to read, but her voice faded before she finished the story. Crane watched over his lowered cup. Her thoughts seemed to be far away as she stared at the fire then slowly closed the book.

"I can't read tonight," she murmured. "My thoughts are too full." The golden light danced across her face. "Seems like a door in my mind has come open, and I can remember all kinds of stuff. Things Ma used to tell me." She turned quickly, fixing her gaze on Ted. "Ted, I don't know what you remember. Seems you weren't very old when Ma started feeling poorly."

Ted's gaze fastened on his sister's face. "I don't remember much."

She nodded. "Sometimes she could barely get out of bed. It was an effort just to talk, but she was always so kind and gentle. I don't ever remember her bein' cross even when Pa was angry with her." Maggie paused to brush an insect from her arm. "I used to think he was angry at her for being sick, but I guess maybe he was angry at the sickness for what it was doing to her." She looked deep into Ted's eyes. "You remember that?"

He shook his head. "I only remember Pa bein' mad."

A flash of pain crossed her face. "You missed the best years."

Maggie leaned back, a gentle smile on her lips. "Ma used to tell the best stories. Stories from the Bible, but lots of stories about her life, too."

Betsy shifted toward Maggie, her elbow digging into Crane's leg, but he welcomed the feel of her against him.

"She told about going to church in the old country."

Betsy's head jerked up. "What's church?"

Maggie laughed low in her throat. "It's where you go to worship God and learn about Him."

"How do you do that?" the child demanded.

"You sing songs about God, you read from the Bible and talk about what it means, and someone prays."

Betsy eased back down. "Sounds good."

"Ma told one story over and over about how she heard what she called 'the truth about God.'" She leaned over her knees, a soft expression on her face. "There was a roving preacher who walked about the country with nothing but an old bag holding a change of clothes and his Bible. He'd sit in the center of town and begin to talk, and soon a crowd would be gathered." Maggie chuckled. "Ma said he'd gather a crowd then preach them into the kingdom."

Crane lay back against the tree trunk maintaining a casual pose, but inside he was hanging on to every word as eagerly as the children.

"How'd he do that?" Betsy asked.

"Ma said he opened his Bible and read verse after verse, telling the people

God had given them a gift of salvation. We didn't need to work for it or pay for it. Then he offered a coin to anyone who would come and take it. Ma said only one little boy had the nerve to go up and take it. Then the preacher said, 'That's exactly how it is with God's gift. You just have to take it.' " Her voice drifted off, and Crane could see she was deep in thought.

Betsy sighed. "I wish I'd been there to get the coin."

Maggie fixed her gaze on Betsy. "But don't you see what he was trying to do?"

Betsy shook her head.

"After the little boy got the coin, a bunch crowded around him saying they wished they'd gone and taken it. But what God offers is so much more than a coin. And all we have to do is take it. 'A gift beyond compare,' Ma always said. It's for everyone who decides to become a child of God."

Betsy sat up. "Then I got the gift?"

Maggie laughed. "You do indeed."

Betsy flopped down on her back. "Ain't I happy?"

Later that night, the four of them stretched out side by side. Crane looked up at the stars, his thoughts going round and round on what Maggie had said. Words he was sure his mother would have agreed with. But he couldn't just take a gift. Not from anyone and certainly not from God. He had learned a long time ago to stand strong and alone. Somehow, to take a gift made him beholden to the giver. But that didn't make sense in God's case. After all, didn't he believe God had a hand in the events of people's lives? Then he already was beholden in some fashion. Or was he protected and blessed?

It made his head ache trying to sort it out, so he turned his thoughts toward another matter: Maggie.

At that moment Maggie sat up. "Crane, you sleeping?"

"No," he whispered.

"I want to thank you properly for rescuing Ted."

"You already did." Had she forgotten or—a little pulse thumped inside his head—did she have something more than words in mind?

She flopped down on her back. "I guess I did, but I want to be certain you know how grateful I am."

"I do."

She reached across Betsy's sleeping form, found his hand, and squeezed it. Crane thought his heart would explode at her touch. It was all he could do to lie there when every inch of his body ached to pull her into his arms and cradle her.

"I care about the boy, too," he muttered, his tongue feeling as if he'd been on a long trail ride without a canteen.

"I know you do. You take good care of us all."

"Yup." His mind refused to work.

She lay there, silently holding his hand; then, sighing, she pulled away. "I wanted you to know."

The sun poured down on them day after day. What energy the sun didn't soak up, the wind blew away. The grass on the prairie was as high as the horses' bellies, but it was a lone, echoing place with no appeal for him.

"The wind sucks at my soul." Maggie shuddered. "I wouldn't want to live out in the open like this."

Crane nodded. They would continue west until they crossed the wide stretch of flatland. "West of Calgary we'll find trees and foothills," he said.

"I can hardly wait." She rubbed a rag across the back of her neck. "This heat is about more'n I can bear."

"Can't we stop?" Betsy whined.

Ted answered before Crane could. "You see a place where it's gonna be any cooler?"

"We'll stop early tonight," Crane promised.

The heat had taken its toll on everyone. Only Cat, curled up on the saddle in front of Ted, seemed unaffected.

"Maybe we'll find someplace close to water so we can take a dip." Not for the first time, he regretted leaving the river.

They rode another hour without seeing anything big enough to squat beside, let alone provide shelter from the sun. Finally, shading his eyes against the glare, he saw a structure against the sky. "There's a water tower ahead."

Water had taken a role the size of the wide sky as they crossed this barren land. The heat waves shimmered along the horizon. Dust wrapped around the wooden tower. A train came toward them, belching and snorting as it slowed.

"Take it easy," he ordered Rebel as he reined in and dismounted.

The others watched Crane with languid interest as he reached toward the spout. He was about to release the water when the engineer blew the whistle. It shuddered down Crane's spine.

Rebel took off as if he'd been shot, Betsy clinging to his back.

"You jughead!" Crane shouted. "Get back here!"

He had his hands full holding the packhorse. Maggie struggled to keep Liberty under control. Cat yowled and scampered up the side of the water tower.

The little Morgan Ted rode seemed to be the only horse with any sense in his head. He sidestepped twice. His nostrils flared, but he didn't bolt. Before Crane could react, Ted kicked his horse into a run and took off after Betsy.

Crane stared after Ted. "He ain't got a chance. No way that old horse is gonna catch Rebel."

Maggie dropped from her mount and grabbed the reins of the packhorse. "Take Liberty!" she cried. "Catch them before someone gets hurt."

Crane leapt into the saddle, reining the horse after the pair, though he was doubtful he could catch them. Betsy bounced madly on Rebel's back, her hair flying out like a spray of yellow straw.

"Hang on!" Crane called, knowing she couldn't hear him.

Ted bent low over the saddle, going for all he was worth, but he wasn't gaining on them. Behind him the train screeched to a stop, and steam whistled out. Liberty jumped sideways.

"Settle down, you knothead," Crane growled. "We got things to do." He struggled with the horse a few minutes, muttering under his breath.

But he could see Rebel was slowing down. Rebel didn't often act so silly and was probably beginning to feel a bit foolish about now.

Ted drew abreast of the bigger horse and caught the reins. Both horses stopped, their sides heaving. By the time Crane caught up, Betsy had crawled off Rebel's back and into Ted's arms, sobbing against his chest. Ted had his arms around the girl, an expression of mingled shock and awe on his face.

Crane grabbed Rebel's reins. "Betsy, are you okay?"

"Yes," she sobbed. "Ted saved me."

"Come on—I'll give you a ride back."

She shook her head, clinging to Ted.

"It's okay," Ted murmured.

They plodded back to the water tower, where the train crew had joined Maggie. One man stepped toward Crane. "I'm sorry. I didn't mean to cause you a problem."

"No harm done."

Maggie rushed to the children. "Are you all right?" Betsy fell into Maggie's arms, sobbing. "Shh. Shh." She reached out and patted Ted's knee. "I'm real proud of you, Ted."

Crane waited until the boy got down to put his hand on his shoulder and say in a low tone, "You did a right fine job, son."

If they hadn't been so desperate for water, they would have left the place; but surrounded by curious, apologetic men, they led the horses to the trough. Maggie insisted the children strip to their undergarments and allow her to splash them with the tepid water. Then they filled the canteens and prepared to leave.

"You folks looking for a place to camp?" the engineer asked.

"Yup." Crane secured the last canteen.

"Ride north." He pointed across the flat prairie. "There's a nice grove of trees. Good camping spot."

"Thanks." Crane reached for Betsy, but she stepped away.

"I want to ride with Ted."

Crane raised his eyebrows, but Ted nodded. Betsy grinned widely as she sat in the saddle, Ted's arms around her as he took the reins.

They found the spot the man had told them about. The poplars were thin but tall enough to shade them from the lowering sun.

The children got their bedrolls shortly after supper and spread them out, Betsy's next to Crane's as always. But when Ted started to spread his on the other side of Maggie's, Betsy said, "No. You sleep here," pointing to a spot between Maggie and her.

Crane watched the pair, waiting to see how Ted would respond.

The boy hesitated, looking at the spot he'd chosen then at the place Betsy indicated. The bedroll draped from his arm. He didn't move.

"Please, Ted. I want you to." Betsy sounded as if she would cry any moment, and the boy flipped his blankets open where she pointed. A deep sigh shook her small frame, and smiling her satisfaction, she sat down on her blankets, petting Cat. "You can read now, Maggie."

Crane laughed. The little minx had a way of binding people close to her then basking in their closeness. She'd succeeded in drawing Ted into her circle.

Maggie grinned at him. He held her gaze until her cheeks darkened, and she lowered her eyes. He kept hoping they would find a way of getting closer. Instead, the children succeeded in pushing them farther apart. He supposed he should be grateful she hadn't found half a dozen waifs to rescue.

He rubbed his chin. Someday he and Maggie were simply gonna have to talk.

It was ten o'clock before the sun dipped behind the horizon, but the heat refused to abate. The children had fallen into a restless sleep, but Crane found it too hot and his mind too active as he tried to sort out his feelings.

He was drawn to Maggie in a way that took his breath away. He hadn't expected this sort of reaction. A "godly woman" to help build a new home, he'd decided, never clearly seeing in his mind where it could lead.

He stared at the star-studded sky. In his schemes the woman had been a silent, shadowy figure—he grinned up at the sky—not this fireball. He ached to tame her. No, he amended, he didn't want to tame her; he loved the spit and fire of her. He only wanted some of that passion turned toward him. His hungry hollowness tore at his gut.

Purposely he turned his thoughts toward the things she'd said about God's love and trusting Him to receive the gift of salvation. She made it all sound so easy, but it didn't feel easy to him. Was his pride getting in the way? But he'd never considered himself a prideful man.

Fear, Maggie had said. But what was there to be afraid of? He wasn't afraid of God.

He was desperate for coffee and pushed to his feet.

"Something the matter?" Maggie called.

"Think I'll build a small fire. I want coffee."

She rolled off her blanket. "Too hot to sleep, isn't it?" She waited as he put the coffee to brew.

He could feel a tension in her, and he knew she would soon express it.

She leaned forward. "I'm sorry. I know this isn't what you expected. It's not the way we should be."

The coffee boiled, and he pulled it from the fire and poured her a cup. "Tell me—how should we be?"

He handed her the cup, taking in the way her hair caught the fire's light, the way her skin glowed. He didn't need to see the darkening of her cheeks to sense her discomfort at the way he stared.

She angled toward the fire. "You know—man and wife."

He grimaced at the way she gulped the hot liquid. He turned his own cup round and round, letting the silence force her to explain herself.

"You said the very first day you didn't expect romance but wanted a real marriage."

"Yup." It wasn't exactly how he had put it but close enough.

"I know what that means," she whispered.

"Good." He downed several swallows

"It's just that with the children and all—" Her voice trailed off.

He studied the flames without answering.

"You"—she gulped—"you aren't wishing they weren't with us, are you?"

"Me?" He jerked to his feet. "Ain't I been good to them? Can't you tell I care about them?"

"Yes."

"Well, then?" What more could he do? What did she want?

She shrugged, a helpless little gesture that made him want to kick himself for his outburst.

"Sometimes I think—I wonder—" She took a gusty breath. "It's so different from what I imagine you expected."

He chuckled. "Are you gonna tell me it's what you expected?"

She shot him a startled look then slowly grinned. "Not in my wildest dreams," she admitted.

Her mischievous look did wild things to his pulse rate, but he corralled his thoughts and held her gaze. "So what do we do except take each day as it comes?"

He heard her swallow. She blinked and opened her mouth twice before she got the words past her lips. "Nothing, I suppose."

But he heard the doubtful tone in her voice and searched his mind for some way of letting her know he was willing to wait for the right time—and some indication from her as to when she was ready. But before he could find the words, he heard a rumble.

"Someone's comin'." He stood and reached for his rifle.

She edged over to stand close to him.

"Hello, the camp!" a man's voice called as a wagon drew near. A man and woman sat on the seat. "Any objections to us joining you's all?"

"It's as much your right as mine," Crane replied, studying the pair—a middle-aged couple with a weathered leanness that made him uneasy.

"We was looking for a nice place to stop and saw your fire," the lady drawled.

The man took in the sleeping children and nodded to the other side of the clearing. "We'll park over there." He swung the wagon around.

Three youngsters sat on the end gate, two good-sized boys and a half-grown girl.

Crane glanced toward Ted and Betsy. Although Ted lay motionless, his eyes were open. Crane sank to the ground next to the children, and Ted whispered, "I don't like them."

"No reason not to," Crane whispered. "They're heading west same as us. And they're minding their own business." In fact, since they'd entered the camp, they'd turned their backs and kept their distance.

He waited until the other family settled down then slipped into the darkness to check on the horses, leading them closer for the night. He moved the packs next to the bedroll.

"Crane?" Maggie whispered.

"Just being cautious," he muttered.

He slept with one eye open and his rifle at his side and woke at dawn. A quick glance assured him their neighbors were still asleep, and nothing had been disturbed. *Gettin' jumpy,* he scolded himself, rising to build a small fire and put the coffee to boil.

Maggie uncurled from her bed and joined him. "Should we call out to them?" she asked.

He shook his head. " 'Spect they'll get up when they got a mind."

"I don't mind telling you I'm anxious to get moving." She rubbed the back of her neck.

Crane straightened and studied her. "You sleep all right?"

She grimaced. "I must have slept crooked. My neck is hurting."

"Let me rub it." He placed his hands on her taut shoulders, his thumbs on her neck. He knew the moment he touched her, he'd made a mistake. Fire flared up his limbs and grabbed his throat so he couldn't breathe. His arms felt like wooden posts. He rubbed firm circles along her shoulder muscles and up her neck.

"Good morning, y'all."

At the sound of the other man's voice, Crane dropped his hands, pressing his palms to his hips. "Morning." He stepped toward the man, extending his hand. "Name's Crane. This here's my wife." He nodded his head toward Maggie then indicated the children. "These are our young 'uns, Ted and Betsy."

Ted kept his stare on the strangers, while Betsy, bleary-eyed and half-awake, struggled to a sitting position.

"Hiram Johns." The man shook his hand. "Wife, Jean, and my youngsters. That there is Billy." He indicated the bigger boy who was rolling up his blanket. "That's Joe." The other boy was almost as tall and a bit on the pudgy side. "The gal is Annie." The girl was still curled up on her blanket. "She ain't been feeling too well."

"Coffee?" Crane held out the pot.

"Don't mind if I do. Say, but ain't it been a hot one?" The man settled down to visit, while his boys ran into the bush for more wood and the missus gathered up food for their breakfast.

Crane scowled at the man, wondering why he wasn't helping with the camp chores, but the man talked on about weather and horses and trains and too many things for Crane to keep track of. He helped Maggie prepare oatmeal porridge, and while they ate, Hiram Johns talked nonstop.

Finally Crane interrupted. "Guess we best get packed up." He tromped toward the horses. "Talks more'n an old woman," he muttered under his breath as he fixed the pack on the horse.

Usually Ted helped with getting the horses ready, but this morning he had run off with the other youngsters to explore the grove of trees. Crane had no mind to rob him of a few minutes of play.

A noise skittered through the air. Crane stopped and listened. It sounded like Betsy. Then he heard it again, small and thin, like Betsy in a panic.

He dropped the saddle and headed toward the sound, sliding soundlessly between the trees. The children were ahead of him. Billy, the older boy, had Betsy by one arm. She grunted, trying to free herself. Crane's jaw tightened at the way Billy's hand squeezed her thin arm.

Billy threw something.

"Stop that." Betsy squealed and tried again to pull away.

Then Crane saw why Betsy was so upset. Cat was up the tree, hissing as Billy threw stones at her.

"You leave my cat alone," Betsy demanded again, tears running down her face as Billy squeezed harder. "Let go of me. You're hurting."

Billy laughed, a sound that made Crane grit his teeth. "What's the matter? Does the little baby think I'm gonna hurt her poor little kitty?"

The other boy chanted. "Poor kitty. Poor kitty. Hit him again, Billy."

And the half-grown girl muttered, "Aw, who cares about a cat? Let's go get somethin' to eat."

"In a minute," Billy growled, raising his arm again.

Crane was about to break into the clearing when Ted ambled over to the bigger boy. Calm and quiet, he stepped to Billy's side and clenched the boy's wrist. "Think you better go now. And you can let Betsy go now, too."

Billy pushed his face close to Ted. "You gonna make me?"

Ted glared into his face. "If I have to."

The other two gathered close. "Fight. Fight," Joe chanted.

Ted did not back down. "Let her go."

Crane took two steps and dropped his hand on Billy's shoulder. "Best do as he says."

Billy jerked away as if Betsy's arm had scalded him, and all three children spun around to face him, their eyes wide with fright.

"Best go on back to your folks."

His eyes wide, Billy dashed after his brother and sister.

"Betsy, get Cat and go stay with Maggie." His gaze lingered on Ted as Betsy ran to the tree to call Cat. "I'm proud of you, son."

A shudder crossed Ted's shoulders. "Now let's get those horses ready and get outta here."

Crane and Ted quickly got the horses ready and led them to camp. "Let's get moving." He waited for Maggie to mount then lifted Betsy up.

"I want to ride with Ted."

"Not today."

"Aww." She prepared to protest, but Maggie interrupted.

"Not today, Betsy." There was a hard note in her voice.

Crane quirked an eyebrow at her.

"Betsy told me what happened," she muttered. "Let's get out of here."

"I'm with you." He was about to kick Rebel's sides when the sound of metal on metal made the hair on the back of his neck stand up.

Chapter 8

Crane lifted his hands several inches into the air and slowly turned to face the Johnses. A pistol glared from the man's grubby fist. Crane sensed a meanness that accompanied cowardice. "What's this I hear 'bout you giving my boys a hard time?" If Crane had been alone, he would bluff his way out, but with Maggie and the children—he swallowed hard. "What is it you're wanting, Johns?"

The man's look darted to Maggie, a few feet away.

Crane's hands squeezed into fists as rage flooded through him. He wanted to trample the man under Rebel's hooves.

Maggie shot Crane a hard look. He knew she knew. She held his gaze, tipping her head so slightly he knew no one would have noticed but him. Instantly he understood her intent, and he twitched in his saddle. *No, don't do it!* But he couldn't scream the words at her.

He widened his eyes, signaling he understood, and almost choked when her lips twitched.

Her hands tightened on the reins. She yelled and kicked Liberty's sides. The horse lunged forward, right into Johns, who threw his arms up to shield himself. Crane jerked the gun from the man's hand.

Maggie reined in, glowering down at Johns. "You're lucky I don't let my horse tromp all over you."

Crane hid a grin. Maggie would have taken great delight in doing so. He tucked the gun into his waistband and turned to face the man.

"Next time you feel like gettin' all hot and bothered about them sons of yers, you best make sure to get the story right." He nodded for Maggie and Ted to ride. "I'll be leaving yer gun out there." He nodded toward the road. "You can go and get it when it suits ya."

He reined around and paused. "Y'all have a nice day now," he said and trotted after the others.

As they rode away, the humor of the situation hit him, and he roared with laughter.

Maggie crunched her brows together. "What's so funny?"

"You. You're somethin' else." He couldn't stop grinning at her, enjoying the way her eyes widened at his words.

"What do you mean?" Her tone held a note of belligerence.

"Ain't you scared of nothin'?"

Her forehead furrowed. "I vowed I'd never turn away from nothing."

He chuckled. "Well, so far, I'd say you got a pretty good record."

Her eyes rounded. "You laughing at me?"

His grin widened. "Could be." He scratched his neck. "Or could be I'm just tickled."

Her gaze held a challenge. He knew his grin was as wide as the open prairie, but he couldn't seem to help it. And for the life of him, he couldn't say whether it was amusement or admiration that had him staring at her like a moonstruck cowpoke.

"Crane," Betsy sobbed. "I'm scared." Her eyes pooled with tears then overflowed in a glistening trail down each cheek. Her distress was like the sting of a whip.

"They ain't going to hurt you. Isn't that right, Ted?"

"You bet," the boy grunted.

Crane saw a reflection of his own concern in Maggie's eyes. Betsy had more than her fair share of scares in the past day or so. She'd do with some careful watching. On the other hand—he slanted a look at Ted—the boy was proving he had plenty of guts.

"They'll never catch us," he assured Betsy. "Not in that old wagon of theirs and with that old moth-eaten bag of bones pulling it."

Betsy giggled at his description of the horse.

"Why, I've seen better horses put out to pasture." Crane increased their pace a fraction. It was true—the Johnses didn't have a hope in the world of catching them, but he wasn't a man to test his luck.

"She puts me in mind of an old horse we got in a trade one time when we picked up a bunch for Mr. Burrows. I don't know how they slipped her in." He chuckled. "Turns out it was the same old crock Burrows had included in a trade three years earlier. I think she made the trip around a number of traders before someone finally took pity on her."

He amused them with more stories of his cowboy days until the sun hung high overhead. "There's another water tower."

They filled their canteens and watered the horses; then, remembering the roaring train of yesterday, they rode a distance from the tracks before taking a noon break.

After another cold lunch, Ted stood. "Think I'll take a walk."

"Where's Ted going?" Betsy asked, jumping to her feet as Ted and Cat sauntered away.

"He's stretching his legs for a bit."

Crane studied the child more closely. She rocked back and forth on her feet, twisting a corner of her skirt, her face screwed up with worry.

"We can see him real well." He waved his arms. "You could walk for a week without getting lost."

But she didn't relax.

Maggie eased to his side and leaned close, grabbing his arm to pull herself up to whisper in his ear. "She's been tense and restless all morning."

He broke into a cold sweat at her touch, and for a split second, he forgot his concern for the child. Then with iron self-control, he pushed aside his reaction to Maggie to focus on Betsy. "I don't know what we should do about her."

He held to his self-control by a thread as he breathed in Maggie's scent—rich with the smell of sage and fresh grass. A strand of hair wafted across his cheek. He closed his eyes and sucked in heated air.

"I don't see what we can do except let her know we'll take care of her."

He knew the minute she stepped away. It made it possible for him to breathe again.

Betsy remained fretful all afternoon, crying when they rode too fast, moaning that she was tired, and screaming in alarm when a rabbit bounced across the trail.

More than once Maggie gave Crane a worried look. He shrugged. He was worried about Betsy, too, but he didn't have a notion what to do about it.

Several times Crane caught a glimpse of a dark fringe off to the right. "You keep to the trail," he told Maggie. "I'm going to see if there's a creek over there." After ten minutes' riding, he suddenly overlooked a narrow, green valley with a band of dark water winding through it and trees crowding down the banks.

He pushed his hat back. "I'll be a skinned snake. If that ain't the nicest thing I've seen in many a day." He pushed his hat down firm on his head and raced back to the others.

"There's a good spot for camp over here," he called. It was early to stop, but maybe Betsy was plumb tired. She fussed as they set up camp and prepared a meal.

"You want to help cook some biscuits?" Crane asked her.

"No. Where's Maggie?"

"She's gone to get water."

It was the first time Betsy hadn't hung over his shoulder drooling as she waited for the food to cook.

When Maggie returned, Betsy grabbed her hand, pulling her close to Crane so she could hold his hand, too. "Ted, where are you?" she called. And when he answered, she insisted he sit in front of her.

"I have to get up to get the food." Maggie laughed, and Betsy reluctantly let her go. But as soon as they each had a plate, the child again insisted Maggie sit close. She only let go of Crane's hand to allow him to eat. His concern deepened considerably when she picked at her food.

Maggie noticed, too. "Betsy, aren't you hungry?"

"Not much." The child pushed her plate away. "I keep thinking I hear those people coming after us."

"Oh, sweetie." Maggie set her plate down and pulled Betsy to her lap. "You remember what I told you about God?"

Betsy pressed into her embrace. "What?"

"He'll always take care of us. Remember?"

The child tipped her head so she could see Maggie's face. "Was He taking care of us back there?"

Maggie stroked the tangled blond locks. "Well, we was scared, but nothing bad really happened. So I guess He was."

Crane considered her answer. Maybe he'd been thinking the same thing as Betsy, doubting as much as she, but what Maggie said made sense.

Betsy thought hard for a moment. "I was so scared. Especially when that bad man had a gun."

Crane laughed. "I don't think you need to worry, Betsy. Maggie will always come to our rescue." He sobered. "I'll never let anything happen to you, either, if I can help it."

"Me neither," Ted murmured.

A pleased look on her face, Betsy cuddled against Maggie. "I'm not so scared now."

Crane mussed her hair. "Good, 'cause it's hard to do anything with you holding on to us all."

She giggled a little and let Maggie set her aside to clean up.

That night, the four of them lay side by side. Maggie had read until Betsy fell asleep.

Ted's voice came out of the darkness. "Where was God when Pa sold me to that man?"

Crane tensed. How would Maggie explain this?

At first she didn't answer. Then she sighed deeply. "I don't know why bad things happen. I just know they do. Ma used to say it was because everybody can choose whether to do right or wrong, and when someone chooses wrong, then it starts a whole chain of events. And sometimes innocent people get hurt."

"You mean 'cause Pa did something wrong, I had to pay for it?" Ted's voice rose.

Crane felt the same incredulous disbelief. Why should Ted or, for that matter, Betsy pay for something they had no part in?

"Guess maybe whatever we do affects somebody else." Maggie's voice grew stronger. "But we needn't use it as an excuse." She wasn't making any sense.

"What do you mean?" Crane asked.

"Sometimes people say they're mean because someone was unfair to them. Or they say, 'If you had to live like I did, you wouldn't be so nice, either.' I don't think one has to lead to the other. Do you know what I mean?"

He grunted. "I guess."

"And don't you think God played a part when we 'happened' to ride down the road that 'happened' to go past the farm where Ted was and that we 'happened' to stop there to buy some food? Ted, what are the chances, do you suppose?"

"Not very good," the boy mumbled.

"Not a chance in the world we would have found you except for one thing." She paused for effect. "God. God led us there."

Crane let the thought settle into his mind. She had a point. Fact was she had made several of them that somehow managed to upset the way he figured things. He looked at the sky. The stars were so close, he felt he could reach out and grab a handful. Somehow God seemed just as close and real. The idea of God being close enough to touch made him feel warm and good inside.

Before it was light, he wakened to a strange sound. Immediately he recognized it was Betsy moaning in her sleep. She flung her arms out and moaned again. She must be dreaming.

He reached over and shook her. "Betsy, wake up." He jerked his hand back and sat bolt upright.

"Maggie." He reached over both children to shake her shoulder. "Maggie, wake up." But she shrugged. "Maggie," he insisted, shaking harder. "Come on—wake up."

She opened one eye slowly. "It's still nighttime." She pulled the covers to her chin.

"Maggie," he growled, trying to keep his voice down so he wouldn't disturb Ted. He shook her hard, like a dog shaking an old boot.

"What's the matter with you?" she groaned. "Can't you let a body sleep?"

"Not now. I think Betsy's sick."

Covering her eyes with her arm, she groaned. He watched her fight her way to consciousness. Slowly she sat up, leaning over her knees, her head lolling almost on her chest. "What did you say?" she finally managed.

"It's Betsy. I think she's sick."

"Oh."

He shook his head. It was a long ways from her ears to her brain. "Come on, Maggie. Wake up."

"I'm awake," she mumbled. "See—my eyes are open."

He waved a hand in front of her face. "Hello? Anybody home?"

"Very funny," she muttered. "Don't suppose coffee's ready."

"Not yet. I just woke up. Betsy was moaning. I thought she was dreaming, but she's hot."

"Well, why didn't you say so?" She shot him a cross look as she pushed blanket back and struggled to her feet, mumbling, "Life would be a lot simpler if people would just say what they wanted."

"What's the matter?" Ted sat up.

"I think Betsy's sick," Crane said. "Could you get up and get the fire going for coffee? I think your sister could use some."

Maggie bent over Betsy and felt her forehead. "She's fevered all right. Here, sweetie—let me check you over."

In the flare of Ted's fire, Maggie checked Betsy's back and tummy then looked over her legs. "I don't see any rash." She straightened. "I don't know what's wrong with her, but we won't be traveling today."

Of course they couldn't travel with a sick child. "How long do you suppose she'll be sick?"

She shrugged. "Your guess is as good as mine. That coffee ready yet, Ted?"

Crane took the cup of coffee Ted offered and sat deep in thought. Laying over gave the Johnses a chance to catch up. Then there was the problem of food. He had hoped to purchase some more supplies soon. He eyed the creek. A good place for game. He'd go hunting instead.

"I'm going to check on things," he announced and climbed the steep bank, lying on his stomach to watch the trail. He had a good clear view of the trail for miles. He turned toward the camp. It was down far enough that he was certain it would be invisible from the trail. "I'll just have to keep a careful watch," he muttered.

Returning to the camp, he found Maggie giving Betsy some water. "Food's ready," she murmured, nodding toward the fire.

He helped himself and, when he finished, said, "I'm going hunting." He turned to Ted. "I want you to climb that draw." He pointed toward the narrow vee leading to the crest of the bank. "Keep down but look sharp to the trail. Let Maggie know if anybody heads this way." He dug the pistol from his saddlebag and handed it to Maggie. "I need the rifle, but I'll leave this with you."

"We'll be fine."

Betsy slept, her cheeks flushed, her arms flung out.

"You sure?" He didn't mean only the risk of strangers.

Maggie gave him a direct look. "Sleep is probably the best thing for her." She waved a hand. "You go on now."

He hesitated, torn between the desire to guard them and the need for food; then nodding, he headed into the slight breeze. He saw evidence of abundant game but knew there would be none within sound of camp, so he kept a brisk pace along the bare banks of the creek for a spell then eased into the trees, moving more slowly and quietly. He saw several does with fawns at their sides, but it was some time before he spotted a young buck and brought it down with one shot. He dressed it out, taking as much meat as he thought they could use before it spoiled. Heaving the gunnysack of meat over his shoulder, he headed back.

When he could see the camp in the distance, he scoured the banks and caught a patch of dark indicating Ted's position. *Good boy.*

As he drew closer, he looked for Maggie. She lay close to Betsy, both sleeping. Her eyelashes drew dark half moons on her cheeks. The heat painted dull pink in her face, and her dark hair flung out like a glistening black spray. His steps faltered. She was so beautiful.

The child shifted, and Maggie sat up to check on Betsy. She saw Crane and smiled.

At the look of welcome in her eyes, his ribs clamped tight.

"You did all right." She lifted a finger to indicate the sack over his shoulder.

"Yup." He shrugged from under his burden. "How's Betsy?"

"Sleeping lots."

"That good or bad?"

"Seems good to me."

He washed the meat in the slow-moving water of the creek. Then, ignoring the heat, he built an efficient little fire and set several hunks of meat to roast.

"Broth would be good for Betsy," Maggie said, so he put a slab to boil.

Then he straightened. "I better relieve Ted." He climbed the hill to the boy. "See anything of note?"

Ted shrugged. "A couple of riders headed west. They didn't even look this way."

"Fine. You did a good job, son. Now go down and keep your sister company while I sit guard."

The day passed slowly. Ted brought him food at noon, but still Crane kept watch. Once or twice he thought it might all be for nothing, but he couldn't relax until he had seen the Johnses pass.

It was late afternoon before he heard the creaking wagon. They came into sight. Even without the noise, he would have known them. As he'd told Betsy, the horse was a sorry sight. So was the wagon—the canvas torn and flapping on one side. They ambled past without a sideways look and rattled on west.

Crane nodded. He watched the trail a bit longer. "That's that," he mumbled. Not to say there weren't other people they should be wary of, but he calculated the Johnses were the biggest threat they were likely to encounter for a few days, and he rejoined the others.

Betsy woke off and on during the evening and slept fitfully during the night. Crane got up several times to get her a drink or talk softly to settle her.

The next morning she sat up and said, "My froat hurts." Her hoarse voice was proof of her distress.

Maggie fixed warm tea and fed her several spoonfuls before the child lay down and slept.

Worry made Crane's insides stiff. He knew nothing about children and their illnesses.

Maggie met his searching look, and her expression softened. "Don't look so worried. I think she's some better."

"But her throat?"

"I know. But her fever is gone."

He looked at the sleeping child. It was true; her cheeks had lost the flush of yesterday. "Sure hope she's better soon."

Maggie shrugged. "We'll just have to wait until she is."

The enforced idleness proved difficult to bear. Ted and Crane took turns climbing the hill. Ted took Cat for a walk along the creek.

"I'll sit with Betsy awhile if you want to go, too," Crane offered.

Maggie's eyes lit. "I'd love to." She gave Betsy a long look. The child slept quietly.

"Thanks, Crane." She flashed him a wide smile.

Long after she was out of sight, Crane clung to the thought of that smile, so warm and— It felt as if she'd reserved that smile just for him. He'd been waiting for a sign from her that she was ready for more in their relationship. Was this it? He rubbed the back of his neck. Or was he grasping at straws tossed in the wind?

He had supper cooking when Maggie and Ted reappeared.

"Sorry to be gone so long," Maggie called. "We got to talking."

Betsy wakened and took more broth then drifted back to sleep.

"Ted and I were talking about what it was like when Pa turned to the bottle." Her blue eyes blazing at him made Crane's heart pound as if he'd run a footrace.

"I think about all Ted remembers is how afraid he was. Ma was gone. Pa was suddenly mean and unpredictable. And then I was gone for days at a time." Her voice thickened. "I tried to spare Ted, but it was impossible." She paused. "I will never understand why Pa suddenly turned against us."

Crane knew much of this and wondered why Maggie was bringing it up again.

Her eyes flashed. "I was thinking about how it must have been for you. How you must have felt." She stopped, and in the waiting silence, Crane knew she was expecting an answer.

"I don't remember much. It was so long ago," he murmured.

She blinked. "But you said your ma died this past winter."

He clenched his hands. How was he to explain? "Doesn't seem she was there all that much, then I was away working most of the time."

Her look insisted on more.

"I can't rightly remember a time when I had either parent."

"How did you feel?"

He turned to stare at the fire. "Like I said, it was a long time ago."

"I know." She paused. "But I think some things never let us go. For instance, will I ever really trust someone again after what Pa did? There's a little bit of me that says to watch out when things look good. There might be a sudden stop to it all.

"And Ted. Will he always jerk back when someone raises their hand? Do you suppose that years from now, if someone hurts him someway, he might withdraw into himself like he was when we found him?"

Crane didn't answer. How could he?

"What about you?" Her voice dropped to a whisper.

"What about me?"

She gulped before she answered. "Do you fear getting close to people, thinking if you do, they'll disappoint you, maybe even leave you?"

His fists balled into tight knots. "You crazy? Here I am with a wife and two children, and you say I avoid getting close." He pointed at the bedrolls side by side. "How much closer can you get than that?"

"I didn't mean to upset you," she murmured, her face filled with distress. "But that's not the kind of closeness I mean."

Her words stung. He had shared more of himself with Maggie than anyone before in his life, and here she stood accusing him of avoiding closeness. He shoved more wood on the fire. "I haven't the foggiest notion what you're talking about." Then he stalked to the creek bank.

How could he have hit so far from the mark? Here he was thinking Maggie was as attracted to him as he was to her, that any day now she would indicate she wanted more from their relationship; instead she dealt him a vicious blow to the gut. Where on earth did she get her crazy ideas?

"Crane?" Her worried voice stopped him in his tracks.

"What?" He barely managed to keep the annoyance from his voice.

"Are you really mad at me?"

He could hear the fear in her voice. It drove the anger from him. "I guess not."

"I'm sorry. I don't know what I was doing. Guess maybe talking to Ted started a bunch of fears and worries in my mind." She gulped, and her voice fell to a whisper. "Sometimes it's like I say, I think this is too good and something will happen to ruin it."

"What's too good?"

"Us. You and me and the children. Heading to a new home. All that."

"And what do you suppose could ruin it?"

"You could get fed up and leave."

It was the same old thing—Maggie wanting promises for happy ever after, a promise he couldn't make 'cause he had no way of being sure he could keep it.

"Maggie, I don't know what you want me to say or do. I've been a loner most of my life." He knew she would interpret that as proof he feared closeness, so he hurried on to explain. "Didn't have much choice. Cowboys drift from job to job. It don't give them much chance to make long-lasting friendships. My point is, this is the closest I've been to anybody since"—if he said, since he was a kid, she'd take that wrong, too—"since I left home to work. My point is, I'm doing the best I can." It stung to think it wasn't good enough for her.

"Crane." She grabbed his forearms. She was so close, he could feel her warm breath. "I am very, very sorry." Her arms stole around his waist, and she buried her head against his chest.

With a muffled groan, he wrapped his arms around her, his face in her hair.

"Please don't think I was complaining about anything you do. I guess I really don't know what I was trying to say." She paused. "Promise you won't leave us."

"Oh, Maggie," he groaned, barely able to sort out his thoughts. "I don't intend to leave. Why would I? This is the best I've ever known of life."

He could feel her nodding.

They stood hugging each other, offering comfort in the most basic of ways. But Crane knew a stirring deep within. A longing for more. The urgency of the feeling, the yawning depth of the emotion it exposed, sent a shudder up his spine.

"Maybe we should get back to camp."

Later, after they had all settled down for the night, Crane lay awake a long time. His anger had long ago disappeared; yet his mind went round and round with questions. Did he shy away from closeness as Maggie suggested? Or had she been goading him to make promises of security and happiness?

Why had he pulled away when there was every reason to think Maggie might have welcomed a kiss. . .and maybe even more?

What had she said about some things never letting us go? For the first time in years, he purposely turned his thoughts back to the time his pa left. How had he felt? But it was as he told Maggie; he could barely remember. He did remember how it left him feeling so exposed he'd promised himself he'd never let himself be open to that feeling again.

He folded his arms behind his head. Maybe Maggie was right. He cared about these people, but inside was a part of him he guarded. Put it down to experience, even maturity—a person had to keep back some portion of himself or face the threat of being destroyed.

Something tickled his nose, pulling him from his sleep, and he brushed it aside. A giggle close to his ear snapped his eyes open.

"Hi." Betsy giggled again. "It's morning."

"You must be feeling better."

"I'm hungry."

He snorted. "You're better." His arms snaked out and grabbed the little girl, pressing her to his chest. "And I'm glad."

She giggled and squirmed out of his arms, jumping to her feet. "Come on. It's time to get up."

He laughed as he jumped up. "And time to get breakfast?" he teased.

"Uh-huh."

There was a festive feeling as they broke camp and returned to the trail.

Chapter 9

They stopped early in the afternoon at a grove of trees set back from the road. Crane unsaddled the horses while Maggie and the children gathered wood. Later he and Maggie lingered over coffee while Ted and Betsy chased Cat through the trees.

"They both seem to be happy now, don't they?"

"Yeah, I reckon." He listened to their laughter and the rustling of the leaves. Didn't seem to take much to make them happy—full tummies and safety. "What about you, Maggie?"

"Me, what?"

"Are you happy? What does it take to make you happy?" He'd been aching to know. It festered that he seemed to have fallen short.

She stared at the fire a long time. He could tell by the way she pressed her finger to her bottom lip that she was thinking. "After Ma died, I didn't know if I could be happy again. I learnt to take care of myself. I could find a way to earn enough money to buy my food, and I made it clear I didn't put up with no nonsense. I was careful, too. But you know—"

She was sitting a few feet from him, but now she turned and leaned toward him, almost touching his knees, her face turned up at him. The light danced in her hair and slanted across her face, and he caught his breath at her beauty. All he had to do was lift his hand and cup her chin. But he kept perfectly still, wanting something more from her, though he couldn't say what.

She continued. "It wasn't enough."

It was as if his body acted of its own accord as he leaned forward, resting his elbows on his knees so their noses were but a few inches apart. Their gazes bridged the distance until he felt her intense stare reach down into his soul and stir a cauldron of emotions.

She swallowed hard and moistened her lips. "I guess part of it was I'd forgotten about God. But I think there was more to it. I found what I want right here."

His lungs felt like wood. His heart thundered in his ears. A silent cry called from deep inside. He didn't know what it was he wanted or how to still the cry; all he could do was wait for her to explain herself.

"It's this." She circled her hand to indicate the camp. "It's you and the children." Her gaze returned to him. "The people I care about."

His throat constricted for a heartbeat, then a warm feeling flooded upward. For the first time since last night, he could fill his lungs without his breath catching.

"How about you, Crane?"

"Huh?" Her question pulled him from his jumbled thoughts.

"What does it take to make you happy?"

"I'm easy to satisfy. My needs are simple, my wants few."

Happy wasn't something he'd given much thought to in the past. About the only dream he'd ever had was to move west when he was free to go.

Several days later, the sun was high in the brazen sky, pouring its fury upon their heads, when Ted, riding at Crane's side, mumbled, "Wagon ahead."

"I see." He'd seen it for a mile or so. "Slow down a bit. We'll take our time about catching up."

It was possible they had caught up to the Johnses, but he heard no ominous screech, and two horses seemed to be pulling the wagon. Besides, it rode with a certain grace the Johnses' wagon lacked.

Slowly they closed the distance until Crane could see two young boys perched on the tailgate. One turned to call something over his shoulder, and a man's head appeared around the side of the wagon. He waved a greeting.

Crane could now see the two boys well enough to make out that they were as alike as peas in a pod, the same sandy hair, the same blue eyes. He was sure every freckle matched.

"Twins." Maggie edged her horse closer to his side.

"Yup." He couldn't remember seeing twins before and forced his gaze away so he wouldn't be guilty of staring.

A quick glance to either side and he knew Betsy and Ted were as tense as broncs in a corral. He pushed his hat back and scratched his head. "You hold back while I ride on ahead." He slapped the reins and trotted up beside the driver. It was a young man and, at his side, a young woman with a babe in her arms. "Howdy," he called.

The man pulled the wagon to a halt. "Howdy. Saw you coming up behind us." He held out a hand. "Wally Strong. Pleased to meet you."

Crane shook hands as he made a quick assessment of the pair. They had frank, open expressions, friendly eyes, and wide smiles. He decided he liked them.

"My wife, Sally Jane." The man put an arm around his wife, pulling her close. Crane motioned the others forward and introduced them.

Matching faces poked out on either side of the parents, and Sally Jane laughed. "My boys, Matt"—she nodded to the one on her right—"and Mark"—she smiled at the one on her left.

Crane wondered how she could tell one from the other.

The infant squirmed, and Sally Jane sat her up. "And our daughter, Sarah."

The little one's eyes widened at the sight of so many strangers; then she saw Betsy and gurgled, reaching out her arms.

Betsy beamed. "She's so sweet."

"We were thinking about taking a noon break," Wally said. "Perhaps you folks would like to join us."

Crane felt everyone's gaze turn to him and nodded. "Why not?"

Over their meal Crane asked, "Where you headed?"

Wally looked thoughtful. "I've been looking for land that's good for farming." His gaze swept the horizon. "This appeals—no trees, level."

Crane nodded. "We're thinking to go as far as Calgary before we look for something."

As he talked, he watched Maggie holding the baby and talking to her. It looked so natural. Then Maggie lifted her head and met his eyes. A deep yearning stirred in the pit of his stomach. It looked so right to see Maggie with an infant. *If only it was mine.*

He swallowed hard. Where had that come from? He was grateful when Wally's voice drew him back to reality.

"We'll be settling before that. As soon as we find land close to the rail line."

"Wally," Sarah Jane called softly. "Ask them to ride with us for a spell."

He smiled at her across the clearing. "The very thing I was thinking." He held her gaze a moment more before he turned to Crane. "How about it?"

Crane saw the eager flash in Maggie's eyes. Perhaps it was just the thing they needed to erase the remnants of fear left by their encounter with the Johnses. "Sounds good." He was rewarded by a warm smile from Maggie.

They hadn't gone far when one of the twins crawled to his father's side. "Pa, can we get down and walk?"

"Us, too, Crane?" Betsy asked.

Wally reined in the wagon. "It's fine with me, if Crane approves."

"I don't know." Crane stared down the trail, pretending reluctance. "You might not be able to keep up. Or"—he rubbed his chin—"you might get lost."

"Aww," Betsy slumped.

"He's joshing us," Ted muttered, but the worried look didn't leave his face until Crane grinned and nodded.

Whooping, Ted jumped down, and Crane tied Ted's horse to the back of the wagon.

Ted raced down the road, shouting over his shoulder, "Can't catch me!"

The twins barreled off the wagon and tore after him.

"Hurry, Maggie," Betsy begged as Maggie reached around to hand her down. The child barely waited for her feet to touch the ground before she lit after them, calling, "Wait for me!" Cat raced after her.

Wally chuckled. "Could be we'll be the ones having to hustle to keep up." And he clucked at the horses. Maggie rode at Sally Jane's side. Sally Jane turned to her. "I can't help but notice the children call you by your first names. It seems a little unusual."

"They aren't our children," Maggie hastened to explain. "At least not in the usual way. Ted's my brother, and Betsy—"

"Betsy was a waif we found on our travels," Crane supplied.

"First day we were married." Maggie chuckled.

Crane pressed his lips together. He wished she hadn't said that. It was like begging for more questions. And he was right.

"Really." Sally Jane perked up. "How long have you been married then?"

"Almost a month." Maggie's tone said she regretted having opened the door to their curiosity.

Silence followed Maggie's answer. Crane stared straight ahead. He could almost hear their questions.

Sally Jane nodded. "Newlyweds then. Congratulations to you both."

Maggie murmured her thanks.

"A waif? Such a beautiful child." The young woman shifted so she could see Maggie better. "Tell me how you found her."

"Now, Sally Jane, it's none of our business," Wally warned.

"You're absolutely right. Forgive me, Maggie." She dipped her head to Crane. "You, too, Crane."

" 'S'all right," he murmured, feeling tight inside at her embarrassment. Suddenly he hooted with laughter. "But truth is—it's too good a story to keep to ourselves."

"Crane," Maggie muttered. Her cheeks stained dull red.

"You should have seen her square off against—" He searched for some way to describe Bull without being indecent. He finally said it the best way he could find. "Betsy has no parents, and this man thought he owned her."

Wally shot him a shocked look.

"Anyway, didn't matter to Maggie that he was bigger and meaner. She marched up to him bold as could be and ordered him to drop the child."

Sally Jane stared at him. "And did he?"

"He took some persuading." Crane chuckled.

"I threatened to shoot him," Maggie muttered.

Crane's smile deepened. Despite Maggie's uncomfortable squirming, he was afraid he'd pop the buttons on his shirt.

Then Wally chuckled, too. "Bet she led you a merry chase before you caught her."

Crane's mouth tightened. He wondered what they would say if he told them he met her, married her, and rode out with Betsy all in the space of a few hours.

"Don't remember her putting up much of a fight," he mumbled and, glancing out of the corner of his eyes, saw the tips of Maggie's ears turn bright red.

They overtook the children at that point.

"Cat keeps yowling to be carried!" Ted called.

Wally slowed the wagon. "Put her in the back."

Ted set the cat inside, and the children dropped behind, skipping along in the dust.

They rode together the rest of the day and by mutual consent pulled into a treed area for the night.

"Boys, gather up some firewood," Wally told the twins.

"Come on, Ted," one of them called, and the boys scampered away.

Betsy hung close to Sally Jane. "Can I hold the baby?"

"Of course you can." Sally Jane patted the ground beside her. "You sit right here, and you can hold her as long as you like."

The baby stared at Betsy then cooed. Crane had heard others speak about heartstrings being tugged, but this was the first time he'd felt it.

He turned to Wally. "Let's go find some fresh meat."

"Do you need anything before I go?" Wally addressed his wife.

Sally Jane waved a hand, her focus on the baby. "You go ahead."

They found partridges and a couple of rabbits. As they returned, the smell of wood smoke and coffee greeted them. Maggie and Sally Jane looked up as the men approached.

Crane watched the eager way Sally Jane's gaze sought her husband. It brought a hollow feeling to his chest. He turned his eyes in Maggie's direction. She smiled at him. It wasn't the same intimate kind of look the other couple had exchanged, but it was warm and welcoming, and it made him want to laugh out loud.

"This is real nice, isn't it, Sally Jane?" Wally turned to Crane to explain. "She's been missing home and wishing she had someone to visit with." He chortled. "Guess she's getting tired of what I have to say."

Sally Jane laughed. "I never get tired of you, and you know it." Then she sobered. "But sometimes I think I've heard all I want about the virtues of plows and wheat and oxen." Her eyes twinkled at her husband. "It's nice to talk to someone about other things."

Crane fixed the carcasses on a spit, but his thoughts tumbled over each other. He knew he wasn't real good company on the trail, content to ride for hours without saying a word. Until now it hadn't mattered. But suddenly he wondered if Maggie wished for better company. He promised himself he'd try harder to find things she liked to talk about.

Wally turned to Maggie. "How are you enjoying the trail?"

She seemed surprised he had asked.

Crane's hands stilled as he waited for her answer.

"Just fine."

Her words sounded sincere, and Crane bent over his task, pleased he had passed muster.

"Maggie's made of pretty tough stuff," Sally Jane murmured. "She was telling me some of the things that have happened to her recently."

Crane perked up. Was their marriage one of the things that had "happened" to Maggie?

"What things?" Wally asked kindly.

Maggie swallowed hard and explained about her mother's death, her father's changed behavior, and how she'd lost track of Ted for a while.

"Wow!" Wally rubbed his chin. "You really have been through the rocks, haven't you?" His expression gentle, he asked, "How are you doing now?"

Crane watched the expressions play across Maggie's face as she considered Wally's question. "I still miss my ma." Her voice thickened.

At the sound of her distress, Crane took a step toward her then halted, crossing his arms over his chest.

"But my anger at Pa has gone, and it's left me able to remember all sorts of good things. We were a happy family until Ma died. I don't want to forget that. And I especially don't want Ted to forget."

"You young folk have a mighty lot on your plate," Wally murmured. "We wish you all the best." He hesitated. "And if we can help in any way, you let us know."

Maggie murmured her thanks.

Absently, Crane mumbled agreement. It was the first time he'd realized that acquiring two children carried such a heavy load, and he wondered if he'd grabbed himself a wild bronco. Then he relaxed. He'd always been the one to go for the rankest horse in the outfit 'cause he'd sooner have a horse with guts and spirit than a lead-footed nag. As he turned to check the meat, he grinned. Guess he was the same way about life. Somehow he knew he'd never have a dull moment with Maggie at his side.

After supper Sally Jane brought out a pair of scissors. "Come on, you two." She nodded at the twins. "I want to get rid of some of that hair while there's still light enough to see." She wrapped a towel around one boy and set to work cutting his sandy locks. Then she did the same to the other. Finished, she held the scissors toward Maggie. "Maybe you'd be wanting to borrow these."

Maggie's head jerked up, then she grinned at Crane. "Sounds like a good idea." She crooked her finger at him.

"Me?" He needed a haircut. Had for weeks. But it never crossed his mind he'd get it from Maggie. The idea of her hands in his hair made his mouth go dry.

"Why not? I used to cut Ted's hair all the time."

He purposely looked at Ted. The boy's hair was only getting long enough to be sure it was light brown.

"You can't blame me for that." She waited, a towel in one hand, those wretched scissors in the other. "Not afraid, are you?" she jeered.

He narrowed his eyes. "Of you or those scissors you're holding like a branding iron?" She shrugged as Wally chuckled.

Knowing he was beat, Crane pushed to his feet. He could use a good diversion right now. Say a stampede.

The fire crackled like an old woman laughing. The children squealed and laughed as they chased through the trees. But nothing came to his rescue.

Forcing his lungs to expand and his eyes to obey, he lifted his gaze upward.

Fascinated, he watched a small pulse throbbing in Maggie's throat.

He tried to quiet the pounding from a surging pulse deep in his chest. Despite his determination to breath normally, his throat tightened, and he could barely suck in a gasp. His ears pounded with a deafening roar. Was it desire he saw in her eyes? Or—he forced a shaft of air into his lungs—was it simply a challenge?

He felt Wally and Sally Jane watching him and forced himself to lumber to the stool. Stiffly he sat on the smooth wood, bracing the toes of his boots in the dirt. She wrapped the towel around his shoulders. He could feel her warmth as she stood behind him. Then she ran her fingers through his hair. Fire ignited his nerves.

"Been awhile?" Her low voice fueled the fire.

His thoughts choked. *Your hair, you idiot, she's talking about your hair.* "Yup," he croaked.

"How short you want it?"

"Short." *Short enough so I never have to go through this delicious torture again.*

"Short it is."

Her hands lifted a strand of hair, and she snipped it. Other sounds faded. There was nothing but the *snip, snip, snip* of the scissors. And her nearness.

He was drowning in her nearness. Her arm brushed his shoulder. Her thigh glanced across his knee. She reached out and touched his chin with a fingertip.

"Let's see how it looks."

His lungs like steel bands, he raised his head. But he looked past her shoulder. If he met her eyes, he would lose all control.

"Not too bad so far," she murmured, her breath grazing his face, sweet as honey, warm as the summer's breeze.

Betsy skidded into the circle of light. "Whatcha doing, Crane?" She leaned against his knee.

"You're gonna get hair all over you."

She grabbed a handful as she straightened, stroking it with her fingers before she pulled a lock of her own hair forward and lifted Crane's to it to compare. "Same as mine."

Betsy's was much lighter and curly, but Crane agreed. "Just about."

Satisfied, she scampered away.

Maggie stood in front of him now. "Just about done." She leaned across his knees. He felt her muscles tense and shift as she lifted her arms and took a handful of hair. She was so close. She smelled of coffee and supper and the baby she'd held. He wanted to tell her to stop. To leave the rest uncut. He wanted to beg her never to stop. He closed his eyes, wishing his ordeal was over.

By the time she finished, his muscles ached. He jerked to his feet to brush the hair off then grabbed a cup of coffee, desperate to relieve the parched feeling in the back of his throat.

Wally stood and stretched. "Just look at that sunset!"

Flames of pink and orange and red flared across the sky.

"It's beautiful," Sally Jane murmured, going to her husband's side, leaning against him as he wrapped an arm around her shoulders.

" 'The sky is the daily bread of the eyes,' " Wally quoted. "You don't see much more sky than you do out here on the prairies."

Crane met Maggie's gaze and knew she was thinking the same as he: a bit too much sky, a bit too much nothing.

They called the children in.

"Can we sleep over there?" Matt, or was it Mark, pointed toward a clump of bushes.

"As long as you stay where we can see you." Wally handed them each a bedroll.

Crane handed Betsy her roll, but she looked up at him. "Where you going to sleep, Crane?"

"Right here." He grabbed his bundle and flipped it open a few feet from the fire.

She nodded and unrolled her bedding next to his then stood over it, waiting for Ted to put his beside hers. "Now you, Maggie." Maggie silently obeyed.

Crane saw the glance that passed between Wally and Sally Jane, and he knew they must be wondering about the sleeping arrangements, but he didn't offer any explanation.

Maggie waited until the children were settled then turned to the Strongs. "Crane brought his ma's Bible with him. I've been reading aloud from it every night. Do you mind?"

Sally Jane swallowed hard. "My father always read aloud at suppertime. I miss it."

Wally stared at his wife. "Why, dear, you never told me that."

She shrugged. "Maybe it's leaving them all behind that makes me remember little things we used to do." She patted his knee. "Don't look so worried."

Silently he squeezed her hand.

Maggie waited while Crane filled his cup and got comfortable on his bedroll before she began. He didn't mean to be irreverent, but he found her voice settled through him, like sand filtering through water, until it reached its limit. A hundred things rose and flitted away before he could grab them and figure them out. Longings. Wishes. Waiting.

She closed the Bible. He hadn't heard a word.

Sally Jane sighed. "That was nice."

Ted sat up. "What does it mean?"

"It means God loves you so much He sent His only Son, whom He loved, so we—you—could live with Him forever. That's what eternal life means."

"Did He love me when I was at Dobbs's place?"

Crane had never asked, and it was the first time Ted had referred to the man by name.

Maggie wrapped her arms around him. "Of course He did." She brushed his hair back. "Did you think I had stopped loving you?"

He shook his head. "But you couldn't find me."

"That's right. Sometimes things keep people apart, but it doesn't stop their love. Same way with God. He doesn't stop loving us because somebody does something bad to us."

"You sleep now," Maggie said. She walked to the fire. Crane joined her, filling her cup then his own.

Sally Jane sat nearby, nursing the baby. Wally took her a cup of coffee then sat beside her.

"I can't tell you how good it's been to find you people," Sally Jane murmured.

"It's been good for us all," Maggie said. "I think Betsy and Ted have finally forgotten the Johnses."

"The Johnses?"

Maggie and Crane filled them in on their experience.

"You surely must have God's hand of protection on you," Wally said, shaking his head. "Otherwise, I don't know how you manage to get yourselves out of so many scrapes."

Maggie agreed. "I'm beginning to see that God works in many ways—big and small—when we aren't paying the least bit of attention."

Wally stretched. "Well, my dear, I think we should go to bed." He took the baby in one arm and pulled his wife to her feet, wrapping his other arm around her as he led her to the wagon.

Long after he settled down for the night, Crane heard the other couple murmuring together. *They have something special,* he thought. Something he wished he had with Maggie. He tucked his arms under his head and reminded himself he and Maggie were just beginning. They could afford to take their time. He could afford to wait for Maggie to show she was ready for more.

Chapter 10

They rode with the Strongs the next day.

"Any objection to stopping?" Wally said when they saw a line of trees.

"Nope," Crane conceded. They'd made good time all day. Besides, he wasn't in a tearing hurry.

"It's beautiful," Sally Jane said as they pushed their way through to the clearing and saw a grassy slough. "Now I can wash a few things."

The boys gathered wood, while Crane and Wally hauled water.

A little later Crane stretched out, enjoying his coffee. Maggie sat on a stool, bent over the baby, crooning. Garments of all descriptions hung on the bushes and branches. Wally and Sally Jane had gone for a walk.

He sat down beside Maggie. The baby looked at him and gurgled. When he held his hand toward her, she grabbed his index finger and pulled, chuckling.

"She likes you," Maggie said.

"She likes everybody." But he grinned, pleased at the baby's friendliness and Maggie's assessment.

"We're back," Wally called, stepping from the trees.

"How's my sweetie?" Sally Jane asked, her attention on the baby.

"Happy as a lark." Maggie reluctantly handed the infant to her mother. "She's a real sweetheart."

"I know." Sally Jane buried her nose against the baby's neck, and Wally stroked the tiny head.

"The children will be clamoring for something to eat soon," Wally said, and he and Sally Jane began preparing supper.

After the meal the children did not disappear into the trees. Crane decided they must be tired after a long afternoon of play. Several times he thought a look passed between one of the children and Sally Jane. He couldn't rid himself of the feeling that something was up. Something he should probably know about.

He was reaching for another cup of coffee when Ted sidled up to him. "Crane," he began, "Betsy and me, we'd like to sleep with Matt and Mark tonight. Can we, please?"

Crane looked at Betsy.

"Please, Crane?" she begged.

"It's fine with me," Sally Jane said.

He studied Betsy and Ted. "You sure?"

They both nodded.

He turned to Maggie. "What do you think?"

"We'll be right here if they need us."

Crane nodded, and the children sprang to get their bedding. He turned to Maggie, muttering, "I'm betting they don't get much sleep."

She nodded.

Their beds ready, the children came back to the fire.

Wally cleared his throat. "You folks can enjoy an evening to yourselves." At the twinkle in Wally's eyes and his kindly smile, Crane's cheeks grew hot.

He heard Maggie's sharp gasp, but he dared not look at her.

"It's a surprise," Betsy said, her voice high with excitement.

Ted pulled at Crane's hands. "Come and see."

Sally Jane smiled widely. "We all worked on it."

Crane's insides felt brittle as he rose and let them lead him away from the fire. Maggie followed, as mute as he.

They circled the slough water and turned around a large clump of bushes.

"There it is!" they called. "Just for you."

Crane stared. A pile of wood lay ready to light. A coffeepot sat on a rock. A small lean-to of willow branches squatted within comfortable distance of the fire. He narrowed his eyes. Someone had placed their bedrolls in the tiny enclosure. His mouth turned as dry as sand as he understood their intent. He wouldn't deny he'd been longing for this day, but to be railroaded into it made him feel as awkward as a gangly newborn colt.

"Come on, children. Let's go back to our fire." Wally shepherded the children away.

Crane couldn't bring himself to look at Maggie. She cleared her throat, a grating sound screeching through his mind. "Might as well start the fire."

The fire caught and flared upward, and he stared at the flames. Ignoring the steel bands that had once been his ribs, he stepped closer. A pair of logs had been placed to sit on. He thought of sitting but couldn't seem to get the message to his legs.

The fire crackled, and a log snapped, the sound thundering along his nerves. The sharp smell of wood smoke filled his nostrils. It was all as familiar as his own name; yet tonight the scents and sounds tugged at his senses, stirring reactions totally unfamiliar. The coffee bubbled, and the smell flooded his brain.

"Coffee smells good." Was that croaking sound his voice?

She reached for the cups, and the movement drew his gaze to her. Her hair hung over her shoulders like a shiny curtain; the fire flared, sending shafts of light through the dark strands. He closed his eyes. His heart beat a tattoo inside his head.

"Coffee?"

Her voice started a riot along his nerves. He blinked and managed to take the cup she offered. Their glances touched then danced away.

She sat on one of the logs. Coffee sloshed over the edge of his cup and stung his hand. He sucked in his breath, welcoming the pain that forced him to breathe again.

He heard her sigh softly. It was all he needed—that little sound of distress. He dropped to the other upturned log and immediately wondered if it had been wise. They were so close, he could feel the warmth from her body, smell her sweetness. As he lifted his cup to drink, his elbow brushed hers. He gulped the scalding coffee.

"I had nothing to do with this," Maggie murmured, her words so low Crane could barely hear them. Or was it the pounding of his thoughts that almost drowned out her words?

"Me either."

"I suppose you can't blame them for thinking we'd be pleased."

"Yup." Was she pleased?

"After all," she hurried on, "they don't know that we've never. . ." She shrugged. "That with the children and all. . ." She trailed to a halt.

A smile tugged at the corners of Crane's mouth. Maggie, his sweet, innocent bride, always ready to state the facts boldly, was suddenly unable to speak her mind. The tension in him eased, and he leaned back. He was not one to bulldoze his way through life. The strain fled from across his shoulders. He was more than willing to let Maggie set the pace tonight. Whatever she wanted was fine with him. They had a lifetime to learn about each other and to find what pleased the other. He had no need or desire to break down gates.

"I hope the children will be all right," she said.

"They'll miss you reading to them, I expect."

"I expect." Silence settled around them, easy and comfortable.

"They sure are enjoying having some playmates," she said after a spell.

"They're a good bunch."

It had grown quite dark. To the east Crane saw a fork of lightning. "Looks like a storm building."

Maggie's head jerked up. "Where?"

Another jab of lightning was followed by distant rumbling. "It's a ways off," he said.

Flash followed flash. The thunder rolled and echoed across the plain, and the storm drew closer. Leaves rustled, and the trees bent low, creaking under the force of the wind. Off to his right, Crane heard a branch crack.

The lightning was spectacular, forking across the sky in vivid paths. As the storm approached them, the thunder increased in volume. Maggie clamped her hands to her ears.

"Does it scare you?" he asked after the noise had rumbled away.

"I hate thunder." She shivered.

He reached for her then pulled back, afraid she would find his touch as frightening as she found the thunder. Then it boomed again. She turned into his arms, her face against his chest. His nerves echoed the flash and roar of the storm.

It was only that she was afraid of the thunder, he warned himself. Her quivering body in his arms had nothing to do with him.

The wind carried a sprinkle of cold raindrops.

"We better get out of this." He eased her toward the tiny shelter. She followed without protest. Each roar of thunder sent a shudder through her, and she clung to him. His heart thundered its own response.

He pulled her inside and eased her to the ground, lowering himself beside her. The willow branches gave off a fresh smell. The enclosure was very small. He closed his eyes. A chill wind tore across the clearing and into the shelter. "It must have hailed somewhere," he said.

Maggie shivered in his arms. Her teeth rattled. "I'm so cold," she said, chattering.

He threw more wood on the fire. For a moment the logs lay dark and dead then flared into flames that threw a blanket of warmth toward them. Crane studied the sky. "I believe the storm is moving away."

But despite the passing storm and the increased warmth of the fire, Maggie continued to shiver. "I can't seem to get warm," she said.

"Crawl between the blankets." He pulled her boots off and helped her slide down into the bedroll. "Is that better?"

Her teeth rattling, she said, "I'll get warm in a bit."

He threw more wood on the fire, poured himself another cup of coffee, then huddled back in the shelter, his knees brushing her shivering form. "You still not warm?"

"No."

He squeezed the cup until his knuckles cracked. The storm had passed, circling to the south of them, so the thunder he heard had to be inside his head. He filled his lungs then held his breath for a heartbeat. And another. Slowly he let the hot air escape through his open mouth. He eased down beside Maggie, his body matching hers, legs to legs, hips to hips, shoulders to shoulders, separated by the layer of blankets. His hand shaking like leaves in the wind, he lifted the covers.

"Come here—I'll warm you up." He pulled her into his arms.

She came willingly.

His senses flooded with her scent and the feel of her small, lean body. Her hair whispered against his cheek. He closed his eyes. She would never guess how much he ached for them to be truly man and wife. It would take every ounce of his self-control, but he clamped down on his back teeth, promising himself he would not allow his needs and wants to rule his actions.

Slowly her shivering subsided, and she lay soft and relaxed in his arms.

"I've wondered—" She broke off quickly.

"Wondered what?"

She swallowed loudly then rushed on. "How it would feel to be in your arms like this."

Blood surged through his veins. "I've wondered—" Dare he say anything more? Would she jerk away and retreat to the far corner of the lean-to? He smiled. Not that such a move would put much distance between them. He began again. "I've wondered what your lips would taste like."

She slowly lifted her face. In the golden glow of the fire, he could see her faint smile. His heart threatened to explode, then, accepting her unspoken invitation, he found her lips. It was a gentle, chaste kiss, but he discovered her lips were cool and yielding.

"Soft and sweet," he said. And driving him to want more.

She gave a short laugh. "Warm and cozy."

He knew she was referring to his arms, and he laughed deep in his chest. He felt her straining toward him and took her lips again, this time his kiss deeper, firmer. Her arms stole upward to encircle his neck. He buried his hands in her thick, silky hair.

❧

Crane woke the next morning as pink light gently colored the sky. Maggie lay curled beside him, her hands bunched together under her chin. He filled his senses with her, taking in every detail—the dark fringe of eyelashes across her cheek, her complexion as pretty as the morning sky with the first rays of sunshine.

He'd never seen a sight that gave him more pleasure. He'd never been happier than he was right now, and he breathed deeply, filling each pore with joy.

He took his fill of watching her then eased himself from under the covers, humming softly as he rekindled the fire and put on a fresh pot of coffee.

"Crane." A little whisper came from some nearby bushes.

"You can come out now, Betsy." He'd known she was there for several minutes. She hurried to his side, leaning against his shoulder.

"What are you doing up so early?" he asked.

"I missed you."

"I missed you, too." He hugged her.

"Was it a good surprise?"

"A very good surprise."

"Then I don't mind missing you for one night."

He smiled. "Do Mr. and Mrs. Strong know you're here?"

She nodded. "Mrs. Strong was feeding the baby. She saw me go."

The coffee boiled, and Crane reached around the child to get a cupful.

"When's Maggie going to wake up?"

Crane shrugged. "I don't know. Do you suppose we should help her?" He had to hold the child back. "Maybe we should do it together." Not for anything would he miss the chance to see Maggie's expression when she first opened her eyes.

He hunkered down at her side, releasing Betsy, who threw herself across Maggie's chest.

"Maggie, wake up." She patted Maggie's cheeks.

Maggie's eyes opened slowly. Crane couldn't breathe as he waited for that moment when she'd see him. She saw Betsy first and groaned. "Who let you in?"

The child leaned back. "Crane did. He said I could wake you up."

"He did, did he?" And her gaze found him.

His heart slammed into his ribs. Half-awake, her eyes dark as deep water, she looked so kissable he could hardly stand it. He smiled, not caring that he probably looked like a love-struck fool.

Her cheeks darkened, and her gaze danced away.

"Come on, Maggie—get up." Betsy shook her.

Maggie tried to pull the covers to her chin. Crane caught a glimpse of her bare shoulder, and his mouth dried. Perceiving her difficulty, he caught Betsy in his arms. "Come on, little Miss Betsy. Let's go see how Mrs. Strong is doing."

As they ducked into the open, he whispered over his shoulder, "We'll give you a few minutes."

He and Betsy returned to the main camp. Sally Jane was leaning over the fire, frying bacon. "There you are. Join us for breakfast."

Crane waited for Betsy to settle beside Sally Jane, then he headed back.

"Good morning, Maggie." She sat next to the fire, nursing a cup of coffee. She lifted her gaze. Dark, questioning, and—dare he hope—warm with a just-kissed, just-loved, and mighty-happy-about-it expression.

"Did you have a good night?"

"Slept good." She swirled the coffee around in her cup then nodded toward the others.

"How are things over there?"

"Good." He held himself tight, wanting her to say something about last night, wanting her to give him some indication of how she felt. But she only tipped her mug back and forth, studying the dark liquid.

There's time, he warned himself. *Plenty of time. Give her all the time she needs. She's such a young thing.*

The smell of bacon wafted through the trees and made his mouth water. "They said to come for breakfast."

"Guess I'm ready." She went to the shelter and rolled up the bedrolls.

Crane stared after her. Guess that's that. Unfolding arms that were suddenly stiff, he doused the fire and gathered up their few items.

Her arms loaded with bedding, Maggie headed toward the other campsite without looking back. With his heart suddenly cold and heavy, he followed.

Sally Jane looked up, smiled, and ducked her head. Crane wondered what Sally Jane saw that made her look so pleased.

Maggie plunked down and grabbed another cup of coffee. Ted sidled up to her, and she rubbed his hair.

Betsy danced to her side. "We're having bacon and hotcakes. Don't they smell good?" She turned to Sally Jane. "How long 'til it's ready?"

Sally Jane laughed. "Quick as a wink. That is, if Maggie doesn't mind holding Sarah so I can use both hands."

Maggie's smile returned as she reached out and took the baby.

Everything was back to normal, Crane thought later as he threw the saddle over Rebel's back. But things had changed. Even if Maggie seemed set on showing she preferred things to be the same.

He slapped the saddlebags on. Rebel snorted and backed away. "Sorry, old boy. Didn't mean to take it out on you."

If that was the way Maggie wanted it to be, well, so be it. It took time to become truly man and wife. One night alone under the stars didn't make it signed, sealed, and delivered.

He finished with the horses and paused, resting his hands on the worn, bulky pack. He was balking because she'd pulled at the reins.

He slowly filled his lungs. *Let her set the pace,* he cautioned himself. A colt broken with patience and gentleness was always a better horse than one broken by force. He figured people weren't all that different.

His laugh was more snort as he thought of how Maggie would react if she knew he'd compared her to a horse. Quite sure of her outspoken reaction, he grinned as he led the horses to camp.

Maggie's eyes widened as she stared at him.

He pushed his hat back from his forehead and grinned at her, delighting in the emotions racing across her face. Surprise, wonder, and a flare of something he decided he would take as interest. There was a definite crackle in the air between them.

As he turned to get organized to hit the trail, he hummed tunelessly.

Chapter 11

The sun was hot and the sky so bright it hurt the eyes. The children rode quietly in the wagon. Even the adults made little conversation, the heat sucking at their energy.

Crane watched Maggie out of the corner of his eye. As the morning progressed, she slumped over her chest. He dropped back until he was at her side. "Are you all right?" he murmured, touching her arm.

She jolted up, blinking. "Just hot and tired."

"Maybe we should pull up for the day and wait this heat out." He studied the landscape but saw nothing offering relief.

"No. I'm fine. Besides, how do we know how long it will last?" She glanced at the horizon and shuddered. "Let's keep going and get out of these prairies as quick as we can."

"I'm with you on that," he muttered.

Wally, overhearing part of their conversation, said, "This heat is good growing weather."

Wally could be right for all Crane knew, though he wondered about the lack of rain. Even the thunderstorm last night had produced nothing but a few drops.

By noon the heat was almost unbearable. They pulled to the side of the road and sought the shelter of the wagon.

Baby Sarah fussed.

"Poor wee mite can't take the heat," Wally said, his look forbidding the twins to complain. "Sponge her off, and see if that will help."

Sally Jane did as her husband suggested then nursed the baby.

"We might as well push on," Wally said. "Sally Jane, you and the baby stay in the wagon, out of the sun."

She climbed in back, and the twins sat on the tailgate.

Crane helped Maggie and the children mount.

"I don't blame Sarah," Betsy whispered as he lifted her up behind Ted. "I'm so hot I want to cry."

"I know, little bit. I promise we'll stop if we find some trees or water."

But by late afternoon they had found nothing but a solitary water tower. Crane opened the spout, letting the water cascade over the children. They filled their canteens and watered the horses.

"There must be a dam close by to fill this tower." Wally shielded his eyes against the brittle glare and studied the lay of the land.

"There's a furrow where the pipeline runs." Crane pointed to the north. "But

I see nothing but flat prairie."

Wally shrugged. "It could be miles."

"I'll ride over and have a look-see."

Crane rode three miles or more before he found the dam tucked in a deep coulee. Plenty of water was there, but not so much as a twig of a tree. Nothing but scrub buck brush and wild rose bushes loaded with blossoms from white to deep pink. He breathed deeply of the sweetness then turned back. "We're just as well off here."

Maggie sighed. "Then let's get set up."

Wally pulled the wagon off the trail, angling it to provide a band of shade. He pulled a tarp from the back. "Let's tie this to the side of the wagon. It will help some."

It was too hot for a fire, and with nothing but twigs to burn, they settled for cold meat and biscuits. Crane opened two cans of peaches.

Ted leaned against a wheel, casting a dark look toward the twins. Even Betsy looked fit to go bear hunting.

"You probably won't believe this," Crane began, "but I'd sooner ride in this heat than in a cold rain." He leaned over his knees. "I recall a time we was trailing cows north from down in the States, and it had been raining for five days."

The children faced him.

"Have you ever tried to build a fire in the rain? Or cook a pot of stew with water pouring down into the pot?" He shook his head. " 'T'weren't Cookie's fault, but he was getting the butt of all the complaints."

He glanced around at his listeners. "I want to tell you—you don't want to run into a bunch of cold, wet, hungry cowboys who haven't had decent coffee in days." He chuckled.

"Well, sir, a couple of the boys was really riding Cookie. He threw down his spoon in disgust and muttered, 'Don't see none of yous doing anything but bellyachin'.' And stomped away. But don't you think them old boys had heard the last of it. Cookie waited until they had gone to sleep then scraped out the pot and dropped a good-sized spoonful of stew on a couple of pairs of boots." Crane grinned at the boys, who sat forward, hanging on his every word.

"Seems Cookie knew some coyotes were slinking about and figured he'd get the last laugh. That night the coyotes found the stew."

Wally started to chuckle.

"What happened?" Ted asked.

"They licked up the stew clean as a whistle then went for the boots. Well, you can imagine what the boys had to say when they woke up and found their boots half-chewed up."

The children stared at him, wide-eyed, their mouths hanging open. Betsy was the first to laugh, then the twins joined in.

"I bet they was real mad," Betsy said.

"Serves them right," Ted muttered. Then a slow grin crossed his face. "I'd like t've seen it."

Crane shrugged. " 'Course they could never be sure it was Cookie's fault."

"You wouldn't have had anything to do with it, would you?" Maggie asked.

He shrugged, barely able to think with her eyes sparkling at him. "I was just a boy. Just the cook's helper."

"Great story," Wally said. "Bet you got a dozen of them."

Crane tore his gaze from Maggie. "You hear a lot of things around a campfire."

"No doubt." Wally turned to the boys. "You two get ready for bed."

Crane nodded at Betsy and Ted. "You, too."

After the beds were rolled out, he took the Bible to Maggie. "Might be a good time to read about the flood," he muttered. "All that water sounds good in a place like this."

She choked back a laugh. "You think I should avoid stories of fire and brimstone tonight?"

"Good idea," he murmured.

Her gaze held him, unblinking and dark. And questioning. He was caught in a rushing stream of emotion. What was she wanting? He waited, hoping she would explain.

"You going to read, Maggie?" Betsy's voice rang across the narrow space.

Maggie blinked and lowered her eyes, but not before Crane got the feeling he had disappointed her.

He turned away, crossing his arms over his chest. He was no good at guessing games. She should know that. In fact, one of the things he'd grown to appreciate about her was her directness. Now all of a sudden she had this—this something she wasn't being direct about.

She read the story of Abraham sending his servant to find a wife for his son, Isaac. At the words about Isaac taking Rebekah to his tent and making her his wife, her voice trembled and she hurried to the end.

Crane kept his head lowered, watching from under his eyelashes, barely hearing the last few words. Something about Isaac loving her and being comforted.

He chewed his lip. It hadn't been a tent, only a tiny shelter built from willow branches. But he'd made her well and truly his wife. And it could be comforting if only he knew what she thought.

Sally Jane's voice interrupted his thoughts. "Read again the part where the servant said the Lord had led him."

Maggie found the place and read it again.

Sally Jane sighed. "That's comforting to know God will lead us to the right spot."

Maggie looked up. "I remember a picture Ma had. Probably still hanging up at home. It was of the good shepherd rescuing a lamb that had fallen over a cliff."

Crane could hear the smile in her voice.

"Ma used to say sometimes we don't follow so good and get ourselves into trouble, but even then God doesn't leave us. He comes and finds us. You remember that, Ted?"

"Uh huh."

"I guess that's what He did."

Sally Jane leaned closer. "What do you mean?"

"I'd lost my way. There's no other way to say it. Then God sent Crane, and Crane had this Bible, and I remembered all the things I'd forgotten."

Crane looked at his boots. It wasn't the first time she'd said something that made him feel as if she were calling him some kind of savior. And he wasn't. The idea made him twitch.

Sally Jane spoke again. "God's made you into a special and unique family."

Crane looked around. She was right. They were a family. He and Maggie, Ted and Betsy. A different kind of family but for sure a family. And they'd find themselves a place out West and make a new life. No looking back.

Maggie put away the Bible.

"Let's do like Abraham's servant and ask God to guide us." Sally Jane reached out to take Maggie's and Wally's hands.

Maggie took Crane's hand. A shock raced up his arm. He steadied himself as he reached for Betsy's hand. The children joined hands until they formed a circle, then Wally prayed aloud for God's guidance and protection. A gentle quietness held them after his "amen." Without speaking, they found their bedrolls.

Crane heard Wally whisper, "Good night, dear," and kiss his wife.

Betsy shuffled and squirmed, trying to get comfortable.

A light wind came up, carrying the heat of the day, but it stirred the air and eased their discomfort.

Maggie sighed.

Crane ached to ask her what was troubling her, but every word would be overheard. He turned on his side and waited for sleep to come.

❧

The heat still hung over them the next morning. They stopped at noon for another cold meal. Shortly after their noon meal, they saw a town in the distance.

"I've got some things to look after," Wally said as they passed the first scattered buildings.

"A woman's store!" Sally Jane cried. "Could I at least look?"

Wally chuckled. "Look all you like."

"Maggie, I'll get the supplies," Crane offered, "if you want to go with Sally Jane."

The twins and Betsy followed the women; Ted trailed after Crane. He clomped up the steps to the general store, pausing at the doorway to let his eyes adjust to the gloomy interior. The air inside was as hot as outdoors with the added weight of cinnamon, linseed oil, and turpentine smell. Flies buzzed against the grubby window and swarmed across every surface.

Crane stepped up to the counter, took off his hat, and swept the flies away. He reached out and took four cans of peaches and a half dozen cans of beans. He ordered cornmeal and flour then circled the store, selecting more items he needed.

One corner held a selection of books. He glanced over them and turned away when something else caught his eye. He bent over the display and studied the fine black pen, remembering Maggie's desire to write her father.

He nodded at the man tallying his purchases. "I'll take that." Crane pointed at the pen. "And that." He indicated some ink. "And some paper suitable for letter writing."

A few minutes later, he stepped back into the sunshine, pulling his hat low to shade his eyes. Ted followed at his heels.

They crossed to where the wagon and horses were tied. Maggie, Sally Jane, and the children waited in the shade. Wally hurried toward them then climbed into the back of the wagon with Sally Jane to put away their purchases.

As he half-listened to Betsy's chatter, Crane wondered what took them so long to stow a couple of parcels.

When Wally climbed down, he turned to Crane. "I've been asking around. There's lots of land around here. Sally Jane and I agree this is the sort of place where we want to settle. So we'll be stopping here." He cleared his throat and looked from Maggie to Crane. "How about you folks? Why don't you stop here, as well?"

Crane met Maggie's gaze, reflecting the blue of the sky. A man could drown in eyes like that. "I think we'll be moving farther west," he murmured.

Sally Jane touched Maggie's shoulder. "I'm sorry. I'll miss you."

"We must at least spend the night together before you move on." Wally called the twins. "We're going to find a spot to camp. This will be the last night we'll all be together."

"Pa, why can't they stay with us?" one twin asked.

"Why don't we go with them?" said the other.

Wally shook his head. "This is as far as we go together."

They camped a stone's throw from town, next to a sluggish creek. Three large trees and a handful of bushes were all that relieved the relentless sun.

Long after the children had fallen asleep, the adults sat drinking coffee and visiting.

Finally Crane pushed to his feet, stretched, and yawned. "I'm for getting some sleep."

"You're right." Wally stood and pulled Sally Jane up beside him. "I'm eager to see if I can find us a homestead tomorrow."

Sally Jane hesitated. "We'll say our good-byes in the morning." Then she let Wally help her into the wagon.

"Good night all," Wally called before he pulled the canvas over the opening.

Maggie stared into the flames then sighed heavily as she got to her feet, found her bedroll, and, despite the heat, pulled a blanket up to her chin. He drained his cup before he headed for his own bedroll. But sleep didn't come easily. He sensed Maggie was unhappy and put it down to having to part with their newfound friends. He wished he could offer her comfort. His arms ached to hold her, but his mind warned him to caution. She had come to him before, and he figured, if she wanted comfort from him, she would come again on her own.

Next morning they said their good-byes.

"Be sure to write," Wally said. "Let us know where you settle."

Sally Jane and Maggie hugged a long time. When they broke away, Sally Jane dashed tears from her eyes. "If you ever need anything, you let us know."

Maggie stepped away and pulled herself to Liberty's back. She and the children turned around and waved several times, but Crane did not look back.

With every passing mile, the heat grew. They rode all day without finding a place to hide from it. Crane's gaze constantly swept the horizon, hoping to find anything that would provide a bit of shade. It was late afternoon, the sun still blasting at them from high in the western sky, before he saw a stand of trees promising relief. It wasn't far from the trail, and he pulled up. "Let's stop here."

The others followed without speaking. The temperature dropped a degree or two as they entered the protection of the trees. The clearing in the center was filled with knee-deep grass. He let his breath out in a whoosh when the horses' hooves sucked at the ground. A step farther and water splashed through the blades of grass.

"Last one in's a rotten egg!" he called.

The children barreled off Ted's horse, whooping.

"Take off your clothes," Maggie ordered.

"Aww," Betsy whined, but Ted had already stripped down to his undershorts and was pushing his way through the grass.

Betsy forgot her annoyance and pulled her dress over her head, tossing it to Maggie.

The children stomped in the water, screeching when it splashed up in their faces. Ted lay down. The water left a circle of flesh on his stomach dry, and he cupped his hands to wet his entire body.

Maggie watched Crane through narrowed eyes then dropped from her horse. "There's no way I'm passing this up," she muttered and, turning her back to him, pulled her dress off and stood before him in that same skimpy, lace-trimmed garment he'd seen before.

His throat had been parched for some time, waiting for a drink, but the dryness he'd been nursing was nothing compared to the way his tongue felt now.

She jerked off her boots and marched toward the children, her head high.

"Come on, Crane," Betsy called.

"Not now." He turned to set up camp.

Crane watched them as he worked. Maggie spread her arms wide and belly flopped into the water, sending a wide spray across the children, causing Betsy to shriek and Ted to laugh.

Crane swung the saddles off each horse and led the animals to water, leaving them to graze. He trampled down grass and dug a hole for a fire. He didn't care how hot it was; he was going to have coffee tonight.

He tried to ignore sounds of splashing as he gathered wood. Sweat dripped from his chin and soaked his shirt.

Suddenly his nerves zinged. Then three shrieking, wet bodies grabbed him from behind. He staggered and flung them off. Maggie snagged a cup and tore back to the water, where she scooped it full. Crane knew what she intended, but before he could escape, Maggie tossed the water across his chest, soaking his shirt.

"You need to cool off, too!" she yelled, grinning widely. "No point in sitting there hot and miserable when you could be having fun."

The children dropped hold of his hands and raced to scoop up water, flicking it in his face.

"I'll show you fun." He lunged for Maggie, but she darted away, laughing.

Shrieking, the children raced after her to stand in the ankle-deep water.

"Think that will save ya?" He tromped after them. The water didn't even come over his boots.

Betsy sat down with a plop. He grabbed her head and pushed her into the puddle, at the same time snagging Ted and flipping him off his feet.

Growling, he headed for Maggie.

She backed away.

He scooped her up in his arms, ignoring how his nerves hummed, and raised her high. "Say uncle," he ordered.

"Never," she sputtered.

"Then you pay." He threatened to drop her. "Uncle?"

She clutched at his arms. "Never."

He uncurled her fingers. "Last chance."

"We'll save you," Ted called.

Two bodies slammed into Crane's legs. He staggered but couldn't regain his balance. He pulled Maggie to his chest, fearing he would fall on her, and landed heavily on his knees, water splashing up.

Maggie scuttled away, turning to face him, her eyes wide. She swallowed hard, then a grin spread across her face. "You're still too dry." She sprayed water on him.

The children tackled him again.

"What's the use?" he muttered and flopped down in the water, rolling over and over until he lay looking up at the bright sky.

The children piled on his chest.

Maggie sat close, her wet garments clinging to her. "Now doesn't that feel better?" she asked. "I bet you're a whole lot cooler."

He swallowed hard. There was no way he was going to tell her a fire was burning in his heart. He stood up, shaking the water from him, wiping his hands across his hair. "Come on—let's make supper." He emptied the water from his boots before he lit the fire.

Betsy kept up her usual chatter as she knelt beside him, but Crane heard little of what she said. His nerves crackled as Maggie sat nearby, combing the tangles from her hair.

She gasped as the comb caught. "Crane, what's in my hair?" she grumbled.

With his legs feeling as if he'd run a mile, he moved to her side. "Looks like you was rolling in some weeds," he muttered, barely able to speak.

"Can you get it out?"

He opened his mouth, but nothing came out except a strangled croak. He rubbed his palms against his wet trouser legs. His movements stiff and jerky, he plucked at the leaves and grass tangled in her hair. His heart thundered in his ears.

"Got it," he murmured, stepping back so he could breathe.

He cast a desperate look at the puddle of water. He steadied himself and returned to tending the meat.

"We were sure lucky to get so many good things at that town, weren't we, Crane?"

Betsy's thin voice pulled him back to reality. He knew she meant the food and mumbled agreement, suddenly remembering the gift he'd bought for Maggie. In the confusion of parting with the Strongs, he'd forgotten it. He wondered how to present it to Maggie and what she'd think of it.

That evening Maggie read about Jacob's sons and the birth of Joseph. As she explained that it meant Rachel had a baby boy, Betsy started to sob.

"Whatever is the matter?" Maggie asked.

"I miss Baby Sarah," the child sobbed, flinging herself in Maggie's arms. "Don't you?"

"Of course I do. I 'spect we all miss the family."

Betsy put her face close to Maggie's. "Maggie, can we have a baby?"

Maggie gasped.

"Can we, huh?"

Crane tried to choke back his laugh.

"Yeah, maybe, sometime." She threw him a desperate, half-angry look.

Still chuckling deep in his chest, Crane reached out for another cup of coffee. He was about to say something about the fun they could have at that when he saw the tightness around her eyes and bit back the words. He'd almost done what he promised himself he'd never do—say or do something to rush Maggie.

Crane stared into the fire. He'd always considered himself a calm, methodical man who didn't let anything upset his reasoning or set him charging after some fanciful idea. But Maggie had him spinning like a top. It was a lot like getting bucked off a bronc.

Maggie shifted position, and he pulled himself back into control. He went to his saddlebag and pulled out the parcel for Maggie. "Got you somethin'." He handed it to her.

"Me? What would you get me?"

"Guess you'll have to open it and see."

She nodded, but her gaze never left his face.

"Go ahead," he urged.

She ducked her head and untied the strings then folded back the crackling brown paper.

Crane stood back watching as the paper, pen, and ink lay open on her lap. She didn't say anything. She didn't raise her head. He crossed his arms over his chest.

"Crane, thank you." Her voice was low and thick. "Now I can write Pa." She swallowed hard. "And Sally Jane."

Crane caught the glisten of tears on her cheeks.

He straightened up and took a step toward her.

"No, no," she murmured. "I'm all right. It's so thoughtful of you to get me this." Her eyes shone. "You are such a kind man."

He dropped his arms to his side. Kind? He? Byler Crane? Had anyone ever said that about him before? He opened his mouth to protest, but he couldn't make his lips work. Probably no one would agree with her, but suddenly it didn't matter. Maggie had said he was kind, and that made him feel like something.

He wrapped the feeling around him.

Chapter 12

The feeling lasted all the next day.

Crane found ways of watching Maggie without her being aware of it. It surprised him that she seemed unchanged.

"Will it always be this hot?" Betsy whined.

Crane pulled his thoughts away from Maggie. "Sure hope not."

The day had dawned hot as an oven and had unrelentingly baked them as they plodded down the dusty trail. He'd thought of waiting it out at the campsite, but as Maggie pointed out, "No telling how long this will last. We're just as well off to ride it out. Maybe there'll be relief soon."

But despite the heat, his heart was light.

And the countryside had changed. They saw more trees now, and the land rolled along like folds in a length of cloth.

"I'm going to ride over there and have a look around." He rode to the top of a hill and looked west. For a moment he stared then yelled, "Come up here and see!"

When the others joined him, he pointed west. "See the mountains! The Rockies." They looked like a jagged saw's edge topped with clouds. His heart swelled at the sight. He was finally seeing them.

"They aren't very big," Betsy said.

Crane laughed. "We're miles away yet. Wait until we get to Calgary. I hear they're big as giants."

He stared and stared, unable to get his fill. "Let's have dinner here," he said, never taking his eyes off the horizon.

They didn't stop long before they returned to the trail. In the middle of the afternoon, the sky to the east darkened and lightning zigzagged across the sky. Cat, who had been riding in front of Ted, stood, arching her back, her tail like a bottlebrush.

Betsy laughed. "Cat's scared. A scaredy cat."

Maggie frowned, her eyes on the sky. "It looks like a thunderstorm."

"It's a long ways off," Crane said. "Can't hardly hear the thunder."

"Could move this direction."

He grinned at her. "Guess you're right. We best find a place to stop."

She wrinkled her nose. "Not out here. Not in the open." She nodded toward the hills. "Let's find shelter up there."

By the time they climbed the hills, the storm was close enough to make Maggie shudder at every thunderclap.

"These trees will do," Crane called, reining in at the closest bunch.

"Trees aren't safe in lightning." Maggie refused to follow him. "I'm sure we can find something better."

At the look on her face, he decided not to argue. "Let me know when you find what you're looking for." And he let Maggie take the lead.

"There." She pointed. It was a ledge high up the hill.

He nodded. The storm was catching them faster than he'd guessed.

He handed the lead rope of the packhorse to Maggie. "Here—you go on ahead while I get some firewood."

He had his arms full of wood when a flash of lightning almost blinded him. Thunder roared down the side of the hill. With it came a flood of rain, soaking him in a matter of seconds. He heard the frightened whinny of a horse.

Wrapping a piece of canvas around the wood, he secured it to the saddle then headed for shelter. Water poured down the side of the hill. Rebel struggled to keep his feet under him. Again he heard a horse whinny.

"Come on, boy. You can do it," Crane urged Rebel upward.

"Maggie!" Ted's yell sent shudders racing down Crane's spine, and he pushed the horse harder. The rain sheeted down so he could hardly see Ted holding Liberty and his own mount. Betsy stood back a few feet, her hair clinging to her head, clutching Cat in her arms.

"Maggie's down there!" Ted yelled, pointing downhill.

Crane's heart leapt to his mouth. "What happened?"

"The packhorse spooked. She tried to hold it. They went down there."

Crane followed the tracks over the edge of the hill. He scrubbed the rain from his eyes and squinted into the murky distance. He could make out the horse, shuddering on the slope.

"Keep back from the edge." He handed Rebel's reins to Ted then slid down the slope, digging his heels in to slow himself. A flash of lightning allowed him to see through the shroud. Maggie lay face down in the mud. "Maggie!" he yelled, his heart clenching like a fist. "Maggie, answer me."

Water poured down the slope, parting around her body then cascading past. When she wiggled in the mud, the rain and misery disappeared.

"Give me your hand," he barked.

"No. Take the horse." Her voice was muffled against the ground.

"Forget the horse. Give me your hand."

"The horse," she insisted, turning her head toward him.

They were wasting time arguing. He grabbed the reins, but it was impossible to force the animal up the slippery slope. He skidded down to the trees and tied the animal securely.

"Maggie, I'm coming." But he slid back a foot for every step he made. Digging his hands into the mud, he clawed his way to her side, grabbed her around the waist, and lifted her. His feet slipped. He threw himself sideways, landing on his backside, Maggie in his arms, her icy fingers clutching his shirtfront.

They slid downward. Lightning filled the sky. Moaning, Maggie buried her face against his chest as the thunder echoed and reechoed across the hill. They ground to a halt a few feet from the horse.

Maggie was muddy from head to toe, drenched like a little rat. He didn't want to leave her, but he had to go back for Ted and Betsy. He gently removed her from his lap and set her on the ground. "Wait here while I get the children."

She huddled there, spitting mud from her mouth.

Ignoring the pain under his rib cage, he jerked to his feet and found a grassy spot that gave him better traction. He crawled back to the spot where he'd left the children. Betsy threw herself at him, clinging to his muddy knees. "I fot we was lost."

"We have to go to Maggie," Crane said. "I'll take the horses. Ted, you and Betsy stay close."

Ted nodded, swallowing hard.

"Put Cat down," he told Betsy. "She'll have to follow on her own."

Betsy did as he said. Cat pranced from paw to paw but stayed at their side.

"Now hang on tight," he said, knotting the reins in his fist and taking a child in each hand. Betsy shrieked as her feet went out from under her, then they skidded down to the trees.

Water running down her neck, Maggie sat huddled in a heap just as he had left her. Betsy flung herself at her, but Maggie only shuddered.

Ted stood over the pair. "Maggie?"

But Maggie only tightened her arms around her knees.

Crane looked at the miserable trio. The rain fell in buckets. He shook his head, wiping water from his eyes. A fire was impossible, and there wasn't a dry inch where they could find shelter. He pulled a piece of canvas from the pack, keeping it folded against his body as he returned to the others. He edged his legs between Ted and Maggie and pulled Betsy to his lap then flipped the canvas open covering Maggie, Ted, and Betsy. The rain ran off the canvas, washing down his back. Lightning blinded him, accompanied by a roar of thunder. The smell of gunpowder filled the air. Maggie shuddered and moaned while Betsy clawed at his chest and Ted pressed into his side.

"We're safe," he murmured.

Cat pushed her nose under a corner and crawled into Ted's lap.

At that moment Maggie moaned, pushed aside the canvas, and dashed away.

"Maggie?" Crane called, but she didn't answer. He strained to hear and thought he caught the sound of someone being sick.

She returned and crawled back under the protection.

"You all right?" he asked.

She shuddered. "Think I swallowed some mud. My stomach doesn't like it."

He pulled her under his arm, wrapping the canvas as tightly as possible around her shivering shoulders, but again Maggie pushed away and fled for the trees. He lost count of the number of times she made the trip. He didn't know how long they sat huddled in the rain. It seemed like hours. Finally the rain slowed to a drizzle then quit. It was so dark, he couldn't make out the horses tied a few feet away.

"I'm going to see if I can get a fire going." He found Rebel and untied the bundle of wood he'd gathered earlier. He spaded the wet sod away to form a circle of bare ground and carefully arranged the wood. It took several tries before he got the fire started.

Steam rose from the wet ground. Warmth curled toward the others, and slowly the canvas lowered.

Crane couldn't remember when he'd seen a sorrier-looking bunch—Ted pale, his hair plastered to his head; Betsy's eyes round as saucers, her hair hanging in dark tangles, mud clinging to her face and hands.

Crane's chest tightened. Maggie looked the worst, her face streaked, her clothing covered with mud, grass, and leaves. But it was the pinched look around her eyes and the tightness of her lips that made Crane clench his teeth. She lurched to her feet and dashed into the stand of trees.

Crane stared after her before he turned his attention to Betsy, stripping her down to her undergarments, rubbing her down with a towel, removing mud and water in one operation, then finding her dry garments.

Maggie returned as he finished, and he said to the child, "Stand here and stay warm while I take care of Ted."

When both children were cleaned and dried as best he could, he spread the canvas on the ground and, finding a dry blanket in the pack, had them lie down. Before he was finished, Maggie had disappeared into the trees again, clutching her belly. He set water to boil and waited for her to return.

The children fell asleep. Cat sat by the fire cleaning her fur. Crane stared into the trees. Maggie had been gone a mighty long time. He wanted to go to her but was afraid he'd embarrass her. He washed the worst of the mud off himself and put on a dry shirt then hooked the wet blankets and clothing over branches near the fire.

Still Maggie hadn't returned. He called her name. Only the crack of the logs in the fire and the drip of water from the leaves answered him. He grabbed a piece of wood from the fire, a flickering circle of light landing ahead of him.

"Maggie," he called, following her tracks. "Maggie, where are you?"

The trees rained on him, soaking his shirt again, but he merely shook his head and pushed on. "Maggie." *What could have happened to her?*

He saw her curled up on the wet ground and sprang to her side.

"Maggie." But she didn't answer. He touched a trembling hand to her shoulder.

She moaned but didn't open her eyes. He scooped her into his arms and hurried back to the fire. His heart thudding thickly, he snagged one of the damp blankets, throwing it on the ground. Gently he laid her on it. She curled into a ball.

She wouldn't thank him for moving her about, but he couldn't leave her in her wet clothing. His fingers clumsy, he unbuttoned her dress and pulled it off. It was soiled with mud and sickness. Her undergarment was soiled, as well, and he struggled to remove it. Tenderly he sponged her face, her hands, her trembling body.

She moaned and drew her knees to her belly. He wrapped a towel around her, holding her in his arms, trying to warm her with his body, trying to calm the shudders shaking her small frame. Warmth slowly seeped into her. Still he held her.

It had been some time since her body had erupted. He decided the worst of the stomach upset was over. His arms cramped. His back ached. Pins and needles raced up and down his legs, but he did not lay her down.

Although he sat as still as a rock, his mind raced. "Maggie mine, do you have any idea how much I love you?" he murmured. "I can't stand to see you suffer like this. I wish it was me instead."

He would do anything for her. The knowledge of his love seared through his body. He'd loved her since she faced Bull. He loved the way she said what she thought, the way she tended the children so gently, the way she teased. He loved everything about her. If only he could make her see that.

He remembered when she had asked about the future. He knew she'd been seeking assurances from him, and he had refused to give them. He stared at the fire without blinking.

Sure, he excused himself. He didn't believe in making promises he couldn't be sure of keeping, but it wouldn't have hurt him to give her something to hang on to.

He vowed he would find a way of telling her how much she had come to mean to him.

Not until he felt her body relax, not until her legs no longer pulled up to her midsection, did he carefully lower her next to the children.

He couldn't bring himself to dig through her clothes, so he pulled one of his shirts from the saddlebags and eased her arms into the sleeves. A pulse thudded in his temple as he fastened the buttons down the front.

Her head lolled in exhaustion. He covered her warmly then leaned against the nearest tree, watching her sleep.

To the east the sky was already turning gray. He turned his face upward. *God, it's been a long time, but here I am. I guess I never quit believing in You. But it's like Maggie says—I got lost somewhere.*

More of Maggie's words filled his brain—like how God sent His Son, Jesus, so he, Byler Crane, could have his sins forgiven. And how it was as easy as accepting a gift. Just like that little boy who took the coin from the preacher man.

So here I am, God. Ready to accept that gift. Ready to trust You. He'd never been good at trusting, but this time it was easy. He remembered when home had meant feeling good. That same feeling settled into the edges of his heart. He filled his lungs slowly before he continued.

Maggie's always saying how You're ready to help us anytime, so I could sure use some help right about now. Not for myself, you understand. But for Maggie.

Crane woke with a beam of sun in his face and jerked upright. Everyone else still slept. Maggie, dark shadows under her eyes, moaned.

He tried to decide what was best to do. Only one canteen of water was left. Either he would have to go and find water, or they would have to move camp closer to water. But Maggie and the children were still exhausted. Maggie wouldn't be strong enough to ride today.

They had the added threat of another storm. The idea of being caught in another like last night was enough to make him shudder.

He eased to his feet and crept away to a spot where he could study the surrounding land. For a long time, he gazed at the scene before him. The mountains weren't visible today, hidden in the misty horizon. To the north he could see a heavy shower, then a spear of sun broke through and painted a rainbow across the sky. He could hear the distant wail of a train.

He returned to camp and quietly saddled Rebel.

"Where are you going?" Maggie's weak voice spun him around. She watched him with shadowed eyes.

His throat tightened. "How are you feeling?"

"Like a wet dishrag." Her voice cracked, and he sprang to get her a drink.

Her hands shook as she took the cup, and he steadied it, wrapping his fingers over her cold ones.

She lay back, panting.

He grabbed one of the dry blankets and wrapped it about her.

"Were you going someplace?" She sounded weary.

"We need water." He rubbed his neck. How could he leave her? Yet they had to have water.

"How far do you have to go?"

He shrugged. "Can't say for sure."

She tried to sit up. "It might storm again."

"Lay down and keep covered."

She shook his hands off and pushed the covers down. "I don't want to spend another night here."

Both children wakened and listened to the exchange.

"Crane, it was so awful," Betsy whispered. "I was so scared, but I kept thinking of that picture Maggie told us about." She touched Maggie's face. "You know. The one where Jesus reached down and helped the lost lamb."

She shuddered. "I know He helped us, but I don't want to stay here."

Ted nodded.

"I suppose it's best if we stay together." Crane sighed. "On one condition." He gave Maggie his fiercest look. "You don't do anything."

Her eyes narrowed, and he feared she was going to argue, but she sighed deeply and flopped down. "I don't think I'll mind taking things easy for a bit."

"Betsy, you gather up all the stuff hanging on the trees. Ted, you help with the horses."

The children scampered to do his bidding. He couldn't tear himself away from the look Maggie gave him. How much did she remember from last night? Had she heard his confession of love? He waited, hoping she would somehow let him know, but instead she sighed and turned away.

"I know I'm causing you a lot of trouble—" Her voice trailed off.

Laughing, he stood to his feet. "This is nothing." He wanted to make light of it, tell her a story about trying to corral some wild cows, somehow convince her he'd handled much worse situations, but he felt hollow inside. He knew he'd never faced anything in his life that made his nerves shake the way they did as he thought of making Maggie ride in her weakened condition.

As soon as they were ready, he lifted her to the saddle. She gripped the saddlehorn so hard her knuckles turned white.

"Are you sure you're up to this?"

She gritted her teeth. "I can do anything I make up my mind to do."

"No doubt," he muttered, leading them down the hill.

By the time they reached the bottom, Maggie's lips had a strained white ring around them. It wasn't a hot day; yet beads of sweat stood out on her forehead. He opened his mouth to say something, but she glared at him and muttered, "I'm fine."

He turned away mumbling, "Of course you are. And I'm the king's brother."

"What'd you say, Crane?" Betsy called.

"Nothin'. Just thinkin' out loud."

"I'm hungry."

"I know." She'd done well to be so patient. "Just a bit longer."

A glance over his shoulder at Maggie clinging bravely to the saddle sent a squeezing tightness around his ribs.

A bunch of trees came in sight. He glimpsed a reflection of a stream through the trees and heaved a sigh. "We'll set up camp here."

He soon had a fire going, and while Ted tended a pot of oatmeal, he built a shelter and carried Maggie to it. By the time he'd tugged her boots off and pulled the covers around her shoulders, she was asleep.

"Is she all right?" Ted asked, his face creased with worry.

"I 'spect so. Just a little weak from being sick." He said the words with a lot more conviction than he felt. "We'll stay here until she feels stronger."

Satisfied with his answer, the children played with Cat.

Maggie slept the rest of the afternoon and into the next day. Crane stayed close by, trying to hide his worry from the children. He sat nursing a coffee, staring at the flickering flames, when he heard her clear her throat.

"Got any more of that?" She nodded toward his cup.

He leapt to his feet and took her some coffee. "You feeling better?"

She drank several swallows before she answered. "Better'n what?"

He laughed. "Guess you must be."

"You going to stand there gawking or get me something to eat?"

He laughed again. "What would madame like?" He was so relieved to see her awake, he would have gone bear hunting if she'd asked.

"Food would be good," she muttered.

His shout of laughter brought the children running.

He cooked her oatmeal, figuring it would be easy on her stomach. By the time she finished, her eyelids were closing. He eased her back to the bed. He could barely breathe. *Thank You, God, for her strength. And her beauty.* He sat there a long time.

When the coffee boiled the next morning, she rolled over so she could watch the fire. "I'm feeling much better today."

"I'm glad." He sat beside her.

"I mean we should be moving along today."

He stared at her. He knew better than to argue when she had that look, but he had no intention of dragging her across the country, wilting like a flower in the sun.

"I mean it," she mumbled. "What's the point in sitting here staring at the sky day after day?"

"The point," he ground out the words, "is in letting you get your strength back."

"I think I'm fit to be the best judge of that."

"You'd think so."

She didn't blink before his glare. "I think I am." She smiled.

Maggie could have asked for anything at that moment. He clamped his mouth shut and tried to think of something halfway intelligent to say. And failed.

She continued to smile at him as she called, "Ted, Betsy, up and at it. We're heading out as soon as we're ready."

Betsy erupted from her blankets. "Good. I'm tired of waiting around. What's for breakfast?"

Ted emerged more slowly. "I'll go get the horses."

Crane had lost the battle. He prepared to leave, but his thoughts troubled him. How was he going to tell Maggie how he felt about her?

For days Maggie was exhausted after a few hours in the saddle, and they stopped early; but as she said, they were making progress slowly.

Crane wished he could likewise feel he was making progress with Maggie, but with each passing day, they slipped back more and more into the roles they had before the storm. He sighed. It wasn't that he didn't enjoy the way they had been; he simply wanted more.

He practiced how he would tell her he'd changed, but the time never seemed right. And it grew more and more difficult to find the words.

Days later, with the sun glistening off the Rockies, they rode down the streets of Calgary. The children couldn't stop staring at the elaborate sandstone buildings, some three stories tall.

Crane had heard about the fire of '86 that had taken out a large part of the town. After that the town fathers had encouraged the use of sandstone for building.

He saw a sign that said ATTORNEYS AT LAW and marked the spot in his mind. Maggie swayed in the saddle. They needed to find a place soon.

He reined in at the general store and hurried inside. "I'm looking for some temporary quarters."

The pot-bellied man eyed him up and down. "Rooms for rent at any of the hotels." Crane shook his head. "Don't want a room. I need a place my wife can rest for a few days." He jerked his head toward the door.

The man shuffled over to peer out the window. "That your family?"

"Yup."

"I see what you mean. Your wife looks done in."

"She's been sick."

Bushy eyebrows jerked up. "She still sick?"

Crane shook his head. "Just tired of riding."

The man hesitated then gave a brisk nod. "I don't usually do this, but I have a house on the edge of town that's empty. You're welcome to it as long as you need."

" 'Preciate that."

They made arrangements, and Crane bought supplies. Then he led the tired trio to the house.

"We'll be staying here for now." He took in the upturned chairs, the mattresses rolled up on the two sets of bunks. It was dirty, but nothing that couldn't be swept up. "It'll do."

He set one chair upright and pushed Maggie to it. "You sit," he ordered, "while we get things cleaned up."

She nodded.

He figured it was a good measure of how poorly she felt that she put up no argument.

"Ted, there's wood out back. Let's get a fire going and heat some water. Betsy, get the broom I bought."

He cleaned the beds first, then unrolled some bedding and lay Maggie down. She was as limp as a rag in his arms. She curled on her side, bunched her hands at her chin, and slept. The dark circles under her eyes troubled him.

Hours later, with the children's help, he'd gotten rid of the cobwebs and crud. He brought in the saddles and packs. Ted pumped water into the trough at the back for the horses as Crane prepared supper.

Maggie stirred long enough to eat a few mouthfuls of stew then fell asleep again.

"Maggie's sure tired a lot." Betsy's voice was thin with worry.

"She just needs some rest," Crane assured the child, praying he was right.

"She was pretty sick after the storm, wasn't she?" Ted asked.

"Guess she got some dirty water in her stomach."

"She's going to be all right, isn't she?" Ted asked as he perched on the edge of his chair.

"I'm pretty sure she is." Crane chuckled. " 'Spect she'd skin us alive if she could hear us talking."

Ted smiled. " 'Spect you're right."

Betsy leaned against Crane. "Nobody's read to us for days."

He wrapped his arm around her. "I do believe you're right. Do you know what?" She shook her head.

"I bet I could read you a story."

She turned her big brown gaze to him. "For sure?"

"Yup. I believe I could. As soon as you're ready for bed."

She didn't have to be told twice. "Can I sleep here?" She pointed to the other lower bunk and, at Crane's nod, spread her bedroll. "Will we have a house as nice as this when we get where we're going?"

"Yup. Maybe even nicer."

Ted looked thoughtful. "We just about there?"

"Yup."

He sighed. "Good."

Crane studied the boy. He'd never complained or shown any sign of being tired. Crane shook his head. If the truth be told, he guessed he was about ready to settle down, too.

Betsy handed him the Bible. In the far corners of his mind, he remembered something his ma had read and found it.

" 'The Lord is my shepherd; I shall not want.' "

He read the whole psalm then closed the book. The room was quiet as Crane searched for the words he wanted to say.

"You know, everything Maggie's been telling us about God is true. I think I always knew it, but somehow I figured I didn't need it. But it's like she says, even when we forget about God and get lost, He finds us and helps us back."

He thought of how easy it was to come back. "I remember my own ma saying how God loved us so much He sent Jesus, His Son, to be the way back to God." Maybe Ma was like Maggie; she got so lost in her hurt and anger after Pa left that she forgot about God's love and only remembered it just before she died. That was what she'd tried to tell him. That was why she was so all-fired set he take the Bible.

"This story we read about the Shepherd," he patted the Bible, "it's a story that tells us how He leads us and guides us and takes care of us."

Betsy's muffled voice came from her bunk. "Is He taking care of Maggie right now?"

"I'm sure He is, but it doesn't hurt to ask Him."

All was quiet.

"You mean pray, don't you?" Ted asked.

"Yup."

"I don't know how to pray," Ted whispered. "All I know how to do is cuss."

His words startled Crane. Apart from the first day or two, he'd never heard the boy cuss.

"I do it inside me."

Crane took a deep breath, wishing he was better at finding words. "I 'spect praying is as simple as talking to God."

"Crane." It was Betsy. "You pray."

He almost choked. But he couldn't refuse. He swallowed hard. "God," he began, "thank You for finding us when we're lost. Now we're needing a Shepherd to help us and lead us. And most of all we need You to make Maggie better." He fell silent. Suddenly he had so many things he wanted to say, but he couldn't find the words.

"Now I know she'll be fine." Betsy's voice was full of confidence, and she shuffled around in bed, getting comfortable. "Good night, Crane," she called. " 'Night, Ted."

Long after the children had settled, Crane sat up. Somehow, he promised himself, before they left this place, he would find a way of telling Maggie he loved her. His heart lurched as he remembered their agreement—no romance, just partners. What if she preferred to keep it that way?

He pressed his forehead to his palms. If she did, then he would accept it, living his love out quietly, but he could not let it go on without telling her.

If only he was better with his words.

They stayed in the little house several days. Crane waited and watched for a chance to tell Maggie how he felt, but the chance never seemed to come. The children were always close by or Maggie was tired, though he was pleased to see her gaining strength every day.

He'd made several trips downtown, visiting the lawyer, asking where the best land was, and purchasing supplies and equipment to set up a new place. Returning from one of his trips, he paused to look at the house. Smoke snaked up the chimney. He smelled savory meat and fresh bread.

He opened the door. Maggie sat peeling potatoes.

"Crane! Crane! You're back!" Betsy wrapped herself around his legs.

He scooped her up and tossed her high.

She giggled. "Do it again."

He tossed her up again then tucked her under his arm like a sack of potatoes.

Ted got up from the floor where he'd been playing with Cat. "I took care of all the chores you gave me."

"Good boy." He ruffled the boy's hair.

He crossed to the table. "And how about you, Maggie? What have you been doing with yourself?"

She glanced up. "Nothing much." She ducked her head again but not before Crane caught the sheen of unshed tears.

He waited, but she kept her head down. He set Betsy on her feet. "Ted." He didn't take his focus off Maggie. "Take Betsy outside for a bit." He waited for the door to close behind them.

Still she didn't lift her head, and the knife in her hand remained idle. He knelt, trying to see her eyes, but she pressed her chin down.

"Maggie." His throat tightened. He swallowed hard and tried again. "Maggie. What's the matter?"

She shook her head.

He tipped her chin up. Tears trailed down each cheek. "Are you sick?"

Again she shook her head.

He jiggled her chin until she lifted her glistening eyes.

"You've got to tell me what's wrong."

She took a long, trembling breath. "I've ruined it all, haven't I?"

He blinked. What on earth was she talking about? He glanced around the room half-expecting to see a torn blanket or a failed cake, but he saw nothing. He wanted nothing more than to kiss away the tears and hold her tight. Instead he asked, "What are you talking about?"

"First the children. Then insisting we go up to the hill." She sobbed once then continued. "Now on top of it all, after agreeing our marriage was going to be businesslike, I've gone and fallen in love with you." Her words ended in a wail.

She pulled away and hid her face. "I'm sorry," she whispered. "I never meant to say that."

His heart thudded against his ribs as if it'd been shot from a cannon. He couldn't move. "Are you crying because you love me?"

Her head jerked up. "No, of course not. I'm crying because I'm so tired of keeping it a secret."

He laughed low in his throat.

She blinked and narrowed her eyes. "Why are you laughing?"

"Because, my dear sweet Maggie, I love you and have been trying to find a way to tell you and wondering if you'd be angry at me." He chuckled and leaned forward, resting his forearms across her knees. "Doesn't it strike you as the least bit funny that we both felt the same way?"

She smiled. "Guess you were as foolish as me."

"Foolish and crazy," he agreed. "Crazy in love with you, Maggie mine."

Her cheeks turned rosy. "I can't believe it."

He caught her chin and waited for her gaze to stop its restless darting about. When it did, he almost fell apart at the love he saw.

"When did you first know?" she whispered.

"I admitted it when you slid down that muddy slope and got so sick." He shuddered. "You had me worried, I'll say." He chased away that dark moment. "But I think I fell in love the day you stood up to Bull." He grinned. "Knew then I'd found me a real woman."

"A real troublemaker, you mean," she muttered.

"Just someone willing to help another even if it isn't easy." He trailed his finger along her jawline. He wanted to run a path of kisses along the same line, but first he had to know. "When did you fall in love with me?"

Her cheeks glowed. Her eyes were dark and shiny.

He could feel his heart pulsing in his throat at the way she looked at him.

"That night."

His breath exploded from him. He knew she meant the night they'd shared the little willow shelter. He wanted to laugh and yell and dance around the room. Perhaps he would later, but there was something he wanted even more than that. He leaned closer but found he didn't have to lean very far, for she met him halfway.

He found her lips. At the same time, he found the love he'd wanted all his life.

Later, after the children were put to bed, Maggie climbed into her bunk and patted the space beside her.

Grinning, he crawled under the covers and took her in his arms. "I love you, Maggie mine."

She laughed against his chest. "And I love you, Byler Crane."

A warm feeling filled him. Except for his ma, no one had called him Byler since he was a youngster.

She tapped his chest with one finger. "We've had some good experiences on this journey."

"And a few bad ones." But lying with her in his arms, he had a hard time remembering them.

"And I've found God again."

"Me, too."

She squeezed him, making it difficult for him to keep his thoughts on the conversation. "And now it's time to finish our journey and build ourselves a new home."

He was quiet a moment, trying to find the words he wanted. "Our journey won't be over," he said. "It will be only starting."

"You're right."

He half-sat. "I almost forgot."

She pulled him down again. "I'm sure it will wait until morning."

He laughed. "It will. It's only another part of the beginning of our journey together."

"Umm. What?"

"I knew you wouldn't be able to let it go." He chuckled.

"I can, too." She snuggled close.

He pressed his face into her hair, breathing in the scent of her, and waited.

"I think maybe I want to know." Her voice was muffled against his chest.

He laughed, pleased with his knowledge of her. Then he murmured, "I went to see a lawyer here. To find out about the children. He says you can apply for guardianship of Ted and name me as joint guardian, or if your pa will relinquish his rights, we can adopt him."

He felt her waiting stillness. "That's up to you. He'll act on your behalf if you like.

"I told him all we know about Betsy, and he sent out some letters. He says there shouldn't be any problem with us adopting her."

"I'm glad. It's the beginning for all of us."

"Tomorrow, if you're feeling up to it, we'll head north. I hear there's fine land available up there."

"I'm up to it." Before he found her lips again, he breathed a silent prayer. *Thank You, God, for this family. For the children. But especially for Maggie, my bride.*

The Heart Seeks a Home.

Dedicated to my sister, Leona,
who listens to me talk about the people in my books as if they are real
and accompanies me on research trips and into used book stores;
and to my sister-in-law, Shawna,
who listens to me talk about my stories,
provides kind and construtive feedback, and shares my love of writing.
They say you can pick your friends but not your relatives.
For both of you, if it had been up to me to choose,
I couldn't have picked anyone better. Thanks.

Chapter 1

She should have known better. The instant she saw them lounging at the edge of the railway platform and studying her from under wide-brimmed cowboy hats, she should have been warned. Certainly when they ambled over to ask if she was Miss Lydia Baxter, and their startled looks when she said she was, should have given her cause for concern. When they announced they were to take her to the Twin Spurs Ranch, she should have grabbed her valise and stepped back on the train.

But now it was too late.

"There must be some mistake," she murmured, her voice catching deep in her throat. *Mistake!* If what they said was true, the word didn't begin to address the magnitude of her situation.

Quivers raced up and down her body. If she didn't sit down right now, she was going to fall on her face. Her distress must have been evident to the two men, for one of them—the shorter, heavier one who had introduced himself as—but she couldn't recall his name—grabbed a chair and shoved it under her. She sank into it, her limbs shaking like straws in the wind, her face burning hot then, seconds later, cold and clammy.

"I'm sorry. I can't stay. You'll have to take me back." Her teeth rattled as she talked, and she gripped her hands in her lap to slow their shaking.

The men exchanged looks. The taller one shuffled his feet and looked around the room. The other leaned back against the door, twisting his hat in his hands.

"Y–you must ta–take me back to town. I—I can't possibly stay here." She prayed they would not see how frightened she was. "I thought I was going to work for a family."

"A nice family for you," Reverend Williams had said. "You'll have a good home."

Suspicion burned at the back of her mind. Had he knowingly sent her to this situation? Immediately she dashed the thought away. It wasn't possible. He and Mrs. Williams would be as shocked as she to discover there was no family, only two young bachelors who steadfastly refused to look at her or respond to her demands to be taken back to town so she could get back on the train and go—

Go where? She had no place to go.

It didn't matter. Anyplace was better than this.

She cleared her throat. Two pairs of eyes flicked toward her. "Did you hear me?" she demanded in stronger tones. "You must take me back."

The one at the door straightened. "Well now, I don't rightly see how we can. You can see it's already dark out. And no trains run tonight. Guess you'll have to stay."

Lydia stared at him long and hard. Matt Weber. That's what he'd called himself when he sauntered up to her at the train station and hoisted her trunk on his shoulder with an ease that made her gasp. His brown mustache twitched under her scrutiny.

The other man stepped forward, and Lydia shifted her gaze to him. His name returned, as well. Sam Hatten. Taller and slighter, his blue eyes met hers for a moment, then he looked away, rubbing a hand over his thatch of blond hair.

"I'm sorry, ma'am," he said. "This really is as much a surprise to us as to you." He cleared his throat. "We were expecting a spinster, not. . ." His gaze darted to her face and then past her shoulder. "But we decided we might as well make the best of a bad situation. Besides, it really is too far to go back to town now, and it is, as Matt says, already dark."

She shrank inward and hugged her arms around her. This was the worst situation she'd ever been in. There was no one in these hills to come to her rescue.

Matt jammed his hat on his head. "I'm going to put the horses away." And he fled out the door.

Sam turned and lifted the stove lid to stir the fire. "I think we should have tea," he mumbled.

Lydia couldn't breathe. Her heart thudded so loudly, she was sure it drowned out the noise of Sam dipping water and pouring it into the kettle. She stared at his back as he stood over the stove waiting for the kettle to boil and then poured the hot water over the tea leaves in a squat brown teapot.

She couldn't think what she should do. These men were certainly not prepared to take her back to town. She studied the door, but it didn't make sense for her to walk out into the dark. A shudder raced across her shoulders. From what she'd seen as they drove up to the house in the dusk, it would be worth her life and limb to wander around these hills in the dark. And heaven knows what sort of wild animals would share the night. She shivered and looked again at Sam's back. Animals outside; two men in. What was the difference?

Sam set a teacup in front of her and filled it. He poured himself a cupful, sitting opposite her. Still not speaking, he added two spoonfuls of sugar.

The door rattled open and Lydia jumped.

Matt entered, grabbed a cup, and joined them at the table.

Sam stirred his tea and sighed. He looked long and hard at Matt then turned to Lydia. "I'm sorry, but I think you really will have to stay." He sipped his tea. "No doubt things will look better in the morning." Suddenly he rose to his feet. "I'll take your things to your room, and you can make yourself comfortable." He scooped up her bag and headed to the doorway of the next room.

She gulped her tea and lurched to her feet, hesitating as she struggled to think what she should do. Stay? Go? Sit? Follow her bag?

Her bag and the small trunk on the wagon contained all that remained of her life, so she hurried after Sam.

He stepped into a dark room.

She hung back while he lit a lamp then turned to leave, pausing at her side to look down and say, "You'll be perfectly safe, you know." He waited for her to step into the room then pulled the door closed as he left.

She stared after him. *Safe? Hardly!* There wasn't a place in the world where she could feel safe. For a while she thought she'd found a place with the Williamses. But that, too, had come to an end.

She dropped to the edge of the bed and hunched over her knees.

Oh, Mother, if only you hadn't left me I wouldn't be at the mercy of others. Thinking of her mother brought a measure of calm.

A great weariness overcame her, but she commanded her leaden limbs to move. The first thing she must do was secure the room.

She checked the door, but there was no lock or key.

A straight-backed chair sat in the shadows by a desk, and she carried it to the door and shoved it firmly under the knob. It wouldn't stop much but would at least warn her if someone tried to intrude.

With arms that seemed too weak to function, she opened her bag and removed her brush. She pulled the hairpins out and let her hair fall loose down her back, brushing it with little care then braiding it into one thick plait for the night. Her thoughts unraveled as she twisted the braid.

Was it only this morning she had said good-bye to Reverend and Mrs. Williams and kissed the children?

How could they have sent her to this place?

She had trusted them when they brought her with them from England to Canada, promising she would always have a home with them. A bitter taste rose in her throat. A promise easily forgotten after two short years when Mrs. Williams's niece, Annabelle, wrote asking if she could stay with them. It was clear she was a hired servant easily disposed of.

She choked back tears. As she returned the brush to her bag, her hand touched her Bible, and she brought it out, tenderly stroking its soft cover. At the end of a day, Mother would sit in her rocker and, no matter how weary, she'd read a chapter to Lydia.

"Lydia," she'd say in her gentle voice, "I want you to remember God is faithful. He cares for you in a special way. He will never leave you nor forsake you."

It had been easy to believe those words while Mother was alive. Lydia shuddered, remembering some of the unwelcome surprises the world had offered a young girl alone in the world.

She looked at the Bible on her lap. "You were wrong, Mother," she whispered.

"God doesn't care about me. No one does."

With trembling hands and aching heart, she pushed the Bible back into the valise and, without removing her clothes, crawled into bed. For a moment she thought about leaving the lamp on then sighed and turned it down until it died. Her eyes felt too large for her face as she stared into darkness that reached past the walls of this room into her future and down to her inmost being. She lay tense and wide-eyed as the night deepened, afraid to shut her eyes in case. . .in case. . .

Light glared through a large square window. Lydia blinked and shot up to a sitting position. She hadn't expected to sleep so soundly nor to meet the morning unharmed.

Beyond the walls of the room, muted noises warned her there were still two men in the house. Boot-clad feet thudded across the floor, sending echoes of dread into the pit of her stomach. The sulfur smell of a match was followed by the pungency of wood chips burning. The aroma of coffee called her to get up.

Instead, Lydia lay down and drew the covers up to her neck. Bits of conversation drifted to her.

". . .can't keep her. . ."

". . .until something else. . ."

". . .misunderstanding. . ."

She was sure the soft voice belonged to Sam, the blue-eyed one, and the deeper voice to Matt, the stockier one.

A knock at her door sent her scurrying deeper under the covers. She lifted her head enough to see the chair still hooked under the knob then lay in a quivering huddle.

"Miss Baxter? Lydia Baxter? Are you there?" It was Matt outside her door. A louder knock and another call. "Lydia Baxter?" Then a call to the other one. "She's still in there, isn't she?"

Sam's voice joined Matt's. "Miss Baxter? Are you in there?"

Her eyes widened as they rattled the knob, and she clutched the covers to her chin. Any minute they would break down the door.

"If you're there, please answer."

They wouldn't hear if she screamed. Nobody would.

Suddenly the chair jumped, and Lydia screeched. The door opened a crack, and two heads appeared in the space. She shrank back, her hands knotted along the top of the quilt.

Matt chuckled. "I see you're all right. Breakfast will be ready in a few minutes." He ducked out of sight.

Sam hesitated for a heartbeat then, letting his breath out in a whoosh, silently followed his partner.

Lydia waited for her trembling to pass then swung her weak legs over the side of the bed and reached for her bag. Her hand touched the Bible where she had shoved it last night, and she jerked it out. It fell open to the bookmark. Mother's words came to her.

Read a few verses every day; then pray about your day, expecting and trusting God to guide you.

Lydia's hand hovered over the pages, but it was a habit too old to ignore. And somehow to do other than Mother had instructed made Lydia feel guilty, so she read Psalm 54, the reading for the day. The words so perfectly fit the ache in her heart that she bent closer and read them again. *"Save me. . . . Hear my prayer. . . . Strangers are risen up against me. . . . God is mine helper. . . . He hath delivered me out of all trouble."*

She closed her eyes and breathed the words deep into her soul then whispered a prayer for God's help and intervention.

Only then did she return the Bible to her bag and pull out the pink and blue printed shirtwaist. It was dreadfully wrinkled, but she shrugged out of the soiled and equally wrinkled white one she'd slept in and pulled on the clean. Freeing her hair from its braid, she brushed it quickly, with little regard for the results. Not bothering to check for a mirror, she simply twisted her hair into a knot at the back of her neck and pinned it in place.

At the door she took a long, shaky breath. She must convince these men to take her back to town. Immediately. She lifted her chin and stepped into the kitchen. In order to keep her hands from trembling, she clasped them together at her waist.

Matt sprang to his feet. "Here, have a chair." He pulled one from the table then straddled his own, arms resting on the runged back.

"How about some coffee?" Sam held a steaming cup toward her.

"Thank you," Lydia whispered, welcoming the warmth as she clutched the cup in cold hands.

"Well now," Matt began. "Let's talk about your job."

Lydia cleared her throat. "Excuse me." It was barely a whisper, and she tried again. "Excuse me. This really is impossible. You must take me back. I thought I was going to work for a family. Not for two—" Her voice faded again. "Bachelors."

Matt looked at her with narrowed eyes. "We understand that. And you can bet we were equally surprised."

His unblinking stare made Lydia duck her head. He continued. "Where were you planning to go?"

She jerked her head up and met his unwavering brown eyes. "I. . .it's. . .there. . ."

"Do you have a place to go? Family in this country?" His dark eyes probed for answers.

Mutely, she shook her head.

"What about money? You got enough to get you someplace and take care of yourself until you find something?" Again that probing, prodding look.

She thought of the twenty dollars Reverend Williams had given her as a farewell gift and wondered how far that would take her.

Sam leaned over the table and fixed her with his blue eyes. "You see, we're finding we have too much work to do outside to look after things in the house."

Her gaze swept around the room, and she knew at a glance that he spoke the truth. The whole room was littered several feet high and wore a grimy coat.

Sam smiled acknowledgment of her silent assessment. "So this is what we have in mind. You stay here and work." He leaned back and before she could answer, added, "We'll pay you well, and when you find another place or a job you think is as good as here, we'll take you there immediately. Deal?"

Matt leaned forward on his arms, a lazy expression on his face, but Lydia guessed he was waiting for her answer as anxiously as Sam, who tipped his chair back and kept his eyes on her.

"Seems to me it would help us all out." Matt's low drawl filled the silence as Lydia stared from one man to the other.

"What will people think?" Lydia blurted out the thing uppermost in her mind.

Matt sat up, a scowl drawing his brows together. "I do not think right and wrong are determined by what people think or even what they say."

She shrank back from the anger in his voice.

"If people want to find something awful to say, then they will whether or not you or I give them cause." He jerked to his feet and rubbed his thick black hair into a mass of curls.

Lydia glanced nervously at Sam, but he rose and went to the stove to stir the porridge, seemingly unaffected by Matt's reaction.

Matt rested a foot on his chair and turned to face her, a half smile on his face. "The way I see it is we need a housekeeper. And you need a place to stay."

Lydia stared at Sam's back and again at Matt's crooked smile. She certainly needed a place to stay, but Matt's words were only partly correct. It sometimes mattered a great deal what people thought. And she didn't need a third opinion to know it was wrong to live here alone with two men.

Matt nodded, taking her silence for consent; but from someplace deep inside her, Lydia discovered an inner strength that surprised her. She pulled herself straight in the chair and pushed her back against the hard rungs. "I'm sorry," she whispered. "I understand your predicament, and I'd like to help out." Her voice grew stronger with each word. "But I cannot stay here under these circumstances—" she threw her hands in the air "—without some sort of chaperone."

Sam turned and stared at her.

Matt dropped his foot to the floor with a resounding thud that jarred up Lydia's spine, but she did not shrink back or lower her gaze. These men must understand that she would not allow herself to be put in such a situation.

Sam turned and filled bowls with steaming porridge and carried them to the table along with a pitcher of milk. Lydia's mouth watered when she saw the thick layer of yellowish cream floating on top of the milk. It was breakfast-time yesterday that she had last eaten, and suddenly nothing seemed as important as food. She pulled a bowl close.

"Help yourself." Sam pushed the cream and brown sugar close. Matt spun his chair around and sat down.

Lydia paused, glancing from one man to the other. From that same unprobed strength, she smiled and, keeping her voice soft, said, "Perhaps someone should give thanks first."

Matt's eyes narrowed. Sam practically jolted in his seat. Silence hung over the table. Finally Sam cleared his throat and mumbled, "Go ahead."

She nodded and bowed her head, murmuring a short, simple prayer. "Amen." She reached for the pitcher and poured a generous amount of cream into her bowl. There was sweet comfort in the warm, rich food, and for a moment Lydia forgot her predicament.

Sam pushed aside his empty bowl and stared into his coffee cup. Suddenly he slapped the table with his open palm, almost causing Lydia to jump from her chair. "I got it!" he shouted. "Granny Arness!"

Matt glowered at him. "What about Granny Arness?"

"I was talking to Eldon Reimer in town awhile back, and he said something about not needing her anymore, but there didn't seem to be any place for her." He shrugged. "Don't rightly remember all he said. I wasn't paying much attention."

Matt sat back, his face thoughtful. "It just might work."

Lydia leaned forward. "Who is Granny Arness?"

They both spoke at once. "She's—" Matt sat back and waited for Sam to explain. "Granny is a widow with no home of her own. She helps out at different places." He grinned smugly.

"If she could come here. . ." Matt nodded. "Sam, I think you've hit on a good idea."

Two pairs of eyes regarded Lydia. She studied the tabletop, running her fingernail along a crack in the wood. Despite the prospect of a chaperone, her mind was still troubled.

She slowly raised her head, looking at Sam first. "I still don't know anything about either of you." She turned from blue eyes to brown. "Apart from your names."

Matt's expression hardened a moment; then he smiled, the change making him seem suddenly younger and not so formidable. "Fair enough. I'm more than twenty-five and less than thirty."

Sam snorted. "Who you trying to kid? I'm guessing if you're less than thirty, it's only by a sliver."

Matt cocked his head. "A very large sliver if you must know." He pushed back from the table and, tipping his chair back, hooked the heel of his boot over the bottom rung. "I'm not married. Never have been. I've never been in trouble with the law. I pay my bills on time, and that's about it." His gaze moved to Sam.

Sam nodded. "I'm twenty-three this summer. Haven't had time to get married. Running this ranch leaves time for little else."

Matt nodded.

Lydia gave the crack in the table her full attention. Neither of them had mentioned God or church or family. A dark and familiar feeling hovered at the edges of her mind. She recognized it from the past. The sense of having little choice in the direction of her life. She sighed and the shadow receded. At least she'd gained one victory. Granny Arness.

Matt broke the silence. "Let's make a deal. We'll get Granny Arness to come. You help us for a few days—say until we get the cows moved to spring pasture—and then we'll discuss it again."

They took her silence for consent and pushed back from the table. Sam donned a worn denim coat. "I'll get the wagon ready."

Matt nodded. "I'll empty out the little room and put up a bed."

"Wait," Lydia squeaked, but Matt had already disappeared into the doorway next to the kitchen.

Sam turned at her call. "You'll do okay," he said before he left.

For several seconds she stared at the closed door then clamped her teeth tight. It seemed there was no choice but to stay. She was trying to trust God to take care of her, but sometimes it was hard to see how He was doing it.

She unclenched her jaw and rose to do the dishes.

Matt came through the room, struggling under a load of crates and lengths of leather. "I've uncovered the cot. I'll store this stuff in the barn."

She waited until the door closed behind him before she turned and gave the room a sweeping gaze then looked beyond to the far room. If she were to be stuck in this place, she would at least have a good look at it.

Three doors stood along the wall of the far room. The first was the room for Granny Arness. Lydia peeked in. It was a narrow room with a cot on one side. The long, narrow window looked out over the green hillside.

The far door she guessed to be the men's bedroom, and she averted her eyes and retraced her steps to the middle one, stepping into the room where she'd spent the night. A glance revealed a desk and chair beneath the window, the tousled bed, and narrow wardrobe. She stooped and smoothed the covers then turned to face the front room, which was slightly less messy than the kitchen. The oiled logs of the wall held a surprising array of objects.

She circled the room to better see the mounted deer heads, deer horns sporting a variety of hats, a rifle hanging across two hooks, and on a nail, a gun belt with the initials MW. She paused before a series of pictures mounted in plain black frames. One was of a man and woman standing beside a stately brick house. The next showed a young man in a school uniform holding a parchment in his hands. She leaned closer. The boy held a definite resemblance to Sam.

With brisk steps she moved to the other side of the room. Light bathed her as she stood in an alcove encircled by windows. Even the door contained a long window. She closed her eyes, letting warmth flood her, then stepped forward for a better look, gasping as a wave of dizziness swept through her. The house was set on a couch of green grass that dipped and rolled until it came to a white-ringed lake far below. The distance had laundered the greens to a smoky gray.

Her head swam as she stared. She grasped the window frame to steady herself but could not tear her eyes from the scene. Something stirred in her. A nameless feeling. A sense of discovery. Of being uncovered. It was not altogether an unwelcome sensation mounting inside and calling to her.

Lydia tore herself away and hurried back to the kitchen, where she looked about in dismay. Piles of neglected belongings filled every corner and swarmed over every surface. She wrinkled her nose and identified the brown puddles under the coats as the source of the pungent aroma.

Fresh panic assailed her.

How was she to bring order to this chaos?

Where did she begin?

She sank into a chair. She knew how to clean and how to cook a few simple things, but that was all. A smile tipped the corners of her mouth. It was what they deserved—an inexperienced housekeeper. She sniffed. She'd never been in charge before, but on the other hand, she'd never seen such a mess, either.

A quick inspection of the cupboards revealed the cleaning supplies she needed, and she tackled the smelly corner, throwing the boots and coats out of the way. The smell was enough to make her eyes water. She was on her knees, head-first in the corner, when the door opened. Lydia sat back on her heels, feeling trapped. She blinked at the pair of legs that moved toward her.

"Well now, what are you doing sitting on the floor?" Matt asked. He dropped something on the table and hunched down beside her. "I didn't mean to startle you," he said, his voice deep. He waited and watched.

Lydia swallowed three times and blinked her eyes.

"Here, let me help you up." He rose and offered his hand. She looked at it, big and strong, then gingerly reached up and allowed him to pull her to her feet. "You're sure a timid young thing," he said as she pulled her hand away.

Her cheeks warmed.

Matt turned to the table. "I thought you might need some meat for dinner so I brought in some pork."

She looked at the raw slab of flesh on the table. It didn't look like anything she was familiar with. Did she fry it, roast it, or boil it? At Matt's sudden shout of laughter, she looked up.

"Do you know how to cook this?"

The corners of her mouth drooped. "I'm afraid not."

"Do you know how to cook anything?"

"One or two things." The Williamses had always had a cook.

He laughed again. "Well, don't that beat all. We've looked for a housekeeper for months. Some refused to live so far from town. One had a passel of young 'uns. Another had a dog she had to bring. There was one sounded pretty good, then she sent a letter full of 'house rules' as she called them. No smoking. No drinking. No swearing." He snorted and rolled his eyes. "She had more rules than most mothers. We finally get someone to come here, and it turns out you don't want to be here. On top of that, you can't cook. If that don't beat all." He laughed. "Well now, I guess I came along just in time to give you a cooking lesson."

He pulled out a bin to reveal a mixture of vegetables. He strode back and forth showing her where to locate flour, pans, salt, sugar, and more. He sliced the meat for frying, measured flour and lard for biscuits, and then scooped up his hat.

"Do you think you can manage?"

She drew a deep breath and glanced around the kitchen, trying to recall all the instructions he had rattled off. She looked at him with a sense of awe. "How did you learn to cook?"

He chuckled in deep, rolling bursts. "I've been on my own a long time. It was a matter of survival."

She smiled shyly. "Thank you for helping."

"Sam's gone for Granny Arness, and I'm headed to check the far fence line." He backed from the room. "I expect it will be almost suppertime before either of us is back." He paused. "You'll do fine." The door closed behind him.

Lydia smiled. He'd been so kind and helpful. She hummed as she returned to cleaning the corner.

Chapter 2

S he worked steadily all afternoon, finding a soothing calmness in the physical effort. So intent was she on her work that the sound of a wagon rattling to the door made her jerk up in surprise.

Sam stepped through the door bearing a wooden rocker in his arms. "Wait there," he called over his shoulder. "I'll be right back to give you a hand."

He set the chair to one side then went back, his voice coming to Lydia. "Here now." And then, "Take my arm."

Lydia stared at the door, waiting for her first glimpse of Granny Arness. Sam returned, his steps measured and slow, a small woman clutching his arm. Lydia's first impression was of a rounded back and coarse gray hair bundled into an untidy bun.

Her mouth hanging open, Lydia stared. She didn't know what she had expected but certainly not this frail, half-crippled person who with Sam's help hobbled to the rocker, groaning as she eased herself into it. Any thought of a bustling, kindly, helpful sort of mother-figure immediately vanished.

Aware of Sam's scrutiny, she jerked her mouth shut and met his eyes. He shrugged then bent over the woman. "Granny, this is Lydia Baxter, the girl I—"

Granny waved a hand. "I know who she is." Her voice rasped.

Lydia blinked. The sharp tone could be from pain, for she was sure every move the older lady made must hurt, or—trepidation rushed to her heart—it could be irritability.

"You can call me Granny. Sam here said he was in need of a chaperone." Granny sniffed, leaving Lydia no doubt how she felt about the living arrangements. "I explained to Sam my rheumatism has gotten so bad this past winter, I can't do much work." She groaned again.

Sam edged toward the door. "I'll bring in your bags."

Granny nodded, her faded blue eyes studying Lydia. "Child, could you get me some tea?"

"Of course." Lydia sprang to do as she was bid.

A few minutes later, she handed Granny a steaming cup. Something had been bothering her since Granny hobbled through the door, and she rested her hands on the arm of the chair. "I'm sorry to be adding to your discomfort."

Granny's gnarled fingers clasped Lydia's hand. "Don't be thinking any of this is your fault, child. I've been in pain most of the winter." She clucked her tongue. "The wagon ride didn't help, but I'll get over that soon enough." She patted Lydia's hand. "I'm afraid I'll be more trouble than I'm worth. I have so many poor days."

Lydia blinked back a sudden sting in her eyes. Granny was homeless, too—depending on the wants and charity of others for a roof over her head. Right there and then, Lydia promised herself that, no matter what, she would do all she could to make Granny comfortable.

Sam came through with a small trunk, which he carried to Granny's room. He stepped back into the kitchen; his gaze rested on Granny a moment, then he sought Lydia's eyes. "Will supper be ready in an hour or so?"

Lydia nodded, stilling the panic at trying to remember what Matt had told her. She studied the top of Granny's head, knowing she would benefit from the older woman's experience. But Granny handed her the empty cup and said, "I'd dearly love to stretch out for a few minutes."

"Of course." Lydia sprang toward the door. "I'll make the bed."

"Thank you, my dear. I brought my own sheets. You'll find them on the top inside my trunk."

Lydia quickly made up the bed as Granny, groaning with each step, hobbled toward the room. Lydia waited as Granny eased herself to the narrow bed and pulled a pink afghan around her shoulders then slipped away, hurrying to peel the vegetables and work on supper preparations. She couldn't remember how long Matt had said to cook everything and wished she had thought to ask Granny before letting her escape to her room; but now it was too late, and she would have to do her best.

Granny shuffled out when the men returned. They seated themselves around the table, and Matt reached for the bowl of potatoes.

Sam cleared his throat.

Matt jerked back and glanced at Sam.

Sam nodded in Lydia's direction, and Matt mumbled, "Forgot." Then he smiled thinly at Lydia. "Would you like to pray before we eat?"

Lydia nodded and again said a quick prayer of thanks.

Granny barely waited until Lydia said, "Amen," before she began.

"I declare. Mr. Arness always said the grace." She glowered at one man and then the other. "It just isn't fitting for a young gal to be saying the prayer when there's two perfectly capable men here. Why don't one of you give thanks?"

Sam drummed his fingertips on the tabletop and stared out the window.

Matt glowered at Granny. "Well now, I expect I could say the words as well as anybody. I just don't care to. Lydia, on the other hand, said right up front she thought it should be done, so I'll leave it to her." He grabbed the potatoes and spooned some onto his plate.

"Well, I do declare. It just doesn't seem right."

Lydia shrank back, wishing the floor would swallow her. She hadn't intended to start a fuss. She was quite sure it didn't matter to God who said what, but it didn't seem right not to say grace, seeing they were dependent on God's provision.

The meat was tough, the biscuits underbaked, and the potatoes still hard in the middle, but the men ate the food without complaint. Granny only pecked at hers, her tongue stilled for the time being.

When the men were done, Sam held his coffee cup and smiled as he glanced around the room.

"I'd forgotten there was a desk under that pile of papers." He nodded. "Good-looking desk, too." He slanted a look at Lydia. "What'd you do with all the papers?"

She guessed they'd be nervous about her throwing out something important. "I sorted them into piles. Anything that looked like business, I put into the drawers." Most of the drawers held odd bits of tools and hardware, and she'd put that in a box and shoved it under the bottom shelf in the pantry. "I put all the old newspapers in a bundle." First, she'd gone through the newer ones, hoping to find someone needing a housekeeper or nanny or companion; but there was nothing, and she had swallowed her disappointment.

Matt stretched and yawned. "What do you think?" he asked Sam. "Have I got time for a nap or shall we go finish that fence?"

Sam jumped to his feet. "The fence." And he grabbed up his hat and headed for the door.

Matt chuckled. "Wouldn't do to spend the evening lollygagging about," he explained to Lydia, winking as he followed Sam out the door.

Lydia pressed her palms to her hot cheeks, hoping Granny had not seen. *What would Mrs. Williams have said?* Then she stiffened and carried the dishes to the basin. *Who cares what Mrs. Williams and her husband might think? They hadn't cared much for propriety when they sent me to this job.*

Granny nursed her tea and watched as Lydia cleared up and washed the dishes. Lydia finished and hung the rag over the basin.

Granny spoke without breaking the rhythm of her rocking. "You didn't rinse that rag out."

Lydia stared at it then, sighing, poured a little cold water in the basin and rinsed it well before she again draped it over the edge.

"How did you manage to get yourself into this mess?" Granny demanded as Lydia cut the leftover meat into a large pot and set it aside to stew.

Lydia stiffened. Granny made it sound like it was her fault. Remembering her vow of kindness, she took a deep breath before she answered. "I understood I was to be working for a family."

Granny snorted. "Two less family-minded men you couldn't have found."

Lydia turned to stare at her. "What do you mean?"

Fixing her pale eyes on Lydia's face, she answered, "From what I hear of them, they don't have time for anything but work." She paused and added darkly, "I've heard other things, too."

Lydia's stomach lurched. They seemed pleasant enough young men. "What have you heard?"

Granny appeared to think better of what she had begun and pressed her lips tight.

Lydia persisted. "If there's some dark secret, I should know about it."

Granny shook her head. "It's no dark secret and, besides, now that I think about it, it was a long time ago. Before Sam came." She halted, but when Lydia continued to stare at her, she went on. "I can't say for sure if it was right or not, but I heard stories about Matt being a bit wild. But like I say, that was awhile back. Haven't heard any rumors recently, so maybe it was an exaggeration or could be he learned his lesson. Many a fine man has had a wild youth." She rushed on. "In his favor, I understand he is honest and hardworking. The men all speak highly of him. And the women find him charming."

Lydia tucked away a smile at the way Granny said the final words—like it was something to dread.

"And Sam?"

Granny shrugged. "My guess is Sam isn't interested in much but work." She pursed her lips. "Maybe he's running from a broken heart or something."

This time Lydia made no attempt to hide her grin. She was beginning to suspect Granny spent a great deal of her time speculating about other people.

Granny seemed inclined to linger and watch Lydia work. With several hours left before dark, Lydia decided to keep working on the kitchen and heated a bucket of water then set to work scrubbing the rest of the floor, the rhythmic creak of Granny's rocker keeping her company.

"Sam tells me you came over from England."

It wasn't a question, but Lydia recognized the bid for more information. She worked as she talked. "That's right. I came with Reverend Williams and his wife and children, Annie, Harry, and Grace. I've worked for the family since Gracie was a baby." She missed the children so much, she ached.

Grabbing the scrub brush with both hands, she shoved it back and forth, back and forth, determined to ignore the pain their memory brought.

Granny grunted. "At least you're young. No doubt you'll find someone to marry you and take care of you. Me, I'm too old for that. Besides, I could never stand to live with another man. Not after my Will." She sighed. "But it's no fun depending on others to provide you with a home."

Lydia sat back on her heels and flexed her aching arms. She wished she could offer some sort of encouragement, but Granny's words came too close to echoing her own feelings. Yet hearing the bitterness in the older woman's voice made her think. She didn't want to end up a prune-mouthed old maid. "I'm sure God will provide something for you." She dipped the brush into the hot water and mumbled under her breath, "And me."

"Yes, yes, of course." The chair rocked faster. A few minutes later, Granny pushed to her feet. "It's time I put these old bones in bed." She left with a muttered good night.

Lydia had dumped out the last of the dirty water and rinsed the rags before Sam and Matt tramped back in.

They jerked to a stop.

"I guess we should clean our boots before we come in," Sam mumbled, and they went back out, returning in a few minutes with most of the dirt scraped off.

Matt grinned as he hung his hat on a nail. "You sure are making progress getting this place cleaned up. It looks good."

"Thanks," she mumbled, a great weariness falling about her shoulders. She looked longingly at the bedroom door. Was it polite to excuse herself and go to bed? She yawned and rubbed her eyes and decided she couldn't wait another minute to think about the correct thing. "If you'll excuse me, I'm going to bed." She left without a backward look.

A few minutes later, she heard the men cross to their room.

In her nightdress, she sat on her bed, loneliness pressing into her chest. *If only there were a place where I belonged. A little corner of the world I could call my own.* When her mother was alive, they'd had two little rooms of their own. Now she had nothing. She would go from this house to another and another, always moving when her services were no longer needed. She ached for a family where she could become a permanent part.

Granny had predicted marriage would end her dilemma, but she knew it was a futile dream. No man would ever look at her and choose her for a wife. Not with her plain brown hair, her pale gray eyes, and her equally plain face. Mother had often said she had a face that would stand the test of time. "You'll only get more and more beautiful," she'd said, but Lydia knew she saw with eyes of love.

She picked up the Bible. Mother had told her over and over that God would take care of her. Lydia sighed. She knew she should be grateful for small mercies, and in a sense she was. This place was pleasant enough, it felt safe now that Granny was here, and the men seemed to appreciate even her faltering efforts.

But despite her attempts to remain strong in her faith and trust God to provide what was best, she couldn't stop the emptiness that sucked at her strength. Shivers raced up and down her arms, and she crawled into bed, pulling the quilt tightly to her chin.

She slept poorly and woke with little energy.

Granny snored softly from her bedroom during breakfast.

Matt glanced at the door. "Is she going to sleep all day?" he muttered.

"I don't think she had a good night," Lydia murmured. "I heard her up several times." Her head ached. She was grateful the men hurried out without wasting time with conversation.

She forced her weary limbs to do her bidding as she cleared up the kitchen and set to work scrubbing walls. She'd added vegetables to the leftover meat, and the mixture simmered on the stove.

Granny hobbled from her room as the men returned for lunch.

Matt took a deep breath as he pulled a chair to the table. "Smells good in here." She noticed he picked up a biscuit and opened it gingerly. When he saw it was cooked clear through, he nodded. Looking up, he caught her watching him and grinned. "You're a quick learner."

With an answering smile, she said, "Thank you." Then as a warmth crept up her neck, she dipped her head.

Sam sighed as he tried a spoonful of stew. "Excellent," he mumbled. "It is great to come in to a hot meal."

They truly seemed to appreciate her efforts, and smoothness settled into the pit of her stomach.

Sam pushed to his feet. "We'll be gone most of the afternoon checking fences. Don't work too hard." He smiled at Lydia before he ducked out the door.

Matt grinned at her as he slapped his hat on his head. "Well now, Miss Lydia, Sam's right. You don't need to do everything the first day or two. There's plenty of time. You might as well enjoy life. Go outside for a walk or read a book or something."

Granny snorted as they left. "Men. What do they know about a woman's work?" She glared at the living room that Lydia had yet to tackle. "It's obvious these two think a house cleans itself." She pumped back and forth in her rocker. "Get me my knitting bag, Lydia. It's by my bed."

Lydia blinked at Granny's command. Not even so much as a "please." But she dredged up a smile and hurried to do as ordered. As she watched Granny's gnarled fingers plucking at the yarn, she forgot her resentment. Granny was right. At least Lydia was young and strong.

She hurried with the dishes then turned to face Granny. "Matt's right. The housework will keep. I'm going to go outside for a while."

Granny frowned. "Neglected work multiplies," she muttered, but Lydia smiled.

"I'll get it done soon enough." She hurried outdoors before Granny could say anything more.

A few steps from the house, she halted and turned full circle. The cloudless blue sky was almost blinding in its brightness. The sunshine warmed her veins.

She'd always lived in town, and apart from glimpses from the train window, this was the first time she'd seen such an expanse of space. She was a dot in the vast panorama of rolling green hills. She looked about and, seeing no one, lifted her hands above her head and twirled. Breathless, she paused and, catching a glimpse of purple down the slope, slid down to investigate, sinking to the soft grass where downy, bell-like purple flowers waved in the breeze. As she marveled at their grace, a rustle startled her, and she turned to see a motionless tweed-brown rabbit with flattened ears. Lydia laughed.

At the sound of her voice, it bounced away.

She looked at the lake far below, its surface rippled by a tickling breeze. Big Spring Lake—she knew from listening to the men. She threw back her head to take a deep breath of the cool air laden with spicy grass smells and, drawing her knees to her chest, hugged her arms around them.

For the first time in so long she couldn't remember, she found her world worth embracing.

She breathed deeply. If only she could feel this way every day. If she could feel this good about the future. She sat still and quiet for a long time then rose and ambled back to the house.

Granny had gone to her room when Lydia returned. Humming quietly, enjoying the solitude, Lydia set to work washing the kitchen windows. That done, she began removing items from the wall in the living room and dusting the logs.

Lydia stood washing dishes the next morning, thinking about meal preparations and the work she'd do today as Sam and Matt sat at the table discussing their plans. Granny had again failed to come to breakfast.

Sam's voice startled her from her contemplation. "Why don't you take Lydia with you? I'm sure she'd enjoy it."

"Good idea!" Matt turned to her. "Would you like to come?"

Lydia looked from one to the other. "I'm sorry. I wasn't listening. Where are you going?"

"I'm headed up in the hills for some firewood. Do you want to come along and see the best part of the countryside?"

She hesitated for a moment, finding herself tongue-tied at the thought of being alone with him. But the beauty of the outdoors called. She wanted to see more of this country. "I'd like that." She kept her head down to hide the color she felt rising in her cheeks.

"Good." Matt rose to leave. "I'll be back as soon as I hitch up the wagon."

Lydia hurriedly scribbled a note telling Granny she was going exploring. A few minutes later, she sat high in her perch on the wagon seat, turning from side to side trying to take in everything. Matt was quick to notice her interest.

"See the crocuses over there?" He pointed to her side of the wagon. "They're like a bridge between winter and spring. Seems like they come out before winter decides to leave and stay until spring is really here.

"Look, there are some buffalo beans." He stopped the wagon and jumped down to pick a handful of lemon-colored flowers, handing them up to Lydia.

A lump swelled in her throat as she buried her face in them and peeked at him from under her eyelashes. He climbed back to his place beside her, the seat bouncing as he sat down, but he didn't spare her a glance before he flicked the team into a steady walk. Despite his impersonal interest, she couldn't help feeling it was a special time as he continued to point out plants of the area—the silver willow bathing them in spicy perfume, the olive-colored sage, the wild pussy willows, and the poplars dressed in palest green buds.

Granny was right. Matt could be quite charming when he chose.

The trail grew more uneven, and he fell silent, concentrating on guiding the horses over the rough ground.

"Where does this trail go?" Lydia asked as it grew more rugged.

"It's the trail we made last summer to get logs out of the hills to build on to the house."

The living room with its logs was quite different in construction from the frame kitchen, Granny's little room, and the long bedroom the men shared. "You built the log part of the house after the rest?"

"Well, the house was pretty small when we bought the place from Old Man Burrdges. We wanted more room for ourselves and a room for a housekeeper, so we split the house in half and added the front room and your room in the middle."

"How long have you and Sam been living here?"

"I was here before Sam, running horses in the hills and helping Old Man Burrdges. We bought the place over a year ago now."

"Where did you come from before that?" Suddenly there were so many things she wanted to know about him.

"From a lot of different places." Matt said it like it was all the explanation necessary, but Lydia persisted.

"Like where, for instance?"

"Well, I worked for a rancher in North Dakota for a while. Before that I did some tinsmithing. I even helped build bridges for a while."

Lydia turned on the hard seat to look at him more carefully. He kept his eyes on the horses, giving them more attention than she thought they needed.

"Where did you come from to start with?"

Matt's face hardened. "I was born in Wisconsin."

"Is that where your family is?"

"I have no family ties." He shook the reins as if to indicate that the conversation was over.

She folded her hands in her lap and stared straight ahead. Many times she had experienced the same reluctance to discuss her family with strangers. Her hands clenched in her lap. Perhaps he was hiding a shameful secret.

For a few minutes, they rode in silence; then Matt leaned back and looked at Lydia. "What about you; where are you from?"

She didn't mind telling him and relaxed. "I was born in Witnesham, Suffolk, England."

"I understand that you have no family. I'm sorry. What happened?"

The kindness in his voice brought tightness to Lydia's throat. She swallowed hard then told how she had lost both parents, then about living with the Williams family and coming to Canada with them. She explained how she'd had to move on when Annabelle decided to emigrate.

"That must have been hard after so long with them and no family here." Matt shook his head. "No wonder you were angry at ending up with us."

"Well," Lydia tilted her head and considered him, "one good thing came out of it."

"What would that be? Perhaps that you have two fine fellows to look after you?"

"Nooo. That's not what I had in mind." She shook her head and looked around at the beauty enfolding them. "I got to come to Canada. It is such a wild, free land." She sighed. "I'm just glad I could come."

"Then I think you'll enjoy what I have to show you."

The wagon climbed a steep grade with trees pressing in on either side.

"It's just over that rise." He pointed toward the break in the trees.

"What is it?" Excitement touched Lydia's voice.

"You'll see in a minute. It's worth waiting for, you can be sure."

They broke through the trees and drove a few yards more before Matt pulled the wagon to a halt. He jumped down and ran to help Lydia. Grabbing her hand, he pulled her toward the edge of the hill then stopped. "Look." He waved his arm.

Before Lydia lay a scene so enormous that she gasped and stared open-mouthed.

The tree-covered hills fell away before her in gentle waves to the deep blue of Big Spring Lake, surrounded by its collar of white. Beyond lay the plains, rippling on and on until they disappeared into a smoky gray line at the horizon.

Lydia's eyes felt wide. "I think I've just seen infinity," she whispered.

"Come, that's not all." He turned her around and pulled her past the wagon to the other side of the plateau. Again she saw the vast landscape open before her. This side of the hills lacked the beauty of the lake, and the plains were dotted with dark patches of bushes, but again, Lydia felt she could see forever.

After a few minutes, she swallowed and glanced toward Matt.

He was staring at the scene before them. Sensing her eyes on him, he turned. "You are standing on the Neutral Hills. They are called that because the Cree Indians lived to the north." He pointed to the plains before them. "And the Blackfoot to the south." He pointed to the far edge. "From these hills the tribes could come and spot game—deer, buffalo, whatever—then go out and hunt it. For that reason, they agreed this would be a place either tribe could come without fear of attack from the other.

"Come on. There's more." He pulled her after him down the trail. The plateau widened, the trees still sheltering the edge. Matt stopped. "See those circles of rocks?"

Lydia nodded.

"Those are tepee rings. They're the rocks the Indians used to hold down the edges of their tepees."

Lydia looked about her. There were several rings where she stood. "Do the Indians come here anymore?"

"No. Not since the buffalo disappeared and they signed treaties agreeing to live on reservations." He stood pensive for several seconds. "It's too bad to see a way of life end like that."

As she followed Matt back to the wagon, Lydia thought of the mysterious inhabitants who had lived in such a different way. It seemed strange to see signs of them, yet not one living being.

They continued along the hill to a small draw, where Matt pulled the wagon to a halt. In the trees was a pile of logs, all trimmed and neatly stacked. Matt jumped down and crossed to Lydia's side. "I'll be busy awhile if you want to go exploring."

Looking down on his broad smile and twitching mustache, Lydia felt a warmth building in the region of her heart. Whatever secret his past held, he was an interesting man with a kind, generous way about him.

And right now he'd be wondering what took her so long to respond. She allowed him to grasp her around the waist and lift her from the wagon. She stood facing him, his hands still at her waist, and breathed deeply, her senses assailed by the masculine scent of him. And then he released her and strode to the pile of wood and heaved an armload into the wagon.

Her gaze followed him, lingering on the muscles that bulged in his arms and down his back. Then she shepherded her thoughts and set off to explore.

She found many spots where she could view the plains below. She thrilled to the majesty before her. She was looking down a narrow valley with a stream glistening like a silver ribbon when she heard the wagon approach.

"It's a great view, isn't it?" Matt called out as he waited for her to join him. "I never get tired of it. Sometimes I come up here just to have a look. Never fails to make me feel better somehow."

"It's wonderful. I'll never forget it." Lydia faced Matt. "I want to thank you for bringing me." Without waiting for a reply, she turned quickly and let him help her up, smoothing her skirts neatly around her as she sat.

Before he flicked the reins, Matt nodded toward her. "I'm glad you enjoyed it."

The ride down the hill was more difficult because of the decline and the load in the wagon. For a time, neither of them spoke, but crossing the same ground took Lydia's thoughts back to the conversation they had on the upward trip.

"How did you and Sam meet?"

"Sam was looking for someplace to start a farm or ranch and met Old Man Burrdges in town. They got to talking, and Burrdges invited him to come to his ranch. That was when Sam and I met. Turns out Old Man Burrdges thought this country was getting too civilized. Said he wanted to go west and live out in the mountains, so we decided to buy him out."

"Where did Sam come from?"

"Little Miss Curiosity!" He smiled as he said it. "I know he came from England and has family back there. 'Fraid I don't know too much more about him. We sort of agreed to mind our own business with each other. Guess if you want to know, you'll have to ask him yourself."

Lydia lapsed into a thoughtful silence. She would, indeed, find a time to talk to Sam about his family and background, and hopefully he would reveal more than Matt had.

Matt circled past the house and let Lydia off before he drove to the shed to unload the wood.

The house was quiet when she entered; Granny, no doubt, was sleeping in her room.

Humming, she put on the coffeepot and went to the pantry to get vegetables. As she moved about, she decided she liked Matt. She was pleased that he'd been willing to share his favorite place with her.

She heard the wagon rumble across the yard then the barn door squeal as it was opened. The coffee boiled, and she pushed it to the back of the stove. A few minutes later, Matt entered and bent over the basin to wash. He was drying on the towel when Sam burst through the door.

"Matt, come quick! Queenie's had her foal, and she's brought him to the fence to show him off." He hurried back outside then stopped and called. "He's a beauty. Hurry before she leaves."

Matt grabbed his hat. Sam shifted from foot to foot, his gaze roaming restlessly around the room and, seeing Lydia standing at the stove, said, "You, too, Lydia. Come and see the foal."

Lydia didn't need a second invitation and hurried after them.

At the pasture fence stood a black horse, neighing as they approached. Lydia and Matt held back as Sam went to her, murmuring compliments. He climbed the fence slowly and stepped down on the other side. The foal skittered away on long, awkward legs then stopped and watched as Sam stroked Queenie and talked to her, all the while keeping his eyes on the nervous foal. For a few minutes, he watched, his eyes reflecting his pleasure. Then he quietly backed away.

"Isn't he a beauty?" he asked, his voice warm and rich.

"Looks like he's got the makings of a good horse," Matt agreed. "You did okay with that mare."

"She's got good bloodlines." He turned to Lydia. "Isn't he something?"

"He sure is." But she watched Sam, not the foal. His blue eyes sparkled, his face shone with pleasure, and he bounced on the balls of his feet. She had never seen him so animated. It filled him with a vitality that made her throat constrict.

After a few minutes, they returned to the house. Lydia poured coffee for the men and drank hers as she continued supper preparations.

Sam talked more than she'd ever heard him, racing on about the shed they would build, the fences that needed to be extended, and the herd of horses that would result from Queenie and her foal. There was a timbre to his voice that plucked at Lydia's heartstrings. She stole a glance at him. He scrubbed his fingers through his hair as he talked, the movement highlighting strands streaked with sunlight. His eyes flashed. She hadn't noticed before what a vivid shade of blue they were. She blinked. He was quite handsome when he was excited about something.

Chapter 3

The next morning, breakfast cleaned up, Lydia carried a bucket of hot water to the living room and tackled the smoke-grimed windows. She completed the first one and leaned against the sill, letting the morning sunshine warm her. The outdoors danced with light, making her feet restless. Sighing, she turned away and, squeezing her rag out, began scrubbing the next pane. Each swipe made the outdoors appear brighter and closer and let in more of the enticing sunshine.

"Come here," Granny called from her room.

Lydia dropped the rag and stepped to the door. "Good morning. What can I do for you?"

Granny groaned. "There's a hot-water bottle at the bottom of the bed. Fill it up again." She tipped her head back. "My old bones are making a real fuss today. I doubt I'll be able to get out of bed. You'll have to bring me my tea."

Lydia blinked. Annoyance threatened to erupt into anger until she saw the sun glaring under the lowered blind. She smiled, promising herself to let nothing ruin her enjoyment of the day. "I'm sorry you're feeling poorly," she murmured as she retrieved the hot-water bottle.

Granny groaned. "Sometimes I think I must have done something really bad to have to suffer so. God is punishing me."

Lydia gaped at the older lady. If Granny had decided suffering meant God no longer loved her, it was no wonder she was often cranky. She thought of her mother, who had suffered so much the last year of her life but still had remained sweet and gentle. Feeling half-guilty, half-pleased, Lydia knew it was because Mother was so intent on preparing Lydia for the future that she didn't have time to linger on her pain. *No, it was more than that. Mother never wavered in her belief that God had a bigger picture in mind. "Troubles can either make us bitter or better,"* she'd said.

Lydia looked down on Granny, wanting so much to communicate the assurance of God's loving control that she'd learned from Mother. "My mother used to tell me that our lives are like a weaving. We see only the bottom side, but God uses the dark strands, as well as the light, to create a beautiful picture."

Granny grunted. "Just get me what I asked for."

As Lydia filled the bottle and made a pot of tea, her own words circled round and round in her head. For a while, she'd forgotten to trust God's love, but she promised herself she would not let her light and momentary troubles push her away from God but, rather, draw her closer to Him.

She left Granny settled with the hot-water bottle at her back and a tea tray on a low table next to her bed and returned to her task to find the water had grown cold. As she dumped it out, Matt came to the door and called, "We're heading out to the pasture. Could you throw a few things together for a lunch?" He hesitated at the door, his wide smile lifting the corners of his mustache. "I don't suppose you know how to make bread?" Then he shook his head. "No, I suppose not, and I'm guessing Granny won't ever feel up to giving you a lesson, either." His dark gaze lingered on Granny's closed door. "Fresh bread would sure be welcome around here." He shrugged and nodded toward the pantry. "Throw in a handful of those dried apples from the corner cupboard." The door banged and he was gone.

Lydia slapped together biscuits and jam. She wrapped a handful of dried apples and threw everything into a sack. When Matt came to the door, she handed him the bag.

As soon as they rode out of sight, she set aside the bucket. Windows were easily forgotten when the outdoors called, and being careful not to disturb Granny, she slipped into the sunshine.

She hurried toward the hill, where she slid down the bank to a ledge and sat in the fragrant grass, staring at the lake shimmering in the bright sun. A gentle breeze lifted her hair and filled her senses with a mixture of alluring scents: sage grass and the nectar of flowers, the dry heat of the distant prairie, and the warmth of the sky.

The first words of the Bible sang through her mind, *"In the beginning God created the heaven and the earth."* The words echoed like a drum beat. *"In the beginning. . . In the beginning. . ."* They pulsated through her until the assurance that God was there from the beginning and would certainly be here for her now beat into her heart.

The words grew louder and louder until she realized it was the sound of wheels she heard. A wagon drove into the yard. Her gaze darted about, searching for a place to hide; and with a mouth gone as dry as cotton, she settled for huddling down in the grass, hoping she was invisible from the house.

The rattle of the wheels, the snort of a horse, and a sharp "whoa" came to her. A pause and then Lydia heard the rap of knuckles on the door. She huddled down as far as she could, hardly daring to breathe.

"Hello, is anyone home?" It was a woman's voice, and Lydia released a ragged breath, jumping to her feet to climb the hill.

Her visitor's voice rose as she called again, "Hello? Where are you? I'm your next-door neighbor come to visit." She turned and saw Lydia. "There you are!" In the yard stood a sturdy young woman.

Lydia walked across to her. "I'm sorry I wasn't here when you knocked." She reached around the girl and opened the door. "Won't you please come in and have tea? I'm Lydia Baxter."

The girl removed her bonnet and shook free her blond hair. "I'm pleased to meet you. I'm Alice Young, and I guess I'd be about your nearest neighbor. The boys stopped by this afternoon and told me about you coming here."

"The boys?"

Alice nodded. "Matt and Sam. They came by on their way up to the pasture. Said they thought you could use some company." She hurried on before Lydia could answer. "I know I sure can." She glanced around the room. "I thought they said Granny Arness was here."

Lydia jerked her head in the direction of Granny's room. "She's feeling poorly today and said she was staying in bed."

Lydia tried to sort the information Alice had imparted. "Where do you live?"

"Down the road a bit. You pass our place on the way to Akasu."

"I don't remember noticing it."

"No, you wouldn't." Alice smiled. "You can only see it from the other direction." Then she rushed on. "Norman and I have been married three months. I'm happy to be married, but I still miss my folks and the younger ones. It's the first time I've been away from home." Her face grew wistful. "I wish it weren't so far. It would be nice to visit them." She sighed and shook her head. "I'm sorry. I shouldn't be troubling you with my homesickness. Tell me about yourself. How old are you? Where you from? Where's your family?"

Lydia began. "I'm nineteen—"

"Same as me."

Lydia nodded. "I have no family. My father died when I was a baby. I don't even remember him. My mother died six years ago. Since then I've been a servant for a number of families. I came to Canada two years ago with the Williams family."

She told Alice about having to leave when a niece wanted to come to Canada.

Alice, in turn, told about being the eldest of six children and how she had met Norman while he worked for a neighbor. She told how Norman came to Alberta, picked out a quarter of land, and built a sod shanty before going back to marry Alice.

For a moment, neither spoke, lost in memories of the separate roads that led them to their present situation.

Lydia gasped. "I'm sorry, I haven't made us any tea yet." She jumped to her feet and scurried around.

Alice opened the bag on her lap. "Sam said he thought you could use some help with recipes so I brought along my cookbook." She held a worn book with loose pages bulging out. "It used to be my mother's." She dashed away a tear then dipped into her bag and drew out a small paper-wrapped package. "I hope you don't mind," she murmured, glancing at Lydia. "I thought I would give you a lesson in making bread."

Lydia laughed. "Matt's suggestion, I suspect."

Alice giggled. "It was indeed."

Tea was again forgotten as Alice showed her how to make bread. It was a lot more fun than Lydia expected as Alice took her through every step. Lydia laughed as she watched the yeast foam up as if it had a mind of its own. Alice said helping Lydia reminded her of some of her own disasters, and as she shared her experiences, she had them both giggling.

It was only after the dough was set aside to rise that they finally had their long-awaited tea.

"We have church in Akasu every Sunday now," Alice began. "We'd be glad to take you with us if you could get one of the boys to bring you over."

"Why, that would be lovely, but—"

"I'm sure they'd bring you if you ask."

"Perhaps."

Granny shuffled from her room at that point, demanding more tea and a bite to eat. She glanced at the dough rising. "I see you've done something useful with your time."

Alice looked startled as she met Lydia's gaze. Lydia shrugged. She was quickly learning to ignore Granny's sharp comments.

Her newfound friend left soon after leaving instructions on baking the loaves.

Shivering, Lydia lit the lamp and placed it on the table. The golden, fragrant loaves lay on a cloth at the other end. Darkness had closed in around the house. Granny had grunted, "Those two scallywags are up to no good. Mark my words," before she had shuffled off to bed two hours ago.

Matt and Sam had still not returned.

Lydia's fears circled round and round at a fevered pitch. What had happened to them? Maybe they met an outlaw up in the hills. Or been attacked by a bear or a wolf. What if they didn't come back? What would happen to her?

Suddenly she gave a short, bitter laugh. She, who had feared the presence of the men, now feared they might not return. She admitted the second possibility held far more dangers than the first.

Unable to sit idly staring into the lamp, she jumped up and went to the stove to lift the lids on the pots. Quiet pride flowed as she stirred the mashed potatoes, now growing dark and sticky. Meat stewed in thick, rich gravy.

She dropped the lid back on the pot and turned away. She'd made such a nice meal, and it was going to go to waste if they didn't get home soon. She paced to the window to stare into the blackness outside, straining to pick up some sign of movement. After a moment, she returned to the table to sit huddled in front of the lamp.

Was that the sound of horses in the yard? She stood frozen while the door opened and two figures entered. Her fright changed to shock at the sight of the men.

Pale mud clung to their chaps and boots, the color reflected in their fatigue-lined faces. Matt threw his wet cowboy hat at a hook, where it rested for a minute then plopped to the floor. Sam grabbed two chairs, offering one to Matt.

"Is there any hot water?" Matt asked in a voice thick with weariness.

Lydia hurried to pour water into the basin while the men unbuckled their chaps and dropped them to the floor. Matt tugged at his boots.

"Here, I'll help." Sam got up and straddled Matt's leg. He pulled and grunted, assisted by Matt's other leg pushing at his backside until the boot came off, trailing muddy water in its wake. Another struggle and Matt's other boot hit the floor. The men reversed positions, and Matt pulled off Sam's wet, muddy boots.

"Lydia, run to our room and get us some dry clothes, would you?" asked Matt as he pulled off his wet socks and began to unbutton his shirt.

Her face burning, Lydia lit another lamp and went to fetch the needed items. Both men were stripped to their jeans when she returned. For a moment, they looked blankly at her, then Sam said slowly, "Maybe you should wait in your room until we get changed and washed."

She fled, waiting in the darkness until Sam called, "It's all right now. You can come out."

He lay sprawled in the big armchair in the front room. Matt stood before the corner cupboard pouring amber liquid into two small glasses. He offered one to Sam and kept the other as he sank into the soft couch. He took a slow drink from his glass, meeting Lydia's eyes as he lowered his hand. She knew by the twitch of his mustache that he'd heard her sniff of disapproval and could read the severe expression on her face. She bit her tongue to keep from pointing out the evils of drink.

"I have supper made if you care for some," she said, her voice tight.

Sam sighed wearily. "I'm too tired to eat. Give us a few minutes to rest." He sank farther into the chair. "A cup of tea would sure taste good about now, though."

Matt put his glass on the floor beside his feet and slouched down, his legs stretched out in a long, lazy line. "I think coffee would better fit the bill, but make the Englishman his tea, and I'll share it with him."

They remained motionless, heads back and eyes shut, as Lydia hurried to boil the water.

"I have never seen such a stupid cow in all my life," Matt said, his voice low and lazy.

"The way she acted, you'd think we were trying to butcher her not rescue her." Sam moaned as he shifted, turning to Lydia with an explanation. "A rangy old cow got stuck in a mud hole. Looked like she'd been there since yesterday. But she put up such a fight when we tried to get her out, I thought we'd all three end up drowned in the mud before we could free her."

"She sure took off in a high fury when she got free," Matt laughed. "I expect she'll stay clear of us for a long time."

"Suits me just fine." Sam stretched and moaned again. "Think I'll have some supper then go to bed. I'm completely exhausted."

Lydia hurried to the stove to serve up plates of food. The men ate quickly and silently then shuffled to their room.

Deciding it had been a long day for her, as well, she put the dishes in the basin and poured water over them, leaving them to soak until morning, then dragged herself to her room and crawled into bed, where she lay staring into the dark. Matt's drinking disturbed her, and she couldn't understand why. She'd been in homes before where it had been a part of celebrations, and she had simply turned away and ignored it, so why should this time be different? Why should it make her want to cry?

Next morning, the men moved slowly, rubbing sore spots on their legs and stretching their back muscles.

"Did you have to use up all the hot water?" Matt shook the kettle and stared down its spout.

"Sorry. Put some more on. It'll only take a few minutes."

Matt grumbled to himself as he filled the kettle and put it on the hottest spot on the stove.

"My boots are still wet," Sam grumbled. "Now I'll have to wear my good ones."

"Ain't my fault," Matt retorted.

"Never said it was."

"Breakfast is ready," Lydia murmured, hoping they wouldn't turn their grumbling to her.

They hunched over their places, eating in grumpy silence. Lydia watched them warily, almost expecting them to growl over their food.

"If we had a dog, he could've chased that old cow out all by himself." Sam kept his head bent over his bowl.

Matt slammed his fist into the table. "I won't have a dog on the place. They can be more trouble than help." He shoved his chair back and gathered his coat. "You know how I feel."

"Yeah. I know." Sam sighed, making no effort to hide his exasperation.

Lydia had been about to mention how pleasantly the sun was shining, and didn't it look like a nice day? But she bit back her comment, remembering how often she'd let herself think there was nothing to be happy about.

She stood gazing out the window with her hands in warm dishwater and examined her thoughts. How often had she turned her face from what was good to hunker over the bad, tending it like a reluctant fire?

Too often, she admitted. It was a lovely day with the sun on the spring-green hills, and the view from the window was pleasant. She breathed a prayer of thanks.

The following days could have been cut from the same cloth.

Each evening the men returned late—tired and dirty, though never as late and dirty as the first evening. In the morning, they were short-tempered and testy with each other. Lydia was thankful they chose to ignore her except to call for hot water or give instructions for the evening meal.

Granny spent most of each day in her room, nursing a hot-water bottle, or shuffled out to sit in her rocker, picking at her knitting and offering dire comments about life.

Lydia found the days long and boring.

The sun was almost directly overhead several days later, when Lydia heard the rattle and creak of a horse and wagon entering the yard. A quick glance out the window showed Alice stopping in front of the house. Before she could step down from her perch, Lydia threw open the door and bounded out. "Am I ever glad to see you! I was getting very bored with my own company."

Alice laughed. "Sounds like the lament of many a prairie woman. Have the boys been away?"

"Well, not exactly." Lydia pulled her toward the house. "They've been moving cattle up to the pasture in the hills and have been gone all day. And when they are home, they're as cross as a couple of dogs with noses full of porcupine quills."

Alice laughed at the wry face Lydia pulled. "I wondered what happened to you yesterday. I fully expected to see you for church."

Lydia felt her mouth drop. "I plumb forgot what day it was. Fact is, I've hardly spoken to either of them, nor they to me. It doesn't seem to be worth it. Neither of them has said a polite word in days."

"That's a bit odd. They're always pleasant to be around and seem such good friends. Perhaps they're having some problems."

Lydia nodded. "They've said something about having trouble getting some cows out of a coulee. I think the side of a hill slid down in the spring rains and trapped them. They sounded like they might finish up today or tomorrow, though."

From what Lydia could gather from overheard comments, that would complete the task of moving the cows to spring pasture. Her heart swelled, knowing they would soon have to make good on their promise to take her back to town. Perhaps Alice could suggest a better position for her.

"How did your bread turn out?"

"It was fine. I've made it three times now, and it's turned out good each time." She shook her head. "Not that anyone seems to notice. Neither of them said a word, though they manage to eat large quantities of it."

"Then it's being appreciated, isn't it?" Alice smiled.

"I suppose you're right. Now tell me about church."

Alice entertained Lydia with comments about the people at church and the happenings of the small town of Akasu.

"I'm curious," said Lydia. "Akasu is such an unusual name. Where did it come from?"

"Norman tells me it's a Cree word meaning sick. He says it's because the water from Big Spring Lake is full of alkali and makes animals and people sick if they drink it."

Lydia nodded. "Matt told me a bit about the Cree and Blackfoot."

"Far as I know there aren't many around anymore. Now tell me what you've been doing."

Soon Lydia was telling how she had spent the long, lonely afternoons exploring the countryside just outside her door. The wide-open spaces stirred something deep within her soul. She couldn't describe the feeling, not even to herself. She felt her heart expanding as if to embrace the vastness of the landscape.

The view from the hills continually beckoned. She could look down on the lake and watch both cattle and wild animals grazing nearby. She thrilled to the delightful surprises she found hidden in the grass. "The crocuses are beautiful."

"I know. They turn whole pastures into a purple carpet in the spring. And it doesn't have to be very warm, either."

"Matt says they're the bridge between winter and spring."

Alice laughed. "I didn't realize he was so poetic." She shrugged. "I guess I shouldn't be surprised. He does seem to have a way with words, though in the time I've known him, I still don't really know a lot about him." Her expression grew thoughtful. "It's like he has this surface that is all charm and good cheer, yet sometimes I get the feeling that's all it is—surface—and underneath it all is a very serious, deep-thinking man." With a little chuckle, she shook her head. "And here I am writing my own story as my mother often said."

Lydia blinked. She got much the same feeling with Matt. "Sam is quieter but doesn't give away anything more than Matt."

Alice nodded. "The strong, silent type—both of them, but someday each of them will find someone they know they can trust their hearts to, and that's when they'll be willing to open up." Her gaze settled thoughtfully on Lydia for a moment; then her expression grew soft. "That's the way it is with Norman. He tells me everything."

Long after Alice had left for home, the conversation stuck in Lydia's mind. Alice's words had stirred up restless longings. When Mother was alive, Lydia had known the kind of relationship Alice meant. Lydia stared out the window, rubbing her palm over the ledge. Her chest muscles tightened so she could barely breathe. She exhaled loudly and jerked away, rushing to find some pressing task.

Early the next afternoon, the men rode into the yard, laughing companionably together, all impatience forgotten. Alice was right. They had been concerned about the cows; their friendship had survived the strain of the last few days.

They leisurely unsaddled their horses and spent a good half hour rubbing them down before they treated them to a bucket of oats. Lydia smiled. It looked like they were apologizing to their horses for their recent bad behavior.

In the house, they filled a boiler with water and put it on the stove. When it was hot, they carried it to their bedroom.

"Who goes first?" asked Sam.

"You go ahead while I clean my boots and chaps." Matt was already gathering up leather soap and rags for the job.

After Sam came from the bedroom, his hair wet and slicked back and his skin noticeably pink, they emptied the tub and refilled it for Matt.

A little later Matt emerged, his dark hair likewise wet and slicked back, his mustache trimmed and neat. Within a few minutes, his hair lost its prim look as it dried into a wavy mass.

Their good humor with each other seemed completely restored.

"I feel like a new man," boasted Matt.

"Sure hope you smell like one, too," Sam teased, punching him playfully on the shoulder. "It was getting pretty painful riding downwind from you."

Matt grabbed his shoulder in mock pain. "Why do you think I was always upwind? It weren't roses I smelled coming from your direction."

They took the coffee Lydia offered and sat at the kitchen table.

Granny, hearing the noise, had come from her room and sat rocking. Lydia put a cup of coffee close to her. Her mouth pursed, Granny studied the two men. "Am I to assume you have the cows moved wherever it was you had to move them?"

"Yes, ma'am." Sam sighed. "And mighty glad I am to have the job done."

"And all the cows safe and sound," Matt added.

"Humph. Seems like a lot of fuss and bother for some old cows."

Sam leaned back and grinned at her. "With cows, you get out of them what you put into them."

Her lips tight and working in and out, Granny turned back to her knitting.

For several minutes no one spoke as the men enjoyed their coffee and Lydia continued with supper preparations.

"Lydia?"

She jumped when Matt called her name.

"I sure hope you've got more of that homemade bread. You know, I think it's what kept us going the last few days."

Lydia felt a blush sweep up her cheeks as he continued in a teasing voice. "Just knowing our lunch would contain thick slices of it and waiting until supper for some more was worth all the hard work of the last few days. I expect we would have wasted away without it." His tone grew more serious. "Much obliged."

Sam joined in. "Yeah. Thanks for everything. You've been patient with us when there were times we were pretty awful."

Lydia mumbled, "You're welcome," and began to turn away, then paused. With a spark of boldness, she said, "There were times I felt a good spanking for you both would have been in order."

The men gaped at her. They turned to each other and blinked, then both let out a shout of laughter. They laughed until they had to wipe their eyes. Then, slapping their legs, they laughed some more.

Lydia kept her back toward them, her shoulders shaking as she chuckled.

Over supper Matt announced, "We'll be going to town tomorrow. We can take you with us." He turned toward Granny. "You, too, of course."

Granny snorted. "And why would I be wanting to bounce myself all the way to town? I'll just make out a list and one of you can get what I need."

Chapter 4

M att turned back to Sam, and they continued discussing nails and lumber for a shed while Lydia's thoughts buzzed.

She'd had the barest glimpse of the town when she arrived on the train, but it appeared a thriving center. *Surely I will find someone who needs my services. I could work in a store, help look after children—*

"Could you make a list of supplies for the house?" Sam asked.

Startled out of her thoughts, Lydia eyed him with surprise. He regarded her with a wariness that reminded her they would be left to fend for themselves after tomorrow. The idea made her insides feel tight, and she glanced around the room, now tidy and clean. How many days would it be until it was back to its former state?

She sat straighter. It didn't matter. "I know what's needed. I can make a list before we go."

"Good." His gaze rested on her for several seconds. Lydia wondered if she imagined he was waiting for her to offer to stay, but he turned to Matt without saying anything. "We better get some more paint, too."

Sleep was slow in coming that night as Lydia wondered about taking her trunk then decided to take only her valise and make arrangements for the trunk later.

God, You are finally providing a way out and I thank You. I hate to ask for more, but a job with a loving family would be nice.

She finally fell asleep with a smile on her lips, dreaming of life with a happy, generous family. She awoke with a bubble of anticipation tickling her throat and paused while making her bed to listen to the sound of birds outside the window.

Leaving her room, she saw Matt at the table, his chair tipped back as he drank a cup of coffee. She glanced back at the bedroom the men shared.

"Sam's gone to hitch up the wagon," Matt drawled, apparently enjoying his leisure while Sam did the work.

By the time Sam returned, she had made a hasty breakfast. After they'd eaten, she hurriedly washed up the dishes, knowing they would otherwise sit for days and grow so hard it would be a chore to wash them. For a moment she wondered what would become of Granny. She shrugged. That wasn't her concern.

As soon as she finished, they were on their way.

"It's another nice day, isn't it?" Lydia asked as they rumbled toward town. The sun shone in a cloudless blue sky. A soft breeze teased the waving grasses, lifting the faint scent of spices. Patches of blue, yellow, and purple dotted the rippling golden-fringed grass.

The men grunted agreement.

A few minutes later, Matt raised his hand and pointed to their left. "That's where Alice and Norman live."

At first Lydia couldn't see anything; then she remembered Alice said they lived in a sod shanty and realized that the brown humps were actually the house and barn. Her eyes widened and a shudder hurried up her spine.

I would hate to live in such a small, ugly house. She immediately scolded herself. Alice seemed content enough, even happy, so it couldn't be too bad. But Lydia turned away and looked straight ahead down the road. In the distance she could see a turn in the trail and strained forward, trying to see everything at once.

By the time they turned the final bend before Akasu, Lydia was perched on the edge of the seat. As they drew near the town, she saw it bustled with activity.

Matt stopped in front of a building with a large wooden sign saying BEAVER MERCANTILE STORE and helped her to the sidewalk. Across the street two ladies were deep in conversation as they entered the post office. A man laden with parcels came out of the pharmacy and crossed the street. Children ran along the sidewalk making drumming sounds with their feet. She pulled her attention back to Matt as he spoke.

"Here's twenty dollars for your wages." He handed her the bill then pointed across the street. "Sterling's Department Store carries a nice selection of ready-made ladies' wear. Why don't you go there and buy yourself a new dress—something pretty?" He climbed back onto the wagon seat and guided the horses toward the lumberyard farther down the street.

Lydia looked down at her plain, practical brown dress. She stared at her brown shoes. Suddenly she wished for a shiny black pair with fancy bows.

Sam reached out to take her elbow and Lydia jumped.

"Would you mind getting the supplies?" He guided her into the store.

"No, of course not." She'd never had the freedom to select items and relished the idea.

"You'll be able to get everything you need here."

As he went to make arrangements with the store owner, Lydia thought he must be right. Her eyes swept the shelves lining the store. They were laden with everything imaginable.

An hour later she emerged into the bright sunlight.

"I'll have it all ready to be loaded when Sam comes back," the storekeeper promised. "Thank you for your order. It's been a pleasure doing business with you."

Lydia thanked the man and allowed the door to close behind her. It had been a pleasure for her, too. She smiled and fingered the twenty dollars in her pocket. For a moment she stood and stared across the street at the sign above Sterling's Department Store.

She hesitated. What if she needed her wages to live on? But she couldn't remember ever having a new dress. She was accustomed to hand-me-downs. Her eyes narrowed, and she straightened her shoulders before stepping into the street and crossing to the department store.

Inside, the ladies' wear was displayed discreetly toward the back. Lydia hurried the length of the store and lingered over the selection of dresses, hats, coats, and shoes.

"May I help you?" asked a salesgirl.

Lydia wavered for a minute then replied, "Yes, I'd like to purchase a new dress and a pair of shoes."

The girl picked out a number of dresses for Lydia's inspection.

"Let's go in the back where you can try them on," she invited. Lydia found herself in the back room being encouraged by the vivacious salesgirl, who introduced herself as Lizzie. Lydia's cheeks grew hot with the exertion of changing outfits. She studied herself in the full-length mirror. The bright dresses emphasized her gray eyes and accented her ivory complexion. Strands of dark hair had come loose from the tight roll she kept it in and softened her face. She hardly recognized herself.

"I think I like the blue one best," she said much later, indicating a soft lawn dress in light blue with darker blue flowers tumbling down the skirt. A crisp lace collar circled the neckline while dainty tucks embellished the bodice.

"You wait here, and I'll find you the nicest pair of shoes you could ever want." Lizzie hurried to the front of the store. She returned as quickly as she left, bearing a pair of black patent leather shoes with an attractive square heel and—Lydia drew in a sharp gasp—the daintiest black lace bow.

"Aren't these just perfect?" Lizzie asked as she slipped them onto Lydia's feet.

"Oh, yes. I'll take them."

"Why don't you wear your new dress and I'll wrap up your things?"

Lydia wavered. Before she could decide, Lizzie made up her mind for her. "Here, I'll help you." She tucked the old dress inside a brown wrapping.

"You sit here, and I'll have your hair fixed in no time," Lizzie told her.

"Oh, that isn't necessary," Lydia protested, but Lizzie gently pushed her into the chair and removed the hairpins as if Lydia hadn't spoken. Submitting, Lydia relaxed as Lizzie brushed her hair out and worked it back into place. In the mirror, she watched Lizzie pull her hair into a loose roll circling her face and secure it with a few hairpins. It gave her a soft, classy look.

"How do you like that?" asked Lizzie.

Lydia turned her head side to side, admiring the results. "I like it. Lizzie, how can I thank you? You've been such a help."

"It was fun. I like helping people find what suits them. Now away you go and have a good day."

"Wait." Lydia grasped Lizzie's arm. This was her chance. Lizzie would know where she could get a position. "Lizzie, I need a job. Do you know someone who could use my services?"

A surprised look crossed Lizzie's face. "But you have a good job."

Lydia nodded. She had told Lizzie much of her story as she tried on clothes and had her hair fixed. "I never intended to stay."

Lizzie rubbed her chin and stared at the ceiling. Lydia held her breath. There had to be something somewhere. Then Lizzie shook her head. "There's not much call for a young woman to help. Most women get married and have their job cut out for them." Her eyes narrowed as she studied Lydia carefully. "Seems to me that would answer your problem." She tipped her head and grinned. "And with that new look, I'm guessing you shouldn't have any trouble."

Her jaw slack, Lydia stared at Lizzie. She wasn't ready for marriage. Why, that would mean she would have to look after a house, plan meals—she swallowed loudly. All the same things she'd been doing. But marriage? She turned and studied her reflection in the mirror. Was it really possible someone could look at her and think she'd make a good wife? As she turned from side to side, she admitted she wasn't that hard to look at. Plain and practical, but weren't those desirable qualities in a wife?

Lizzie peered over her shoulder. "And you have the two most eligible bachelors in the country to choose from."

Lydia met Lizzie's eyes in the mirror. "Sam and Matt?"

Lizzie giggled. "Have you looked at them? They're so delicious-looking."

Lydia pressed her finger to her chin. Sam with his fair hair and lightning-blue eyes, Matt with that riot of dark curls and laughing mouth, yes, perhaps they were worth a second look. She grinned at Lizzie. "I guess they aren't too bad." But there was a major flaw in the whole idea; neither of them had expressed an interest in spiritual things. Mother had drummed into her that marriage was one of the biggest decisions she would ever make.

"As a Christian," she'd said, "you will never know happiness if you marry an unbeliever."

Lizzie pulled Lydia about to face her. "Where have you been, girl? Forget trying to find a job. It's next to impossible. Go take advantage of what's right before your nose."

Lydia shook her head. "No. They aren't for me."

"Why ever not? What more could you ask for?"

Lydia jerked to her feet. "When—and if—I ever marry, there will be two requirements. I will have to love the man, and he must love me. And he will have to be a church-going believer." She sighed as she picked up her bundles. "Unfortunately, Sam and Matt are not." She headed toward the counter to pay for her purchases. "Perhaps you could keep an ear open for something and let me know."

At her side, Lizzie nodded. "But what about the other?"

Mystified, Lydia looked into the other girl's mischievous eyes. "What other?"

"Do you love either of them?"

"Of course not. I hardly know them."

They paused at the door, and Lizzie chuckled. "I'm guessing you know them better than most people do."

Lydia shrugged. "Perhaps. I couldn't say."

Lydia stepped to the sidewalk with the paper-wrapped bundle under her arm. *Why haven't either of them married? A wife would certainly solve their need for a housekeeper,* she mused.

Across the street she saw Sam and Matt loading the supplies into the wagon. For a minute, she watched them work.

Sam, tall and wiry, moved with a quickness she had come to expect of everything he did. It seemed Sam wasn't about to waste his time at anything. His hat was pushed back, and as he swung a box over the side of the wagon, she caught a glimpse of his blond hair combed back from his forehead as always. She couldn't see his eyes from where she stood, but she knew the intensity of the blue gaze that seemed to pierce right through a person. She knew he was steady, pleasant, and hardworking.

And Matt? She shifted her gaze to the other man. What did she know about him? His back was to her as he hoisted a five-gallon bucket into the wagon. Even across the distance, she could see his back muscles ripple. He was stockier than Sam, more muscular. She'd had a glimpse or two of his arms and knew they were thick as fence posts; she'd seen them bulge when he bent to pick up the bucket of water to add to the boiler on the stove. He had warm brown eyes that could probably melt a young lady's heart with their softness. He had a ready sense of humor that hovered just below the surface. Not as quiet as Sam, he had an easiness about him.

She sighed. *If only they had a Christian faith.*

The creak of an approaching wagon caught Lydia's attention, and she stepped back as it passed, wrinkling her nose at the strong smell of sweating horses.

As the wagon passed, Sam glanced up and saw her. Slowly he straightened and murmured something to Matt. Matt turned. They stared for a moment then headed in her direction.

Lydia took a deep breath and waited for them.

"Well, don't you look fine," said Matt as his gaze skimmed her from head to toe.

She smoothed her skirt and ducked her head. "Thank you," she managed, her tongue suddenly thick and cumbersome.

"Nice," Sam murmured his agreement. "Were you able to get the supplies?"

"Oh, yes." She glanced up in time to see how Sam's eyes lingered on her hair. She coughed a little. "Mr. Smith said he'd have it ready for you to load when you came by."

"Great. Thanks." Sam sounded like he had a lump of mud stuck in his throat. He turned to Matt. "Shall we?" And he stepped off the sidewalk and headed for the wagon.

Lydia wondered why Matt chuckled as he started to follow.

"Wait," Lydia implored, and both men turned to her. "I didn't. . .that is, I couldn't. . ." She stopped and took a deep breath. "I wasn't able to find another job."

Sam grinned at Matt then said, "Does this mean you're coming back to the ranch with us?"

"If it meets with your approval."

Matt grabbed his hat and slapped it against his thigh as he let out a whoop that made Lydia jump and glance up the street to see how many people heard him. Two ladies coming out of the mercantile looked their way then bent their heads together. "You can count on it!" he roared. "I thought I was going to have to give up homemade bread." He threw his hat in the air. "This calls for a celebration." He turned to Sam. "How would it be if we all have supper at the hotel before we head home?"

Sam, heading for the wagon, called over his shoulder, "Fine with me."

"Would you like that, Lydia?" Matt asked.

"Yes, I would."

"Give us a few minutes to get the supplies, then we'll be ready."

Content to watch the activities of the busy little town, Lydia leaned against a post and waited. As soon as they were loaded, the men tied the wagon in an alley and strode down the sidewalk toward her, their boots thudding against the boards. In their denim jackets and wide-brimmed hats, they radiated power and a sense of wildness that was an echo of the land they rode.

Matt hooked his hand around her elbow and escorted her across the street and down the sidewalk to the Empress Hotel. Sam dropped her parcel in the wagon and followed in their trail.

Her steps faltered as they entered the dining room, and she stared. Snow-white tablecloths were the background for sparkling china and crystal. Lydia drank in the air of luxury as Matt led her to a table and Sam held the chair for her.

Lydia couldn't shake a nervousness that made her want to turn and run. She was a servant girl. She didn't belong in such surroundings except to fetch and carry. She choked back a giggle, thinking how offended some of her former employers would be if they saw her here.

A leather-covered menu was placed in her hands. A sigh escaped her lips, and she settled back into her chair. This was an experience to be enjoyed not questioned, and she glanced at the selection.

What would she choose from so many good things?

Oysters, duck, salmon, or turkey?

Sam turned his blue gaze upon her, and she felt her cheeks warm. "Do you see something you'd like?" he asked kindly.

It was a moment before she could answer. "I don't know. It all looks so good, but I'm not familiar with many of the dishes."

Matt pushed her menu down so he could see her face. "Are you brave enough to try something completely new?"

She almost choked. "I think so. What do you suggest?" Matt leaned toward her, pointed to the menu, and made a few suggestions.

She stared at his blunt fingers skimming the items on the menu and caught the scent of grass-covered hills. Her own senses were swept with the feel of a warm prairie breeze.

Only half-aware of what he said, she settled for letting him order for her.

In a few minutes, they placed their order, and as they waited, Lydia unfolded the white napkin and placed it on her lap, suddenly so shy she couldn't look up for fear of meeting a pair of blue or brown eyes. She curled her fingers until the nails bit into her palms. Her insides quivered uncertainly. It was all this talk of marriage, she decided. Granny, Alice, and now Lizzie planting thoughts she was trying hard to ignore.

Marriage was, of course, out of the question, yet the remarks had accumulated until she was acutely aware of the two men.

Sam tipped the water jug to fill her glass and smiled slowly.

She nibbled her food, but it could have been anything under the sun. For the life of her, she couldn't seem to keep her mind on the meal.

Her fork slipped from her hand and landed on the carpet. She bent to retrieve it at the same time as Sam; their fingers brushed as they reached for the utensil. She jerked back, her nerves twitching. *This is ridiculous. Lizzie and her crazy ideas.*

But it wasn't the idea that was crazy. It was her silly response to it. She was so aware of every move the men made that she rattled like a wind-driven pile of junk.

The rest of the meal passed in a fog. Lydia didn't know what she ate or when the dishes were changed. Matt's boisterous chuckle made her jump in alarm, and Sam's quieter laugh tickled across her nerves.

They finished their meals and drank their last cup of coffee.

Lydia forced her wooden tongue to speak. "That was wonderful." She folded her napkin and laid it beside her cup. "Thank you."

"It was our pleasure." Matt grinned. "Umm, um. Homemade bread. Hot meals when we get home. Clean clothes. I'd say we got the better end of the stick."

Lydia's face grew hot as she met Matt's eyes. The look in them warmed her insides in a way she didn't understand.

Sam pushed his chair back and moved to hold hers. As she stood, she could feel the warmth of him. She breathed the scent of him—a clean, masculine smell of the outdoors. His arm brushed hers as he guided her from the table. Her rib cage tightened. Taking a steadying breath, she murmured her thanks and walked toward the door with legs that were stiff and unreliable.

Both men reached to open the door. Stepping back to make room for them, Lydia bumped into Matt's chest.

"Careful there," he murmured, grabbing her to steady her.

The tips of her ears burned, and she realized Sam stood at the door waiting. Barely able to speak, she mumbled her thanks again, praying she wouldn't trip. Never had she felt so awkward.

She'd spent the better part of a fortnight in the presence of these two men. Why should she suddenly be so self-conscious around them?

Matt jumped into the wagon and took the reins while Sam held out his hand to assist her. She rested her hand in his palm and gripped it as she stepped up. Determined to ignore the way her heart lurched at the feel of his strength, she quickly withdrew her hand and sat stiffly on the hard seat. She would face forward all the way home, she decided, and pretend Sam and Matt were strangers.

As they turned toward home, the sun tinted the scattered clouds with a golden underlay.

The sky is wearing a gold crown, thought Lydia. *A golden crown for a golden day.*

"Look at that sunset," Sam said. "Looks like the promise of a good day tomorrow."

"Yep," Matt drawled. "We should get a good start on that shed."

The men discussed their plans for the morrow, but Lydia didn't listen. Her thoughts were on Sam's words. The promise of a good tomorrow. It had a nice sound to it. Anticipation swelled inside until it caught in her throat. Tomorrow and tomorrow. Life was a bright promise, and she vowed she'd enjoy it fully regardless of all the uncertainties.

As the men's voices rumbled around her, she silently spoke to God. *Lord, it's been a good day. There have been times I wondered if You were looking after me; if You truly cared, when all the time You have kept me safe. Help me to trust You for each day.*

Chapter 5

Supper was quiet that evening. Sam seemed lost in his thoughts. Matt twirled the ends of his mustache and stared into space. Even Granny, after asking about acquaintances in town and reading her handful of letters, lapsed into silence.

Lydia sat up straight. "Alice says they have church in Akasu every Sunday." Her words came out in a breathless rush. "She says I could go with them if I had a ride to their place."

Sam's head jerked up. Matt dropped his chair to all fours and stared at her.

"Would you like to go?" Matt's voice reflected his surprise.

"I have always gone to church on Sunday. It just seems like the right thing to do—to get together with other believers whenever possible."

"Then you shall go." Matt looked toward Sam, but Sam stared at the wall behind Lydia. Matt raised his eyebrows briefly then shrugged his shoulders. "I'll take you myself." He tipped back in his chair again and turned his attention to the study of the ceiling. "And I'll take you right to town."

"You don't have to do that," Lydia protested, but when he didn't answer, she murmured, "Thank you."

Later she finished her bedtime rituals and went to the small desk in front of the window. The silvery moonlight bathed the scene outside in tinsel hues. She took out her Bible from the drawer, opening it to Psalms. She turned to Psalm 19, recalling how Mother helped her memorize these verses so many years ago, and she read the first verse, "The heavens declare the glory of God; and the firmament sheweth his handywork."

She stared out the window at the trees and hills bathed in moonlight.

Living here, she had seen so much of the beauty of God's creation. *Thank You, God, for that beauty.*

With a contented sigh, she turned back to the book and lifted the worn leather of the front cover to the tattered picture of Mother. How she would have enjoyed the beauty. If only Mother were here to offer advice in dealing with her feelings. Since Lizzie's remarks, Lydia hadn't been able to stop thinking about marriage—how it would provide her with a home where she belonged and someone to love her. *Neither Matt nor Sam is for me, but surely there is someone. . . .*

Mother's voice came to her, reminding her of God's care. God would lead. God has the answers.

Lydia shut the Bible and closed her eyes. In the quietness of her room, she committed her desires to the Lord.

Sunday morning Lydia put on her new dress and lingered in her room trying to recreate the softer hairdo Lizzie had fashioned. She found she was better at recapturing the enjoyment of the day. At the sound of Matt bringing the wagon to the house, she hurried from her room.

"Everything seems so crystal clear today," she told Matt as they rumbled along the trail. The sky was a flawless blue, the sounds of the birds clear and sweet; the spicy scent of the grass tickled her nose.

"It's one of those rare prairie days when the air is still and pure."

"Of course. There's no wind." She had come to expect the varying levels of it.

The town was muted as they traveled Main Street, every business closed, the sidewalks quiet. And then she saw the steeple of a church.

Matt pulled to a stop in front of the building and jumped down to offer her a hand. Lydia's feet had barely touched the ground when Alice rushed to her side.

"I'm so glad you came." She threw her arms around Lydia in a quick hug. "Come, I'll introduce you before we go in."

Lydia glanced over her shoulder. Matt was already back in the wagon.

"I'll be back to get you." His hat hid his eyes, but his lips formed a firm line under his mustache.

"You aren't coming in?" Alice tugged at her arm, but Lydia hung back.

"No." And with a flick of the reins, the wagon rumbled away.

Alice pulled at her arm, but Lydia watched Matt over her shoulder until he turned into the street. Only then did she follow Alice toward a group of people, a heavy lump settling around her heart. She had assumed Matt would accompany her to church.

"This is Mrs. Esther Johnson," Alice said, pausing in front of a woman surrounded by four little girls with large eyes and long black hair. Lydia wondered if the infant in her arms was a boy.

As they edged toward the church, a man joined them.

"Lydia, this is my husband, Norman." Alice looked at him proudly.

Norman had sandy-colored hair and a generous case of freckles; he smiled gently at his wife before he turned to Lydia and held out his hand. "I'm pleased to meet you. Allie has told me much about you."

"We'd better hurry," Alice said, and with Norman on one side and Lydia on the other, drew them through the doors and toward the front of the church.

Lydia settled herself and looked about. To one side of the platform, an older lady pumped the organ. Her graying hair bulged out from below a very ugly black hat with a frayed feather swaying in rhythm to her pumping feet. The familiar hymns had a startling quality as the organist struck several wrong notes.

"That's Reverend Arthur Law," whispered Alice, indicating the man seated on the platform. "He came in January. Seems to be a very ambitious young man."

Lydia studied the man. His fair hair dipped in a wave across his forehead. He had a fine, straight nose and a narrow chin with the most appealing dimple right in the center.

"I expect he's set a few hearts fluttering," Alice whispered in her ear.

So that's what you call it, and Lydia attempted to calm the trembling inside her chest as she turned to grin at Alice. "Do you really think so?"

Alice giggled behind her hand.

"Could you open your hymnbooks to number ninety-seven for the opening song?" asked a deep, well-modulated voice.

Reverend Law had taken his place while they whispered and giggled. For some unfathomable reason, it struck Lydia as funny, and she lifted the hymnbook to hide her face and hoped he wouldn't be able to see her shaking shoulders.

She lowered her book as Reverend Law raised his rich voice to lead the singing. The words squeaked out of her throat as she tried to join in. She realized she was staring. He was the best-looking, best-sounding man she'd ever encountered.

She hung on his every word as he gave the sermon, uttering familiar words of God's care and all-seeing knowledge, but the sensations racing up and down her spine at the sound of his voice were totally unfamiliar.

Even after he closed in prayer and walked to the back of the church to greet the members of the congregation, Lydia stared at the pulpit. Alice nudged her and giggled.

"Fluttering heart?" she whispered.

Lydia jerked her gaze away and blinked. "Something like that," she mumbled and rose to follow Alice and Norman. At the back, Alice pulled her forward, her eyes twinkling.

"Reverend, I'd like to introduce you to my friend, Lydia Baxter."

He gently took Lydia's hand between both of his. "I noticed you sitting with the Youngs." His warm voice seemed to suggest his notice had been more than ordinary. "I'm very pleased to meet you." He bent closer. "Are you new to the community?"

Alice pushed in. "She's been here a few weeks. She lives at the Twin Spurs."

"Then may I welcome you? And please extend an invitation to the rest of your family."

"But—"

Alice grabbed her arm and pulled her outside, calling over her shoulder, "Thank you, Reverend Law."

Outside she turned to face Lydia. "That was close."

"What?"

"I don't think the Right Reverend Law would consider it proper conduct for you to be keeping house for two bachelors who don't attend church. Even with Granny Arness's critical supervision."

Lydia stared and then narrowed her eyes. "You're right, of course, but how do you suggest I keep it a secret?"

Alice shrugged. "I don't rightly know." She grinned. "I don't suppose we could lie?" And she giggled.

Lydia's jaw dropped and then she laughed. "I wouldn't have imagined you could be so wicked."

Alice tossed her head. "As if I'd really do it." Her smile didn't fade one inch, and Lydia knew there was a wide mischievous streak not far below the surface of the efficient Mrs. Young.

Matt pulled the wagon into the yard, and Alice gave Lydia a quick hug before Matt helped her to the hard seat. Lydia was still smiling as they headed toward the ranch.

"Looks like you enjoyed yourself."

Lydia wriggled. "I did." Her thoughts lingered overlong on Reverend Law. The unmarried, handsome Reverend Law. She filled her lungs and let her breath out slowly. Was it only last night she had asked God to provide a suitable candidate for marriage?

She turned to look into Matt's face. "I thought you would attend church."

"It wouldn't do me any good. Besides, I can't see any difference between those who go to church and those who don't."

The words stung Lydia. Even though she sometimes harbored doubts about whether or not God cared, she didn't wish to be told she didn't act any differently than some heathen. "God commanded us to meet together." Her lips puckered as she spoke.

"Well, I think the outdoors is a better place to worship than some dark, musty building."

Lydia plucked at a flower in the material of her skirt. His words made her twitch. "Don't you believe in God?" She held her breath, certain that he would admit a deep knowledge of God's love even amidst his doubts—a mirror of her own situation. And if she were honest with herself—she prayed he would reveal the sort of growing faith she hoped to find in the man she married.

"Not a whole lot. I can't see how a loving God would allow awful things like floods that leave people homeless or fevers that kill whole families."

Her body was numb with the hopelessness of his words.

"I learned a long time ago it was safer to believe in myself."

"Was it flood or fever?" she whispered.

"What?" His voice crackled with tension.

"That took your family." It hurt to say the words, but something had happened to his family that left him angry and defensive. And blaming God.

"What makes you think it was that?"

"Your anger." The words fell into a long silence.

His hands clenched on the reins, and he stared ahead. Lydia stole a glance out of the corner of her eye and flinched at the tightness of his jaw. The silence deepened until she could feel it pulsating.

He made a sound like a muffled moan and mumbled, "It was a fever."

"I'm sorry," she whispered, but wondered if he heard her as he continued to speak, his voice rumbling deep in his chest.

"Everyone died but me. Even my baby brother." He stopped as if he could not go on.

"How old were you? What happened to you?"

"I was fourteen. The bank took the farm and I found a job. Been working ever since."

"Matt." She touched his arm. "I'm truly sorry. I know how much it hurts to have no family."

He turned to her and looked deep into her eyes. She couldn't breathe. His expression softened, and she remembered she once thought his eyes would have the power to melt a young lady's heart and knew she was correct.

"I guess you would at that." He smiled crookedly then shrugged. "I learned to live with it a long time ago."

She nodded, her throat too tight for her to speak.

He turned his attention back to the horses. *We share a common pain.* Lydia ached to be able to comfort him even though he made it clear he didn't think he needed it.

If only he would allow God to comfort him.

❦

Lydia tucked damp strands of hair behind her ears before she bent to open the oven, flinching as the blast of hot air struck her. She sighed her relief. Now that the meat was cooked and the bread baked, she could let the fire die down. She hurried to the open window, fanning her face with her apron. A dust devil skittered across the pathway and fluttered to death in the wilting grass. Heat waves shimmered across the land. But no breeze sighed through the screen.

Only June yet, and the heat wave sapped her energy as much as it parched the land. If only she could do as Granny had and move outdoors to a shady spot.

Wearily she moved to the other side of the house to look at the lake far below. In the bright sun, its hard surface gleamed like a mirror. Matt said when it got hot enough, people swam in the water despite the alkali.

I think it's hot enough.

She went to the basin and splashed water on her face before dipping the dishes into the water. She paused frequently to fan her face, but she grew hotter by the minute.

Throughout the afternoon the kitchen hoarded the heat, storing it in cupboards to blast in her face when she opened a door, chasing it into corners to throw at Lydia when she picked up a dish. Exhausted, she sank into a chair.

Matt and Sam stomped into the room, faces glistening, shirts damp with sweat.

"It's hotter than an oven out there," said Matt, fanning his hat across his face.

"Whew." He gasped. "It's even hotter in here! How do you stand it, Lydia?"

"I try not to think about it. I just keep doing what I have to." Her voice reflected the weakness she felt throughout her body.

Sam paused to call over his shoulder, "Granny, you want something to eat?"

"You won't catch me in that stifling heat. Tell Lydia to bring me something. And some more water."

Sam reached for a milk bottle. "I'll do it." He filled the bottle with water, scooped small portions onto a plate, and carried it outdoors to Granny.

The men ate lightly, explaining it was too hot to eat. Lydia filled the water pitcher three times.

She drooped over her own plate, staring at the food but unable to eat.

Sam shoved his chair back. "We're going to do something about this. Lydia, don't build another fire in the stove. Come on, Matt."

"What do you have in mind?" Matt filled his water glass and drained it before he followed Sam.

"I'll show you."

The screen door rattled shut behind them.

Lydia stared after them a long time before she forced herself to get up and get at her work. As she gathered up dishes, she saw them crossing the yard with armloads of lumber, which they piled outside the kitchen window. She poured water from the kettle over the dishes and watched the men pacing out some sort of measurements. The drum of hammers accompanied the swish of her broom.

Finished, she fled outside to escape the heat and sat in the shade a few feet from Granny's rocker, watching the men make a frame and nail it into place.

"You'd think those two had enough to do without dreaming up work," Granny said, rocking slowly and fanning herself with a piece of paper. "What are they trying to prove?"

Lydia shrugged.

Soon a shell of a room stood on the grass. Her curiosity stirred. What were they up to?

The shadows lengthened, and a gentle breeze drifted across the hills, thinning the heat as the men continued to work.

Granny pushed to her feet and shuffled to the house mumbling, "As if the heat isn't bad enough, how's a body supposed to sleep with all that racket?"

The sweet fragrance of wild roses perfumed the air, and Lydia reached over and plucked one of the flat, waxen blossoms from a bush growing tenaciously along the edge of the house. As the evening shadows lengthened, the men continued to pound and saw, the fresh wood smell mingling with the scent of roses.

"We'll have to quit now," Matt called, throwing his hammer on a pile of wood scraps. "We'll finish it in the morning, then I'll go to town."

"It should only take a couple more hours." Sam stood back and surveyed the shell, its roof sloping one direction, its walls naked uprights. "I hope a wind doesn't come up in the night and take our roof off."

Matt removed his hat to mop his brow with his shirt sleeve. "If I hear the wind during the night, I'll get you up and you can sleep on the roof."

"But if you went to sleep on the roof right now, you wouldn't have to worry," Sam replied.

Matt swung his hat at him. Sam ducked and pretended to throw a punch at Matt.

How can they find the energy? Lydia wondered as she dragged herself to her feet and went to her bedroom.

Despite her exhaustion, she tossed and turned, unable to find relief from the heat.

Dawn brought a blast of already overheated air. Lydia lay staring through her window at the brassy sky. She was tired and her head still ached. She tossed aside the sheet and struggled out of bed, pulling her nightie away from her sticky body. She straightened the bed covers before pulling on a worn cotton dress, the coolest thing she had. Already weary, she sank into the chair, pulling her Bible toward her. It fell open at the crocheted bookmark Mrs. Williams had made for her when she first began to work for them.

She wondered how Annabelle was doing as a nanny and whether Gracie and the other children missed Lydia. Then she read a few verses. But her foggy mind refused to concentrate. Finally she closed the Bible in defeat and let her head fall into her arms.

Lord, I can't take this heat. I'm so tired I feel sick. Please, could You send some cooler weather? And give me strength to make it through today.

She heard Sam and Matt cross the kitchen and the screen door slap shut. Almost at once she heard them hammering outside her window.

I suppose they want to work before it gets any hotter. Though if it gets any hotter, I'm sure to melt into a little pool of butter right in front of the stove.

Then she remembered Sam told her not to light another fire in it.

I don't know how I'll make them their porridge or heat water to wash dishes. She dragged herself to the kitchen, took out bread, sliced it, and set out butter and jam.

The rose blossom lay on the table where she'd dropped it last night. It was still fragrant but shriveled and ugly. For a moment she looked at it, wishing she could put it in water and restore it, yet knowing it was beyond help. She felt a sharp pain at the destroying power of the heat.

She called the men. They hurried in and quickly spread generous amounts of butter and jam on thick slices of bread.

Watching them gave her a queasy feeling.

"I think you can finish by yourself," Matt said to Sam as he tipped his chair back. "I'll go into town and get the things we need."

Sam nodded. "I'll get at it before it gets any hotter out there." The men rose and left. Lydia heard the rattle of the wagon as it left the yard and then more hammering.

With little work to do in the kitchen, she went outside.

Half the building had walls right to the ceiling; the other half had waist-high walls. Sam nailed a ledge on top of one of the shorter walls.

"Come over here, and I'll show you what we've done," he called.

Lydia did so.

"The stove will go here," said Sam pointing at the tallest of the walls. "These walls will allow the heat to escape and any breeze to blow through." He pointed at the partial walls. "We'll build some shelves and a table for you. Then you will be able to cook without heating the house up."

She turned full circle, admiring the construction. They had thought of everything. Sam beamed as she smiled and nodded. She turned her eyes toward him, letting his piercing blue gaze reach into her mind. Today he seemed tall and comforting and thoughtful.

"What a good idea! Thank you for thinking of it." She forced the words past a tongue that had grown stiff.

"I'm sorry and ashamed we didn't think of it sooner. Most farms have a summer kitchen, but we were too busy with our own concerns to think about how hot the kitchen gets in a heat spell like this." The color in his eyes deepened as he shifted his stance and crossed his arms. He seemed reluctant to tear his gaze away, and she couldn't find the strength to do so. As they looked deeply into each other's eyes, something warm and golden began to swell behind her heart, and she found it difficult to breathe.

"I sure hope this doesn't build into a hailstorm," Sam murmured.

Lydia blinked and filled her lungs. With limbs that felt borrowed, she crossed to one of the open walls, where she strove to pull her thoughts into order. Any form of relief from the heat would be welcome, but then she corrected herself, knowing how devastating a storm could be.

She looked into the overly bright sky, wondering if the blue of Sam's eyes was embedded in her brain. Thinking of the way he'd looked at her, she grew even warmer.

"Come, I want to show you something." Sam took her hand and led her out of the summer kitchen and away from the house.

The heat rushing up her body was suffocating. "Where are we going, Sam?"

"Just over that little hill." He pointed to the rise north of them.

Hand in hand, they crossed the yellowed grass, kicking up dust. *We're kicking up more than dust,* Lydia thought as shivers raced through her stomach.

A brown bird with a long, curved beak flew around them calling, "Pivot, pivot."

"What kind of bird is that?" she asked, hoping conversation would calm her nerves, knowing that nothing but dropping his hand would do so. Yet he showed no sign of releasing their grasp.

"Most people call him a curlew. He's trying to chase us away. Probably has young ones nearby."

A second and then a third bird joined the first, circling and squawking. Then a fourth bird came.

"It sounds like he's got a cold," Lydia said as the bird flew around them. They stopped to listen, laughing at the raspy voice. As Sam lowered his eyes, a shaft of sunlight flashed across his face and lit his eyes with an intensity that made Lydia gasp. For a heartbeat, she thought her chest would explode.

It's only the enjoyment of a shared moment, she told herself, forcing calmness to return. *Simple pleasure in a simple thing.*

Sam led her to the top of the hill. "Look below you," he said.

"Oh," Lydia gasped, "it's beautiful!"

The bottom of the hill was a mass of orange flowers so vivid she could hardly believe they were real. She picked up her skirts and, momentarily forgetting the heat, ran the last few yards to kneel among the cup-shaped orange stars. Sam squatted down on his heels next to her, his eyes on her face as she tenderly touched the blossoms.

She raised her face to him. "Oh, Sam, they're like china teacups. What are they called?"

His expression was gentle. "They're wild tiger lilies," he said softly, his low voice swelling in her mind until—

She gulped. "Is it all right if I pick some?"

Sam pulled out his pocketknife. "Here, let me. They have tough stems." He handed her the handful of blooms. Their hands touched. A shock ran through Lydia's body.

They stood. She raised her eyes to his. They were inches apart, both clasping the bouquet. Lydia's heart refused to function. She held her breath, aware of the intensity of his blue eyes; then he dropped his arm and turned away, shoving his hands into the back pockets of his pants.

"We better be getting back," he said. "I need to finish up the summer kitchen before Matt returns."

Lydia inhaled the subtle fragrance of the tiger lilies.

Sam strode up the hill as if his pants were on fire. Sweat poured down Lydia's face as she struggled to keep up. At the top, he stopped and turned, waiting for her. As soon as she caught her breath, she said, "Thank you for the flowers, Sam."

He smiled. "You're welcome. I thought you would enjoy them."

Lydia nodded then hurried toward the house.

Granny watched them the whole time. "Don't let a few flowers make a fool of you."

Lydia bit back the sharp retort that sprang to her lips and rushed inside to find a container. Granny's words burned in her mind as she lingered over arranging the flowers. *No, I won't let a few flowers, or even a few warm glances, sway me from my decision to wait for the right man—the man God will provide—before I fall in love.*

She made sandwiches. They were on a plate covered with a clean tea towel when Matt drove into the yard and over to the summer kitchen. The men unloaded a new stove and pipes. In a few minutes, they had the stove set up and the pipes running through the wall. Matt gathered kindling and coal while Sam wiped the stove off. They lit a fire and stood back. As soon as they were certain it was working well, Matt drove the wagon up to the door of the house.

"It's all ready to go," he announced, carrying a large box to the table. "Wait until you see what else I got."

Sam followed him, each carrying a box.

"The Johnsons, from south of town, were there. They'd picked saskatoon berries and brought them to town to sell, so I got some." He indicated two of the boxes full of small purple berries mixed with leaves and twigs. Two more boxes contained jars.

Matt proudly stated, "I thought you could can them and we could have fruit this winter. I just love fruit of any kind. I expect there will be peaches in pretty soon, too. We got that summer kitchen built just in time."

Lydia stared at the fruit and the jars. She understood she was expected to can them, but how did one can fruit? She dropped to a chair and gaped at the boxes on the table.

She was aware of Sam watching her.

"I guess I'll put the horses away before I eat." Matt left.

Sam twisted his hat in his hands. Finally he spoke. "Lydia, are you all right?"

She raised her head, but his face wouldn't focus; and she dropped her gaze back to the box of berries.

"Lydia, what's the matter?" Sam persisted. He followed her eyes to the berries. "Don't you know how to can?"

She shook her head.

He turned to Granny. "I suppose you know what to do?"

Granny snorted. "Young man, if you'll stop and think, you'll recall I said from the outset that I was too old and crippled to do heavy work." She picked up her knitting as if to dismiss the whole idea. "Lydia will have to learn on her own just like I had to at her age."

Chapter 6

Lydia lifted her head and watched Sam.

His eyes darkened, and his mouth drew to a hard line as he glowered at the older woman. Turning on his heel, he mumbled something under his breath then filled the kettle and took it out to the summer kitchen.

Lydia picked up a jar, examining it closely, hoping for a clue. Desperate for help, she determined to beg Granny to tell her the essentials, but Granny scurried into her bedroom mumbling something about needing a rest.

Sam returned with a pot of tea. "Leave the berries for now. I'll get Alice to come. She'll be able to show you what to do." He poured a cupful and handed it to her.

She swallowed the lump in her throat. "Thank you, Sam." Her voice wobbled noticeably. After he left she got the recipe book Alice had lent her and hunched over the pages but could not find any instructions for canning fruit. It must be something a person was supposed to know, maybe learning it from her mother.

Mrs. Williams's cook had done up jars of fruit and pickles and vegetables. Lydia squeezed her eyes tightly, trying to recall if she'd seen how it was done, but all she recalled was the steamy kitchen, the way her nose twitched from the smell of simmering vinegar, and rows of jars cooling on the table. Cook had not allowed anyone to linger when she was busy.

She paged through the recipe book again. It yielded no more information the second time through. Nor the third.

Lydia stood and stared into the box of berries then leaned over the box of jars and blinked. Did she expect to get inspiration from their contents? She took out a jar, turned it round and round, and shook it. She exhaled sharply. One would think instructions would be included. She took out each jar and examined the interior of the box. The only words she could find were the names on the sealers.

She paced the room then fled to the summer kitchen, where she ran her fingers over the ledges and the square wooden table, white and pure. Nothing yielded any information.

Desperate, she hurried back indoors, not slowing until she stood in the doorway of Granny's room.

But Granny lay with her back to the room, snoring softly. Lydia didn't know if the old lady was asleep or pretending, but it was obvious she didn't intend to help.

With heavy steps, Lydia returned to the kitchen and plunked down on a chair.

A suffocating sense of despair had gripped Lydia by the shoulders when the screen door squawked open.

"Well, what do we have here?"

Lydia sagged with relief at the sound of Alice's voice.

"Am I glad to see you! I hope you can tell me what I'm supposed to do with these saskatoons."

"That's why I'm here." Alice crossed to the table and peered in the boxes. "Sam told me you needed some help. I'm an old hand at this sort of thing. I've helped my mother since I was old enough to carry a pail of water."

"Thank goodness. You'll have to tell me everything. I've never done this before."

"First, let's take it all out to the summer kitchen. By the way, when did the boys build that?"

"They finished it this morning. Fact is, I haven't used it yet."

They carried out the boxes of fruit, the cases of jars and lids, buckets of water, and the pots and pans, while Alice kept up a steady stream of instructions.

Lydia strained to remember it all, hoping it would make more sense once she'd done some of it.

"There, that's the first batch ready," said Alice a few hours later as she lowered a jar of purple fruit into the boiler of hot water. "We'll sort some more berries while they boil."

Lydia sank to a chair by the plank table, the new white wood now stained with saskatoon juice. She scooped some berries into her bowl and proceeded to pick out the leaves and twigs as she listened to Alice's chatter.

"This heat has sure been hard on my garden. I don't know how many more days it can take before it dies. I've been giving it as much water as I can spare, but I don't know. . . . I remember one year Mother. . ."

Her voice faded as Lydia concentrated her energies on the tedious job of removing debris from the berries. Canning was a chore she wouldn't classify as easy work.

"We'll take these jars out now and set them to cool."

As Alice hurried to the stove, Lydia's head jerked up. Lost in her thoughts, she'd heard nothing of what Alice said.

"I'll help you get the next batch in, then I'll have to get home. It looks like there might be a storm coming up."

Lydia looked up. Far to the west, she saw a white-tipped, dark cloud churning. But the air drifting through the little shack was still oven hot.

A little later, Alice gathered her things and tied a bonnet over her flyaway blond hair. She paused. "I hate to leave you to finish this alone." She cast an anxious eye at the sky.

"I'll be fine. You get on home, and thanks so much for your help." Lydia remained seated, sorting berries, pausing only to wave good-bye and call her thanks.

"Anytime," Alice called. She hesitated a moment more then climbed into the wagon and rattled away.

As Lydia turned back to her task, a refreshingly cool breeze rippled across her neck, teasing her damp hair.

Cook the berries in the syrup, pour them into the jars, screw the lids down—not too tightly—and carefully lower them into the boiling water. Lydia repeated each instruction as she finished up the last of the saskatoons. *Now wash up the dishes, throw out the garbage, and put everything away.*

A blast of wind rattled the walls. Lydia looked up to a black, foaming sky. She shook her head, letting the cool air sweep her neck. Then she quickly covered the hot jars, making a dash to the house for more tea towels.

"You'd do well to hurry up," Granny said as Lydia raced into the kitchen. "I can't imagine what's taking you so long. Why, I remember when I did two hundred jars or more on my own."

Lydia paused, her hands full of towels, and stared at the older woman. "I'm sure you did." Her voice was strained. She took a deep breath to calm herself. "But don't worry. I'm just about done."

Granny's eyes widened and her mouth dropped open, but Lydia hurried from the room without waiting for a reply. She shook her head. She shouldn't let Granny's comments get to her. After all, the old lady was in pain and alone in the world despite Lydia's attempts to befriend her.

Lydia lifted the jars from the hot water and carefully arranged them on a piece of wood on the floor, hoping it would be enough protection from the cool breeze. Alice had warned her the hot jars wouldn't seal if they were bumped or cooled too quickly.

Lightning flashed across the sky and thunder rumbled over the hills as Lydia prepared supper then carried it indoors.

As the men crossed the yard, she heard them discussing the storm, wondering if it would bring hail or rain.

Sam paused at the door. "Did you get the saskatoons done?" The gentleness in his voice made her eyes sting.

"Yes, I've just finished."

"How many jars did you get?" Matt's voice was muffled by the towel as he dried his face.

"I think it was forty jars."

"Good job," Matt said, looking pleased. "It will be great having fruit next winter."

"You did great," Sam added. "But it was a lot of work." He looked at her closely. "You look tired."

His concern and the expression in his eyes lifted her fatigue. Suddenly she felt like singing. She smiled at him. "I'm fine."

It didn't rain or hail, but the heat ended. The following days were more tolerable, and Lydia breathed a sigh of relief.

"It's early," Matt warned. "We could see lots of hot weather yet."

But Lydia didn't care as long as it remained bearable for the time being.

Sunday morning broke with a cloudless sky, a gentle breeze promising moderate temperatures. Lydia fussed over her hair, wanting to look her best for church.

Sunday after Sunday Reverend Law asked about her well-being. Lydia liked to hope his questions and the way he looked at her with such a kind smile meant he was developing something more than pastorly interest.

She tucked in a strand of hair and studied herself in the mirror. She was being foolish. Reverend Law had been nothing but a perfect gentleman. There was no reason to pin her hopes in that direction. No reason—except for Alice's constant remarks.

"He's smitten with you," Alice had whispered as they parted a few Sundays ago.

"Me?" She wished Alice was right.

Alice leaned closer. "He'd have to be blind not to have taken notice of you as more than another warm body in the pew. Blind and a little deficient." She winked at Lydia. "And we know he's neither."

The way she waggled her eyebrows made Lydia giggle. "There's no reason for him to notice."

Her expression gentle, Alice grabbed Lydia's arm and walked her to the wagon, where Matt sat waiting. "Don't sell yourself short," she ordered.

Matt waited until Lydia was seated before he asked, "Sell yourself short at what?"

Lydia almost choked, thinking how Matt would react to the truth. The idea made her giggle.

"Now you have to tell me."

She turned to see his lips twitching under a mustache that wiggled like something alive. It made her laugh harder, so she couldn't speak. He shook his head, but as he drove from the yard, he growled, "Are you going to tell me what's so funny, or do I have to squeeze it out of you?"

His words interrupted her laughter; her mouth was suddenly as parched as the prairie grass. She stammered, "Alice th–thinks I'm too hard on myself."

He slanted a look at her. "Could be she's right." He paused. "You're an interesting young woman."

She'd stared at the horse's ears trying to think what he meant. *Interesting? In a good way or a strange way?*

The next week, as soon as the last elderly couple had shaken hands with the pastor, Reverend Law hurried down the steps toward the small group where Lydia stood.

Alice winked at Lydia, sending Lydia's thoughts into confusion.

Reverend Law paused at Lydia's side. "Would you care to stroll around the yard?"

Lydia glanced toward the street. Matt had not arrived yet. She had a few moments to enjoy a stroll. "I'd like that."

"How are you finding your new home?" Reverend Law bent closer, making her feel like he couldn't wait for her answer. His dark blue eyes were gentle, and she lowered her lashes before she answered.

"I enjoy the beauty of the prairies. I only wish. . ." She paused, thinking how much Mother would have enjoyed the details of color and texture and movement.

"Wish what?"

"I wish my mother could have seen it." Her throat was so tight, she could barely speak.

"Is your mother back in England?"

She had told him very little about herself. "My mother passed away a few years ago."

"I'm so sorry."

She was sure Mother would approve of Reverend Law. He was so refined, so cultured, so handsome.

"How are you doing otherwise?"

Her thoughts had run away. "I'm sorry. I'm not sure what you mean."

"I like to pray for you during the week and wondered if there was anything special I could pray for."

She lifted her face to him then and met his eyes, feeling as if she soared, so great was her joy. No one had offered to pray for her since Mother had died.

Afterward she couldn't remember her answer. All she could remember was how she'd seen him as if for the first time. A glowing light seemed to radiate from him.

That was a week ago, and as she prepared for church now, her hand trembled at the thought of seeing him again. It had taken several tries before she got her hair pinned in place—just in time, for she heard the wagon and hurried from the house to join Matt. There was only one dark spot in her day—despite her asking him repeatedly to attend the meeting with her, Matt continued to drop her at the church door and drive away. And Sam refused every invitation to accompany them.

When the final "amen" was said, Lydia turned to Alice. "It was a lovely sermon."

Alice laughed. "And what was it about?"

Lydia gave a toss of her head. "God and love and Jesus."

Her friend giggled. "I'm sure it was love you were thinking about."

"Was not. You're way off." She'd been thinking about the way Reverend Law's hair seemed to catch the rays of sunlight. She'd been wondering if he would draw her aside again.

But when she got to where he stood, a family clustered around him talking earnestly. She hurried outside, swallowing her disappointment.

The family must have had a lot to discuss because the parishioners left one by one until Lydia was alone in the yard. She had stared down the road for ages waiting for Matt, but there was no sign of him.

The door behind her clicked shut, and she turned. Reverend Law stared at her. "I thought you would have left by now," he said. "Where is your brother? Why hasn't he come for you?"

"He isn't. . .I don't. . .I don't know what has become of him." At first she'd welcomed Matt's delay, hoping it would give her a chance to see the pastor again, but now she was really and truly concerned.

Reverend Law hurried down the steps to her side.

"Where does he usually go while he waits?"

"I. . .I don't know." She'd never asked.

Reverend Law pulled his watch from his pocket and studied it. "I'm sure he'll be here soon. In the meantime, why don't we sit down and relax?"

She should have welcomed the extra time, but she could feel trembles starting in her legs. What could possibly have happened to Matt? She envisioned the wagon overturned and Matt injured.

Finally the pastor checked his watch again. "I think I'd better get a buggy and take you home. Perhaps your brother has forgotten you."

She shook her head. Matt wouldn't do that. But she didn't bother to say so. Somehow it was more important to find a way to set him straight about Matt being her brother.

Before she could decide the best way to say it, he rose.

"Perhaps you should wait inside until I'm ready to go."

"Of course." The building seemed dark and moody with no other occupant, and shivering, she huddled on the edge of a pew.

At the squeak of the door, she jumped to her feet.

"I didn't see any sign of your brother in town," said Reverend Law as he escorted her outside and helped her to the seat of the rented buggy.

"He's not my brother." But he seemed not to hear as he pulled himself up beside her.

"You'll have to direct me, as I have never been to the Twin Spurs Ranch."

Lydia indicated the direction. "I can't imagine what has happened to him." She twisted her hands.

"Not to worry. I'm sure there's a reasonable explanation. Now tell me about the ranch."

Grateful for his attempt to divert her concern, she said, "It sits in the hills looking down over the lake with the most wonderful colors that can be rich and vibrant one day and muted the next, depending on the weather."

"It sounds like you're very fond of the place."

"I guess I am." She hadn't thought of it before, but there was something about the ranch that made it special. It almost felt like home. "Tell me about yourself," she said.

"I was born in eastern Canada and came west with my folks when I was almost grown. I'm a graduate of the University of Alberta and of Alberta College, where I got my degree in theology."

Lydia was impressed. Such a well-educated man. "Your family must be very proud of you." Her voice revealed her awe.

"My family has always encouraged me."

"Where do they live? How many brothers and sisters do you have?"

"My family still lives in Edmonton, or at least my parents and my youngest brother do. My older brother is a lawyer, and my sister is a teacher."

He turned to Lydia. "Is there just you and your brother in your family?"

She studied her hands grasped tightly in her lap. Things were going from bad to worse, but she had no choice but to answer him honestly.

"Matt's not my brother," she whispered, not daring to look up.

"Your cousin then?"

"No. . .no, he's no relation," she blurted.

"I don't understand."

Lydia sighed. He might as well know the truth. Surely he'd understand. "You see, I was employed by Reverend Williams to help his wife care for their children. That's how I came to Canada. But then Annabelle, their niece, wanted my job. I had to find another position, or rather, Reverend Williams found it for me. I thought I was coming to care for a family. It wasn't until I got here that I discovered I was going to be housekeeper for two bachelors. I told them it was an impossible situation, so they got Granny Arness to move in with us." She thought she'd said it rather well and held her breath waiting for his reaction.

"Two!" His voice was sharp.

Her shoulders drooped. She'd forgotten he didn't know about Sam.

"Yes, there's Sam, as well."

His fine eyebrows drew together.

"I've tried to find something else." Her spine seemed to have lost the ability to support her body, and she slumped over her knees. "There doesn't seem to be anything."

"Why, Miss Baxter. What an intolerable position."

"They've treated me kindly. And don't forget Granny is there. She's a very capable chaperone." Sam or Matt would have smiled at that. Granny was everything any parent could ask for in that capacity—sharp-eyed, suspicious, and critical.

"Would you like me to see what I can find for you?"

She nodded, unable to speak around the lump in the back of her throat. His voice was so gentle, his concern so evident. She indicated the trail to the ranch house.

As they approached the house, Reverend Law patted her hand. "Now don't you worry about it anymore. I'll find you something."

Lydia stared straight ahead. Was it possible he could find her a new job when no one else had been able to come up with anything? But maybe he was thinking of something different. A pulse thudded under her jaw. There was one position she would jump to have—that of his wife. Could that be what he was hinting at? But he said nothing more as they neared the house.

Sam was at the corrals cleaning a saddle when the buggy entered the yard. He looked up at the sound, and when he saw it wasn't Matt escorting Lydia, he vaulted the corral fence and strode across the yard.

"Where's Matt? What's happened?" he demanded.

"I don't know," Lydia murmured, her thoughts in too much turmoil to do more than stare at him.

Sam's eyes narrowed as he watched her, blazing as he turned them on the man beside her.

The reverend jumped down from the wagon and came around to help Lydia, but Sam had already reached up.

Reverend Law faced Sam. "You must be Sam," he said. "I am Reverend Arthur Law." He drew himself up to his full height but still had to look up to meet Sam's eyes.

He took Lydia's arm and escorted her to the house, promising, "I will see you very soon," before he closed the door between them.

Chapter 7

Lydia fell against the door, her legs too weak to hold her. The buggy rolled out of the yard. She waited, wondering if Sam would come to the house. After a few minutes, she realized he had gone back to work, and she straightened. Crumbs indicated Sam had been in to make himself a sandwich. She should eat something, as well, but she had no appetite and simply stared at the top of the table.

Granny, moaning, hobbled from her room. "Well, what kept you so long? You'd think a good Christian could get home in time to look after her work."

Lydia clamped her mouth shut and remained quiet.

"What does a body have to do to get fed around here?" Granny plunked down in her chair and glowered at Lydia.

Lydia sighed. There was no point in responding to Granny's comments. "Would you like a sandwich and some tea?"

"Certainly I would."

As Lydia worked, hurt edged her thoughts. How could Matt forget her so easily? Though perhaps she should count it as a blessing, seeing as it provided the opportunity for her to enjoy a buggy ride with Reverend Law. His promise to help her seemed to carry a special meaning.

She put Granny's lunch before her and hurried outdoors to the edge of the hill; gathering her skirt around her legs, she plunked down on the grass.

In the background she heard Sam moving about in the barn and wondered if he waited for Matt's return with the same mix of emotions she felt. But then he was more familiar with Matt's habits and perhaps didn't find this unusual.

It stung to think Matt would treat her this way. She clenched her hands around her knees. Just when she thought things were going well, something went wrong. It seemed to be the story of her life. She longed to bury her head in Mother's lap and let her calm voice guide her. There was no one else she could turn to for comfort and advice.

God, You are the one I must depend on.

For a long time, she sat huddled over her knees, staring at the lake until the scents and sounds of nature seeped into her thoughts and she began to relax.

The sound of a wagon brought her stumbling to her feet. Her legs had gone to sleep, and it was a few minutes before she could walk. By the time she crested the hill, she saw Sam facing Matt, shoulders squared, his fists clenched.

She couldn't hear Sam's words, but she understood Matt's reply.

"I had something I had to do. It took longer than I thought." He turned to walk away. Sam grabbed his arm and jerked him around.

"You left her at the mercy of every Tom, Dick, and Harry in town." His voice rang across the yard.

Lydia had intended to confront Matt herself, but at Sam's angry words, she drew to a standstill.

"The preacher man said he'd taken her home." Matt rolled on the balls of his feet.

"That all he said?"

Matt shrugged. "Nope, but I didn't pay much mind to the rest of it."

Sam glowered at Matt and snorted. "He intends to find a more suitable job for Lydia."

"I wish him the best of luck." He paused to rock back on his heels. "You know he'll be scraping the barrel to find anything." He stretched. "And if he finds anything better, she'd be foolish not to go."

Sam's shoulders relaxed. "Yeah, I suppose so." Then he stiffened again. "Where the scratch were you?"

Matt shrugged and turned away to unhitch the horse. "Just something I had to look after."

Sam stared after him a moment then stomped away.

Lydia waited and, when no one noticed her standing at the crest of the hill, hurried toward the house. Too confused to face either of them, she hoped she could slip by without being noticed. When Matt called her name, her heart sank. Slowly she turned to face him.

He strode over and looked down in her face. "I didn't mean to leave you like that." He lifted his hands. "I plumb forgot the time." His brown eyes begged for understanding.

"Of course," she murmured, dipping her head.

He waited, but there didn't seem to be anything more she could say.

"Fine then," he said at last.

She headed toward the house, her heart heavy with disappointment. She couldn't so easily dismiss the knowledge that he'd forgotten all about her.

Granny sat knitting in her rocker. "I see the scallywag decided to return. He was up to no good, you mark my words." She rocked harder. "So he left you to your own resources to find a way home?" When Lydia didn't answer, Granny continued. "I expect you found a substitute easily enough."

Lydia kept her back to Granny and stared out the window. Granny made it sound like Lydia had done something wrong. She blinked back tears. Had everyone turned against her?

She mixed up johnnycake, shoved it in the oven in the summer kitchen, then returned to the house, where she sat down to wait for the men to come for supper.

Matt entered first and threw his hat at the hook, where it swung for a few seconds then settled. He draped his vest beside it before he bent over the basin. He was scrubbing his hands when the door opened and Sam came in.

Sam took his time hanging his hat and tugging off his boots then sat and waited for Matt to finish.

Matt looked over the top of the towel as he scrubbed his face dry. "Still mad?" he asked Sam.

Sam drew himself up. "I am not mad."

"Right, and I'm the preacher's wife." Matt flicked the towel at him.

Sam yanked it from his hands then marched past to plunge his hands into the water.

"It won't happen again," Matt promised.

"No, it won't," Sam muttered, drying his hands and face and bunching the towel over the hook.

By the time supper was over, the men were laughing and joking again, but the whole business stuck in Lydia's gut. *They are no different from Reverend and Mrs. Williams and all the others before them, forgetting me as easily as one forgets yesterday's yawn. A person should be important enough to be remembered!*

She took her hurt and confusion to bed with her, tossing all night as she turned her thoughts over and over, telling herself it didn't matter what anyone thought. Not Sam or Matt or Reverend Law. Certainly not Granny. God had not and would not abandon her. She would trust Him and Him alone.

Next morning, she looked at herself in the mirror and saw her eyes red-rimmed, her complexion wan.

That's what comes of thinking of yourself more highly than you should. She had to live with what she was—a servant girl with no home of her own.

A quick breakfast soon had the men outside working. Lydia turned to her own chores. Several times she looked out the window to see why the sun felt so cold. Even the color of the trees and flowers had faded.

Granny ventured out of her room, mumbling something about the pain in her back, waiting only long enough for Lydia to refill her hot-water bottle and make a pot of tea before she returned to her bed.

By dinnertime the darkness in her heart had not lifted, and Lydia served the meal with limbs that seemed heavy. The men said little, though she noticed the look they exchanged before they quietly rose and left the house. She turned back to the table to clear it and stopped like she'd been lassoed. In the center of the table lay a bouquet of wildflowers. There were brown-eyed Susans, harebells, and others she couldn't name. And loads of wild roses. Gingerly she scooped them up, avoiding the thorns on the roses, letting the sweet scent wash through her. A ray of sunlight gleamed through the window and caught the water jug, spraying a burst of color across the table.

Lydia held the flowers to her face for a long time before arranging them in a pitcher. Even then her fingers lingered at the blossoms. The men had cared enough to try to cheer her up. Her heart sang so she could hardly contain it. Her feet skipped across the floor as she did her afternoon chores.

Five days later, Lydia heard the rumble of an approaching wagon and hurried to the window.

Reverend Law sat upright on the seat.

She'd thought it might be Alice. In fact, she'd wondered if she would see the reverend again before Sunday. She assumed he'd been no more successful at finding her something than she had.

Realizing she was rumpled, she pulled off her apron and patted her hair.

The wagon stopped. She waited for his knock before she opened the door. "Reverend Law, what a pleasant surprise. Do come in." Her heart fluttered like a trapped butterfly.

"Good afternoon. I'm glad to see you're at home. I have good news." He glanced around the room. "It appears you are alone so I will remain here to speak to you." He stood with the door open. Lydia opened her mouth and shut it again, her heart racing too hard to be able to speak. It was almost more than she could do to keep from throwing herself into his arms saying, "Yes, yes, yes! I'll marry you!"

"I have found you a new job." He beamed. "It's with Karl Laartz and his family. They have five young ones, and his wife could use some help." He paused and leaned forward, waiting for Lydia's response, but all she could manage was a nod as her limbs wilted.

"The Laartz family lives about fifteen miles south of town," Arthur continued, unaware Lydia was finding it difficult to remain on her feet. "I'm afraid they won't be able to pay you very much—just room and board. And you'll have to share the room where the children sleep. Maybe you can help them learn English at the same time." He finally stopped talking and looked at her. "I know you're surprised I found you something. But where there's a will, there's a way." He grabbed the doorknob. "I'll wait out here while you get your things ready."

He walked to the wagon and leaned against it.

Lydia closed the door softly and fell against it, staring across the room. A job looking after a bunch of youngsters who didn't even speak English. It was hardly a proposal of marriage. She struggled to catch her breath.

And yet, wasn't it what she wanted? A job with a family?

She pushed herself away from the door. There was much to do.

In her room, she took her valise from the wardrobe and placed it on her bed. She looked about trying to decide where to begin. Moving to the desk, she took her Bible from the drawer and stood holding it. Suddenly her eyes focused. She sank down on the bed, the Bible in her lap.

I asked for a way out, and now I have it. God, You've answered my prayer when I didn't believe You would.

With renewed purpose, she pulled out her trunk and folded her belongings into it then rose and glanced about the pleasant room with the large comfortable bed, a desk under the window that seemed to invite her to sit and enjoy reading or writing, and—she turned full circle—complete privacy.

But it was time to move on. God had provided a way.

She grabbed her packed valise and walked out of the room to grind to a halt in the living room.

She'd cleaned and polished every piece of furniture. The desk Sam brought from England was over a hundred years old. For hours, she'd labored over it with rags and lemon oil until it reflected her face like a mirror. She scanned the objects hanging on the wall then stiffened her back and walked into the kitchen.

A possessive feeling tightened inside her. She'd brought order to this house. She had given it its sparkle. How could she bear to leave, knowing the disrepair that would soon sweep over it? Her eyes settled on the bright bouquet that had replaced the one the men left a few days ago, and she dropped her valise, hurrying over to bury her face in the flowers.

Would she find another view like the one from the top of the hill? Would she have time to admire flowers or pick them?

Matt and Sam. How could she leave them? She'd been so afraid of them at first. But now she looked forward to Matt's ready smile and the way he told her the names of the flowers.

And Sam. Sam was quiet and always kind. He offered encouragement with a soft word or two.

Even Granny. What would happen to Granny if she left? The men wouldn't be around to fill her hot-water bottle or make her tea in the middle of the morning. And she had no other place to go. How would she manage?

They needed her. They all needed her.

What had Reverend Law said? She would have to share a room with five children! And teach them English! She would be crowded into a corner without any privacy or space and yet—she shuddered—she would be so alone. It would have been different if he had even hinted at marriage. But he'd said nothing.

Lydia lifted her head. Her eyes felt hollow. *I got what I prayed for, but maybe. . .* She hesitated. *Maybe. . .* She drew a deep breath and closed her eyes. *Maybe what I asked for is not what I need. Or want.*

She squared her shoulders, picked up her valise, and marched into her room to drop it on the bed. With fingers that moved with firm purpose, she pulled out her Bible and returned it to the drawer in the desk.

With growing conviction that she knew what she wanted and where she wanted to be, she headed for the door and threw it open. Only one thing would change her mind. And that was up to Reverend Law.

He looked up as she stood in the doorway. "Are you ready?"

Lydia faced him squarely. "I've decided I'm not going." She met his eyes without blinking. If he had any interest in her as a woman, this was the time to proclaim it.

His mouth dropped, and he gathered himself up. "You've what?"

"I've decided I'm not going. At least not to the Laartz's." Would he understand her meaning? She waited. *Give me a better offer, and I'll jump at the chance.* But he simply stared at her.

"Lydia, you can't be serious. You're alone here with two unmarried men. Think how it looks. Your reputation will be ruined."

"I'm very serious. Besides, you keep forgetting Granny." She stiffened her spine. Perhaps she had imagined that his kindly interest meant more than it did. "I have a pleasant home here, and I have a job to do. I'm going to stay and do it."

"Lydia, you're making a big mistake."

"I'm sorry you came all the way out here for nothing, but I'm not leaving." She blinked hard, determined her eyes would not glisten with tears. If only he would say something that gave her reason to hope he had plans for the future.

A frown drove deep creases into his cheeks. "As your pastor, I must warn you that this is a foolish and dangerous choice you're making."

Unable to speak, she swallowed back the deep, empty feeling.

Finally he turned on his heel and swung up into the wagon. "I can see you're not about to change your mind." He looked down on her with a sad expression. "I hope you don't come to regret your decision."

She watched him drive from the yard. Had she thrown away her future? A deep ache filled her.

She watched until he was out of sight; then she fled to the shelter of the house, thankful to hear Granny's muffled snores.

Maybe Reverend Law was right. Maybe I don't belong here. But I don't belong anywhere else.

She looked about the kitchen, taking in all the things she had learned to love. *Yes, love. This is my place as much as any. Maybe not forever, but until I have to leave, I might as well enjoy it.*

She began the evening meal and was rolling piecrust when Matt came into the room. He skidded to a stop and looked at her, astonishment blazing from his eyes. Lydia blinked before his stare.

"What. . .what are you doing here? I saw Law drive into the yard. Didn't he come to take you away?"

Lydia laughed at the bewilderment in Matt's face. "Yes, he came to get me, but I'm still here," she teased, enjoying his confusion.

"What happened?"

"I just decided I didn't want to go." Lydia turned back to her piecrust.

Matt crossed the floor in two strides and, grabbing her arm, spun her about to face him. "What do you mean, you decided you didn't want to go? Isn't that what you've always wanted? Some way to get out of here?" His voice had grown hard.

Lydia wiped her hands on a towel before facing him squarely. "I guess I made it plain I wanted out; but when the chance came, I realized I wanted to stay. And so I told Reverend Law I wasn't going." No point in telling him the reverend had been appalled at her decision.

Matt didn't say a word. Suddenly he grabbed her about the waist and swung her around the room. "Whoopee!" he yelled as he twirled her. "This is the best news I've heard in a long time!" He sobered and set her down. "I thought you would be gone when I came to the house."

The door flung open and Sam charged in. "I just saw Reverend Law driving down the road. Was he here?"

"He was here and gone already," Matt answered, grinning.

Sam stared at Lydia. "I thought. . .we thought. . ."

Matt and Lydia laughed together.

"You thought I was going to leave with him, didn't you?" Lydia asked.

"Well, yes, I did," Sam sputtered. "He said he would be back to take you away. What happened?"

"I decided I didn't want to go. I'm staying here." Lydia grew serious and looked from Matt to Sam. "That is, if you still want me."

Matt took his hat off and threw it in the air. "Yahoo!" he hollered. He looked at Lydia, a wide grin lifting the corners of his mustache. "Of course, we want you." He punched Sam's arm. "Boy oh boy, did we strike it rich today!" He hollered again and the three of them laughed.

Granny limped from her room. "What's all this racket about? You'd think a body could sleep in peace, but no."

"You can sleep anytime." Matt grabbed her arm and guided her to her chair. "Fact is, you mostly do, so it won't hurt you to listen to us once in a while."

Granny snorted. "Such carryings-on. It's not decent."

Matt clapped his hands. "Seems you don't think having any sort of fun is decent, but it don't matter. Lydia's just agreed to stay on, and that's news worth making a fuss about."

"Humph."

Lydia wondered if she'd seen the ghost of a smile as the old lady rocked back and forth, her attention on her knitting.

But smile from Granny or not, Lydia couldn't remember feeling so warm inside since before Mother got ill. It stung to think Arthur could so easily dismiss her, but at least there were two—probably three—people who appreciated her.

❦

The next Sunday, Lydia prepared for church as usual. Although nothing more had been said, she hoped Matt would still take her. She stepped from her room and came face-to-face with Sam, resplendent in a navy suit and white shirt. His hair, the color of a ripe wheat field, was still damp. "I've decided to take you to church this morning."

Lydia swallowed hard, her thoughts colliding. She tried not to stare. "Where's Matt?"

Sam shook his head. "I'm not sure. He rode out a little while ago. Didn't say a word to me." He led her to the wagon, helped her to the seat, and climbed up beside her. "I don't know what he's got up his sleeve right now. Guess he'll tell us when he has a mind to."

Lydia settled back, her head buzzing with questions. Had Matt decided he couldn't be bothered to take her anymore? Or had Sam offered because of Matt's forgetfulness last week? She was pondering what this meant when Sam pointed to some cows grazing close to the road.

"See those cows, Lydia? They belong to the Schmidts. Notice how small and speckled the calves are? Now look over there." He directed her gaze to the hills above the lake. "See those pretty red, white-faced calves running about? Those are my cows with their Hereford calves."

She could almost see his chest swell.

"With the animals I imported from England, I'm going to have the finest herd in all of Alberta." He paused. "And the biggest ranch."

Lydia turned so she could see his face. "That's a pretty big goal."

"One I aim to reach." The muscles in his jaw rippled.

"I'm sure you will." She'd seen enough of him to know he would succeed if it depended on hard work and determination. Where had he learned such dedication to a task? Perhaps at home. "Are your parents farmers?"

"No." He shook his head, his voice growing hard as he stared across at the distant hills. "My grandfather—my father's father—used to own a good farm. It had been in the family since my great-great-great-grandfather's time."

"What happened to it?"

"My father decided he had more noble things to do than farm and advised my grandfather to sell it when I was just a boy." He spat the words out.

Lydia shrank from the vehemence in his voice. "What. . ." She hesitated, wondering briefly if it was a subject that should be avoided, then plowed on with her question. "What was it your father wanted to do instead of farm?"

"Preach!"

"Your father is a preacher?"

"No, not really." Sam sighed. "But he probably wishes he were. My uncle is, though. I think he calls himself an evangelist. They—and my mother—were involved in a revival about twenty years ago. That's when they decided they had a calling to preach. They left my grandfather on the farm alone. My uncle works in a mission in the slums of London, and my father took a job at the mill in town so he could be free to travel around and preach on Sundays. Eventually Grandfather's health gave out, and he had to sell his land. He died six years ago."

Lydia stared at Sam. She would never have guessed his calm exterior hid all that resentment. She turned her gaze back to the road as she said, "And you came to Canada to build a new farm to honor your grandfather?"

"No!" he exploded. "I came to prove I can make it on my own. I can succeed and be happy without the religious fervor they think is necessary."

Lydia nodded. "So that's why it's so important you have the best ranch and the best cow herd."

"And I will have!"

They were turning the corner before Lydia spoke again. "What about their beliefs? Did you never share their faith in God?"

"I suppose I did at one time. I was taught that God loves us but sin separated us from Him and that Jesus died to take care of my sin so I could reestablish my relationship with God. I believed it and accepted it as applying to me personally. But," his voice grew hard, "I've decided to be a rancher—and a good one."

Lydia studied his face. "Isn't it possible," she asked, her voice low, "isn't it possible to do both?"

He turned and held her with his intense blue gaze. She tried to understand what his look meant. She couldn't decide if he was startled at her statement or thought her daft for thinking such a thing.

Then they were in Akasu, and Sam turned away. Lydia sucked in a deep breath.

In front of the church, Sam helped her down then turned back to the wagon, but instead of driving out of the yard, he tied the horses to the fence and strode across the yard to join her. At her questioning glance, he smiled and said, "I might as well go in out of the sun as wait around town." He gently took her elbow and turned her around, escorting her across the yard and into the church.

Lydia was relieved that Reverend Law was already on the platform. As he rose to announce the opening hymn, his eyes swept the congregation, lingering on her a moment then widening as he saw Sam seated beside her. A smile twitched the corners of Lydia's mouth as she picked up the hymnbook.

After church, she paused and wiped her damp palms on her skirt, and then there was no one between her and Reverend Law.

"It's always a pleasure to have you with us, Miss Baxter." He lowered his voice. "I hope you've had time to reconsider."

Lydia shook her head.

"Well, if you do, the position is still available."

She nodded and joined Sam outdoors.

People gathered around him.

"Sam, it's good to see you here."

"How are the calves doing?"

"Did you get that heavy rain?"

The men and women flocked around him, welcoming him and seeking his advice.

Lydia had never seen this side of Sam and was amazed at the way in which he was accepted, even admired. Rather than rushing off as she had imagined, they were among the last to leave. Norman and Alice had been gone several minutes when Sam finally turned to her.

"Shall we be going?" he asked.

Nodding, Lydia hurried toward the wagon.

Driving down the street, Sam asked, "Do you have something ready for dinner?"

"I have some cold meat for sandwiches. And there's still some rhubarb pie left." She hoped he wasn't wanting something more substantial, as she hadn't prepared anything.

"Then I suggest we have our dinner here." With a decisive flick of his wrist, he turned down the street to stop beside the hotel. He reached up and lifted Lydia down as easily as he would swing a child. It made her pulse break into a gallop despite her vow to treat the men like she would any other employer.

She hid her confusion under the pretext of smoothing her skirt.

Inside the dining room, the light was muted by the heavy curtains and dark wood of the room. Sam touched her elbow lightly to guide her to a small table overlooking the veranda then pulled out a chair for her.

Lydia found herself very interested in the three horses tethered outside. Suddenly a menu was set before her.

"Well, now isn't this a surprise!"

Lydia jerked up and saw Lizzie. "Why, Lizzie, how are you? But I thought you worked at the store."

"I do. But I work here some of the time, too." She passed a menu to Sam, who was watching them with open curiosity.

"Lizzie, this is Sam Hatten from the Twin Spurs Ranch."

Lydia turned to Sam. "This is Lizzie, who works at Sterling's Department Store. She's the one who helped me buy my dress and shoes."

Sam rose quickly and held out his hand. "Pleased to meet you, Lizzie. You did a good job of helping Lydia select her dress. It's very becoming to her."

"Thank you, sir."

Lydia bowed her head to hide the warmth flooding up her cheeks.

As they waited for their orders, Sam pointed out people he knew and told her more about the town. Later, after the meal arrived, he asked if everything was to her liking. He called Lizzie over to refill her coffee. He was very attentive, but Lydia had difficulty concentrating on what he said.

"Have you always gone to church, Lydia?" They were bumping along on their way home—full of good food—the sun warm on their faces.

"Well, I spent the last two years working for a reverend so I went every Sunday." She smiled at the thought of deliberately missing church while in Reverend Williams's home.

"Before that, I went when I was given the opportunity, and seeing it's considered proper etiquette to allow servants to attend Sunday services, I usually managed to go."

"What about before that? Before you started work. Did your family go to church?"

So Lydia told him about her mother's death. "Mother spent a lot of time reading the Bible to me and talking to me. When I look back, I realize she was trying to prepare me. I think she knew she wouldn't be around to see me grow up, and maybe she knew things would happen that wouldn't be pleasant. So she tried to tell me ahead of time how to deal with them."

They were silent for a while.

Finally Sam spoke. "I'm trying to imagine how your mother must have felt. What sort of things did she say to you?"

"Maybe it was more her message than her words, but I do recall a few things she said, like, 'Give an honest day's work for an honest day's pay.' And she would read me verses such as, 'Seek ye first the kingdom of God, and His righteousness; and all these things shall be added unto you.' " Lydia gazed at the fluffy clouds sailing overhead. "I remember one saying she had." Lydia's voice was tremulous. " 'Remember, no matter how cloudy the sky, the sun is still shining. It's the same with God's love. No matter how awful our circumstances—' " Lydia's voice broke. She took a deep breath and continued, her words barely a whisper, " 'He still loves us.' "

"I'm sorry." Sam touched her arm. "I didn't mean to stir up painful memories."

She shook her head and tried to smile. "Thanks, but it isn't that. I've just realized how little attention I've paid to her words, and I feel like I've let her down."

"How could you have let her down? I'm sure you've always done what's right."

"Maybe I've done what looked right on the outside. That was easy when I lived with a preacher and his family, but I haven't always believed the way I should."

"What do you mean?"

"Remember what I said Mother would tell me? That God's love is always there even when things seem troublesome, like a storm blotting out the sun? I'd forgotten she said that until right now, but. . .well, when things haven't gone as I think they should, I've doubted whether God loved me. I just realized how childish an attitude that is. It doesn't show any trust at all. I must believe God cares about me all the time if I believe He cares at all."

This time the silence lasted much longer. Then she sighed. "I remember something else she said a lot. 'It's not nearly as important what happens to us as how we react to what happens.' I guess my reactions have been wrong. Maybe it's time for me to grow up and stop looking for someone to be responsible for me. It's time I was the one responsible for me."

Sam nodded. "In a way it reminds me of my mother. Only I always thought she and Dad were preaching at me. I never thought they might be trying to prepare me for some of the problems and decisions I would have to face." His voice deepened. "I felt I had to do things their way or it was wrong."

"And you found their way to be different than yours?"

"You might say that. I'm sure they thought I would follow in my uncle's footsteps and become a preacher, but I had no such desire. I always thought they were disappointed in me when I decided to come to Canada and become a rancher."

"You keep saying you thought they thought this or that. Did they say anything about your choice?"

"Well." Sam shifted uneasily. "No, not really. They helped me pack and ship the things I wanted. In fact, they arranged to have my bull shipped over here. But I knew what they were thinking." He blurted out the last words.

"I wonder if you could have been wrong."

Sam rubbed his jaw. "I don't think so." He shifted on the seat like he was suddenly uncomfortable. "I don't know."

Lydia twisted her hands. "Now it's my turn to apologize. I'm sorry. It's really none of my business."

"No need to apologize. I thought I had everything figured out. Maybe I need to do some more thinking."

The house lay ahead of them. The sign to the right of the lane proclaimed Twin Spurs Ranch and bore the brand of the twin spurs.

Sam reined in at the sign. "I love this place. It's what I've dreamed of owning. I want to make it into a place known far and wide." He stared at the sign for a moment then flicked the reins to hurry the horses home. "I'm not prepared to give this up." His words were blunt. His voice final.

Lydia longed to be able to tell him God's love was worth everything else. But she wasn't sure she could. Not without dealing with her own foolishness first. Even though she had no words to offer him, she knew he was making a big mistake if he chose a piece of land—no matter how pretty—over God. It gave her goose bumps to think of him turning his back on God. Though she had often doubted God's love, she couldn't imagine planning Him right out of her life.

Sam would have to find a way of reconciliation with God if he were to be happy. She felt certain that success without God's blessing would be hollow.

Chapter 8

Matt, having declared a holiday to celebrate Lydia's decision to stay, sat in the back of the wagon on a box while Lydia and Sam perched on the seat. At first Sam had hedged at the idea of taking a day off then, his glance lighting on Lydia, he shrugged and agreed it was time for some fun.

Pulling the box close, Matt leaned forward. "You're going to enjoy your visit to the lake."

Lydia caught her breath. He was so close, his face practically touching her shoulder.

"People come from all over in the summer. Everything from family outings to political conventions. You should have seen the one last year. All the fancy duds and all the bigwigs. And the food! It was. . ."

She didn't hear the rest of what he said. His breath against her cheek was like the playful teasing of a feather, only the thrill it brought was to a place deep within.

Sam chuckled at something Matt said, and Lydia met his blue eyes, the expression in them as warm as the smile on his lips.

Lydia thought the men seemed different since the day she had refused to leave with Reverend Law. They were more attentive, more considerate. Sam brought a bundle of flowers almost every day, and several times she'd caught him watching her as she moved about the kitchen.

She stared at the twin tracks disappearing under the horses. Maybe it was her imagination.

They pulled into the Youngs' farm, and Lydia plunged her errant emotions into hiding, determined to keep Alice from guessing the confusion in her heart.

Norman helped Alice into the back and climbed up to sit beside Matt. The conversation turned to weather and crops and community events, leaving no time for Lydia to dwell on her circling thoughts of Matt and Sam.

It was ideal picnic weather with a bounty of warm sunshine and cool breezes. They had barely stopped the wagon beneath some trees when Sam, Matt, and Norman produced a ball, a bat, and gloves. Out on the sand, they tossed the ball back and forth for a few minutes, then Sam batted the ball for Matt and Norman to catch.

Lydia sat on a blanket beside Alice, swaddled in lazy contentment. She leaned back to enjoy the sunshine.

"Let's have a game of scrub ball," said Matt.

"Come on, ladies, you'll have to help us out," Norman called.

Alice jumped to her feet. "I think they're in for a surprise. I was always a good ballplayer at home. Could beat out all my brothers."

"Wait," Lydia begged as Alice jogged toward the men.

"What's the matter?" Alice asked over her shoulder.

"I don't know how to play ball. I've never, ever played it before. I can't do it." Lydia's voice rose in panic.

Alice rushed back to Lydia, grabbed her arm, and pulled her to her feet. "You'll learn. There's nothing to it."

The men gathered round.

"Sure, we'll show you what to do," Norman assured her.

Matt and Sam nodded in agreement.

The idea of being at the receiving end of a spinning ball made Lydia want to run in the opposite direction, but the others hurried to spots on the grassy sand. Sam pounded the ball into his glove; Norman hunched down with his glove raised in front of him. Alice moved out to the right then turned and hollered, "All right! Let's play ball!"

Matt tipped a bat toward Lydia.

"What do I do?" she asked, her voice a thin squeak.

"You take this bat and hit the ball when Sam throws it to you. And then you run like the fury to the base where Alice is standing."

Lydia took the bat like it was a bad smell and dragged it across the sand. "Where do I stand?"

"Here, let me show you what to do." Matt turned her about, wrapping his arms around her, and lifted the bat in front of them. The pressure of his chest against her back and the warmth of his hands over hers sent a shivering shock through her body. A warm flush spread up her face. His sudden indrawn breath made her wonder if he, too, felt the shock of being so close.

The moment passed quickly as Sam called, "Are you ready?"

The ball whizzed toward them. Matt swung the bat, guiding Lydia through the motions. She felt the shudder and heard the crack as the ball arched through the air.

Matt grabbed the bat from her hands and pushed her toward Alice. "Run, run!" he shouted. "Go to that piece of wood!"

Lydia ran. At the marker, she tripped and tumbled in a heap on the warm sand.

"You're safe. Good run!" Matt called.

Lydia looked up and saw Sam and Alice both lying on the ground. Alice rose and dusted herself off. "I'd have gotten it, if you hadn't run into me," she said with disgust.

Sam got up, rubbing a spot on his arm. "What did you hit me with?"

Norman threw his glove on the ground. "Where's the ball?"

It started as a tickle in her stomach and burst forth like the ringing of bells.

The others stared as her laughter rippled across the sand. They looked sheepishly at each other, then they were all laughing.

Lydia couldn't seem to stop laughing all afternoon as they played ball on the warm sand, the gentle breeze cooling them. The others seemed to have caught the same tickle, for they laughed, as well.

"I've got to have a drink," Matt called at last, ending the ball game. The others joined him at the wagon for cool lemonade.

Resting on the grass, listening to the others laugh about the ball game, Lydia felt a wonderful sense of ease with them, and she let contentment envelop her.

She turned on her side to stare at the lake, fascinated by the glisten of the water, sparkling like coins tossed into the sunshine. She grew aware of a deep calm. She couldn't remember ever feeling happier than she did at that moment.

She turned to study the others.

Matt and Sam lay with their hats covering their eyes. Alice was on her stomach next to Norman, who chewed a blade of grass as he gazed at the leaves overhead. Suddenly Lydia knew why she felt so pleased with life. It was the first time she had friends her own age or felt she was part of a group.

Her gaze roamed the hills above the lake until she found the green-roofed house. How fortunate she was to have such a lovely home. A rush of warmth filled her as she studied it nestled in the hills. Of course it wasn't really her home; she only worked there.

She lay on her back and gazed at the leaves dancing against the sky. A leaf flitted down and landed beside her. *Drifting aimlessly like my life.* She jerked convulsively. *No. Not like my life. As long as I don't leave out God, my life has purpose. It has meaning. God, I will trust and follow You.* She allowed His love to flood her heart until she thought she would burst.

Even if it meant moving to another place. Even if it meant moving on and on for the rest of her life. For a moment, she lay still; then a surge of renewal jolted through her, and she jumped to her feet. Four pairs of eyes jerked open to follow her sudden movement. "I'm going to walk along the shore," she announced and marched toward the water's edge.

"Wait." Alice ran after her. "I'll come with you. This is the first time I've been to the lake. I want to explore, too."

Behind them they heard grunts and moans as the men struggled to their feet and followed.

On the lake, several brown baby ducks swam in a V-path behind their parent. At their approach, the adult bird flew quacking into the air while the young ones darted into the reeds and hid.

"We should have brought swimming suits and gone in the water," Alice said.

"I wish we had. It would be fun to see the expression on your face," Matt teased.

"Why? What do you mean?" Alice turned around to face him.

"That's alkali water and it tastes terrible. I've seen men bring up their dinner when they got a taste of it."

"Can't you swim in it then?"

"Oh, yes. You just have to be very careful not to get any in your mouth. And you have to wash when you come out or your skin turns all white. I guess that's why people only swim here when it gets really hot."

Lydia's nose wrinkled as the breeze drifted across the water. "Phew. What's that dreadful smell?"

The three men laughed as if it were some special private joke.

"That's the water. Doesn't that make you feel like jumping in right now?"

Lydia shook her head in disgust. She couldn't imagine it getting hot enough to enter water that smelled so bad.

"Look!" called Alice, her voice high. "It's a boat!"

A cumbersome structure, looking more like a floating cabin than a boat, was tied to a post.

"It belongs to some people in town," Matt said.

"Would they mind if we looked?" asked Alice.

"I'm sure they wouldn't."

They found a narrow dock leading to the side of the boat and climbed aboard.

"Let's take it for a ride," said Matt as he helped Lydia over the side. She shut her heart to the pleasure springing to life at his warm touch and turned her attention to the boat.

The front part was a small room, more roof than walls, and inside a waterwheel had attached pedals.

Matt and Norman sat on small benches on either side of the wheel and began to pedal. The waterwheel turned and the boat eased forward.

Sam and the two women sat on the benches built along the back. Lydia lifted her face to the sunshine and listened to the rush of the water. The spray cooled her warm face. For a moment a sense of loneliness welled up inside her. She acknowledged it briefly before she dismissed it, resolving she would let nothing steal away her newfound peace and assurance.

She opened her eyes to meet Sam's steady blue gaze, gentle and kind as always. A slow smile crossed his face as she held his gaze. Shyly, she returned Sam's smile then turned to look across the lake. They were in the middle and no longer moving.

Matt and Norman joined them in the sunshine. Even nature was still as they sat contentedly soaking up the sun and the peace.

"I wish we'd brought our picnic out here," Alice sighed. "It's so pleasant, I hate to go back."

"Today is a holiday. We can stay here as long as we like," Sam said, still watching Lydia.

"I think I could stay forever," Alice said.

"Well, I couldn't." Norman was emphatic. "My stomach is already beginning to tell me it's suppertime."

"Oh you!" Alice moaned. "You have a stomach like a clock. It's never late for a meal."

Norman sighed in mock resignation. "I guess I can wait if I have to."

No one answered. For several drowsy minutes, no one spoke.

"I'm sure the food must be getting overly warm by now." Norman spoke, his voice sad.

Finally Sam roused himself. "Okay, Norman. I'll help you power this boat back to shore."

The others remained quiet, their eyes closed, as the boat moved slowly toward shore—the lap of water spilling from the waterwheel soothingly hypnotic.

The sun was already kissing the treetops when they got back. Lydia and Alice put out the food while the men gathered up pieces of wood to start a fire. With an ease Lydia admired, Matt prepared a pot of coffee and set it over the fire to brew.

While they lingered over the food and washed it down with the almost-bitter coffee, the sky performed for them. To the music of the water lapping against the shore and the birds calling in the reeds, a medley of pinks and oranges danced across the sky and rippled over the lake. The dance slowed and the colors faded, almost disappearing, then sprang to frenzied life in the firelight. Lydia sat mesmerized as the flames twisted and danced. Glancing around, she saw the others also stared into the fire.

Matt rose to get himself another cup of coffee and throw some more wood on the fire. "I remember the first time I saw this country." He hunched down on a log. "I was driving fifty head of horses north from Montana, needing a place to winter them, when I saw a ridge of hills to the north of me. It had snowed the day before and then melted, except in the hollows on the hills. I thought it was one of the prettiest sights I ever saw." He took a long drink from his cup, wiping his mouth with the back of his hand before he continued. "I left my horses in someone's corrals and just started riding for these hills. When I got here, I just kept riding higher and higher until I was right at the top, where I could see both ways for miles."

Lydia knew it was the same spot he had taken her and cherished the memory even more, knowing it was where he had begun.

"That's when I saw Old Man Burrdges for the first time. He was getting a load of firewood. He was a bear of a man. Not very tall but with shoulders like an ox and a big, bushy beard. Anyway, I got down and helped him. Could that man work! He kept a steady pace all morning; then we rode down to the cabin. He asked me some questions and I asked him some. That's how I ended up running my horses in his pasture and helping him."

Matt fell silent then sighed. "It's hard to believe that was almost four years ago, and now Burrdges is gone."

319

"I was sure sorry to see him go," Sam agreed. Turning to Norman and Alice, he explained, "Burrdges thought this country was getting too civilized for him, so he went to live in the mountains. You know, he used to be a Northwest Mounted Police officer. Sure told some fascinating stories."

Norman was watching Sam. "Sam," he asked, "how did you come to be in this part of the country?"

Sam took a long drink of coffee before he answered. "I left England when I was seventeen. I had decided I wanted to join the adventure of 'opening up a new land,' as they said in the advertisements. I worked my way across Canada, doing whatever I could, saving my money and learning as I went. It took me three years to get to Alberta and another year of working farther north of here before I found this spot. As soon as I saw it, I knew it was what I wanted, so when Old Man Burrdges decided to sell, Matt and I bought him out."

"This is nice country for sure," agreed Norman, "but one of the prettiest sights is those white-faced red cows of yours. That was a smart decision, bringing Herefords from England. A real smart decision."

"I still think horses are better," Matt said. "At least they drive better and you can sell them anyplace."

"I don't intend to drive my cows anywhere 'cept to the rail yards in Akasu," said Sam.

Matt shifted restlessly. "Sometimes I understand how Burrdges felt. There are other places to see; new grass for the horses."

"Well, I intend to stay right here and build the biggest ranch in the area and raise the finest cows, too. And I'm willing to give whatever it takes to do that." Sam's voice held a brittle edge. He threw the rest of his coffee into the flames, raising a hiss.

A protest sprang to Lydia's lips, but before she could voice it, Norman rose. "You can stay here if you wish," he laughed, "but I need to get some sleep, and I prefer my bed to this hard ground."

"I guess we should be heading home," agreed Matt.

In a few minutes, they were riding down the road with only the moon to light their way.

Later, pleasantly tired, Lydia reviewed the events of the day as she prepared for bed in the soft glow of the lamp. It had been fun to learn to play ball, but the memory of Matt's arms around her sent a shiver through her stomach. Shaking aside the memory, she pulled the chair out and picked up her Bible. Her thoughts wandered as she opened the pages at the marker. Life was good and pleasant right now, despite her confused feelings about Matt and Sam. But she must set those feelings aside and let God lead her where He would.

She turned her eyes to the open pages before her and read Isaiah 26:3: *"Thou wilt keep him in perfect peace, whose mind is stayed on thee: because he trusteth in thee."*
The ache that had been building behind her heart melted away to be replaced

with a swell of gratitude. God knew and understood the longings of her heart. His way was best. She read the verse several times.

Her heart filled with peace, she climbed into bed to fall instantly asleep.

"It's a good thing we had that picnic when we did." Matt wiped sweat from his face and neck as he watched Lydia working in the summer kitchen. "It's been so hot since that we would have burned to a cinder on the sand."

Lydia sighed and pushed back strands of damp hair. Even with the summer kitchen, making bread and cooking meals left her gasping from the heat. "I hope this breaks soon."

Matt shrugged. "Never can tell."

"What are you planning today?" She hadn't meant to sound so sharp, but his comment about the weather made her cross. You'd think he could come up with something a little more encouraging than "never can tell." She didn't think she could survive another day of crushing heat.

He shrugged. "Don't know. Seems too hot to do much of anything. Maybe I'll go lay in the shade."

"Think again."

At the sound of Sam's voice behind them, Matt spun on his heels. "Where did you come from? You trying to scare the liver out of me?" Matt growled.

Sam grinned. "Would you call that a chicken liver? How come you're so jumpy?" He chuckled as Matt's expression grew fierce.

"I'm not jumpy, and I'm not chicken. Why are you sneaking around like a weasel headed for the henhouse?"

Sam laughed and playfully punched Matt's arm.

Lydia shook her head and turned back to the meat she was browning, knowing they could tease each other for hours. Usually she found it amusing, but this morning she wished they would take their noise elsewhere. Her head felt like it was going to explode. No wonder Granny had shuffled back to her room saying she would lie in bed and melt; the heat was so bad, it made no difference whether she was inside or out.

"I told Norman we would come over and give him a hand with the last of his hay," Sam said as he ducked a swat from Matt.

Matt stared like Sam had suddenly lost his head. "In this heat? You must be loco."

Sam shrugged. "His hay is burning up on him. Of course, if you can't handle it, I guess it's okay if you lay in the shade." He stepped back. "Maybe Lydia could even lend you a dress."

Matt exploded. "I'll dress you for that!" He lunged at Sam, but Sam was already racing across the yard.

He called over his shoulder. "We won't be back until dark."

A few minutes later, she heard them ride out and heaved a sigh. The bread had to rise before she could bake it, but after that, she would find something to do that got her away from the hot stove.

She tidied the summer kitchen; then as the bread baked, she returned to the house and quickly dusted. There seemed to be a never-ending supply of dirt drifting into the house as the heat sapped the moisture from the land. She couldn't imagine how dry everything would be if this kept up. And the bulk of summer was still ahead. Matt had assured her it was unseasonably warm.

"More like August weather," he'd said. Then he'd grinned and quipped, "There's one thing about prairie weather you can count on and that is that you can't count on it. It can change as quickly as a woman changes her mind."

She'd grinned and waved a towel at him at the time, but it didn't seem funny anymore. She looked to the sky. She'd liked to see one of those sudden changes right about now.

Somehow she got through the morning, but the afternoon loomed like an over-heated furnace, and she decided to take a blanket and sit in the scrap of shade provided by the scraggly trees on the hillside. Perhaps a whisper of breeze would drift over the slope to cool her. Or maybe she could imagine relief by looking at the lake.

Nauseated and exhausted, she drifted into an uneasy sleep.

Something broke through her troubled dreams, and she sat up to lean her throbbing head against her knees. There was a difference in the air. The lake had turned inky black and churned like a madly boiling pot. Black clouds twisted like rags in a froth of white soapsuds. A chill wind raced up the hill, and Lydia pulled the corners of the blanket around her. The wind increased, tearing at her scalp until the pins fell out and her hair whipped free.

Lightning streaked across the hills; thunder rolled like the beat of a thousand hooves. It was exhilarating, and Lydia stood to throw back her head and let the wind tear through her hair. The bolts grew closer, momentarily blinding her as they zigzagged earthward. A crash shook the ground. A prickly sensation skittered up the back of her neck, and she could smell gunpowder. She hugged the blanket around her shoulders. The sheer power and volume of the storm held her spellbound. So this was what Matt meant by a sudden change in the weather.

Suddenly an angry voice demanded, "Have you lost your mind, woman? Don't you see how close that lightning is?"

Stilling the alarm that skidded across her shoulders at Sam's unexpected intrusion, she turned to meet his flashing blue gaze. Before she could gather her thoughts, he grabbed her hand and almost jerked her off her feet. She clutched at the blanket, but he yanked it from her and half-dragged her toward the house. She scrambled to keep her feet under her. He didn't slow until he slammed the door shut behind them.

"What do you think you're doing?" Lydia yanked her hand away and glared at him.

"Maybe trying to save your skin. You make a lovely target sitting on the side of the hill. Don't you know anything?" Sam, breathing hard, stood with his legs apart and his hands on his hips.

"I was just watching the storm."

Sam shook his head and turned to hang up his hat. "Lightning isn't particular about where it strikes, and it was getting pretty close to you."

Lydia didn't know which of her churning emotions was most predominant. Anger at his high-handedness or gladness at his concern.

She murmured, "Sam, I'm sorry. I didn't realize there was any danger. Thank you." He met and held her gaze. Lydia felt herself being drawn into a bigger, perhaps more dangerous storm.

"Well, I wouldn't want anything to happen to you." Sam's voice sounded gruff. "I. . ."

The door flew open and Matt strode in. "Here it comes. I made it just in time. Listen." He looked upward and pointed toward the ceiling.

Granny stumbled from her room. "There's nothing like a summer storm to shake things up." She settled in her rocker.

What had begun as a light patter quickly crescendoed into a deafening beat upon the roof. "Look." Matt snaked his arm out and pulled Lydia to the doorway, where the three of them crowded to watch the rain falling in sheets.

"It looks yellow!" said Lydia, awed by the sheer abundance of water pouring down.

"Must be something to do with the light," Matt suggested.

"Have you ever seen so much rain? It's like someone is pouring barrels of water over the house."

A trickle started at the barn and ran down the pathway to disappear over the hillside. It increased to a steady stream more than three feet wide. They were about to turn indoors to wait out the storm when the yellow light faded, and as quickly as it had begun, the torrent slowed to a light sprinkle then ceased.

Lydia looked at Matt and Sam, wondering if they felt the same amazement she did. Matt's face wore a faint smile. Sam's eyes gleamed.

She stepped outside. A fresh, clean smell filled the air. The stream running through the yard had already died away, leaving nothing but a sandy, smooth trail. Lydia went to her favorite position on the slope overlooking the lake. The water radiated a silvery sheen repeated in glistening beads of moisture on every blade of grass. The whole world was highlighted in silver. The sun shone forth in blinding brilliance and painted a rainbow from the hills to the lake. Its colors were as bright as if one of the Williams children had used his paints to brush them there.

"I will never leave thee, nor forsake thee." She spoke the words aloud, her heart swelling at the beauty around her and God's words of promise. A light touch on her shoulder made her jump.

"It's beautiful, isn't it?" Sam asked.

Lydia could only nod.

"Do you see why I care so much about this place?"

She wanted to say the right thing and sorted her thoughts carefully before she answered. "I can understand how you could love this place, but. . ." It wasn't his love for the ranch or this country that bothered her. She could understand that. But he seemed to think his love must exclude devotion and commitment to anything else.

"But what?" His question interrupted her thoughts.

How could she answer him when she had so often faced the same dilemma of trying to reconcile her wants with God's leading? Yet she was convinced that to pursue a course apart from God would lead to all sorts of disasters, and somehow she had to try to make Sam see that.

"Sam," she began in a faltering voice. "I. . .I, well, I can understand your devotion to this ranch and this country. It's a beautiful place. I find myself drawn to it more all the time." She turned from the majestic view to face Sam. "It's just that you talk as if there is nothing else in life for you. You talk as if God can't be part of your goals. That makes me uncomfortable." She wrapped her arms around herself to still the ache as she understood that not only was God left out of his life; he seemed to think caring about anything or anyone else would get in his way, as well.

They stood looking at each other. His eyes darkened, and she felt a power like lightning zinging through her veins.

A shuttered look fell over his eyes. He stuffed his hands in his pockets and turned toward the lake.

"This ranch is the most important thing in my life!" His voice was hard. He turned on his heel and strode across the yard to the barn.

Lydia watched him go. His words left her with a knot of inner turmoil, and she ached with a sense of loss she couldn't explain. *I will trust God,* she reminded herself and gathered up her skirt as she crossed the damp grass, planning what she would make for supper.

Over the meal, she tried to catch Sam's eye. Afraid she had offended him or hurt his feelings, she longed to make amends. The meal itself was a peace offering. She prepared all his favorites: fried steak, mashed potatoes, gravy, turnips, and bread pudding. But Sam steadfastly refused to meet her eyes, even when she passed him a generous-sized dish of pudding.

Matt pushed his chair back from the table. Oblivious to the strain between the other two, he sighed. "I feel better now. Not quite so hungry." He laughed at his own joke. "I was beginning to get a little gaunt before supper."

When the other two didn't respond, he continued undaunted and unaware. "We had to do some repairs in the corrals. The water washed right through one section and loosened some posts, but we got it fixed already."

He rocked back and forth on the chair legs, contemplating the ceiling. "I think we better ride up to the pasture tomorrow and see if there's any damage up there." He addressed this to Sam then turned to Lydia.

"We'll have an early breakfast and take our lunch." He crashed his chair down on all four legs, rose, and stretched. "Let's get everything ready tonight." He snagged up his cowboy hat and hurried from the house.

Sam pushed his chair back.

Lydia looked up. His face was set in hard lines.

The silence echoed with things she longed to say, and Lydia sighed. She must try to mend what she'd mangled. "Sam," she began, hesitated, then hurried on before she could change her mind. "I'm sorry. I didn't mean to upset you. I was only trying to help." She ducked her head and concentrated on her hands.

"It wasn't you," he said. "I made a choice when I came here. I chose to work at being a rancher—the best rancher in Alberta. Then you came along. You don't say much, but the little things you say and do make me question my choice. Was it the right choice? Can I change my direction even if I want to?"

She jerked her head up, but he looked past her as if his thoughts were far away, then his eyes narrowed.

"Right now I don't want to." Again his face grew hard. "I still want to be the best. And I don't think I can do that if I let anything get in the road."

Lydia felt his withdrawal like a blow to her stomach, and aching to see him change his mind, she put her hand on his wrist as he twisted his coffee cup round and round. "Sam, there's nothing wrong with having dreams and goals. We all do. But what about people and what about your faith? Aren't they important, too? Can't you pursue your dream of being a big rancher and still retain your faith?"

Sam stopped twisting the coffee cup and stared at Lydia's hand upon his wrist. Slowly he raised his eyes to hers. Her cheeks burned, and she jerked her hand back and hid it beneath the table. His gaze never faltered.

"What dreams do you have?"

His question skidded across her thoughts. "Why I. . .I. . .have dreams. Lots of dreams."

"Tell me what they are," he insisted.

She twisted her hands and looked about the room. She hardly ever looked at her dreams. Dare she take them out for public view?

"Tell me," he said again, his voice low and demanding.

Lydia glanced at him. Something in his eyes tugged at her. She lowered her eyes and, in a barely audible voice, she began, "Ever since my mother died, I've dreamed of having a home where I belong." Her voice grew stronger. "Not just some place where I work until I'm not needed anymore before going to another set of strangers."

"A home like this?"

Lydia avoided looking at him as she glanced around the room. It was familiar and comforting to her. She had cleaned it till it shone, mended the curtains, and filled the rooms with warm smells of spicy cookies and fresh bread. She turned her eyes toward the window. Beyond lay the hills and the lake, the flowers, and the immense sky. She felt her heart twist as she realized how much she cared for this house and this ranch. It would hurt tremendously to leave it. But more than that, she cared about Matt and Sam. They had become very special to her. It would hurt even more if she were never to see them again. They were like family now.

With a loud swallow, she got rid of the lump in her throat and answered Sam. "Yes." Her voice trembled. "A home just like this."

"What would you do to get such a home?"

"I. . .I. . .there's never been anything I could do." Pain swelled within her. "I have no family, and I belong nowhere. I go when I'm told to go." She felt tears threatening at the back of her eyes and swallowed quickly.

"I'm sorry." Sam's quiet words threatened to undo the last of her self-control. "But perhaps you can understand how important this place is to me."

Lydia didn't answer. She realized how important it was to him. She understood his feelings but. . .is it possible for a place to be more important than anything else in life?

It felt like someone had jabbed her with a knife. She would not think about it anymore. As Mother always said—

The door banged open. Matt looked in surprise at Sam.

"I thought you'd be out to help get ready for tomorrow! What's the matter?"

Lydia jumped to her feet and began to gather the dishes. *What have I been thinking of? Dishes to wash, lunch to get ready for tomorrow, and many other chores. And here it is almost bedtime.*

Sam rose more leisurely, stretching his arms overhead and yawning widely. "I guess it is getting late. I'll just get my things ready then go to bed."

Matt shook his head as Sam gathered up his rope, his chaps, and a jacket.

Chapter 9

July first. Dominion Day. Canada's birthday and a good reason to celebrate, or so Sam and Matt had been telling Lydia for days, and she was prepared to believe them. Nor were they the only ones planning a day of celebration. For the past month, the local paper had run full-page advertisements informing one and all of the upcoming party to be held in town. RACES. BALL GAMES. LIVE ENTERTAINMENT. FIREWORKS. PICNIC. BRING YOUR OWN BASKETS.

By the time July first rolled around, despite the lingering fatigue the heat had left behind, Lydia was bouncing with excitement. She'd been to fairs before, but this time she would not be in charge of children or tending a booth or serving tea. This time she was going to be free to enjoy every activity while being escorted by two handsome young gentlemen.

Even Granny had decided she would go to town with them. "I'll go visit my friend, Martha," she announced. "I hear her husband is doing poorly. Maybe I can cheer her up."

Lydia grinned as she recalled the conversation. She couldn't imagine Granny cheering anyone up. She shrugged. Granny probably hadn't always been sharp-tongued and critical. Lydia wished, as she often did, that she could share the joy and peace she had learned in letting go of her troubles and letting God be in control—and trusting Him to do what was best.

But today she would let nothing steal from her happiness, and dancing a jig across the kitchen floor, she hurried to pack the food she'd prepared yesterday—fried chicken, potato salad, a pot of baked beans, and a loaf laden with raisins and cinnamon. All night the food had cooled in the cellar. She packed it into a large box and tucked layers of newspaper around the food then covered everything with a blanket to keep it cool for the picnic tonight. The cutlery, plates, and cups were already in a box, but she turned back to the shelf for a final check. Satisfied she hadn't forgotten anything, she grabbed up her skirts and hurried to her bedroom to change.

She was going to wear her blue dress. It was the most becoming thing she owned. And today she wanted to look her best. After she changed, she twirled around the room until she skidded to a stop before the mirror. Grinning at her reflection, she brushed her hair into the soft roll Lizzie had shown her and stood back to admire the effect.

Her black shoes beckoned from the closet. She looked at the brown ones she wore. They would be more comfortable and decidedly more practical. *Practical?* The very word decided her. *Why must everything be practical?* She would wear the black ones and endure the discomfort of wearing them all day.

"Lydia," Matt called, his voice vibrant with excitement. "Are you ready? Hurry. We don't want to miss anything."

"I'm coming." She hurried out, breathless and flushed.

"Good," he greeted her. "Let's be on our way."

"Don't forget our picnic." She pointed toward the box on the table.

"Good thing you reminded me. Sure would hate to think of this sitting on the table while we went hungry tonight."

Granny had insisted she would ride to town in her rocker and was already seated there, facing backward, her mouth tight.

Sam helped Lydia into the wagon while Matt shoved the box to the front. Matt's horse stood tied to the wagon.

"You really don't need to take your horse," Sam said. "You can ride in the wagon."

"I know that," Matt replied as he swung up into the saddle and waited to ride beside them.

As Sam clucked to the horses, a wagon rumbled past on the road. Dust from another wagon rose farther down the hill. At the last turn before Akasu, Sam pulled the horses to a halt and waited for a wagonload of waving, cheering party-goers.

They stopped long enough to unload Granny and her chair at a white house with a white picket fence.

Then they passed the elevators and headed for the fairgrounds. The last time Lydia saw the open area, it was empty and overgrown with grass. Now it was crowded with wagons, tents, and throngs of people.

She gaped. "Where did all these people come from?"

"Everyone within driving distance is here," answered Sam.

"Be careful; you'll wind your neck like a spring," Matt teased.

Lydia giggled. She was craning from right to left at a pace that left her dizzy. Matt pointed and waved. "It's Major Davey."

Lydia saw a man in a dark green uniform sitting stiffly in his saddle.

"Who is he?" Sam asked.

"Major Davey. He's in charge of the militia for this area."

Lydia's eyes found another man resplendent in a red jacket. Yellow stripes edged down the side of his pants. Sam followed her gaze.

"Why, it's Sergeant Baker, the Mountie. Don't he look like something else, though?"

Sam pulled into a grassy spot and unhitched the horses then led them to the fenced area. Meanwhile, Matt tied his horse to the back of the wagon before taking the lunch box and placing it underneath the wagon, where it would be in the shade for the better part of the day.

"I wish people who own dogs would leave them at home," he grumbled. "They'll be over here sniffing at the food, but at least they won't be able to get into it." He had tied a rope around the box and lid.

Throngs of people hurried past, and Lydia stretched on tiptoe to see where they were going.

"Shall we go see where everyone is headed?" Matt's voice close to her ear was teasing, full of laughter.

She jumped at his nearness and asked, "Where's Sam?"

"Here I am." Sam's voice came from directly behind her, and she jumped again. Sam and Matt laughed loudly.

"You two are rotten," she muttered, but her grin took any venom from her words.

"May we escort you to the festivities?" asked Sam as he and Matt each gallantly offered her an arm.

"Why, thank you, kind sirs," she responded in exaggerated politeness as she took their arms. Marching abreast, they crossed the trampled grass, laughter trailing in their tracks.

The crowd gathered like a flock of hungry chickens around a newly painted white bandstand festooned in ribbons of red and white. Banners on the roof fluttered in the breeze, whispering enticements to the people to come and see.

The squawk of the band as it warmed its instruments formed the backdrop for the voices raised in greeting, the shrieks and shrill laughter of the children.

The bandmaster tapped his stick sharply, a drumroll drew everyone's attention, and as the band played "O Canada," the crowd grew silent; men held their hats over their hearts, and women hushed the little children.

Lydia felt the tears pooling in her eyes. Her chest was so tight, she could hardly breathe. It felt so good to be part of this country and part of this celebration while accompanied by two men who meant a lot to her.

Following enthusiastic applause, a gray-haired man in a pin-striped suit and top hat stood at the podium.

"I'd like to welcome everyone to Akasu's Dominion Day Celebration. We are proud to be part of this great country of Canada. As is fitting on such an auspicious occasion, we have planned a day of festivities. It is our hope that. . ."

"That's Mayor Wright," Sam whispered in her ear. "He tends to be a bit of a windbag. Let's hope he'll cut his remarks short, or we'll be standing in the sun for the rest of the day."

Lydia hid a giggle behind her hand, but soon clapping and cheering announced the end of the speech and the beginning of a program. A young girl sang, a gray-haired man gave a funny recitation, a group of schoolchildren sang, and then a stately older gentleman stepped quietly to the front and began to play his fiddle. When he finished, the mayor signaled for a drumroll as he stepped again to the podium. "Ladies and gentlemen. Boys and girls. Thanks to the generosity of the good citizens of Akasu and my own personal efforts, we are pleased to present to you a magician of some renown. Right from the city of Ottawa, I give to you Mikal the Mighty."

A dark, mysterious man clad in tight pants with a full-sleeved white shirt ran onstage. A bright red cape billowed out behind him. He stopped abruptly, twirling his cape to reveal a woman dressed in a similarly bright red dress. Lydia blushed to see how much of the woman's shoulders and upper body were revealed. She glanced out the corner of her eye. Sam was watching intently, seemingly unaware of the woman's indiscreet state of dress. She turned toward Matt. His eyes restlessly searched the crowd at the side of the bandstand.

Lydia soon forgot everything but the magician as he produced balls where there had been none, pulled feathers out of a little boy's ear, and made scarves disappear into thin air. Then he swallowed a burning sword.

"How did he do that?" Lydia turned to Matt, but Matt was not there.

She turned to Sam. "Where did Matt go?"

Sam peered around Lydia. "Humph. I wonder what he's up to."

Then he turned his attention back to the stage as Mayor Wright announced in his stentorian voice, "Ladies and gentlemen. Boys and girls. We are privileged to have in our presence Major Davey of the militia. D Squadron, of the Twenty-first Alberta Hussars, under Major Davey, will now honor us with a parade. I direct your attention to the field directly behind you."

Lydia turned, and her attention was riveted on the horses carrying stern-faced, stiff-backed men. Four abreast, they marched around the perimeter of the field, a thin screen of dust rising from each hoof. The musky smell of warm horseflesh drifted over the crowd. Lydia stood on tiptoe, her hand resting on Sam's arm. The movements of the horses were precise and measured. She studied the faces of the men. Their expressions were so serious. Suddenly she gasped. Matt sat on one of those horses. What was he doing riding with the militia? He raised his hat to her and waved a solemn salute.

Lydia fell back on her heels with a thud. Mouth half-open, she turned to Sam. "Sam, did you. . . ?" Her words died. She knew by the set of his face he had seen Matt and wasn't pleased.

"Well, I guess that explains where he has been disappearing to." He shrugged, but his expression was guarded; and he quickly looked away.

The column of horses and riders swung down the pathway between the wagons. As the last pairs exited, the men all raised their hats and waved them over their heads then suddenly galloped away. The crowd cheered and clapped.

Lydia grasped Sam's arm. "What does that mean?" she asked. "Matt riding with the militia?"

Again Sam shrugged. "I don't know if it means anything. As far as I know, they just meet to practice drills and do some target shooting."

"Then why are you angry?"

Sam turned and looked her straight in the eye. For a moment he didn't speak. "I don't exactly know." He sighed. "Maybe it's just that he kept it a secret, and I'm wondering why he did."

"Don't let it spoil the rest of the day," begged Lydia, remembering the silence and anger she had previously witnessed between the two men.

Sam stared toward the now-empty field. Lydia gently touched his shoulder. "Sam?"

He took her hand and turned to face her. The stubbornness melted from his features, and he smiled gently at her. "You're right. Let's have a good time and not worry about it."

The blue of the summer sky reflected in his eyes until she grew quite dizzy. She started to pull away, but Sam grabbed her hand.

"Come on, let's go see what else is going on."

There were races for the children and a baby contest. There was a horse race in which the contestants rode down Main Street, around a wagon half a mile out of town, and back to the fairgrounds, skidding to a halt in front of the milling crowd.

Sam and Lydia stopped in front of a booth.

"Throw the ball. Win a Kewpie doll for your lady," the man in a black-and-white striped shirt called, offering a ball to Sam.

Sam pulled Lydia to a stop and studied the stack of milk bottles.

"Let's see how we do on this," said Matt from behind them.

Lydia spun on her heel. "Where did you come from?"

Matt grinned and dug into his pocket for a nickel, stepped up, and threw a ball that tumbled the bottles. The attendant presented him with a Kewpie doll.

"For you," he said, handing it to Lydia. He was so full of vitality as he stood watching her, his hands on his hips, his dimples flashing. Lydia thought he had never looked more handsome.

He turned to Sam. "Now it's your turn."

Lydia saw the flash of his eyes before Sam turned and picked up a ball. His throw caught only a corner of the pins and failed to knock them down. Muttering, he picked up a second ball and threw it with vengeance. The pins tumbled down and scattered across the ground. Sam grabbed his Kewpie doll and stood staring at it. Then he stepped to Lydia's side.

"Another doll for you," he said. "That makes two."

He strode away, Lydia hurrying to catch up, Matt strolling after them.

"Thank you," she murmured when she was close enough for Sam to hear. The sudden change in his attitude confused her.

Sam slowed so she could walk beside him, and Matt fell in step.

"I'm getting hungry," Matt announced.

Lydia shook her head. Where had the day gone? It seemed like only a few minutes since they'd left home. In silent agreement, they turned their steps toward the wagon. Alice and Norman joined them as they passed the bandstand.

Dust rose with every step, clinging to her clothes, sticking to her skin. She was glad to see one of the men had thought to put a cream can of water in the wagon. They took turns washing and having a long drink, then Lydia spread the blanket out and passed the food around. They were licking the fried chicken from their fingers when a man passed by shouting, "Ball games to start in half an hour."

The men hurriedly reached for slices of the raisin loaf then helped Alice and Lydia tidy up.

"Come on, girls," Norman urged. "We don't want to miss the ball games. This is what we've been waiting for."

Matt slapped Norman playfully on the back. "Yup, this year you have to play on the married men's team. It's sad," he said as he pulled a long face, "to see a good man go downhill so fast."

Norman remained serene. "I wouldn't count my chickens before they hatch if I were you," he warned.

"We'll soon see who's gone downhill," Alice added.

At the edge of the playing field, Lydia and Alice spread a blanket. Teams were already drawn up, the married men against the single. The married men were up to bat first. Sam stepped into place as the pitcher.

Lydia flinched as the ball sped past the batter. As a single woman, she knew she was expected to cheer for the singles team, but when Norman hit a grounder that had Matt and two other men chasing it with their gloves to the ground, she jumped up alongside Alice and yelled encouragement.

Then the single men were up to bat. Back and forth it went, accompanied by a chorus of cheers and jeers. The score was tied, five each, when the single men came to bat again.

The first batter struck out; then it was Sam's turn. He stepped to the plate, confidently swinging the bat, insolently tapping it on the wooden plate.

"Do your best!" he called to Norman at the pitcher's mound.

"You won't even see it!" Norman called back.

"Try me."

"Play ball!" yelled the umpire.

Norman wound up and let the ball whistle across the plate.

Sam swung. The crack brought the crowd to their feet, some cheering for Sam as he ran for first, the others cheering for the fielder as he backed up, preparing to catch the ball. Then the fielder tripped in a gopher hole. The ball bounced across the ground, where it was scooped up by another fielder and winged toward second. Sam rounded second and headed for third before the ball arrived. The second baseman threw the ball to third. Sam skidded to a stop— trapped between bases.

The crowd roared. Sam faked toward second, but as soon as the ball left the third baseman's hand, he dashed for third. He dived the last few yards, landing with his hands on the base.

The crowd was screaming, "Run, Sam, run!"

Sam picked himself up, saw the second baseman had dropped the ball, and raced for home. The ball spun through the air toward the catcher. It smacked into the catcher's mitt, but Sam slid into home plate under the catcher's legs before the tag could be made.

"Safe!" the umpire yelled, and the crowd was on its feet screaming.

Lydia, her voice hoarse from yelling, grabbed Alice, and they jumped up and down together. Sam raised his arms in a victory salute as he ran off the field toward the girls. Lydia ran out to greet him, throwing her arms around him in her excitement.

"You made it! You made it! It was so exciting!"

Sam draped a hot, sweaty arm around her shoulders as they walked back to Alice. "Thank you, Lydia. For a few minutes, I wondered if I would." He sank down beside her on the blanket and wiped his face on his shirttail.

Then she realized what she'd done. Her ears burned, and heat crept up her neck. She dropped her eyes, sure everyone was looking at her, shaking their heads, and whispering to the person next to them. What was she thinking? She had just run out and hugged him! And in public! She pressed her palms to her cheeks to cool the burning.

A young boy carrying a bucket of water and a dipper ran toward them and offered Sam a drink. Sam drank several dippers full then offered a full dipper to Lydia. She took it without looking up; but as she tipped her head back, she met his eyes and saw a warm expression. She lowered the dipper and handed it back to the boy. Almost afraid to look at Sam again, she darted a glance from under her eyelashes and almost choked at the smile he gave her.

The crowd's cheering saved her from doing something stupid like falling into his arms, and she turned to watch as Norman delivered three fast throws and struck out a man. Then Matt was up to bat.

Two times he let the ball streak by him and held his stance. On the third, he connected, sending the ball soaring into the air. He had reached first base when the ball thudded into the fielder's glove.

Amid calls of "Too bad" and cheers from the married segment, Matt walked back to retrieve his glove.

"Too bad," Lydia commiserated.

"There's always next time," he said, winking at her as he and Sam returned to the field.

The first man to bat for the married men's team struck out. The crowd cheered Sam for his good pitching, but the next man drove the ball high into the sky. Matt and another fielder ran across the grass, looking skyward as they judged where it would descend. Neither saw the other as they raced for the ball. Lydia shuddered as they collided, the impact sending both men backward to the ground. The fielder rose, shaking his head and dusting off his pants, but Matt lay still.

Lydia strained forward, wanting to run out and see if he was injured, but she stood rooted to the spot, her hands clenched at her side, forgetting to breathe.

Sam was the first to arrive at Matt's side and knelt over him. He spoke to Matt and ran his hands over his head, his arms, and legs, but Lydia could not hear their words or guess what Sam discovered. Matt lifted his head.

Lydia let out a slow, shuddering breath and sank to her heels. Matt sat up, Sam's arm supporting his back. They stayed crouched, heads almost touching; then Sam stood and pulled Matt up. The deathly silence was broken by a rippled murmur; then the crowd clapped their approval. Lydia shuddered, watching Matt push Sam's hands away, lifting his hands to indicate he was all right.

Sam spoke to him again, but Matt shook his head. Sam nodded and turned to walk slowly back to the pitcher's mound.

The game resumed, but Lydia sank to the ground, her limbs rubbery. A drumming echoed inside her head. A spinning sensation whirled in the pit of her stomach. Gradually her body returned to normal, but Lydia could not seem to regain her interest in the game. A great weariness filled her, and she heaved a sigh when there was an announcement that the married men were victorious by two runs.

"Matt, are you okay?" Lydia asked as the group walked to the wagon.

"I'm fine."

But his words were sharp, his gait stiff.

Sam and Lydia exchanged glances.

Back at the wagon, the men washed off the dust and sweat. Lydia eyed the lump over Matt's left ear. A bruise darkened his forehead and edged toward his eye. She longed to apply a cold cloth, but his countenance forbade her making such an offer.

Sam met her eyes as he lowered himself to the ground and settled into a lazy sprawl. Lydia understood his unspoken message and sat with her back resting against a wheel. This way they could keep a guarded watch on Matt. Out of the corner of her eye, she saw that his color had paled and his face looked drawn. She ached to say something, but his fierce expression made her shiver, and she held her tongue.

Sam shook his head. "Matt, I think we should go home now. We're all tired and dusty and ready to call it a day."

"That sounds like a good idea," Lydia added, a tremor of fear skittering through her at how much the bruise had swollen.

Norman and Alice had joined them and murmured their agreement.

"No." Matt's voice was firm. "Not until after the fireworks. Thanks for your concern, but I'm fine."

Lydia glanced at the sky. Although it blushed a soft pink, it would be at least an hour before darkness fell.

The others sank back like wilting flowers, except for Matt, who pulled himself to his feet.

"There's no point in sitting around here with long faces. Let's see what's going on." He began to walk away. The others jumped to their feet and followed.

They circled the grounds, stopping at the booths, visiting with the neighbors, buying lemonade from the Ladies Aid stand, but Lydia thought of how quiet they were compared to earlier in the day. They walked slower, talked more softly, and huddled together. Each in his or her own way was trying to protect Matt. It seemed they all sensed he wasn't feeling as he should. She would have gladly settled for going home for her head had begun to ache. But the determined set of Matt's jaw made her keep silent.

Dusk descended, and they hurried back to the wagon and climbed aboard to wait for the fireworks. In spite of her fatigue and the throbbing in her head, Lydia cheered and clapped with the rest of the crowd at the display. Her enjoyment was dimmed further by the knowledge that Matt winced at every explosive sound.

They were the first to pull out of the fairgrounds.

They stopped to get Granny. She looked at Matt sprawled in the wagon box and sniffed. "I told you no good would come of frolicking all day."

"He got hurt playing ball," Lydia said in a low voice.

As Granny settled into her rocker, Lydia asked, "How was your day, Granny?"

"Fine, thank you." Then she added in a more pleasant voice. "I had a lovely visit with Martha. It was just hard seeing her Tom so sick."

Darkness wrapped about them as Sam turned the wagon homeward. Lydia wished it wasn't so rough. What if Matt was hurt worse than he would let on?

"You're awfully quiet." Sam's words broke into her thoughts.

She glanced at Matt, his hat over his face. His horse followed obediently behind the wagon. "Do you think he's all right?"

"I'm fine," came a lazy rumble from behind. "Just a bit of a headache, but, Lydia, I wanted you to see the fireworks before we left. Weren't they great?"

"They were wonderful," she agreed, but she wasn't thinking only of the fireworks. His voice sounded stronger, and the tightness that had burrowed into her stomach when he fell finally eased. It had been thoughtful of him to insist on her seeing the fireworks. Both Matt and Sam had been especially attentive and kind today.

Life was just plain wonderful.

Too bad it couldn't always be like this. But she pushed away the thought, determined not to let anything spoil her pleasure.

Chapter 10

They headed toward home, a cold wind tearing at them. Lydia shivered. She hadn't thought to bring a shawl, and Granny huddled under the only blanket. Icy splatters of rain stung her skin.

Sam wrapped his arm around her shoulders and pulled her close. "Let me keep you warm," he murmured.

Embarrassment burned through her veins, but the wind was unmerciful, the rain like sharp arrows against her skin.

"Thanks." She shivered so hard, she could barely form the word.

By the time they turned into the yard, ice water ran through her veins and her teeth chattered until her head echoed with the sound.

Sam lifted her from the wagon. "Hurry and get into something warm and dry." He scooped up Granny and carried her to her bedroom.

Matt hunched at the doorway. "I'm soaked and cold," he moaned.

"All I need is for all of you to get sick," Sam muttered.

"The l–lunch," Lydia stammered.

"I'll tend to it. Now go get changed so I can look after the horses."

She needed no more urging and hurried after Matt. She didn't even wait for him to light a lamp but crossed to her bedroom in the dark and stripped off her wet things, piling them in the middle of the floor. Her flannel nightie was tucked in the bottom drawer. She found it in the dark and shrugged into it. With shaking fingers, she loosened her hair and blotted it with a towel.

She ached with cold. Her insides were numb. Weakness flooded through her, and she thought she was going to be sick to her stomach. Moaning, she crawled into bed and pulled the blankets up, praying for warmth to return. She piled the covers over her head but continued to shiver. Her throat scratched and her head drummed.

Finally she drifted into a restless sleep, tortured with dreams of being chased by indistinct figures. She moaned and tossed as she tried to reach out to the figures. Her attempts were frustrated by a shadowy barrier. Voices called to her. She tried to answer but couldn't make a sound.

She felt something on her brow and forced her eyes open. A shadowy figure bent over her, and she tried to move, but she was tangled in covers. Someone spoke her name, and she realized she was only dreaming and sank back into her troubled sleep.

Again something cool brushed her brow. She tried to open her eyes but could only lift her lids enough to see through the curtain of her lashes. A lamp cast its warm glow over the bed to show Sam standing above her.

Sam. She struggled to understand why he was in her room and why there was such a worried look on his face yet his eyes were so gentle. Calm settled over her mind, and she slept.

Someone pulled a nightgown over her head and insisted on washing her face. Lydia moaned and clutched the covers to her.

"Well, well, so there is a little fight left."

"What are you doing here?" she asked Alice.

"I've been helping nurse you."

Lydia lay still, letting her mind analyze her body. Everything seemed to be whole but extremely weak. She wondered if she had the strength to pull her nightgown over her knees. "I've been ill, haven't I?"

"That you have. I guess you caught a chill in that storm. And maybe you were a bit rundown and overtired."

Lydia nodded. "How long have I been sick?"

"Three days."

"Have you been here all that time?" She could remember bits and pieces. It seemed there had been someone sitting with her, offering sips of water, murmuring comforting words. She knew she had clung to those words and found strength in that presence.

"I came over the morning they found you sick."

"You must be tired." Lydia sighed, thinking how weak and tired she felt.

"No, I'm all right. Sam took turns sitting with you."

Lydia turned to look Alice full in the face. "Sam sat with me?" Was that what she remembered? She searched her confused recollections and found glimpses of Sam holding a glass of water to her lips, wiping her brow, leaning over her, murmuring words of comfort. She felt again the peace offered by the soothing rumble of his voice and hugged the memory close. "I don't remember seeing Matt." She didn't realize she had spoken the words aloud until Alice answered.

"Matt said he wasn't any good in a sick room, but he took care of the cooking and the chores and hung around the house like an overanxious father."

Alice lay aside the washcloth. "You really had all of us worried for a while." She bent and brushed Lydia's cheek with her lips. "Now, I'll leave you to sleep."

Lydia closed her eyes. But she didn't sleep. Something inside would not settle. She longed to see Sam. To hear his voice.

The orange glow of the late evening sun filled the room when she again opened her eyes. She lay staring at the golden window, then feeling someone in the room, turned to see Sam in a chair beside her bed, his head bowed, her Bible on his lap. He turned a page and glanced up, his eyes locking with hers. Mesmerized by their warmth, she could not tear her gaze away. A gentle smile widened his mouth.

"Hi." His voice was low. "It's good to see you feeling better."

"Thank you." An emotion jolted through her. She turned away and picked at the covers. "I understand you helped look after me. I want to thank you."

When he didn't reply, she slowly raised her eyes again. He smiled, his blue eyes brilliant in the fading light. "Actually, it was quite interesting."

She looked at him with a measure of alarm. Had she been delirious and said foolish things? She glanced away in embarrassment. "What do you mean? What did I say?"

"Wellll. . . Nothing really." He emphasized the "really."

Lydia began to squirm. Sam's hand came out to rest over hers where it lay picking at the cover.

"I'm sorry. I was just teasing, and that isn't fair when you're not feeling well."

She blinked. It was difficult to breathe and even more difficult to think. His hand was warm and comforting and did strange things to her emotions. She wanted to turn her palm over and twine their fingers together. This lurching of her insides at his touch, this ache to look at his face, this strange fluttering in her stomach frightened her.

"You didn't say anything, though you did moan a lot. I'm just glad you're going to be all right." He squeezed her hand then rose to his feet. "I'd better go and let you rest."

He slipped out, leaving her with a head full of confused thoughts.

The next morning, Lydia insisted on joining the others for breakfast. Alice pushed her into a chair and hurried to fill her cup with coffee. Lydia barely had time to lower the level before Alice jumped up and refilled it. Lydia stared after her friend. "You act like I'm going to collapse if I so much as lift a hand."

Alice ground to a halt. "I guess I am acting like an old hen."

"Alice. I didn't mean it like that. It's just that I feel a little awkward having you wait on me." Lydia drank slowly, watching Alice over the rim of her cup. "Besides, you must be exhausted."

"Of course I'm not. I'm as sturdy as a fence post, and I'm used to hard work."

But as they lingered over coffee, Alice cleared her throat and looked from Matt to Sam. "I think you can manage now. As long as Lydia doesn't do too much, she'll be fine." She pushed her chair back. "So, if that's all right with everyone, I would like to go home."

Matt sprang to his feet. "Of course. You must go home and look after that man of yours. I'll go hitch up your wagon."

Sam helped Alice gather her belongings. "You've been a godsend, Alice. We all thank you, but I especially want to thank you."

Alice patted his hand. "I know, Sam. I know." She gave Lydia a hug. "Now you take it easy. You hear?"

"I hear." Lydia grinned at her friend. "Thank you so much for helping."

Alice nodded; then amid a flurry of good-byes and more thank-yous, she drove away.

Sam and Matt stood at the closed door while Lydia sat silently at the table.

"I'll clean up and make some sandwiches if you. . . ," Sam began.

"Why don't I go and saddle. . . ," Matt said.

"I don't know what. . . ," said Lydia.

They laughed.

"You clean up here; I'll saddle the horses," said Matt.

"I'll help—" Lydia began.

Sam said, "You'll do nothing!"

Matt nodded, his look stern.

Lydia sighed loudly, sinking back into her chair, and watched Sam dip the dishes into the soapy water then slice bread and meat and make sandwiches. He talked as he worked. "Lydia, we'll be out haying most of the day. There'll be nothing for you to do but rest. Go back to bed, and don't worry about supper. Alice left food cooked. We'll get by on our own. We did before you came, remember?"

She sighed again, feeling guilty, yet at the same time relieved, for she was already tired, and looking forward to her bed.

Matt stepped inside, addressing Lydia. "You are not to do any work today. Not even run Granny's errands. She'll have to look after herself. You go back to bed and stay there. Do you hear?"

He waited, looking at her sternly, until she raised her head and nodded.

"I hear and I'm already looking forward to obeying."

He smiled, his dimples winking. "Good. See that you do. You're weak as a kitten. It wouldn't take much to have you sick again."

"I promise to be good," Lydia said demurely.

Matt nodded his head, jammed his hat on, and left.

Sam hesitated at the door, twisting his hat in his hands. "I hate to leave you alone, Lydia. What if you get sick again? Or need something?"

If he knew how much I want him to stay. But it wasn't possible. He had work to do and couldn't be at her side all the time. "I'll be all right," she assured him. "I plan to sleep the whole day away. You'll probably be back before I wake up again."

He still made no move to leave. "I wish. . ." He stopped then jammed his hat on his head. "I have to go. Take care."

She finished her coffee then returned to her bedroom. But despite her weariness, sleep did not come immediately. She didn't know how to explain the way her thoughts clung to Sam. Shadowy memories of him hovered just out of reach. She sat bolt upright remembering his cool lips kissing her brow.

Or was it part of a dream?

Sucking in a deep breath, she lay down, trying to relax. Everyone had been so good. It was wonderful to know people cared enough about her to worry when she was sick. And to sit by her throughout the night. In her mind, she could still see Sam sitting at her bedside, the light illuminating his face while his body blocked out everything else—even her concerns and worries. She felt protected. Safe.

With a little mew of serenity, she slipped into a dreamless, peaceful sleep.

Lydia sat at the table sipping her cup of tea when the men returned later that day. They stopped inside the door and stared at her.

"I thought you would be resting," growled Matt.

"If she sleeps any more, she'll end up like me," Granny announced from her rocker.

Lydia giggled. Granny had surprised her by saying how glad she was to see her up and feeling better. Then she'd added: "It's about time."

Lydia grinned at Matt; then she looked at Sam, drinking in his kind, gentle expression.

She gulped. "I slept almost all day, and all I've done is make myself some tea while I wait for supper. I'm starved. Who's cooking?" She looked back and forth at the men, her gaze lingering a second longer on Sam. He hadn't spoken yet but smiled at her, and her heart soared.

Matt looked to Sam. "Pamper a woman a few days and what do you end up with? A tyrant! That's what. What do you think we should do with her?"

Sam rubbed his chin and appeared to give the question serious consideration. He stared long and hard at Lydia, his eyes sparkling with diamond flashes of blue. "Well, looking at the dark circles under her eyes and the deep hollows in her cheeks, I suggest we feed her." He punched Matt on the shoulder as he said, "It's your turn to cook."

Matt put his fists on his hips and glared at Sam in mock anger. "And I thought Lydia was getting demanding!" He quickly began pulling things out of the cupboards. "But I'll do the cooking tonight." His voice was resigned. "After all, Alice left everything ready." His voice filled with mirth. "You'll have to take your turn tomorrow."

Sam looked disgusted then burst into laughter and began setting the table. Matt continued to gloat as he finished setting out the dishes Alice had prepared.

"If you ask me, that young lady was awfully anxious to get back home. It was downright unneighborly of her to leave before Lydia is back on her feet." Granny stopped her rocking and looked at the others as if demanding a response.

Lydia sputtered. "But Granny, she has her own home to look after, and I certainly don't need any more nursing."

"Well, I'd like to know who's going to make my tea?"

Matt's expression darkened, but before he could say anything, Sam spoke in a low, lazy voice. "We aren't that busy. I suppose Matt could stay around the house and run errands for you." He bent close to Granny. "Do you have an apron he could borrow?"

Granny gaped. Matt growled. Lydia giggled.

"I was thinking a nice one," Sam continued, "with frills over the shoulders." He ran his hand up his chest and around his neck to show what he meant.

Matt planted his fists on his hips, glaring at Sam. "I'll not be wearing any apron." He turned toward Granny. "As for your tea—"

Granny shifted back in the rocker to face Matt squarely. "Never mind my tea, young man. I'm perfectly capable of getting it myself." She jerked her head for emphasis then resumed rocking. "Impertinent young man," she muttered under her breath.

Ignoring Matt's sullen stare, Sam slouched his shoulders. "Does this mean you won't be lending him a pretty little apron? I'm so disappointed."

Matt stomped to the cupboard for a bowl. "You'll pay for this. See if you don't. You'll have to watch your every move. Check under your saddle for burrs. Look in your boots before you pull them on." A lazy smile twitched Matt's mustache. "Don't forget to look under your covers before you crawl into bed."

Lydia grinned. Matt was enjoying this every bit as much as Sam was.

The good-natured teasing continued throughout the meal and while the men cleaned up afterward. Lydia smiled and chuckled often.

That night she went to bed smiling, the laughter and teasing ringing in her ears as she fell asleep.

Next morning, she lay in bed and stretched lazily, contentedly listening to the sounds of the men preparing breakfast. She rose in time to have coffee with them, lingering over her own breakfast while they prepared their lunches. They left, and Lydia returned to her room. A glow of well-being warmed her heart as she sat peacefully at her desk, cradling her Bible in her hands and studying the picture of Mother. Suddenly she understood her glow of contentment. She was feeling cared for in the same tender, gentle way Mother always cared for her. Again that ache in her heart called. Was she simply looking for security? She admitted she ached for a permanent home, a place where she belonged. She forced her attention back to her Bible. She'd been through this struggle before and had promised she'd trust God to take care of her needs. She tried to shepherd her thoughts back to the words on the page, but her mind was especially willful today. Over and over, like a wayward child, her thoughts turned to recollections of Sam leaning over her, his expression tender, sitting beside her reading her Bible. He seemed different.

She shook her head. *There I go again, dreaming up "happily-ever-after" endings for my life. Hoping someone will rescue me from my lonely existence and give me a pleasant, permanent home. It's time I grow up and stop daydreaming.* She gave herself a mental shake, but even as she did so, another image of Sam flashed into her memory. *Enough,* she scolded. Until Sam allowed God to control his life, Lydia knew he was not the man for her.

God, You are my comfort and guide. Help me to trust in You and stop looking for mankind to provide my needs.

She rested three more days before she grew so bored, she couldn't stand it and made a batch of bread.

"What do you think you're doing?" Matt roared as he walked in the house and saw the fresh bread, but his eyes lingered hungrily on the warm loaves, and she laughed.

"Don't go getting all worked up. It's time I started doing a few things."

"You sure?" Sam ran his gaze over her as if checking to see if she'd done any damage.

"Very sure." Tipping her head, she grinned at him. "I promise I won't do anything stupid."

And so they allowed her to begin work again.

Slowly, as July passed into August and then September, she regained her strength. The long evenings of summer were a special delight, and as autumn approached, she discovered new pleasures in the season—the golden wheat in Norman's field, crisp grass underfoot, yellowing leaves rustling on the trees. The countryside was golden in color, and she felt a golden glow of serenity. But as the grain ripened, the days grew busier. Sam and Matt joined the neighbors going from farm to farm to help with threshing.

While the men were away, Lydia dusted the logs in the front room, scrubbed walls in the kitchen, and washed the windows throughout the house, scolding the flies that buzzed about soiling her clean walls and windows.

Saturday evening the men returned for a late supper. Sam's face was set in grim lines. Matt studiously avoided looking at him.

Lydia wondered what had happened.

The men sat down and began to eat without speaking to each other. Finally Sam growled, "You shouldn't have left Price's this afternoon." His voice was tight. "You left us short a man and cost us a lot of time."

"You got by without me." Matt's voice was cool.

"But it wasn't right. Everyone was tired. They didn't like you leaving us shorthanded."

Matt bent over his plate without answering.

Sam glowered at him, hands clenched into fists on either side of his plate. "What was so all-fired important you had to leave in the middle of the afternoon?"

Matt placed his fork carefully beside his plate then leaned back in his chair. "I had an important meeting in town that couldn't be postponed." He stared at Sam for a moment then picked up his fork and resumed eating.

Nothing more was said, and silence descended for the rest of the meal. The disagreement hung like a wet blanket over them throughout the evening.

Next morning Lydia woke wondering about church. Would either of the men be prepared to take her? After the strain of last night, she was reluctant to leave her room and ask; but when she finally gathered up the courage to open her door, she found Sam dressed and ready to go. There was no sign of Matt, and she refrained from asking where he was.

As they drove down the road, Lydia longed to speak from her heart; but how could she find the right words when she couldn't even identify what she felt? Was it gratitude? An ache for permanency? A desire for things that couldn't be? She was glad Sam filled the silence with stories about the threshing crew.

As they pulled to a halt in front of the church, she pushed her confusion into a corner of her heart.

The days were busy as Sam and Matt turned their attention to the fall demands of their own ranch. Lydia welcomed the time alone to examine her thoughts. Something had changed since she'd been sick, but she could not put her finger on what it was. All she knew for sure was there was a void inside her crying to be filled. Over and over she turned to prayer, seeking God's strength in dealing with her troubled emotions.

She had just finished telling herself again she would forget all about it when she was startled to hear a horse racing into the yard. She hadn't expected either of the men back until suppertime, but before she could cross to the window, the door flew open and Sam raced in.

Her jaw dropped at the sight of him. Flecks of foam from a well-lathered horse clung to his pants. His eyes brushed over her then scanned the room. He kicked the door shut and dropped his gaze to her. "Are you all right?"

His look ignited her senses, and she forced her answer past a dry mouth. "Of course."

"Where's Granny?"

"Sleeping."

He strode to the windows and pulled the blinds down. "Is Matt here?"

"I haven't seen him since he rode out this morning. Sam, what are you doing?"

He hurried to her side and grasped her arms, pulling her close. "I was afraid I'd be too late."

Chapter 11

"Too late?" His hands were warm and possessive on her arm, turning her insides upside down. "Too late for what?" She couldn't keep the wobble from her voice.

But instead of answering, he pulled her to the front room. "This is better." He felt along the ledge about the door until he found a key and hurried to lock the back door.

A shiver skittered up her spine. "Sam? What are you doing?" His strange behavior was unnerving.

"Get Granny from her room."

Granny had heard the commotion and hovered in her doorway. "What's all the ruckus?"

But Sam didn't answer. He dragged Granny's rocking chair to the living room then rushed around the room pulling blinds and closing the bedroom doors. All the while the tension mounted in Lydia until she felt ready to explode.

Finally he pulled two chairs close to Granny, pushed Lydia into one and perched on the other, every movement so tightly controlled, she knew he was holding himself in with a harsh rein. Coiling and uncoiling one fist, he looked into her eyes, something dark and probing in his steady gaze.

Her alarm increased, and she studied his face for some clue about his behavior.

He took a deep breath and said, "There's a crazy man loose. He was seen headed this way." He scrubbed a hand over his hair.

"A crazy man? Who?"

Sam shook his head. "Some fellow living behind the hotel. He lived in a little shack with his wife and son. He shot them!" His voice trembled.

"Oh!" She couldn't think of anything else to say as wave after wave of disbelief surged through her.

"Some people heard gunshots early this morning and ran to check. They saw this man running down the street waving a gun. He shot at Mr. Church, the postmaster, but missed. He ran into the post office and threatened to shoot anyone who came near.

"Someone ran to get Sergeant Baker—you remember the Mountie? He sneaked in the back door of the post office, but the man must have heard him coming because he bolted out the front door, took the handiest horse, and rode out of town. In this direction." Sam sprang from his chair. "Did you hear that? Did you hear a horse?" He grabbed the rifle off the hooks and filled his hands with shells from the corner cupboard before he strode to the window to pull back a corner of the blind.

The sound of air escaping over her teeth rasped in the quiet room, and Lydia held her breath as Sam watched out the window.

Granny groaned. "I knew no good would come of living here."

Lydia wondered what living here had to do with a madman in town, but she only shook her head, still watching Sam.

He dropped the blind back into place and slowly turned. "It must be my horse. I didn't stop to unsaddle him."

"Sam, what happened to his family? Are they dead?" She had to know before the pounding in her side would stop.

He shook his head. "I think they'll be okay. Someone sent for the doctor. Things were kind of crazy in town with everyone running around yelling." He moved toward the door. "I'll have to slip out and put my horse in the barn."

Lydia leaped to her feet, clasping her hands at her throat. "Don't leave us. What if that crazy man comes here? He must be demented." She rushed to his side and clutched his arm. "Don't leave us here." Her voice ended on a squeak.

His arm snaked out and pulled her close. She leaned against him, her knees as weak as wet rags.

Granny folded her arms over her chest. "I don't aim to move. If some crazy fellow wants to bother me—well, let him try."

Lydia turned from Granny to Sam, torn between wanting to be with Sam and knowing she should stay with Granny.

Granny gave a little wave. "You go with Sam. You can watch his back. I'll be fine."

"Well, I guess it is best to take you with me." Sam's warm breath whispered through Lydia's hair. "We're going to run for it, so you stay close, hear?"

She nodded against his chest but didn't move until he pulled her to his side, braced the rifle in the crook of his other arm, and opened the door. He dashed for the horse, scooped up the reins, and headed toward the barn without slowing his steps. Lydia skidded after him, clutching his sleeve.

They ducked into the darkened interior of the building and stopped. Lydia panted as she kicked her tangled skirts from her ankles. Her heart racing, she looked about at the dark shadows and gasped.

Sam sprang to her side. "What?"

"What if he's hiding in here?" She wanted to bury herself in Sam's arms but restrained herself, forcing herself to be content with wrapping her hands around his wrist.

They huddled together in silence. "I don't hear anything," he whispered, turning away to uncinch the saddle and throw it in the corner, then quickly pulled the bridle over the horse's ears. "Let's get out of here."

They crept to the open door and halted. Sam studied the open yard, his gaze probing each clump of trees. "Lydia, did I leave the door open?"

She stared at the house. The door gaped like the mouth of a snake. "I don't know. Maybe."

They pulled back into the shadows.

"We can't stay here," Sam hissed in her ear. "He could be hiding in the loft right now. Besides, we can't leave Granny."

She nodded.

"Come on." He grabbed her hand. "Let's go."

Her heart beat a rapid tattoo as they inched around the barn and halted at the corner.

Preparing to leave the shelter of the building, she filled her lungs and gripped Sam's hand, then her feet were tripping over the ground in a desperate race for the house.

He pulled her to the wall next to the open door. She leaned against the rough wood, too weak to hold herself up. He signaled for her to wait. She stifled a cry of protest as he tore his hand from her death grip and edged toward the open door, rifle poised as he ducked inside.

No longer able to see him, her insides froze. She closed her eyes and prayed.

"Everything's okay." His whisper close to her ear sent a spasm through her body, and she jerked her eyes open. He beckoned her to go inside.

Almost falling into his arms, she dashed through the door, and Sam quickly locked it.

"My heart's about ready to burst," she groaned.

Granny called, "Everything all right?"

Assuring her it was, they gathered in the living room. The rifle hanging from his hand, Sam paced back and forth. "Where's Matt? He should be back by now. It'll soon be dark." He spun on his heel. "Maybe I should go look for him."

Lydia jerked to her feet. "No." He didn't even know where Matt was, and if that lunatic had found Matt, well, Sam could easily become another target. Besides, that would leave her alone. Except for Granny. A spasm clenched the back of her neck, and she moaned again. "No."

Sam seemed not to hear her. "He can probably take care of himself," he mumbled, pausing to lift a corner of the blind. "I'd best stay here."

She was as concerned as Sam about Matt's absence, but at his words, she almost crumpled. If anything were to happen to Sam—

Her thoughts skidded to a halt and she gasped. *I love him.* Her eyes followed him hungrily as he paced. Despite the gloom filling the room and the fear holding them in its palm, her lips softened and a wave of tenderness touched her heart. Sam. Gentle, quiet, thoughtful Sam. Lydia realized how much she'd learned to depend on him. He was the staying sort of person.

"I suppose we should eat."

His words bolted through her thoughts. Lydia was sure she looked like someone caught with her hand in the cookie jar, and she looked away. "I'll see to it," she murmured, her voice distorted like someone talking in a rain barrel. Her cheeks burned, and she was grateful for the darkened room.

Food was the farthest thing from her mind, but she welcomed something to keep her hands busy. Perhaps it would distract her from the tangles in her mind. Her newfound admission of love for Sam seemed ironically at odds with her fear of a madman on the loose and her worry about Matt's absence. It was difficult to sort out such a differing array of emotions.

She stared at her hands moving without conscious thought on her part and took a shaky breath. Nothing could come of her love for Sam unless—until he gave up resisting God. It would remain a secret locked securely in the depths of her heart.

The floor in front of the stove creaked, the blind flapped against the window, the wind whispered across the shingles. Never before had she noticed how many noises the house made, but now each one jolted across her nerves.

"Sam," she murmured, "the food is ready." The sound of his name on her lips was so unexpectedly sweet that her throat tightened until she could hardly speak, and her hands shook as she set the plate of sandwiches before him.

He placed his hand over hers. "We'll be safe here."

She nodded, grateful for his comfort. "Granny?"

"I don't aim to move my bones again. Bring me tea and a sandwich after you've eaten."

Sam sat across from Lydia, the rifle between them on the table. Its presence drove thoughts of love from her mind. Fear rose to predominance.

"Sam," she whispered, "how will we know if he's been captured?"

"Sergeant Baker promised he would let us know when it was safe. Until then he warned us to stay indoors and out of sight. This man is extremely dangerous."

A shudder raced down her spine at his words. She tried not to think of Matt out there unaware of the danger, but her mind flooded with pictures of him being held at gunpoint—or worse—and hot tea threatened to splash from her cup. She set it down hard, waiting for the trembling to pass.

Darkness closed in around them, but no one made any move to light the lamp. Sam yawned and pushed his chair back. "Why don't you try to get some sleep," he said. "I'll keep watch."

She jerked to her feet. "I couldn't," she murmured. She could hardly bear to have him move about the room without clinging to him. The idea of being alone in her bedroom brought a cold sweat to her whole body, and she shivered. "I'll wait here. Granny, you lie on the couch."

Moaning, Granny did so, pulling a quilt around her shoulders. Lydia sank into the rocker, suddenly cold and weak.

Sam stopped pacing and sat on a hard chair, the rifle across his knees.

Her eyes felt gravelly as she kept them wide, promising herself to stay alert, straining for sounds in the dark.

"I pray Matt is safe," she whispered.

"Pray for us, too," Sam answered.

Slivers of light fractured the dimness of the room. Lydia stared at them, wondering why the blinds were pulled. She jerked wide-awake as she remembered why she was in the darkened front room. How long had she slept? Sam's head lolled back. The rifle lay at his feet.

Her veins turned to ice. What if that madman had found them sleeping? She edged to her feet, pushing aside the quilt. Her hands lingered on the warm cover. Sam must have placed it over her while she slept. She wished she'd been awake to enjoy his hands pulling it around her shoulders. She straightened. There was no time to think about such things. She crept to the doorway and darted a look around the kitchen but saw no threatening stranger. She turned back to Sam, watching him sleep, his face soft and relaxed, his hair mussed. She longed to brush his hair from his forehead. An ache tugged at her innards. She loved him so much, she could stand there looking at him for hours.

But she jerked away. She dare not let her emotions get out of control, nor could she ignore the reason for the thread of fear tightening the muscles of her neck. Gently she touched his shoulder.

"Sam." She spoke his name quietly, hating to wake him.

He erupted from the chair as if shot from the rifle at his feet. "What is it? Are you all right?" He grabbed her shoulders and shook her.

"I'm fine," she answered. *Except for the way my heart is acting.*

He scooped up the rifle and stalked across the room, opening the bedroom doors to peer in, lifting the blinds, and peeking out the windows. When he had toured the entire house and satisfied himself that no one hid in a corner, he returned to her side, running his hand over his hair to further muss it. The shadow of whiskers on his jaw gave him a rugged appearance, which Lydia found disturbingly appealing.

"I must have dozed off at sunrise."

She nodded. His bleary eyes revealed it had been a long night for him.

Granny snored softly on the couch.

"Any sign of Matt?" asked Sam.

"I'm afraid not." She refused to think about it. All she could do was pray again for his safety. "You look like you could use some coffee." She hurried to the kitchen and stirred the fire to life.

Sam moaned and stretched. "Sounds good."

She made hot porridge as well. He ate quickly then continued prowling the house, periodically lifting the blinds to check outside. Several times she caught him yawning and rubbing his eyes.

"Sam, you're so tired you can hardly see. Give me the rifle, and I'll watch while you sleep."

Their eyes locked, and she felt his inner struggle; then he smiled and relinquished the gun. "Thanks."

Moaning, Granny struggled to her feet. "You can lay here, lad. I'll be more comfortable in my chair."

Nodding his thanks, Sam lay on the couch, his legs bent to accommodate his length, and closed his eyes. In minutes his breathing deepened, and Lydia knew he was asleep. Still she stood watching him, drinking in every detail of his features, letting her newly acknowledged love wash over her heart in thudding crashes. Then she forced herself to turn away.

"I'll make you tea," she mumbled to Granny. She did so quickly then padded across the floor to check out the windows as she had seen Sam do. Everything looked peaceful and ordinary, and after a few minutes, she settled into the armchair. Despite her resolve to keep her mind on other things, her gaze returned to Sam. What would it be like to wake every morning to the sight of him sleeping beside her? Heat sizzled through her veins. She loved him so much.

She strangled a cry. It was impossible to imagine life without him. She tried to pray, but all she could think was *O God, I love him. I love him.* Her eyes were dry, but great teardrops flooded her heart.

She ached so badly for love. Only now she knew it was Sam's love she wanted.

She longed for a permanent home where she belonged, but it was his home she wanted to share.

But he had said so plainly there was only one thing that mattered to him. The ranch. His words echoed like tolling bells. Love and marriage. God, church, friends. None of these would he allow to interfere with his pursuit of success.

She knew he was mistaken in his thinking. He would end up alone and disillusioned, but he would have to come to that conclusion on his own. If she or anyone else tried to reason with him, she knew he would clench his jaw, his eyes would grow hard, and he would refuse to listen.

It was several minutes before Lydia realized Sam's eyes were open and gazing at her. She imagined she saw tenderness in his expression. Embarrassed to be caught staring, she jerked away.

"Did you have a good sleep?"

"Umm." He sat up and stretched. "I feel like a new man." He reached toward her. A dull roar filled her eardrums, but he took the rifle from her lap, and her senses settled into a rapid beat.

Sam prowled the room, checking doors and windows, then perched on the arm of the couch.

"If Matt doesn't show up soon. . ." His voice trailed off, and he pushed his hair back. "I don't know what we should do."

Lydia shivered. "I can't bear to think what might have happened to him."

Sam jerked his head up. "Listen," he warned. "Did you hear something?"

She held her breath and tilted her head to listen.

"There it is," Sam whispered hoarsely.

She heard it. She thought she would suffocate from the fear lodged in her throat. A scratching at the outer door sent shivers through her body. There it was again. Her eyes felt as large as saucers.

Sam jerked to his feet and padded silently toward the kitchen. Lydia leaped up and followed on his heels. He stood in the doorway, rifle poised. A scuffling sound grew louder, followed by a grunt.

A heavy weight descended upon her chest, making it impossible to breathe. The room tilted. Sam reached behind him and pulled her to his back. She leaned into his warmth, drawing strength from his nearness.

The doorknob rattled. Thuds shook the door. Sam lifted the rifle and aimed it directly at the door.

Lydia's legs turned to rubber. She was afraid her weight against his back would affect his aim, but she didn't have the strength to pull away.

A muffled voice called through the door.

Sam stiffened.

The voice outside rose. "What's the big idea? Open the door."

Lydia jerked. Sam half-lowered the gun.

"It sounds like. . . ," she whispered.

"Matt, is that you?" Sam called.

"Open the door." Matt's voice was muffled yet unmistakable.

They rushed to the door. Sam unlocked it and threw it open.

Matt crashed to their feet.

For a moment, shock rendered them motionless. They stared at Matt, his clothes torn, one eye swollen, dried blood caked on his pant leg. Then they bent and pulled him inside. Sam closed the door and relocked it.

Granny called, "What's going on out there?"

"It's Matt," Lydia replied. "He's hurt."

They turned Matt on his back. "Take it easy," he muttered.

Lydia gasped, her mind feeling separated from her body.

Matt's left leg was crusted with blood.

Sam pulled off the boot and ripped the pant leg to the waist. "Get me some scissors. And get water and clean rags. This cut needs attention."

She raced to obey him. A ragged gash on Matt's thigh oozed blood. She bent to sponge the wound.

"This looks dirty," she murmured.

"Use some disinfectant, then we'll bandage it up."

She brought another clean cotton rag and poured disinfectant in the wound before she covered it.

"That hurts, you know," Matt growled.

"Let's get you into bed." Sam helped Matt to his feet. They hobbled to the bedroom. Lydia waited outside while Sam helped him into bed.

As she stepped into the room, Sam asked Matt, "Did you run into that crazy man?"

Matt opened his eyes and stared at them. "What the scratch are you talking about?"

Sam and Lydia took turns telling Matt what had happened. An amused look crossed Matt's face.

"So you thought I was some lunatic, and you were prepared to shoot me? That's a fine welcome home."

Sam's expression grew fierce. "You had us some worried. What happened to you?"

He smiled weakly. "Nothing very heroic." He closed his eyes.

Sam and Lydia exchanged a look and quietly rose.

"No, don't go. Let me tell you what happened."

They waited.

"I rode up to check the cows in the north pasture. On my way back, I came through the trees rather than go around by the trail." A sheepish look crossed his face, and he grimaced at Sam. "I know. You've warned me about it, but I wanted to see if there were any berries.

"It was getting kinda dark, and I never saw the hole. Neither did my mount. She fell in it and threw me. I tore my leg on a tree branch." He swallowed hard. "The mare broke her leg. I had to shoot her." His voice deepened with emotion, and Sam clucked.

"I knew no one would find me, so I crawled back to the trail and waited until morning. Took me this long to make it back."

Tears stung Lydia's eyes as she thought of him hobbling home with his injuries.

"Sure is good to be home safe and sound." His eyes flew open. "Or am I safe and sound? You greet me with a gun and tell me there's a lunatic on the prowl." He groaned. "Could be I was safer out on the prairie."

"You're safe enough," Sam said, patting his shoulder. "They've probably caught the fellow by now and just haven't been able to get word to us."

Matt nodded. His eyes closed. Lydia and Sam watched until they saw the steady rise and fall of his chest and knew he was asleep.

Granny gave them a sharp look as they slipped out of the bedroom. "I suppose he was up to some foolishness."

"His horse fell in a hole," Sam answered, a hint of annoyance in his voice.

Granny blinked once then studied her knitting.

There seemed to be little to do but wait. Lydia went to the kitchen and made coffee, breathing a silent prayer of thanks for Matt's safe return.

She and Sam lingered over coffee. Lydia turned the cup round and round, starting as Sam set his cup down. The waiting was making her jumpy. She thought she could hear hooves drumming across the yard.

Sam jerked to his feet, grabbing the rifle and heading for the door.

A voice called out, "Hello, Twin Spurs! Anybody home? It's Sergeant Baker."

Sam threw the door open. "Come on in, Baker. Sure hope you've got good news."

The Mountie strolled into the kitchen, removing his broad-brimmed hat. Lydia felt a twinge of sympathy at his red-rimmed eyes and the dark smudges under them. He sank into the chair Sam pulled out for him.

"We got the man two hours ago," he said. "He's on a train to Calgary with two armed guards. His wife and son have only flesh wounds, but they'll be safe now." He looked around the room, alert to every detail. "I don't see Matt."

"He's here but I tell you. . ." Sam launched into a tale of Matt's adventures.

"I'd better take a look at him in case he needs a doctor." The Mountie rose to his feet. "I could send one out from Akasu if he does."

Matt woke as they entered the room. One eye was swollen and surrounded by purple bruises.

As he examined the injuries, Sergeant Baker kept up a stream of small talk. Lydia understood it was his way of distracting Matt as he probed the leg wound.

"Haven't you anything better to do than poke at a fellow when he's down," Matt grumbled, glaring at the man.

"Everything looks like it will mend." Baker straightened. "But I see his temper hasn't improved."

"Aren't you supposed to be looking for a madman or something?"

The Mountie smiled. "I've been working while you slept. He's in custody."

Matt glowered, but with one eye swollen half shut, it lacked fierceness.

Lydia grinned.

Sam choked back a chuckle.

Chapter 12

What do you think you're doing?" Sam's angry voice rang from the bedroom.

Her hands poised above the pancakes she was frying, Lydia stopped to listen. Matt's rumble carried to her, but she couldn't make out his words.

"You're staying right there." Sam stomped from the room. "Take him some breakfast and make sure he stays in bed."

Lydia finished the breakfast tray and hurried to the bedroom. She set the tray on a stool. "Here's your breakfast."

"Take it back to the kitchen. I'm getting up." Matt glared at her.

She sat on the edge of the bed and crossed her arms. "I'm staying right here. Eat."

Their eyes locked.

"Pass the food." The expression on his face remained cross.

"That's better." She moved the tray closer. "I'm to keep you in bed today."

"How do you propose to do that?"

She shrugged. "Any way I can." Her voice softened. "I'm not about to let you take any chances. Do you have any idea how worried we were?"

He looked at her crossly. "At least you were with Sam. Seems that's the way it should be."

"Whatever do you mean?" She stared at him.

"Oh, come on. I've seen the way you look at him. You can't keep your eyes off him." He lifted his fork, eyeing her grumpily.

"Oh, Matt. I—" She fled the room and his knowing look. Her feelings had been riding high since she'd acknowledged to herself how much she loved Sam— a love that swelled and grew as she rejoiced over it. At times she could barely keep from dancing across the floor.

Now her joyous emotions collapsed. She had to keep her love hidden. How long, she wondered, could she keep it a secret? Forever, she vowed. Sam must never guess. She pressed her hand to her chest.

Somehow she had to get Matt to agree to keep her secret. She retraced her steps to the bedroom.

"I'm done. You can take the tray," he mumbled.

"Matt," she began, forcing the words past the tightness in her throat. "Promise you won't say anything to Sam."

"You should both come to your senses," he said crossly.

"I don't know what you mean."

"I know you don't." He waved her away. "But don't worry." He closed his eyes.

He hadn't given his promise; and she hesitated, wanting him to say so much more. But she knew he had said all he intended, and with her insides feeling like shattered glass, she left the room.

The day passed in a fog of worry. If Matt had read her face, Sam could do the same. She'd have to be a lot more careful, learning to disguise the way her heart lurched when he came in the room, the way her eyes sought him when he was near, the ache she felt when he left. If she didn't—if he guessed how she felt—her mouth dried so suddenly, she almost choked.

The next morning Matt limped out to the table despite the heated words Lydia heard from the bedroom.

"Man can't eat lying on his back," he grumbled. "Besides, it's only a little scratch."

Sam glowered at him, but Matt stayed seated until Sam left the house, then he rose and grabbed his hat.

"Matt, shouldn't you be taking it easy?"

"Got things I gotta do," he mumbled and left the house. A few minutes later, she heard a horse ride from the yard.

She stared around the room, her thoughts jerking from Matt's foolishness at not resting his leg to Sam—she closed her eyes. She wouldn't let her thoughts dwell on him and what she wanted but couldn't have. Perhaps work would take her mind off her worries. She got out her cleaning supplies and attacked the stove. But all too soon, she forgot the brush in her hand as she mentally listed things about Sam she found appealing—his strong jaw, his heavenly blue eyes, his slim build, his quiet strength, his deep sense of devotion. She sighed. That deep sense of devotion would mean her love would go unrequited. Sam had made it plain nothing would take the place of the ranch in his heart and mind. There was no room for God and certainly no room for a little servant girl with nothing to offer.

Picking up her forgotten brush, she returned to her task, determined more than ever that she would never let her guard down.

She scoured the stove until it shone.

With the same frenzy, she scrubbed the floors.

She was peeling potatoes when the door opened.

Matt entered, carrying a squirming black pup.

She sprang to her feet. "What a cute little fellow!" The pup wriggled wildly, licking her fingers and trying to reach her face to lick it. She laughed. "Who owns him?"

Matt placed the puppy in her arms. "He's yours."

She stared at him and then at Sam, who entered behind him. Sam shook his head. "I don't understand. You always said you wouldn't have a dog on the place."

"I never had much use for a dog," Matt admitted. "But I thought it was a good idea for Lydia to have a watchdog." He paused and stepped aside so he could see them both. "Especially now."

"Now?" she asked, lifting her head from rubbing against the puppy fur.

He nodded. "Sit down. Both of you. I have something to tell you."

Lydia took a chair, more curious than anything. What could Matt have to say that made him twist his hat so badly?

"Remember when you were mad because I left the threshing crew?" He addressed Sam, who nodded without speaking.

"I said there was something I had to take care of."

Again Sam nodded.

Matt took a deep breath. "I signed up to join the army."

Sam half-stood. His mouth opened and closed, and then he dropped back to the chair.

Matt hurried on. "I'll be leaving as soon as I can make arrangements. I'm off to Ottawa for my training."

The silence greeting his words went on and on.

"What about the ranch?" Sam pushed his hair back from his forehead.

"I'll leave you in complete control." Matt spoke softly. "You can run it as you see fit."

Sam shook his head. "I don't understand. How can you just walk away from everything?"

"I'm not walking away," Matt protested. "I'm doing my duty as I see it." He gulped and hurried on. "I think we're about to see problems in Europe."

"It's halfway around the world," Sam almost shouted.

"Yes, and your family may well be in danger."

At Matt's words, Sam subsided.

When Matt spoke again, his voice was low, tight with emotion. "I thought you'd understand." He rose and stared at Lydia. "That's why I got Lydia the pup."

She lifted her face to him, but his features were blurred behind a veil of tears. Everything was changing so fast, she couldn't breathe. She choked back the tears pooling in her throat. She wanted to grab hold of time and force it to stand still. She blinked hard. She didn't want Matt to leave. She feared for his safety.

And it meant she'd be losing Sam, as well. She couldn't stay now. She'd have to find another place. A moan tore at her throat. She failed to stifle it completely.

Matt watched her through narrowed eyes, and she lowered her gaze to hide her pain.

"Sam," Matt began, his voice hard, "if you're half the man I think you are, you'll marry Lydia and give her the protection of your name."

A roaring sound filled Lydia's eardrums. She couldn't breathe. She couldn't move. "That's not necessary," she muttered.

"You're both daft," Matt muttered. "Your love for each other is as plain as the pink tongue that pup is scrubbing Lydia's face with." He jammed his hat on his head. "You've hid it from no one but yourselves." He marched to the door. "I'm riding to the top of the hill."

The door closed behind him. Unable to face Sam, Lydia buried her face against the squirming puppy.

Suddenly Sam squatted in front of her and tipped her chin up with his finger. "Is it true?"

Avoiding his gaze, she asked, "Is what true?"

He clasped her chin more firmly, forcing her to look into his eyes. She held her breath at what she saw. "I love you, Lydia. Do you love me?"

His blue eyes pierced through her defenses and melted her embarrassment as quickly as snow before a fire. She nodded.

He leaned toward her and covered her lips with his. A shock raced through her veins, freeing the love she had tried to hide.

But she couldn't let it have free rein.

"I don't understand," she murmured, turning her face away from the temptation of his lips. "You said there was room for nothing but the ranch."

He laughed, the sound rippling through her veins until she was sure she quivered all over.

"I did say something like that, didn't I?"

She tipped her head back to look in his eyes. At his warm look, her heart somersaulted and danced, but she forced herself to forge ahead with her question. "You did. What happened?"

"I guess it started when you were sick." He kissed her cheeks, then sighing deeply, pulled away. "I was so worried about you. I knew then that I loved you. I wanted to pray for you to get well, but I knew I didn't have the right after I said I didn't want God anymore. I thought being a rancher was more important than knowing Him." He kissed her on the temple and pulled her toward him.

Reluctantly, she pulled away. "You were saying?" The words practically strangled in her throat.

He laughed low, and she knew she hadn't fooled him. "I wanted to change, but it was hard. For years I lived thinking all that mattered was being the best rancher. And all of a sudden, I knew it wasn't enough, yet it wasn't easy to change. I guess I finally gave in the other night as you slept in Granny's chair and I kept guard. As I watched you sleeping, I realized the ranch would mean nothing without you and that God was calling me back to Him through you. That's when I quit fighting God and said I wanted Him back in my life. I meant it."

He jerked a chair out with his foot and sat down, pulling her to his lap. His arms tightened around her. "And life has been a lot more beautiful since I gave up trying to have my way."

She could no longer contain her love. It burst free like a thousand blossoms touched by the sun opening to release their perfume. The puppy slipped from her lap, and she leaned into Sam's embrace, wrapping her arms around his neck, letting her fingers explore the silkiness of his hair. He tasted like every sweet thing she had ever tasted. Hungrily she returned his kiss, telling him in the only way possible how much she loved him and ached for his love. She snuggled against him, reveling in the warmth of his arms.

When he pushed her away, she mumbled in protest.

He laughed and shook her gently. "I want to see your face when I say this." He lifted her chin with his finger. Their gazes locked. "Lydia, I love you. Will you marry me?"

She nodded, unable to speak. Tears flowed down her cheeks.

"Don't cry," he begged.

"I'm not," she laughed, the tears continuing to flow.

Someday, when she could talk without laughing and crying at the same time, she would explain her joy. God had answered her prayer for a home of her own in a way far beyond her expectations.

Not only had He given her a home, He had sent her Sam.

Silently, she thanked God for the gift His perfect love had supplied. Then her thoughts were swept away as Sam's lips captured hers.

Epilogue

It was the brightest day in October, and Lydia couldn't stop smiling as she clung to Sam's hand and buried her face in the bouquet of wildflowers he'd picked.

He'd shaken his head over it. "Not much left this time of year."

She'd laughed. "Heads of wheat and a bundle of cattails would make me happy." Flowers were nice, but now that she was secure in the knowledge of Sam's love, she needed nothing more to make her happy.

The skirt of her white lawn dress caught in the breeze, tickling her legs.

Everything had happened so quickly.

Matt had agreed to wait a few days before leaving for Ottawa. "As long as it's by the end of next week."

Lizzie had found the perfect dress for her.

Reverend Law had agreed to do the honors.

And so this very morning, she and Sam had been joined in holy matrimony.

There'd been only a handful of people at the wedding. Matt, of course, Alice and Norman, Lizzie, and Granny.

Now Granny was with her friend, Martha. Despite Granny's sharp tongue, Lydia knew she would miss the older lady.

"I wish you all the best," Granny had said when Lydia told her she and Sam were to be married in a few days. "You deserve it." She'd rocked hard for a moment then added, "It works out for me, too. Martha's been after me to come and live with her ever since Tom died, but I said I couldn't leave you alone with those two scallywags."

Lydia hugged Granny. "Thank you for being here."

"Go away with you, child."

Lydia was sure she saw the glisten of tears in the faded eyes. "I'm glad for you." She squeezed Granny's hand. "Just don't shut out God's love."

Granny stared straight ahead, as usual ignoring Lydia's attempts to tell her about God. But suddenly Granny faced Lydia squarely.

"I've always been a believer, but I guess I let bitterness creep in until it pushed everything else away." She nodded, her eyes shining. "You made me see it didn't have to be that way."

The wail of the train whistle echoed down the tracks, and the engine huffed and puffed to a halt.

Matt stood before them. "I guess this is it."

Sam handed him a parcel. "This is from Lydia and me."

Matt raised his eyebrows. "What is it?"

"Open it and see."

He tore the paper off. "A Bible?" He turned it over several times. "Thank you." His voice was strained. "I've been thinking I might need more than my wits and good looks," he winked at Lydia, "to keep me alive."

She threw her arms around him. "Matt, I'm going to miss you so much. We'll pray for you every day. You take care, hear?"

He hugged her tight. "You, too, Mrs. Hatten. Mrs. Hatten—sounds good, doesn't it?"

She nodded, holding him a moment more before he freed her.

He turned to Sam and gripped his hand. "You take care of things now."

"I will. You take care of yourself."

A lump grew in Lydia's throat as the men gripped each other with both hands.

"All aboard!"

The handclasp ended. Matt picked up his gear. "I guess this is it." With a crooked smile for Lydia and a sober-faced nod for Sam, he climbed onto the train, pausing for a final wave.

The train snorted, belched smoke, and jerked away.

Matt was gone.

Sam grabbed her hand as they watched the train fade out of sight, then he pulled her around to face him.

"Well, Lydia Hatten, let's go home."

At the look of love and pride in his face, Lydia's sadness fled. Together they would face the future and build a home filled with love and laughter.

Unchained Hearts

To Sharon, who was there from the beginning.
Thank you for never-failing support and encouragement.
Your friendship makes my life richer.
God bless.

Chapter 1

Abby turned her face heavenward and laughed. She liked the way her voice drifted across the waving grass. She still couldn't get over the breadth of the sky, which seemed to spread from one week to the next, nor the beauty of the Rocky Mountains, jagged and mysterious against the western horizon. While Andrew was away overnight checking on some brood mares that he hoped to add to their herd, she was going to allow herself some time to explore this inviting countryside. Longing to run in wild abandon across the vast meadow, she hugged herself, and her heart bounced like the grass dancing in the wind.

Andrew had promised her a trip to town after he returned. She had to admit that living twenty miles from the nearest settlement took a little getting used to, and she longed to check for letters from home and have a visit with Sarah. How blessed she was that God had provided a friend like Sarah in this new land.

First, though, she would take the laundry off the line.

Scooping up the empty wicker basket, still yellow in its newness, she sauntered across the yard, smiling as her eyes continued to drink in the scenery. A thicket of aspens sheltered the house and yard, but from where the clothesline stood on the edge of the slope, she could enjoy an unobstructed view of the hills drifting into the blue distance and disappearing in the shadow of the jagged skyline to the west.

The sheets snapped in the brisk wind, and Abby shook her head, letting the warm breeze sift through her hair and whisper in her ear. There was no one to notice that most of the hairpins had fallen out, letting her hair escape the bun she had wound up tightly a short time before. Another pin fell to the ground, and her hair whipped against her cheek. She bent and retrieved the bit of hardware and dropped it into her pocket. It was useless to try to put the bun back in place. Her hair was such a nuisance—thick and wiry, with enough curl to make it impossible to control. If there were one thing she could change about herself, it would be her hair. She had often wished for smooth hair and plain brown rather than the copper color of an old penny.

As she grabbed the clothesline and pulled off the pegs, she forgot the vexation of unruly hair. The sun was so bright, she couldn't help but hum along with the wind.

The breeze caught the sheet, blowing it against her body. Straining against the white waves, she laughed as the material skipped free. Suddenly her arms were pressed to her side. Gasping, she looked down to see black-sleeved arms wrapped around her. Her heart kicked against her ribs, and she screamed. The arms tightened against her, jerking her off her feet. She choked, and the wind sucked away her screams. Feeling like a fist had slammed into her heart, she gasped for air, her mind racing with frightening images. She steeled her racing thoughts. Was someone playing a cruel joke? Her throat clamped shut as terror flooded through her.

Her captor turned and hauled her away from the edge of the hill, jolting her like an awkward sack of corn. She flailed her feet against her assailant's legs, her heels thudding against solid bone, but the man didn't slow. She squirmed upward, desperate to escape the viselike grip that pressed her into his warm, solid chest. Uncoiling every scrap of strength, she flung herself backward. Her head connected with a sharp chin, and she felt a puff of satisfaction at the grunt from her captor.

Her efforts to break his grasp increased, but his hold tightened. A low growl rose from her throat—a sound totally unfamiliar to her. With her mouth now as dry as old grass, she continued to twist against the steel-like arms. His grasp tightened further.

Gritting her teeth, she stiffened her shoulders and strained upward against his arms. His grip tightened until she could barely breathe. A great knot seemed to have lodged in her chest, the pain shooting blinding spears to her mind. She was wallowing in the pain, the tightness, the terror.

Unaffected by her weight or her struggling, her captor continued his jerky journey. His fists, digging into the soft spot just below her breast bone, felt like heavy iron weights squeezing the air out and compressing her lungs. Every time she released a breath, the fists pushed in farther until she was suffocating.

Twisting her arms, trying to free them from the mighty trap, only caused the pressure to increase. If only she could wrench a hand free. If she could manage to jab an elbow into his ribs. . .

She panted, her lungs screaming for release, her heart thundering for oxygen, her brain knee-deep in flashing stars.

The world blackened and tilted. From the edges of her mind, she was aware they had entered the shelter of the trees. A tall, black horse lifted its head to watch them. Then the arms loosened, and she sucked in air, gasping it into her starving lungs. The darkness receded, and the world righted itself. Feeling him strain to one side as he reached for the reins, she squeezed her eyes into slits. She had to get away. *Escape.* The word blazed through her brain. The best time would be just as he reached out to flip the reins over the neck of the horse. She would not miss her chance. She breathed a silent prayer. *God, help me.* Coiling her muscles, she counted the seconds. *One, two, three. Now.* She flung her muscles into action, throwing her hands upward, heaving against the arm that girdled her to his chest, her feet searching for traction.

A muffled grunt echoed above her head, and his arm tightened, swinging her off her feet. She was heaved upward and thrown into the saddle in front of him, molded to his legs and chest.

At five-feet-six, Abby did not consider herself tiny. She wouldn't have thought anyone could swing her into the air like that. Her helplessness against such strength seared her thoughts. Terror—red hot and suffocating—flashed through her mind, erupting in shrill, panic-laced screeches that came out the top of her head, rising, rising, rising until she was consumed by them.

A hand clamped over her mouth, and her terror increased as her lungs again fought for air. She twisted her head back and forth. Drawing back her lips, she buried her teeth in his palm. He grunted and cupped his hand to escape her bite, but his fingers continued to dig into her cheeks. He pressed her head to the hollow of his neck and dug his chin into the top of her head, making it impossible for her to move her head. She squirmed, twisting her torso, scraping across the rough horsehide. The horse pranced nervously, but her captor held the reins firmly, completely in control, and the horse calmed. The man crushed her to him harshly, almost raising her off the saddle. She pounded the horse with her heels. Without a word, the man took his feet from the stirrups and covered her legs with his own so it was impossible to move her legs. His silence was unsettling. It triggered tremors in her limbs, and she clenched her teeth to keep them from chattering.

Firmly encased in his grasp, all she could move were her eyeballs. Finding no outlet in shrill screeches or frenzied physical acts, her terror gelled into something deeper and more awesome, coagulating into a solid mass settling into her stomach. She had always thought one's heart turned to stone in times of shock, but now she knew it reverberated with depths she could never have imagined. Each heartbeat felt like a tear inside her ribs, ripping her heart to shreds. She had no idea what her captor planned, but her imagination skittered across the likelihood of what lay ahead. Would he rape her and leave her to perish, lost and alone in the thick forest? Would he do the deed and murder her? Who was her captor? Was he an Indian? She'd heard of the tortures of some of the Indian tribes. She squeezed her eyes shut, trying to ease the pounding behind them. Then another, even more terrible idea emerged. She had heard the words whispered behind hands and even then had recoiled in disgust. White slavery. *Oh, God!* she silently cried. *God, my shield and defender. You promised You would never leave me nor forsake me.*

The flashes of light inside her head faded. She was able to suck air past her pounding heart and fill her lungs.

The arm of her captor relaxed slightly, allowing her to settle in the cramped saddle she shared with him. An evil man should have a repugnant smell, but this man bore the smell of pine needles and freshly cut hay. Odd how her senses seemed so sharp. Was it fear or lack of air that made them so, she wondered. Every sensation was magnified—the scratch of the horse's mane against her hands, the taste of salt on her lips, the grunt of the horse as its hooves struck the ground, the rise and fall of the chest at her back.

"If you won't scream, I'll take my hand from your mouth."

Those were the first words he had spoken. His voice was gravelly and low, like water running over a rough stream bed.

She considered his offer. Why should she agree? She must use every means at her disposal to escape. On the other hand, they had been riding through the thick pine forest long enough for her to know that the chances of anyone hearing her screams were remote. Unless she were to count the deer and other wild animals. Yet something deep within her knew that if she gave her promise—even by silent consent—she would feel honor bound to keep it, even in this situation. She heard her father's gentle voice telling her, "Let your yea be yea and your nay, nay." The habit of speaking honestly was too deeply ingrained for her to be able to ignore it. Barely able to move her head, she managed a slight nod, and he slowly lifted his hand.

Her mouth felt wooden, and she stretched her cheeks and grimaced.

He let his arms slide down her body, freeing her. She flexed her fingers to restore circulation and rubbed her mouth.

"What are you going to do to me?" Her lips were wooden.

"I mean you no harm." Again the low voice, almost a growl.

Twisting in the saddle, she tried to catch a glimpse of her captor, but he leaned forward, pressing her against the saddle horn.

"Don't turn around," he ordered and by a touch of the reins turned the horse onto a narrow, almost invisible trail.

Was it just this morning she had waved good-bye to Andrew and laughed at the thought of a day to herself? She could remember congratulating herself on how perfect life was. In a matter of minutes, her life had cartwheeled into disaster. She choked back the bitterness rising in her throat.

The words, *I will never leave thee* drummed inside her heart. For a moment, she resisted their message of assurance. Where was God now? But they echoed again, and she allowed the thought to calm her as she recalled the little game Father had taught them.

"Hold up your fingers," he had told them. "Now use each one for a word." And he had marched his fingertip over their fanned fingers, at each saying a word, "I—will—never—leave—thee."

"Never forget it," he had admonished.

She tightened each digit against the palm of her hand as she forced herself to repeat the words over and over.

They rode slower, ducking under low branches. Once he reached out to lift a heavy bough, and they bent low to avoid it.

As the darkness of the thick woods increased, so did Abby's fear. It rose in her stomach and puckered her mouth like a long drink of sour milk. It rolled inside her belly on a wave of nausea; and she gritted her teeth, as much to keep them from chattering as to quell the urge to vomit. She would not let him know how afraid she was.

Around her clenched teeth, she demanded, "If you mean me no harm, then take me back home."

She felt him shake his head, and for a minute, she couldn't control the rattle of her jaw. "Take me home," she pleaded. "I won't tell anyone." She had not seen his face. It would be impossible to identify him. She babbled the words, desperate for him to see this was to his advantage. But again, she felt the shake of his head.

"I'm not taking you home." The words vibrated along her spine, racing through her body like a fever.

"Let me go," she ground out, flailing her legs and arms like a flapping towel in the wind. The horse tossed his head and whinnied. A branch slapped her in the face, and she whimpered. Again he pressed his legs over hers and pinned her arms to her side so she couldn't move.

"Settle down," he growled. "Just settle down."

"No," she panted. "I won't settle down. Let me go." Her words turned to a sob. "Please, let me go."

"I can't."

She stiffened, every nerve alert to his meaning. "Why? What are you going to do?"

He was picking his way through a thick tangle of trees and didn't answer. They broke into a small, sunless clearing, completely shrouded by tall pines. A fine-boned, black horse matching the one they rode was tethered at the far side. In a flash, Abby took in the details. The rolled-up bedroll and saddle on the ground, a piece of canvas draped over. The saddlebags high in the trees beside two canteens. This had been his camp for at least two days, she guessed by the tripod over the dead ashes. He looked to be supplied for many days in the wilds.

"No." The moan came unbidden to her throat, and she struggled against his arms. "What are you going to do?" She was drowning in her own panic, and she felt her limbs go rubbery. "What do you want?"

The horse snorted and pawed the ground, restless to be free of its unpredictable burden. The man shifted in the saddle, and for a minute, Abby thought he was going to step down without answering her. Then he grunted, a sound that might have been him clearing his throat.

If only he would get down first, she would have a few seconds to grab the reins and kick the horse into flight. If she could just get into the bush. . .

She stared at the mass of dark trees. The forest was thick and moody, and she trembled at the thought of being lost in its gloom without provision or protection, but it was preferable to what lay ahead here. He must have guessed her thoughts, for he stiffened and his arm tightened painfully.

"We're gonna get down," he growled, and she heard and understood the warning note in his voice. "You aren't gonna try and run away, or I'll have to tie you up." He paused and she waited, but they stayed seated in the saddle. "One more thing. When you see me, you better not scream."

She shook her head, wondering at his warning.

"Ready?"

Before she could nod, he swung his leg over and lifted her from the saddle. Gasping at the pressure against her rib cage, she was dragged off the horse and set on her feet. It was the longest she had ever been on the back of a horse, and the insides of her legs screamed a protest. Her knees threatened to buckle. His arm steadied her until her rubbery limbs took her weight, and then he stepped back.

She spun on her heel and stared at her captor.

Draped in a long, black slicker, he gave the impression of power and—she struggled for the right word—it wasn't evil she read in his face, though she had no doubt his intentions were just that. It was more a sense of warning, a belligerence accented by the dark scowl on his face. His face might have been called handsome apart from the brooding scowl and a scar puckering his left cheek. He turned his head slightly; and under the shadow of the battered, black cowboy hat that hid all of his hair but a thick black fringe at the nape, she caught a glimpse of dark, hazel eyes, veiled and unfathomable. It was hard to guess his age—somewhere in his late thirties, she thought, though it could be the hardness in his face that made him look that old.

"Who are you?" she demanded in a strong, clear voice that revealed none of the inner terror making her arms feel extra long and her hands seem detached from her body. Her feet had the same not-quite-there feeling. "What do you want?"

He settled back on his heels, his stance wide, his arms loose at his sides, yet she sensed his steady gaze and knew he watched her with the sharpness of a hawk. "My name is Brewster Johnson." He nodded. "And you are Abigail Landor."

Her eyes widened. "How do you know my name?" At the same time, her mind was searching for a tidbit tucked away. She knew she had heard that name before. Suddenly she remembered Sarah's words.

"You have a neighbor west of you," she had said. "A dark, brooding man. He rides into town with his hat pulled low, gathers up what he needs, and rides out again, as silent as the morning mist."

What else had Sarah said about him?

Abby remembered thinking at the time that he lived too far away to be making social calls. A shudder wriggled up her spine. One could hardly call this a social visit.

"I know lots about you. You have a brother, Andrew, and you arrived here a few months ago."

"He's my twin brother." It seemed important he get the facts right.

"Yup. Know that, too."

"What do you want?" She almost choked on the words.

"We're going to get married."

The ground swayed beneath her feet, and the trees closed in as she struggled to retain control of her swirling senses.

"Married?" She could barely whisper.

"Yup." He rolled back farther on his heels and rested his hands on his hips. "Haven't got time to run the house. Too busy with the ranch. I need a woman."

Her cheeks sagged, and she felt the blood drain away. She was sure her face had lost all its color. Then red-hot anger raced upward, burning her cheeks and flooding her brain with such force that words rushed from her mouth. "You think you can just grab a girl and plunk her on your horse and race off with her and announce you're going to get married? Just who do you think you are anyway, Mr. Brewster Johnson? This is a free country. Slavery is not allowed." Her mouth was so dry, she choked and was forced to stop and swallow hard. The infuriating man stood there scowling at her, his eyes shadowed by his hat, his mouth tight. She glowered at him. "If you're so all-fired anxious to get married, why don't you court a girl like anyone else?"

He dropped his hands to his sides and hunched forward. "Wouldn't work."

"How do you know?" She spat the words at him. "Have you tried?"

"I just know." His jaw tightened, and his hands closed into fists.

"How can you be so all-fired sure?" She saw him tense. Not knowing what to expect if she angered him, she backed away, her insides fluttering as her gaze darted around the clearing. There was no place to run.

"You see me," he growled. "I'm ugly. What girl in her right mind is gonna take a second look at me?" His fingers touched the scar on his cheek.

She took a step back. She didn't know what she had expected, but not that. Ugly? No, she wouldn't call him ugly, at least not his features. What made him unattractive was the way he scowled. Her anger mounted. She could feel it spark in her eyes. "Mr. Johnson, it is not your face I find objectionable. It is your high-handed attitude. You can't just grab a girl and force her to marry you."

He laughed. At least she supposed she could call his snort of derision a laugh. "Maybe I'll forget the preacher bit and just take you to my cabin. We don't need to be married for you to cook and clean."

"You—that's not—" She paused and swallowed. "You can't make me marry you." She sought for control. How dare this man think he could choose a wife this way? Was he crazy? Her heart ticking in her throat, she gathered up her skirts and dashed for the deep woods, only steps to her right. Being lost in the woods was preferable to whatever this lunatic had planned.

Behind her, she heard his angry growl and then his thudding footsteps. She increased her pace. Parting the bushes, she dived under the branches, jerking her skirts as they caught. Keeping low, she scooted through the thicket until the forest closed around her. For a ragged moment, she forced herself to remain still as she gathered air into her aching lungs and calmed her breathing.

Twigs snapped and branches cracked as he thundered after her. Knowing his noise would hide the sounds of her escape, she grabbed her skirt and pulled it between her legs, tucking it firmly into her waistband. Dropping to her hands and knees, she scurried deeper into the forest, pushing her way into thick growth, wriggling under the low branches and tangled brush. The underbrush scratched her face, but she pressed on, deeper and deeper into the protection of the thicket. When she was sure she was hidden from view, she huddled into a ball and held her breath, listening. The forest was silent. A beetle scurried across her arm, and she choked back a sob. A seed pod snapped, loud as a drum beat in the damp silence. She didn't dare take a breath. It would signal her hiding place like a red flag. She forced herself to ignore the burning in her lungs. A branch snapped so close, she could feel the sound. Rustling sounds of boots on a leafy forest floor moved past her and faded. She dropped her head to her knees and drew a shaky breath, letting the air seep into her famished lungs.

Andrew, she silently called, *I need you.* It wasn't unusual for them to be able to communicate without using words, and she prayed this would be one of those times. Even as she thought it, though, she knew he was too far away to help. He wouldn't even know she was gone until tomorrow. Hot tears puddled on the back of her hands. How long would she have to huddle here until it was safe to make her way home? How long would he wait for her to crawl out? The forest floor was cold and damp, and she shivered.

Again and again she repeated the words, *"I will never leave thee nor forsake thee."* Another verse Father had taught them tacked itself to her litany. *"What time I am afraid, I will trust in thee. I will not fear what flesh can do unto me."*

No matter what happened, she had the assurance that God would be with her to help. Her breathing deepened. Was Sarah praying for her now?

She remembered her pleasure the first time she met Sarah. Sarah had been helping her husband, Tom, in the general mercantile store in the fledgling settlement of Pine Creek. The plain, young woman had a spark that drew Abby's interest. Similar in age, there had been an immediate sense of kinship between them despite the infant Sarah carried in one arm. It didn't take either of them long to discover that they shared the same faith in God and excitement in this wonderful, new land. When Sarah had suggested they pray for each other, Abby had readily agreed.

She drew strength from the thought that Sarah would be upholding her before God and centered her thoughts on Andrew. He wouldn't know what to think when he returned and found her missing. If only he wouldn't blame himself. But she knew he would. He had always been protective of her, just as she felt it was her responsibility to care for him. It came of being motherless since they were three. Father had been there, quiet and loving, but she and Andrew had given each other the affection and understanding their mother would have provided if she had lived. Being twins only strengthened the bond between them. They were like matching bookends.

They even shared the same dreams. For three years, stirred by the stories Cousin James had read in letters from a friend in Canada, they had worked and saved and planned for this move. And now, just months after they had found the ideal spot in the foothills west of Fort Calgary, this madman had ridden in to ruin their lives.

What would Father say when he heard of her disappearance? Closing her eyes, she thought of his pain. Father had planned to come with them, but as the time drew near, he had gently said he didn't think he could stand to be so far from Mama. He still went to her grave every week. It was the only thing that marred their happiness, but Abby knew he was right. He would never have been content leaving Mama behind.

But if something were to happen to Abby, she feared it would drive him to an early grave.

Her jaw tensed as she huddled in the damp forest. How could this madman think he could force her into marriage? Why, it was barbaric! Had he escaped from the Dark Ages? She shuddered and drew her knees closer to her chest, promising herself she would perish in the gloom of the forest before she would let him find her.

Poor Andrew. He would never find her hiding place, either.

A spasm clawed at her neck and ran its sharp talons into the small of her back. She stiffened against the pain. How long could she stay in this position? Already she could feel pins and needles jabbing in her thighs. She shifted her weight to her right, but even that little bit of movement set the leaves dancing and jingling. She forced herself to remain motionless, letting her breath slide silently in and out. The stillness was alive with normal forest sounds—birds gossiping in the foliage, pine needles whispering in the treetops, wind sighing through the branches. She strained to catch a sound that would provide a clue to the man's whereabouts. Her ears hummed from listening, but she could not detect anything out of place.

The talons in her back dug deeper. Her legs twitched, and she grasped them tighter to keep them from jerking outward. How long had she been hiding? She tried to measure the day, but it had occurred in flashes of fear and tension rather than in minutes and hours. They had ridden far enough to penetrate the pine forest. She estimated that would have taken at least an hour, probably longer. She had been huddled here long enough to make her limbs cramp. Probably another hour. It was hard to tell by the light because it would be dull under the trees even at midday, but she guessed it had to be late afternoon. She hadn't heard a sound from her captor in a long time. Every nerve in her body cried for relief, but she kept her head lowered to her knees, her heart surging against her chest, as she contemplated the noise she would make if she moved. Finally she couldn't stand the discomfort any longer. Moving with the speed of Old Lady Sparks, who was so crippled she could barely inch her way across the street, she lifted her head.

Her heart almost exploded. A scream rose in her throat, unfolded in the air like a thin piece of paper, then tucked into a moan and dropped to the pit of her stomach where it lay like a cold rock.

Like some monstrous bat, silent and unnatural, her captor leaned against a tree, his black slicker draped at his sides. His eyes, guarded by his hat, didn't so much as twitch. His arms were crossed over his chest. One scuffed, worn, black boot rested against the instep of the other as he waited, as still as a shadow.

Chapter 2

He uncoiled with deliberate slowness.

"I could track a mouse up a tree in a rainstorm." His voice was deep and ominous.

She tried to swallow, but her throat closed up. She was paralyzed before his unblinking watchfulness—fearing he would strike; not knowing when. Her heart turned cold. This staring, unmoving stranger was more frightening than when he had crushed her in his grip.

"You can come out, or I can drag you out."

Her fear ignited, jolting her into action.

She staggered upright, gritting her teeth as daggers stabbed through her feet and legs. It took a full minute before she could straighten herself completely. She looked him squarely in the eye. She didn't say a thing. She didn't need to. Her clenched jaw and the defiance that made her eyes feel brittle were all that were necessary. He may have prevented her escape, but he didn't have her beaten. No amount of force or threats or torture could make her give in to his demands. She would never give in!

His eyes darkened to match the green of the pine needles behind him, and she knew he had read her message and understood it. Just as surely, she understood his answering certainty.

"Back to camp," he ordered.

She glanced around her. It all looked the same, but she stepped to the right.

He grabbed her upper arm and tugged her to the left. "Wrong way," he growled. She lurched after him, dragged along by his hand. His grasp was firm enough to warn her that if she tried to run, he would jerk her to a stop before she could go half a step, but she had no intention of running again. Not right now. The darkness of the forest was rapidly closing in on them. She could hardly see where to put her feet. And with the deepening gloom came penetrating cold. No, she would sit by a fire and get warm before she made another attempt.

They burst into the clearing. Black shapes loomed across the patch of pine needles. A shudder shook her body. He felt it.

"I'll light the fire soon as I tie you up."

She tried to wrench free. "No." It was bad enough to be kidnapped and held in this black hole in the forest. She couldn't bear being tied up, as well.

"I warned you." He dragged her toward the horse. She dug in her heels, but he continued, almost jerking her off her feet. As he uncoiled a rope from the saddle, she twisted her hands and wriggled her wrists like a snake squirming out of a hole. His thumb burrowed deep into her flesh, and his grip tightened until her bones ached from the pressure.

"Please, don't tie me up." Her exertions had left her breathless and her voice whispery.

"I can't spend all my time hunting you down." Without looking at her, he pulled her hands together in front of her and wrapped the rope around each wrist, the coils digging into her tender flesh. With a flick of his wrists, he knotted the rope between her hands and pulled both ends into his palm, leaving five feet of double-stranded rope between them. Although he had secured her wrists well, he had left her hands loose enough to allow movement.

"You can't do this." Clamping her jaw, she flung herself backwards. The rope tightened around his fist, and his slicker flapped in the shadows. Her teeth rattled as the rope snapped taut.

"Settle down," he growled. "Follow me. I'm going to build a fire and make something to eat."

He couldn't make her settle down. She'd fight him at every opportunity. She tugged at the rope, forcing him to keep his fist tight around his end. She dipped to her right, intending to fling herself on the ground. What would he do if she lay there and refused to move? Her throat tightened as she remembered his plans for her, and she straightened, knowing she would be at a terrible disadvantage flat on the ground. And as long as he was expecting her to try to break loose, she realized, he would not slacken his hold on the rope. If she could get him to let down his guard, perhaps he would forget about clutching the ends. Trotting after him, she decided to wait her chance.

Settle down. Silently she repeated his order, forcing her fear back, back, back until it was like a sleeping bear in a cave. She filled her lungs and held her breath for the count of two and let it ease past her clenched teeth. A fragile calm seeped through her limbs.

Wood was already laid ready for a fire, and it started instantly when he put a match to it. "We need more wood." He strode toward the forest with Abby scurrying in his wake. "Hold out your arms. I'll fill them."

Separated by the slender strands of rope, she stared at him as he bent to pick up deadwood. Anger choked at the back of her throat, and her eyes were tight with fear; but she blinked back her emotions and waited as he piled several small pieces of wood in her arms. Perhaps her silent consent would do what she could not trust her voice to do—convince him she was prepared to cooperate. The rough bark burned at the tender flesh of her inner arms, and the rope tightened around her wrists as she strained to hold the weight of her burden close to her body so the coils wouldn't bite so harshly. He bent to pick up wood to fill his own arms. As he straightened, she gritted her teeth to keep from showing her discomfort. She was aware of his scrutiny, but it was too dark to be able to make out the expression in his eyes. Did he have any idea how painful it was for her to have her wrists bound? She bit her bottom lip.

They piled the wood close to the fire. Brewster bent and pulled a blackened cast-iron pot out of the saddlebags.

"Can I help?" she croaked.

"Can you make mush?"

"Of course."

He poured a handful of meal into water and set the pot on a rock near the fire then handed her a spoon. She stirred until the gruel thickened, all the time keeping her head turned away so he wouldn't see the desperate fear making her limbs feel like string. If only she could poison the pot. She'd gladly die to escape what lay ahead.

Turning back to the saddlebag, he poured a scoop of coffee into a blue enamel coffeepot and hung it over the fire then opened a can of baked beans and set it between two rocks near the flames. The aromas blended and wrapped around her, making her forget the dark shadows sucking the light from the clearing and the rope that bound her wrists. As the smell of beans, cornmeal, and coffee rose on the thin twist of smoke, she sank to the ground.

Filling a battered tin plate, he handed it to her. She felt resentment flare in her eyes and lowered them, waiting until he turned back to the fire before she pulled the plate to her chin and shoveled the food into her mouth with short, jerky movements. When she finished, he took her plate and handed her a cup of coffee. She savored its warmth. As comfort spread outward to her limbs, she allowed herself to relax. Out of the corner of her eye, she watched Brewster cleaning his plate. The rope tying her to him rested in his fist.

Taking a deep breath, she turned to him. "Do you live close by?" She hoped he would enjoy talking about his place as much as she and Andrew did about theirs.

"Up the mountain some," he grunted, not bothering to lift his head.

"What sort of place do you have?" *Keep pressing him to talk. Get him to let down his guard.*

"Just a small place."

"A log house?"

"Of sorts."

He was as closemouthed as he was unsmiling. "You originally from around here?"

"Nope."

"Where are you from?"

"No place in particular."

She stared at him. His expression never relaxed. The lines in his face were as deeply engraved as the scar. His left side was to her, and she studied the scar. Whatever had happened, it was not a clean cut. The edges were puckered like he had caught his cheek on something sharp. It was an old injury, she guessed, for the scar was silvery white and almost invisible except when he turned and the light caught it as it did now. He met her gaze with dark, motionless eyes. She knew he had seen her studying his scar, and she read the challenge in his eyes.

Blinking before his stare, yet determined not to be intimidated, she asked, "What happened?"

He turned away and ducked his head, hiding his face under the brim of his hat. "Got cut." His voice was hard as rock.

It seemed the more she asked him questions, the more he tightened up. She lighted on another topic. "Do you have family? Parents, brothers, sisters?"

"None." His voice was so deep, it bounced against her chest.

"None?" Thinking of Andrew and Father, she couldn't imagine the loneliness of no family. "I'm sorry," she murmured.

He didn't answer. Instead, he took her plate, set the dirty dishes in the pan she had used for mush, and filled it with water.

"I'll do that," she offered and hunched down on her knees. Swaying slightly, she stiffened her spine to steady herself. Using her hands as one, she scoured the dishes, shaking the water from them and letting the heat from the fire dry each item before she passed it to him. Silently he took each dish and tucked it inside the saddlebags. She could feel his eyes watching her, measuring her. Was he questioning her change of attitude? Or—her throat tightened—was he assessing her qualities as a wife? A shudder rippled up her spine and blurred her vision. He had made no secret of what his intentions were.

The rope chafed her wrists as he stood. Her heart fluttered, and she jumped up, rocking on the balls of her feet. Lights flashed before her eyes from the sudden movement. She bunched her hands into a fist. But he turned away and bent to untie a bedroll from the saddlebag.

"Here." He handed it to her then turned to get the other roll.

She stared at the bundle in her arms. Questions raced through her mind. When? Where? How would he force himself on her? She clenched her teeth until her jaws ached and answered the question herself. *Never.* She would find a way to stop him. But he was so strong. How could she protect herself?

Another verse she'd learned slipped into her mind.

"He will not suffer thy foot to be moved: he that keepeth thee will not slumber."

It was a verse from one of Father's favorite psalms. She clung to the comfort of the words and thoughts of her father's love.

Brewster was spreading the blankets on the ground next to the saddle, the rope between them hindering his movements.

Staring at his back, she tried to still the panic shaking her knees. The rope between them meant she had to place her own blankets less than five feet away. She shuddered. Everything in her cried for space.

Tugging the other saddle as far from him as the rope would allow, she let the bundle drop in a heap. Gritting her teeth, she settled herself on the blankets, sitting stiff and upright against the saddle.

Turning away, he pulled the slicker around his shoulders. He could have been made of stone for all the movement she saw after that. Stubbornly she kept her face toward the fire, determined to ignore him, yet sharply aware of him. He was so close, she could have reached out and touched him. Every nerve in her body was taut with apprehension.

"You might as well get comfortable." At the sound of his deep-voiced rumble, her nerves twitched. "We got a long ride tomorrow."

Crossing her arms across her chest, she squirmed down until her head rested against the saddle. Let him think she was settling down to sleep. She'd lie quiet and relaxed until he fell asleep, then. . .

Her head toppled toward her chest, jerking her to dull awareness. The fire had burned down to twisting, glowing embers. She held herself still for several thudding heartbeats, watching Brewster's back for any sign of wakefulness. His shoulder rose and fell with soft regularity. Filling her lungs slowly, Abby eased the blanket down to her ankles and drew her legs close to her body, tensing her muscles. Inch by cautious inch, she pulled the slack rope toward her until it hung between them in a gentle curve. It poured from Abby's hand, bridged the space between them, and crossed his body. Although she couldn't see it, she knew it was wrapped around his fist. She watched it sway hypnotically with the motion of his breathing and held her breath, waiting, her heart pounding in her ears. Slowly, silently, she eased air into her lungs. With trembling fingers, she inched the rope into her palm until it grew taut. Tugging very gently, she tried to free it from his grasp, but it grated against the slicker. Stifling her disappointment, she let the rope relax, gathered her feet under her, and pushed herself up like a silent puff of smoke. Leaning toward him, she lifted the rope until it swayed above his body. Again, she raveled it in until it was taut and gently tugged. The rope came alive in her hands, jerking her off balance. Reaching out to steady herself, her bound hands clawed at his shoulder. The fabric of his slicker, stiff and rough, rasped at her skin, and she could feel his warmth beneath her palms. Gasping, she teetered on her feet, scrambling to keep from falling on top of him.

"You'll never get away." His voice rumbled beneath her fingertips, and she fell back to her heels. Turning, he flipped the rope, and it snaked between them like a living thing. "Now settle down."

She turned and met his eyes. His hat had fallen off and lay between them. For the first time, she saw his face without protection; but it was too dark for her to make out anything but a shadowy outline.

He leaned forward and hissed, "I don't sleep much." There was no mistaking the tone of his voice. "Besides." He held out his open hand, and she saw that the rope remained secure. He had tied it to himself.

Her chest collapsed as hope died; and she shuffled back to the blanket, edging as far away as possible before she flipped on her side to stare into the darkness. Her pulse was still beating erratically, and she concentrated on calming her breathing.

He made no move to touch her, but she fancied she could feel his hot breath against the back of her neck. She could sense his eyes boring into her, and she suppressed an urge to whimper. To bring her breathing back to normal, she filled her lungs and exhaled quietly in a slow, steady rhythm. She had to calm herself so she could think. Running had proved a disaster. Trying to gain his confidence and make him careless seemed futile. The permanent scowl sculpting deep creases in his face reminded her that he seldom let down his guard. There seemed little she could do while it was still dark and he had her shackled to him. Perhaps tomorrow would bring more opportunities. Surely he would release her for a little privacy. She remembered what he had said about riding a long distance. The second horse gave her hope she would have her own mount. She would stay alert and grab whatever chance she could find.

The darkness swirled and throbbed around her, but she could not relax. When she closed her eyes, a dark-cloaked figure loomed above her, intimidating and silent. The rope chafed at her wrists, and her neck hurt from using the saddle as a headrest. She was tired and knew the next day would be even more exhausting than this one had been, but she was afraid to fall asleep. As long as she stayed awake, she could see and hear his every move. If she slept, she was easy prey. She prayed for morning to come. She prayed for someone to rescue her. She prayed for mercy.

A sharp rock jabbed into her hip, and she shifted to find a smoother spot on the cold, unforgiving ground. An owl hooted, its low, mournful voice sending a shudder through her body. There was a quick rustling in the underbrush, and she peered around the clearing for four-legged intruders. The tall pines were black giants moaning high overhead. The saddle under her cheek smelled of old leather and horse sweat. It wasn't an unpleasant smell, because it reminded her of her father. Often he'd come home with the smell of leather and warm horseflesh clinging to his clothes. After supper, it was his habit to sit in the rocker and read. She could picture him now with a book in his lap. Whenever she needed comfort or just his company, she would drop to the floor at his knees. He would put his finger in the book and lift it off his knee to make way for her to press her head to his lap. Father would pat her head as he rocked. Even now, she could feel the rocking motion and hear the chair's creak. Funny she should think of Father and the comfort of his rocking chair now. It would have made more sense to think of Andrew astride his horse riding in pursuit of them.

But maybe not so strange after all. Father's quiet presence had been her mainstay during her growing-up years. He didn't say much, but he was there. And it was at his knee that much of her training had taken place. It was there she had learned to trust God's goodness and love. Never had she needed that confidence more than she did right now.

She drifted awake as the smell of coffee tickled her nose. Instinctively she reached out to push herself upright and cried out, falling back as pain shot through her wrists. Her arms were cramped from their unnatural confinement, and her wrists were on fire. Suddenly she noticed the rope was slack and the end lay on the ground. Struggling to a sitting position, she awkwardly pushed her hair out of her face. She stared at the end of the rope, possibilities churning through her mind.

"Don't try it."

Flopping back on the blankets, she stared up into the narrow patch of blue. She should have played possum until he moved away. But it was too late now. Sighing loudly, she sat up again and watched him stirring something in the pot. Probably cornmeal again, but what difference did it make? As long as it kept up her strength so she could get away when the time came. And she was certain the opportunity would come.

Feeling like she had been tumbled over a pile of rocks, she pushed herself to her feet. Bending stiffly, she picked up the end of the rope, and with as much dignity as her creaking bones would allow, marched toward the forest, silently daring him to question her.

"Remember, I can track a mouse—"

"I know," she muttered. "Up a tree in a rainstorm."

"Yup. Don't be long."

Gritting her teeth to keep from retorting, Abby pushed her way into the trees until, glancing over her shoulder, she could no longer see him. She leaned against the rough bark of a pine tree, letting the tension drain from her body. The branches caught at her hair. How would she ever get the needles from her curls? She didn't even have a comb with her. Her wrists burned. A tear dribbled down her nose, and she wiped it away. She knew the sun was shining overhead by the bits of brightness flashing through the upper branches, but they did nothing to relieve the gloom on the forest floor. Slowly turning full circle, she studied her surroundings. There was nothing around her but trees and tangled undergrowth. She already knew the futility of trying to make her way through it. Futile or not, she had to get away. Muffling a sob, she bent her head and bit at the rope. Curling back her lips, she used her molars to grasp the coils. The rope burned at the corner of her mouth and her teeth ached. The rope grew wet with saliva, but she failed to loosen it.

"Arrgh." Her voice grew urgent as she continued to strain.

"Time's up." His call thudded into her frenzy.

If her brain weren't laced with spears of panic, she might almost imagine it was a game like one she had played often with Andrew when they were children. "Come out, come out, wherever you are." Only this wasn't a game. Abby had no doubt her life was winding away, and a deep shudder settled in the pit of her stomach.

Wiping her mouth, she flung her way back through the heavy growth, praying that Brewster's mind would be on continuing the journey and not on making good on his threat to take her as his wife. Hah! What a laugh! A wife was loved and cherished—not kidnapped and terrorized. What he planned to do to her had nothing to do with love and marriage or a husband-wife relationship. He could call it whatever he wanted, but it was pure and simple torture. Hesitating as she broke into the clearing, she stared at his back as he hunched over the fire, letting all her anger and fear blaze through her eyes as they bored into his black-shrouded figure. Too bad looks couldn't kill, or he would fall face first into the fire.

"Food's ready." His words made her swallow hard and blink. Handing her a bowl of mush, his eyes lingered on the rope at her wrist where the wetness was plain to see. She met his look squarely. He said nothing, nor did he take the end of the rope in his fist. It was as if he knew she could try whatever she wanted with no chance of success. Her jaw tightened against already sore teeth. If her bound hands hadn't made it difficult, she would have thrown the mush in his face. Instead, she turned her back to him and stomped across the clearing. She bent her head. No words of thanks came to mind as she stared at the food. Then, realizing she would need to keep up her strength for the moment when God would provide a way of escape, she silently thanked Him for the provisions and ate in silence, biting down a cry of pain as she struggled to bring the spoon to her mouth. She let her resentment burn into a roaring fire as rawness stung her wrists. His footsteps thudded across the ground. From beneath his eyelashes, she saw him roll up the bedrolls and tie them to the saddles. Without lifting her head or turning around, she knew when he brought the horses to stand by the almost dead fire and heard him exhale as he tossed first one saddle then the other onto their backs.

"Time to go." She hadn't heard him move toward her, and the sound of his voice just a few inches away made her hands twitch. Why did he have to sneak around like that? She refused to look up. She wasn't going to move from this spot. Let him try to make her.

In a flash, she recalled how he had thrown her into the saddle the day before, and she jumped to obey. Turning her head to avoid him, she marched to the side of the smaller horse. She stared at the stirrup and lifted her gaze to the saddle. She couldn't do it with her hands tied. Unless. . .she swung her wrists over the saddle horn, biting her lip against the pain. The horse sidestepped, and Abby shuffled after it. She could taste blood but kept her teeth clamped firmly. Lifting her foot, she tried to wiggle it into the stirrup but her skirt caught her leg and she struggled to regain her balance, sweat beading on her brow. Before she could try again, he grasped her waist and lifted her. She swung her leg over the saddle and allowed him to settle her.

All the anger and frustration she had bottled up since she awoke, erupted in a burst of words. "If you would untie me, I could take care of myself." She glared down at him, feeling her eyes sting with resentment.

Pushing his hat back so he could see, he looked up at her, eyes dark and measuring. She waited, and when he didn't move away, she held her hands toward him. She could feel her heart beating in her chest as she waited. Finally he dug in the pocket of his denim trousers and pulled out a knife. With practiced ease, he thumbed out a blade. Grabbing her fists, he sawed through the ropes.

She couldn't breathe. His grasp was gentle as he held her hands in his palm. He had enough power in his hands to crush her. She felt dizzy. He cut through the last coil and tossed the frayed scraps into the ashes before folding the knife and shoving it back into his pocket.

"Thank you," she whispered, rubbing her reddened skin. She was grateful that his attention was on coiling up the length of rope so he couldn't see her confusion. She almost wished he had left her bound. It was easier to deal with a man who was cruel and cared little for her comfort.

He tied the loops to his saddle then swung up. Reaching back, he took the halter of Abby's horse.

"Let's ride," he rumbled.

Chapter 3

They rode through the trees into a pocket clearing.

"This here's as good as any." His low, nonchalant growl did not deceive her. She knew he'd picked this place with care, perhaps days ago. Throughout the long, hot hours of the day, she had followed in his wake, climbing hills, skirting rocks, and wading noisy mountain streams. Abby's eyes were sharp enough to recognize the same narrow stream they crossed three times during the afternoon. She understood he was laying a carefully convoluted trail that would confuse the most expert tracker. For the last three hours, they had climbed gradually until they were high into the rocky slopes of the mountains. He was meticulous in the execution of his plan.

She couldn't recall ever feeling such mind-numbing fatigue. They had stopped hours ago for a bit of dry biscuit and warm water. Since then, he had offered her his canteen several times. She had refused until she was almost choking on a combination of dust and fear. She almost gagged now as she thought of how thorough were his preparations. How could she hope to escape? Blinking back tears, she wondered what she had done to deserve such a fate. It hardly seemed fair that he'd noticed her in the short time they had been in the country.

It took her a moment to realize he had pulled his horse to a halt under the trees and had slid down and was now reaching for the bridle of her mount. Before she could think to protest, he came to her side and lifted her from the saddle.

Her legs wobbled with the shock of her weight. She grabbed blindly for something to steady herself, and her fingers brushed against his hand as he reached out to grasp her elbow. Revulsion shivered up her spine, and she twisted away, gritting her teeth as she forced herself to stand unaided.

"I'm not used to riding." She grated the words over clenched teeth, biting hard to keep her teeth from rattling.

Now he'll make good on his threat to make me his wife. Her skin crawled at the thought. She almost gagged again. Apart from the hugs and kisses she'd received from Andrew and her father, she'd never been touched by a man. They had been there to protect her from any passing dalliance. Not that they had needed to. She had never felt the need for romance. Andrew and Father were all she needed. She fixed her eyes on the ground, aware that she was quivering visibly.

"You can help gather firewood," he said in his low, grating voice, and she hurried after him, welcoming the gift of another few minutes.

Swathed in the scent of pine needles, they scoured the forest floor. Soon she had her arms full of dry kindling. He turned toward her, the ever-present slicker swinging out behind him like a billowing tent, filling her nose with the smell of old canvas. She stared at the slicker, wondering how he could stand to wear it everywhere. Despite the heat of the afternoon, he had not once removed it, merely opening it wide so the wind could blow up underneath. He had eaten in it, slept in it, and rode in it. She wondered if it ever came off his body.

Seeing her arms full, he shifted his own load closer and strode back to the clearing. She scurried after him.

Efficiently and quickly, he built a roaring fire; and while waiting for it to burn down to hot embers, he turned to face her.

This is it, she thought. *The moment I pay the price.* And as he moved toward her, a prickling sensation crept across her skin. Despite the evening coolness, sweat beaded on her forehead and dribbled between her breasts.

A shudder raced up her spine as he stood close enough that she could catch the scent of pine and wood from the forest and oil from his slicker. It was all she could do to remain motionless, arresting the screams that roiled in the back of her throat.

"Supper will be a minute, but don't get any ideas. I could track you over a pile of rocks, so don't even think of running," he warned. His words seemed to come from a hollow deep within him. He glowered down at her from under the shade of his hat and then turned away, crossing to the horses to check their tethers.

Shuffling toward the fire, she held her hands toward the flames, as dizziness stole her strength. The heat could do nothing to warm the cold fear in the depths of her heart.

Behind her she heard the rattle of tin dishes. She flinched as he suddenly crouched next to her, fashioned a tripod over the glowing fire, and secured an iron pot full of beans. Within moments the deep, rich smell bubbled up, and she realized how hungry she was. Perhaps eating was of primary concern to Brewster at this moment, too, because he showed no interest in her. Some of the tension seeped away, making room for her to become aware of other sensations.

"I need to go into the bushes," she murmured.

He nodded. "Go then."

Gathering her skirts, she held her head high and walked into the forest.

She felt relief at being alone, and for a few minutes, she reveled in her freedom, acutely aware of the soft beauty of the evening. Beside her, a half dozen leather-colored butterflies clung to a decayed stump. The late afternoon sun poured golden light through the trees, and the air was filled with the sounds of a hundred birds busy in the treetops. Then a heavier sound—the muffled thud and crackling rustle of a larger animal—silenced the birds and sent warning spears prickling across her skin.

For a heartbeat, she hesitated before deciding she preferred a human attacker to the clutches of a wild animal. She turned and hurried back to the clearing, slowing her steps as she broke from the shelter of the trees. Praying that the racing of her heart and the flush of her flight did not show on her face, she stepped toward the fire.

Brewster watched impassively.

What did he see? she wondered. Could he see the fear in her eyes? Did he see her relief at seeing him lounging against his saddle? She turned her face downward, hoping that if he had noticed her reactions, he wouldn't misinterpret them.

"Coffee's ready," he murmured, picking up a cup and pushing himself to his feet. He jerked to a stop. Abby followed his gaze and saw two men creep from the shadows, guns pointing straight at Brewster's chest.

"Don't do nothin' stupid," said one of the men. Behind him, the second man cackled.

Abby's scalp crawled. The flow of saliva that filled her mouth at the smell of coffee and beans drained instantly, leaving her tongue furry and stiff.

This is how the end feels, she thought, wondering at how calm she felt. Whoever these men were and whatever they wanted, she knew she wouldn't live to remember it.

From the corner of her eye, she saw Brewster facing the men, his hands still holding the cup in front of him. The flesh around his eyes was taut. She could almost feel his dark eyes glowering at the men. His rifle was propped like a lazy sentinel against his saddle, just out of reach and unavailable against the rifle and handgun held by the others.

Abby quickly turned her attention back to the two men.

"Get the gun," ordered the bigger of the two, and his sidekick scurried to obey. In the half light, Abby saw his face was pinched and narrow behind grimy whiskers. A sour, acidic smell stung her nostrils—a smell as evil as anything she'd imagined. The skin on the back of her neck crawled.

As slowly as she could manage, she began to back away.

"Hold it." The bigger man spun the gun in her direction, and she stopped. "You watch him, Petey," he ordered the smaller man, nodding toward Brewster, and he took a step toward Abby.

"Well, well. Lookee here," he jeered. "A little chicken ripe for plucking."

"Hee, hee. And yer jest the one to do it. Right, Sam?"

"Durn tootin', I am." He leered, his narrow eyes gleaming, brown tobacco juice drooling out the corners of his mouth.

Every muscle in her body tightened as she measured the distance to the woods.

Understanding her intention, he lunged at her. With a muffled scream, she twisted away; but he caught her arm, crushing it in a cruel grip. "It'd be a shame to let good game like this get away, wouldn't it, Petey?"

Petey cackled his agreement. "Do it, Sam. You first then me."

"No," she moaned, the sound coming from the pit of her stomach. *I'll die first,* she vowed. She turned her eyes toward Brewster in a silent appeal for help, and then Sam's rough hand grasped her and dragged her toward him. He wrapped both arms around her, pinning her to his chest. She exploded in his arms, kicking and thrashing violently, twisting her head wildly until she was forced to stop and catch her breath.

He laughed, his breath rancid against her face. "We got us a real fighter. Some get really feisty in rutting season."

Bursts of red flashed inside her head. His breathing was rapid, and she realized he was excited by her efforts to escape.

With a deep-throated groan, she sank her teeth into the fleshy part of his shoulder and bit so hard she could feel the flesh crunch. She gagged at the overwhelming stench but hung on.

He roared and grabbed her hair, jerking her backwards, sending shafts of light ripping through her brain. She yanked her arm free and slapped him, only distantly aware of the sting in her palm.

With an angry grunt, he trapped her fist and in one quick movement twisted her arm behind her back, pushing it upward until she cried out in pain. He laughed.

"Now that's better, ain't it?" He released his grasp on her hair and trailed his dirty hand down her throat and chest. His skin was rough, scraping her flesh like sandpaper. As he moved to do it again, she spat in his face.

"You ugly, bucktoothed son of Satan," she growled and spat again.

With an angry curse, he slapped the side of her head. Her vision disappeared into flashing, dancing lights, and a roaring filled the air.

Sam released her abruptly, and she staggered, shaking her head in an attempt to clear it. Blinking her eyes to see past the pinprick lights filling her vision, she saw Brewster facing the pair, his legs spread wide, knees slightly bent, arms raised to reveal clenched fists. He roared like an angry bear. Petey staggered backward as Brewster exploded into his face. With a thrust that sent Petey reeling, Brewster leapt across the clearing, closing the distance between himself and Sam, who spun on his heel at the sound of a wild animal charging.

"Why you ugly monster," he snarled and, raising his gun, slammed it into the side of Brewster's head. Brewster staggered, knees buckling, but he did not go down.

"Run, Abigail," he growled. "Take my horse." With an upward jerk, he drove both fists into Sam's chin, spinning him backward.

Abby didn't hesitate. She dashed toward the horses thinking perhaps none of the men would survive. And she didn't care. A burning emotion flooded her brain. Where on earth had such animals come from?

With Brewster's roars thundering in her ears, she darted across the clearing. Brewster's bigger horse was closest. Grabbing the halter, she swung him around. Clutching handfuls of rough mane, she vaulted herself into the saddle. Behind her, the sound of grunts and thuds shuddered up her spine. She hesitated. Should she kick the horse into the forest or try to race across the clearing to the narrow pathway they had followed earlier in the evening? Her heart catching in her throat, she reached down and gathered the halter of the second horse, clucking them both into motion. Ducking under the branches, she paused at the edge of the clearing. Sam lay face down, perilously close to the glowing embers. A motionless Petey stared up at the darkening sky, blood streaming from his mouth and nose. She saw them both in a flash and turned to locate Brewster. He rocked back and forth on his hands and knees, his head hanging almost to the ground. Blood dripped from his nose. Before she could change her mind, she guided the horses forward.

"Get on," she choked out.

Brewster raised his head and looked vacantly at her.

She stared down at him. As he huddled on the ground he looked harmless. Her brain screamed for her to race away, but she couldn't move. Her heart echoed inside her chest, which seemed suddenly hollow. Brewster had risked his life to save her from Petey and Sam—she felt she owed him something for that. But wait! He had placed her in harm's way in the first place.

The urgency to escape warred with the fledgling reluctance to abandon him to his bloody fate. Suddenly—with blinding clarity—she remembered that she was lost in the woods without him.

She slid from the horse and pulled it toward him, reaching one hand out to grab his arm. "Get up," she begged. "Come on, we've got to get out of here." Behind her, one of the men moaned. "Hurry."

Brewster staggered to his feet, weaving unsteadily, and gave his head an unsteady shake. His eyes rolled back, and she grabbed him as he tipped to the side.

"Brewster. Stay with me." She pushed him toward the horse. He leaned his forehead into its flank, and a long shudder raced through his body.

"Get on," she urged, panic making her voice thin.

"Wait," he mumbled. "Guns. Food."

"Never mind that." A grunt behind her made her sure the men would be on them again. "We have to hurry."

"Get them."

Recognizing the stubbornness in his growl, she grunted with exasperation and turned to look for the items. The saddlebags lay close to the fire, and she gingerly picked them up, avoiding looking at the inert men. When Petey groaned, she jumped back.

"The rifle, too," he whispered, taking a pistol from the saddlebags and jamming it into his waistband. Wasting no time arguing, she ran toward the saddle and scooped it up. Spinning on her heel, she hurried back to the horses. Grabbing the saddlebags from his clutches, she flung them over the horses.

"Get on," she ordered, pushing on his back as he tried to lift himself to the animal's back. For a moment, she thought he was going to fall off the other side, but he moaned, shifted his weight, and held on.

Hurrying, she pulled herself on the second horse and clucked the horses into action.

"I'll get you for this." The roar from Sam made Abby kick her horse in the ribs. He bolted down the trail. When they came out of the trees into a narrow strip of grass, she reined her horse in the direction from which they had come.

"Left," Brewster mumbled. "Go left."

Before she could argue, he took the lead, guiding his mount along a trail that rose briskly into the mountains. Her mouth was dry with panic, but she followed closely on the heels of his horse.

They managed to keep up a steady pace, though Brewster swayed, riding with his head bobbing on his chest. He seemed to know instinctively where they were, several times indicating they should veer slightly in a different direction. They entered a rock-strewn hilly area, their progress slowed as they climbed, picking their way over and around rocks often as big as a house. She continually wondered how Brewster could tell where he was going in the moonless night. A few minutes before, he had reached over and taken the lead rope of her horse. Somehow he seemed to be able to find the invisible path, which couldn't have been any wider than the horses' hooves.

Suddenly he lurched to a stop, and the horses waited in single file, the sound of their breathing loud and rough in the still night.

"Get down," Brewster ordered, his words gruffer than usual. She knew he was struggling to remain conscious, and she prayed he wouldn't pass out and leave her alone in the choppy sea of boulders and strange shapes.

Sliding from the back of her mount, she prayed there would be a place to set her feet and discovered a thin strip of gravel behind the horse. She grimaced as she heard Brewster grunt when he slid down. In the dimness, she could make out his shape. He swayed like a pendulum then pushed himself upright and pulled his horse forward. She looked up as her horse followed. Before them were more rocks, seemingly a mountain of them rising right to the sky. Stumbling, she grabbed for support, scraping her palm on the rough boulder at her side. It was surprisingly warm. Suddenly, the ground leveled, and she saw that the rocks gave way to a black wall. Brewster stepped into the blackness and disappeared, pulling the horses in after him.

"Come on," he rumbled.

She stepped forward into the black unknown. Brewster and the horses disappeared in the thick blackness. She stopped. In the darkness, it was impossible to tell if a bottomless pit lay at her feet. With a mouth as dry as desert sand, she felt around with both hands. There was nothing. The air in her lungs rushed to her throat in a lump that almost choked her. She strained to hear a sound that would give her a clue to Brewster's whereabouts.

"Keep a comin'."

She never thought she would feel relief at hearing his rough voice but had to hold back a cry. She stepped forward, hands out to guide her.

"We'll be safe in here. As long as they don't track us across the rocks." His voice was immediately to her right, and she turned, bumping into the broad, warm flank of a horse. A hand came out and grabbed her arm.

"Right here's the wall. Just sit down and keep quiet."

She put her hands against the rough, damp walls and lowered her weary body to the ground, refusing to think about what might be underneath her. Beside her, Brewster shuffled about and grunted. His shape was barely discernible, but knowing he was there made her feel a smidgen safer. Slowly her toes uncurled, and the tension inside her stomach loosened. The muscles in her legs began to uncramp. She was too exhausted to feel fear, even though in the back of her mind she knew that her situation had not improved. Not only was she in captivity to a man who made his plans for her very plain, now there were two men on their trail. Sam did not look like the kind of man who would be happy until he had extracted his pound of flesh in payment for the humiliation Brewster had poured on him.

The clouds sailed away, and the moon dribbled silver light on the rocks outside the cave. She could make out Brewster leaning against the wall, turned toward the opening, watching. He had lost his hat in the fight, and in the wan light, he had a ghostly pallor. He swung to the right, carefully studying the scene, and she saw dark dribbles seeping down his neck.

He'd risked his life for her. Whether to protect his own interests or out of genuine concern for her safety, she didn't know. And it didn't matter. She owed him for what he had done.

Still, she couldn't stop a burst of satisfaction at the sight of his injury. He deserved no less for the misery he had inflicted on her with his crude way of seeking a wife.

A wave of guilt blurred her vision. She wouldn't have left an animal to suffer unattended. And he had been injured saving her.

The scene at the fire raced through her mind. Brewster leaping across the fire to attack Sam, ignoring the risks involved. What had triggered his foolhardy rescue? She shuddered as she remembered Sam's roughness and rubbed the side of her head where he had slapped her. Realization flooded her mind. It had been when Sam slapped her that Brewster roared into action.

She dashed away hot tears and stared at Brewster. A surge of gratitude warmed her. He didn't have to risk his life for her. He could have waited until Sam and Petey were doing what they planned and escaped without their notice. For a moment, her fear of him and her anger at what he had done vanished. She wanted to convey her appreciation.

She shuffled toward him, kneeling close to his side. "You're injured," she murmured, reaching out to touch the wound on his temple.

Her fingers barely touched his brow before he jerked away, turning to face her. His scowl darkened his features. "Leave it be."

"But it should be cleaned," she murmured, thinking she had startled him from his concentration on the scene outside the mouth of the cave. "There's blood all through your hair." Perhaps, she thought, his wound was causing him pain. "I'll be careful."

"Don't bother." He turned away, his words as cold as steel.

His refusal stung her. "I was only trying to help."

"It'll heal without your help."

His tight words were so full of icy dismissal that she felt as if he had hollered at her to get lost. He shook off her offer of help like it was a bad smell. Her eyes burned. This man was as unlikable as any she'd met. He couldn't go around refusing to accept people's kindly offers without offending someone. No wonder he wore a permanent scowl. Her resentment could not be stemmed. "I suppose that's what happened to your face," she lashed out at him. "You got cut in a fight and refused to take care of it."

She sat back on her heels, breathing hard.

Inch by inch, as if turning on a rusty hinge, he pivoted toward her. A lump of dread settled in the back of her throat. She knew she shouldn't have spoken those words. She would have taken them back if it were possible, but now all she could do was wait for the unleashing of his anger.

His eyes were dark and unreadable in the dim light, and yet she felt them boring into her, impaling her with their intensity. He seemed so tense—tightly coiled like a man who is holding himself in, or, she thought in a flash of understanding, like a man holding himself above things.

"You're right on except for a few details." His voice was heavy with sarcasm. "I was five years old, and it was my mother who did this."

Chapter 4

The silence between them was thick in the dank closeness of the cave. Somewhere behind her, she heard a faint rustle. A shiver raced across her neck. She stared at him, certain she had misunderstood the venom in his voice.

"Your mother?" she gasped. "You mean you were hurt in an accident."

Brewster continued to look straight ahead, his eyes dark and empty. She knew he stared right through her.

"It was no accident." His voice was low and flat, but the sound of the pain he tried to disguise tore through her.

"Oh, Brewster." There was so much she longed to say. To ask. Surely, it was a misunderstanding. No mother would purposely injure a child. Especially her own.

Even the black slicker did not hide the hunch of his shoulders or the rigid way he held his neck. "Forget it."

His voice was so deep, it thundered through Abby. She shuddered and pressed her lips together to keep from crying out.

"But. . ." She longed to say she was sorry, but the words stuck in her throat, choked back by her confusion. How could she feel pity for this man?

"Forget it, I said." The brittleness in his voice killed any sympathy that had bubbled unbidden to the surface. She blinked back angry tears.

Fresh blood, black in the dim light, oozed past his right eye. It spread along his cheek over the tracks of the already-dried patches.

Cuts and blood were not unfamiliar to her. She had doctored many wounds for Andrew and Father. Father always said she was a good little nurse, teasing her because she was so particular about keeping even small cuts clean and covered. Swallowing back her revulsion at the thought of touching him, she tried again.

"Please let me clean your wound." She tried to keep her voice from shaking, hoping she sounded pleasant, maybe even cheerful.

He stared out at the moonlit rocks, as impassive as a drugstore Indian.

A shudder raced down her spine. If his injuries were worse than she thought, she could never hope to find her way out of these rocks. And if Sam and Petey were to find them—

She trembled, remembering the stench of Sam's nearness. Nausea welled up, and she forced herself to breathe deeply.

Slowly, as if the movement took all his effort, he nodded. She wondered whether he was agreeing. He leaned forward to rest his arms on his knees.

Not giving herself a chance to change her mind, she bent and ripped a strip from her petticoat. The canteen lay beside him, and she poured a little water on her rag, then edging closer, leaned toward him. Her nostrils flared with the oily smell of his slicker and the metallic scent of blood. And something more. She could smell his warm flesh—pine scent mixed with the salty smell of sweat. For an instant, she wondered what strange mixture composed this man. Then, narrowing her eyes and filling her lungs with the stagnant air that seeped down from the ceiling of the cave, she pressed the wadded cloth to his forehead.

"I'll have to probe around this wound a bit. I'll be as careful as I can." Her nerves were as ragged as the bit of cloth she had torn from her petticoat. In order to keep her fingers steady, she resorted to her usual way of calming herself. She talked as she worked. It was the way Andrew and she had always dealt with pain or problems. They talked to each other. Although there was no twin-bond with this man, she needed the comfort of words.

"I've taken care of injuries before," she murmured. "Andrew seemed to always be getting himself scraped up, falling out of trees, gouging his knees on the gravel, or jamming his hand into something sharp."

Beneath her fingers, the blood was warm and sticky.

"There's gravel in here," she muttered. "You must have rolled in the dirt after you were hit."

He grunted a reply, and as she picked the bits out, she felt him trembling.

"I'm sorry. I'm being as careful as I can."

"It don't bother me."

As near as she could determine in the dim light, the wound was about three inches long. From the width of the gash, she guessed it was fairly deep, but there was little that could be done other than to clean it as much as possible with the limited water supply and try to stop the bleeding. She knew it must be painful. Yet, apart from the slight trembling, he gave no indication—not even a grunt— as she pressed her fingers against the wound, plucking out the bits of bark and rock.

"I wish I had a light," she grumbled, more to herself than for his benefit. "It's impossible to see how clean this is."

"It don't matter much," he rumbled.

"But it does," she insisted. "If I can get it clean, it lessens the chance of infection. Now hang on; I'm going to apply some pressure." She turned the soiled rag over and folded it to a clean side then pressed it to the cut.

Again she felt him quiver, and she touched his shoulder in sympathy. "I know it hurts, but I have to stop the bleeding."

"It doesn't hurt. I never hurt."

It had to hurt like mischief. She glanced down at his fists clenched around his knees. Even in the pale light, she could see the knuckles white and gleaming.

She shook her head. Tense as a cat about to spring, yet silent and stoic about his pain—her sense of who this man was grew more and more confused. Lifting her compress, she leaned close. She heard his breath scraping over his teeth. She guessed that he held himself with a very taut rein, and she wondered at the tension in him.

The bleeding had slowed but not stopped entirely, so she continued to apply pressure. For a moment, she studied his profile, pale in the flat light. His expression was hard, as if etched eons ago in the granite walls of the cave.

Cautiously, she again lifted the cloth and was relieved to see that the bleeding had stopped. Now she could attend to cleaning up the rest of the blood.

"There isn't much I can do about the gunk in your hair until we get more water. I'll just sponge at it a little and do the best I can." His hair was heavy and coarse, matted with dirt and clots of blood.

She dampened the sticky spots with the soiled rag and eased out the worst of the dirt.

"I'll get rid of this mess on your neck." The blood had dried to stubborn crusts, and she had to scrub at the area, resting her hand against his neck to steady herself. His skin was damp and cool. Like the air. Suddenly she realized how cold it was. No wonder he was shivering. The cave had the closed-in coldness of never being warmed by sunshine. Her fingers grew more brisk, scrubbing until the worst was gone.

She was filled with curiosity about this man. His voice was as expressionless as a piece of glass. He claimed he felt no pain. But how could he be as cold and unfeeling as he seemed yet want companionship so badly that he turned to desperate means in order to acquire it? Part of her despised everything he stood for—the selfish hardness of him. But he had risked his life to save her. As if controlled by someone other than herself, she let her fingers slide down his damp neck. It felt strong and surprisingly smooth. A tingling raced up her fingertips, and she shrank back, her cheeks burning. Beneath her breast bone, she felt a quickening, and her breath caught in her throat.

"I'm done." Her words sounded breathless and strained. She plunked down beside him, careful to avoid touching him, and pressed her hands into her lap, trying unsuccessfully to stop the shivers coursing through her body.

She hated this man. It was his fault she wasn't safe at home with Andrew.

Andrew, she silently cried. She hadn't felt so cut off from him since childhood. There had been a time when she cried bitterly if she couldn't be with him. Father used to laugh and say they were like two halves of a ball. Without the matching half, they were nothing. He said it teasingly and lovingly, but she suspected there was a great deal of truth in it. She no longer cried when she and Andrew had to be apart, but with every passing hour, she felt farther and farther from him. She anguished over how he would feel. Would she ever see him again? A dagger pierced her gut and ripped toward her heart. She leaned forward and grasped her knees, stifling a moan.

Brewster turned toward her. "You hurt?"

"No," she mumbled, even as her pain and fear turned to burning hatred of this man. She eased her breath over her teeth and reminded herself that she needed him to get her out of this place.

Besides, she reminded herself, *God loves him.*

It was a strange thought, and she wondered that God's love included both of them despite their vast differences. How could He love such a person? She shuddered as she reflected on the evilness of his plan.

"You're cold," Brewster muttered. "Here." He shrugged out of his voluminous slicker and thrust it around her shoulders.

"No, no." She shook her head, even as she welcomed its warmth. "You keep it." She didn't want to feel any more in his debt. It was hard to be angry at a man who saved your life and then made sure you were warm while he sat stoically ignoring the cold. And she needed to be mad at him. She needed that defense. Something about him called to a place in her heart where she sensed something deep and hungry—she didn't know what. She was afraid to look any deeper.

The smell of the warm canvas stirred a response from some hidden place, but she shrugged her shoulders and shook her head to chase any thoughts away. The slicker fell to the ground.

"You keep it," she insisted. "I'll be all right."

"Don't be crazy," he growled just a breath away from her ear. "The rest of our stuff is back at the campfire. You'll freeze without some protection." He picked the coat up from the floor and once again draped it around her shoulders.

"You'll get just as cold," she argued, still not willing to accept it.

"I don't feel the cold much," he said and turned back to his study of the landscape.

His attention was focused on something in the distance. He seemed to have forgotten her. She waited for a heartbeat before admitting defeat then let her shoulders relax and pulled the veil of warmth about her, sniffing a bit at the canvas smell and then breathing deeply as she searched her senses for the more elusive smells—the scent of old forests and strong dreams. She snorted softly at her thoughts. Determined once again to ignore them, she lifted her head, concentrating on the rocky scene below.

Abby noticed that Brewster was suddenly peering intently toward the horizon, and a pang of alarm raced through her. She followed the direction of his gaze. In the distance, far to the right, there was a flare of orange.

"Is it a campfire?" she asked, almost certain of the answer without asking.

"Yup."

Despite his calm answer, she could sense his intense study of it. He tightened without moving like a man who comes upon a coiled rattlesnake.

She half-rose. "Maybe it's Andrew. I know he's looking for me."

Brewster settled back again. "This brother of yours—"

"Twin," she interrupted.

He continued as if she hadn't spoken. "He done much tracking?"

"No. Why?"

"Then it ain't him. It'd take an Indian to follow the trail I left."

"Then—" Alarm skittered up and down her spine. "Indians?"

"We're pretty far from any Indians I know of."

"Sam and Petey?" A blend of disgust and fear made her voice crackle, and she tried to blink away the memory of Sam's face. His evil gleam seemed branded on her brain, along with the stench, and the way tobacco juice dribbled down his whiskers. Petey's lewd "hee-hee-hee" rang in her ears.

"Yup. That's my guess."

"Will they be able to follow us?"

"Can't say. Didn't take either of them for trackers."

What would have indicated they were? she wondered. But she supposed she knew what he meant. Somehow they didn't fit the picture of keen-eyed, sharp-witted trackers.

He continued staring at the flickering orange spot that was no bigger than a firefly.

"They're too close." Brewster's low, rough voice broke the tense silence. "We'll have to move before light." He hunkered down closer to his knees. "Best get some rest."

She stiffened at his suggestion. As if she could just order up sleep when she was trapped in a living, breathing nightmare. But the night was cool, and her mind refused to face any more problems. She lay down on the hard, cold ground and curled up on her side, pulling the warmth of the heavy coat around her.

Suddenly she bolted upright and stared out at the darkness.

"What's the matter?" Brewster's low voice came from the darkness.

"Andrew," she gasped, too affected by her worry to care what this man might think. "What if he meets up with those two down there?"

"Your brother—your twin," he amended. "Is he a careful man?"

"What do you mean?"

"Would he chase after you without consideration? Would he race down the trail or watch for signs?"

She had to think about it. Andrew was so much a part of her, she couldn't picture how he would act alone. And up until a few weeks ago, their lives had been simple and predictable. She had taken care of Andrew and Father. Andrew had worked at the mill. Suddenly she recalled how he had always checked the belts and gears and warned her to stay back when she had visited him. "Yes, he's careful."

"Then he wouldn't likely ride up to them unawares. They aren't exactly invisible."

His words soothed her fears, and she lay down again, squirming around on the hard ground until she found a place halfway comfortable.

Andrew, she silently called, *be careful. God, be with him. Be with me. Get us all out of this mess.*

"Wake up." A hand jostled her shoulder.

"Go away, Andrew," she mumbled, shrugging away.

"Wake up."

The hand grew more insistent.

The voice! It wasn't Andrew's. She recoiled as all the details of the past two days filled her mind in a deluge of fear and terror, and she retreated into the warmth, wanting nothing more but to sink into oblivion until this nightmare ended.

"It's time to leave."

His deep rumble was firm, but she still huddled in a ball, reluctant to leave the shelter of sleep.

"You planning to be a welcoming party for our two friends down there? If you are, you'll be a party of one. I'm leaving." His boots thudded on the floor of the cave.

Ignoring the chill of the air, she sprang to her feet, clutching the slicker around her shoulders.

"Wait." Her voice broke. Her mouth was so dry, she could hardly swallow, and she wanted to call out for the canteen; but in the darkness, she couldn't see where he was. Afraid he had already left, she stumbled toward the gaping area that was a shade lighter than the rest. "I'm coming." Suddenly his figure loomed against the yawning opening. Her heart somersaulted with relief.

"I'm so thirsty."

"Have a drink, but go easy on it until we can refill."

She groped in the darkness for the canteen she knew he was holding toward her. She found his arm first. He remained motionless as she let her fingers scurry down the length of his limb until she found the canteen and removed it. Eagerly, she filled her mouth with water. It was stale; but it was cool and wet. She kept the moisture in her mouth for several seconds before swallowing. Then she took three more large mouthfuls, screwed the lid on, and passed it back. In the darkness, their hands met. In the blackness that surrounded her, contact with human flesh sent warm trickles up her arm.

She jerked her hand away and rubbed it on her skirt. It might be dark—and the darkness oppressive—and it might be spooky, but she detested this man, and nothing would change that. Not even the shivers racing across her shoulders and the hand begging to reach out and know someone was out there.

"It's pitch dark out." Her voice was sharper than she planned. "How can we go anywhere?"

"You'd rather wait 'til Petey and Sam are at the door?" His voice said how foolish he thought she was.

"No," she answered, stung by his sarcasm. "But neither do I want to fall down the side of a mountain."

"Best stick close then. I know the way." He clucked to the horses, and they shuffled forward. "Come on."

Wondering if he meant her or the animals, she moved to obey and stumbled on the hem of the slicker. "Wait. I can't walk in this thing. What do you want me to do with it?"

His warm hand touched her head and slid down her neck. His fingers dug into her flesh as he lifted the coat from her shoulders. From the sounds beside her, she knew he had flopped it on the back of one of the horses. "You ready now?"

His every action was so sudden and decisive, it left her groping for a response. "Come on then."

His words thrust her into action, and she stepped through the mouth of their shelter.

The forest-sweet air brushed her face, and the stars winked overhead. She lowered her eyes to where they had seen the campfire, but nothing relieved the blackness.

She followed him, sliding her feet past sharp rocks. She stifled a cry as her ankle raked against a razor-edged stone.

"Give me your hand," he whispered hoarsely. "I'll show you the way." He found her hand and gripped it tightly, his warmth a welcome contrast to the cold rocks. Inch by inch, he guided her along the path. She wanted to fling his hand away, yet she clung to his warm, hard hand, trusting him to direct her. The night was as black as the path beneath them. It was an eerie feeling, like walking across the sky.

He stopped. "We'll have to wait a bit. Just until there's light enough to see." He dropped her hand, and she hugged it to her chest, glad to be free of contact yet fighting a spinning feeling of isolation.

The ground was still black, but the stars had been rubbed out by a faint gray line across the horizon. They didn't have to wait long for the sky to lighten, and as it did, the pathway slowly grew visible. Abby gasped. Ahead of them, a sheer cliff rose from the gloom. At their feet, the mountain fell away into darkness.

"We're trapped." She half-turned to see where they had come. "I thought you knew where we were going." Her voice was high with panic.

"Calm down," he muttered, his voice grating in the stillness. "There's a path across the face of the cliff."

"A path?" Her voice rose to a squeak. "You're joshing me." The cliff was sheer rock. Not a twig of branch or strip of dirt. Just straight up and straight down.

"You'll see. Just a few more minutes, and it'll be light enough."

Light enough to die? she thought. If there had been any doubt in her mind about his sanity, it had vanished. "You're crazy if you think I'm. . ."

"Hush. Sound carries for miles in this air."

She sputtered to silence as he raised his hand. He stood with his head tilted as if listening. She tipped her head to match his and strained to catch a sound.

There was nothing but the whisper of the pine branches. The sun edged over the horizon in a shout of orange and pink, filling the world with color, awakening the birds. And awakening the two men far below. Their voices carried to the cliff like echoes in the distance.

Abby's mouth was so dry, her tongue stuck to the top of her mouth. She guessed if they made a sound, it would carry readily to the men below, and she prayed they were too sleepy to look up. She shuddered at her plight, trapped like an animal in a cage. Trapped by the mountain, Brewster, and the dirty men below.

"You'll have to go first," Brewster whispered. "I'll bring the horses."

She hesitated. She didn't want to leave the protection of the shadows. He nudged her gently, and she shuffled toward the cliff, her fingers digging into the dirt at her back. Through squinted eyes, she saw the world drop off at her feet. Her head pounded like a hundred war drums.

"Don't look down," Brewster ordered. His whisper sounded like it came from the sighing treetops down the slope. "Look carefully to your right, and you'll see a narrow ledge."

She followed his instructions. There was indeed a narrow ledge, but she couldn't force herself to step into the blue-gray void. The world swirled and tipped. Brewster's hand caught her shoulder and squeezed.

"It's wider than it looks. I've crossed it and so have the horses."

"I can't." She leaned against the cliff, her eyes closed tightly.

"You can." His words were quiet and firm but did nothing to relieve the quivering in her limbs. "Consider the alternatives."

She swallowed hard.

"You could go straight down. Not a pleasant thought. Or you could go back and wait for Sam and Petey."

"You mean I'm stuck between a rock and a hard place."

He snorted softly—a sound that could have been either mirth or derision. Given her choices, she turned toward the rock wall.

Brewster murmured instructions in her ear. "Take it slow and careful. Slide your feet one at a time." He kept up a slow, steady patter of words, which she clung to like a lifeline as she leaned into the cliff. Holding her breath, she willed her dizziness to stop and forced her eyes to focus on the ledge, telling herself it had to be wider than her fears reported. Hadn't Brewster said the horses had crossed it?

Her heart racing like a hard-run horse, she inched her foot sideways. Every muscle in her body tightened as she forced her leg to extend past her hip. Her chest rose and fell like a churning paddle, but she could not make herself shift her weight to the extended leg.

"Easy now." The words came from someplace to her left, his grating voice jerking her free of her paralysis. "Just another inch and you'll be on the path."

She clenched her toes and leaned into her foot, feeling the coolness of the rocky ledge at her back.

"There you go. You've got it." His voice remained slow and calm, his words pushing her to take that first step and then the next and then another.

She kept her eyes focused on the barely visible cliff, clamping her jaw to keep her teeth from chattering.

Suddenly a rock rolled from under her foot. She gasped as her foot slipped. She felt the color drain from her face, and her stomach churned until she thought she would throw up. The rock skittered down the mountain, bouncing and banging, a sound like bells, announcing their whereabouts.

"Don't move."

He could have saved his breath. Frozen with fear, she couldn't have moved if she wanted.

"Yoo-hoo." The sound was faint, like a distant whisper. Sam's voice was unmistakable as was Petey's accompanying, "Hee-hee-hee."

"Keep moving," Brewster whispered. "A few more feet and we'll be across this cliff. They'll never see us once we reach the trees."

Her muscles, stiff and unresponsive, felt like metal rods as she resumed her shuffling sideways gait. She caught a glimpse of swaying tree branches and slowly lifted her head. Safety and solid ground were just inches away. She threw herself toward the ground, clutching at a tree trunk as she gasped for air, letting the windstorm of fear subside into a sighing breeze. She turned to see what had become of Brewster. He was almost across the rock face, leading both horses.

He turned his head until he could see her. "You okay?" The bright morning sun caught the scar on his cheek. The irregularity of his features made him appear to be part of the rough bank behind him. She blinked to bring him into focus and called a soft, "Yes."

"Lookee, there they is."

Abby's eyes locked with Brewster's as Petey's faint chortle carried to them on the rising morning air.

"Looks like we got us a sitting duck. Too bad, you ugly monster." Sam's words echoed in the stillness.

Brewster's expression hardened. Abby didn't take time to consider his reactions. All she wanted was for him to get to safety.

"Hurry," she called, and he began to move again, but it was impossible to hurry on the narrow ledge.

A puff of dirt exploded beside Brewster's head, followed by a sharp crack.

She stared at him, not wanting to believe what she saw.

He was being shot at. She clamped her hand to her mouth.

Suddenly Brewster recoiled like he'd been slapped and grabbed his left shoulder. From below, she heard another crack of the rifle. Red seeped around Brewster's fingers as he clutched his arm.

He's been hit. She stared openmouthed at him then sprang forward, reaching a hand toward him.

"Brewster," she called, silently willing him to turn toward her. If he passed out and fell—

Her hand quivered. She didn't know how long it would take Sam and Petey to catch up to her, and she didn't dare think about what would happen to her when they did.

"Give me your hand." She strained toward him, but he shook his head. She could feel him take a deep breath and begin to move again. She prayed he would make it.

Another puff of dirt burst from the rocks, this time to Brewster's right. The far horse threw back its head, jerking Brewster's arm. Abby gasped, certain he was going to be thrown to his death. Brewster mumbled something to the horse and continued his snail-paced shuffle. Her pulse throbbed in her temples. Then he was close enough to raise his arm. His hand touched hers.

With fierce determination, she clamped her fingers around his and wrapped her free arm around the trunk of a scraggly pine. He leapt the last foot, crashing into the branches of the closest tree, the horses nearly landing on top of him; and then she yanked him away from the treacherous edge. His weight carried her backward. With a lung-wrenching thud, they landed in a heap on the soft forest floor.

She noted every detail with a sharp precision. His square jaw clenched so hard that the muscles in his face twitched. His scar slashed across his cheek. She had not seen his eyes so clearly before—deep, deep green pools, guarded and secretive. His whole expression was as bleak and hard as the rock cliff he had crossed.

Somewhere, deep in her being, something sparked and flared. Her lips parted as she fought to get air.

She took a long, shuddering breath as he lay beside her for a moment then staggered to his feet and stood gasping. She noticed his sleeve was red with blood.

"You're bleeding."

He glanced at his arm with barely a flicker of interest. "It's nothing. Only a graze." And he turned his back on her, pulling the horses to him.

She sat up, a warm blush of anger racing up her cheeks. He didn't feel pain. He didn't feel cold. He never slept. He never felt anything. She was surprised he bled.

Let him bleed to death or fall off a cliff. It will only make my life easier.

But what about Sam and Petey? And finding your way off this mountain? a little voice nagged.

She stood and smoothed her skirts though they were long past improvement.

Turning, she stared at Brewster's stiff back. She needed him. For now. But not for long.

He wiped his hands on his thighs, leaving dark streaks of blood down one pant leg. Without turning, he ordered her to follow him.

"From here, we climb," he announced over his shoulder.

Chapter 5

Abby staggered along, forcing her reluctant legs to function.

They had spent the day climbing, backtracking, then climbing some more. At one point she looked up from her weary slouch to discover that they were back at the clearing where they had encountered Sam and Petey. She lifted her head and glanced around, afraid they'd ridden into a trap; but as Brewster dismounted and helped her down, there was no sign of Petey or Sam. She collapsed on a log and watched with weak interest as he recovered the saddles and the bag suspended from the tree that contained the bulk of their supplies. He pulled the horses into a thicket and tied them. Before she could fully catch her breath, they were once again on the move, following another nearly invisible trail.

Abby stumbled, but Brewster forged ahead, never looking back. She wondered if she were to collapse in a quivering heap behind him, would he come back for her? She doubted that he would, but she couldn't dredge up enough energy to feel anger or even hatred. Muscles she didn't know she owned screamed for rest.

Brewster's back loomed suddenly before her, and she scuttled to a stop. Thinking they could rest, she sagged with relief and glanced around his shoulder. Above them loomed a shrub-laced hill. In the lengthening shadows, she was certain there was no passage or pathway. Moaning weakly, she allowed weariness to wash through her. Her limbs quivered, and she knew she lacked the strength to retrace her steps.

As she stood trembling, Brewster bent, parted some bushes, then pushed aside a rock. He stared into the shadowy depths then grunted.

"Looks in good shape. In you go." Stepping aside, he waved his arm for her to proceed.

She stared at him, her mouth working in confusion.

"Go ahead. There's a tunnel."

His face floated before her eyes. Too confused to argue, too weary to care where the tunnel led, she dropped to all fours, groaning at the dull ache in her back, and forced her arms to pull her into the blackness. The walls closed around her, damp and musty. The skin crawled on the back of her neck. How long must they be in this shaft, crawling along like animals? It was Brewster's fault. *I wouldn't be here if he hadn't had the notion to kidnap himself a wife.* But the anger she wanted to feel was merely a vague stirring in some distant corner of her heart. All she could think was, *Please, let's stop.* She leaned forward, letting her head almost touch the damp ground. She couldn't move another inch.

As if in answer to her silent plea, he spoke, his voice even deeper and more rasping than it had been in the open.

"There's an opening in front of you. It's a room. You can stand up."

She moved her hand forward slowly and felt empty space. She leapt back in alarm, banging into Brewster. "Sorry," she mumbled, red-hot embarrassment burning her cheeks. She let her hands feel down the walls of the dark room, found the bottom, then lowered herself headfirst out of the tunnel. The darkness was as deep as the inside of a well. It was impossible to fill her lungs.

"Move away so's I can get in."

His voice startled her, and she gasped. Scuttling along on all fours, she stopped when she bumped into a cool wall.

She heard Brewster drop to the floor, then the scrape and thud of his boots on the earthen floor. A match flared, highlighting his features in a yellow puddle of light as he tipped the flame over a stubby candle. Flickering light wavered across the dark walls.

Abby glanced around. It was a very small room. Her gaze lingered on the narrow cot a few feet from where she crouched. She lifted wide eyes toward Brewster. The sputtering candlelight threw dancing shadows across his face, distorting his features, giving him a hawklike appearance. She was beginning to understand that his piercing eyes and forbidding expression disguised a mind like a steel trap. The trail they had left was convoluted enough to confuse anyone. More than once she had been both impressed and dismayed by his cunning and cleverness.

He wiped the back of his hand across his eyes. The wavering light made him look like he was swaying. Reaching into the tunnel entrance, he retrieved the canteen and offered her a drink. She tipped the container back and drank greedily.

He pulled the saddlebags out of the tunnel and flung them open. "You best eat something." He dropped two hard biscuits and a piece of jerky in her lap.

She stared at the food. Never before had she realized how much effort it took to move her head. The food had all the appeal of two rocks and a scrap of leather, and she made no move to pick it up.

"You'll sleep better if your stomach ain't barkin' to be fed."

She lifted her gaze to him again, fascinated by the way his face floated. She wanted to lift her hand and pin it in place but couldn't make her limbs obey.

"Eat," he commanded, nodding in her direction as he bit his biscuit in half.

She lifted her hand and stared vacantly at a biscuit. She absently sank her teeth into the hard exterior. As she chewed and swallowed, her only thought was how much her teeth hurt.

From somewhere, an annoying voice croaked. "Bed," was the only word she understood. When she didn't respond, Brewster tugged her to her feet and pushed her toward the wooden-slatted cot. As she tumbled onto it, she had a drifting feeling that she should be worried about something, but she couldn't remember what and promised herself to think about it in the morning. She felt a coarse blanket across her shoulders.

Someone was fighting close to her bed. Turning over, she pulled the covers closer, wishing the noise would go away and leave her in peace. The commotion only grew louder. Pushing herself out of sleep, she struggled through a sense of weightlessness.

"Go away," she mumbled and sank into oblivion.

A shout jolted her back to consciousness.

She awoke instantly, but nothing seemed right. It was too dark. The bed was too hard and too narrow. The blankets were scratchy. There was an earthy smell in the room. Her senses tingled with alarm.

She heard it again. The rough, fear-laced voice, the indistinguishable words. Then she remembered and bolted upright in bed, straining to see. A thin bar of gloomy light gave shape to the cut log that served as a table. She saw the remains of the candle. Gingerly she lowered her feet to the floor and stepped over to pluck a match from the box and light the candle. The agonized mumbling continued.

Lifting the shaft of weak light, she turned slowly, fearing what she would find.

Brewster lay curled up on the floor at the foot of the bed. Suddenly he flinched and called out in a voice that made her cringe. Holding her breath, she bent closer and saw that he was still asleep. *He must be dreaming. Probably about Sam and Petey*, she decided.

She grabbed his shoulder to shake him. His body recoiled from her as though her hand had seared his flesh, and he cried out, his words plain enough for her to understand.

"Stop. Stop. I'll be good. I promise."

She held her hand above his shoulder, shivering at the fear in his voice. He sounded different. His voice was higher, almost childlike. She wondered if he was dreaming something from his childhood. She trembled as she recalled how she used to wake up crying from a dream that haunted her. In it she was running blindly down a dark hallway calling Andrew's name. It seemed he was just out of her grasp in an open doorway that was always beyond her reach.

A shudder raced across her shoulders. Swallowing her own shadowy terror, she grasped his arm and pulled.

Again he flinched, flailing against the wall in his attempt to avoid her. "No, Lucy. Please, don't hurt me."

Nausea rolled in the pit of her stomach. Someone had hurt him. From the sound of his voice, she guessed it had happened when he was a child. The thought of a child being deliberately misused triggered a rush of emotion. Suddenly she wanted to hold and comfort this man who was her captor, her enemy. But that was impossible, she reasoned. It was the child he used to be that she wanted to soothe. She pressed her fingers to her lips as her eyes welled with tears.

"I didn't mean to. You hurt me." His voice held a note of surprise, and in his sleep, he touched his left cheek.

The pain in his voice tore through her. She had to find a way to waken him—to stop this awful nightmare, but when she again touched his shoulder, he flung her away. She barely managed to keep the candle from being thrown across the room. Reaching out to set it on the table and taking a deep breath, she grabbed his face between her palms.

"Brewster," she shouted. "Wake up." She ducked in time to dodge his outflung arm. But she had touched his skin long enough to realize that he was burning up.

Her thoughts raced into action. Which one of his wounds was infected? How was she to examine them when he reacted so violently to the slightest touch? And how was she going to treat them? There was nothing here. Or was there? She hadn't given the room more than a bare glance last night. Was it still night?

Suddenly the impact of his illness hit her, and she sank to her heels, rubbing her chin. As soon as it was light enough, she could slip away. He was in no shape to stop her or even know she was gone. She could simply walk away.

God had answered her pleas. All day she had comforted herself with the words "I will never leave thee nor forsake thee." Assuring herself that God was with her, she trusted Him to provide a way out of this ordeal. Over and over she had prayed for a means of escape.

And now God had provided the opportunity she'd been waiting for.

But what about Brewster? Could she in good conscience leave him as he was?

Doubts nibbled at the back of her mind. Could she find her way home and, at the same time, avoid running into Petey and Sam? This thought had been the reason she blindly followed Brewster through her haze of exhaustion. But now, escape was finally possible.

She continued to kneel at Brewster's side as her thoughts played tug of war. What would happen to him if she left? Would he die alone except for his tortured memories?

Someone named Lucy had hurt him in the past. But why should she care about his past?

She studied him. What had he been like as a child? Did his face light with innocent anticipation, or did he learn to wear that guarded look so young it had always been there? Had his lips ever softened in a smile, or were they always a straight, tight line? With his high cheekbones and strongly squared jaw, she had to admit his face was handsome despite the scar. He would have been a beautiful child, she guessed. Then she remembered that he had been merely a child, five or something, when he got that scar. Was it Lucy and not his mother who was responsible for it? Who was Lucy, and why did she hurt him? Why would anyone want to hurt an innocent child? Who was this man? Why did he cry out in his sleep like one tortured? What would drive someone to such desperate measures for companionship?

She nodded as she made up her mind. She would stay and take care of him. She would be the opposite of whoever Lucy was. And in the process, maybe she'd find the answer to some of her questions. She would pry the information from him somehow.

Remembering his habit of grunting replies, she knew it would take a lot of prodding to get what she wanted. She chuckled softly, enjoying the thought of the challenge.

She straightened. What she needed right now was some Epsom salts and hot water for compresses to draw out the infection. And maybe a strong pair of arms to hold him down. Lifting the candle, she looked around. Perhaps there was something she could use. In the corner, hanging next to the minuscule stove, were three shelves. Moving closer, she peered at the contents. There was the usual collection of tin dishes and a half dozen books. *How odd,* she thought, *for someone to leave books in a hovel like this.* Next to the books was a small, square box. Pulling it out, she discovered an assortment of items—shoe hook, needle case, a small screwdriver, a pair of scissors—*some sort of survival kit,* she thought, but nothing to meet her present needs.

Then she spied a bottle far back on the top shelf. Straining forward on her tiptoes, she reached for it, catching it as her fingers tipped it forward. A cork had been jammed into the mouth. She tried to pry it free as Brewster's ramblings continued. With a low growl, she bit the cork and jerked it free. It smelled like a home-brewed remedy, and the eye-watering fumes convinced her that the contents were powerful enough to kill any infection.

Returning to his side, she stared down at his restless body, wondering how she would manage to examine him. Setting the bottle and candle at a safe distance, she knelt beside him, gritting her teeth as she grasped his shirt sleeve. With a garbled protest, he pulled away. She pressed her hands to her thighs and considered her options. Ignoring the way her insides twisted and turned, she grabbed his hand and pinned it under her knees.

"No, Lucy. No," he muttered over and over while she checked the wound on his arm. His agonized words forged a deep ache in her heart.

She poured some of the vile liquid on his wound and flinched as he cried out. Tearing a strip from her already ragged petticoat, she sponged the wound and bound it.

The injury on his arm didn't appear to be deep. She doubted it would send him into fevered delirium. Her worry burgeoned. Amid his protests and mumblings, she released his hand. Immediately he scuttled backward until he was pressed into the wall.

She watched, knowing the wound on his head would take a great deal more effort to check than had the arm. How could she restrain him? She considered her few options, and she shrank back before each one. But having cast her lot in one direction, she determined to follow through even if it meant doing things she found distasteful. Gritting her teeth, she swung her leg over his chest, pinning him as best she could.

"I'm not going to hurt you, Brewster," she murmured, hoping her voice would break through his confusion and either comfort him or jolt him out of his ramblings.

Arching his back, he fell silent as though aware that another being had intruded into his delirium. Abby held her breath, waiting to see if he would calm.

"No," he grunted and heaved his body to the side. She braced her hands against the wall and tightened her leg muscles, but her weight was useless against his strength, and she fell to the floor as he continued to protest.

There had to be another way, she determined as she pulled herself to a squat. Hesitating but a moment, she edged around until she faced his head, being careful not to touch him. Murmuring what she hoped were comforting sounds, she positioned one knee on either side of his head, still avoiding any contact. Waiting until he seemed a bit calmer, she clamped his head between her knees.

"Now hold still," she ordered in her firmest voice. It seemed to work better than her soft words.

She grabbed the candle and bent to examine his head. The odor was enough to tell her the wound was infected. Except for the spots matted with blood, his hair was as straight and heavy as the fringes on an altar cloth. So unlike her flyaway curls, she thought with a touch of resentment.

The wound looked like something the dog had dragged around for days and buried a few times. She wished she had checked it yesterday. Then, shrugging, she admitted she had given his injuries no more than a passing thought as the terror of escaping Sam and Petey had consumed her. Hoping she could make up for her neglect, she lifted the bottle and poured on the pungent liquid, gripping her knees as hard as she could as he tried to pull away from the pain. She used another piece of her rapidly shrinking petticoat to clean it. Her knees growing weaker by the minute, she hurried to pour on more disinfectant. Setting the candle a safe distance away, she shifted her weight to her cramped feet and pushed herself up and quickly stepped away. Brewster murmured a protest and lay still.

She brushed her skirt and felt the warmth inside her knees. He was as hot as a washday fire, and she knew if she hoped to see him recover, she had to fight the fever. Pouring a cupful of their precious supply of water into a pan, she added a couple of shots from the jug. With nothing else to use, she tore yet another strip from what remained of her petticoat. Dampening the rag, she knelt beside him, wondering if he would fight like a mad bull. Taking a deep breath, she prepared to duck his flailing arms.

"Lie still," she ordered as she leaned forward. Again, at the sound of her loud words, he tensed but lay still. She ran her rag over his brow and down his cheek. He lifted his chin and turned toward her. *Like a kitten*, she thought, as tenderness swept through her like a wind. She choked back a yearning to stroke his cheek; a great hunger consumed her innards, making her long to weep.

She shook her head in vigorous denial. *He kidnapped me,* she reminded herself. *All I care about is getting away from him. Just as soon as he's well again. I don't feel anything for him but dislike.* Her fingertips burned as she pressed them to her face, and she plunged them into the tepid water. It took several seconds for her breathing to return to normal and her heart to stop its erratic pounding.

It's because I'm so tired, she assured herself. Tired of running for her life. Tired of riding up and down. She was plain and simple tired. That's why she'd reacted to his nuzzling the way she had. *That and a bit of pity,* she admitted. *Pity for his pain, both present and past.*

Chapter 6

Dusty gray light filtered through the room and tickled her nose as her thoughts drifted peacefully like floating dust mites. A muffled grunt slid across her soft wakenings, but it was only an annoying interruption; and she curled tighter and let the lazy drifting continue. Her back was cold, and she snuggled closer to the warmth in front of her.

A sound—half grunt, half growl—snapped her eyes open. She found herself staring into Brewster's dark, watchful eyes just inches away.

"My goodness," she mumbled as she bolted upright. Intense heat flooded her cheeks.

Brewster never blinked, but his eyes grew more wary.

"I must have dozed off," she murmured, her voice thick with deep thirst and not enough sleep. Then she remembered why she was at his side. "How are you feeling?" She cleared her throat as the words stuck.

"Fine." Another grunt.

She pressed a hand to his brow. "You're still hot." She leaned over him to stare at his head wound. His eyes never left her. Unwilling to meet his questioning eyes, she studied the wound. "You were raving last night."

She sat back to see his reaction.

He never blinked, but behind his eyes, she still saw something dark and unfathomable.

"Who's Lucy?" she asked.

The lines around his mouth deepened. He didn't answer.

"Is she someone from your childhood?"

He turned to stare at the ceiling, his jaw clenching and unclenching. "She's my mother."

"Your mother!" She had thought. . . She didn't know what she'd expected but not his mother.

"What did I say?" His voice had dropped to a low rumble.

"Not much," she stammered, but his words rang through her head like stabbing accusations. *Stop. I'll be good. Please, don't hurt me.* She choked back the bitter taste in the back of her throat. She couldn't look at him. Leaping to her feet, she stumbled across the room to pour water into the chipped enamel basin. She plunged the rag into the water, letting her hands spend several minutes swishing back and forth. One burning question blazed across her mind, demanding an answer. She tried to ignore it as she scrunched down next to Brewster and sponged his brow. He closed his eyes, his mouth tight and lipless, the tiny lines around his eyes deepening in pain. *Perhaps,* she thought, *it is only my own distress magnifying what I see.* She wanted to cry out, to protest what he had said. But could she deny it when she suspected he spoke the truth?

Pus still seeped at the edges of the gash on his head, but it seemed less than before.

"Did your mother hurt you?" She paused long enough to watch his reaction, but she didn't need eyes to know she had stunned him. A shudder rippled through him.

"She tried," he muttered, his words almost lost in the depths of his soul.

"Why?" she demanded. "Why would a mother try to hurt her child?" Confusion clouded her mind. "Were you difficult?" She knew that wouldn't make it right.

He flung her away and glowered at her. "I was not 'difficult,' as you say." He chewed out the words like they were full of sand. "I never did anything to deserve what I got." He fell back, crossing his arms, his chin protruding in stubborn defiance.

She couldn't speak, her mind was a bog of sticky confusion of what-ifs and whys and it just couldn't be. Suddenly she realized how slack-jawed she was and clamped her mouth shut, blinking as she tried to sort things out. Her eyes focused on the scar on his left cheek. It flared its way into her thoughts. It was the only concrete thing she could find.

He saw her look at his cheek.

"If I hadn't learned to duck and run, she would have killed me. This," he jabbed his finger at his scar, "is my punishment for not paying attention."

"No." She shook her head. He was surely mistaken. *Children don't always see things the way they are. It must have been an accident. He just misunderstood.* She could imagine his mother—Lucy—trying to console her son, weeping and begging forgiveness, and Brewster, so stubborn and hard, refusing to grant it. "You must be wrong."

He glared at her a minute longer then turned to study the ceiling. "I was watching the dust flecks dance in a bar of sunlight." His voice was a flat monotone, and she thought he was talking about the air above them. Then he continued in the same dead voice, like a child reciting a poem that made no sense to him. "The sunlight crawled up the wall and landed on a pile of crates. I climbed up to see where it went; but the stack tipped over, making a horrible racket. I hurried to the corner, but Lucy's friend came crashing through the door and saw me. I remember how he shrugged into his braces and then smacked them in place. I thought it was strange that his boots were unlaced.

" 'This kid yours?' he bellowed.

"Lucy was standing in the doorway, begging him to come back.

" 'What kind of woman are ya, locking a little kid in this rat hole while you whore around next door?' Then he pushed her away and stomped out.

"I tried to shrink into the corner, hoping I could become invisible, but she grabbed me. She lifted my feet off the ground as she shook me. I kept waving my toes hoping to touch the floor, hoping maybe I could break loose.

" 'I curse the day you was borned,' she screamed. 'Too bad you didn't die.'

"And she threw me into the crates.

"I caught my cheek on a nail."

Abby's chest felt trapped under a heavy stone. His flat, toneless voice did nothing to dispel her horror. She moved her mouth, but no words came out. There were no words. Her mind was black, swirling denial. It wasn't possible for a mother to act that way. Mothers were kind and gentle and protective. She remembered something her aunt Aggie had said about a mother being more protective than a bear with cubs.

"But she couldn't have felt that way all the time," Abby protested.

"She hated me." There was no anger or self-pity in his voice. He could have been saying, "Today is Monday."

"There must have been times when she showed you love."

"Never."

Had he never known what it was to be touched with affection? That would explain a lot of things. "Is that why you flinch when I touch you?"

He turned, his eyes flaring with denial. "I don't. . ." His voice trailed off. "It wouldn't work, would it?"

"What?"

"Me trying to be a husband."

"What on earth do you mean?" What did Lucy's treatment have to do with getting married?

"I thought it would be better if I had someone to talk to." She could hear his loud swallow. "I thought a woman would—if I had a wife, it would be different. But I know nothing about loving and touching."

She heard the defeat in his voice and wanted to protest that he had to give love a chance. She swallowed back a stubborn lump in her throat. How could she? She didn't want to offer him love. She wanted to go home and forget this had happened. "Has no one ever shown you love?" Surely there had been someone in his life who had seen the little boy and known his need.

He closed his eyes as if trying to remember—or was he trying to forget?

"Love?" He snorted. "I don't believe in it."

She was flung back into confusion. "What do you believe in?"

Slowly, as if controlled by a distant force, he turned and stared into her face, his eyes hollow and haunted.

"I don't believe in anything." His words echoed the emptiness of his eyes.

A swirling abyss hovered between them. She wanted to shake him. Slap him. Hug him. She didn't know what she wanted except to prove him wrong. He had to believe in something. Especially love. God loved him. He had to know that. He had to believe it. But when she opened her mouth to speak the words that were hammering in her brain, his eyes glistened and silently denied everything she believed in.

"Seems to me you have to decide to accept love and kindness instead of kicking and snapping when people offer it to you." She saw him recoil at her harsh words, but she was too angry to withdraw them.

"You offering it to me?" His voice was low. When she didn't answer, he continued. "I thought not. Words come easy, don't they? Besides, what would you know? What's the worst thing that ever happened to you?"

"Apart from this little episode?" She paused long enough to see him furrow his forehead; then she hurried on, determined to prove him wrong. "I thought you knew all about me."

He snorted. "Not much. Just that you and Andrew are twins and come from the old country."

"Well, if you must know, my mother died when I was two. But I suppose I couldn't classify that as a deep sorrow. I barely remember her except. . ." She had never told anyone—not even Andrew—of the fleeting memory she clung to. But something in Brewster's expression—a flicker that departed as quickly as it came—made her want to prove to him that all mothers—all women—were not the same.

"I remember being held on her lap and feeling her heart against my cheek. I sometimes think I can hear her humming a song—perhaps a lullaby." So easily she slipped back into her comforting memory. She blinked her eyes and focused again on Brewster. His eyes narrowed, and the shutters fell back in place, yet he watched her intently. She plucked at the hem of her skirt. "I guess I never really missed her because I couldn't really remember her. Father and Andrew were always there."

"So no unhappy memories."

"Just a brief one." Again, she hesitated. It seemed so trivial compared to what he had allowed her to see of his past, yet at the time she had been devastated. His eyes compelled her to continue. "It was when we started school. The teacher thought it would be good for Andrew and me to be separated, so she put us in different classes. I wasn't even supposed to see him during school hours. I thought my world had dumped me upside down and left me hanging. I wept bitterly. I couldn't eat, and if Father forced me to, I threw it all back up again. I don't know what happened to change things. I suppose Father went to the teacher and reasoned with her. Anyway, we were allowed to be together for our classes. After that, I found I liked school." She couldn't look at him, knowing he would surely mock her little bit of trouble. And she couldn't blame him. Yet even now her stomach knotted and kicked at the thought of not being able to see Andrew. Where was he? Was he looking for her? She was sure he would be, but how would he know where to look?

"Is that why you've never married?"

His question brought her back with a thud, and she stared at him. "What?"

"You're too dependent on Andrew. It keeps you from other relationships."

She stumbled to her feet, fighting an urge to throw the basin of water in his face. "How dare you make such a mean accusation! Andrew and I are very close, but that does not keep us from living a normal life."

His expression never altered. Her impassioned response meant no more to him than the anger of an ant.

"Is he as dependent on you?"

"Of course. I mean of course not." He quirked his eyebrows mockingly. "Oh, you're despicable." Her innards twisted like a ride on a bucking horse. "Andrew has always been protective of me. We share everything. He's very kind and patient." She stopped. Why had she said patient? It sounded like she was a pest, but Andrew put up with her. It made her sound demanding. Was she demanding? Was she dependent? After all, they were twins—motherless twins. But was it unhealthy? Had she kept Andrew from pursuing his own life? Did he wish for freedom? She thought of the few girlfriends he'd had and tried to remember whether any of them had visited more than once or twice. She could think of only two who had come to the house three times. Was she the reason?

She leaned forward as pain pierced upward from the pit of her stomach. She would do anything rather than be the cause of hurting Andrew. Out of her turmoil, she saw Brewster, who had flung these darts of doubt into her life. She turned on him, her chin jutting forward. "It's you that has sick emotions. You see the world through a cracked glass. Don't try to make my world look as sick as yours. Andrew and I are twins. Our love is special."

"What would I know?" He shrugged and looked away. "I know nothing about love."

It wasn't the response she wanted. She preferred accusations and arguments to being faced with his disbelief in love. "Listen, God loves you."

"How convenient!" His eyes flared with accusation. "No one else loves you, but God does. What is He, the universal dump for unlovable souls? You should make a banner for Him. 'Apply here for handouts. Only the dregs of society accepted.'"

She wanted to shout a denial, but his words burned into her heart. It was too close to what she had been thinking, and she felt a sting in the back of her throat. "It isn't that way, Brewster."

"How is it then? No kid should ever have to go through what I did. Where was God then?"

She shrank from the pain and anger in his voice even as she realized it was the first time he had allowed himself to express his emotion. Somehow she had to convince him that God did care in spite of what he'd experienced. "He must have sent you someone who showed a little kindness."

"You could also say He sent me Bubba."

"Bubba?"

"Yeah. The guy who beat me until I couldn't walk."

"No. I don't think you can blame God for Bubba. God is a God of love, and I know He hates that sort of thing. I'm sure there's a hotter place in hell for people like Bubba."

"Bubba was just a drunk. He wasn't a mother." His emotions had drained him, and he turned away, his voice back to the flat rumble she'd grown used to.

"Not all mothers are like Lucy."

"How would you know? You never had a mother."

He was as determined to refuse to believe in love as she was to prove it. "Brewster, would you know love if you had it? Would you accept it?"

He closed his eyes and didn't answer. She placed the basin on the table and went to the saddlebags. There were still a few hard biscuits and some jerky. Hardly enough to see them through another day. Where would this day take them? She turned to ask Brewster, but his mouth was slack and his face soft. He had fallen asleep.

He slept long and sound.

She took a book from the shelf and lay on the bed but couldn't get interested in reading *Essays* by someone called Ralph Waldo Emerson. She put the book back and searched the other titles, but none of them caught her fancy. Restless, she circled the room, peering out the narrow slit of a window set into a deep, earthen wall, but all she could see was a patch of blue. A heavy robe had been pulled over the tunnel entrance. Brewster must have done that last night to keep the draft out. Beside the cupboards she had examined during the night, there was only a narrow door about four feet high. A closet, she assumed. She pulled on the leather strap. It stuck. She braced her feet and heaved. Reluctantly it opened, a gush of fresh air sweeping across the room. A short tunnel opened to the outside. Glancing over her shoulder, she saw that Brewster remained asleep. He would be okay now. She could leave with a clear conscience. Gathering up the blanket from the bed, she stuffed four dry biscuits into her pocket. Tiptoeing across the dirt-packed floor, she ducked through the door and pulled it shut behind her.

Five crouching steps took her to freedom, and she filled her lungs, stretching as she studied the surroundings for a familiar landmark. Below her lay a wide, green valley. Nothing looked familiar about the trees or the lay of the land. The mountains lay so close, it seemed she could reach out her hand and touch them, but the peaks and rocky slopes were foreign. She searched the rising skyline for some point of reference, but there was nothing.

A cold wind shivered down her spine, and she spun around to study the sky. Far to her left rolled a black thundercloud, breathing out ice and fear. Lightning flashed, and seconds later thunder bounced back and forth across the valley. Before she could assess the strength of the storm, the sky grew as dark as a winter's evening. Abby began to shiver. The sun ducked behind the mountains, fingering the sky. The storm was about to break.

A cold shudder shook her shoulders. Nature was against her escape. Common sense overcame her urge for freedom, and she retraced her steps to the doorway. It had latched behind her, and in the dark, she could feel no way to open it. Forcing herself to take a deep breath, she examined the door again and with shaking fingers found a bit of protruding wood. Yanking upward, she felt it release. She put her shoulder to the door, heaved it open, and stumbled into the room, kicking the door shut behind her to block the rush of cold air.

Brewster grunted and opened his eyes as the blast of cold hit him. His eyes met hers. "Look what the wind blew in," he muttered.

Self-consciously, she raked her fingers through her hair, knowing it was tangled beyond repair. Not everyone could have smooth, heavy hair like his, she fumed, replying, "You look a bit sorry at the edges, too."

"Feel about the same." There was no rancor in his voice. He started to get to his feet but grabbed his head and fell back with a moan. When he opened his eyes and looked at her, she could see they were dark with pain. "I could sure use a drink," he whispered.

Sighing, she took him the canteen, steadying it as he pulled it to his mouth and drained the last of it. He fell asleep immediately. She knew it was a healing sleep. With a glance at the closed door, she wondered if he would recover before she could escape.

Crossing the room to the tunnel they had entered the night before, she checked the other canteen, letting her breath out through pursed lips when she discovered it was almost full. Turning, she retraced her steps, rubbing her arms as she paced. The room had grown cool, and she wrapped the blanket around her shoulders and stood before the cold stove, toying with the idea of starting a fire. Would the smoke give away their hiding place? Was it possible Sam and Petey still stalked them? She knew they weren't the type to give up easily, but the damp coldness seemed to burrow into her bones. She glanced at Brewster, but he continued to sleep. She knew at a glance his fever had broken, but lying on the cold, earthen floor was certainly unhealthy, she reasoned. Before she could think better of it, she dropped the blanket and grabbed a handful of wood to shove in the firebox. She promised herself she'd keep the fire low. Just enough heat to warm her bones. The kindling caught immediately. She leaned over the first flames, waiting for the heat. It felt so good. She turned and warmed her back. The warm flow of blood in her veins was invigorating. She gathered together the meager ingredients, combining what the saddlebags and shelves had to offer, and mixed up johnnycake. As it baked, she rationed out enough water for two cups of tea.

The fire had burned to flickering embers when Brewster raised his head, pressing a hand to his wound and growled, "Smoke. I smell smoke."

"I fired up the stove," she explained.

He sat up and braced his hands on the floor. His eyes rolled and he swayed, but he gritted his teeth and remained upright. "Sam and Petey will smell it. They'll find us in no time."

"Don't worry. It's raining out. They'll be holed up somewhere trying to keep dry." She picked up a plate of still-warm corn bread smothered in molasses and poured the boiling water over the tea. "This will make you feel better." She held the plate and cup toward him.

He stared at her without taking the plate then shook his head and moaned as the movement brought pain. "I hope you're right, but with their type, I've learned never to assume anything."

"I was pretty close to Sam, and I think it's fairly safe to assume he has an aversion to water." She wrinkled her nose in remembrance.

He didn't smile. He never smiled. But the lines around his eyes deepened, and he snorted softly. It was enough for Abby, and she grinned at him, pleased at his reaction.

He sank back to his elbows and took a bite of food. "Good," was all he said, but she was gratified.

He cleaned his plate and again slept. She blew out the candle and lay down on the cot.

It was dark when she woke to the sound of Brewster moving about.

"Hey," he whispered gruffly. "Let's go."

She startled awake in the cold. "Go?"

"Hurry. Let's get out of here."

She staggered to her feet and followed him blindly, barely able to make out his outline as they slipped through the door. The sky was steel, revealing the faint outline of the two horses, saddled and waiting. Abby blinked as she realized she had slept while he moved about and saddled horses. A burning anger watered her eyes. She had slept through her chance to escape. How could she continue to ask God to help when she failed to take advantage of the opportunities He sent? Now it was too late. She was stuck having to again follow Brewster. But until another chance came along, Brewster was preferable to being in the hands of Sam and Petey. She swung into the saddle without protest.

As they traversed the hill, she called to Brewster. "What is that place? How did you know it was there?"

"It's an old miner's cabin. I stumbled on it a year or so ago. I fixed it up some. I still use it once in a while."

She glanced back, but the entrance had disappeared into the hillside. She turned her attention to staying on the trail.

The cold seeped through her, numbing her brain as she clung to the saddle, her horse patiently plodding after Brewster's mount. The sky turned to gray and then slowly lightened to blue, but the air was damp and did not warm in the early sunshine.

They climbed one slope and then skidded down another. Every hillside looked the same to her, and she wondered whether they were riding in circles. Once, they stopped by a pencil-thin waterfall to drink and fill their canteens.

As it grew warmer, she let the blanket slide from her shoulders. The day grew hot and sticky. She could no longer feel her legs. If only she could say the same for her back. It screamed at every rough step the horse took.

She shook herself out of her weariness as something about her new surroundings stirred her subconscious. They were in the valley now. They climbed less, and there were more deciduous trees. She twisted in the saddle to look over her shoulder. The mountains rose behind them. Her stomach churned as she tried to pinpoint the uneasiness tugging at her.

"Where are we going?" she called to the back she had watched for hour after endless hour until she had memorized the width of his shoulders, the fringe of black hair, the narrowness of his hips.

Brewster raised a hand to signal her to keep quiet.

She swung her head back and forth as her stomach lurched against her ribs. Her neck muscles tightened. Something felt very wrong, but she didn't know what it was.

Brewster reined to a halt and reached for her horse as she drew abreast.

He dismounted, and she followed his lead, paying scant attention to her numb legs as she continued to study the hillside and nearby trees, her glance racing from place to place. She rubbed her breast bone as her apprehension mounted.

"Stay quiet," Brewster whispered as he led the horses into the trees and tied them.

She remained under the shelter of the trees, waiting, watching, but for what she couldn't guess.

"Come on," he growled as he returned to her side. When she didn't respond, he grabbed her hand and pulled her after him. They went about thirty steps before he dropped to his stomach on the ground, pulling her down beside him.

"What are you doing?" she demanded, as her near panic swelled.

"Shh." He held his finger to his lips then began to edge forward. "Follow me."

She obeyed him. They crawled to the brow of a hill. Her stomach banged at her throat. She pressed her hand to her mouth as she stared down the slope at her house—Andrew's and hers. It looked just as she had left it. Somehow she had expected it to be different. Two towels flapped on the line. *They'll be bleached to snowy whiteness,* she thought and then wondered why it mattered. Two horses nibbled at the grass behind the barn. It looked like a peaceful, pastoral scene, but every nerve in her body was screaming disaster, and she twisted around to face Brewster.

"There's something wrong," she croaked.

Chapter 7

Shh." With narrowed, intent eyes, he studied the view below them. "This could be a trap."

"No," she shook her head. "No."

She became the object of his narrow-eyed scrutiny.

"No, what?"

"It's not a trap. There's something wrong." Her words raced out in a tangle. "If I try, I can always feel Andrew, no matter how far apart we are. I can't feel him." She pressed her hand to her chest. "He's not there. He's gone." Staring at the empty yard, she choked back a wail as the ice in her innards roared into flaming anger. She turned on Brewster. "Why are we here? What are you up to? Did you do something to him?" she demanded with piercing intensity.

His eyes darkened, and his expression hardened, but she ignored it. Something had happened to Andrew, and it was Brewster's fault, if not directly, then indirectly.

"I was taking you back. I figured you'd be safer with Andrew than with me." His words were deep and low in his throat. "Besides, without you to watch out for, I could deal with Sam and Petey."

She instantly dismissed the fleeting pang of guilt. She couldn't reason. Panic was drowning her. She sprang to her feet and started running down the hill toward the house.

She stumbled a few feet before Brewster's arms grabbed her around the waist. She tripped, and they fell to the ground.

"Let me go." She spat the words out around coarse blades of grass. She said it again as she tried to untangle herself and get up, but he held her to the ground. Finally she lay still, hoping he would release her if she stopped fighting. He didn't move. His warm body pressed her to the ground. Her lungs ached. "Please, let me go. I can't breathe."

He eased his weight back, but his arms still pressed her shoulders down.

"Please. I must find him."

"First, we make sure it's safe. No point in getting tangled in our own lariat." He uncoiled and stood over her while she scrambled to her feet. Motioning her to follow him, he edged his way down the hill.

She couldn't tell how long they took. It seemed they weren't making any progress, and then, the next thing she knew, they were at the door. Brewster held her back as he eased in and checked the room. She pushed past him and dashed inside.

"Andrew," she called, her voice echoing in the empty room. She paused and listened then dashed to her bedroom, giving it a cursory glance. She didn't need to look to know he wasn't there. She didn't need to climb the stairs to the loft where he slept. Nevertheless, she hurried upstairs. Again, the silent room stared back.

"He's not here." A bitterness burned inside her stomach. "I told you he wasn't."

"When did you expect him back from his trip?"

"The day he left. Or maybe the next if he had to drive some horses." Her eyes continued to dart across the room as if some object would give her a clue to his whereabouts. A fine layer of dust lay on the table like ashes from a cold fire. She wanted to scrub it clean, to somehow reverse the tide of events. Instead, she swiped her finger across the table, leaving a long slash in the sooty layer. She stared at her dirty fingertips.

"Maybe he took longer than he expected."

She scrubbed her hands on her skirt. "No." Her tone indicated her conviction. It wasn't as simple as Andrew having been delayed. There was something very wrong. Her gaze settled on a black, wide-brimmed hat that hung on a nail by the door. She grabbed it. "His good hat. He always wore it to town. He was wearing it when he left." Her fingers brushed the brim, remembering how careful he was to keep this hat in good repair. "No need to go to town looking poorly," he always said as he positioned it on his thick hair—coppery colored like her own but roguishly attractive on him. It was the one thing she had begrudged him, but now she vowed that she would never again complain about him having the nicer hair, if only he would turn up safe. She scurried to the window, knowing without looking that the yard would be empty. Beside her, the flies bounced against the window pane, the noise threading into her ears until it boomed. She turned back to the room, noticing the horses as she spun around. "Besides, there's a bunch of horses in the pasture. He must have bought some and drove them home."

Her footsteps rang hollow as she crossed to the stove and stared at the cold kettle. Something sat uneasy in her brain. When had she first noticed his absence in her mind? She remembered feeling him looking for her the night they spent in the cave. That was almost three days ago. She couldn't remember sensing him again until they were on the hill overlooking the buildings. By then her heart was already screaming disaster.

Her insides were ready to explode. She paced back to the table, almost tripping on the laundry basket. In her mind, she pictured herself dropping it as Brewster's arm trapped her. Andrew must have brought it in when he got home and found her missing. She imagined his distress—a mirror image of her own feelings. She dropped his hat on the table and pressed her hands to her ears to block out the droning that went on and on.

Brewster made a sound deep in his throat. "Maybe we should look around outside."

She beat him to the door and ran toward the garden; then, realizing Andrew wouldn't be there, she headed toward the clothesline. The two tea towels flapped in a gust of wind like thunder in her ears. She snatched them from the line without stopping and spun around to race toward the barn, catching up to Brewster as he pulled open the door. Stepping inside, he paused to study the surroundings. He slowly checked inside the three stalls on one side, crossed the alleyway, and checked the three stalls on the other side.

Rocking back and forth on the balls of her feet, Abby shouted, "Andrew," and cocked her head to listen.

Overhead, she heard the whir of pigeons' wings.

"He's not here." She was breathless. Her tongue stuck to the bottom of her mouth.

"I tell you he's not here anywhere." Her voice rose to a wail. "We have to find him."

Brewster turned his dark, hooded eyes to her. "We?" His eyebrows shot up.

"Yes, we. After all, it's all your fault. If you hadn't. . ."

"Whoa up there now. Guess I acted rashly thinking I could kidnap myself a wife. It was a mistake and all, but I brought you back in the same condition as I found you. I figure that makes things square."

"Mistake. Same condition? What am I? A borrowed saw or something?"

"No, ma'am." He stood motionless, his hands dangling at his side.

"You think you can just grab some poor, unsuspecting girl and ride halfway across the country and back, make me hide in caves and scale cliffs, go cold and hungry, and then change your mind and say things are square and that makes everything fine? Is that what you think?"

"No, ma'am."

"Besides, as I said, if you hadn't kidnapped me, Andrew wouldn't have ridden out. You have to help me find him."

"Now hold on a mite." He rubbed his chin. "You don't even know if he needs finding."

She stomped her foot and blinked back tears. "I keep trying to tell you. I know he needs help. Why won't you listen?"

"Lady," he answered, looking toward the roof and shaking his head. "I am listening."

"Then you aren't hearing."

"You mean I'm not agreeing."

"Oh! Forget it." She stomped from the barn and raced across the yard to the horses tied to the hitching post. Grabbing up the reins of the horse she had ridden all day, she pulled the animal away from the rail.

Brewster stood in her way. "What are you doing?"

"What does it look like? I'm going to find Andrew. If you won't help me, I'll do it alone."

"Aren't you forgetting something?"

She paused, one foot in the stirrup, but her mind was too tightly wound to be able to guess at his meaning. "What?"

"That's my horse."

"Tough." She swung herself into the saddle and grasped the reins, but Brewster reached up and grabbed the chin strap before the horse could move.

"Get off." His voice was deep and low.

Abby shook her head and kicked her heels into the horse's flanks.

Brewster grabbed her around the waist.

"Let go." She squirmed, but his hold only tightened. She barely had time to shake her feet free of the stirrups before he yanked her from the saddle and swung her down to his side.

"This horse is exhausted. He deserves a rest."

"Let me go."

"You bet."

She stumbled away then straightened and stomped to the house, mumbling under her breath, "I'll find Andrew. Somehow. Some way. And I don't need your help. Or permission." She slammed the door behind her and marched to the table, where she stood leaning against a chair. She'd go catch up one of the new horses. There had to be one that was broken. Or she could wait until Brewster was asleep and take one of his. Trouble was, Brewster didn't seem to need much sleep. Her eye caught a movement out the window. It was Brewster walking along the pasture fence, his head bent as though he were looking for something. *Probably making sure I can't take one of the horses,* she fumed and turned her back. She'd find a way to look for Andrew if she had to walk to town to get help. Brewster probably thought her fears were silly, but she knew what she knew.

She stared at the cold stove, remembering the day, in the old country, shortly after Andrew had begun work at the mill. She had been busy making a pudding for dinner. Just as she was about to add currants to the batter, an awful feeling of pain came over her. It was so sharp, she checked to see if she had cut herself. But this pain didn't touch her body. It ripped her heart. She'd called Andrew's name. Father, who had been working at his accounts, looked up and reminded her that Andrew was at work. She'd tried to explain that something had happened to him, but Father assured her she was anxious because he was away while she remained at home. He gently comforted her, saying she would get used to his absence. She didn't argue, but she knew it wasn't that.

When Andrew came home that night, his hand was wrapped in a heavy, white bandage. He had caught it on a sharp corner of a wagon he was unloading and cut it badly. When Abby asked when the accident had occurred, he had given the exact time she had felt the pain in her own being.

There were other times, too. Like the time they were children and his shirt had caught on a limb as he climbed a tree, holding him suspended two feet above the ground unable to help himself. In response to his calls, Abby had looked up from her own play nearby and hurried to rescue him. Only he hadn't called for help.

The only time I've been wrong was when I didn't listen to what I felt.

She heard the door open but didn't bother to look up. She'd find Andrew, she vowed, with or without Brewster's help.

Brewster grunted. "Looks like he rode out three maybe four days ago."

She glared at the silent stove.

"I'll go look for him." His voice was a low rumble.

She spun on her heel and grabbed her coat from the hook next to the door. "I'm coming with you."

He stared at her long and steady. "First we sleep and get some supplies ready." He remained in the doorway, twisting his hat in his hands, feet planted squarely.

She wanted to argue about the delay, but the light was already changing, throwing long, lean shadows on the ground behind him, reflecting in his eyes, making them warmer than she'd ever seen them. She blinked away the thought, knowing it was a trick of the light. Inside he was hard and cold. Maybe even dead. She returned her coat to the peg. "I'll make some supper," she said, turning away. Every minute of delay felt like another death. Hers. Andrew's. But she knew Brewster was right. Nothing would be gained by venturing out in the dark.

Brewster stood shadowed in the doorway, motionless and broad.

"You might as well come in." She spared him a fleeting glance.

"I'll wash up first." Before she could offer him a basin of warm water, he was at the horse trough, working the pump handle up and down. A gush of water poured forth, and he splashed it over his face, spattering a golden spray around him. The warm glow stirred her heart. She slammed her mind shut and handed him a towel as he climbed the steps. His eyes met hers and flashed away.

She retreated to the stove while he continued to hover at the doorway. She could not bring herself to say, "Make yourself at home." She was off balance at his presence in her house. On one hand, she longed to see the end of Mr. Brewster Johnson, to be free of his dark nature and laconic speech. Yet the thought of being alone made her ears pound and her chest hurt, and she wanted to grab him with both hands and bolt him to the floor. She might not like him, she assured herself, but he knew the countryside like the back of his hand, and he exuded a calm, imperturbable attitude that made the future seem less foreboding. Besides, she needed him to help her find Andrew. And that was all, she reminded herself.

Nodding toward Andrew's armchair, she said, "Sit over there." It was all she could bring herself to offer.

He dipped his head and crossed the room, perching in the chair like it had a bad smell. His gaze followed her, his eyes hooded and wary.

He expects to be treated poorly—rudely, she thought with a stab of conscience. She tightened her chest muscles. She didn't care how cruel life had been to him. She wasn't responsible for the guardedness in his eyes. She had no reason to feel guilty. Then she remembered her manners. "Feel free to read the magazines." It was the neighborly thing to do. She was prepared to be polite and neighborly but nothing more.

She turned her back on him and began to peel the basin of potatoes. *God,* she silently prayed, *be with Andrew wherever he is. Keep him safe.* A sudden hollowness in her chest sucked away her breath. *If anything happened to Andrew—* She couldn't think about it. Brewster was right in a sense when he said she was dependent on Andrew. But it wasn't in the twisted, unhealthy way he had made it seem. It was a bond of mutual love. And a closeness that came not only of being twins but having been motherless and looking to each other to supply that lack.

The rattle of paper brought her back to her task. The first potato was still in her hand, forgotten as she stared out the window. She forced her attention to supper preparations, finishing the potatoes and putting them to boil.

As she fried the salt pork, the smell clogging her nostrils, she glanced toward Brewster. His head bent over the paper, he seemed wholly concentrated on his reading.

A few minutes later, she placed the serving bowls on the table. "Supper's ready," she said, pointing toward a chair.

He closed the magazine and rose silently, his gaze sweeping past her to the table. They pulled their chairs to place like a pair of silent actors.

Taking a quick breath, she silently thanked God for the food. In the same breath, she prayed for Andrew's safety.

"Help yourself." Her words dropped like pennies into the stillness as she handed him the platter of meat. Their eyes met. His didn't quite catch the light. It was like looking into the depths of the cave they had shared. What was he thinking? Was he regretting his decision to stay and look for Andrew? Was he wishing he had ridden out while it was still light? Did he find their closeness as nerve tingling as she did? She forced her attention to her own plate, filling her fork with fluffy mashed potatoes, but the food tasted like paper, and her throat closed shut. She almost gagged. Taking a deep breath, she forced herself to swallow. The silence had become an unwelcome guest. She knew she would scream if she didn't drive it away.

"You seem to know this tracking business very well." Polite social noises were better than the breathing silence.

"I had a good teacher."

"Who was that?" Anything to stop her thoughts from leaping back and forth between silently calling Andrew and wishing there was a way to get a better look at Brewster's eyes.

"He was a half-breed. Used to scout for the Mounties before he signed on with the cattle outfit I was with. I watched him lots. Asked a few questions and learned a pile about reading signs." He kept his head down, stabbing the meat with his fork.

Abby would not let herself admit she was disappointed that he didn't look up.

"Was that a long time ago?"

"I was just a kid."

He lifted his head. *Success!* She squirmed at the dark brittleness in his eyes, uncertain as to what it meant. Was he challenging her to probe further or fighting another painful memory? There was a power in his eyes she couldn't look away from.

"How old were you?" The darkness shifted, grew less guarded yet more intense. She couldn't be certain, but she thought she detected sorrow in his expression.

"Maybe twelve."

She blinked, breaking the spell. *Did he say twelve?* "What were you doing on a cattle drive at twelve?"

For a heartrending moment, she caught a glimpse in his eyes of the lonely child he had been, finding an old scout his only company. Her heart held its breath as she slid toward—*stop.* She reined herself in. The shutters closed, and she knew a pang of loss as if she had almost discovered something supremely important.

"It was a job."

"I suppose." She kept her attention on her plate, waiting for her lungs to stop galloping about and fill with air. "I'll clean up." Gathering the dishes, she took them to the washbasin.

Later, after she had shown Brewster the ladder to Andrew's loft and he had taken a lamp and climbed the steps, she closed the door to her own room.

Overhead the floorboards creaked. A muffled thud was followed by rustling noises—all sounds she'd heard before. When it was Andrew, they were comforting—a lullaby that drifted her to sleep; but now, they were different. She lay awake staring at the ceiling, aware of the sigh of the ceiling above her every time Brewster moved. His scent, his movements, his presence dominated the place, seeping through the pores of the house, tingling her nerves until she lay rigid as a piece of glass. *I'm being silly. Why should I be so conscious of him? We've already spent four nights together.*

But, a niggling voice answered, *those nights were out in the open. Not in your own house. And you didn't have a choice. But now he's upstairs at your invitation.*

She'd practically insisted he sleep in Andrew's bed.

I should have let him sleep out in the barn like he suggested, she thought, flipping to her side and squeezing her eyes shut.

Then the shifting above her ended, and all she heard was the wind moaning around the eaves, calling Andrew's name to her. The sound drilled into her heart until she pulled the covers over her head and murmured a prayer. *Lord, wherever he is, whatever's the matter, guard him and lead us to him. Keep him safe. Keep him safe. Lord, keep us all safe.*

Chapter 8

A bby shifted in the saddle, twisting and arching her back, trying to ease the stiffness. All morning she had been leaning into the day. It had been a hurry-up-and-wait as Brewster meticulously studied the signs, examining each blade of grass, each rock, each leaf with total concentration. He was so intense that she imagined him magnifying every item until the tiniest detail spoke its history. She watched him now, down on one knee, studying the grass inch by inch. Then he straightened and looked into the distance.

When they had started out, Abby had repeatedly asked him what he saw. Could he tell if Andrew had been this way? He had merely shaken his head and continued to look. After a few rounds of questions with no answers, however, Abby discovered that, if she was quick enough to catch the expressions that flitted across his features, she could read the answers in his face. If he saw something helpful, there would be a flicker in his eyes, so tiny and brief that at first she thought she had imagined it, but it was there. When he failed to find something that he seemed to be expecting, his eyebrows would arch upward—again, almost imperceptibly—as if surprised that the clue wasn't there. When the trail would seem to grow cold, Brewster would study the ground with such intensity that Abby expected to see the grass at his feet smolder. Constantly watching him to read his expressions gave Abby plenty of opportunity to study him. And to think.

To keep her mind from its endless twisting, she tried to guess where Andrew was. The scenes she imagined were not comforting. Maybe he accidentally ran into Petey and Sam, and they had taken out their frustrations on him. Or maybe this wasn't his trail at all. What if he didn't go this way at all but rode into town for help or was miles the other way?

Yesterday his disappearance had filled her with boiling fear; but today she suddenly realized, even with her "what-ifs," she was less frightened. Today it was more an urgency. As if she knew they would find him and the sooner the better. She examined this feeling. Why was she more determined and less panicked today? Was it because her gut—the same belly-deep feeling that assured her Andrew was not at the house—was assuring her he was at the end of the trail? Had her faith in God grown to give her a resting confidence in His love and power? She knew God would take care of Andrew, and it did help her to stay calm. Or—she tried to stop the thought from blooming—was it Brewster that accounted for her calmness? Was she so trusting of his ability and willingness to help that it eased her mind?

Something between them had changed. She couldn't quite put her finger on what it was, nor was she sure she wanted to. No, that wasn't quite true. She was sure she didn't want to know. It was bad enough that she had to depend on him right now. Bad enough that she had to watch his expression like a hawk. It meant she had no choice but to see the way his eyes captured the blue of the sky or the green of the forest. It was inevitable that she would notice the way the sun caught the planes of his face, reminding her of the strength of the granite cliff they had traversed three days ago. She couldn't avoid noticing the way the breeze trickled through his hair at the back of his neck as he bent over.

He straightened in the saddle, and she blinked, chasing back her thoughts, half-expecting he would face her and read her mind. Her cheeks warmed with a blush, but instead of turning her way, he looked toward the west.

"What? What do you see?" She had stayed back, knowing she could destroy clues; now she urged the horse toward him.

"I've found tracks that might be his. He seems to be headed in that direction." He pointed toward the rising hills that gave way to the towering mountains and heavy forest. Abby didn't remember the exact place they had spent the first night or how they got there, but she did know they had been up in high country. She recalled the thick pine forest and the crisp air. Was Andrew headed the same direction? How would he know? She voiced her questions.

"Maybe he heard you calling him." Brewster gave her a fleeting glance before he resumed studying the land ahead of them, but it was enough for her to see his eyes were as green as the dark forest and as full of secrets. However, she had seen no hint of mockery in his eyes.

"Maybe." She ducked her head, not knowing what to think. No one had ever believed she and Andrew had this connection. Even Andrew, his intuitive awareness less intense than Abby's, doubted the depth of it. That Brewster might accept it made him seem almost likable. She didn't want to like him. This was the man who had kidnapped her, tied her wrists, subjected her to attack by two depraved men. Not only that, he was a man with deep hurts who didn't much trust other people and women in particular. Besides, she didn't want a man. She and Andrew intended to build their new farm together.

Brewster swung into his saddle and rode silently and slowly ahead of her, leaning over his horse, ever studying the trail. He reined in. "Look. Whoever it was got off his horse here."

Even Abby could see the broken blades of grass.

Again, they followed the faint trail.

Brewster stopped. Pushing his hat back on his head, he stared at the mountains, his eyes dark, lines of concentration deepening around his mouth.

"What's wrong?" She couldn't stop the spear of alarm flashing through her insides.

"Nothing, I guess." He rubbed the back of his neck.

"Then what are you worrying about?"

He flashed her a stinging look. "I'm not worried. I'm thinking." He paused. "I'm concerned."

Abby's gaze swept over the countryside. For the first time, she noticed twisting, black thunderheads forming far to the south. A chill wind drove through her shoulder blades. "The storm?" She couldn't keep the thread of fear from lacing her voice. Even a frank greenhorn like her knew that rain would erase the faint trail they were following. For a moment, she resented the frequent showers that poured over the mountains and bathed the land. Knowing that her frustration was futile, she took a deep, steadying breath.

He nodded, his eyes searching her face. "That. And something else."

It was as if he was measuring her ability to be told the truth.

"What else?" Her voice was brisk. Whatever it was, knowing was better than guessing.

"For some reason, whoever made this trail broke into a gallop about here."

She clung to his gaze, drinking from the cool depths. "What does that mean?"

He shrugged. Their eyes held like clasped children's hands. "Can't say for sure, but I'd guess he saw something. Perhaps a rider. Or a fire." The way his voice deepened on the last words, Abby knew he was thinking that Andrew—if indeed it were Andrew—had seen a fire. But what fire? They'd had a small fire the first night, but it was so small and so deep in the woods, she was certain it would have given no sign. The second night they had hidden in the cave. There had been no fire. "Sam and Petey. They had a fire."

"Yup. Could be that's what he saw. He'd have no way of knowin' if it was us or someone else."

She rubbed her chin then pressed her hand to her chest. "If he rode up unannounced, they might—" She choked.

"No telling what they might do. Or if he reached their camp. There's a number of obstacles between here and the mountains."

She shivered at the way he said "obstacles," but before she could press him for an explanation, he cast an eye on the approaching storm and kicked his horse. Talk would have to wait. They had to move fast to beat the rain.

They kept up a steady lope, one that jarred Abby's spine like a hammer. They slowed only enough for Brewster to check the trail by leaning over his horse, then they resumed the jolting pace. Abby clenched her teeth, but not for anything would she call out. She had seen how the lines around Brewster's mouth deepened each time he slowed down. Something had him worried. Something more than what he told her. Her own mouth felt like it was gouged into brittle cheeks. The sound of distant thunder shuddered up her spine, and she glanced over her shoulder to see black clouds churning toward them.

Their path had been as straight as a taut rope in the direction of the granite-faced mountain. Brewster called over his shoulder. "Looks for sure he was leather bent in that direction. We'll pick up the trail when we get to the trees. Let's ride."

She didn't need any urging and clung to the saddle horn as they raced across the meadow.

Brewster leaped from his horse and grabbed her reins as she skidded to a stop. He pulled the horses into the trees and loosened their saddles before he tied them.

"Come on," he urged her, grabbing the saddlebags and canteen. "Let's find shelter." Already the first drops of rain were falling.

"What about Andrew?"

"It's only a summer storm. It will pass quickly."

He'll get soaked. She didn't say the words aloud. She breathed a prayer for Andrew—one in a long chain of petitions she had sent to her heavenly Father—then followed Brewster deeper into the trees.

"This will do." He sat on a log.

She perched beside him. Shrugging out of his batlike slicker, he reached behind her. She jumped as his arm brushed her back.

"I'm just trying to keep you dry," he growled, draping his slicker over them both. She huddled inside the damp warmth of it, holding it close with one hand, forced to crowd next to him so that they could both enjoy the protection of his coat.

She watched him open the saddlebags and noticed for the first time how long and slender his hands were and how deeply browned—almost stained looking—they were from work and weather. One fingernail was blackened and his knuckles were scraped. Likely from his fight with Sam and Petey, she guessed and wondered how much discomfort this adventure had caused him. Punched. Shot. Sick. He'd never said a word about the gunshot wound to his arm, and she hadn't seen it since the night he was raving. He removed his hat to hunker under the slicker, and now she studied his head wound. A blackish scab puckered at the edges. It looked nasty but was healing well enough. Her eyes lowered to study his face. It was so strong. She knew he hated his scar. He said it made him ugly, but as far as she could tell, it only served to make his face stronger.

Brewster pulled some biscuits from the saddlebags, straightened, and turned to her. Their looks collided. Neither of them turned away.

She could swim in his eyes, she decided. They were so deep. Was she swimming? Or drowning? Drowning should be a violent struggle, not a gentle, swaying seduction of warmth and boneless limbs.

The lines around his mouth softened to whispers. His lips parted, revealing even, white teeth like pearls of pleasure. She half-lifted one hand, longing to run her fingers across his lips, to learn them by heart. She leaned toward him as his head began a slow descent. He was going to kiss her, and she welcomed the thought, though the admission was dredged from a place beyond logic and reason.

A crash of thunder made her bolt to a rigid posture. She shook her head. What was she thinking? She was here for one purpose, to find her twin. She wanted only one thing from Brewster—to help her find Andrew. She shuddered as a bolt of lightning shattered the sky and thunder roared across the land. It was the sheer force of the storm that made her heart pound in her ears. Or so she told herself.

Brewster's face was tipped to the sky, his eyes flashing. "Just listen to that thunder roll."

She'd never before seen anyone who liked a thunderstorm, but as the rain cascaded from the leaves in a hundred miniature waterfalls and the wind purred in the treetops, she watched him breathe in its majesty. The earthy aura of mushrooms and wet leaves swelled from the forest floor, mingling with the metallic scent of lightning. The aroma of pine needles, damp canvas, and sweat teased Abby's nostrils. She'd never be able to smell pine again without thinking of Brewster. A chill wind caught at the edge of the slicker. Brewster grabbed it and pulled it closer. Warmth flared into flame, searing through her being, licking at her reason, scorching her ability to think.

Thunder clapped again, reverberating through her senses, making her want to press her hands to her ears. She couldn't breathe. Her lungs grew tighter, and she squeezed her eyes shut. The thunder rolled into the distance, growing farther and farther away.

The storm ended as suddenly as it had begun, sunshine backlighting the final drops of water. The air freshened, and she could breathe again. Opening her eyes, she glanced at Brewster's profile and saw his face still upturned to the elements of nature. She was astonished to realize he was oblivious to her turmoil.

As they gathered up their things, her mind tangled in a web of unfamiliar thoughts and feelings. She slipped out of the protection of his slicker, pulling her own jacket closer around her shoulders.

She waited for him to tighten the cinch on each saddle, glad that his attention was away from her. She needed time to compose her emotions and sort out the ones she wanted to keep from the ones she had to bury. She chose to dispose of most of them.

He held the horse while she pulled herself into the saddle then swung up on his own mount. All he said was, "Let's go," in a voice that was an echo of the fading thunder.

They were riding again, faster, without stopping to check the trail. Brewster had mumbled something about knowing where to look. His eyes continually swept over their path, forever vigilant, lest he miss something.

The hills grew steeper, the trees thicker, the deciduous giving way to pine and spruce.

The sun regained its warmth and then lost it in the slanting evening rays.

Just when she wondered if they were going to ride forever, Brewster pulled up and waited for her to stop at his side. "We'll have to go much slower now." She turned to him, watching his eyes. In their depths was a warning—and something else. Something she shied away from. "The terrain is rough here—dangerous for both man and horse." The roll of grassy hills had given way to clumps of dirt, washouts, and scrubby trees fighting for survival. Abby shivered as she viewed the scene.

Dangerous! The word whirled through her brain. Was this what he had been worried about? She took a slow, steadying breath in a futile attempt to calm the riot of emotions. Her mind was as confused and tangled as the treacherous landscape they faced.

Brewster urged his horse forward through the dwarfed trees and broken branches.

"Wait," she begged, staring straight ahead, not seeing him or the rugged landscape. She was listening to the sounds inside her head. It was Andrew. She felt him.

"He's here," she nodded with utmost certainty.

"Where?" He looked at the maze of dips and hillocks.

"I don't know. But he is. I can feel him."

She met his eyes, daring him to disagree, but he simply lifted one eyebrow and said, "Then we better find him."

Find him. Two little words. It sounded so simple. Abby stared at the maze around her. There were gullies, some higher than a man's head, and mounds of earth like abandoned giant ant hills. Her insides were so tight, she could feel her heart thudding against her ribs and the blood gushing through her veins.

Find him! The words shrieked inside her head.

"Andrew." She called over and over until her voice was hoarse. She knew he was there. Yet after several minutes, they had found nothing to give them any assurance.

Brewster was looking to her right, guiding his horse over the clumps and around potholes.

"Andrew." It was a wail. She nudged her horse forward, skirting a trench that angled westward, twisting and deepening as it went. The stunted trees reached out long, bony arms and dark, gnarled fingers, clutching at the light that was speeding away. Abby wanted to grab the sinking sun and force it to wait—to let them find Andrew before darkness descended. She knew this terrain would force them to call a halt to the search once the light faded. It wasn't worth a man's life and that of his horse to try to cross this at night. Her pulse pounded in the pit of her stomach. She tried to avoid thinking about Andrew. If he had ridden unaware into this insane scene, he might be—

She stopped her thoughts, but she couldn't prevent the pictures that flashed through her mind of Andrew lying twisted and bent, his body broken on rocks and whitened stumps.

"Andrew," she shrieked his name to the sky. And from the sky heard nothing but the mocking of three crows she had frightened from their evening routine.

God, she pleaded. *Where is he? Show us where to look. Please, please, please keep him—alive,* her mind screamed. *Oh, God, please,* she begged.

She let her horse munch a mouthful of grass and closed her eyes, waiting for peace to replace her panicked fears.

"Abigail, over here." Brewster waved at her. She gripped the reins and kicked her heels.

"Be careful."

She nodded and watched the ground, knowing it would take the concentration of both her and her mount to avoid every hole and pile of tangled branches. In the wan light, it was hard to pick out a safe route until it was almost too late. She bit the inside of her lip. Her arms felt ready to snap. She didn't dare think about why Brewster had called her. He watched her until she had gone ten feet then dismounted and disappeared into a gully.

"Wait," she cried, but only the wind answered. She pressed the horse forward. Fifty yards from where Brewster's horse waited, she slid from the saddle and dashed toward the spot she had last seen him.

"Brewster, have you found him? Where are you?" She stumbled, her feet caught in a snarl of branches. Kicking herself free, she didn't bother to straighten but ran with her hands almost touching the ground. Her skirt caught on a bush, and she wrenched it free, clutching it in a crumpled ball. "Andrew," she whimpered his name as she scurried forward.

"Abigail, over here." Brewster's head appeared over the edge. She was almost there. She didn't slow her scuttling gait. Brewster grabbed her arm as she dived over the edge.

"Slow down," he rumbled.

"Did you find him? Where is he? Is he okay?" Her words tumbled out as tangled as the branches at her feet.

Grabbing her by the shoulders, Brewster forced her to stop and face him. His eyes shadowed by the lowering sun were impossible to read, but she saw the tense set of his jaw and stiffened. Her heartbeat filled her like the roar of rushing waters.

"I've found him," Brewster said, his face so close she could feel his breath fanning her cheek.

"Is he. . . ?" She gulped.

"He's alive."

"Where is he? Let me go." She struggled to free herself, but his hands dropped to her upper arms, and he held her so tightly, she couldn't shake free.

"Wait a minute. Listen to me." He held her until she met his eyes. Even in the half light, she could feel them boring into hers. "He's alive, but his leg is broken."

"How bad?" She lost her voice and could barely get out a whisper.

"Bad."

Again she struggled.

"Hold on." He refused to release her. "He's in pain. But we're going to have to move him."

Her thudding heartbeat pooled in a heavy puddle deep in her gut.

He nodded as he saw she understood. "There isn't anyway to do it without making his pain worse."

She moaned.

"Get yourself together. You've got to be strong now."

Forcing air into her lungs, sucking it down to the quivering pool inside, she drew strength from someplace outside herself. A shudder raced up her spine and she nodded.

Still holding her shoulder, he guided her down the bank, steadying her when her foot skidded on loose gravel that scattered before her like dreams exploded by the sound of an alarm clock. Maybe it was all a dream. If so, she wished the alarm would sound now before she had to face Andrew, injured and in pain.

But no alarm sounded. Instead, Brewster's arm tightened around her shoulders, and she knew the next step would take her around the corner of this narrow wash. She clamped her jaw so tight, her teeth squeaked.

Chapter 9

All she could see was a shadowy form. With a cry, she broke from Brewster's grasp and hurried to Andrew's side, dropping to her knees.

He turned to her. "Abby." She had to bend to catch his words. "I knew you would come." His breath smelled like old socks, and she pressed her hand to her mouth then leaned closer, trying to make out every detail in the dusk.

Bruises on his face. *Oh, his face!*

Andrew's eyes were dull and sunken in gray cheeks. Her gaze raced across his body. A deep gash on his forearm. His pant leg—dark with blood—was torn back to reveal a swollen thigh. Even in this light, she could see the dull red of a massive bruise.

"Water," he mumbled.

The canteen lay at his side, just out of reach, but she could see the cap was off. How long had he been without water?

Behind her she heard Brewster leading the horses over the rocks, gravel clattering ahead of them, and then he pressed a full canteen into her hand.

"Just a few swallows to start with."

Andrew's breathing came in gasps, and she hovered over him, wondering where she could touch him without furthering his pain. He lifted his left arm and grabbed for the water. She guided the jug to his mouth. His icy palm against her flesh felt like sandpaper, and she knew there were small stones imbedded in his hand.

Taking the canteen away, she capped it and set it aside.

"Andrew." It was a prayer, a plea. She wanted to touch every part of him to assure herself he was all right, but she was afraid of hurting him. She brushed back his hair, feeling bits of dirt. "I'm so glad we found you. I was so worried." With shaking hands, she trailed her fingers down his cheeks. He winced as she touched a bruise, and she pulled back, but not before she realized that he was as cold as winter snow. He needed to get out of his wet clothes as soon as possible.

Again he grasped her hand. She took his hand between hers. "How long you been here?" she asked.

"I think this is the third day." His voice was reedy. "My horse tumbled into this drop-off and threw me."

She squeezed his hand, but there was no need for more words. They said all they needed to through their hands.

Firelight flared, driving away the shadows. Brewster brushed his hands off and stood over them. She met his eyes for but a heartbeat then turned to study

Andrew's leg. In the better light, she could see it bent unnaturally, and the smell of old blood oozed from a gash close to the knee.

She lifted her eyes to Brewster. She knew her expression must be bleak. It seemed they had found Andrew only to be powerless to help him. How were they going to deal with all his needs, especially out here? They had only a few cups of water. There were no supplies for cleansing the wound. He needed warm, dry clothes. Brewster's steady gaze remained on her. Finally he spoke. "We'll need some sort of bandages."

She nodded, glad to be able to do something, and turning her back to him, slipped her petticoat off and began to tear it into strips. *The second petticoat to be ripped to shreds,* she remembered.

He strode out of the light and was gone for several minutes before returning with several long, straight branches in his arms. Where had he found them? She remembered only bent and tangled wood around them.

He dropped close to the fire and knelt beside Abby. "Andrew." His voice had a ring to it she hadn't heard before. "We're going to have to set that leg before we can move you."

Andrew groaned softly and nodded.

"I expect it's going to hurt some."

Abby was surprised to see something flicker in Andrew's eyes, and she darted a glance at Brewster in time to catch a blaze in his expression. A message had passed between the two men that she didn't understand. Grateful as she was for Brewster's help, she didn't like the silent contact Andrew had shared with him.

How petty, she scolded herself. It was just her reaction to seeing Andrew hurt that made her resentful, she rationalized.

Brewster pulled two of the longer sticks closer, arranging them in neat lines, then tied one of the blankets from the saddle roll across, fashioning a travois. Abby shuddered at the thought of Andrew bouncing across the rugged terrain in this shabby affair. When he was done, Brewster pulled out his knife.

"I'll have to cut his pants."

Before she could answer, he deftly sliced the pant leg from toe to hip, exposing the swollen flesh even more.

In unison, Abby and Andrew groaned.

"You want something to bite on while I do this?" he asked Andrew, offering him a green stick. When Andrew opened his mouth, he placed the stick between his teeth. Turning, Brewster looked at Abby. She read the question in his eyes.

"I'll be fine," she muttered, ignoring the way her stomach rolled.

"Hold his hands," Brewster ordered, and she moved to do so while he moved toward Andrew's feet. Placing his legs on either side of Andrew, he grasped the foot. "Now," he barked and heaved on the injured leg.

Andrew moaned low in his throat, the sound ripping through Abby, tearing her in strips like she'd torn her petticoat. Then his head lolled to one side.

"He's passed out," Brewster grunted. "It's for the best. He won't feel anything for a few minutes." Already Brewster was placing the shorter branches on either side of Andrew's leg. "Help me bind it."

Her head spun, but she forced her fingers to obey, gathering up the strips of cloth. With steady hands, Brewster lifted Andrew's leg so she could wrap it in the splints.

"Tighter," he ordered when her shaky hands let the bandage grow loose.

He held the leg with one hand and helped her wind the cloth, taking the roll from her hand and carrying it under Andrew's leg. Once, Andrew moaned, and she dropped the strip.

"Keep going," he growled. Tears stung her eyes, and she obeyed blindly, hating him for his lack of feeling.

As soon as they were finished, he lowered the leg carefully and pulled the travois closer. "I'll roll him toward me, and you shove this under as far as you can."

"I can't," she whispered. "It will hurt him too much." She shook her head, looking everywhere but at him.

He reached across Andrew and grasped her chin, forcing her to meet his eyes. "He's out," he growled. "He can't feel a thing. Let's get it done before he comes to."

She swallowed hard. Her mouth felt like she'd rinsed it with ashes.

He waited.

She blinked. He braced himself on his knees and eased Andrew to his side. Abby shoved the rough contraption awkwardly under Andrew's back. With infinite care, Brewster eased him down then slipped the travois under him. Andrew remained unconscious.

"Well, let's go for those wet clothes while we have a chance. Get all the blankets from the bedrolls."

She scurried to obey. When she returned, Brewster had slit Andrew's clothes and eased them off, tossing them behind him. Together they tucked blankets around him as tightly as possible, but Abby knew it would do little to ease the jostling when they moved him.

Andrew moaned, his eyes open, pupils wide with pain.

"All done," she whispered.

Brewster hunkered down beside them. "We have to get you out of here," he addressed Andrew. "There's another storm coming up."

Abby heard thunder in the distance. "Where will we take him?" She half-rose, pressing her hand to her mouth. It was miles back to their place. She knew Andrew would never make it.

"I know a place."

She stared at him, remembering the miner's dugout they had shared. *I sure hope it's better than that*, she thought.

Brewster turned away, unaware of her concerns, and murmuring instructions to his horse, he positioned the animal in front of the travois. He uncoiled his lariat, slipped loops over the ends of the branches, and hooked it to his saddle. Slowly he tightened the rope until Andrew's head was halfway up the horse's tail.

For a minute, he studied Andrew. "That was the easy part, I'm afraid." He brought Abby's horse to her.

Her mouth felt slack-jawed. For a moment, she didn't move. It had to be the light, she decided, that made her think she had seen Brewster squeeze Andrew's shoulder in sympathy even as he shoved the reins toward her.

"I think I'll walk behind with Andrew," she murmured.

He nodded and led her horse as he mounted his own.

There was no way any of them could ease the roughness of the ride. Andrew grasped the sides of his conveyance until his knuckles shone white in the dying firelight. He clenched his jaw so tightly, she could see the muscles below his ears quiver.

The firelight was far behind them, no longer giving the faintest illumination to the path. She stumbled on the uneven ground and barely stopped herself from grabbing the travois for support. Her rib cage squeezed painfully at the thought of how much pain it would give Andrew.

"Brewster, I'm ready to ride."

As she sank into the saddle, it finally hit her.

Andrew was hurt. Badly. She couldn't guess how badly, but two nights in the open had made his condition worse.

She couldn't stop shaking. Brewster's low voice reached out to her in the darkness.

"He'll be fine. Hang in there."

Now why did he go and do that? She was doing just fine, but his unexpected kindness jarred the tears from her, and she scrubbed at her eyes.

Either the man has eyes like an owl, or he has memorized every inch of this country, she thought as they plodded one weary mile after another.

Tiredness was long past—something she felt hours ago when her legs quivered and her back screamed for rest. Now she was beyond feeling. All her energies were concentrated on staying upright in the saddle. It was impossible to keep both eyes open at the same time. Her chin kept falling to her chest despite her attempts to keep upright. She felt herself tipping and snapped her head up, forcing both eyes wide open, but she was powerless to keep them open.

"Abigail, we're here."

At his low voice, she lifted her head. When had they stopped moving? Or had they? Her muscles vibrated with movement, but she couldn't hear hoofbeats. In the silvery starlight, she saw Brewster standing at her side.

"You can get down."

"Umm," she sighed, trying to nod her head. But her chin settled into the collar of her coat.

"Abigail. Wake up."

I am awake, she thought, but it took too much energy to say the words.

"Come on. Get down."

She kicked her feet from the stirrups and lifted herself from the saddle. At least she thought she did, yet her hand still clasped the saddle horn. Again she ordered her muscles to complete the task, but they were as responsive as sticks of wood. She felt like a stuffed gunny sack.

"Here we go."

Strong arms grabbed her waist and lifted her from the saddle. She felt so heavy, like a water-soaked log, yet she was floating.

"Hang on there."

The words drifted above her head. Warm breath caressed her face. She snuggled against a comforting chest.

"Umm," she sighed and nestled into the protection of a strong pair of arms.

Sunlight turned her eyelids into a scarlet screen and warmed her cheek, but Abby kept her eyes closed, letting awareness seep in with the scent of pine needles. The first thing that registered was that her whole body ached like it had been through a butter churn. And she had her clothes on, except for her shoes. She reached out her hands and knew instantly it was not her bed.

Then she remembered the long ride and being carried. Her cheeks warmed as she recalled how she'd nuzzled into his embrace like an adoring bride.

She bolted upright and flung the covers back. Flinging open the door of the bedroom, she dashed into the next room and skidded to a halt. Andrew lay on a sofa, his leg cradled on either side by a rolled blanket. She stared down at him. His cheeks were pale in contrast to the purple bruises on them. He slept with his lips parted. Occasionally he moved and groaned. Tears stung her eyes. She wanted to touch him, assure herself he was really there.

His eyelids fluttered and slowly opened. He stared at nothing then gradually focused on her.

"Hi." He sounded like a frog with a cold.

Her legs turned to cotton, and she dropped to the edge of the sofa and touched his cheek. "Hi." She smiled weakly.

"I never got a chance to ask you last night. Are you all right?" He searched her face.

She nodded. "You want some water?" She looked around. There was a cup of water on the table next to the couch. She picked it up and glanced around the room. The kitchen and eating area at the far end were as efficient and clean as a dream. A large cast-iron sink in a row of neat cupboards boasted its own pump. The table was round oak. She thought of how plain their hand-hewn plank table looked in comparison.

Though dusty, the wood floor held a gleam of beauty. She checked over her shoulder and saw a huge field rock fireplace that took up the entire wall behind them. The whole room was beautiful. It glowed with warmth, and she decided it was because of the books. The entire lower half of the room was bookcases filled with books. Two huge paintings hung on the inside wall. One showed a cabin nestled in foothills surrounded by towering mountains. It washed her with a sense of peace. The other picture was a riot of blue flowers parting for a narrow path leading to a wicker settee on which lay a white straw bonnet and an open book as if waiting for someone to return. A surge of joy swept over her at the scene.

There was a thin layer of dust everywhere, suggesting the owners might be too busy to tend to household chores; but whoever built this house and lived in it must be deeply sensitive and refined. She longed to meet them.

"Who owns this place?" she whispered to Andrew as she handed him the glass of water.

Andrew slanted his eyes to a spot past her shoulder. She turned and for the first time saw Brewster stretched out asleep in front of the fireplace.

"Him?"

"Yes."

"You sure?" They were whispering.

"He told me last night."

The travois lay bundled on the floor. "How did he get you in here?"

"He pulled me in on that thing."

"By himself?" She tried to imagine Brewster dragging Andrew into the house and across the room. She remembered how easily he had thrown her onto his horse, but Andrew weighed close to two hundred pounds.

"I helped some getting on the couch."

"Ow. That must have hurt."

"I think I was past caring. Anything that didn't move or bump sounded pretty inviting even if I had to drag my leg to get there."

"I should have helped."

"Yes, you should have, but you were out like a light. Anyway, he was most kind about it. Who is he? He told me his name is Brewster Johnson, but where did he come from?"

"He's the man who. . ." She hesitated, not wanting to upset Andrew.

"I'm the man who kidnapped her." Brewster's deep voice finished her sentence.

Abby stiffened, her cheeks burning at the memory of last night. She prayed he wasn't looking at her. She held her breath, waiting for Andrew's reaction.

"So that's what happened to you. I wondered and imagined all sorts of things." He held her gaze, searching her eyes for satisfaction. "Did he hurt you?"

She shook her head, but it was Brewster who answered.

"I did not. And I brought her back home."

Andrew's lips twitched. "I always knew it would be hard to find a man who would keep you." His eyes closed, and she saw how drawn his face was.

"You rest now." She patted his shoulder and hovered over him, reluctant to face the other man at her side.

"I'd better check that leg," Brewster muttered.

She stepped aside, grateful that he kept his back to her. She forgot everything as she watched him lift the strips of cloth and look at the swollen leg. Straightening himself, he stood looking down at Andrew. She waited, shuffling as the minute lengthened into two.

"What is it?"

He shook his head. "Let him rest for now. I think we could all use a decent meal."

She followed him to the kitchen aware he had not answered her question. Glancing over her shoulder at Andrew, already sleeping, she wondered what had grabbed Brewster's attention; but he refused to meet her eyes, and she knew he would not tell her until he was ready.

Andrew woke long enough to take a few spoonfuls of thin oatmeal and another draught of water; then he waved her away and fell back to sleep.

Brewster left the house as soon as they had eaten their breakfast, but now, as Abby sat watching Andrew, he returned. She met his eyes, trying to find clues about this man who helped a stranger, gave efficient medical help, constructed a home that was much more than a simple cabin, and yet kidnapped a woman for his wife. His hazel eyes darkened as she searched their depths, but his secrets remained hidden. He would reveal nothing.

"Did he eat something?" He dropped his eyelids and looked at Andrew.

"A little. Is he going to be all right?"

He kept his eyes lowered as her heart leapt with fear. Then his eyes, narrowed and hardened, met hers. "I don't know. There was a hand on one of the outfits I worked who had a break like this. He. . ." He shrugged and didn't finish.

Abby's heart turned to stone, and she stared openmouthed at him.

" 'Course every day he got bounced about in the wagon. Don't suppose that did him much good."

She didn't move or blink.

He flung his hat to the floor and strode to her side. "Abigail, snap out of it. He'll likely recover in fine form if he gets proper nursing, and that's up to you." He drew her toward the stove. "There's lots of firewood, and all you have to do for water is pump the handle. Now heat up some water and make some compresses." He opened a cupboard and handed her a small tin. "Add Epsom salts to the water. Keep hot compresses on that swollen area above his knee." Returning to the door, he scooped his hat off the floor and watched her. "I'll be gone a day or so. Two at the most." He jammed on his hat and left.

Chapter 10

The next morning, as Abby waited for the water to boil, she watched as a milky curtain of fog lifted from the valley and honey sunshine poured over the treetops, dipped under the eaves, and flooded the house with warm light.

I wouldn't call this place a cabin, she thought. It was really and truly a house—a warm, inviting home. When he said he had a house of sorts, she had imagined a mean, narrow cabin with a slit of a window and a dirt floor. Not these rich, hand-rubbed planks.

The pot bubbled, and she stirred in the salts, one tablespoon at a time, until it grew murky. Plunging in a clean cloth, she scooped it out with a wooden spoon, laying it in a basin until it was cool enough for her to gingerly pick up two corners and fold it into a neat square. Flipping it from hand to hand, she hurried to Andrew's side. He watched her warily, knowing she would only let it cool enough to prevent a burn before she placed it on his red and swollen leg. His jaw tightened, and he clenched his fists.

Patting the cloth, she decided it had cooled enough and, avoiding his eyes, laid it on the wound with infinite care. He stiffened and moaned. The sound dropped into her stomach like she had swallowed a rock.

"Is it getting worse?" she asked.

His eyes were clouded, and he didn't answer right away. When he did, his voice was thin, threading its way into the depths of her brain. "It's hard to say."

His pain stung her like a dip in boiling water. "If only I could do something. Give you something." Her inadequacy burned.

"You're here." The stabbing pain settled. He unclenched his fists and his eyes focused. "Tell me what happened."

She searched for the end of a thread that went somewhere. "He wanted a wife," she began, plucking at the first loose end. She told him about Sam and Petey and how Brewster had exploded with anger. For the first time, it dawned on her that he might have been killed. She shuddered as she thought what that would have meant to her personal safety.

Bit by bit, she unraveled her story. When she had finished, Andrew, whose eyes had remained fixed on her, said, "Wow. Sounds like something from a book." His hand touched hers. "I'm just glad you're safe and sound."

She nodded, echoing his words in her mind.

"Abby? Did you pray?"

"Like never before in my life."

"Me, too. And even harder when I broke my leg and my horse ran off and I was stranded in the middle of nowhere."

"And our prayers were answered."

He nodded, and she knew his thoughts matched hers. It was the first time they had realized how much they needed God's intervention. And He had proven faithful. She squeezed his hand.

"I'm scared," she whispered. "We're all alone here, and your leg looks bad." She shivered in spite of her attempt to remain strong. She should have remembered she couldn't hide the truth from Andrew.

He nodded and said, "Let's pray together."

She nodded and bowed her head until it almost touched Andrew's forehead. They took turns praying for safety and healing for Andrew's leg. Andrew thanked God for the fact they were both safe.

When they were done, Abby felt her tension ease away.

"One thing I don't understand. Why kidnap a wife? Why not court a woman? Or simply ask her right out?"

She shrugged. "Maybe it took too much effort." The words he had said that first day came to her mind. "Besides, he thinks he's ugly." More things came to her now—the bitterness in his voice when he spoke of Lucy, his avowal that he didn't believe in anything. "Probably most of all because he doesn't trust anyone. This way, he doesn't expect anything so he can't be hurt if he never gets it."

"Strange man, yet he seems so straight." Andrew's eyes drooped.

"Yes," she agreed. She pulled the thick, gray blanket to his chin and slipped away.

Yes, strange, she thought as she circled the room. The collection of books surprised her, but not as much as her discovery that the wide windows gleamed like freshly washed china. Why would he keep his windows so clean despite his confessed lack of time for household chores? And there were so many of them.

The room grew warm. She opened the door and stood gazing out. Birds peppered the sky above the trees, their wings sifting the air. Insects hummed and chattered.

She picked up a corner of the cloth compress, careful not to waken Andrew. Several hours later, the skin of his leg glistened like a polished apple, but she couldn't tell if there was any improvement. Andrew continued to sleep, giving her plenty of time to think.

She recalled how she had one day watched a rope maker at work, twisting long strands until they were taut then joining the twisted strands to make a rope. She felt like one of those strands—and the crank was still turning.

Suddenly one of the strands broke and whirled out of control. How dare Brewster ride away, oblivious to Andrew's pain and her worry. He'd left her with no way of getting help. She didn't even know where she was.

Pressing back the burning in her chest, she continued applying compresses to

Andrew's leg, praying it was enough. There was little else she could do.

The afternoon shadows were growing long when rocks clattered outside and a knock sounded.

Before she could call out, the door flew open and a dark-suited man stepped in.

"I'm Dr. Baker." He smiled without changing the expression on his round face. "Where's the patient?" He saw Andrew and, without waiting for a reply, stepped to his side. "I presume this is where I'm needed."

Abby shook aside her surprise. "Thank you for coming, but how did you know?"

"Mr. Johnson informed me. Fact of the matter is, he rode out with me." As he talked, he pulled aside the compress and probed the reddened area. Andrew flinched. Abby stepped toward the doctor then halted as he grunted and pulled aside the blanket. His hands felt along Andrew's collarbone and down each arm, pausing as Andrew flinched again. He turned Andrew's arm over and examined an ink-colored bruise. As his hands moved, his mouth kept pace.

"Quite the hero, your Mr. Johnson."

Abby met Andrew's eyes and read the warning in them. She pressed back her accusations about Brewster.

"Single-handed, he brought in two ruffians who have been terrorizing the country."

Abby and Andrew asked each other the same silent question. Was it Sam and Petey?

"Seems they've been responsible for robbing the stagecoach, helping themselves to a few cattle, and stealing from some of the ranch houses. I heard tell one of Coyote John's daughters was raped. 'Spect these fellows are responsible." He pulled some bottles from his bag. "Dissolve this in water, and use it for compresses. It will work a little better. Something I mixed up myself." He dropped several small packets into her palm. "Give him this for relief of his pain." He gave her instructions, jabbing his finger at her as he talked as if he were drilling the words into her.

"Yes, sir," he continued, closing his bag. "Must have been quite a thing for that young man to bring those two in by himself. I wish I could have seen it. Fact is, he probably could have sold seats to the event. They were hopping mad. Kept saying as how they would get even. But I don't expect they'll be much threat. They'll soon be wearing neckties so tight, it'll give them a permanent headache."

The door squeaked open, and Brewster faced them, a carpet bag in his hand that she recognized from Andrew's room.

He's brought us clothes! she thought, her cheeks warming as she pictured him entering her room. Yet she had to admit she would be glad for a fresh outfit.

"Why here's your young man now."

He's not my young man, she wanted to scream, but Dr. Baker was headed for the door. "Wait, Doctor. How is he? Is his leg going to be all right?"

He paused and turned to face her. "Looks pretty fair. Pretty fair. Couldn't have set it better myself. Just keep him still. I don't want him moved for six weeks. I'll check on him in a few days."

He passed Brewster in the doorway and squeezed his shoulder. "Good work there, son."

And he was gone as quickly as he had come. If she didn't hold the paper packages and bottle of salts in her hands, she would have thought he was a mirage. Andrew must have had the same feeling for he let his breath out in a whoosh. "Bit like a cyclone, isn't he?"

Brewster closed the door and moved toward the cold fireplace, but no one answered Andrew's question.

"Brewster." At Andrew's call, he turned and faced him. "Was it Sam and Petey?"

He nodded.

Andrew spoke first. "How did you manage to apprehend them so quickly?"

Brewster shrugged. "Didn't take much. I figgered they'd be on my trail, so I circled around them and waited where I knew I could get the drop on them."

No one spoke, and the silence deepened around them.

"I guess that leaves you. What shall I do about you?" At Andrew's question, Abby looked directly at Brewster. He studied the floor at his feet. Finally he cleared his throat and lifted his head to meet Andrew's eyes.

"I think that is up to you."

Her breathing was loud. Neither man looked away, and again she felt alone as she watched them measure each other and come to a conclusion that excluded her.

Andrew broke the silence. "All's well that ends well." Knowing he'd made up his mind, Abby turned away, tears stinging her eyes. *What about what he did to me?* she wanted to scream. *He kidnapped me and dragged me back and forth across the country.*

Yes, a little voice argued, *and he took you home. And then helped you find Andrew.* She clenched her fists at her side, drowning in a flood of emotion.

"You'll stay here as long as you need," Brewster said.

Andrew nodded. "Appreciate that."

So all the questions were answered, Abby fumed. But no one had taken into consideration her feelings or asked her what she wanted. It was one of the rare times in her life that she was truly angry at her twin.

"I need some fresh air," she muttered and marched out, controlling the urge to slam the door. *As if they'd notice,* she raged, feeling as forgotten as yesterday's sunrise.

She hurried down the path, giving no thought to where she went. *How can Andrew so easily ignore the fact that Brewster kidnapped me?* she thought. *Did he not think how frightening it had been? And to dismiss it so simply with "all's well that ends well."* As if the path taken to arrive at their destination was of no concern. Truth was, she decided, her ordeal meant nothing to anyone but herself. Andrew and Brewster had come to some sort of conclusion without speaking a word.

She stomped her foot on the damp grass. *How dare Brewster think he could get away with this? He should have to pay. Like Sam and Petey. Brewster should have turned himself in at the same time.*

Yes, and then where would you be? a little voice nagged. *Stuck out here with an injured brother. How would you cope?*

I'd find a way, she fumed. *Without his help. And how could Andrew agree to staying here after what Brewster has done?*

What has he done? the annoying voice argued. *Rescued both of you, gone for help, seen that your pursuers were in jail.*

As if that cancels out what he did, she argued with the persistent voice.

Maybe you should think of Andrew. He can't be moved if you want his leg to heal properly, the voice insisted.

Fine, she grunted. *I'll stay for Andrew. Just until he can travel. Not one minute more. But I won't change my mind about Brewster. He deserves to be punished.*

For a long time, she stood looking over the valley, refusing to allow the beauty of the evening to soothe her. The shadows turned as purple as the folds in a velvet cape, and the trees whispered secrets.

God loves him. The statement echoed inside her head.

She'd already tried to tell him that.

What had he said about a dump? God was a garbage dump for unloved people. Did she agree? Of course not. It's just that—that—

She crossed her arms and squared her jaw. She didn't want to think about it. She knew God loved her and had answered her prayers to find Andrew. If God wanted to love Brewster, too, that was fine with her. But it didn't change anything.

She yawned, suddenly very tired. It had been a long, tension-wrapped day on the heels of many such days and nights. She turned toward the house.

It took longer than she expected to retrace her steps. By the time she returned, she was too tired to fight. She would, she concluded, be polite, even if he didn't deserve it.

※

It was the smell of coffee that tugged Abby from her sleep the next morning. She sprang from the bed and into her clothes and bolted to the door, where she skidded to a stop. Brewster had pulled a chair to the side of the sofa, and he and Andrew were chatting away like old friends, each enjoying a steaming cup of coffee. It had always been her job to make Andrew his morning coffee, and she wanted to fling away the cups and pour out the pot on the stove.

"Good morning," Andrew said.

Brewster rose so quickly, the chair skidded away. He let his eyes rest on her for a fleeting moment then strode toward the stove. She could hear the humming fire and the purring kettle. The firebox was full of wood. At home she usually got her own wood. Annoyance made her tighten her lips. A flash of color caught her eye, and she stared at the jar of flowers in the center of the table. Red fireweed, orange paintbrush, bluebells, and yellow brown-eyed Susans sang a cheery greeting as gentle perfume bathed the air. Flowers, of all things. Didn't the man have anything better to do with his time? Her gaze lingered another heartbeat, then she turned to Andrew.

"Good morning, and how are you feeling today?"

"Much better. Thanks to those powders the doctor left." The lines in his face had disappeared, but his voice was deep, his eyelids heavy with the effect of the pain killer. Brewster must have given him some earlier.

She would have come if Andrew called, she fumed. It was her job.

Ignoring Brewster, who sprang out of the way at her approach, she hurried to make porridge, sitting at Andrew's side to eat her own breakfast when it was ready. As soon as Brewster wolfed down his food, he grabbed his hat and the rifle from over the door and left. Abby kept her face turned toward the floor. Not even to herself would she admit the tiny pang of loss as the door closed behind him.

It took only a few minutes to clean the kitchen and look after the compresses on Andrew's leg before he fell asleep. Circling the room, wondering what to do with the long hours stretching before her, Abby began to pull books from the shelves. Her wonder grew as she examined them. *He must own every book ever published*, she decided. She spent a long time paging through a set of wonderfully illustrated bird books. Flipping open the pages of *The Last of the Mohicans*, by James Fenimore Cooper, she was soon lost in a world of Indians, settlers, and the wilds of the Americas. A banging noise caused her to clutch at her throat. Had she raced into a trap? Her eyes focused, and she mentally returned to the house in which she sat, staring openmouthed and wide-eyed at Brewster.

"I brought you some meat for supper." His voice was rough and low as he held up two small birds, already plucked and cleaned, then dropped them into the basin. Without another word and before she could find her voice, he closed the door behind him. She could hear his boots thump down the path. In a few minutes, she heard hammering from across the clearing.

She covered the birds with water and set a pot of soup to simmer, then returned to her reading, where she stayed until it was time to serve the soup.

Brewster came slowly through the door. Abby turned her back, busying herself at the stove. She didn't look at him until she set the bowl of soup before him, but he kept his head down so she couldn't see his face. *That's fine with me*, she thought. She didn't want to see his eyes and the wariness in them at her continued coldness. She steeled herself to remain angry.

After she cleaned the kitchen, she changed Andrew's compresses and made sure he was comfortable before she again picked up her book from the shelf. Much later, with reluctance, she set it aside as the afternoon heat crowded in on her, but she knew she must put the birds in the oven if supper was to be ready on time. Despite the allure of the fictional world, she would not allow Brewster an opportunity to think her lazy.

Andrew wakened off and on through the day but seemed disinclined to talk. Knowing sleep would hasten his healing, she left him.

Late in the afternoon, he awoke, his eyes alert as he watched her every move. Something about the way he watched her made her uneasy, but he shook his head when she asked him what it was.

After they had eaten the evening meal in near silence, Brewster left the room with a mumbled explanation about having to check on the horses.

"Abby," Andrew called as the door closed. "Come here."

Drying her hands on a white linen towel, she hurried to his side.

"I've been watching you."

She nodded.

"And something's been bothering me."

Again she nodded as a lump swelled in the back of her throat.

"You've never been an unfriendly person, yet when Brewster's around, you are. What's the problem?"

"I'm not." She protested, knowing it was futile to argue with her twin. She was only surprised he seemed so thick about why. "All right, I suppose I am. But who could blame me? He kidnapped me. And it doesn't seem like anybody cares."

He opened his mouth, but before he could speak, she hurried on. "And it's his fault you're lying here injured. Is it any wonder I don't feel like being friendly?"

"But Abby, I've never known you to be unforgiving." His voice was low, but his words stung like he'd flung acid in her face. "He made a mistake, and he knows it and is trying his best to make it right. What more can you ask?"

What more? she asked herself. *Revenge. Justice. Not to see you and him visiting like old buddies.*

When she didn't answer, Andrew went on. "He seems so lonely. And so wary." He shook his head. "That doesn't seem fair. This is his house, and he's going out of his way to look after us. Can't you try a little harder?"

Her best friend, protector, and defender had become her accuser. She closed her eyes until she could swallow the sting of tears. Was she being petty and unforgiving? Andrew seemed to think so. She couldn't bear to have his disapproval.

Opening her eyes, she whispered, "I'll try."

"Good." He squeezed her hand as the door opened. He held it firmly, expectantly, as Brewster entered the room.

"I want to thank you for your hospitality and kindness," she blurted before she could change her mind, feeling her cheeks warm as she spoke.

Brewster halted midstep and raised his eyes to hers, holding her gaze for a long, tense moment. His expression became guarded and wary.

"You're welcome." His voice was a low rumble that rattled across her mind and tugged at her breast bone. The brittleness that had held her tight all day softened. Nothing had changed, she reasoned. Least of all, her feelings. She would always hate him. Perhaps hate was too strong a word. She would always dislike him, she amended, but being friendly? Andrew was right. It was the least she could do.

Chapter 11

Abby gave Andrew the *Farmer's Almanac* then curled up in the wine-colored armchair with her book. Brewster stared into the cold fireplace while the warm dusk settled around them, a welcome breeze stirring through the open windows, cloaking the room in the scent of wildflowers. Finally, with a deep sigh, Brewster grabbed a chair from next to the table, plunked it beside the bookcase, and lifted the lid of a gramophone. Abby had never seen a gramophone before, and over the top of her book, she kept an eye on Brewster's movements. He put a cylinder on the sleeve then wound a small, black handle before dropping the needle. At first, the music was too fast—thin and reedy—then it swelled into sweetness and filled the room. Abby closed her eyes and leaned back, letting the melody lift her and flood her chest with both sad and joyous emotions. The music died, and she kept her eyes closed, lost in the swirl of emotions. Slowly, as if rising from a coma, she lifted her eyelids and saw Brewster tipped back in his chair, his head resting on the golden logs, his eyes closed, his lashes like a dark fan against his cheeks. Surrounded by the effects of the music and the warmth of logs and book bindings, his face looked younger, softer, warmer. His eyelids drifted upward, and he stared straight at her. The sweetness produced by the gramophone had stripped away his pretenses, broken down his guard, allowing her to see past his eyes into his soul. She saw his naked hunger, his stark longing for someone to care about the unloved boy-man inside. In an instant, his expression hardened, and the shades were drawn as surely as if a hand had reached up and pulled the blinds. He dropped his chair to the floor with a thud.

"That was swell," Andrew sighed. "I've never heard anything like that. Do you have any more?"

"Some." Carefully he removed the cylinder and placed on another then cranked the handle again.

A rousing tune filled the room.

"Camptown races start tonight,

"Do dah, Do dah. . ."

By the end of the song, Andrew was chuckling. "Could we hear it again?"

The second time around, Andrew joined in the chorus of "do dah, do dah" and the third time, raised his hands as though conducting a band. "Everyone sing," he urged.

By keeping her eyes fixed on her brother, Abby was able to forget Brewster's tight look as she sang along. Andrew asked for it again and sang the entire song, with Abby joining in on the do-dahs. She almost lost her voice when a third voice—deep and full—joined her partway through. She and Andrew smiled at each other, sharing a joint victory in knowing they had succeeded in getting Brewster to have a little fun. By the fourth time through, the twins were laughing; and when Abby turned to include Brewster, she was surprised to see that he almost smiled. *At least,* she thought, *if you could call a slight lifting of his mouth and a deepening of the creases at the corner of his eyes a smile.* She had to admit she liked what it did to his features, gentling the hard planes and the slash across his cheek. But it was his eyes that trapped her. They were the color of pine needles and full of deep, dark mysteries.

It is absurd to think about such things, she scolded herself.

Andrew broke the silence. "You have so many books and all those phonographs. I don't think I've ever seen such a lot. Not even in the library back in the old country. It certainly didn't boast a gramophone."

Brewster rose from his chair. "They're my friends." He closed the lid and carefully replaced the cylinders.

"I'll get you settled for the night," Abby said to Andrew. A few minutes later, she was in the narrow bedroom with Brewster's words still ringing in her ears. As she brushed her hair, she felt moisture at the corner of her eyes and dashed it away with the back of her hand. It was due to the music and the scent of flowers and pine needles. It had nothing to do with Brewster's lonesome words now blaring through her head. She was getting far too emotional if his statements got under her skin that easily.

Over the past days, she'd seen a glimpse of his unhappy childhood and how it shaped him as a man who didn't trust relationships. Yet in this house, she had a peek of something else. The music, the flowers, the books all pointed toward fine things. Things, she was sure, he'd deny and reject if she mentioned them.

Was it possible for him to learn to trust people? To love and be loved? Was that why he had kidnapped her? Had he thought he saw in her someone he could trust?

She clutched the hairbrush in both hands, staring out into the silent darkness. Her heart thrilled to think someone would see her in that light.

Then she flung the brush aside. *What difference does it make what he thinks?* she fumed. Despite his comments about needing help, he seemed to manage very well on his own. And with the books and gramophone to enrich his life, he had no need for friendship.

She knew her thoughts were unfair and likely untrue, but she clung to them as she climbed into bed and pulled the covers close. It suited her to think the way she did.

The next morning, she hurried from her room determined to be the first up. Andrew lay asleep on the sofa, his hair mussed and his covers tangled. She felt a pang as she realized he must have found it difficult to get comfortable. Brewster had moved to the smaller bedroom, leaving her the one he normally used. The door to his room remained closed. Moving as quietly as she could, Abby built the fire and put the coffee to boil. Within a few minutes, Andrew stirred and moaned. Abby hurried over to put on a fresh compress, ignoring Andrew's muttered complaints. He was always grumpy in the morning, and she had learned long ago to pay little attention. She was hurrying back to the kitchen with her hands full when the bedroom door opened and Brewster appeared, his dark hair sleek as usual. Determined to establish a friendly atmosphere, she set two places on the table before taking Andrew a cup of coffee.

Filling both mugs on the table, she called, "Coffee's ready. Come and have some breakfast." She sat, her hands folded in her lap, and waited for Brewster to join her.

She prayed silently and began to eat.

Brewster's eyes darted from Andrew to Abby and then to the floor. He pulled out the chair across from her and lowered himself into it as if he expected the seat to drop out.

"Thank you for bringing in the flowers." She would make this a pleasant experience, she decided, even if she had to carry the conversation entirely on her own. If she had any power over the situation, they would all act as if this were a normal everyday event.

"Welcome," he grunted, gulping a swallow of coffee.

She continued. "The mountain flowers seem so bold and showy."

Brewster darted a glance at the flowers. Before she could see what his expression said, he lowered his head and studied his plate.

"Don't you think so?" she persisted.

His fork hovered halfway to his mouth. "I guess so." He gobbled his food then pushed back his chair. "I best get to work."

"What are you doing? For work, I mean?"

He was poised on the edge of his chair, prepared for flight. "Making some fence."

Andrew perked up. "You running horses?"

"A few. Mostly cows. I bought some breeding stock from the Bar U when I bought this place."

"Herefords?"

"Shorthorn." He edged toward the door, eyeing his hat.

"Well, have a good day," she called as he pulled open the door.

He jammed the hat on his head and fled.

"What was that all about?" Andrew demanded.

"What?"

"All that eye batting and moony looks. You scared the man half to death."

She drew herself up. "I did not. You said I should try to be friendly, so I was." She turned away, ignoring his snort.

The first morning set the tone for the following days. Abby set out to draw Brewster into conversation, and when he responded even slightly, she almost cheered. At the same time, Brewster did all he could to ease life for her. Whether he did it intentionally or out of habit, she didn't know. He provided a supply of fresh meat. He kept the wood box full. One day he brought a pan of blackberries and set them on the table. She baked them in a pie. Andrew, whose appetite improved daily, ate two pieces and raved about the treat. Brewster said little but ate three pieces and thanked her hoarsely. Berries appeared every three or four days after that.

The doctor came and checked Andrew's leg, declaring it was healing nicely and said Abby could discontinue the compresses. They all sighed with relief, knowing it would now be possible to let the fire die down during the heat of the day. Dr. Baker also brought the news that Sam and Petey had been transported to Fort Calgary, tried and convicted, and were now rotting in the fort's jail. "The country can breathe easier with those two gone," he drawled, and Abby couldn't help but agree. She knew she would breathe easier and slanted a glance at Brewster. His dark gaze met hers for a moment before he turned away to listen to the doctor.

The days folded into each other, warm and contented.

We are learning to be friends, she thought.

⚭

As soon as she got up, Abby knew the day was different. It started as she left her bedroom.

"About time you showed up," Andrew groused.

"It's barely light. You were expecting me in the middle of the night?" She bit her lip, wishing she had kept silent. She knew responding to Andrew's early morning moods only provoked him. And she was right.

"It's hours since it grew light, and I've been lying here like a sack of potatoes. You know I can't do anything by myself. I'm beginning to think you're enjoying my helplessness." He glowered at her.

"Like I haven't looked after you every hour of every day for the last three weeks. Did you ever think I might want a break?"

"It's me that has the break I might remind you."

"Like I need reminding," she growled.

A thud sounded on the closed bedroom door. "Quiet," a voice grated.

"Humph." She flung her head back and stomped to the kitchen, ignoring Andrew's steaming glare.

Outside, the clouds hung low and threatening, shutting out the morning sunshine. Without the bright morning light, the house seemed dull and lifeless.

Brewster joined them for breakfast, but after glancing at brother and sister and seeing their scowling expressions, he kept to himself.

I'm in such a bad mood, I think I'll bake cookies. Abby threw more wood on the fire and gathered up her supplies.

449

The clouds clung to the treetops like a tent to its pegs. By late afternoon, a fine mist began to descend. Brewster came in and shook the moisture from his hat.

"Looks like it's going to settle in for a good pour."

Great, thought Abby, and she turned to pull a sheet of cookies from the oven. Andrew grunted.

"I'll build a fire in the fireplace. Help take the chill out of the air." In a few minutes, flames danced merrily at the far end of the room. Abby stared at them, feeling the depression lift from her shoulders.

After supper Brewster pulled the sofa closer to the fire for Andrew, and Abby drew the armchair close. Brewster set his own chair a little way from the twins but still drawn up to the fire. Abby set out a plate of cookies and a huge pot of tea.

"This is nice," Andrew said, his earlier peevishness forgotten.

I guess I can't blame him for feeling restless at times, Abby thought. *It's hard for him to have to lie there day after day. On the whole, he's been a good patient. Besides,* she concluded, *it's this rotten weather as much as anything that's making us cranky.*

"You know what it reminds me of?" Andrew turned to her, his eyes sparkling. She shook her head.

"You remember that time when we were about, oh, I suppose six or seven, and Father was cleaning up the garden? It must have been late October. I remember the big pile of leaves and corn stalks and old grass. It was already dark when he lit the fire. Remember?"

She nodded as memories trailed across her mind, warm and cozy as a wool quilt. "I remember how warm it was. Like the night was just a silken curtain. And the flames were orange monsters that licked at the sky. We ran around and around the fire. Widening our circle until we hovered between light and dark."

"Daring the darkness to frighten us."

"Yes. Exactly. Begging to be scared."

"Remember what Papa did?" He had unconsciously shifted to his childhood name for their father.

"I remember." Her voice bubbled with laughter and joy. "It was one of the few times I remember him really playing with us. And laughing so much."

"There were still some corn stalks to be pulled. . . ."

"And we would hide behind them as Papa yanked them out. . . ."

"And he would. . ."

"Lunge. . ."

"And growl. . ."

"And pretend to scare us."

They tripped over each other as they told Brewster their story.

"Then we ran around the fire and he. . ."

"Would wait for us and grab us. . ."

"And throw us up in the air."

Abby and Andrew looked at each other and grinned. "I screamed with laughter until I felt weak," she said.

"Me, too."

"It was the best day of my life. I felt so safe and happy."

"Guess that's why I like a fire so much."

"Umm. Me, too."

She looked at Brewster. His eyes shifted from Andrew to her. Her heart leaped to her throat as she saw his unvarnished longing. Hunger. A dog too often kicked and now afraid to take the bone offered him by a kind stranger.

"How 'bout you, Brewster? You must have sat around many a fire. What memories come to mind when you see the flames?" Andrew asked.

Abby saw Brewster's face drain. His skin was gray and bleak as he stared into the fire without answering. The log cracked. A flame leaped up the chimney. Sparks sprayed against the screen. Rain pattered against the shingles. Still he did not answer. Lost in his own thoughts, Andrew seemed not to notice, but Abby's chest grew tighter and tighter until she was afraid she was going to choke.

Brewster sighed, and Abby eased in a little air.

"I can't say I have any memories that make me feel safe and happy like you do." His voice was almost lost in the depths of his chest. "My earliest memories are of crouching in a corner, straining for the least little sound that would warn me that Lucy was coming. But I did like to watch sunbeams." His voice deepened. "I would find a spot where I could see one. Didn't matter if it was coming through a crack between the boards, or through a bit of glass, or even a door hanging by one hinge. I liked to watch the shaft of light cross the floor and crawl the walls, catching bits of dust that danced and skipped in the light. Guess the firelight sort of reminds me of that." He rubbed his cheek, drawing his finger along the scar as if feeling some deep, driving pain. "Guess I was a bit of a dreamer. No wonder Lucy was always getting mad at me." He shook his shoulders. "I hunkered down around enough campfires over the years trying to stay dry or find a way to get both sides warm at once that I promised myself when I had a place of my own, it would have a fireplace big enough a body could hope to get himself warm clear through."

Andrew had never heard Brewster speak of Lucy and his childhood, and Abby could feel his shock. "Who was Lucy and why were you crouching in corners?" His voice was sharp with horror.

The hardness slipped back into place. Brewster's face looked lean and so filled with pain that Abby bit her lip to keep from crying out.

"Lucy was my mother, and she didn't want anyone to know I was there; so I learned to hide and be quiet. I tried to become invisible, but I never quite figured out how." He gave a twisted smile.

"Why?" Andrew whispered, his voice echoing Abby's incredulity. Although she had heard some of it before, she still shuddered at what he had suffered as a child.

Brewster shrugged, hard planes angling his face. "I guess a kid wasn't good for her business. She used to tell me I should never have happened. I was a mistake. That was in her better moods. Otherwise, she shrieked at me and cursed the day I was born. She said she couldn't count the number of times she wished I'd die, but I was a tough kid. Too stubborn I guess." He stared into the fire. Abby wondered if he even remembered they were in the same room. "I tried real hard to do what she wanted. Figured if I did, then she'd be able to love me." He shook his head slowly. "Never could be good enough. I finally had to accept I never would."

He paused for a full minute and then continued, his voice so low, Abby could barely make out his words.

"I always thought if she'd marry one of her boyfriends and settle down, we could have a real home. A home filled with. . ."

His voice trailed off, the sentence unfinished, but in her mind, Abby supplied the word. *Love.* And she recoiled as she felt the despair he acknowledged in admitting he felt himself unlovable.

It's not true.

She almost bolted from the chair but caught herself just in time and forced herself to sit back and fold her hands in her lap. She felt Andrew's eyes upon her but stared into the fire, afraid to look, knowing he would read what was in her heart. Her thoughts flared, and a fire was kindled inside her.

For a brief moment, she'd seen him with his guard down. She wanted to tell him he wasn't unlovable. God loved him. God loved everyone. He needed to know that and believe it. It would surely chase away all the hurt his mother's words and actions had inflicted in his soul.

Andrew said, "God's love doesn't depend on how good we are. Or whether we deserve it. He gave us the ultimate gift of love—His own Son. It's up to us to choose what to do with it. We can't earn it. We simply have to believe it and accept it. Father taught us many verses like John 3:16, which says, 'For God so loved the world, that he gave his only begotten Son, that whosoever believeth in him should not perish, but have everlasting life.' And there's verses in Romans. 'For all have sinned, and come short of the glory of God,' and 'The wages of sin is death; but the gift of God is eternal life through Jesus Christ our Lord.' "

Andrew paused for a moment, watching Brewster's face, but his expression was unreadable.

Andrew continued, "There is nothing we can do to earn it. He gives it to us freely. We just have to accept it."

Abby saw hope flicker in Brewster's face, then wariness returned so quickly, she wondered if what she saw was simply the reflection of the fire.

"It's easy to believe in love when that's all you've ever known." Brewster rose hastily to his feet and went to his bedroom, closing the door quietly behind him.

Chapter 12

Abby pulled the covers over her ears in a vain attempt to block the sound of rain pummeling the roof and the eaves weeping mournfully. Tonight the moon did not run silver fingers through her window and pull back the curtain of night. She wished for enough light to see the trees outside or to be able to stare at the Audubon prints on the wall. Even to see the shape of the logs so she could count how many were in each wall. Anything was preferable to the sounds inside her head—Lucy screaming her hatred to Brewster; venom-filled words ripping through her mind like gnarled fingers tearing at raw flesh. It was as if a huge canvas had been nailed to the wall next to her bed and Brewster's past slashed across it in blood and tears. The blood still dripped. The tears were still damp.

There had to be people who knew of Brewster's situation. Why had no one reached out a hand and helped?

Words raced through her mind. Where was God?

God is love. The words blasted through her mind.

She believed it with all her heart. *Why, then, didn't God do something? Why didn't He send someone?*

He did. He sent you.

She sat bolt upright in bed and stared out the darkened window. *Me! An instrument of God's love? Impossible.* She couldn't do it. It was preposterous to think of loving him. Wasn't it?

But was that what God was asking?

No, she decided. He was only asking her to show His love. To convince Brewster that love and healing were possible.

The argument continued unabated.

Did love stand a chance? Could she convince Brewster there was love and healing for him? Did she really believe it was available for Brewster?

She lay back against her pillow and tugged the covers to her chin. Of course, she believed it. Without reservation.

But did she want to be the one responsible for carrying the message?

Again the sound of Lucy's words scraped through her mind. *No child should ever hear that message; no person should believe those words.*

God did love him. He forgave freely.

Could she show God's love without forgiving him?

She remembered a portion of Matthew's gospel and pulled her Bible toward her, grateful that Brewster had included it when he gathered up items back at the house for her and Andrew. Tipping it toward the light so she could read the words, she found what she was looking for in the sixth chapter, verses fourteen and fifteen, *"For if ye forgive men their trespasses, your heavenly Father will also forgive you: But if ye forgive not men their trespasses, neither will your Father forgive your trespasses."*

God had forgiven her. She had no choice but to forgive Brewster. She began to pray, and as she did so, slowly her stubborn bitterness melted away.

A few minutes later, filled with a gentle peace, she opened her eyes. Now she could prove to Brewster that love existed. But she would need a plan.

The night deepened, the rain continued, and the rest of the house slept as Abby contrived her plan. Finally she fell asleep, a smile on her lips.

She awoke still smiling and scurried from her bed, shivering in the early morning dampness. She paused to glance out the window and was relieved to see that, though the sky was still dark and lowering, it had stopped raining. The wet weather would give her a chance to implement her plan. She didn't want to waste any time.

She waited until Brewster was seated at the table before she poured his coffee. "I made it especially strong today," she announced, leaning over to fill his cup, balancing herself with one hand on his shoulder. "I noticed you like it that way." He twitched under her palm, but she pretended not to notice. He'd soon get used to it. Since she had become aware of his nervousness at being touched, she had avoided it as much as possible. But not anymore. Touch was an important part of showing love.

Rather than set one place at each end of the table as had been her habit, this morning she set the two places so that she was on Brewster's right. He raised one eyebrow. Ignoring his look, she pulled out her chair and sat down.

"You know," she began, resting her hand lightly on his, "I really appreciate having flowers on the table every day. You must have to search to find so many of them."

He stared at her hand, and when she didn't remove it, he flicked his arm away and picked up his spoon, becoming suddenly very busy stirring his porridge. "I'd have to be blind to miss them."

"Well, thank you anyway. They're especially cheery on a day like this."

He gulped his food and glanced out the window. "I think it's clearing. Sure hope so. There's a lot of work to be done." Dropping his spoon, he bolted for the door.

And you can't wait to escape, she thought, but she smiled sweetly and called, "Have a good morning," as he flung himself out the door.

She hummed as she worked, ignoring Andrew's slanted looks. It had been a good start to her plan, she decided.

When Brewster came in with a plump partridge, cleaned and ready for baking, she was ready. "I really appreciate this fresh meat all the time. You're a very good hunter."

"Comes with experience," he grunted and turned to leave.

"Wait," she called. "I just took these cookies from the oven. Help yourself." She extended a plate toward him.

He paused and studied her with eyes that burned; then he nodded and took one.

All the things she found to say about him were true, but she had a feeling he had never heard them before. Or thought about them. He had never given himself credit for his abilities. And she intended he would never again be able to say he couldn't do anything that earned appreciation. Maybe Lucy had never seen and acknowledged his abilities, but Abby vowed she wouldn't be guilty of the same thing. And there was much to appreciate, she discovered as she looked for it.

He helped around the house, not only providing meat and flowers, but keeping the wood supply up and helping with Andrew's care. He was tidy. In fact, tidier than either she or Andrew, and it made the housework easy.

That evening she waited until he was preparing to read before she crossed the room to the bookshelves next to his chair.

"Which of these are your favorites?" she asked, running her fingers along the spines.

"They're all the same to me."

"You mean you enjoy this medical text," she tipped the book, "as much as this collection of poems by Robert Browning?"

She held the leather-bound book, its cover soft with use, in the palm of her hand.

His eyes narrowed. "They serve entirely different roles. One is factual and informational. The other. . ." He paused. "The other is like music. For the senses."

She handed him the book of poetry. "You must have a favorite."

Their eyes met—hers daring, his seeming to tell her she was playing with fire. *Fire doesn't have to be dangerous,* she thought. *It also warms and comforts.*

"Pass me that medical book." Andrew's voice snapped the spell. "Maybe it will tell me something about a broken leg. I can check up on Doc Baker. Make sure he knows what he's doing."

She pulled the book from the shelf and took it to him then sat in the wine-colored armchair, turning her attention back to Brewster as he sat with his head bent over the pages, turning them slowly, pausing over the passages.

She stared at him until he looked up. "Do you have a favorite?"

He nodded.

"Would you read it aloud?" She held her breath as he continued to stare at her. She could feel him measuring her, wondering why she was doing this, wondering if she were mocking him or was genuinely interested. "I'd really enjoy it." She smiled, hoping he would see encouragement.

His eyes darkened until all she could see was the deep, bottomless void, and then he ducked his head. Softly at first, his voice growing stronger as he was caught up in the words, he read aloud.

His deep voice reverberated in her heart and swept her away in a spell woven by the intertwining music of poetry and his deep tones. He finished with the words, " 'Ah, but a man's reach should exceed his grasp, or what's a heaven for?' "

Barely seeing him, her eyes focused on images floating like dreams. Finally he lifted his head, and their eyes connected. A shock ran through her body, tingling her scalp. This was the first time he had allowed her a view of his soul, and the vista before her was as wide and as vivid as the scene outside his door.

His heart flows with melody, she thought. A man with such depth, such fineness, such capacity to love, and he refuses to believe in it. Lucky would be the woman who was able to unlock that reservoir. She would be blessed with an endless bounty. Abby shivered, feeling empty and alone.

Why, she mused, *should I feel alone?* She would always have Andrew. She shifted her eyes. Her brother watched her with rapt attention, his book resting on his chest, his mouth agape. Andrew swallowed and blinked then flicked his gaze to Brewster.

Glad to be free of Andrew's stare, Abby picked up the book she had selected and opened its pages. She kept her eyes downward, but the words floated before her eyes. She tingled with the power of the poetry. Absently she turned a page, peeking out from under her eyelashes. Brewster, too, had his head bent as if in deep concentration, but she guardedly watched him for several minutes and saw he did not turn a page. He looked up and caught her studying him. Their eyes locked. She searched for more of the depth she had caught a glimpse of but found in its place only reluctance and misgiving. Whatever she had seen or thought she'd seen had vanished behind his perpetual shield, and as she tore her gaze away, a pang of disappointment made her sigh.

Andrew slammed his book shut and yawned loudly.

Abby felt a pang of guilt as she realized how long she had been lost in thought, completely unaware of how late it had grown. Perhaps Andrew would think it was because she had been caught up in her book. Maybe he failed to notice that she hadn't turned a page for a long time.

Brewster stretched and yawned. "I'm off to bed." He let his gaze slide over Abby, not quite meeting her eyes, before he strode purposefully to his room.

Before she went to bed, Abby penned a note to Sarah, hoping there would be a way of getting it delivered to Pine Creek. She told about Andrew's accident and needing to stay at Brewster's ranch but skipped the part about the kidnapping. Later, she decided, when she could sit down with Sarah and explain it properly, she would tell the whole story. For now, she simply wanted to let Sarah know what was going on and ask for her prayers.

"Brewster needs to know God's love," she wrote. "But his background doesn't make it easy for him to trust."

She was sure Sarah would understand.

Later, in her bed, she lay staring up at the ceiling. She had counted the planks on the ceiling: thirty-five. She had studied the botanical prints, memorizing each detail until she could recreate them perfectly in her mind. She had measured the window and figured how many yards of fabric it would take to make three different styles of curtains. She tried to plan tomorrow's chores but couldn't get past breakfast. She counted slowly and lost track at twenty-five. She tried counting backwards and couldn't do it. She recited nursery rhymes, Bible verses, and hymns; but no matter what she did, her thoughts returned again and again to the same place. Brewster.

Brewster, her kidnapper. Her rescuer and protector.

Brewster, who brought flowers, filled his house with books and music, decorated his walls with fine artwork, and read poetry.

Brewster, neglected and probably mistreated by his mother, who vowed he did not believe in love.

How could he make this claim? She was sure he had a capacity to love as big as all outdoors.

She pursed her lips. It was up to her to make him see it.

The next morning, she determined again to implement her plan, but he shrugged out from under her hand as she poured his coffee, wolfed his breakfast before she could catch her breath, and bolted out the door.

There's more than one way to skin a cat, she mused, watching him stride across the grass.

She quickly completed her morning chores then told Andrew that she needed some fresh air and headed outdoors, pausing as soon as both feet hit the ground. The rain had washed the colors so they sparkled like Monday's laundry. There were patches of scarlet, sunshine yellow, and freshwater blue of the wildflowers Brewster picked. The trees were variegated skeins of green. The damp earth breathed a warm, steamy breath. Abby lifted her face to the sky, filling her lungs until every pore was bathed in the clean pure air. Tipping her head, she listened, wondering where she would find Brewster.

She sauntered to the barn and stepped inside but found nothing but silent lattice-work shadows.

Turning to her right, she circled the corrals and almost missed him. The sound of chipping wood led her to the far end of the paddock, where Brewster squatted on his heels, boring a hole in the bottom of a gate post. A gate stood against the fence, and she knew he was preparing to hang it.

He paused and glanced up as her shadow crossed. "You need something?" he asked, leaning his weight into the drill. Sawdust dribbled to his boots.

"No. Just enjoying the fresh air." Clasping her hands behind her, she watched him work.

He glanced at her out of the corner of his eye.

The silence stretching between them grew taut.

He pulled the bit out, shaking the shavings from it as he straightened. His gaze flashed over her face before he turned his attention to the next hole.

"I never have thanked you properly," she stammered, almost choking on the words as he turned to face her.

"For what?" His voice was deep and lazy.

"For finding Andrew and taking care of him. For letting us stay here while his leg mends."

He pushed himself upright from his knees and slowly turned the full force of his gaze upon her. He didn't speak. He simply looked at her with inscrutable sharpness.

It pressed her to fill the silence rather than meet his stare. "I mean, I was really worried there for a while when he was gone. I don't know what I would do if anything happened to him." She rushed on like a barrel rolling down the hill. "I remember a neighbor lady once telling me that if one twin dies, the other can't survive on its own. I guess it's the truth 'cause I know I couldn't survive without Andrew."

"Are you talking about death or just being apart?"

She couldn't look at him. She rubbed her thumb with her other hand and squeezed it until it turned white. "It feels the same either way."

"Seems to me there's a vast difference." He poised the bit against the post and began turning the handle.

"I didn't say there wasn't. I said it feels the same."

"You lost me."

"I don't expect you to understand. It's something special between twins." Her insides began to twist, and remembering how he had already questioned her relationship with Andrew, she wished she had kept her mouth shut. It seemed he was determined to see their twinness as a problem.

He stopped cranking the handle but stayed bent over his task, staring at the post. "Sounds to me like you're saying it would be impossible for you two to live apart. That you wouldn't be able to function. As I see it, things are bound to change."

"Why should they if we're both happy the way we are?"

"Does Andrew feel the same way? What happens if he wants to get married?"

"We'd work it out, I'm sure, but I don't see it's any concern of yours. I just wanted to thank you for your help."

"And so you did. It was nothing. I'd do it for anyone."

Clenching her hands at her sides, she glowered at him. *Why must he be so difficult?* She was simply trying to be friendly and polite, and he had to treat her like a crackpot. Imagine treating her like she was the one who had a problem when it was he who couldn't trust people and didn't believe in love. The man had a real knack for drilling holes in offers of friendship, driving people away when they wanted to establish some sort of trust. Maybe she should just forget her plan. It would serve him right.

She stomped back to the house, pausing outside the door to collect her thoughts, knowing if she didn't smooth her face and calm her breathing, Andrew would demand an explanation.

He's just jealous, she decided, because Andrew and she had always enjoyed the security of their love for each other. No doubt he would have liked to destroy it, and finding it wasn't possible, he was doing all he could to sully it.

Well, he could try as much as he liked. It would never work. She straightened her shoulders and lifted her chin. She would pay no attention to his remarks. She promised herself she would simply act like he hadn't said anything. Certainly she would never let him guess how much his words had stung.

It was easier than she thought to ignore Brewster when Dr. Baker called that afternoon.

"Well, well, well, and how is the patient today?" Dr. Baker bustled in and headed for Andrew with all the instincts of a homing pigeon. "I like the color of your leg. Very healthy looking." He widened his mouth into the shape of a smile, while nothing in his expression changed.

Abby had the feeling he was only pretending to smile to be polite but really found people quite challenging creatures. He seemed more comfortable dealing with a physical need, like Andrew's broken leg. She felt he would have been better pleased if he could have dealt with a leg without actually having to meet the whole person.

"I think it's time to see if this leg is going to do its stuff." He looked up as Brewster came in carrying a pair of crutches. "Good. Good. Here they are now. Let's get you up on these and see how you do."

Andrew swung his legs to the floor as Dr. Baker steadied him. Abby hurried to Andrew's side, and she and the doctor helped him balance on his good leg.

"Aghh. My head feels like a top." Andrew grabbed her shoulder for support.

"Take it easy now. We won't rush things," Dr. Baker ordered.

In a few seconds, Andrew nodded that he was ready to continue.

"I don't want you putting any weight on this leg just yet. Got to give it a chance to heal. That was a nasty break you had. By the way, young man," he turned to Brewster, "where'd you learn to set a bone like that?"

"Seen it done before," Brewster drawled, leaning against the door, watching the proceedings.

"These contraptions take a little getting used to. You put your weight here." The doctor showed Andrew how to use the crutches and helped him walk to the table and back.

"I'm shaking like a leaf," Andrew said and dropped to the sofa.

"Takes time. Takes time. No going out on the rough ground. Too dangerous. It's fine if you want to step outside, though. Just be careful. I think it's safe to take off this contraption." As he removed the splint, he talked, telling them news of the town. "I'll be back in a week. If things go well, we could think about you folks going home."

"Wait," Abby called as he headed for the door. "Could you give this to Sarah Fergusen for me?" She handed him the note she had written.

With a nod of his head, the doctor agreed.

After he left, Abby stood looking down at Andrew. Home at last. It sounded so good. She wanted Andrew to share her joy, but she could see he was too tired. She lifted her head and caught Brewster staring at them. As soon as he saw her gaze, his expression hardened, but not before she caught a glimpse of something that made her wonder if he would miss them when they left.

Chapter 13

For three days after the doctor's visit, Andrew insisted on being outdoors every afternoon, promising he would not go farther than the end of the path. Today he asked Abby to put a chair outside so he could sit and look at the sky and trees and mountains—things he had been missing more than he could stand. After she had him settled, Abby returned to the house, where she prowled the rooms. Soon they would leave here and return to their own house—truly a simple cabin in comparison to this place. She had to admit she would miss many things about Brewster's house. The paintings, for sure. The garden scene had become her favorite, never failing to bring a rush of joy. The flowers on the table had come to mean so much to her that she had already decided to continue the habit once they were back home, though she didn't recall such a variety of flowers down the mountain.

Another thing she enjoyed was the variety of books. *I haven't even had time to examine all of them,* she thought with a pang as she ran her fingers along the shelves. As she surveyed the tidy shelf where her hand now rested, she noticed one book shoved in behind the others.

How strange. She had grown accustomed to the way Brewster kept his books in precise order.

She pushed aside the front books and pulled it out, turning it over in her hands. Across the spine was emblazoned Holy Bible. She stared at it in disbelief. *A Bible? Brewster has a Bible?* By the way he normally reacted when either she or Andrew mentioned God, she hadn't imagined he'd ever seen one, much less keep one in the house.

Opening the front cover, she saw an inscription penned in thick, black strokes:

> *To Brewster,*
> *We pray you will never forget we love you.*
> *Love never faileth.*
> *May the God of all peace be with you.*
> *Mr. and Mrs. Rawson*

She squeezed her eyes shut, then opened them to read the words again. There was no date, but it was a plain, cloth-covered book much like the one she had received in Sunday school, and she thought he must have been a child when Mr. and Mrs. Rawson gave it to him.

Brewster said he didn't know anything about love, that he had never experienced it. Here was proof otherwise.

Dropping the Bible on the shelf, she raced out the front door.

"Where are you going?" Andrew called as she sped past him.

"For a walk."

"Looks more like a run. What's your hurry?"

"Nothing. I'll be back in a few minutes." She ran past the barn to the set of corrals that Brewster was building and skidded to a stop, breathing like a well-run horse.

Brewster faced her over the fence, his expression impassive.

"You said no one ever loved you. You said you didn't believe in love. What about the Rawsons?"

His eyebrows reached for his hair.

She rushed on. "I found a Bible in your bookcase and read the inscription. 'Never forget we love you.' The Rawsons must have loved you."

Brewster was busy weaving rails through parallel posts to make a section of fence, and he bent to pick up another pole without answering.

"Well? What about the Rawsons?"

"They were just some people."

"What happened to them?"

"Nothing, as far as I know."

"You know what I mean."

He gave her an annoyed look. "We lost touch."

"You mean they moved?"

"No, we moved. We always moved."

"And they didn't write?"

"Nope."

"Why not?"

"Probably didn't know where to send a letter."

"Did you write them and let them know where you were?"

"Can't say as I did."

"You mean they're still waiting to hear from you?"

His dark look said it was none of her business, but she plowed on, determined to uncover this bit of mystery. "How long ago was that?"

"Years. Last saw them when I was ten or eleven."

"That's a long time for them to wait for a letter."

"I don't expect they are."

"So who were they? How did you meet them? Tell me about them."

Clearly annoyed, he leaned the post against the existing fence and wiped his hands on his pants.

"They were just an old couple who lived across the back alley from the house where my mother worked."

"There has to be more to it than that." She crossed her arms to show that she wasn't leaving until he told her the whole story.

"They had this nice flower-filled yard. Behind us, like I said. It had a white picket fence around it. I used to sneak up to the fence and peak through the slats. I liked the flowers." He glared at her as if daring her to laugh.

She nodded. "You still like flowers," she murmured to herself.

"If I kept real quiet and hid behind the slats, I could watch this white-haired old man weeding the garden. Sometimes an old lady helped him." His eyes looked past her, as green shadowed as the shaded forest floor, full of history and memories normally hidden except when a flash of sunlight revealed their secrets. Abby knew he had forgotten she was standing there, but she didn't care. To see that ray of sunshine probe into the darkness of his memories and uncover something good was as sweet as finding a perfect orchid growing from the decay of long-dead leaves.

"I didn't think they knew I was there," he continued, his voice husky as distant, murmuring thunder. "But one day, the man was working in the corner and began talking to me.

" 'I see you're a fellow admirer of beauty. How many of these flowers can you name?'

"I didn't answer of course, but it didn't seem to matter. He just kept on talking.

"He went around the garden, naming all the flowers and telling me special things about each. 'These are called angel trumpets,' he said, pointing to some large white juglike flowers. 'Though Mother says they are more like death bells. They aren't your favorite flower, are they, Mother?'

"I hadn't seen the old lady come out of the house, but there she was.

" 'Why I see our young friend has come to visit and just in time for some iced tea. Come in and join us.' She pointed to the gate.

"I wasn't sure what to do. No one had ever invited me to anything before. But before I could find my voice, Mr. Rawson unlatched the gate and waved me in.

"After that I went over quite a lot. Mr. Rawson seemed eager to teach me all about the garden and brought out books full of pictures and drawings."

Abby nodded again. Now she knew where his love for botany had been born. The prints in his bedroom convinced her that Mr. and Mrs. Rawson had not loved in vain. From them he had learned an appreciation for the beauties of nature that had nourished his deprived soul.

"When Mr. Rawson found out I couldn't read, he taught me. He was a preacher man so he used the Bible as my textbook." His expression hardened. Abby's breath stuck in her throat. She hated the way the sunshine faded from his eyes.

"One morning, Lucy said we were going and we did. That was the end of that. I'd known all along it wouldn't last."

"Oh, no. That's where you're wrong." The kindness and love that these two old people had shown to a lost, little boy touched her heartstrings. She wiped the corner of her eyes as she imagined how hurt they must have been by his disappearance. "You can't say their love didn't last when you never gave them a chance to tell you otherwise." How could he cast aside what they offered as easily as tossing out dish water? "You never wrote them. You never let them know where you were. You just decided it was all a fake. You told yourself they never truly cared. Those poor old people. And you did the same with God. You decided you couldn't earn love and you wouldn't accept it as a gift. Even though the Rawsons proved otherwise, you act like everybody is like Lucy."

Her eyes ached with intensity, but when she saw the desperation in his eyes, she blinked aside her anger.

"Don't you think I wanted her to love me?" His voice rasped like a saw catching on a nail. "The only way I could survive was to tell myself I didn't care. And after a while, it was the truth."

The hollowness of his last words settled in her stomach like a lump of unbaked dough. Had he killed the part of him that was capable of giving and receiving love? She shook her head, unwilling to believe it. He still had a living, beating heart flowing with the same needs and desires as everyone else. She was sure of it. There were so many things she saw as proof. Even her kidnapping had been a desperate means to fulfill those desires.

She knew he was equally, and stubbornly, convinced of the opposite. If only he could go back and repair some of the relationships from his past.

"Where's Lucy now?"

"I don't know and I don't care."

She glowered at him, and he lowered his eyes.

"I heard she died," he mumbled.

"Where did you hear that?"

"From some saddle tramp. Probably one of her customers."

If it were true, then all hope of mending that relationship was gone.

"Where do you suppose the Rawsons are now?"

" 'Spect they're still in the same place. Richmore."

"Why don't you write them?"

"Now?" His eyes widened momentarily before he narrowed them to a slit.

She nodded. "I bet they're still praying for you and hoping someday you'll write."

"Yeah, sure. I can see them going to the post office every day checking for a letter from some little kid they knew pretty near twenty years ago."

"Don't be flippant. You know what I mean."

He bent to pick up the maul. "It would be a waste of time." He swung the hammer over his head and brought it down on the top of the post, shutting the door to any further questions.

Abby watched him pound the post into place. *How many minutes does it take to write a letter?* She wanted to knock the heavy hammer from his hand and shout the question in his face. So what if he had to take a risk? He had to take a chance once in a while in order to gain what he really wanted, and she was sure she knew what he wanted. To be loved—completely, unconditionally, unquestion-ingly, through good and bad, day in and day out.

She could love him like that. She gasped and grabbed the gate for support. She loved him exactly like that. She wanted to grab him by the neck and pull his face down to hers and say the words so plain and simple he couldn't misunderstand.

I love you, Brewster Johnson.

She turned and stumbled away, lest he see the blaze in her face. It was use-less, she told herself. Even if she could bring herself to say the words, he would never allow them to reach his brain, let alone his heart. Blindly, she followed the trail past the barn.

When had she fallen in love with him? So many scenes filled her mind: The beauty of his house and the certainty that it was an expression of the real Brewster. Brewster setting Andrew's leg. The jar full of flowers on the table every day. His dark head bent over a book of poetry. His fury exploding into action as he rescued her from Petey and Sam.

Yes, she admitted, *I felt something for him even then.* When he risked his life for her, she knew he was a man who would be prepared to die for her. That's when she had first realized he was a man who was worth loving.

Why then had it taken so long for her to realize the truth?

She supposed it was partly because he made it so plain he didn't want love. He tried so desperately to convince everyone. She wondered if he had succeeded in convincing himself.

She skidded to a stop under the pine trees and turned to watch him as he worked. He paused to wipe his brow then gathered himself and lifted the maul again.

She stood for a long time under the trees. The scent of pine needles mingled with memories of her past ordeal—once so terrifying, but now almost precious when viewed from the vantage point of love. If only she could make him believe in love.

She hugged her arms around her. How would it feel to be loved by this man? To share a faith in Jesus Christ. To fight the elements side by side and carve out a place in this beautiful land. To have someone she could truly give her heart to. She had no doubt that once Brewster gave his heart, it would be well and truly given. She allowed her imagination to soar until she could see his house filled with love, a baby in her arms, another at her feet. Her legs grew rubbery, and she sighed.

Until he allowed God's love into his heart, she knew he would not be ready for the kind of relationship she ached for. Without a shared faith, all her hopes and dreams were useless.

Please, God, work in his life. Help him to accept Your love.

Even if Brewster never loved her, she knew he needed the healing power of God's love.

She started back toward the house.

If only he would believe in love.

Chapter 14

"You're fit as a fiddle," the doctor said, slamming his bag shut. "Go on home and behave yourself. You're one lucky lad, you know. Most legs broken as bad as that one was would never be good as new again."

"You mean I'm all mended?" Andrew asked, his voice revealing his surprise.

"Throw away the crutches, boy. You might find your leg a little sore at first, but take it easy and you'll be fine."

Andrew stared at him a moment longer then tossed the crutches at his feet and whooped. "We're going home, Abby." He limped to her side and grabbed her hands. "I can get our place ready for winter and begin breaking the horses I bought. About time, too."

Dr. Baker shook his head and smiled his paper-thin smile. "Take it easy, son."

Andrew nodded, but his grin threatened to split his face in two.

Abby managed a wan smile, but she knew her effort was wobbly. She was overjoyed that Andrew was better, and she was ready to be in her own home again, but her pleasure was marred by Brewster's stubborn indifference. Avoidance was more like it. She hadn't been able to break through his tough veneer and convince him to believe in love. More than once she had almost blurted out the words, "I love you," but no good opportunity had arisen, and something told her that he wouldn't believe her anyway. And now, if they left, when would she have another chance?

It wasn't that she hadn't tried. The evenings had been long and warm, and they had spent many hours reading and discussing things. Having discovered that both Andrew and Abby enjoyed it, Brewster often read bits of poetry aloud. Andrew, especially, had taken every opportunity to tell Brewster about God's unconditional love, and Abby had added her agreement, but Brewster remained adamant. He'd survived so far, he insisted, and he wasn't about to change.

"It's too hot in here. I'm going for a walk," Abby announced, her fingers clutching the letter Dr. Baker had brought from Sarah. As she strode down the path, she was aware that Andrew was watching her intently. She'd caught him studying her often in the past few days, and she knew he was attuned to her inner turmoil. Unfortunately he was as powerless as she to do anything. Thank goodness he didn't feel it necessary to say something. Knowing that he knew and understood comforted Abby. She knew he wanted only to see her happy because that was what she wanted for him. She had tried to explain that to Brewster, but his doubts about their dependency on each other never faltered.

It's simply another way of shutting himself away, she thought with startling clarity. In the face of Abby and Andrew's love for each other, Brewster determined it excluded others. She wondered if he really did have feelings for her and was using this argument as protection.

A spark of hope stirred inside her, and she hurried down the path in search of him, determined to convince him that love was available for him.

As she followed the narrow ribbon of the wagon trail, Abby thought about a future without Brewster and saw it as gloomy as the dust-mottled leaves of the trees.

But even worse than her own sense of loss was the sorrow of Brewster's self-enforced loneliness in refusing to accept love. Not only her love for him, but more importantly, God's love for him. She wanted to wrap her understanding of God's full and free love in a gift box and hand it to Brewster. If he would only open the box, God's love would flood his soul and melt his heart.

Sighing, she wiped the beads of sweat from her forehead and admitted her powerlessness to change his hardened heart. She had hoped that forcing Brewster to acknowledge a love for her would erase his pain and enable him to accept God's gift of love.

Only God could do that!

Hope blossomed anew. Nothing was too hard for God, and she closed her eyes and prayed for Him to break through Brewster's strong defenses.

"That he might know the strength of your love," she whispered.

As she hurried on, the heat of the day was a heavy blanket on her shoulders. If only there was a cool breeze. She lifted her hair off her neck and poked it back into a bun, securing it with the few hairpins she hadn't lost. Heat waves shimmered across the face of the mountains. Underfoot, the grass crackled. A thudding sound in the distance made her back teeth tighten.

A trail parted the trees, and she turned under the shade, but even there the heat clung to her. A few feet more and she came to an open field. Across the clearing she saw Brewster, his back to her, his shirt off as he set posts for a fence. His stance wide, he braced himself and dug a hole with an auger, his back muscles rippling and his biceps bulging with the effort. Sweat rolled down his bronzed back. Dropping the auger, he reached out a gloved hand, snagged a post, and dropped it into the hole. Widening his stance again, he grasped the handle of the heavy maul with both hands. The muscles in his arms bulged, and his back muscles swelled and corded into a deep vee. Abby marveled at the crescendo of power as he swung the hammer over his head and slammed the top of the post. She saw the hammer bounce before she heard the thud. Her legs quivered.

He dropped the maul to the ground, and as he turned to grab the next post, he saw her. He leaned forward, catching his breath, his hands resting on the handle. He didn't say anything. She knew he couldn't, or wouldn't. He had to maintain his posture of indifference. But she was convinced that his facade hid a dawning knowledge of her love for him, and she was equally certain that the feelings were mutual. She knew that it scared him to death, because it would make him vulnerable. She had to convince him that love was worth breaking down his brick wall. Without love, his heart would remain forever an empty void.

Her legs unsteady, she walked toward him.

Every detail of his features seemed magnified as she drew closer—the dark shadow that his whiskers drew along his chin, the way his hair clung in damp tendrils to his neck, the trail of sweat trickling down his chest over sun-kissed skin. She stopped her eyes from trailing farther down his chest and felt her cheeks turn to fire.

He pulled a rag from his back pocket and wiped his face.

"Pretty hot, isn't it?" she murmured, her tongue thick.

"A mite."

"Hard work for a day like this."

"One day's the same as the next."

Something inside her exploded. "Why do you do that?"

He raised his eyebrows. "Didn't notice I was doing anything."

"You always act like you've got no feelings. You don't feel heat. Or cold. Or pain. Or love." The words dropped into the heat like hailstones.

His jaw tightened. "I just tell the truth." He lifted a canteen from the ground and took a deep drink.

A drop of water trickled down his chin onto his chest. The words that had been forming in her mind disappeared in a flush of longing. If only he would admit that he loved her and take her into his arms. She understood that somehow accepting her love and believing in God's love were intertwined. She knew she could never give herself fully to this man until he had found his way to God, yet she longed for things that could not be. Blinking, she forced her thoughts back to what she wanted to say.

"You don't know the truth." Would he hear it if she told him? She rushed on before he could answer. "I don't know about Lucy. Maybe she loved you. Maybe she didn't. I do know that if a mother doesn't love her child, it is the mother who is sick. Not the child." She held up her hand to stop him from interrupting. "And I do know the Rawsons loved you. And I know God loves you." She took a deep breath and faced him squarely, her eyes refusing to let him look away. "And I love you." Her firm, solid words rang across the pasture and disappeared into the trees. He stared at her, the expression in his eyes never changing even though a muscle along his cheek twitched. With a dismissive wave, he turned to pick up an iron bar and began tamping the dirt around the post.

She stared at his bent head, anger and embarrassment raging a war. "Brewster." She touched his arm and heat raced up her fingers.

"I don't want to hear it," he growled.

"Hear what? That somebody loves you? Does that shoot holes in your self-protective beliefs? How are you going to insist you don't believe in love when the evidence is standing right in front of you?" She placed herself squarely between Brewster and the post, her arms jammed on her hips.

He straightened his back and met her eyes. His eyes were as cold as stone. "I guess we all have our little pretenses, don't we?" His voice was like tumbling gravel.

"I don't." Bright lights flashed through her brain.

"Yep. You do." His voice slow and lazy. "You talk about God and how much He loves you. But it ain't God you depend on. It's Andrew. If something happened to Andrew, I wonder, would you still believe in love?"

Her jaw dropped and she stared at him. How could he possibly have misunderstood? Yes, she'd said she couldn't imagine life without Andrew, but she hadn't meant it would make her doubt God's love. She knew God loved her. Why was Brewster always harping back to the subject of Andrew and Abby? It was like he couldn't believe they truly cared about each other.

Suspicion germinated in her mind. Was he jealous? Did he think love for one person excluded love for a second? Did he think Abby's love for him would play second fiddle to her love for Andrew?

She grabbed his shoulder and forced him to look at her again. "You don't understand," she whispered. "Love doesn't divide when you love another; it multiplies. Don't you see?"

Something flashed behind his eyes, and she held her breath, waiting for him to soften, but the hardness descended, and he shook his head.

"There's nothing to see. Love doesn't last. It's not real."

"Brewster, that's just not true. You've told yourself lies and believed them for so long, you're convinced they're true. But believing a lie doesn't make it true."

He picked up the auger and bar in one hand, grasped the handle of the maul with the other, and walked toward the next fence post a few feet away.

Abby watched him until he set the auger in the ground and began turning it. He never looked back. The rigid set of his shoulders told her he wouldn't.

A lump the size of a large rock settled in the pit of her stomach, and Abby turned and retraced her steps to the house, admitting defeat. She had tried to prove to him that love was worth believing in, and she had failed. There was nothing left but to pack her few things and return home to pick up the threads of the joy and peace she had known before she met Brewster.

She was almost back to the cabin when she remembered Sarah's letter and pulled it out of her pocket.

"Dear Abby," she read. "I was shocked to hear all that's happened to you. Not a very warm welcome to your new home, I fear.

"I know little about Mr. Johnson. I did not even know his given name until you told me in your letter. He sounds a very lonely man. I know he appears rather unsociable when he comes to town, but I'm sure he has his reasons.

"I'm continuing to pray for you and for healing for Andrew's leg. May God give you strength and wisdom, and do His work in Brewster Johnson's life."

Abby folded the page and dropped it back in her pocket. They were the words of encouragement and direction she needed. She would trust God to do the work needed. Humming, she returned to the house.

Abby leaned against the window, staring at the mountains. Somewhere high in their invincible heights was Brewster's house. She knew it lay south of the saw-toothed peak, but she couldn't pinpoint the exact location.

She let her eyes drift down the deep green of the pine forest to the aspen woods closer to the cabin she and Andrew shared. It still surprised her to see the leaves dancing in their flashy golden gowns. A blue jay parted the leaves and disappeared.

"Abby?" Andrew's voice broke into her thoughts. "Are you all right?"

She wondered if he had spoken before and she hadn't heard. Without turning, she nodded. "It's just the season. Fall is so melancholic."

"You're really missing him, aren't you?"

She turned, letting her back rest against the wall. Brown eyes met brown eyes. "Yes, I suppose I am." They had never spoken directly about it. Hadn't needed to. Andrew had seen for himself the way Brewster stood stiff and cold in the open door of his house when they had said good-bye and thanked him for his help. Andrew, feeling Abby's misery, had taken her hand and helped her onto the horse.

"Maybe he'll change his mind," he said now.

"I don't think so." Brewster had what he wanted—a place in the mountains where no one would ever invade his privacy. And a barred heart that allowed no one to share his emotions. He'd had a chance to choose otherwise and had chosen not to. Abby had to live with the reality that Brewster could not—or would not—allow love to enter his life.

"You never know." Andrew rose from the table. "In the meantime, I've got work to do." He paused at the door until she nodded.

Long after he was gone, she sat staring at the dirty dishes. Even after all she had eaten, Abby still felt as hollow and empty as a rain barrel during a drought. She knew the hungry emptiness could not be filled with food. It was Brewster shaped. And she knew it would never be filled. How then was she to deal with the stirring inside that leaped at the sound of a horse riding into the yard or the outer door opening, yet curled into a knot when it was only Andrew? How was she to stop her heart from fluttering at the scent of pine needles? Or when she caught the brightness of a patch of wildflowers? How was she to silence the unending wail of pain burrowing into her soul?

Shaking her head to clear her thoughts, she slowly gathered up the dishes and lowered them into the hot, soapy water. When she had finished, she went to her room.

Brewster had been right about one thing. She had never before separated God's love and Andrew's love in her mind—until recently, when she found Andrew's love was not enough to ease her pain. She opened her Bible and began reading where she had left off yesterday. The only thing that helped ease her pain was casting herself on God's love. Reading her Bible had become a balm to her bleeding heart.

She finished the portion she had chosen and bent her head in prayer, asking God to heal her wounds.

As peace stole into her heart, she set aside the Bible and knelt in front of the trunk where she had left her winter things. Cold weather would soon be upon them, and she needed to be prepared. She removed a gray wool dress that had been her favorite last year. The color made her feel warm and alive, and she admitted it was because the soft gray made her hair glow with rich highlights. Beneath it lay a black skirt and two flannel nighties. She shook them out and laid them on the bed. Returning to the trunk, her fingers touched something hard and cold. She pulled out a framed picture of Father in front of their house in England. She had forgotten it in her excitement of unpacking and settling into her new home in a new country. She pressed her finger to his likeness. The old country seemed so far away, another lifetime. She was glad Father wrote regularly to assure them he was well and happy.

Smiling, she withdrew a bundle of material from the trunk. She'd been saving these pieces for a quilt. She loved the colors and textures of cloth and was suddenly glad to have this project to help pass the long winter days ahead.

Unfolding the material, she caressed the soft, brown flannel from which she had made shirts for Father and Andrew two winters ago. There were pieces from her gray dress and her pink print nighties. She rubbed a bit of heavy, green brocade between her fingers. Mrs. Olsen had given her that. She folded back some more pieces and gasped, falling back on her heels.

She'd completely forgotten the scrap she had tucked into this bundle so it wouldn't be damaged or lost. Slowly, almost not breathing, she withdrew it as her thoughts fled back to the day she had discovered it.

She could no longer remember why she had gone to the attic. Nor what she was looking for. Or why she had chosen that particular trunk to look through. What she did remember as clearly as if it happened this morning was discovering the square of blue cloth. It was the color of deep, calm water, rich and smooth, the finest quality wool Abby had ever seen. It felt like velvet between her fingers, soft as a cat's fur, and she caressed it hungrily. But her mind hadn't been on the bit of cloth. Rather it had flooded with memories. She had been crying about some small injury. Seems like it was a bump on the head. Gentle arms had pulled her to a comforting lap and pressed her head to a warm breast. She could feel a lullaby beneath her ear and smell roses. And she had pressed her face into warm, soft, blue material. Exactly like the scrap she had found.

It was the only real memory she had of her mother, and she had taken the square of blue and hidden it under her pillow, clutching it in her fingers before she fell asleep. As she grew older, she had tucked it safely in the top drawer of her bureau right next to the small photo of her mother. Only on really bad days did she pull it out and bury her face in its softness as she did now. She breathed its soothing familiarity as tears flowed unchecked, soaking the cloth while the smell of wet wool wrapped about her.

She cried for a mother she could barely remember and who could not comfort her now, when she needed it most. And she cried for a love that would never be because another mother, whose arms had never comforted, had left behind a legacy of fear and mistrust rather than the gentle, warm memory she had.

Chapter 15

Abby stood at the clothesline, the wind tearing at her skirt, biting her skin. She glanced at the sky, half-expecting to see snow, then turned her attention back to getting the clothes off the line before her fingers froze. It was only October. Surely, she thought as she struggled with the wind-whipped articles, it wouldn't snow this early. But Andrew had warned her that winter came early in the foothills.

"I'm told that it often snows much sooner than this." He'd shaken his head, but when she asked if he was sorry they'd chosen this particular place, he had brightened. "Nope," he said. "Still the prettiest bit of land I ever saw."

She had nodded and agreed.

Yet there were times she wished they'd chosen a spot to the south, or perhaps to the north. Any place where Brewster's path wouldn't have crossed hers. Over and over, she reminded herself she would never see him again, but she hadn't been able to silence the longing in her heart.

She continued to pray for God to send healing into his heart and consoled herself that whether she ever saw him again or not, God would work in his life.

Dropping the sheets in the basket, she picked it up and turned toward the house. Her hair, tugged loose by the teasing wind, blew across her face and obstructed her view. Balancing the load on her hip, she scooped her hair back and almost dropped her basket. The wind sucked away her startled scream.

Not fifteen feet away stood Brewster, twisting his hat in his hands, the wind sifting through his hair.

She couldn't speak. She couldn't breathe. The basket creaked as she clutched it in her arms. She blinked, expecting him to disappear, but he was still there, his feet planted firmly on the ground. She let her glance skim over his face then ducked her head, hoping against hope he was real, yet afraid it was only her imagination running wild. How often in her thoughts had she heard his voice across the yard? Or looked up, thinking it was his footsteps. Slowly, her heart pounding in her ears, she raised her head and looked deep into his uncertain eyes.

"Have you come to kidnap me again?"

"No." A spear of darkness flashed through his eyes. "I have something to show you," he growled.

Nodding, she moved toward him. "Come to the house. It's too cold out here." He took the basket from her as he turned. Together they crossed the yard. Neither spoke until the door closed behind them.

"I'll take that." She set the basket by the stove before she faced him. Now that the initial shock of seeing him had passed, she studied him, drinking in every detail. His hair was a little longer, strands of it blown across his cheek. Her fingers twitched, longing to catch them and tuck them into place. His face seemed leaner, but it was more than a little thinness that made him seem different, and she strained to grasp the difference. It was something in his expression, she decided. Something hovering just beyond her grasp. His eyes, too, were different. *Almost inviting,* she thought and knew it was only her own desperate longings making her see something that wasn't there.

He cleared his throat, the sound snapping her out of her preoccupation.

"Have a seat while I make coffee." She nodded toward the table.

"Thanks." He sat on the edge of the wooden chair, twisting his hat between his fingers.

"It's a cold day for a ride," she said, trying to fill the silence.

"It'll get colder." He glanced around the room. "Where's Andrew?"

"Gone to bring the horses closer to home. He's worried it will snow."

"Feels like it could." He set his hat on the table and then seemed to think better of it and picked it up again.

She filled two cups and placed them on the table and sat on the chair across from him. She couldn't quit looking at him, filling her mind with the shape of his brow, the slash across his cheek, the jut of his jaw. She wanted to gather enough looks to last the long winter.

"I did what you said."

She startled in her chair, surprised by his voice. She'd been so busy stocking her larder of memories that she'd forgotten his reason for being here. Not that it mattered. It was enough that he was there, if only for a few minutes to conduct an errand. But she couldn't remember saying he should do something. "What did I say?" Only part of her mind was on the question.

"About writing the Rawsons."

"Oh yes." Guess she had said something of the sort, but all she could think right now was how soft his eyes were, how dark the fringe of eyelashes.

"They were still in the same place. They wrote me a reply." He waited, but when she didn't answer, he continued. "You want to read the letter?" Pulling an envelope from his breast pocket, he offered it to her.

The sound of paper rattling forced her back to reality. She let her gaze linger on his strong mouth a heartbeat longer then blinked away her dreams. "Thank you." She pulled out three sheets of well-thumbed pages and read the words slowly. It was as she guessed. The Rawsons wrote they had never stopped praying for him. Their greatest desire was that he would remember what they had told him about God and His love and not forget their love. She flipped a page and continued to read the bits of news. Mr. Rawson had recently celebrated his seventieth birthday and could no longer look after the flowers as well as he wanted. Somehow she had assumed that the Rawsons had been in their seventies at the time Brewster knew them, but then she realized that to a youngster anyone past the age of sixteen was old.

Abby gasped as she read the next line. Lucy had come back in the hope that the Rawsons would know where to locate Brewster. Lucy had tried to find Brewster before she died.

By the time Abby reached the end of the letter, her vision was so blurred, she could barely make out the words.

"Oh, Brewster. What a lovely letter."

"You were right. They prayed for me all those years." His face grew serious. "Lucy knew it was the only place I would ever return to. That's why she went back when she knew she was dying. I can't believe she tried to get a message to me."

"She did get a message to you." She blinked back the tears and read from the last page.

" 'Your mother made us promise we would give you this message if we ever got a chance. She even asked us to write it down so we would get it right, so these are her exact words. She said, 'Tell Brewster I know I wasn't much of a mother. He was a good kid. He deserved better.' "

Abby's voice shook so much, she had to stop. "I'm so glad for you," she whispered when she could speak again.

He nodded. "When I got this letter, it set me to thinking about some of the things you said."

She had said a lot of things and thought even more. Things such as how compelling his eyes were when they flashed shards of green like they were now; how she longed to feel his hair, knowing it was silky and smooth; how warm his skin looked, like it carried the touch of summer sun. But she had never said those words aloud, and she couldn't think what things he was referring to.

"You kept hounding me that I had to be willing to give love a chance."

She wouldn't have called it hounding, but yes, she had challenged him not to throw love away.

"You said love was worth a few risks."

I would gamble my life for a chance to share your love, she thought, her eyes lingering on his lips, fascinated with the way they formed each syllable.

"I thought about that lots," he continued. "That's why I wrote that letter in the first place." He arched back in his chair and lurched to his feet to pace the floor. "I'd shut myself up. I figured if I didn't believe in love, I'd never be hurt or disappointed that no one loved me."

Turning, he strode back to the table and stared down at her. "Then you said what you did."

"What did I say?"

"You know." His gaze settled on something above her head. "What you said about loving me." His voice dropped to deep within his chest, and she strained to catch the words.

He stood so close, she could smell sawdust and pine needles. Her throat constricted so her words were a mere whisper. "What I said was, I love you."

"Yeah. And I didn't know what to say or do. I didn't know how to feel." He was pacing again, crossing the room in long strides and spinning on his heel to return.

It wasn't hard to know what to do, or say, she wanted to scream at him. *All you had to do was pull me into your arms and promise me you'd love me until forever.* She couldn't sit any longer. His pacing made her feel like exploding. She hurried to the fireplace, pressing her back to the cold rocks, and turned to watch him.

He rubbed his jaw. "After you and Andrew left, I was so alone. I kept telling myself I'd get used to being alone again. But I didn't. I even thought of riding over."

"Why didn't you? You knew you'd be welcome." A hollow ache echoed in her chest. So many times she stood at the window wishing he'd come. She wanted to tell him, to repeat her vow of love. But she couldn't. She still didn't know why he had come or what he wanted. It seemed there was more on his mind, yet he seemed unable to say what it was.

"I knew you'd be hospitable, but I was too confused. I had to sort out all that stuff twisted up inside me."

"Such as?" Narrowing her eyes, she wondered what he meant.

"Why wasn't I loved by my mother?"

"It wasn't your fault."

"It's easy to say that. I told myself the same thing all the time. But it didn't help." He ceased his pacing and stood directly in front of her, his eyes boring into hers.

There was an expression in his eyes she couldn't fathom, and she tore her gaze away, uncertain where to look. Finally she settled for looking at the letter where it lay on the table.

"The letter helped, didn't it?" she asked, understanding suddenly that the words contained in it had helped him sort out some of his confusion.

Something warm and eager flashed across his face. "Yes. It was like a door had been stuck for years and finally swung open. When I read her message, all of a sudden I remembered all sorts of little things. Like wherever we went, there was someone who watched over me—usually the barkeep. And I can see now that Lucy sent me to that person." His voice rang with freedom. "I think it was her way of seeing I was kindly treated. It was the only way she knew of taking care of me."

He paused. "I know now she did the best she could for me. I never saw it that way before."

Abby could see he was bursting.

"It's like my whole life has been filled with closed doors that suddenly opened wide. I saw all the good times I'd had at the Rawsons. I remembered how special

I felt. How good it had been when they told me God loved me." His eyes shone like the sun was trapped behind them. "I began reading the Bible. I found so many answers there." He straightened and shook his head as if to clear his thoughts. "I can't tell you how much my heart has changed." His expression hardened ever so slightly. "Sometimes I'm afraid it's too good to be true and I don't deserve it." He strode away and stood with his back to her.

She half-stepped toward him then stopped. Clasping her hands in front of her, she spoke softly to his back. "How many of us deserve the love we're given? Sometimes we accept it. Sometimes we don't." She still didn't know how far he'd come in accepting it himself. Had he healed enough to believe in her love?

"I still have so much to sort out." Slowly he turned toward her. "Remember what you said to me?" He took a step toward her.

She shook her head. How could she know what he meant?

A waiting, longing expression filled his eyes, and then she knew. A tiny bubble of joy began to swell upward from the pit of her stomach. "Brewster Johnson, I love you yesterday, now, and forever." Her smile reached for her ears.

His eyes filled with flashes of happiness. He took another step toward her until they could have touched each other, but neither did. Brewster's mouth opened and closed, and then he said, "I have something I want to say to you." His voice was so deep, it plucked chords of pleasure in her chest. His Adam's apple plunged up and down as he struggled for the words he wanted. "Abigail Landor," he began, "I love you." The tension drained from his face.

Knowing how difficult it was for him to say those words aloud, Abby found them extra sweet. Her bubble of joy exploded in a shout of laughter, and she flung herself at him. He caught her in his arms and crushed her to his chest, where she heard a rumble of laughter. She couldn't remember hearing him laugh before, and she tipped her head back to watch as his face creased in a smile that transformed his whole countenance. She was reminded of the way the early sunshine flashed off the mountains, filling them with diamond-sharp brightness.

He looked deeply into her eyes, searching them in a way he had never done before. "There's still a lot I have to work out," he warned.

"I know." And she did something she'd wanted to do for such a long time. She lifted a finger and trailed it along his jaw line, thrilling at the roughness of his whiskers.

He caught her hand and pressed her palm to his lips, his eyes never leaving her face.

"I'm not very good at this loving business. I don't know how to go about it."

Her other hand sought the back of his neck, where she could tangle her fingers in his silky locks. "I'll help you all I can." She lifted her face toward him.

He gave a sound halfway between a gasp and a sigh before he lowered his head, catching her lips with his. He held her so tight, she could barely breathe, but she didn't mind. She wrapped her arms around his shoulders and allowed the kiss to start fires inside her. Her toes were tingling, and her knees shook when he lifted his head.

He had a smile that would melt snow, she decided.

Suddenly his eyes clouded, and he softened his grasp on her. "What about my scar?"

"What about it?" She trailed a finger from where it began at his bottom eyelid to where it puckered to an end just above his lower jaw.

"You don't find it repulsive?"

Her fingers stopped moving, and she stepped back, forcing him to drop his arms to his side. "Brewster Johnson. How dare you ask me that!"

He looked sheepish, but his eyes remained insistent.

She grasped his face between her hands and met his eyes boldly. "I think this scar has become a symbol for you. A physical reminder not to trust love." She pulled his face closer. "From now on." She began to trail kisses along his cheek. "I want you to see it as a reminder of how much I love you." She continued to kiss his scar line. "Consider it a flag of love."

A deep rumble filled his chest as he swept her into his arms and covered her face with kisses.

"I have so much to learn," he murmured against her mouth.

She enjoyed the touch of his lips a moment longer then broke away long enough to whisper, "But what fun to learn together."

A Letter to Our Readers

Dear Readers:

In order that we might better contribute to your reading enjoyment, we would appreciate your taking a few minutes to respond to the following questions. When completed, please return to the following: Fiction Editor, Barbour Publishing, Inc., P.O. Box 719, Uhrichsville, OH 44683.

1. Did you enjoy reading *Alberta Brides*?
   ❏ Very much—I would like to see more books like this.
   ❏ Moderately—I would have enjoyed it more if _____
   _____
   _____

2. What influenced your decision to purchase this book?
   (Check those that apply.)
   ❏ Cover   ❏ Back cover copy   ❏ Title   ❏ Price
   ❏ Friends   ❏ Publicity   ❏ Other

3. Which story was your favorite?
   ❏ *Chastity's Angel*   ❏ *The Heart Seeks a Home*
   ❏ *Crane's Bride*   ❏ *Unchained Hearts*

4. Please check your age range:
   ❏ Under 18   ❏ 18–24   ❏ 25–34
   ❏ 35–45   ❏ 46–55   ❏ Over 55

5. How many hours per week do you read? _____

Name _____

Occupation _____

Address _____

City _____ State _____ Zip _____

E-mail _____

HEARTSONG
PRESENTS

If you love Christian romance...

You'll love Heartsong Presents' inspiring and faith-filled romances by today's very best Christian authors...DiAnn Mills, Wanda E. Brunstetter, and Yvonne Lehman, to mention a few!

When you join Heartsong Presents, you'll enjoy 4 brand-new mass market, 176–page books – two contemporary and two historical – that will build you up in your faith when you discover God's role in every relationship you read about!

Imagine...four new romances every four weeks – with men and women like you who long to meet the one God has chosen as the love of their lives...all for the low price of $10.99 postpaid.

To join, simply visit www.heartsong presents.com or complete the coupon below and mail it to the address provided.

✂ -

YES! Sign me up for Heartsong!

**NEW MEMBERSHIPS WILL BE SHIPPED IMMEDIATELY!
Send no money now.** We'll bill you only $10.99 post-paid with your first shipment of four books. Or for faster action, call 1-740-922-7280.

NAME _____

ADDRESS _____

CITY _____STATE_____ ZIP_____

MAIL TO: HEARTSONG PRESENTS, P.O. Box 721, Uhrichsville, Ohio 44683
or sign up at **WWW.HEARTSONGPRESENTS.COM**

ADPG05